"The world-building is as solid as a rock. Altogether, the reappearance of these novels can only enhance the author's high reputation for intelligent storytelling among readers familiar primarily with his recent fiction."

Publishers Weekly on *Empire & Ecolitan*

"L. E. Modesitt, Jr., is a writer deeply concerned for the impact of humanity on the world. This concern shows clearly in fantasies such as *The Order War* and science fiction such as *The Ecologic Envoy*."

Analog

Praise for *The Ecolitan Enigma*

"It is thoughtful, well written . . . an accurate and disturbing portrait of the dark side of humanity. . . . *The Ecolitan Enigma* can be enjoyed as a first-rate political-adventure tale, as a continuation of the long-running SF conversation, or as an examination of human nature. . . . It's an outstanding work, and I plan to reread it."

SFSite.com

"Revel in the delights of another L. E. Modesitt science fiction adventure. . . . Modesitt provides the very best in science fiction—thrilling adventure viewed through the crucible of the human spirit."

Romantic Times

"In this exciting SF adventure, Modesitt puts his characters through all the right paces, creating a rising tension that's sure to keep action-oriented readers nailed straight through to the explosive conclusion."

Publishers Weekly

"Plot and characters are always intelligent, and the climax is thundering and action filled."

Booklist

TOR BOOKS BY L. E. MODESITT, JR.

THE COREAN CHRONICLES
Legacies   *Darknesses*

THE SAGA OF RECLUCE
The Magic of Recluce   *The Chaos Balance*
The Towers of the Sunset   *The White Order*
The Magic Engineer   *Colors of Chaos*
The Order War   *Magi'i of Cyador*
The Death of Chaos   *Scion of Cyador*
Fall of Angels   *Wellspring of Chaos**

THE SPELLSONG CYCLE
The Soprano Sorceress   *Darksong Rising*
The Spellsong War   *The Shadow Sorceress*
Shadowinger

THE ECOLITAN MATTER
Empire & Ecolitan
(comprising *The Ecolitan Operation* and *The Ecologic Secession*)
Ecolitan Prime
(comprising *The Ecologic Envoy* and *The Ecolitan Enigma*)

THE FOREVER HERO
(comprising *Dawn for a Distant Earth, The Silent Warrior,*
and *In Endless Twilight*)

TIMEGODS' WORLD
(comprising *Timediver's Dawn* and *The Timegod*)

THE GHOST BOOKS
Of Tangible Ghosts   *The Ghost of the Revelator*
Ghost of the White Nights

The Hammer of Darkness   *The Green Progression*
The Parafaith War   *Adiamante*
Gravity Dreams   *The Octagonal Raven*
Archform: Beauty   *The Ethos Effect*

*forthcoming

CONTENTS

THE ECOLOGIC ENVOY   7

THE ECOLITAN ENIGMA   217

THE ECOLOGIC ENVOY

For Susan,

gymnast, supporter, and daughter,

who liked this book from the first draft.

"You get what you can, and you call it honorable."

L. deLewis Spragg, *Politics of Trade*

"Trade is too important to be left to politicians."

Variation on Twentieth Century (A.D.) saying

"Politics is too important to be left to the traders of votes or to the traders of tangibles."

G. Wu-Reginald, Farewell Address to the
S. A. Guild

"Trade and Commerce are merely another form of war. At least, the warriors admit their calling is war."

Fleet Admiral Gorham, *Memoirs*

"True trade is honest, but not merciful. Politics is dishonest, no matter how merciful . . . and war is neither honest nor merciful . . . therefore, choose trade above politics, but politics above war . . . "

Anonymous

THE NEEDLE-BOAT blinked out into norm-space. Both high and low wave detector plates flared.

"Flame!" The pilot scanned the board, jabbed a series of control studs to put all energy radiating equipment into a passive mode, and waited for the picture to build on his screens.

Energy concentrations peaked around the fourth planet, Haversol, then spread to a standard picket line and deep warning net typical of an Empire operation.

Whaler's fingers flickered over the control studs as he took in the information flowing from his receptors. While all the material would stay on tap for the Institute to dissect after his return, his own survival might depend on a nearly instantaneous understanding of the tactical pattern.

"Ten stans, max," he muttered to the controls, eyes darting from screen to screen. The needle-boat itself was a single pilot craft, jammed with sophisticated sensors and communications equipment, and made possible only through a combination of thin hull, minimal support and backup systems, and overpowered drives.

At the upper left of the board in front of Whaler, a flat panel flashed amber twice, then settled into a steady glow. He touched the panel and listened to the direct feed of the Imperial comm net through his own implant.

"Seven . . . clear on grid november five . . . interrogative . . ."

"That's negative."

"Angel four . . . negative on survivors . . . send the junkman."

"Hawkstrike! Hawkstrike! Gremlin, Arthur class, vector zero eight five, radian one three three, ecliptic plus two."

"Hawkstrike, gremlin acquisition, closing."

The Imperial Fourth Fleet was obviously mopping up the scattered remnants of the Haversolan system defense forces.

"Class four on radian two five seven. Hotspot three. Interrogative waster. Interrogative waster."

"Waster's down. Negative."

Screeeee!!!!

"Unscramble, Northwave. Unscramble."

"Gremlin secured, Hawkstrike. Repeat, Gremlin secured."

The needle-boat pilot shook his head and touched the pale green panel to start the power-up for nullspace reentry.

The return coordinates for his out-space base flashed across the display. The Institute maintained its own forces independent of the Coordinate. So independently, thought the Ecolitan who was the needle-boat's pilot, captain, and crew, that the government itself had no idea of the Institute's strength.

"Sooner or later, they'll need us again," murmured the pilot. "Sooner, if this is any indication. Much sooner."

Nathaniel Firstborne Whaler, sometime scholar and full-time practicing Ecolitan, automatically squared himself within his seat cocoon and cleared the board readouts, returning all the data to the coded master disc in the center of the boat.

As the bell chime sounded in his ears, Whaler tapped the sequencing plate, and the needle-boat vanished from the norm-space where the Imperial detectors had failed to notice the discrepancy in the energy levels that had been the only sign of its presence.

■■

THE ADMIRAL GLARED around the conference table that circled an empty space, then tapped the flat control panel.

The panel flashed twice before settling into a steady amber glow to signify that the full security screens were on-line and functioning.

A tap on another panel stud brought the holo star map into being in the once-vacant center of the encircling table.

The Admiral lifted the light pointer from the console and rapped the table. Once. The low murmur from the dozen senior officers died.

Guiding the pointer into the holo map, the Admiral focused the tip on a G-type system on the far side of the Rift.

"Accord. You can see how it controls the trade lines. Particularly since the Secession."

The pointer tip moved from the holo and jabbed at the Commodore. "Let's have your isolation strategy report."

The Commodore stood stiffly and gestured at the blank wall to the right of the senior officer. A segment of the holo, blown to larger dimensions, appeared. On the inner edge of the Rift, the Imperial side, three stars appeared in red.

"Haversol, Fonderal, and Cubera. Until the success of our recent operation, Haversol was the largest out-Rift trade staging point on the

Imperial side dealing with the Coordinate traders. The economics dictated that we hit Fonderal first, and that was completed before we even planned the Haversol campaign. The embargo on Fonderal was a simpler matter, of course, because of its lack of an internally supported infrastructure. Even *they* couldn't tackle that kind of rebuilding job, not in the short run, and especially with Haversol still open.

"Next came the flanking movement. We managed to get adequate support to the statist insurgents, who, in turn, were able to topple the monarchy. Of course, the new provisional government asked for Imperial assistance, and the Fourth Fleet was close enough to provide the necessary support."

"That left Hernando and Haversol along this corridor, and we've just about completed the establishment of the military support agreement with the new government of Haversol."

Another system on the holo blowup began to alternate flashing white and red.

"That leaves Hernando."

The Commodore coughed twice, reached down, and took a sip from the tumbler before returning to the presentation.

"Obviously, this is all just a sketch, but the next step will be harder. Hernando is considerably more stable than the other systems. Still . . . if we can get a more favorable government in the upcoming elections or, failing that, generate enough civil unrest to demonstrate a certifiable lack of control, we would have the basis for another control action, citing the threat to Imperial commerce. That would just about close down Accord's access to the Limber line."

The Commodore looked back at the Admiral.

"Any questions, Admiral?"

"What's the best possible time line?"

"The midterm elections on Hernando are more than a standard year off, and to generate any real results will be hard in such a short frame, but we intend to try. Certainly, by the next elections after the midterms—"

"Aim for the midterms. Giving Accord time to react could put us on the defensive."

The Commodore nodded. "Full speed ahead on Hernando it is, Admiral."

■ ■ ■

TIPSY, THAT THE man definitely was.

Otherwise he would not have staggered down the hallway and elbowed his way through the heavy wooden door into the private party in the second dining room of the Golden Charthouse.

Twenty people, fourteen men and six women, sat around the two rectangular tables, enjoying the first course of dorle soup and the thin and genuine wheat crackers and anticipating the days of power to come. Only six weeks remained before the upper chamber elections.

A tall man, clean shaven and attired in a formal, deep blue tunic and contrasting cream sash, was standing to make the first toast.

"To the people of Hernando and to the Popular Front, the government to be."

The drunk, a sandy-haired fellow, lurched inside the room.

"Sir, this is a private party." The guard moved away from the curtained archway to block the intruder. His partner approached from the other side.

Neither thought to reach for the illegal freezers in the belt holsters they flaunted.

"So . . . want to join the celebration . . . see the new masters . . . see what kind of government the Empire bought . . . how much the sellout cost . . ."

The sandy-haired man stood almost as tall as the two guards. All three were nearly half a head taller than the men seated around the tables, even than the toastmaster.

"Sir!" protested the lead guard, stiffening.

The interloper stumbled backwards, then kicked the heavy door shut. The toastmaster jerked his head toward the noise.

"Sorry, friends!"

With his right hand, the intruder launched an aerosol into the space between the tables. Simultaneously, a backhand slash casually broke the neck of the guard on his left.

The right-hand guard grabbed for his freezer, too late, and had no second chance as he doubled with a crumpled windpipe and a smashed kneecap.

Even before the aerosol had landed and come to a full stop, the Ecol-

itan had returned his full attention to the diners, with a small dart pistol in each hand.

The toastmaster in blue was dragging a stunner from his waistband
when the first dart caught him in the throat.

"Help!"

"Security!"

"Flamed greenie!"

"Get him!"

"You do!"

A black man with flaming golden hair dove from the top of the nearest table but fell short of reaching the attacker, and was rewarded with
a dart in the neck and a kick snapping his collarbone.

The shouts and sounds, already muffled by the private dining room's
heavy insulation and rich hangings, began to dwindle under the effects
of the darts and the aerosol.

The Ecolitan calmly continued to shoot anyone trying to reach him
or to escape until there were no living figures in the room. None had
escaped. Then he checked the bodies, methodically studying each face
and comparing it against his memory, and insuring that every member
of the Popular Front present was indeed dead.

The sometime Ecolitan professor who bore the unlikely name of
Nathaniel Whaler disliked the necessity of the assignment but continued to move with measured and deliberate speed, touching nothing
except with his gloved hands as he turned each still form. Last, he
replaced the aerosol in his tunic, concealed the dart guns in his boot
sheaths, and opened the heavy wooden door, staggering out as he closed
it behind him. Weaving back and forth, he stumbled back down the
hallway and out into the main corridor from the hidden Charthouse.

Three levels down, he disappeared into a public fresher stall. In time,
a blond man in a dark blue business tunic crisply strode out.

After descending yet another level to the open square, the Ecoli-
tan/businessman sat down beside a fountain on an empty pseudo stone
bench, apparently admiring the interplay of the golden water with the
crimson spray curtains.

In time, a young woman, low-cut blouse revealing her profession
and assets, sat down next to him, thrusting her chest at him with an
artificially inviting smile.

"Complete?"

"All but Zeroga," answered Whaler. "Not at the dinner. You try the
firm. I'll hit his quarters."

As he spoke, Whaler let his eyes range over the woman, as if appraising what she offered.

She rolled her eyes in exasperation.

Whaler shook his head vigorously, and the woman pouted publicly before standing with a flourish and mincing her way from him and the fountain.

The Ecolitan shook his head again and stood.

Finally, with a last look at the fountain, the blond man who had been sandy haired and would be again walked down the corridor to the flitter stand, where he dialed for public transportation.

IV

THE COMMODORE STOOD more stiffly than usual, waiting to report to the Admiral and the other members of the Ministry's strategy board.

"I understand we've run into some difficulties on Hernando, Commodore."

"Yes, Admiral. A major stumbling block, though you will recall that my last report to the board indicated the lack of time facing us."

"I recall that. However, would you please provide a fuller explanation for the record." The tone of the request sent shivers down the back of the senior Commanders in the briefing section. Several others shifted their weight quietly.

The Commodore turned to face neither the audience nor the Admiral and pointed at the lit screen, which displayed a chart.

"As you can see, the Conservative Democrats, with the help of the seven seats held by the Socialist Republicans, control the Upper Chamber, and thus, the executive branch of Hernando's government. The Popular Front, with some outside technical support, had identified the most vulnerable Conservative Democrats and targeted them. We also targeted those strong opinion leaders opposed to a greater Imperial presence along the Limber line."

The chart shifted.

"This indicates the probable election outcome, including deaths and retirements, which we had predicted last month."

"That doesn't look like a problem," commented a junior Admiral to the Commodore's right.

"It wasn't . . . until some mutant form of A-damp virus wiped out the entire Popular Front planning group and the ten leading candidates—all on the same night ten days ago."

"Accord?"

"The Institute. No way to prove it, but the signs all point that way."

"Such as?"

"First, both security guards were taken out by hand. One had a broken neck and the other a crushed windpipe." The Commodore cleared his throat before continuing. "Second, it was done quietly. No guns, blaster bolts, slug throwers. And virtually no traces left."

The Admiral studied the faces around the conference table. Several expressed open doubt.

"Why do you think those are enough to point at Accord and at the Ecolitan Institute, Commodore?"

"Well . . . we don't deal with biological weapons, especially tailored ones. Imperial intelligence, as well as the Ministry's teams, indicates that only Accord has a capability sophisticated enough to develop and deploy individualized weapons—"

"Was this really a weapon?" snapped a senior Fleet Admiral.

"Admiral," answered the Commodore, "have you ever run across a swamp fever virus that killed an entire room full of people within a unit or two, simultaneously? At the same time when two armed security guards were killed by hand?"

The silence dragged out. Finally, the Commodore turned back to the Grand Admiral.

"That brings up the hand-to-hand ability. We might have a dozen men with the ability to disable a pair of two-meter-tall armed guards in seconds. Several other terrorist groups might have a handful spread across the Empire. None of us have anyone with that ability also immune to swamp fever, mutated or not, or with the ability to walk through a crowded restaurant into a private dining room and assassinate twenty people and then leave without even being noticed."

"Not even noticed?"

"Not so far as we can determine."

The Admiral surveyed the faces again. "You might ask why this all points to Accord. I'll tell you. What the Commodore has not said is that all members of the Institute are either naturally immune or immunized against swamp fever and a number of other fast-acting diseases. He also has not mentioned that the Ecolitan Institute maintains the most intensive hand-to-hand combat training in the civilized worlds, along with a special corps that is little more than a crack terrorist unit."

"Can we prove any of this?"

"That's not the point. Accord wanted to send us a message. They sent it, and we've received it. It doesn't change a thing. Single individuals, no matter how gifted, cannot stop the massed force of history that we will bring to bear."

The Admiral frowned slightly after finishing the declaration, then touched the control console. The holo star map and the wall charts vanished.

"We can't wait for another set of elections on Hernando, not with this kind of a challenge. How soon can we go with Plan B?"

The Commodore cleared his throat. "That's already underway, but the flagship won't be ready for about three standard months—"

"See if you can make it two."

The Commodore nodded.

The Admiral touched the amber stud, and the security screens winked off.

"Adjourned."

RESTINAL PAUSED OUTSIDE the open door.

"Come in, Werlin. Come on in."

Restinal didn't recognize the voice, but it was apparent from the cheerful tone of the invitation that the speaker recognized him.

He shrugged, took a tighter grip on his datacase, and went in.

The room was paneled in lorkin wood. The desk and chairs were all carved from it as well. Restinal noted that the furniture all matched, each piece done in the spare style termed Ecolog.

Behind the desk, which was really a wide table with a single drawer, sat a silver-haired man, laugh lines radiating from the bright green eyes. Restinal mentally compared the face against the ones shown him by Delward before he'd left Harmony. He struggled momentarily before realizing that the man was the Prime Ecolitan himself, Gairloch Pittsway. For some reason, Restinal hadn't expected to be met by the Prime himself, much less in an empty office without aides.

"You wonder about the absence of subordinates?"

"Exactly," responded the Delegate Minister for Interstellar Commerce.

"You shouldn't, not if you've followed the precepts of the Institute. Unnecessary subordinates are a sign of weakness. Our fault that most no longer know the precepts, no doubt, since the Iron Rules are no longer popular in the schools' curricula."

Restinal didn't have the faintest idea what the Prime was talking about. He kept his face blank.

"I realize you don't understand what I'm jabbering on about, Werlin, but don't worry about it. If you don't understand it instinctively, it would take more time than either of us has for me to explain what I mean. Power is the question now.

"Neither the Orthodoxists nor the Normists have the power to force their choice for Trade Envoy to New Augusta upon the other. The Supreme Justiciary passed the choice back to the House, ruling that the selection has to be made by the political arm of the government. You're stuck. And you don't like the Institute all that much, since we are the sole remaining traditional structure still respected by the masses you professional politicians cultivate so assiduously. Both you and the Orthodoxists would like to reduce the influence of the Institute more than the passage of time and the ravages of peace have already done.

"Forcing a choice upon the Institute, with the attendant publicity, solves all your problems. Neither party has to take responsibility for the choice. If our selection succeeds, then you will take credit, and if he fails, we take the blame."

"That is conjecture, respected Prime," responded Restinal.

"Gairloch or Prime. None of that 'respected' hypocrisy, please." The Ecolitan smiled, the open smile of a man at peace with himself or as if at a child's joke, before he went on. "The Institute attempts to minimize dealing with speculations or conjectures. I doubt that my analysis is anything but factual. I respect, however, the position in which you have been placed by the operation of the political machinery."

The Prime Ecolitan stood and walked from behind the table toward the still-standing Restinal.

"Please sit down. I forget that politicians all too often stand on ceremony."

Restinal's knees felt rubbery, and he eased himself into one of the carved high-backed chairs. Although the chair was not upholstered, the flowing curves of the wood seemed to welcome him.

The Prime poured a cup of water from a crystal pitcher and placed it on the table next to Restinal before he returned to his chair behind the desk.

Restinal picked up his case, placed it on his lap, opened it, and pulled out the carefully drawn list the Elders Quaestor and Torine had hammered out in the short hours before he had been dispatched.

"Keep the list. The names on it are predictable. They begin with Tormel, Reerden, and Silven."

Restinal kept his mouth shut. The list began with Tormel, Reerden, and Silven. But there were only two copies of the list—the one he had and the one Torine had kept. He, Restinal, had handwritten both.

"I can see you haven't had that much contact with the Institute, Werlin, and I'm afraid that will make your acceptance of your role that much more difficult.

"In answer to your unspoken question, none of us has seen the list, but we do know the personalities of the individuals who made the choices and the parameters for selection. I'll admit, in candor, that I would be hard-pressed to name the next person in order on the list, although we could probably pick eight out of ten."

Restinal allowed his features to express mild interest. "Perhaps you have already made a choice, then?"

"As a matter of fact, I have. But the name is not one on your list."

The Minister for Interstellar Commerce suddenly felt sticky in his formal blacks, as if he had been placed squarely in the Parundan Peninsula rain forests.

"If you would explain—"

"Werlin, the Institute is not obligated to explain anything, but since you are intelligent and informed, I will put it in simple terms. The same reason why the House of Delegates cannot select any Envoy is why anyone chosen from that list will not succeed."

"I fail to see that. Most governments select their Envoys." Restinal was beginning to see why Elder Torine had delegated the job to him and why few of the older Delegates cared much for the Institute.

"Most Envoys fail. We do not care to be associated with failure. The question is not political. The question is power. Politics is a system of using nonovert force to work out an agreeable compromise that does not lead to violence. The more equal the base of power, the more political the means of agreement can be."

Restinal was lost, and he knew his face showed it.

The Prime shook his head.

"Let me attempt to explain by analogy. When two torkrams contest for superiority, do they fight for blood? Of course not. They fight until one loses his footing. In fact, the amount of violence is minimal. If a prairie wolf should wander into the hills, however, the torkram becomes a merciless attacker. The first is an example of near equality of force, as well as an example of similar social behavior which allows what might be called a negotiated settlement. The second is a struggle for survival.

"You and the other Delegates are assuming that in negotiating with the Empire the basis of force is equal and the social behaviors behind the political structures are alike. Both are questionable assumptions."

"Are they really?" questioned Restinal. What did torkrams have to do with the picking of Envoys anyway?

"As a consequence," continued the Prime, "we have picked our own nominee."

Restinal repressed a whistle. Elder Torine didn't like being crossed, and neither did Elder Quaestor, and the Prime was blithely crossing them both.

"Do you honestly think the Delegates will agree?"

"Yes. They have no choice. They don't want to take the blame if things go wrong. Elder Torine knows that. Did you ever ask yourself why you were chosen to present the list and bring back our reply?"

Restinal had wondered but had dismissed it in the face of Torine's encouragement and insistence. He nodded at the Ecolitan.

"We are not unaware of the impact this could have on your career, Werlin," continued the Prime. "But you should be able to surmount any difficulties. If not, it is doubtful your career would have lasted much longer."

Delegate Minister Werlin Restinal was getting the picture, and though the outlines were blurry, he didn't like the view. The Delegate Minister for Interstellar Commerce was about to become Elder Torine's scapegoat unless he could turn the announcement to his own advantage.

"Who is your choice?"

"Nathaniel Firstborne Whaler."

The name meant nothing to Restinal.

The Prime lifted a thin folder from his desk and slid it across the flat surface to where the Delegate could reach it.

Restinal opened it and scanned the background on Whaler.

Nathaniel Firstborne Whaler—senior fellow of the Ecolitan Institute; 38 A.T.U.; 191 centimeters; fluent in the eight leading tongues of the Empire, plus Fuardian and ancient English; Class B scout pilot; combat master; Class C energy tech; noted economist and recognized authority on infrastructure economics.

His single previous tour with the government had been as the Ecolitan Special Assistant to a previous Minister of Commerce.

Restinal was impressed, in spite of his skepticism.

"Are you sure he's the best choice?"

"Do you have anyone who can match half his qualifications?"

Restinal repressed a sigh. There it was, in green and black. Take Whaler or go without the blessing of the Institute . . . and anyone to blame things on if the talks fell through.

VI

THE TALL WOMAN was the Special Assistant. Although the meeting was in her office, she waited for the Admiral.

"The Admiral, Ms. Ku-Smythe."

The Special Assistant acknowledged the faxscreen with a curt nod and stood to await her visitor.

"You look very professional, Marcella."

"Thank you." She gestured to one of the two chairs in front of her desk.

The Admiral sat, erect with the military bearing that could only have come from years of training.

"Have you reconsidered your position on the Coordinate issue?" The Admiral's gray hair glinted in the indirect light. Although, as Defense chief, the space officer could have obtained the best of rejuve treatments, the gray added yet another touch of authority.

"Commerce will support the Emperor. That has always been our position."

"I know that. You know that. What other official position could you have? Why all the reservations?"

Marcella shifted her weight before answering, then coughed softly to clear her throat.

"Sooner or later, you'll push Accord to the point where the Institute will gain control of the situation. That point is closer than anyone on your staff is willing to admit. It's almost as if they're pushing you toward military action. On the other hand, we've worked to make trade the tool for expansion. Without the right kind of legal background and the impression that Imperial commerce is jeopardized, you're taking the unnecessary risk of pushing the independent out-systems to support Accord.

"And that's totally unnecessary. None of them really like the Coordinate. You want to act before we can neutralize Accord, and right now Halston and the Fuards, at the very least, will regard your plans as a danger to all the out-systems—"

"Since we're being candid," interrupted the Admiral, "aren't they?"

"Why broadcast it? If we can get Accord to agree to a trade agreement with Commerce, that becomes a legal document admitting greater Imperial sovereignty—the very sort of legal sham that the out-systems will buy." The Special Assistant frowned, pursed her lips, and waited for the Defense chief to reply.

"Why did you support our action on Haversol?"

"Because we had a previous trade agreement and because Haversol was stalling on renegotiating to avoid complying with the terms. That provided the justification the Emperor needed."

"What's the difference for Accord?"

"You know the difference very well. We don't have a trade agreement with Accord, and, currently, we recognize the Coordinate's full independence. Unlike Haversol, they've the means to fight, possibly to cost you a great deal more than you expect."

"With what? Three small fleets that don't total the Fourth Fleet?"

"Remember how we lost the Rift in the first place?"

"That was nearly four hundred years ago."

"After four hundred years, we still haven't repaired the damage to Terra, and we still don't have all those systems back. You have ten major fleets and are building another. With all those ships, we only get systems back through the combination of trade and force. And here you are, trying sheer force again. It hasn't worked before, and it won't work now."

"Marcella, we've discussed this before."

"You asked—"

"I know. I know. I asked. You still feel that the urgency of the situation is not great enough?"

"Not nearly great enough."

The silence grew as both looked away from each other.

"Well . . ." began the Admiral. "I do value your opinion."

"I understand." The Special Assistant's voice lowered, softened. "Enough so you make your staff wait outside. You've always listened, ever since . . ." She paused, then continued, "but you do your job the way you see it, and you're usually right. Not always, but usually. And we'll support you, whatever you decide."

"I know. I wish I had your personal support as well." The Admiral stood and turned to leave, then half faced the woman again. "Take care, Marcella."

"Thank you."

The Special Assistant looked across the wide and empty office at the closed portal for a long time before returning to her console, where the panels flashed, each light clamoring for her attention.

VII

BEST SIMULATION RESULTS indicate forty percent probability of successful trade negotiations; twenty percent probability of failure; ten percent probability of direct armed conflict; thirty percent unquantifiable." Despite the pleasant sound of the terminal, the evenness of the word spacing rendered the report mechanical.

The Director turned to the three people at the conference table. "Forty percent chance that the situation can be resolved without war. If we can come up with these figures, so can the Admiral's staff. What's the chance of success if the present Envoy is removed?"

"Personality profile not a major component of success probability. Personality profile is a major component of unquantifiable component."

The Director frowned.

"What that means," offered the dark-haired woman across the table from the Director, "is that the personality of the Accord Envoy will shift the unquantifiable component into other areas. The current success probability is based on the structural situation. In short, we could still get a peaceful solution, though that could change at any time."

"What would happen if Defense could assassinate the Envoy?"

"Probability of war rises to fifty-five percent," answered the computer. "Probability of Imperial victory twenty-four percent. Probability of significant loss to Empire approaches unity; probability of destruction of Accord approaches unity."

"Any other significant probabilities?"

"Probability of loss of Rift and Sammaran Sector approach unity; probability of survival of Ecolitan Institute approaches unity."

The Director leaned back in her swivel.

"So . . . if Defense is allowed to force the issue, we're all likely to get blackholed."

The man in the group cleared his throat.

"That assumes one thing . . . that Defense can successfully operate a covert assassination. How likely is that if we oppose it, and if External Affairs is opposed, and if their Envoy is warned?"

The Director tapped the table to still the quick rustles.

"You forget that we cannot officially oppose Defense. Nor could we directly ever feed that kind of information to an Envoy from Accord. That sort of behavior would have even the Senate slapping riders onto our authorization, and we've avoided that for too long to go back to that sort of interference again."

"Could I have an answer to the probability questions?"

"Yes. Let's have the readout on those," the Director agreed.

"Probability of successful assassination not quantifiable under first order assumptions. Under second order, probability twenty percent, with a standard deviation of not more than twenty percent."

The Director smiled.

"All right," she said. "You've got the verification that to warn their Envoy will alter the probabilities along the lines we think would be desirable. How can you warn him, clearly, and yet in a way that will convey the absolute seriousness of the situation?"

"That's simple. We try to assassinate him first."

VIII

NATHANIEL WHALER TOOK another full step in front of the Imperial Marines to survey the entrance to his Legation.

The New Augusta tower corridor was nearly as wide as the average street back on Harmony but without the more elaborate facades that graced the capital of Accord. On New Augusta, each address within the towers or tunnels merely seemed to have a standard portal. The portal to the Accord Legation, aside from its green color and gold letters proclaiming the LEGATION OF ACCORD, differed little from the others he had passed.

As high as he was in the Diplomatic Tower, there was considerable foot traffic, along with numerous automated delivery carts.

Nathaniel half turned toward the bystanders who watched his honor guard with a mixture of boredom and indifferent curiosity. As he did, the sight of an all-too-familiar object coming to bear on him sent him into a diving roll behind the still-standing guards.

Scritttt!

The splinter gun fragments shattered across the portal facing and skittered along the corridor.

"Spread and search!" snapped the Marine Lieutenant.

"He's gone already," observed Nathaniel, dusting himself off.

The Marine officer ignored the Ecolitan's observation and sprinted down the corridor. Two ratings closed up next to Nathaniel, each scanning the corridor in a different direction.

"Sir? Don't you think you should get under cover?"

"Little late for that."

Most of the bystanders had scuttled out of the path of the onrushing Marines or had found they had business elsewhere.

Nathaniel scanned the faces that remained. Two of the handful still in the corridor struck him as possibilities, and he committed their faces to memory before turning his full attention to the narrow scratch on the portal.

"Hmmm . . ." he murmured. The splinter had barely scratched the permaplast. He checked the corridor floor and tiles for nearly twenty meters but could find no trace of the splinter fragments he had heard.

What with the apparent attack and all the Imperial Marines, the Ecolitan felt more like he had been leading an expedition through Accord's southern forests than arriving in New Augusta.

Finally, he touched the Legation entry plate, and the door slid open. The two Marines marched in and stationed themselves in front of the entry desk. Nathaniel followed.

The decor of the receiving area that was supposed to represent the decor and ambience of Harmony didn't. The gargoyled lorkin wood hanging lamps were Secession Renaissance. The woven wheat grass entry mat was Early Settler. The inlaid blackash tea table was pre-Secession, and the likes of the long maroon and overupholstered couch had never been seen in Harmony or even in the depths of the Parundan Peninsula.

As Nathaniel refrained from staring at the mismatched furniture, three more Marines quick-stepped in with his field pack and datacases, deposited them next to the entry desk, and marched away to reform outside the Legation.

The Lieutenant stepped up and gave the Envoy a stiff salute.

"Further instructions, sir?"

"Dismissed," Nathaniel responded in Panglais.

"Yes, sir. Thanks to you, Lord Whaler, sir."

As the door noiselessly closed, the Ecolitan turned his attention to the woman at the desk. She wasn't from Accord, and his change of attention caught her intently studying him.

That was to be expected. The Empire supplied, without charge, space in the Diplomatic Tower and paid up to twenty assistants or technical specialists for each Legation. A planetary government, hegemony, federation, or what-have-you could send as many or as few nationals as it desired for Legation staff, and use any or none of those paid by the Empire.

The catch was the cost. If the Legation were located in the Diplomatic Tower, the Empire paid for the space, the power, and the Empire-supplied staff. If any out-system government chose to put its Legation elsewhere in New Augusta, then the Empire paid none of the costs. While the richer or more militaristic systems, such as Olympia or the Fuardian Conglomerate, had separate Legations staffed strictly by their own nationals, most non-Imperial governments availed themselves of at least the space in the Diplomatic Towers.

The House of Delegates of Accord, not known for its extravagance, had accepted quarters in the Diplomatic Tower and had sent only three people to New Augusta: the Legate, the Deputy Legate, and an Information Specialist.

Just prior to his arrival at the circumlunar station, the copilot of the *Muir* had handed Nathaniel a stellarfax.

WITHERSPOON EN ROUTE ACCORD FOR CONSULTATIONS. WHALER CONFIRMED ACTING LEGATE DURATION, SGN. RESTINAL, DM, IC.

The rest had been confirmation codes.

So now he was standing in the entry of a Legation he was in charge of, looking at a clerk/staffer/receptionist who had never seen him but who worked for him, theoretically, but who was paid by the Empire. And just before that, the message had been delivered by splinter gun that someone wanted him dead.

Hardly the most encouraging beginning.

Nathaniel drew out his credentials folder and presented it to the young woman.

She took it, with a hint of a smile, studied it briefly, then greeted him more officially with a gesture that was nearly a half bow, half curtsy.

"At your service, Lord Whaler." Her greeting was in the old American of Accord, but with an accent and a stiffness that demonstrated practice, but not fluency.

"And I at yours, in the service of the Forest Lord and the Balance of Time," he returned in the archaic format that was no longer used, even in the deepest forests of Accord. While he spoke, he studied the woman's face. She did not understand.

"I don't speak Old American as well as I should," she admitted in Panglais, the standard tongue of the Empire. With her long red hair, freckles, and boyish figure, she might have reached his shoulder.

"I understand. You are called?" asked Whaler in the accented Panglais he had decided to use.

"Heather Tew-Hawkes, Lord Whaler. Would you like to see your quarters?"

"Shortly."

He took another look around the entry hall. Small and crowded with the three hanging lamps, the long couch, an imitation strafe chair, the tea table with the faxmags on the lower shelf, and the entry desk itself before the closed interior portals which presumably opened onto the rest of the Legation.

"The rest of the staff I would like to encounter," he announced.

"Yes, sir. You know that Legate Witherspoon has returned to Harmony. The Deputy Legate, Mr. Marlaan, had already taken leave. And Mr. Weintre is out for the day."

Forest Lord! What was going on? All the natives from Accord were fleeing like troks at his arrival.

"I see. The rest here will I see . . . and my office . . . before I go to my quarters. Can you arrange for my . . . my . . ." Apparently struggling with the Panglais word, he pointed to the field packs.

"Yes, sir. We can take care of them."

Heather gave him a questioning glance before speaking again, tossed her flowing red hair back over her shoulder with a flick of her head.

"Will you be having any assistants coming from Accord?"

Odd question right off the bat, reflected the Ecolitan.

"Final arrangements will I announce shortly," he temporized.

Heather handed him a small folder.

"You might want to look through that first, Lord Whaler."

The file was scripted in the Old American of Accord and outlined the names and functions of the staff. At the end was a map of the Legation spaces.

He glanced through it quickly, storing the information for full recall later.

"Read this later, I will. You may begin."

Heather touched a stud on the console at her desk, and one of the doors behind her opened.

Nathaniel stepped through after memorizing the location of the panel stud that actuated the entry.

The Accord Legation occupied half the three hundredth level of the Diplomatic Tower.

Heather led the way through the spaces.

The tower was divided into four wings joined by the central lift/drop shafts. The official working spaces of the Legation were in the west wing of the tower. Nathaniel's office and the trade talks section had been placed at the right, almost into the north wing of the tower. A spacious private suite adjoined his office, and both were on the outer edge of the tower, with floor to ceiling windows overlooking the hills to the west.

In turn, the trade talks staff suite adjoined his office. His private quarters could be entered from his office or through a separate door, since the private apartment was actually in the north wing.

Because the tower was actually a square, the north, east, south and west designations really indicated onto which public corridor an office or private quarters opened. All the Accord natives from the Legation had their quarters on the three hundredth level, but the local staff lived elsewhere. Wherever they could or wherever they wanted? Which? wondered the Ecolitan without asking.

"This is the travel/visa/quarantine/health section," stated Heather without taking a breath.

A man and a woman, obviously high-paid professionals, looked up from their consoles.

"Harla, Derek, this is Lord Whaler, the Trade Envoy and Acting Legate in the absence of Legate Witherspoon. Lord Whaler, Harla Car-Hyten and Derek Per-Olav."

"Pleased am I to meet you," announced Nathaniel in Panglais.

"And I you," the two chimed in ragged unison.

"How long for Accord have you worked?"

"Three standard years."

"Just over a year."

"Why for a foreign Legation do you work?"

"The Empire itself has a limit to the number of, if you will, travel generalist professionals that it can use," answered the woman, Harla Car-Hyten, "and takes only the most experienced. Working for Accord provides a solid foundation. We have to work somewhere."

"Accord is far enough out on the Rift," added Derek, "that we get to learn more than with an inner system."

And, thought Nathaniel, with the small number of tourists and the restrictive policies of the Delegates and of the Empire itself, the work couldn't be all that demanding.

"I thank you," he finished politely as he turned to continue the tour of the official spaces.

"Lord Whaler, Ms. Da-Vios."

Mydra Da-Vios was the Empire-supplied and paid "office manager" who had been Witherspoon's personal clerk and who would supervise the staff of his trade talks section, according to the briefing file which had been dictated by Witherspoon himself before he had left. That was the same folder Heather had handed Nathaniel right after he'd arrived.

Mydra looked up at him from her console openly but did not attempt to stand. Brown eyes so dark they verged on black, short dark brown hair, and a plain brown tunic piped with yellow, cloaked her with an air of competence.

"Any questions you might have?" he asked.

While his question was partly a pleasantry, her answer might give him a lead. So far everyone was acting as if he were to be humored, not that he'd done much to discourage the impression.

"Mr. Marlaan did not convey how the talks would be structured or staffed. While I have detailed another assistant, I do not know if this is the proper arrangement nor with whom I should coordinate further."

Nathaniel kept his mouth shut, while nodding gently.

Heather's question about staff made sense, too much sense. So did Marlaan's position as Deputy Legate. The briefing officer at the Institute had concluded that Marlaan's psy-profile wasn't suited to being a mere executive officer type. Yet Marlaan had stayed in New Augusta through a second tour, against all odds.

Mydra was asking politely who was going to do the real work, implying that it couldn't be Nathaniel.

"Lord Whaler?" prompted Mydra.

"The current arrangement is proper." He smiled again.

"Would you like to see your office and quarters, Lord Whaler?" interrupted Heather softly.

"That would be pleasing."

The corner office was bigger than he had expected from the plans in the folder Witherspoon had left, with a large reclining desk swivel surrounded by an impressive communications console. The recliner easily could have swallowed a man twice Nathaniel's size.

On the inside wall of the office, away from the panoramic window, was a conference table flanked with upholstered chairs. The far interior corner contained cabinets and counters, including a fully equipped autobar.

The casements to the portals, one to the office, the other to the private quarters, were the heavy-duty type, indicating that the doors were likely to have endurasteel cores under the wood veneer.

Interesting, thought Nathaniel. Is that to keep someone out or me in?

Heather pointed to the far door.

"That's to your private quarters. The locks will key to your palm print, if you'll just touch each of them right now."

Heather gave him a quick tour and explanation of the near-palatial quarters—separate private den/library with comm console, bedroom complete with oversized bed and sheensilk sheets, a guest room, a compact kitchen, two complete hygleniariums, a dining room with space for eight at table, and a living room centered on a full wall window overlooking the lower towers of New Augusta.

"If you need anything, Lord Whaler, just let me or Mydra know. If I'm not on desk duty, whoever is will take care of you. If you want to eat here, just order up dinner from main service. The number is in the folder, but tower information can also provide it. If you feel more adventurous, you might try the Diplomat's Club in the dining area. It's reserved for Legates, Ambassadors, and Envoys."

Nathaniel nodded.

"Tomorrow's the last day of the week, and some of the staff had already arranged leave, since you weren't expected until next week. But I'll be in early if you need anything."

"Too kind you are, but if I question, I will call."

Heather left through his private office.

Really make you feel like some kind of idiot, don't they? Are all Empire women like that?

He wandered through the rooms, apparently just taking it all in, looking at this and that, occasionally picking up an old-fashioned book, a miniature fire-fountain, touching a cushion, his fingers straying to his old style wide belt from time to time.

The multitector in the belt registered four snoops, but from the energy level and the pattern, all but one were audio. The one in the living room was video as well.

Probably more sophisticated equipment on the way, not ready because I arrived early, he mused. Or snoops good enough that I can't detect them.

Nathaniel put the datacases in the study, lugged the field pack into the bedroom and began to unpack. Some of the diplomatic blacks he'd never even worn, except when they'd been fitted at the Institute. Several of the outfits were special, but not in any way an Imperial would suspect from either a visual inspection or an energy scan.

In theory, all he had to do was present some terms of trade, bargain a bit, and see what developed, while staying alive and in one piece. That was theory. Practice usually required a great deal more effort.

IX

THE SCREEN BUZZED twice.

"Corwin-Smathers," answered the Staff Director, as she tapped the acceptance.

The faxscreen remained blank, but the green signal panel lit. The dull gray of the screen indicated either a blank screen call or the caller's inoperative screen.

"You alone?" The mechanical tone signalled that the caller was using a voice screen.

"Yes."

"The Senator should take an interest in the Accord affair. External Affairs is outgunned, by those who control the guns especially."

"The Accord affair?"

Too late, the director realized that the connection had already been broken.

Why Accord? Why a blind call?

Virtually anyone could make such a vidfax call. More interesting was the fact that it had come in on her private line, unlisted and unregistered either in the official listings or the office's confidential listings.

The I.I.S.? Or could it be a double blind, with someone trying to set up the Senator? Or discredit Courtney herself?

She frowned, then tapped a call panel.

The portal at the far end of the office irised open and shut behind the woman who entered. "Yes, Courtney?"

"Would you please dig up anything that's pending with regard to Accord, probably something to do with Commerce or Defense, I would guess."

"The Senator's off on another crusade?"

"No . . . trying to figure out whether he should be."

The dark-haired woman turned to go.

"Sylvia," added the director, "you might ask some of your former colleagues if they've heard anything. Nothing classified, you understand, just rumors, odd information."

"I'll do that. How soon?"

"Yesterday, if you can."

The portal closed behind the staffer, and Courtney Corwin-Smathers leaned back in the swivel, ignoring the softly blinking lights on the console that had automatically prioritized the pending messages.

She wondered who Sylvia really worked for. Certainly it wasn't just for the Senator, for all the salary she drew. Still for the I.I.S.? Halston. The old devil Admiral?

She tapped her fingers on the genuine gorhide antique blotter.

Should she key in Du-Plessis?

Shaking her head in response to her own question, she touched the top console stud to call up the messages awaiting her.

STANDING IN FRONT of the hygienarium mirror, Nathaniel straightened the collars of his formal dress blacks. The uniform displayed no ornamentation. Buttons, belt, and boots were all black. The square belt buckle bore a green triangle, and his formal gloves were a paler shade of green.

He half wished that he had some sort of insignia to put on his collars, as so many of the military and diplomatic personnel from other systems seemed to have.

The irony of it struck him even as he thought of it, and he grinned at himself in the mirror. Not in New Augusta an eight-day and wanting some tinsel to dress himself up.

With a last look at his wide-angle, full-length reflection, he turned and waved off the lights.

Once out of his private quarters and into his office, he palm-locked the quarters' portal, then walked across the dark green carpet to the console. The message light was unlit.

Outside, through the window, he could see dark and swirling clouds, scarcely much above him, and some of the towers' tops were lost in the mist. Hoping that the rain wasn't an omen of the day to come, he marched through the portal into the staff office.

"Good morning, Lord Whaler." Mydra greeted him as the portal whispered open.

"A good day also to you," he replied, trying to remember to keep his syntax suitably tangled.

"The honor guard should be here shortly."

"An honor guard for me? Unbelievable that seems, for a poor fumbler of figures such as me."

"A matter of protocol."

"I know, but for a professor unbelievable it seems."

At the far side of the office sat Hillary West-Coven before her console, industriously plugging figures in. Nathaniel hadn't figured out what she did, unless it was some sort of backup for Mydra.

Waiting in the silence that had followed his last remarks, Nathaniel looked over the staff office again. Three consoles: one which was vacant, one for Mydra, and the last for Hillary. All the consoles were pale green, which toned in with the institutional tan fabric covering the walls and with the deeper green of the carpet. The office retained a faint scent of pine, or a similar conifer, though no greenery was in sight.

No pictures hung on the walls, unlike the other staff offices in the Legation.

He shifted his weight, looked down at Mydra, and asked, "What did you before I arrived on New Augusta?"

"I'm in charge of Legate Witherspoon's office normally, but we didn't see any sense in doubling up on personnel, since he will be absent for some time, or so I was told"—she paused—"and since you will be assuming some of his duties."

Nathaniel nodded, his eyes lifting as Heather stepped through the portal from the corridor leading back to the receiving room.

"Mydra . . . oh, Lord Whaler." With a flip of her long red hair back over her shoulder, she finished, "Your escort has arrived."

"Thank you."

Nathaniel swung the genuine black gorhide folder containing his official credentials under his arm and marched across the staff office to follow Heather, bunching the pale green gloves in his left hand to give the impression he was clutching them tightly.

He reached the reception area right behind Heather.

"Tenhutt!" snapped the squad leader. Four Imperial Marines in their formal red tunics and gold trousers stiffened even straighter.

"Lord Whaler, sir?" questioned the leader, who couldn't have been as old as most of the first year Ecolitans Nathaniel had been training less than two standard months earlier.

"The very same I am."

"Yes, sir. Would you please, sir, please allow us to escort you to your audience with the Emperor?"

"Honored I would be."

From that, Nathaniel decided he was the one to lead the parade and marched out.

The Imperial Marines, caught by his sudden departure, slipped into quick-step and fell in behind him before he was ten meters down the corridor to the drop shaft.

Not too bad, he decided. But he wondered how they would have held up in the outback of Trezenia.

Nathaniel marched right into the high speed drop lane without hesitation. The four Marines angled themselves into a hollow square above him, allowing each to cover a quarter of the shaft.

They carried stunners, and each wore a belt commpak.

Two electrocougars waited in the private concourse. The first was crimson and displayed the Accord flag on a staff over the left front wheel panel. The second car was, surprisingly, a dull brown.

One of the escorts held the rear door of the crimson vehicle open for the Ecolitan. After seeing him seated and closing the door, the Marine eased into the front seat across from the driver, a woman Marine. Belatedly, on noting the driver, Nathaniel realized that at least one of his escorts had been female.

The squad leader and the other two escorts used the brown car to follow his into the tunnel.

"How often this do you do?"

"About eighty systems with Legations here, I'm told," answered the nondriving Marine. "I'm new, three weeks here. This is my second assignment for escort duty. Some of the other teams have had five or six in the past month."

"Just for diplomats seeing the Emperor?"

"No, sir. All sorts of functions—parties, reviews. You name it, and we're on call."

The driver glanced at the escort Marine. The young man stopped talking.

"Many functions and reviews there are then?"

"I really don't know about that, sir."

"What after this duty will you do?"

"That's up to the assignment branch, sir."

"No desire for other duty have you?"

"Whatever the Service needs, sir, that's where I'll be."

Nathaniel leaned back into the cushions. Information wasn't likely to be any more forthcoming.

He recalled the map he'd called up on his console. The Imperial Court had been placed on the high plain east of the main part of the underground city and towers, while the Port of Entry was to the south.

Had he been the Emperor who'd set it up, Nathaniel would have put the court and palace in the hills to the west.

As the tunnel car swept up from the depths into the concourse of the Imperial Palace, Nathaniel leaned forward to get a better look.

Fully fifteen different tunnels merged into the entry area, though he could see only two other limousines.

When the electrocougar glided to a stop, the escort snapped out of the front seat and had the rear door open for Nathaniel instantly. The other three squad members were formed up and waiting before Nathaniel's black-booted foot touched the golden tiles.

A red-coated woman, a striking figure with black hair, black eyes, and a deeply tanned face, stood at the head of the ramp from the concourse.

"Lord Whaler?"

"The very same."

"I'm Cynda Ger-Lorthian, the Emperor's Receiving Auditor. Would you be so kind as to accompany me to the receiving and waiting room?"

"That is where the Emperor receives?"

"Oh, no. That's where you will wait until the Emperor is ready to receive you and where you will be briefed on how the presentation of your credentials will be conducted."

"Sounds like this is done most regularly," the Ecolitan observed as he fell in behind the Receiving Auditor.

"Really quite simple, but we do like to make sure there are no mis-understandings and that everything goes according to plan."

The receiving room, about the size of his office at the Legation, featured a semicircular table surrounded on one side by comfortable padded swivels. The table and chairs faced a blank wall.

"If you would sit there, Lord Whaler, we'll go through the procedures."

Nathaniel's fingers flicked to his belt. The chair was snooped to the hilt, with virtually every kind of gimmickry that could be crammed into it. He turned toward the chair beside the one he'd been offered. It was rigged the same way.

Nathaniel kept the smile from his face. One purpose of the room wasn't exactly to impart information. He eased himself into the larger chair.

Cynda Ger-Lorthian sat next to him and pulled a small panel from the drawer of the table. She pressed a stud.

The mist of a holoscreen appeared on the other side of the table.

"Here's the way the receiving hall looks from the portal."

Nathaniel watched the view, as if he were looking into the enormous room, a gold-tan carpet leading from his feet out toward the throne of the Emperor.

"This is the actual floor plan," continued the Receiving Auditor as the holo display changed. "You can see you have almost fifty meters to walk before you reach the bottom step of the throne.

"You're scheduled for a ten minute presentation. That's longer than average, which means that the Emperor will have something more than the formalities."

"When starts all this?"

"At the time the previous appointment is complete, I'll give you a signal. You walk in the portal and stand. After you are announced, the Emperor will recognize you, and you walk to the throne. Stop at the bottom and make some acknowledgment to the Emperor, a bow, head inclined, whatever is customary for you, which the Emperor will return. You climb to the fourth step, and the Emperor will come down to meet you."

"Here's the way it will look. He is addressed as 'Sovereign of Light.' "

The holo projection showed a still version of the Emperor greeting someone on the wide steps below the throne.

"Do you have any questions?" she finished up with the rush of someone who has repeated the same words time after time.

"When is the audience completed?"

"The words used to signify closure will be something like 'May you enjoy the peace of the Empire.' It is never quite the same. The Emperor enjoys minor deviations from the protocol."

Ger-Lorthian checked her timestrap and stood up.

Nathaniel followed her example, and the two of them were rejoined outside the briefing room by his escort of four Imperial Marines.

The portal to the receiving hall extended high enough to admit a full-sized combat skitter, and the closed, gold-plated portal was obviously backed with endurasteel. With the depth of the casements, Nathaniel doubted whether that Imperial combat skitter could have dented the surface of the portal.

"When the chime sounds, Lord Whaler, the portal will open. Please step through and wait."

A deep bell echoed from the top of the portal casement. The doors recessed into the massive casements without so much as a whisper.

Nathaniel stepped through and placed himself squarely in the middle of the ribbon of carpeting that ran toward the throne block.

Five portals studded the immense circular hall of equidistant intervals, and a similar carpet ran from each toward the circular stepped structure on which rested the Throne of Light.

In all probability, the throne rotated to face whatever portal the Emperor wished or protocol demanded.

Empires need Emperors, and the bigger the Empire, the more impressive the Emperor should be. As a practical matter, reflected the Trade Envoy for the Coordinate of Accord, Emperors only came in one size—human. At least, human emperors did. His Royal and Imperial Highness Jostan Lerann McDade N'troya, while white-haired and close to 196 centimeters, was only human.

The Emperor of the Terran Empire, the Hegemony of Light, the Path of Progress, compensated for his mere humanity by wearing an unadorned and brilliant white uniform that cloaked him in light, making him the focus of the receiving hall in which a full-sized Imperial corvette could have been hangared.

A crowd, gathered around and on the lower steps of the throne pedestal and large enough to comprise several subotta teams, was lost under the sweeping lightstone buttresses, and the height of the ceiling swallowed the pulsing beams emanating from the Throne of Light.

Nathaniel waited on the tan carpet, as he'd been briefed by the majordomo, Receiving Auditor, whatever she was called.

Several of the group gathered below the throne, a good stone's throw away, glanced at him and pointedly turned their heads.

The Imperial hangers-on all affected light-colored clothing. Only the Emperor wore out-and-out white, and no one wore a predominantly dark outfit.

Nathaniel wore Accord's diplomatic blacks. If he had worn the greens of the Ecolitan Institute, the effect and impact would have been the same. In the bright universe of the Imperial court, two colors were absent. Solid green and solid black—the colors of Accord, the colors associated with the Ecologic Secession.

"The Lord Nathaniel Firstborne Whaler, Trade Envoy from the Coordinate of Accord. Presenting his official credentials to His Imperial Highness, Provider of Prosperity and Sovereign of Light."

The announcement stilled the hall for less than an instant.

"We await your arrival." The Emperor's voice filled the hall, over-toned and benevolent.

Nathaniel marched up the tan carpet, which gradually lightened into gold as it neared the Throne of Light. The throne itself stood higher than he'd realized from the holo projection.

Stopping before the bottom step, the Ecolitan bowed once.

"Lord Whaler, the Empire is pleased at your presence."

Nathaniel climbed four steps. The Emperor stood and descended.

From the corner of his eye, the Ecolitan could see that the Empress, who had remained in her seat below and to the left of the Emperor's, was not in the slightest interested in Accord or in credentials. She continued her conversation with a blond man dressed in a peacock blue tunic belted in scarlet.

"Lord Whaler." The Emperor addressed the Envoy.

"Your Highness."

A minor murmur circled the crowd on the throne pedestal. Protocol required the more formal "Sovereign of Light."

But, thought Nathaniel, we provincials can't be expected to know everything about the delicacies of court etiquette.

Nathaniel handed him the credentials case.

"My credentials, my writ to the Empire. May we all live in peace and prosperity."

"On behalf of the Empire and its peoples, I accept your credentials and your wishes for peace and prosperity."

The smile the Emperor N'troya gave the Ecolitan was genuine

enough, and so were the tiredness and the thin lines radiating from the corners of his dark eyes.

"Was your trip pleasant, Lord Whaler?"

"To reaching New Augusta, I looked forward. Seeing your receiving hall, disappointed I am certainly not. Most impressive and suited to you."

The Sovereign of Light chuckled.

"I gather that's a compliment, Lord Whaler, and in our position as royalty, so shall we take it."

The royal chuckle effectively stilled conversation around the Emperor for several instants, except for the fragment of small talk which drifted upward.

". . . so devilish in that outfit, but what could you expect from Accord—"

The speaker, a lady in rust and yellow with a neckline which barely cleared her ample breasts, broke off in mid-sentence.

"Lord Whaler," continued the Emperor as if he had not heard the interruption, "your frankness is refreshing. What do you really think of the Empire? Honestly now?"

Nathaniel could sense the indrawn breath from those listening around the throne.

"Your Highness, large groups of systems organized must be. People accept the government they deserve, and many systems accept the Empire. Wise is the Empire to accept and govern wisely those who wish such governing. Wise too is the Empire which only extends its rule to those who wish it."

He bowed slightly to N'troya as he finished.

"Well chosen words, Lord Whaler. Well chosen."

"Your service, and looking forward to these talks on trade I am."

"So is the Empire. We trust you will fulfill our confidences." The Emperor straightened. "During your stay in New Augusta and thereafter may you enjoy the peace of the Empire."

The Emperor nodded dismissal.

Nathaniel bowed and waited.

The Emperor turned and climbed back to the Throne of Light.

At that, the Ecolitan marched back down the carpet toward the massive portal. Before exiting, he faced back to the throne and bowed again.

When the portal opened, he exited the receiving hall.

"Lord Whaler, your escort."

The same Receiving Auditor waited as the portals shut behind the

Envoy. The same four Marines swung in behind him as he walked back the way he had come.

"I didn't catch your conversation with the Emperor, Lord Whaler, but you must have a way with words. That's the first laugh I've heard during an audience in months."

"Truth only I spoke."

He didn't offer more, and Cynda didn't ask as the short procession made its way back to the Imperial concourse.

Once more the charade with the guards was repeated as he entered the crimson electrocougar. The car whisked him back into the depths and to the Diplomatic Tower.

Nathaniel sank into the red cushions.

Smoothly as things seemed to be going, he had the feeling that pieces to the puzzle were missing. Which pieces? That was the real question.

XI

A MUTED BROWN tunic, slashed with irregular gold stripes, and matching brown trousers—with a sigh, the Ecolitan pulled the outfit from the closet. The clothes were common enough not to draw attention, and his utility belt was compatible.

Once he had the outfit on, he checked himself in the hygienarium mirror. The looseness of the tunic gave him an informal appearance, almost touristlike.

He straightened the belt before heading for the private exit.

Probably Mydra or someone would wonder where the Envoy had gone for the afternoon, but a little mystery would brighten their lives, if they even bothered to check. Besides, he was bored. Bored with waiting for things to happen.

He laughed. "With one take-out aimed at you, you're bored."

All told, the trip from his quarters down the drop shaft to the tunnel train level took less than fifteen minutes. Best of all, no one had given him a second look.

Like virtually everything else he'd seen, the tunnel train level was immaculate, sparkling and shimmering in the indirect light.

All the same, he missed the outdoors, the scent of rain or dusty air, the openness of a horizon stretching into the sky.

The second train was the one he wanted, running south toward the shuttle port. The short train—only four cars—whispered into the concourse so silently it nearly caught him by surprise.

Each car contained twenty-four individual seats and twice that space for standing room. Roughly half the seats in his car were full.

Nathaniel sat opposite the rear portal, where he could observe the entire car without seeming to.

Two seats away, carrying a slim folder, sat a blond Imperial Sublieutenant with her eyes fixed on the panel at the end of the car.

She had not looked up when he had taken his seat, nor did she move a muscle until the second stop after Nathaniel had boarded. At the Ministry of Defense concourse, the Sublieutenant snapped out of her seat, walked past Nathaniel and through the portal before it was fully open.

Nathaniel stretched, ambled to his feet, and barely escaped the train before the door shut behind him. The train was whispering its way out of the concourse toward the shuttle port within instants of his departure.

Muted brown with scarlet trim struck the color scheme for the Ministry of Defense concourse.

Unlike the Diplomatic Tower, the Defense Tower had two lift/drop shafts, one guarded by a full squad of armed soldiers, the other apparently unguarded and open to the public.

Nathaniel watched as the Sublieutenant marched toward the guarded shaft, flashed something, and was waved through. Then the Ecolitan settled down on one of the scattered wall benches, one that had a view of the approaches to both sets of lift shafts, with a faxtab in hand, giving the impression of scanning it while waiting for someone.

Within minutes, he could sense the pattern.

Younger Imperial citizens drifted in and out, seemingly at random, and took the public lift shaft. For all their leisurely appearance, a certain tenseness underlay their casualness, showing in a quietness, a lack of chatter.

Scarcely a handful of individuals presented themselves to the brown-clad guards at the smaller lift/drop shaft, and of that scattering, Nathaniel saw only one other person in uniform, another woman. Two other civilians were quietly turned away.

After a quarter of a standard hour, one of the guards glanced over at Nathaniel, studied the Ecolitan, and returned his attention to the console.

Nathaniel did not react, but kept his nose in the faxtab, with an occasional look around for his "appointment" while he continued to track the comings and goings.

Another quarter hour passed. The guard who had first noted Nathaniel looked him over again, this time giving him an even closer scrutiny and keying something into the console.

Nathaniel went on recording the arrivals and departures into his belt storage.

A quarter hour later, almost to the second, the guard at the console looked up and toward Nathaniel. At the same instant, one of the patrols turned toward the console operator.

The Ecolitan dropped the faxtab and folded it. Unhurriedly, he rose, stretched, peered around, looked at his wrist, shook his head, and finally crumpled the faxtab in apparent disgust.

He stalked away toward the tunnel train stage.

It hadn't been necessary to stay quite so long, but he had been looking for a reaction.

Once in the train, decorated in pale golds and off whites and filled with the low murmur of music, he again took an end seat, this time to see if he could spot a tail. The train was half full, about as crowded as he'd seen any public transport in New Augusta, and he decided, since no one else had joined the small group waiting on the stage, that a tail was unlikely.

Back in the living room of his private quarters at the Legation, he first dialled some juice from the dispenser, then settled himself into the deep chair facing the window. He felt more at ease in the living room than in the expanse of the official office of the Envoy.

People assumed that you had to get inside a building to find out what was going on. Not always so. Sometimes a fairly good picture was painted just by who came and went.

Item: Very few military personnel arriving.
Item: Fewer still in uniform.
Item: Virtually all public access was by young Imperials—student age—and on a continuing basis, as if by appointment.
Item: Military access more tightly guarded than anything else seen in New Augusta.
Item: No discernible patterns in sex of either military personnel or students.

Item: Guards not only tracked loiterers, but maintained voice-
less communications with the central communications
point.

What conclusions could he draw?

Despite the low profile the military seemed to have assumed on New
Augusta, they possessed a great deal of real power.

Further, the "student" appointments implied one of two things:
either the military career was respected and desirable or it was required
of at least some of the population. The lack of uniforms also intrigued
the Ecolitan.

New Augusta, in spite of all the apparent freedom, was a tightly
controlled society.

How tightly remained to be seen.

XII

THE MAN IN black stepped into the drop shaft, angled his body out
into the high speed lane, and watched the levels peel away.

Mydra had told him what she thought of the idea.

"After someone shot at you . . . going out alone, unescorted, Lord
Whaler, is foolish. Very foolish."

Foolish perhaps, but a Marine escort with crimson uniforms would
have been like dropping a location flare.

On the way down, he smiled faintly as a Fuardian Military Attaché
tripped over his dangling sabre and pitched headfirst into the slow drop
traffic, almost colliding with a Matriarch from Halston.

Accord didn't have lift/drop shafts, or the towers with hundreds of
levels running from deep in the ground up into the lower cloud levels.
For the scattered communities of Accord, such towers would have been
an energy waste. Harmony was the only city of any size throughout the
Coordinate, and the capital had fewer people than any single one of the
New Augustan towers.

As the Ecolitan dropped toward the concourse level, he edged himself into the slower lanes, finally swinging off onto the orange permatile
of the exit stage.

He walked briskly toward the private side of the concourse where the official tunnel cars and diplomatic vehicles waited. His eyes never stopped their continuous scan. His ears listened for any untoward sound.

"Lord Whaler?" called a young driver.

"From whom?" he asked noncommittally, still scanning as he approached.

"Lord Rotoller at Commerce." She gestured toward the car and the seal on the open passenger door.

As he bent to enter the vehicle, he checked the energy levels but could find nothing overtly suspicious.

He settled himself into the overpadded seat as the electrocougar dipped noiselessly into the tunnel on its trip from the Diplomatic Tower to the Imperial Ministry of Commerce.

"How long have you worked for the Commerce Ministry?" he asked the driver.

"Two standard years, sir."

"Like it do you?"

"It's part of training. If you're a student at one of the professional or nonmilitary service schools, you're assigned a part-time job as well."

"What school for you?"

"Government Service Academy."

"A specialty you have, a favorite course of study?"

"Political theory's the most interesting. But I like economic history the best." The young woman half turned in the seat, without taking her eyes totally off the controls and guidelights. "Do you think the Ecologic Secession was based more on the imperatives of Outer Rift trade or on the political restraints imposed by the Empire?"

"An interesting question," temporized the Ecolitan. "The factors which to the Secession led as in so many conflicts were doubtless many. Some of them are lost, I would suspect, and today scholars and politicians focus on what they see as important, not on what those involved saw as important."

"That's what Professor Har-Ptolemkin says, that we project our own motives back onto history too much." The driver stopped talking, waiting for a response.

"Trade, the political reasons, the personal heritages, all factors have to be considered. No one sat down and said, 'For these reasons will we rebel.'

"No . . . doubtless said they something more like, 'We are tired of the Empire and want to be free.' And each had a somewhat different reason."

"Do you think they really knew that clearly what they wanted?"

"People say they know what they want, but often when they must choose, they choose not what they asked for."

The student driver did not continue the conversation, and the electrocougar began to slow and climb. After a sharp turn, the vehicle came to a halt. A man clad in a gold jumpsuit opened the door, and four others, wearing identical metallic uniforms, stood by the underground carved stone portal, ramrod straight in the artificial light.

At 191 centimeters, the Ecolitan didn't consider himself particularly tall, but he stood nearly a full head above the five gold-suited guards. Two were women, and all wore long knives in silver scabbards and silver-plated stunners in gilded holsters.

A man and a woman near his own height waited for Whaler inside the portal. Both were dressed in the maroon of the Imperial Commerce Ministry. The man stood in front of the woman and, abruptly, raised his left hand in the open-palmed symbol of greeting used on Accord, almost as if he were being coached.

Whaler returned the greeting.

"Alden Rotoller, at your service, Envoy Whaler. May I present my Special Assistant, Marcella Ku-Smythe?"

"At your service," Whaler returned stiffly in Panglais.

As he acknowledged the introduction with a slight bow and a direct look at Marcella, he was struck by the contrast between the two. Marcella was not beautiful, though her features were clear, clean, and attractive in a strong way, with a nose more aquiline than pert. Her eyes focused with an intensity common to few. Rotoller's face was essentially dead by comparison.

"Your staff?" inquired the Lord Rotoller.

"The full disposal of the Legation for the purposes of any negotiation has been accorded me."

"Of course," responded Rotoller. He turned and motioned toward the ornate private lift shaft.

The dimness of the shaft surprised Nathaniel as he followed the Terran Minister, since the public shafts in New Augusta were so brightly illuminated.

Beyond the white tiled exit stage was a stark, semicircular hallway decorated with a maroon and white tiled chessboard pattern. The walls were white, trimmed with thin maroon molding that shimmered.

Two guards, facing the lift exit, wore stunners in black functional throw holsters and tunics and trousers of solid maroon.

Off the hall were four portals, but only the one on the far left was open. As soon as Marcella Ku-Smythe stepped onto the exit stage tiles, Lord Rotoller turned and walked through the open doorway.

Nathaniel followed. So did Marcella and the guards.

Did they think he was an ogre left over from the Ecologic Secession?

The chamber they entered resembled a private club in Harmony far more than a meeting room for the Deputy Minister of Commerce. Three deep chairs, each with a side table, were drawn up around a light fire, itself contained within flux bricks in the middle of the room. Each side table contained a napkin, real cloth, and a mug holder.

Rotoller suddenly dropped into one of the chairs.

"Take your pick."

Nathaniel bumped into the one closest to him, trying to see if the furniture was either anchored or snooped. Neither seemed to be the case, and he eased himself into the maroon cushions.

The room was decorated in shades of cream and maroon, and the light fountain flared maroon intermittently.

"Would you care for something to drink? Some liftea, cafe, perhaps some Taxan brandy?"

"Liftea, it would be fine."

Rotoller tilted his head at Marcella.

"Cafe," she ordered.

One of the guards disappeared through another portal that had opened from a seemingly blank wall, to return a moment later with three beverages and three identical plates of pastries.

The guard, a woman with closely cropped brown hair, offered the pastry tray to Nathaniel first, letting him choose one of the three plates. She placed his liftea on the table, then served the Taxan brandy to the Deputy Minister before finishing up with Marcella.

Silence stretched out before Whaler realized that the other two were waiting for him.

He picked up the heavy mug and lifted it toward his host.

"For your hospitality and courtesy."

"And for your kindness in coming," the reply came automatically.

The Ecolitan took a small sip of the steaming tea and set the mug back in its holder.

"Such courtesy, for one such as I, most overwhelming is."

"No more than you deserve, particularly when it is you who do us the honor of coming so far."

"And on a small courier at that," added Marcella.

"How was your trip?"

"As expected." Actually, he had enjoyed it and the chance to compare the courier with similar class ships of the Institute. His enjoyment had been heightened by seeing the Imperial battlecruiser tagging along as an official escort.

"Long trip, I imagine," responded Rotoller. "Can't say I've been out to the Rift. In this job, you get tied to the faxwork, in the details, not that it all doesn't have to be done. Marcella does all the real in-depth work, though, and I don't know what I'd do without her."

The Lord smiled faintly at his assistant, who smiled faintly back.

"Lord Mersen will be pleased to know you have arrived safely and will take great interest in what you have to offer."

"Most kind, most kind," returned Nathaniel.

"Did you bring any staff with you?" Again, it was Marcella.

"Ah . . . the question of staff. Such a joy, and so helpful are they, and so determined. A thousand pardons to you, Lady. Would I not mean to offend, in any circumstances."

"No offense, Lord Whaler."

"But your question . . . no . . . answer it I did not. Staff, besides that of the Legation, as you meant, have I none at this moment."

Before the growing silence became totally oppressive, Rotoller jumped in.

"Guess something like New Augusta must be a new experience for you. Understand your government isn't fond of large bureaucracies or diplomatic establishments."

"Our government has not the numbers or the systems with which to deal as does the Empire. Our Envoys are not numerous but deal with more than diplomacy we do. Some other cities and systems have I seen, but none so large and impressive as your capital."

He inclined his head toward the light-haired Special Assistant. "And none with officials so enchanting."

Nathaniel took another sip of the liftea and began the last pastry, interposing nibbles with broad and idiotic smiles.

"Haven't spent the time we should have," continued Rotoller, "since matters between Accord and us have been going so smoothly recently. This trade imbalance thing sort of crept up on us, and I gather that's been the same sort of feeling in Harmony, from what our Legate's reported."

"True. One hesitates to rock a boat floating with a smooth tide, not when so many other disturbances evident are. The Delegates were not aware of the extent of the problem facing the Empire and so the request caught many unprepared. Trade can be the lifeblood of an outer system, and what is a small imbalance to the Empire reflects more heavily for us."

"Do you think some of the other systems are waiting to see what happens?"

"Trade affects us all, and Accord understands such effects, as do you and others in your Ministry. One thing does lead onward to another. That is known. Most important will be these talks to those affected."

The pattern continued.

"Can't tell you how pleased we are to have a chance to chat before the talks get underway . . ."

"Is your Legation here much different from the people back home, really?"

"Understand Accord hasn't changed too much lately . . ."

"Is the Ecolitan Institute an all-around university now?"

Nathaniel responded in kind.

"Pleased am I to have such opportunities . . ."

"People they are people, and much help can be anyone."

"The changes, they happen. Everywhere are changes, but on Accord we take the best of the old, we hope, and the best of the new . . ."

"Ah, the Institute . . . not exactly what you would call a university . . . nor even a training school . . . more an experience, a way of combining a look at the past and the knowledge of today."

The atmosphere changed ever so slightly, and while Nathaniel couldn't pinpoint it, the tête-á-tête was over.

"Regret we couldn't talk all day, Lord Whaler. You've given us a most fascinating insight, but there's far too much waiting for both me and Marcella at our consoles."

The guards stiffened as the two Commerce officials rose from their chairs.

Nathaniel followed.

"So kind have you been in your courtesy, and much too much of your time have I taken today."

"Our pleasure, Lord Whaler. Our pleasure."

While the guards were alert as the three drifted to the drop shaft, their hands poised near their stunners, the Ecolitan almost found himself shaking his head at the sight. If he'd really wanted to dispose of the pair, holding their hands near their weapons wouldn't have done them a bit of good.

"Hope to see you soon," finished off the Deputy Minister as Whaler climbed back into the electrocougar.

"And I you."

Ignoring the frescoes in the tunnel and the driver, an older woman who seemed to want to ignore him, Nathaniel leaned back in the cushions and tried to think.

Why had the two Commerce officials wanted to meet him?

He shook his head and waited until the limousine came to a stop in the private concourse. Rather than using the front entrance of the Legation, he took the back side exit from the lift shaft which led to his private quarters.

The corridor was nearly deserted. He passed a woman and two men on the way to his private door. The belt detector showed the snoops on the portal were still operational.

From the entry, he walked to the study where his datacase had been left. As he half expected, someone had been through the material, despite the privacy seals on the suite locks and on the datacase itself.

What surprised him most was that only a rudimentary effort had been made to replace the case and the material within in the same positions where he had left them.

On the one hand, great technical sophistication had been involved in analyzing the palm-print codes to open the doors and the datacase without destroying the locks or triggering any alarms. Yet the material had been replaced carelessly.

By angling his belt light at the smooth surfaces of the cases, he could tell that fingerprints remained, without any evidence that the intruders had attempted to wipe them off.

That confirmed the general identity of the intruders as government operatives of some sort or another.

He shrugged.

At the moment, there was little enough he could do.

XIII

NATHANIEL SET HIS mental alarms for 0700. The switch to Terran standards hadn't affected his own internal timing. He was awake at 0659.

Once in his office, he tapped several studs on the massive desk console. He hadn't figured out all the possible button combinations yet, but with the aid of the local directory he'd called up into the console memory, he was managing to make direct calls without having Mydra or someone else place them.

"Sergel, come on over, would you?"

"Envoy Whaler, with the other Accord staff gone, matters are somewhat involved . . ."

Nathaniel knew he was lying. The entire Legation staff was grossly underworked.

"I can understand that. This won't take long. I'll be expecting you in fifteen minutes."

Sergel Weintre arrived on time. Nathaniel couldn't miss the dampness on his forehead.

He pointed the younger Information Specialist at one of the deep chairs. Perching on the edge of the desk, the Ecolitan stared down at the man and began in the Old American of Accord.

"First, the situation stinks. I know it stinks. You know it stinks. Second, I don't have time to play games with you. Third, everything we say is being monitored by at least two different groups. Fourth, it doesn't matter. Is all that clear?"

Weintre screwed up his face into a puzzled look.

"No, Envoy Whaler. I'm afraid I don't understand."

Nathaniel ignored him.

"I realize the position you're in, but that's between you and them. I have several questions I expect you to answer."

Weintre shifted his weight, expression blank.

"Who stirred up the question of revision of Accord's trade terms with the Empire?"

"It was the Emperor's decision."

"As I recall, my official presentation of credentials to the Emperor was largely ceremonial. And somehow I doubt that the Emperor could be greatly concerned about the terms of trade with a small third-rate system, even a former colony."

The Ecolitan smiled pleasantly at Weintre.

"So . . . someone had to push. Who?"

"The order was signed by the Emperor."

Nathaniel repressed a sigh. He pulled a compucalendar from the console drawer.

"Weintre, I really don't have time for polite evasions. This is a lie detector, new and improved model. Now . . . why is the Imperial Ministry of Commerce—or is it the military crew—supplementing your already too-generous stipend?"

The Information Specialist swallowed, just once.

"This is totally out of hand, Whaler, totally. You think you can just walk in and threaten? You may have some authority, but you can't do that!"

Nathaniel let the all-wooden dart gun slide into his hand. The weapon would not register on any known detector.

"You know, Weintre, it's too bad you sold us out."

"You wouldn't . . ."

"I not only would, but will. . . . Have you ever studied the Articles of Ecological Warfare of Accord? They've never been suspended, you know. In matters of State, they may be called into force by any Legate or accredited representative of Accord outside the Coordinate . . . and executed by any Ecolitan. Not that they ever expected one to be both."

"I don't believe you."

Nathaniel cocked the dart thrower and fired in one fluid motion. The dart buried itself in the chair less than a centimeter from Sergel's left ear.

"The next one will be closer . . . a lot closer."

"The Empire—"

"Can't do a thing, except declare me persona non grata and deport me to stand trial in Harmony, where I'd be acquitted."

Sergel needed more of a push.

"Weintre, I'm truly sorry . . ."

"No! Reilly-Shiroka contacted me. Aide to Lord Mersen. Helmsworth wants to throw a slide-strip into the talks, hold them up to get better terms for the Empire."

It was the Ecolitan's turn to frown.

"You're making no sense at all, Sergel."

"Look . . . Corwin-Smathers, staff director for Helmsworth, is out to get Commerce. We're just a pawn to force Commerce to deal with Helmsworth's problems."

Nathaniel waved a halt to the flow of words.

"So why involve you? Why pay you off?"

"Helmsworth is supported by the Noram Micronics Association and Corwin-Smathers used to be liaison for External Affairs."

"Look, Weintre," snapped the Ecolitan, leveling the dart gun, "ignorant I may be, but not stupid. Not one word you have said makes any sense. Try again."

"Power struggle between Commerce and External Affairs, but Witherspoon didn't believe me. He's just here for ceremony. Marlaan told me to stay out, do nothing. I've just tried to stay out of trouble."

Nathaniel sighed deeply.

"You still haven't answered anything. Why have you sold out to the Defense crowd? Why do you keep avoiding the military aspects? Which Admiral bought you?"

Sergel looked down, twitched as his ear brushed against the dart.

"The Ministry of Defense . . . uh . . . obviously has some interest . . . and their . . . uh . . . pride . . . their defeat by the Ecologic Coalition . . ."

"Pride?"

"The Ministry of Defense has always felt the responsibility for the loss of Accord and the Outer Rift."

The Ecolitan shook his head. He didn't want to start with a corpse. Not when corpses only led in one direction. Sergel's death would only complicate matters. Besides, the Institute taught that murder out of frustration was clearly futile, and Sergel was definitely frustrating.

"All right, Sergel. You obviously haven't thought this out. I want a written report on the situation, including a listing of all the contacts you're so cleverly avoiding."

"I didn't realize—"

"You didn't think! I want that report in my office here by tomorrow, and it better have those details." He lifted the lethal dart gun.

"Yes, sir."

"Get!" snapped Nathaniel.

Weintre got.

The Ecolitan stood and turned to stare out the expanse of permaglass. What next?

Should he have Mydra try to reach Lord Rotoller? Or the Special Assistant?

He tapped the console plate. Mydra's face appeared.

"Would you get me Marcella Ku-Smythe? She's the Special Assistant to Lord Rotoller."

"I'll see if she's available, Lord Whaler."

Mydra's image disappeared, and the screen blanked.

From the depths of the swivel, Nathaniel tried to figure out why Mydra's mannerisms bothered him.

"*Cling!*" chimed the console.

Nathaniel tapped the acknowledgment.

"Lord Whaler, Ms. Ku-Smythe's staff indicates that she is unavailable."

"Fine. Get me the staffer who told you so."

"Lord Whaler?"

"The staff member who said thus. To that person would I speak."

Perhaps inverted syntax would make the point that a simple command hadn't.

Mydra tightened her lips before finally answering, "Yes, Lord Whaler."

The screen returned to its slate gray color.

"*Cling!*"

The Ecolitan tapped the plate. Another face appeared, that of a tanned and blond young man.

"Nathaniel Whaler, Trade Envoy for Accord, I am. For Ms. Ku-Smythe."

"Lord Whaler, I am so sorry. She is not available, but I know she will be so pleased that you called." The receptionist smiled engagingly, showing even white teeth that seemed to sparkle even through the screen.

"So sorry am I, also. For if she should think to talk trade, available she should be. I had wanted to talk with her first, but since available she is not, perhaps with the honorable Corwin-Smathers I will start."

"I do know she would like to talk with you. Maybe she could break free for just a moment. Please let me check."

The screen went blank for an instant before the image of the blond receptionist was replaced with the visage of Marcella Ku-Smythe.

"Marcella Ku-Smythe."

"Nathaniel Whaler."

"I'm rather flattered, Lord Whaler, that you would call personally. Flattered, and surprised that you would be so insistent."

"Are you alone at the moment?"

"Why, yes, but why do you ask?"

"Because, Ms. Ku-Smythe, I really don't have time for fencing, even if that is the normal mode of negotiating. Now, if you want that, fine; Lord Rotoller, Lord Mersen, and I can mumble polite phrases to everyone's heart's content, and I'll see what I can work out elsewhere."

He could see her stiffen, even on the console screen.

"Aren't you being a bit precipitous?"

"Presumptuous, perhaps, but not precipitous. The Empire is precipitous, which is why I'm presumptuous."

A trace of a smile flitted across the Special Assistant's face.

"This is the Empire, you know, and not exactly a back cluster planet."

"You're deliberately missing the point. I know and you know that the official posturing and positioning may take months. But I'm no smooth-talking diplomat. Nor is Accord a rich system. So it's to everyone's interest to get an early resolution."

He was already in too deeply too quickly, but he had to get things moving before Weintre's military friends sunflared the process.

"Let me think about it." She broke the connection.

For a moment, he stared at the blank screen, puzzled at the abruptness of the sign-off.

Then he chuckled.

He tapped the screen stud to get Mydra.

"Mydra, who is the Special Assistant for Lord Jansen at External Affairs?"

"I'll find out, Lord Whaler."

"Do that, and to that person would I speak."

Would any of it do any good? He shrugged and turned to take another look at the western hills in the morning light.

The screen chimed.

"Lord Whaler, Janis Du-Plessis is the Special Assistant to Lord Jansen. Her assistant says she is unavailable, but I have the assistant waiting."

"Talk with the assistant I will. Thank you."

The assistant to the Special Assistant was a young woman, dark haired and thin faced.

Nathaniel went through his introduction and veiled threat.

"I'm so sorry, Lord Whaler, but she is truly not available, and neither is Lord Jansen. I'll pass along your message, and I am sure Ms. Du-Plessis or Lord Jansen will get back to you as soon as one of them possibly can."

"Most important this is," pressed the Ecolitan.

"It's important to us as well, I'm sure, and I will let her know as soon as I can."

"Thank you."

As the screen blanked, Nathaniel frowned.

External Affairs ought to be far more interested than Commerce, yet they showed little or no concern.

He tapped the comm plate to get Mydra. This time he wanted the top assistant of Senator Helmsworth, one Corwin-Smathers.

"Lord Whaler," Mydra informed him, "Ms. Corwin-Smathers is not available, but the person who is handling the Accord sector is."

Nathaniel swallowed a gulp. He'd assumed that Corwin-Smathers was a man.

"Who is such person?"

"Sylvia Ferro-Maine, I believe, is the name."

"Talk to her I will."

"Lord Whaler?" Sylvia Ferro-Maine was dark haired, fine boned, and extremely competent looking on the fax screen.

"The same. You are Ms. Ferro-Maine?"

"I prefer Sylvia, Lord Whaler. The Senate is quite a bit less formal than the rest of the government."

"About formal matters I had called, such as trade . . ."

"Courtney and the Senator are interested in everything that impacts trade."

"Because of such interest, with them, I had thought to talk . . ."

"Well, Courtney would be the one to see about meeting with the Senator, although he's scheduled for months in advance. As for seeing her, I think, if you didn't mind coming over here, she could see you around 1040 tomorrow."

She waited for Nathaniel to answer.

He didn't like the setup. In essence, he would be packing off as an Envoy to see a mere staff director of one Imperial Senator. On the other hand, it was obvious that the assistants controlled the access.

So . . .

"Appreciate I your accommodation in such haste, and prevail further upon you could I."

"Upon me?"

"So helpful you have been, and so little know I, would you consider lunching today with me? Such short notice it is, but appreciate it I most certainly would."

"Lord Whaler, I don't know what to say."

"Yes, I believe, is the proper word."

"I couldn't possibly get there before 1300."

"That would be fine. At the Legation at 1300, and looking forward to it am I."

Why did she accept? Why had he asked?

He shook his head and tapped the screen plate that stored all the pending messages, waiting for them to flash onto the screen. The wait was short, since he didn't appear to have any messages.

He thought about screening Mydra, decided against it, and walked to the portal, thumbed it, and waited as the heavy door irised open.

Mydra and Hillary, who had been talking, jumped as he approached.

"Lord Whaler, is anything wrong?" asked Mydra.

"Nothing, I think, but a small lunch for two would you please order? For my office at 1300."

"Are you expecting a guest, or is it for a working lunch with someone from the Legation?"

"A lunch for work, but with someone not of the Legation."

Mydra was all business as she entered whatever she thought necessary into her console.

"Do you have any preferences?"

Nathaniel almost laughed. After the years in the Ecolitan action forces, he could eat anything his system would take.

"Something light, I would think."

"Will you notify the front desk, or should I?"

"If you would be so kind . . . the name is Ferro-Maine."

He turned toward Hillary. Her blue eyes met his levelly.

"How long for Accord have you worked?"

"Five standard years."

Nathaniel nodded and turned away.

Back in his office, he tried to take stock. But the answer was simple. He still didn't know enough.

"*Cling.*"

"Nathaniel Whaler."

The caller was Marcella Ku-Smythe.

"Lord Whaler, I've thought it over, and tonight would be fine."

"Tonight also would be fine, but for what is it fine?"

"For dinner and for getting to know you better."

"Would you suggest somewhere?"

"Why not in the Diplomatic Tower?"

"Dear lady, so little I see of your city. Would you have me cooped into an even smaller orbit?"

That created a smile from the sandy-haired Special Assistant.

"Do you know the Plaza D'Artin?"

"I can find it."

"How about 1930 at the Golden Nova?"

"Twenty-thirty."

"Fine."

And that was that.

Except . . . Nathaniel was ready to swallow hard at the aggressiveness of the woman. Not only the aggressiveness, but . . . he couldn't place it, except that he was missing something so obvious he shouldn't be.

He had nearly two hours before Sylvia's presumed arrival, not enough time to go anywhere, had he anywhere to go, and decided the time had come for some faxwork.

"Mydra?"

"If to be effective I am, I must know the people. Would you access the personnel records of all Legation employees to my screen?"

"Now, Lord Whaler?"

"Now is when I need them."

By the time he had reviewed all the records in the personnel files, he was convinced.

Everything was too perfect, and because it was, he hadn't the faintest idea which of the professional staff were planted. The safest assumption was that they all were.

XIV

"MARTIN," ASKED THE woman behind the desk, "anything new?" She nipped a bite from a thin taper of cernadine, then another. With each chew, the room grew more redolent of the spice drug.

"There's a call from the Trade Envoy from Accord. Whaler, I think his name is. Nathaniel Whaler."

"What's his problem?"

"That's the Rift thing."

"Oh . . . and they didn't like our proposal and actually sent an Envoy. How charming." Janis Du-Plessis swivelled her seat to view the western hills, turning her back on the aide. "Do we have a counterproposal from them yet?"

"I suspect that's why he wants to meet with Lord Jansen. Probably wants to present it."

"You know, Martin, I'm not terribly fond of provincials, especially from places like Accord. They even turned down my visa." She turned back toward the console and tapped the lock panel.

"We're in conference, Martin, and that's far more important than appointment scheduling for Lord Whaler. Far more important."

Her eyes were bright with the effect of the drug, and fixed on the wiry blond man.

"Why don't you demonstrate how important?"

"Now?"

"Why not now? Lord Jansen is skying, and Lord Envoy Whaler can certainly cool his provincial heels a bit longer."

She looked from Martin to the long couch next to her console and back to him. As she tilted her head, he stood to accept her invitation.

The console panels continued to blink, unanswered.

XV

THE PRIVATE SCREEN chimed, twice.

The Special Assistant scanned the office out of habit, although she was alone.

"Ku-Smythe."

"Marcella, is your dinner engagement wise?" The Admiral's voice was level.

"How much of the Accord Legation's fax system do you have controlled? All of it?"

"Why do you think that?"

"Unless my techs are totally incompetent, everything here is blocked. That means it can't be snooped until the reception point. Accord doesn't have first-class equipment, I'll admit, but it's good enough to block anyone but your crew. Besides, you've got most of the plants on the staff. So even good equipment wouldn't keep you from finding out . . . but not this quickly."

The Admiral smiled. "It's a pity you wouldn't go the Service route. You're wasted at Commerce."

"Could I have gotten as high at Defense?"

"The man is dangerous, Marcella. Dangerous. Don't forget it."

"You're exaggerating again. No man is that dangerous."

"I wish I could show you how dangerous."

"Why do you care? If you're right, that would give you all the pretexts you need, not that you seem to mind the lack of political concern you've demonstrated so far."

The Admiral frowned. "You continue to believe that politics is more important than military capability?"

"No. Your kind of military capabilities are irrelevant, I suspect. That's more the kind of judgment the I.I.S. should make. But you don't trust them either."

"Marcella . . ."

"Why don't you ask yourself why Accord wants to negotiate?"

"I have. They don't want to fight. Neither do we, but we need the trade routes to the Outer Rift."

"Nonsense. You're still trying to prove that you can undo the Secession with pure military applications. Besides, Accord has never blocked the trade routes. It just happens that we can't compete, not unless Accord is no longer a factor."

"As I said, Marcella, it's a pity you're wasted at Commerce."

The Special Assistant just looked through the screen at the Defense Chief.

Finally, the Admiral looked away, and the screen blanked.

XVI

"*CLING!*"

"Whaler."

"A Sylvia Ferro-Maine for lunch, Lord Whaler."

"Yes. Please send her in." He paused. "And how soon will the food be ready?"

"Shortly, Lord Whaler. I just checked on it."

He stood and moved toward the entry portal, which was opening as he approached.

The woman, who at first glance might have passed for a girl, was dark haired, a brown nearly black, almost as tall as he was, well muscled, but fine boned, with the look of a dancer. Her fair complexion added to the chinalike impression.

"Lord Whaler?"

"One and the very same, Lady dear," he replied with a broad accent. "And you are fine?"

"A little rushed, Lord Whaler, but fine."

He gestured toward the deep office couch.

"You have very spacious quarters here."

"Spacious? I had not thought about the matter, but would such as this be considered spacious here? In New Augusta?"

"Quite comfortable." Sylvia looked around the office, her eyes lingering at the vista of the western hills. "Quite comfortable."

As she sat down, he plopped himself into the chair across from her.

"Know you much about Accord?"

"Only the standard. What should I know?"

Nathaniel shrugged. "So much there is to say. Where would one start? Not at the beginning, for too long that would take. Not in the middle, for too confusing that would be. And at the end, nothing would I be saying. So . . ." he dragged it out, "at the beginning will I start, but more quickly."

"Before start I, hospitality should I offer. Alas, however, my resources here limited are. I have ordered lunch, and arriving in a while it will be. Now I offer you liftea, cafe, or the wine white. You would like which?"

"If you don't mind," the woman responded, carefully crossing her trousered legs, "I think I'll wait until lunch arrives. But do go on with your story . . . I mean, your history."

The Ecolitan cleared his throat.

"In the start, Accord settled was by those fleeing after the fall of the first Federation, and with special skills. The Ecolitan Institute founded shortly thereafter to further and to hand down those skills. All citizens must take Institute training to some degree. Fortunate enough was I to be selected for full training and later to teach there."

He paused to clear his throat again and study Sylvia Ferro-Maine. Odd combination, with the slate gray eyes, dark hair swept up like a dancer's, and the light complexion. She conveyed an impression of fragility.

"Institute does not play now so large a part in our history as once it did, though this time, at crossroads in trade talks, the Institute was indeed consulted. For that I should be most grateful, for that has allowed me the opportunity to see New Augusta."

"Was the Institute the same as the 'Black College' that trained the ecological terrorists of the Ecologic Rebellion?" Her tone was casual, curious, almost uninterested.

"All citizens of Accord did rally together at that time, but the question you have asked, dear Lady, presupposes the Empire was right and Accord wrong. If I answer at all, then I justify your assessment of us all." He shrugged as if puzzled.

She laughed, and the short, sharp sound was nearly musical. "I surrender. Let me put it in another way. Did the Institute play the key role in the Ecologic Secession, as I believe you call it?"

"Most key role, since only the Institute at that time had all the necessary skills gathered under one roof. Times have changed, now, with the five colleges, and the outworld learning centers, and there is less reliance upon the Institute."

He leaned back in the low chair, almost losing his balance as he discovered that the chair reclined and swivelled simultaneously.

"What changes do you see as the most important?"

"Already lengthening what I promised would be short, dear Lady. After Accord was settled and the Institute founded, the government created emphasized self-sufficiency, balanced use of resources, and independent means of interstellar travel. All with good results, until the Empire became most insistent on taking a control over us and over our uninhabited systems. We resisted. Others understood our plight and joined us."

He shrugged. "Now, once again, the Empire has questions about trade and commerce and what systems belong to whom, and here I am to mediate if possible what can be done. Accord is older, and wiser, I am told, and would rather talk this out. So we hope the Empire will talk in good faith as well."

He looked away from her and out through the wide permaglass at the vista of the mountains, sharp and barren, even in the distance.

"Accord like Terra is," he said softly, "with a gravity a touch stronger and a sky that is more green and near the same land masses with oceans as well. Less salty are the seas, and thicker is the air. Accord is younger, and that may be an answer. Our sun is whiter."

The Ecolitan shrugged again.

"Scarcely it seems know I what else to say or what you wish to hear."

"What do you all do? A dumb question, I suppose, but none of your occupations are listed in the socioeconomic breakdowns."

Nathaniel repressed a whistle at the thought of the Empire's collecting socioeconomic data on Accord.

"Like all people everywhere, we work. Some farm, some craft, some heal, some in industry, some in trade. A small microprocessing industry we have, and some small shipyards, but not on large scales, not like New Glasgow or Halston. I had limited scientific talents, and so came into the Institute."

A discreet tapping sounded.

Nathaniel rose.

"Our lunch perhaps arrives."

Standing at the portal was a waiter, trim in solid tan, and guiding a fully set glide table.

"Lord Whaler, your order."

After watching the waiter set up the table in quick and measured movements and ushering him out, Nathaniel gestured toward Sylvia.

"At last . . ."

He sat Sylvia at one side, and pulled the bottle of sparkling white wine from the ice bucket.

The traditional plastic cork would have come out easily, but the Ecolitan struggled with it as if it were difficult, and in the process aimed it almost at Sylvia. The small missile exploded out of the bottle neck and zipped by her face with a centimeter or two to spare. She jumped.

"Ah, dear Lady. I am sorry."

He handed her the glass into which he had dumped the colorless and tasteless powder before filling it.

"Really, I shouldn't."

He poured himself an overflowing glass and sat down across the table from her.

"But you have not explained your presence, your kindness in lunching with an unknown Envoy."

"No kindness, really. Courtney had already asked me to look into the Accord situation. What better way to start?"

Sylvia smiled faintly, faintly enough to chill Nathaniel, and took a deep sip of the wine.

He frowned and pulled at his chin.

After Sylvia had taken a few more sips, the fidelitrol should take hold. The tricky drug left the victim unable to withhold the truth but had its disadvantages. First, the victim remembered everything, and second, any agent could be trained to minimize its effects.

He took another sip of his own wine.

"With a poor diplomat like me? A mere fumbler of figures?"

Sylvia wrinkled her nose . . . then sneezed. Once! Twice!

Her glass nearly tipped, and Nathaniel reached out to steady it.

Sylvia leaned forward in reaction to her sneeze until, off-balance, her hand almost hit Nathaniel's wine glass as she groped to steady herself.

"Oh, excuse me, Envoy Whaler. Please excuse me." She dabbed at her face with a tissue.

Nathaniel took another sip of his wine, waiting for Sylvia to recover. At last, she finished dabbing and took another sip, more like a mouthful, of the wine.

"You're fresh from Accord," she observed, "and who else would be a better source here in New Augusta?"

"But you? What role do you play in this?" He hastily added another sentence to restrict the question. "For the Senator, I mean?"

"I'm the principal investigator for the Committee, dear Envoy, and look into all sorts of things. Now I'm supposed to look into you."

A puzzled look crossed her dancer's face.

"And how did you come to such a distinguished position?"

"Because the Service thought the Senator needed looking after, and because he has a weakness for good-looking women, and you know, dear Envoy, you beat me to it." She smiled, and this time the smile was resigned in nature.

"Beat you to what?" Nathaniel asked. The conversation had taken a decidedly bizarre turn.

"Slipping something into my drink. I've never told anyone that about the Service, nor would I under anything remotely resembling normal circumstances."

Nathaniel realized she was stalling, stalling until whatever had ended up in his own drink took effect.

He laughed.

"Why did you drug my drink?" he asked, jumping to the obvious conclusion.

"Because you aren't quite what you seem, and there doesn't seem to be any other quick way to find out what I need to know."

"Which is?"

"The details of your mission, or missions, including the reasons and rationale . . ."

Nathaniel chilled. He wasn't sure he could fight the fidelitrol as successfully as she was, and he only had a question or two left before her drug, whatever it was, took effect.

"Who sent you? Who is the Service, and what can I do to get a trade agreement?" He snapped out the questions like arrows.

"Courtney Corwin-Smathers sent me because the I.I.S. set her up to have me sent, and the Service is the Imperial Intelligence Service, and the best way for you to get a trade agreement is to keep everyone off balance, wouldn't you agree?"

Nathaniel tried to frame another question, but instead found himself answering hers.

"That was my initial reaction, but it's difficult to know how to do that when you don't know the real players—"

"What's your real purpose, dear Envoy?"

How was he going to turn the tables on her?

"My real purpose is to get a trade agreement favorable to Accord and to continue to block Imperial expansion back into the Rift and to do both while avoiding any sort of direct armed conflict between the Coordinate and the Empire, which complicates things greatly, don't you think?"

There! He'd thrown his own question on the end.

If it hadn't been so serious, he could have howled. Both were compelled to tell the truth, and both were trying to get the other on the answering side of the questions.

"Greatly, but doesn't that mean that Accord is out for territorial expansion?"

"Only in the commercial sense and not in governmental terms because the Institute doesn't believe in large government, but aren't several factions within the Empire out to crush us anyway? Which ones? Why?"

"Not all the Empire; mainly the Admiral and the Ministry of Defense, probably because they're still smarting over the loss of the Rift, and can't we stop this farce?"

"Yes, if we agree not to ask questions."

"I agree."

Nathaniel looked up to see the fine beads of perspiration on Sylvia's forehead, wiped the dampness off his own brow with the back of his sleeve.

He cleared his throat, meeting her slate dark eyes again.

"How . . . I'd like to offer a compromise. I'll tell you what I can, and you can ask me one question afterwards. That question will ask me if what I said is true. Then you say what you can or will, and I ask you the same question."

She laughed.

"For a man with such a dangerous reputation, you're certainly being straightforward, and I'd even drink to that, but I'd rather not prolong the agony."

Nathaniel coughed, looked down at the linen on the table, and then back at the slender woman.

"My story is simple, as much of it as you probably want to hear. I am an Ecolitan, a professor at the Institute, selected because of my overall qualifications to figure out how to negotiate a trade agreement with the Empire before the Empire can employ the lack of such an agreement as an excuse to justify widespread military action against the Coordinate. The job is complicated because we can't politically accept a degrading agreement. The Institute couldn't accept any agreement whose terms might be difficult to keep because we frankly believe that some segments of the Empire don't want any agreement. At the same time, I should reinforce the idea that armed aggression by the Empire would result in catastrophe for the Empire itself. That will be difficult because no one in the Empire really believes that Accord has that kind of ability. Nor do they want to believe that. It's true, unfortunately."

He spread his hands. "I'd be happy to add any more if it's a suggestion and not a question."

She grinned. "Do you trust me that much? Or do you think you could avoid answering?" She put her hand over her mouth. "Oh . . . I'm sorry."

"No, but I have to trust someone, at least to some degree. It's probably better to trust a professional. I could probably avoid revealing anything I really wanted to."

Sylvia opened her mouth, closed it, then began again. "You seem to have a great deal of confidence, a great deal of faith, in your ability to wreak havoc upon the Empire without taking much in the way of losses." Her expression was calm and composed by the time she finished the statement.

"I did not say that. All-out war would probably destroy Accord totally. It would not destroy the Institute nor its capability to devastate the Empire. There is a difference."

"Is all this true, and do you believe it?"

"Yes . . . to both . . . with the qualification that any prediction based on assumptions of human nature has a certain potential for error."

Her laugh was a breeze of freshness. "My . . . you do sound like the professor you are!"

He couldn't help but return her humor with a short laugh of his own.

"I didn't mean to sound so pedantic, but the way you asked the question . . ."

The silence following his words lengthened.

Nathaniel half turned to stare out the wide window toward the foothills and the mountains behind. High white clouds were approaching from the west.

As he brought himself back to meet Sylvia's eyes, he realized he had not even touched the food on the plate before him. Nor had Sylvia.

He gestured.

"Perhaps you'd like a bite or two before you begin . . ."

Looking down, then lifting his fork, he raised his eyebrows, asking an unspoken question.

"No . . . I didn't drop anything in the food, suspicious man. Did you?"

"No, suspicious lady."

Surprisingly, the fish was still warm, and the sweet-sour sauce and a spice he failed to recognize added pungency to the white meat's delicate flavor. The side dish, some sort of vegetable, was soggy, bland, and smelled like overdone seaweed.

It also tasted like seaweed, though Sylvia ate her portion with scarcely a shiver.

He finished nearly all of what was on his plate before realizing she had done the same, and neither had said a word.

"You know . . . Sylvia . . . I wonder if anyone will really believe what I've said after you walk out and tell them."

"Dear Envoy, it's a relief to hear I will walk out." Her smile was teasing.

"Unlike Imperials," he returned, "we don't tease and obfuscate issues, which often leaves us at a great disadvantage."

"The Service already believes you." Her face smoothed into a professional mask. "For various reasons, no one else wants to. In that sense, we're allies. But we can't lift a hand in any direct way to help you make your case."

"Why not?"

"Since I don't seem compelled to answer that, I won't, although I will point out that no military bureaucracy has ever lost the opportunity to destroy rival intelligence sources."

"The Institute faces some of the same problems, and I would guess the same problem occurs in more cultures than not." He cleared his throat. "What else can you, or will you, reveal?"

"You probably won't get much help from the Ministry of External Affairs . . . we feel that Commerce will try to take control."

"You paint a less than optimistic picture."

"Should I distort it, Lord Whaler? No one really likes Accord. Even the Service only supports the idea of a completed agreement because we like the alternatives even less."

Nathaniel shrugged. "What can I say?"

"That you're sorry for the underhanded tactics you use . . ." suggested Sylvia with a twinkle in her eye.

"When I am not . . . when the tactics hurt no one, except the pride . . . ?"

"Touché!"

"After all, Lady, my pride also was damaged." Nathaniel managed to keep a straight face despite the outrageous statement.

The Ecolitan looked down at his empty plate, wondering why he was regretting that the lunch was nearly over.

"Why the frown?"

"Oh . . . nothing. Things are never quite as they seem, but why that should surprise me I can't quite say."

Sylvia pushed back her chair and stood, catching Nathaniel with the quickness of the movement, although he was standing next to her within instants.

"You recover quickly," she observed, still bantering.

"One tries."

Inclining her head to the right, she gave him a quizzical look, her gray eyes clouding momentarily. "Like you, I find things are not quite what they seem. Nor are you."

"I am what I am."

She was already departing. As the portal irised, she turned back toward him.

"Time is running against you, you know, particularly if you have to react to others." She paused, then continued with a brief smile, "But I did enjoy the lunch."

With that, she was gone.

Nathaniel shook his head as the portal closed behind her.

Only a faint scent, similar to the orange blossoms of his father's orchards, hung in the air to remind him that Sylvia had been there.

XVII

NATHANIEL STUDIED HIS reflection in the mirror. The shimmering tan of the semiformal tunic was not all that flattering, made him look even a bit beefy.

"Can't have everything," he muttered as he tapped the plate to dim the quarters' lights.

Was it wise to go out the way he was?

Probably not.

Instead of leaving by the private exit, he decided on going through the Legation. The staff offices were deserted except for the duty desk, captained by Hillary West-Coven, the lady whose purpose he had yet to discover.

"Oh, Lord Whaler. You surprised me."

Several emotions flashed across her face, one of which Nathaniel thought might be guilt.

"That I did not mean," he pontificated. "Just departing am I."

With that, he hurried out, checking the area outside the portal.

The corridor was nearly deserted, but the faint shadow along the far side corridor piqued his curiosity. He eased himself against the wall and slipped toward the side branch, the one that would eventually lead to the private entrance to his personal quarters.

After dropping into a crouch, he darted a look around the corner, in time to see three plain-suited figures heading crisply toward the exit portal from his quarters.

Nathaniel straightened, checking behind himself instinctively, and frowned.

The military bearing of two of the three was obvious, despite their civilian attire. But who was the third figure? Somehow the gait had been familiar, almost like an Ecolitan . . .

"Whew!" A soft whistle escaped his lips.

If he'd seen what he thought he'd seen, he was headed for real trouble. The next question was how to defuse the trap without letting onto the deception.

If the three didn't discover one Nathaniel Whaler exiting his quarters shortly, they would go searching, as well as alert their superiors at the Ministry of Defense.

Nathaniel weighed the options, and as he weighed, checked the few items he always carried.

From the inside of his belt he pulled a thin, golden film cloak and a filmy golden privacy mask. While such masks were not normally worn on New Augusta, his real purpose was to confuse his identity for a few individuals for a limited period of time.

Next came the wooden dart pistol with which he had attempted to persuade Sergel. In addition to the lethal darts were those that sent the victims into a delirium and effectively scrambled their memories from several minutes before they were shot until several days later. The Ecolitan opted for the nonlethal variety.

An unseen attack would be best, but if that couldn't be arranged, surprise would substitute nearly as well.

The corridors narrowed as they approached his private quarters, but Nathaniel trailed the three until it was certain they were staking out his quarters' exit.

From the corner behind which he waited, the range to the nearest "sentry," a blond man perhaps six centimeters shorter than the Ecolitan, was roughly eight meters. The other military operative was stationed to guard the cross corridor, and the third, the one who also wore a privacy cloak, the one whose face and bearing resembled the Ecolitan himself, stood by the exit portal with a drawn stunner.

Nathaniel eased the dart pistol around the corner and fired.

"Thwick!"

"Thwick!"

The nearer sentry pulled at his neck, twice, before dropping his hand to look at the dissolving residue of the dart.

His left arm twitched, followed by his right leg.

The further sentry, the dark-haired and taller woman, had already snapped her head around.

"Thwick!"

"Thwick!"

The first victim began to thrash on the corridor tiles, dull thuds echoing down the long and otherwise empty passageways.

Nathaniel wondered at the man's self-control. By now, most would have been raving wildly.

The woman looked at the disintegrating splinters of the dart which rested in her hand, her eyes widening. Before she could analyze the pattern, in turn, she shuddered as the neural disruptor began to take effect.

Four shots to hit two sentries. Lousy shooting, Nathaniel thought as he reloaded the dart thrower.

The remaining Imperial, the bogus Ecolitan, turned his head from one side to the other as if to determine from which of the two intersecting corridors the shots had come.

Finally, the man made the right decision and dashed for the corridor where the woman lay thrashing, the one farthest from Nathaniel.

The Ecolitan snapped the dart gun together, waited until the other had cleared the corner, and sprinted nearly noiselessly after the man.

As he came around the corner, he saw the fleeing Imperial collide with a passerby, a mid-aged man, and knock him to the tiles. Nathaniel didn't hesitate but used a single dart on the bystander as he passed at full sprint.

The Imperial stopped at the next intersection, the one perhaps thirty meters from the main corridor leading to the lift/drop shaft, and turned to level his stunner at the oncoming Ecolitan.

"*Thwick!*" Nathaniel triggered the dart pistol, knowing the distance was too great but anticipating the other would flinch. He did.

"*Thrummm!*"

The stunner bolt passed over the Ecolitan's left shoulder.

Nathaniel dove to the right and into a roll. He came out still running.

His right hand went dead, but that didn't stop him from firing the dart thrower.

Another advantage to being left-handed, he noted absently as he closed on the Imperial.

"*Thwick!*"

The dart caught the Imperial agent full in the throat, the only area unshielded by clothing. The man staggered momentarily, just long enough for Nathaniel to slash away the stunner and follow through with a quick elbow across the man's jaw.

Without hesitating, Nathaniel pocketed the dart pistol, retrieved the stunner, and hoisted the unconscious but twitching form of the other over his shoulder. In less than a minute he had stowed the man in the public call booth near the lift shaft.

Only one passing couple caught his transit, the woman quickly turning her head, the man still peering back as the two descended the drop shaft.

As he tapped out the codes he wanted, Nathaniel stood to shield the body from full public view.

"Senator Helmsworth's Office."

The respondent was not the urbane male receptionist, but a woman, dark haired and slightly disheveled, in a pale blue tunic.

"Nathaniel Whaler for Sylvia Ferro-Maine."

"Let me check."

The screen blanked, only to be replaced with Sylvia's slate gray eyes and dark hair. She still wore the green and gray she had worn to lunch.

"Lord Whaler . . . what a surprise."

"Not so much as what I have for you." He stepped aside and dragged the unconscious Imperial agent into the focus of the screen.

"Oh . . . and why are you faxing me?"

"I had thought that some of your friends might want to have a chat with this gentleman before he wakes up. You'll note his remarkable similarity to me. That is, your friends might enjoy the conversation if they could pick him up before his dispatcher does."

"Where on earth are you?"

"In the main corridor pubcomm station, right beyond the lift shaft, where you had lunch."

"In that case, something might be arranged. Will you be there?"

"Not for long. I'll call you later. I've probably been available all too long in any case."

"I understand."

The screen blanked.

Nathaniel shook his head. As quick as he thought he was, she was even quicker.

He let the agent slump into a heap in the back corner of the booth, hardly noticeable from outside, and strolled out and toward the drop shaft and his dinner engagement with Marcella, hoping the I.I.S. could retrieve the imitation "Nathaniel" before the military could.

XVIII

AFTER THE QUICK drop the public shaft to the tunnel concourse, Nathaniel summoned a public tunnel cab to take him to the Plaza D'Artin, the Golden Nova, and Marcella.

As he sat in the back of the cab, he flexed his right hand, squeezing it with his left. Some of the feeling was beginning to return.

Was the lady responsible for his recent reception committee? If not, why the coincidence?

He shrugged and took a deep breath, shaking himself slightly to relax muscles that were too tight.

Despite its name, the Golden Nova occupied a quiet corner of the multileveled plaza. Nathaniel was amused to note that his choice of dinner wear, while commonplace among the younger men, was definitely in style.

"I see you found it without trouble." Marcella Ku-Smythe was waiting for him in the restaurant's anteroom.

She wore an amber outfit with a high neck, narrow waist, and slightly flared pants. Much more becoming to her light skin than the maroon of the Imperial Commerce Ministry, he reflected. He didn't miss the bulge of the stunner tucked into the waist folds of her jacket.

A waiter materialized and led them to a corner table. The dining area was filled, obviously with wealthy souls. The use of waiters alone attested to the price levels. So Marcella was well-off in her own right. Or the government was picking up the tab. Or both.

After they were seated, he asked that question.

"You're too forthright even for me. Let us poor Imperials have a few secrets."

"You're more of a mystery to us," he protested. "So many things puzzle me. Terra is the center of the Empire but few live here. You build towers into the sky, but seal them off and travel underground."

"You should know." It was the first trace of hostility he'd heard in her voice. "Or have they forgotten to teach all the history on Accord? Or don't you recall why the war was called the Ecologic Rebellion . . . pardon me, the Ecologic Secession?"

"Forest Lord! Still?" he asked apologetically. The history tapes mentioned the use of ecological weapons against Terra itself by the Institute, and the techniques were still taught. But Accord had long since recovered from the war's effects.

She waved his apology aside.

"I suppose you wouldn't have any reason to understand the lasting impact. Terran ecology was so fragile at the time. We never really recovered from the Age of Waste and the first planetary wars. Yes, we could go outside, and some are allowed, but we're erring on the side of caution. If you notice, all the towers—a necessary requirement of Empire—are within New Augusta. Elsewhere we try to minimize any adverse impact on the environment."

After that exchange, he was more on edge.

"For a man so intelligent, so ostensibly open, you reveal little of what you are."

He spread his hands. "My life is an open book."

"Of blank pages," she added with a wry laugh, "or pages written in an ancient and unknown language."

He looked around the dining area from his position against the wall. Something about the seating arrangements bothered him, but he couldn't pin it down.

"Marcella, you are a witty and brilliant lady, and you entertain me marvelously. Can you entertain me further and tell me how and what I need to do to follow through on the trade agreement talks?"

The smile disappeared from her face.

"Not here. Come see me tomorrow. Say around 1400."

Question asked; question answered.

"I bow to your superior wisdom, and speaking of wisdom, can you enlighten me on what should be ordered."

When he had seen her earlier on the vidfax screen and in person at the Commerce Ministry, she had worn her hair up and more severely. Now, with the swirl of sandy hair across her shoulder, with the light tan of her skin and the dark amber of her outfit, he tabbed her more as a golden girl, mature woman or not. Her green eyes were a shade less intense than in full daylight, but she still missed nothing.

"Their specials are always good, but I'm fond of the flaming spicetails."

"Then I'll have the flaming spicetails."

"You'll actually take the word of a hard, hard, Imperial bureaucrat?"

"On this small matter, at least."

A brief shadow flickered across her face, so fleeting the Ecolitan wondered if she were aware of it, but it brought him back from the edge of relaxation. Marcella Ku-Smythe was not used to having her word doubted—on anything.

"How did you find your way into the bureaucracy?" Nathaniel figured it for a safe question.

"In the same way as any other bright student of applied political theory from a nonnoble family. Took the Emperor's exams, passed with distinction, and was placed in the Commerce Ministry." Marcella furrowed her brows briefly, as if the beginning of a career which had led her to becoming one of the top assistants in the Imperial bureaucracy was nothing unusual.

"Your family?"

"My mother was pleased, although she's from the Eagles and would have preferred me to take a commission. My father, well, he just wanted me to do what I wanted. Nothing any different about me from any other aspiring assistant.

"You, on the other hand, embody romance, mystery, and a hint or so of danger."

"Why? Because I'm from the nasty planet of Accord?"

Marcella was spared an answer by the arrival of a purple clad waiter.

Nathaniel nodded at Marcella.

"Two of the flaming spicetails, Imperial salads with Maccean nuts, and a carafe of Kremmling." She looked at the Ecolitan. "Do you want anything else?"

"I'll leave that up to you."

"The cheeses as a mid-course," she added to the waiter.

"Honored guest . . ." she started, with an appealing lilt in her mocking tone.

"Damn it! I'm Nathaniel. Always was. Always will be. None of this 'honored' this or 'honored' that. Honors never did the work."

"Nathaniel, then. You still haven't answered the question you haven't let me ask."

"Which was?"

"Why you seem to personify the whole concept of mystery."

"There's nothing mysterious about me."

"Oh?"

"I'm thirty-eight standard years old, sandy haired, and I've been employed in some capacity by the benevolent Institute for the past fifteen years."

"Ah, yes. Combat arm of the Institute, but a renowned economist.

Highly rated scout pilot, but a teacher. You're pulled out of the Institute and thrown to head a trade delegation at the last minute. That's not mysterious?"

Nathaniel was impressed with Marcella's ability to tap into the pipeline, particularly since the information existed in written form only on Accord.

He shrugged.

"What can I say?" He forced a grin. "I thought you weren't going to mix business with socializing."

She had the grace to smile back, and the coldness left her eyes for a moment.

"You win."

Nathaniel opted for generosity.

"Not that it's not a good observation, Marcella. But I could say the same about you. All I know is that you are extraordinarily talented and that you work for Lord Rotoller, and that . . ."

"And what else?"

"That I'm perilously close to mixing business and socializing. No sense in drawing a second reprimand."

He took a sip of the Kremmling, a light white wine with a hint of a sparkle, and waited for Marcella to taste the salad which had just appeared.

Was she waiting for him to take the first bite? Style be damned. He picked up the fork.

After the first three bites, Nathaniel decided there was a solid reason why the salad was termed "Imperial." It was too rich for anyone but an Imperial.

"What do you really think of New Augusta?"

An innocently loaded question, but Nathaniel decided to be as truthful as possible under the circumstances.

"I haven't had a chance to see a great deal, but already I feel cramped by not being able to get outside. I suppose that's one reason why you've made the effort toward high-ceilinged architecture."

"You'd have to confirm that with the Imperial architect, but it's as good a reason as any. We just accept it because that's the way it is."

"What happens if someone doesn't accept things?"

Marcella shrugged. "Every society has some who don't fit in."

"I can't say that I've noticed an overt police system, but I have the impression that things are definitely under control."

"As well as could be expected."

"Do the unhappy ones get mental treatment or what?"

"Not necessarily. That's the beauty of having an Empire. If they don't like it on New Augusta or elsewhere on Earth, they can outship to a good hundred planets."

"And you encourage that migration?"

"Yes . . . since we're being frank. The fewer bodies here, the less strain on the ecology and the lower the population dissatisfaction critical point."

"Isn't that merely a mythical assumption, that population densities and comfort levels really have a bearing on civic harmony?"

"The original Living Space Riots, the work of your own scholar Vonderjogt, and the experiments of Kliemersol all would indicate otherwise. Practically speaking, no government could ever let the situation deteriorate that far, not and retain any pretense of civil liberty."

"Isn't dealing with such theoretical matters ranging a bit out of your field?"

"Not really."

He dropped the questioning to concentrate on the flamed spicetails.

"Very good."

"You haven't tasted them before?"

"No. Our fare is much simpler."

"What's Accord really like? I don't mean to ask for a travelogue. We've seen the standard reference works, the tapes, and the footage from back to the Secession, but what is Accord today? What are your candid impressions of the differences between the Empire and Accord?"

"I'm not sure I can answer with any great accuracy."

"I'll take an inaccurate impression." She laughed and her voice relaxed. "You know, you're very careful. I can't blame you, but let go a little."

"First, then, I'll say that you can see the sky. It's a shade greener than yours and our sun is whiter . . ." Nathaniel turned up his hands. ". . . but all the comparisons are conjectures. I see your sun through permaglass, and I see mine in my gardens and in the woods. I know everyone in the town where I grew up, and here I don't see how anyone knows anyone. On Accord, everyone produces something. Even our bureaucrats grow their own vegetables, or write, or compose, or sing . . ."

"You make it sound like utopia."

"Far from it. We're a young society. People have to work hard at two or three jobs. It's only been in the last generation or so that we've been able to afford career politicians and bureaucrats. I'm not convinced that change has been good."

Marcella frowned.

"You picture Accord as a young society. Nearly four hundred years ago, which is a long time for a small political and social system like Accord, Accord was advanced enough to foment, direct, and successfully coordinate a multisystem revolution which cost the Empire all chance of immediate expansion into the Rift area. In addition," she added drily, "roughly fifty systems discovered they would rather not pay levies to the Empire. I'm not sure how you can describe any society that effective as young."

Nathaniel shrugged. "What can I say? You asked for my impressions. Compared to the Empire, we're mere babes."

"You still haven't written much on those blank pages, Nathaniel."

"What blank pages?"

"The ones that compose the open book of your life."

The Ecolitan finished off the last spicetail rather than attempt an answer. The lady knew far more than any mere assistant to the Deputy Minister should. The question was why.

"Is everyone from Accord so reserved?"

"No."

"What's an Ecolitan?"

That was one question he definitely didn't want to answer. It sounded so simple, but trying to give any real answer would create more problems.

"I really don't know how to answer that one."

"You can't be serious." A touch of sharpness crept into her voice.

"We Ecolitans keep pretty much to ourselves. So it's hard to make comparisons. Originally, we were a totally separate and unified force which represented the bulk of Accord's military capability. That is no longer true, although we do keep a number of ships. We are still totally independent of the Coordinate government and don't have all that much to do with them. Call us scholars with the power to remain independent of any government."

"Scholars are usually considered peaceful, and somehow I don't see the Institute as a peaceful force or the selection of an Ecolitan as a peaceful move."

"Scholars shouldn't necessarily be regarded as pacifists. You also have to remember that I was a compromise selection, since neither the Normists nor the Orthodox opposition could agree on one of their own candidates for the position. Besides, any compromise reached by an Ecolitan could not possibly be questioned by even the most fanatical Orthodoxist."

Marcella nodded slightly.

"Put in that light, your position becomes clearer. Only slightly clearer, I might add."

"Whereas yours is still totally unclear."

"What kind of art is most popular on Accord?"

Nathaniel accepted the abrupt changes in subject matter as an indication that Marcella had found out what she wanted to know . . . at least for the moment.

The only other awkward moment came after dinner.

"Excellent dinner, Marcella. May I see you to your quarters?"

"Perhaps it would be better if I did the escorting."

"Is that the Terran custom?"

"Usually," she noted, "but with diplomats, one can adjust to almost anything."

"How about a compromise?"

"Leave as we came?"

"Just this time."

"All right. But I promise I'll hold you to your word."

"In the meantime," Nathaniel concluded, as he turned to go, "I'll see you tomorrow."

XIX

NATHANIEL TOOK ANOTHER tunnel cab back to the Diplomatic Tower, alert for another possible attack. Both the trip and the walk back to his private entrance were uneventful.

The stunner he had taken from the Imperial ready, he touched the lockplate and let the door dilate.

The silence was an alarm in itself. He had left the music on. Instinctively, he dropped to his knees and fired the stunner around the edge of the door into the blind space he couldn't see, following the shot with a quick dash from the corridor into the quarters.

The anteway was empty, as was the living area. So were the cramped kitchen area, the dining area, and the second sleeping quarters. But someone was still in the quarters. An almost imperceptible rustle from beyond the bedroom confirmed his unease.

He surveyed the dimly lit main sleeping quarters again. If anyone were still in the quarters, he or she was probably in the hygienarium or behind the bed.

No sense in being any more of a damned fool.

The Ecolitan sat down noiselessly on the plush flooring, shielded completely by the bedroom door edge, stunner resting on his knee and leveled at the half-open door to the hygienarium. He set it at half charge and went through the drill to sharpen his vision.

After ten minutes, he heard a shuffle. He didn't move.

Close to an hour later, a face peered around the doorway across the room.

Nathaniel got him with a single shot.

Something about the falling figure struck him as familiar, but he couldn't place it. Another stifled gasp announced a second intruder.

The waiting trick wouldn't work a second time, and, besides, who knew what the other snooper might try?

Slowly, he eased the flat pressure foil tube from his belt, nicked the seal, and tossed it gently onto the far side of the bed.

"Hssssss . . ."

A stunner pointed over the top of the bed. The Ecolitan stayed behind the wall as the useless charges struck.

A few minutes later, he stood and slowly edged around the wall.

Now two figures were sprawled on the bedroom floor.

The closer, the one he'd gotten with the stunner, was Sergel Weintre.

The second was a younger man, black haired, olive skinned and clean shaven, perhaps 160 centimeters from head to toe.

A quick but thorough search of both revealed nothing. Sergel had carried only the stunner and a few personal items. The stranger had no identification whatsoever, but the standardized singlesuit and new stunner announced all too clearly his military connections.

In turn, the Ecolitan dragged each to the private exit and dumped them outside.

He returned to his quarters and faxed the tower's emergency number.

"Envoy Nathaniel Whaler am I, and a disturbance has occurred. Outside my door. My composure has gone."

"Lord Whaler, I'll send the Domestic Protective Service up immediately. You say, outside your private suite?"

"Outside. That is correct. A fight, I think. Or several."

"Is it still going on?"

"No. But loudly it ended. A large noise. Someone falls, but check I wish not to do in person."

"Don't worry, Lord Whaler. We'll take care of it."

"I thank you."

So much for that. He made sure both doors were locked with the handbolts and stretched out on the rumpled bed, slipping the stunner under the pillows.

Going back to the disciplines of the Institute, he concentrated on the sleep-time exercises, telling himself to wake at the slightest sound or in five hours.

Five hours and ten minutes later, he woke abruptly. Instantly alert, he listened. No sounds. Apparently, the Diplomatic Police had come and carted Sergel off without much noise, although he wouldn't have heard if they'd brought an entire blasthorn section. The soundproof nature of the walls and doors was a flaw in his story, but he doubted anyone would call an Envoy on such a minor discrepancy.

Nathaniel took his time about freshening up, showering, and dressing for the day ahead.

The last item before entering his official office was a quick fax to one Sylvia Ferro-Maine.

"Lord Whaler . . . and what can I do for you this early in the morning?"

"I had wondered if perhaps your friends had received the package I had left . . . or if you knew."

"My understanding is that the pickup went smoothly, but that they have not had the chance to evaluate the value of the shipment." Sylvia's face was without emotion. "Is that all?"

"I would hope that we could get together again before too long . . ."

"You honor me, Lord Whaler, and I will certainly await your call. And I must be going, but thank you."

Nathaniel was left staring at the blank gray of the faxscreen.

He shook his head. Now what had he done wrong?

Why did he imagine the scent of orange trees?

"Ridiculous . . ." he muttered. "Absolutely ridiculous."

Maybe Sylvia was worried about the leaky nature of the communications at the Accord Legation. He'd have to check back later . . . from somewhere else.

In the meantime, he had the rest of his job to do.

He marched from his quarters into the official office, sat down behind the console, and tried to review the incoming messages that awaited him.

Within ten minutes the intercom chimed, and Mydra's face appeared on the faxscreen. He punched the Accept stud.

"A call from the Diplomatic Police."

"I'll take it."

The young officer who waited on the screen was stern faced and female.

"Envoy Whaler? You complained about a disturbance last night?"

"Yes. There was a fight in the corridor, I believed."

"Lord Whaler, as you mentioned, there was a disturbance. Some of our normal public monitors were apparently damaged. We also found one man lying in front of your private entrance, stunned out. He claims he works for the Legation. His name is Sergel Weintre. The documentation matches, but we thought you as the Envoy should know."

Interesting, thought Nathaniel. I dump two men, and they only find one. Or find two and only let me know about one.

He frowned at the officer.

"Well . . . we do have a Sergel Weintre who works here as an information Specialist. Let me see if he has shown up."

He put the black-haired and square-jawed officer on hold and rang Mydra.

"Has Sergel Weintre come in this morning?"

"No, and that's very unusual. He's usually the first one here. If he's ever late, we all are notified. The main desk says he doesn't answer his quarters' number either."

How interesting, reflected the Ecolitan. Everyone knows everything about everyone.

He went back to the Diplomatic Police officer.

"Mr. Weintre has not shown up this morning and cannot be reached at his quarters. So quite possible it is that Sergel Weintre you do have. Do you have a visual?"

She split the screen, and Weintre's image filled the right half. He was scowling, and his right eyelid twitched above a clinched and unshaven jaw.

"I would say that is Mr. Weintre. Is any way there that he could be released to the Legation?"

"That would not be proper procedure."

"I understand. On the other hand, the Legation is most short staffed at the moment, and I would certainly appreciate any suggestions you might have about how to accomplish Mr. Weintre's speedy return."

"Once a complaint is made, sir . . ."

"Since the complaint was made by the Legation, so to speak, could not I have that complaint withdrawn?"

"That would be most unusual."

"But not impossible?"

"I'll have to check on that, Lord Whaler."

"I'll be happy to wait."

Nathaniel flipped through one of the trade folders while the faxscreen displayed the emblem of the Diplomatic Police.

"Lord Whaler?"

"Yes."

"I understand you made a complaint about Mr. Weintre's creating a disturbance?"

"Concerned was I about the noise and merely reported it and did not charge anyone with anything."

"Under those circumstances, I believe we can release your employee directly to you, but we will still have to continue our investigation into the broken monitors."

"I understand, but I appreciate your consideration of our short-handed state."

After signing off with the Diplomatic Police, Nathaniel caught Mydra on the faxscreen.

"As soon as Sergel gets back, I would like to see him."

"Yes, Lord Whaler, I'll tell him."

Two to one, thought the Ecolitan, Sergel isn't going to get that message.

In the interim, he decided to check the trade figures and review the presentation materials he had brought with him. Not that he expected anything to be overlooked, but the way things were going, who could tell?

After spending close to an hour rechecking the quota figures he worked out before leaving Accord, he took out the "confidential" briefing folders and placed them on the top of the pile inside the datacase he was going to leave by the console. He set the internal counters, and locked the case.

Then he took the "official" briefing folders, three sets worth, and placed them inside the case he planned to take with him.

The "confidential" figures showed the same basic statistics on trade flows between the Coordinate and the Empire, but the projections showed a far more adverse effect on the economy of Accord than the set he was going to present to both Corwin-Smathers and later to Marcella.

He wondered who would get the confidential figures first. If he had to bet, his choice would be on the military types who were slinking around.

That brought back the question of Sergel. Sergel didn't seem to understand that the third-ranking officer of the Legation of a third-rate power didn't rate the kind of attention he was getting merely for his irresistible charm.

He shook his head and looked at the western hills.

With all the angles subdivided by angles, he had the feeling he'd be fortunate to find out all the real questions in six years, let alone in the few weeks he probably had.

Could it be done before Witherspoon wandered back, before the political compromise on Accord eroded, before the Empire figured out a way to militarily moot the whole question?

The second time around, after the experience of the Secession, the Empire just *might* be willing to sacrifice a fleet or two and several dozen planets for a millennium or two to eliminate permanently a thorn in its side.

He brought himself up short and checked the time. 0940—almost time to depart on another trip through the tunnels for his appointment with Corwin-Smathers.

Sergel still hadn't called in.

He flicked the code for the Information Specialist's quarters.

"Weintre," a sullen voice responded. The faxscreen remained blank.

"Whaler here. Let's have the screen, Sergel."

The picture came on. Sergel stood there, stripped to the waist, showing a small paunch over the black waistband of his too-tight rust trousers.

"Why didn't you answer my message?"

Sergel's mouth opened, moving back and forth soundlessly. Finally, he sputtered. "No message . . . I mean . . . no one left a message for me."

"The way everything else works around here, I can't say I'm surprised. Not that important, but what I have to say now is. I don't know what you were doing prowling around my quarters last night, but you'd better have a damned good explanation. I don't want any more phony answers. Face it, Sergel. You can't lie to me and make it stick."

He glared through the faxscreen at the younger man to reinforce the growling tone of his lecture.

"Well . . . umm . . . I hate to say it, Lord Whaler, but I got pretty stung. Thought I was somewhere else. I really did."

"Sergel, you're lying. Don't try to bluff through it again. If an explanation of what you were up to and the report I asked for aren't both on my console by the time I get back this afternoon, you're leaving on the next ship for Accord. Even if it's via the Alparta and takes two years objective. Is that clear?"

"Yes, sir. Perfectly clear."

Nathaniel could almost see the thoughts in his head. Sergel was wondering who had caught him out. He *knew* Nathaniel would have dispatched him, possibly without a trace.

Let him stew, thought the Ecolitan. He deserves it, and then some. In the game of mass confusion, perhaps some by Nathaniel might give Sergel, and his underground paymasters, some second thoughts.

"Remember, Sergel, those reports or you're on your way."

"Yes, sir."

The look on the Information Specialist's face told Nathaniel one more thing. Sergel was more afraid of someone else, much more afraid.

He broke the connection and looked at the blank screen a moment before returning his attention to the datacase he intended to take with him. The locked case was still beside the desk console.

He finally marched out into the general staff office.

"Mydra, sometime this afternoon will I be back."

"Is there anything else, Lord Whaler?"

"Not at this moment."

Nathaniel waved pleasantly to Heather Tew-Hawkes as he left the Legation and strode down the main corridor to the drop shaft.

He wondered if he were being tailed. It didn't matter at the moment. He slid into the high speed section and savored the fall. Almost like using a jump belt, except there was no risk in the drop shaft, no worry about enemy fire.

Out in the underground concourse, he caught a public tunnel cab driven by a man with long and silver-glittered hair.

XX

"WHAT WERE THE results of the interrogation?"

"He'd been totally blocked. If we'd gone any deeper, it would have turned his mind to mush. Didn't want to risk that, particularly since it's obviously a Defense conditioning job. So we released him, ostensibly after treating and detoxifying him. And we sent a confidential report on the detox results to the Ministry of Defense."

"Detoxifying?" asked the Director.

"Whatever Whaler used, we couldn't analyze. Even with a blood sample as soon as we got him, all we had left was molecular soup. Could have been a dozen things, but we think it was a short-term synthetic virus that acts as a temporary neural disruptor."

"How can you have a temporary and synthetic virus? And how could you develop one that wasn't fatal?"

"Damned if we know, but that's what it looks like." The Research Chief shook his head slowly.

The Director turned in her swivel. "That's the sort of weapon we'd give a dozen agents for, and Whaler doesn't mind using it right off. That says a couple of things. First, that it's something that they don't mind revealing. Second, that the trade talks or whatever Whaler is really doing is more than just important to Accord. And third, that Defense doesn't understand what we're up against." She snorted. "And Admiral Ku-Smythe thinks that we could win a war with Accord."

The Research Chief nodded, then added, "There's one other item. Their agent—and his profile matches Idel's, but who can tell—says he hit Whaler with the stunner. Not full, but enough to deaden one hand, maybe part of the arm."

"So?"

"Idel used a military stunner, set close to a lethal jolt, and Whaler still ran him down, apparently slugged him unconscious, and called Sylvia without betraying any discomfort."

"He can override pain to a fantastic degree . . . or our stunners just don't affect him . . . is that it?"

"Those are the only two explanations I can think of. Do you have a better one?"

"Idel missed."

"When was the last time a military Defense agent totally missed a target running straight at him?"

The Director shook her head. If only the Defense Ministry would understand, but that was like asking a tunnel roach not to scavenge.

XXI

THE OFFICES OF the Imperial Senate occupied an entire tower of their own, Senator Helmsworth was listed as having half the two hundred and third level to himself.

Nathaniel swung out of the lift shaft with fifteen minutes to spare and studied the directory before realizing that Corwin-Smathers' office was only fifty meters from the drop shaft.

The young man sitting at the front console of the staff office labelled External Relations Committee Staff greeted him eagerly.

"Lord Whaler! What a pleasure! Ms. Corwin-Smathers is tied up, but she'll be right with you. You know, it's a pleasure to meet someone like you. It really must be different outside the Empire, to be from a faraway system like Accord, and to be a Trade Envoy." He smiled brightly.

"Now, Charles," interrupted the dark-haired woman as she appeared from the side office, "you'll have Lord Whaler teaching you all the secrets of his success, and then what will I do to replace you?"

The Ecolitan offered the finger touch gesture he'd seen used. He thought it was between equals, and that wouldn't hurt.

"I'm the one who should be honored," she replied, "but I do appreciate the flattery."

"Only according you your due," he replied, suppressing a wince at his unintended pun.

She motioned toward a portal at one side of the reception office—not the one from which she had emerged a moment earlier—and paused, waiting for him.

From what he had seen thus far in the Imperial bureaucracy, her office was modest, although not a great deal smaller than his.

Restrained browns, contrasted with touches of brighter colors, set the tone. The console, chairs, and receiving table were modeled along the clean lines of fortieth century functionalism, but the dark shade, similar to stained lorkin, indicated it was from a later period.

Nathaniel selected the nonreclining pilot chair, rather than one of the deeper, ostensibly more comfortable sink chairs, but stood beside it for a minute, studying Courtney. By her posture, he could tell she was waiting for him. After standing for a few seconds longer, he settled into the pilot's chair.

"I appreciate your courtesy in seeing me on such short notice and for understanding the peculiar situation."

"Peculiar?"

"Peculiar to us. First trade talks with the Empire in seventy years, and only the second in over four centuries. I forget this sort of thing goes on day in and day out here in the Empire."

"Scarcely that often, and certainly not with an out-system with the, shall we say, prestige of Accord."

"Now you're overdoing the honor business," protested the Ecolitan.

"I don't think so. For a system which has but three nationals here normally to send such a highly qualified individual for trade negotiations honors us greatly. The fact that you have also contacted one of the most interested Senators shows how close you are to the pulse of things."

"We're just trying to chart all the orbits."

Courtney did not reply. She smiled.

A hush, almost absolute silence, settled on the office.

"I assume you do have a reason for asking to see me."

"Alas," began Nathaniel, "a glib charmer like most Envoys, I am not. Someone who can say nothing while saying everything, that I am not."

"That's a pretty good start."

He shrugged. "I have come to talk about trade. And what Accord would like is clear. Clear it has been from the beginning. So why no one will talk is difficult to understand. All tariffs? Are they the question? Or trade policy? Perhaps the overall trade balance? I know not."

"Are we talking appearances or realities? Politics or economics?"

"I don't know your politics. From outside New Augusta how could anyone really know? And why on poor Accord does the Empire center? After seventy years of quiet, we are protested, instead of I Found It!, the Fuardian Conglomerate, Halston, or other independents.

"As for economics—we do produce a few microcomponents for export, but by themselves why such a fuss they would create I cannot see."

"Really, Lord Whaler, dealing with the Empire is not that difficult."

"About that, you might ask the former Envoy from Haversol. His negotiations, they did not go well, and that precedent worries Accord."

"If you are that worried, why doesn't Accord merely accept whatever proposal the Empire has offered?"

"As I recall, dear Lady, the Empire has offered nothing. Nothing except the declaration that the present terms of trade most unsatisfactory are. So here we are, and I am here also."

"That puzzles me. You are a full Envoy. You have had lunch with a staffer of mine, then requested an appointment with me, prior to any substantive talks being started. Why not the Senator? Why not the government?"

"When requesting an appointment of the Senator, I was told it might be some time before he was free. Some time no one has, whether they know it or not. Also I have had some talks with the government, so far going to no destination."

"Why are you here? Really here?"

"To see you." She was so intent he couldn't resist the jab.

"Lord Whaler, while I appreciate the flattery, you have not told me what you want, why you want it, and why I should help you, if indeed that help is what you want."

Her sharpness brought Nathaniel up short. He looked at Courtney, evaluating what he saw.

The dark eyes, deep set under heavy black eyebrows and lashes, dominated a smooth white face and pale lips. The tightness of her skin and the fine lines radiating from the corners of her eyes emphasized the energy she contained. Her black hair, cut short well above the standard Imperial collar, showed silver streaks. Since standard cosmetology treatments allowed anyone to retain their natural hair color for life, either Courtney didn't care or hadn't had time for recent treatments.

"As you know," he went on, "Haversol refused to negotiate, and the result we all know. We would be willing to negotiate, within reason. Profession of willingness appears with the government, but no negotiation, only buildups of the Imperial fleets. While diplomacy has not been a strength of Accord, try it we would hope, even though some members of the House of Delegates are opposed. We judge that Senator Helmsworth might play a critical role, perhaps in creating momentum. You are the critical assistant to the Senator."

The Ecolitan waited.

"Lord Whaler, one thing comes through clearly. You are racing against time. Why?"

"Dear Lady, perhaps I continue to underestimate you. You have said nothing, committed nothing, and demanded everything. For that, I must have underestimated your power."

"You do me far too much credit."

"Only that which you are due."

"Perhaps, also," she returned, "I have not been as courteous as I should have been, but on the surface there seemed to be no problem, and I hope you understand that right now, particularly with all the Parthanian Cloud questions, the ad valorem tax changes, and the Force Command tax proposal, things have been a bit hectic."

"I understand, but much lies beneath the surface. And everyone avoids what lies there."

"And just what do you mean by that?" A frown creased Courtney's forehead.

"I doubt that the Empire wants another ecological war. While it would mean the end of Accord, history shows that the Empire as you know it could not survive another such conflict. Now, I'm not advocating anything, just pointing out that failure to reach an agreement could lead in that direction."

"What do you suggest?"

Rather than answer directly, he handed her one of the folders.

She looked it over, then laid it down.

"It appears rather generous on the surface. That means there's more to it than meets the eye."

"We can make concessions now that would be somewhat more difficult two years from now when the one-year Delegate selections take place. Economically, it doesn't make that much difference, but . . ." he dangled out the implication.

"You're implying the present political conditions on Accord will turn for the worse, from the Empire's point of view, after the next elections. Is that a fair assumption?"

"Obviously, any prediction of any election result more than a year in the future is little more than a guess, but recently the Orthodoxist extremists have been making a comeback. The failure of the more moderate Normist majority to obtain a trade settlement might well increase the appeal of the Orthodoxist party."

"Isn't that blatant pressure?"

Nathaniel cleared his throat.

"Ms. Corwin-Smathers, it is obvious that talks we are approaching from totally different backgrounds. For you, trade with small systems can be pushed into the background. You view Accord as a fifth-rate outsystem with no real right to question the almighty Empire, and with no real military options."

For the first time, Courtney leaned forward, as if she were interested.

"Let me assure you, madam, that while Accord would be the first to wish to avoid the use of military means, ecological or not, ethical or not, we have the means to prevent the Empire from making us another dependency. We will not be bullied, and we will not hesitate if pushed to the brink.

"The Empire has made such a mistake once. I sincerely hope, for all our sakes, you do not try again. We would prefer to negotiate, and we will, if anyone is willing."

He pointed to the folder she had laid carelessly across her console.

"Those are the facts as Accord sees them. If you feel otherwise, then I am certain you and the Senator will indeed let us know."

Nathaniel ended with nearly a military snap.

"Accord is fortunate to have you, Lord Whaler." She smiled coldly. "I wish you luck in all your contacts. I trust you will be as forthright with them as you have been with me. Who do you plan to see next?"

"The Ministry of Commerce. Then the Ministry of External Affairs."

"I assume you're seeing Marcella Ku-Smythe."

Courtney's statement was not a question but a declaration.

"Before I leave," Nathaniel added in a softer tone, "do you or your staff have any changes you would like Accord to consider?"

She shifted her weight. "It's not really up to us, you know. Ms. Ku-Smythe could endorse your terms, and the Commerce Ministry would approve her recommendations, if that's what you wanted."

"I would prefer your candid appraisal," responded the Ecolitan, backing away from the implications of Courtney's comments. "At the moment, we do not feel anyone should be excluded, since a consensus agreement would raise fewer objections. For example, if we had chosen to exclude you and the Senator, you could easily have suggested a long and drawn-out investigation and hearings that could block any agreement. Drawing things out would not help anyone, except the Federated Hegemony, Halston, the Fuards, or anyone else who was left to pick up the pieces.

"Your candid recommendations could ease the way for a more easily accepted settlement."

"Wait a moment," she commanded as she picked up the folder and rose from behind the console.

Nathaniel nodded, but as she left, let the stunner slip down from inside his wide cuffs to a point above his left wrist.

Courtney was on her way to contact Imperial Intelligence, the Noram microprocessors, or both.

While she was gone, with one eye on the portal, he studied the office in detail, from the Cereberium eternal clock to the real leather desk pad to the all-wooden desk and matched credenza. He also took the liberty of leaning forward slightly and memorizing the two private line numbers on the console.

Again, the nagging questions were piling up, but behind them was an obvious fundamental assumption, something so glaring he was overlooking it, something so common he couldn't see the swamp for the water. He knew it was there. He just couldn't put his finger on it.

It wasn't the arrangement of the office or Courtney Corwin-Smathers herself, as arrogant as she seemed to be.

Courtney was absent fifteen standard minutes. By the end of the fifteenth minute, Nathaniel was ready to leave.

She returned with a smile.

"I was able to reach the Senator, and the general terms of your proposal, provided the facts are as we think they are, will probably be acceptable to the Senator and the External Relations Committee as a sound beginning point. The staff will have to work out more specifics, but by tomorrow I should have a better idea. Can you give me a fax then?"

"That should be no problem. Do you have any objections to my giving the same information to Commerce?"

"Why should I? We're poor innocent bystanders as far as Commerce is concerned."

Nathaniel rose to his feet and gave Courtney a half bow.

"I appreciate your candor and your willingness to work toward a mutually acceptable agreement."

"Lord Whaler, you have been most forthright and very gallant under what I know must be very trying circumstances. Appearances in and among the various bureaus and Ministries can indeed be complicated and deceiving."

That was the second double message.

"I'm learning that." He laughed as he turned toward the portal, keeping an eye on Courtney.

"I hope we'll have a chance to talk again before long."

"Sure hope you'll come to see us again, Lord Whaler," chimed in Charles, the receptionist, who brushed against Nathaniel as he returned to his console just as Nathaniel was trying to get past.

For some reason, the Ecolitan felt on edge, the same way he had during jump training or when he'd been in the Trezenian Police Action, the time he'd avoided leading his patrol into ambush.

This is the Empire, he told himself, not the outback of Trezenia. Out of habit, he checked the people in the corridor as he left the Senator's office.

Only a handful were in the throughway to the drop shaft.

Dropping quickly into the high speed section, he plummeted toward the concourse level where the tunnels cross connected.

The drop shafts were one of the few things he enjoyed about New Augusta.

Swinging out onto the permatile of the bottom level, he looked for the flashing indicators of the tunnel cabs, rather than heading for the tube system. The tunnel trains reminded him too much of the Institute's fast troop carriers.

As he walked toward the tunnel cab dispatching point, which superficially resembled organized chaos with the cabs flicking in and out of wall tunnels in some sort of nearly random order as the passengers inserted their universal credit cards into the dispatch gate, he wondered how the system really worked.

The tunnel cabs worked—no doubt about it—but the intricate traffic patterns leading up to the dispatch stations seemed decorative rather than functional.

Nathaniel inserted the Legation credit card into the slot, punched in his proposed destination, the Ministry of Commerce, and waited.

A silver electrocougar glided out of the third portal and whispered to a stop directly in front of him.

The driver was a woman, dark hair severely cut, the Ecolitan noted as he bent and eased into the rear seat.

"Ministry of Commerce?"

"Right. Main Tower."

The electrocougar pulled away from the silver walls of the Senate Tower concourse and dropped into the cab tunnel.

Nathaniel looked at the back of the driver's head. From the back seat, he could see the high, dark brown collar of her tunic, so plain it almost resembled a uniform, and the squarish cut of her hair. She was nearly as big as he was, far bigger than any of the cab drivers he had seen so far.

Something was wrong. Of that he was convinced, and it was linked to the growing feeling he had overlooked something so incredibly basic that he and everyone else in New Augusta took it for granted, whatever "it" happened to be.

As the tunnel cab hummed through the frescoed tunnel toward the Ministry of Commerce, he tried to take stock, mentally ticking off the possibilities.

Both Marcella Ku-Smythe and Courtney Corwin-Smathers were more powerful than their titles would indicate. Everyone deferred to a limited degree to him as an Envoy, but no one seemed to expect much from him.

A small flashing light interrupted his reflections.

"Destination approaching. Please insert credit card."

He complied, and the dispenser promptly burped the card back into his hand. He slipped the square plasticard into his belt pouch.

Abruptly, the cab halted.

Already tense, Nathaniel flipped open the door and stepped out before realizing he was not in the concourse area of the Ministry of Commerce, but in the flat area outside the tunnel, a good hundred meters away from the brightly lit portal where other tunnel cabs were entering.

As quickly as he turned, the driver had been quicker and was pulling away before the cab door was fully closed.

The spot where he stood, datacase in hand, was lit sporadically, patches of light and shadow alternating.

A low scrape registered. He ducked and whirled, dropping the case and letting the combat training assert itself automatically. Without thinking, he kicked aside the forceblade, grabbed the other's arm, momentarily paralyzed the hand nerves with a grip above the elbow, snapped his left hand across the opponent's opposite wrist in time to send a small hand weapon skittering across the plastistone pavement.

He finished by sweeping the other's feet and leaving the would-be mugger in a heap. Only after the fact did he realize his assailant was a woman almost as tall and heavily muscled as he was.

He reached down and ripped the belt pouch from her jumpsuit, kicked her feet out from under her again, and flipped through the contents.

Miniature knife, tube stunner, Caesar notes, change . . . nothing.

"Any reason why I shouldn't break your leg on the spot?"

"Just like all men. If you're going to do it, do it. Otherwise don't talk about it."

Why hadn't he seen it? In this crazy Imperial society, the women held all the real power. Why hadn't he noticed?

He gritted his teeth, pulled the woman to her feet with his right hand, keeping his weight balanced and ready for any trickery. As soon as she had full weight on both feet, he let go of her hand and with a fluid kick-through shattered her left knee.

She collapsed without a sound.

Deciding that retreat was the better part of valor, he pulled the tube stunner from the attacker's pouch and turned it on the woman, who slumped back into a heap. He then wiped off all the items he had touched, replaced them in the belt pouch, and dropped it by her feet.

Shrugging and taking a deep breath, he picked up his discarded datacase and moved quickly toward the tunnel portal.

Was Courtney out to get him? Or had she been trying to warn him that the situation was beyond her control?

As he edged through the cab portal, narrowly avoiding a speeding tunnel cab whose small driver gaped at him open-mouthed, he wondered just how many people wanted him out of the way.

Several cab passengers stared at him as he vaulted over the barrier where they waited by the dispatch stations. Someone would doubtless report the incident, but, one way or another, his mission would be over before any investigation could be concluded.

XXII

THE LAST THING Nathaniel wanted was to stay around long enough for some public-spirited citizen to link the unconscious woman in the tunnel with the character in black who vaulted the public barrier in the concourse. Not that the linkage wouldn't occur, but the later, the better.

Cowardice was the better part of valor, and he walked quickly toward the lift shaft.

With the time only 1200 local Imperial, he needed to kill some time before appearing on Marcella's doorstep. And he was hungry.

His stomach rumbled as he strode into the circular take-off area for the Commerce Tower lift shaft. He paused, turning his head to search for the directory. Surely, there had to be a directory for services in the tower.

He found it on the far side, flashing in muted maroon, the ever-present color of the Commerce Ministry.

Advertised on the directory were both a public foodomat and an official servarium. The public foodomat had the advantage of speed and relative anonymity. At the servarium, if he could use his official Accord credentials to get in, he'd have more time to think things over and a somewhat quieter atmosphere.

Acutely conscious that he was beginning to react to situations rather than controlling them, he decided on the servarium, listed as being on the forty-first level.

As he eased into the upward lift, he felt watched.

"Come on, Nathaniel," he muttered to himself, "you're getting paranoid."

He shifted his weight enough to turn his body.

Three quarters of a turn and ten levels later, he spotted the woman, rising in the slower outer lane. She was now wearing a light blue cloak, but the squarish face and dark severe haircut were the same. She had been the driver of the tunnel cab that had dropped him off outside the concourse.

"Don't they ever give up?"

Before he finished mumbling the question, he realized the stupidity of it. And the irony. Here he was, trying to get the Empire on edge, and already they were harassing him, trying to get him on edge.

One thing was becoming clearer and clearer. There were more players and higher stakes than Accord had anticipated. When he had a moment, if he ever had one again, that should be conveyed to the Prime.

For the time being, he had another problem. First, was whatever faction of the Empire trailing him going to be content with merely keeping tabs on him, or would they attempt another put-away action? Second, was the driver an attempt to divert his attention from a more immediate and closer danger?

He shifted his weight again, leaning to let himself slide into the highest speed central lane. Shifting lanes in mid-level was frowned upon but not forbidden.

With half an eye on the well-built woman driver, he began to study the others in the shaft both above and below him. A front tail was certainly possible.

Only a thin young man who was squirming into the high speed lane had showed any possible reaction to Nathaniel's shift.

As the Ecolitan passed the fiftieth level, he jumped onto the high speed exit stage and trotted straight down the walkway toward the drop shaft on the other side.

Coming up on the drop side, he studied the drop lane, then jumped to the top of the side barrier, rather than walking all the way around to the entry point, and took a running dive down through the traffic.

"*Clang! Clang!* Danger! Danger! Unauthorized entry!" screeched the automatic warning devices, slowing the drop shaft speed momentarily.

Nathaniel let his momentum carry him to the far side of the shaft, reaching the exit stage and an upright position and the forty-first level all at the same time.

He saw neither the woman nor the nervous man.

The public fresher on the corridor to the official servarium served several purposes—letting him relieve himself, allowing him to catch his breath, and affording him some privacy while donning a thin gold film cloak to reduce the impact of his diplomatic blacks.

Before leaving the fresher stall, he took from his inside thigh pouch a small wooden tube, a smaller version of the dart gun he had used earlier but with the same type of dissolving needle darts that rendered the victim delirious within seconds and which dissolved within minutes.

The drug wore off within two or three hours but left the victims with scrambled memories and intermittent headaches for days.

If those tailing him were as persistent as he suspected, at least one would be waiting somewhere.

Both were—right outside the servarium and seemingly oblivious to each other.

The woman stood by the main entrance, visibly consulting her timestrap and pocket calendar as if to call attention to the fact that her friend, contact, or lover had been delayed.

The thin and nervous man, now wearing a rust cloak, sat on a public bench several meters away reading a faxtab. Neither had noticed him.

Since the servarium was close to the lift shaft, the corridor was wide and foot traffic frequent—perhaps several people moving past the entrance every few seconds—but the spaciousness of the ten-meter width and the high ceilings reduced the visual impact of the numbers.

Nathaniel didn't hesitate. If the Empire wanted to play hardblast, he'd oblige them. Placing his locked datacase against the corridor wall, he slipped the tranquilizer tube, good for two shots, one from each end, just so he could trigger it without the action being obvious to others.

The way the woman was positioned, the Ecolitan should be able to get within a meter or so before she would be aware of him.

She saw him in the wide-angled mirror attached to the calendar and twisted it in an effort to line up the long axis of the calendar toward him.

Nathaniel dropped, triggering the tube with the facility of long practice.

The needle caught her in the neck and began to dissolve. At the same time, he was inside her guard and knocked aside the pocket calendar and whatever weapon it concealed.

"You . . ." she muttered, as she began to shudder. "Told me you were slick . . . devils! Get the devils!" Her voice mounted to a shriek.

She began to convulse. Nathaniel knew the muscular contractions were not exactly convulsions, but anyone not versed in the depths of Coordinate military medicine would not catch the differences soon.

Three or four passersby immediately gathered. A chime in the corridor began ringing.

Nathaniel had already left the woman and had covered half the distance to the bench and to the thin man.

The nervous Imperial agent was better than the woman or took advantage of the slight warning he had. The glint of metal as the angle of the faxtab held by the sitting man shifted indicated he held something ready.

Nathaniel stretched his arm toward the man, triggering the tube from three meters. On the range his accuracy was only about eighty percent. Here he needed one hundred percent.

The Imperial twitched as the needle whistled by his ear, losing his concentration momentarily. Long enough for Nathaniel to cover the last meter at full dash and knock aside the short barreled weapon with his right hand as it discharged. The Ecolitan felt the surge of nerve pain in his right shoulder but clamped down on his reactions.

Jabbing his left hand with force just short of crushing the larnyx, he silenced the bench sitter, who was trying to get to his feet. Despite the waves of pain radiating from his shoulder, he snapped three fingers of the man's right hand in forcing him to drop the nerve tangler.

A knee to the groin left the Imperial agent retching on the ground. After taking only seconds to snap another needle into the tube, Nathaniel fired it into the man's neck while bending down as if to help the poor unfortunate.

As the emergency medical unit, a low-slung silent cart, pulled up, he kicked the tangler under the bench and slid the faxtab over it.

"Here! Here!" he called.

A health officer and a medtech appeared.

"What happened?"

"I was walking up to get something to eat. This man started yelling. He threw down what he was reading, got sick, and went into convulsions."

"May I have your name, citizen?"

The new voice belonged to an Imperial Monitor, otherwise known as the Emperor's Police, who was dressed in a silver tunic with gold piping and brandished a computab, all with the bored look of all police in all eras.

"Not a citizen am I, but a visitor, and quite surprised, officer. I have an appointment up-level later, but I wanted to eat. This man goes crazy. Then somebody behind me yells and screams. I just don't understand. Now you want to know who I am. He's the one who started this business."

"I understand that, sir. But could I please have your name for the record? In case we need witnesses."

"Of course. Nathaniel Whaler."

"Whaler?"

"W-H-A-L-E-R."

"I.D. number?"

"Don't have one, Diplomatic number." Nathaniel pulled out the diplomatic I.D. "A-C-O-3."

"Very sorry to bother you, Lord Whaler. Can we call you if we have further questions?"

"Certainly. I'll be back at the Legation after 1500."

By the time the few questions had been answered, the two Imperial agents, if that had indeed been their calling, had been carted off in small and silent corridor buggies.

Luckily, his datacase was where he had left it, apparently untouched.

Getting into the servarium wasn't nearly so hard as getting there had been.

"Do you allow diplomatic credentials?"

"Of course, sir. Of course."

Most of the clientele seemed to be mid-level junior bureaucrats. Two women to every man. Servarium was a fancy name for self-service off a compuchef, but the odds were that his food at least wouldn't ambush him.

Settling on an elaborate omelet and liftea, he gave the machine his credit card, took it back, and made a hornetline for a small corner table where he couldn't be approached from behind.

"You're getting paranoid again," he said to himself.

After a minute, he decided he needed to answer himself. "Just because you're paranoid doesn't mean that they aren't all out to get you."

He wasn't sure he believed himself, but he dug into the omelet anyway, which seemed half real, half synthetic, but filling all the same, and polished it off.

The lemony taste of the liftea relaxed him fractionally, just enough to lower his pain threshold and bring the throbbing in his shoulder back to his attention. He let his fingers run over the shoulder, but there was no exterior soreness, and the nerve twinges would probably pass within a few hours. So he hoped. Two shots to his right arm and shoulder area in a matter of days wasn't helpful.

If the nerve tangler had hit him full in the chest at that power, he'd have been the one carted off, with an emergency sheet over his face and the diagnosis of coronary arrest.

Checking his other shoulder and the rest of his blacks, he'd noticed a black bump on the fabric behind his upper arm almost impossible to see. He recognized the snooper instantly.

When had anyone touched him? Not Courtney. She'd kept her distance. The Imperial crowds were sparse and avoided each other. No one had come within body lengths.

Charles! The friendly receptionist had brushed him when he had left Courtney's office.

That was how he'd been tracked. The only question was for whom Charles worked.

He resisted the impulse to crush the bug on the spot. Instead, pretending to adjust his cloak, he worked it free and slipped it onto a scrap of plastic.

He studied the others eating in the servarium, listening while he looked, finally zeroing in on an obnoxious-sounding man who was complaining to his tablemate, another man, about the unvarnished ambition of his boss, a woman.

Nathaniel headed from his table toward the exit. Stumbling slightly as he passed the complainer and banging the datacase against the table, he brushed against the man and left the snoop affixed on his shoulder.

The stumble had gained him a momentary dirty look, but so intent was the man that he scarcely let up on his tirade. The switch would only deflect things for a few minutes, and he'd have to be even more on guard from now on.

Outside the servarium, in the same relative positions as the previous team, were another man and woman, both consulting pocket "calendars" which presumably indicated that Nathaniel was still inside. Neither reacted as he passed.

Checking as he went, he could find no one tailing him as he took the lift shaft to the one hundred fourth level and to the office of Special Assistant Ku-Smythe.

The exit stage time readout indicated 1410 when he walked off and toward the directory. Marcella's office was down the branch corridor to the right.

Before he got close to her office, he ran into a security gate and a console with maroon clad guards sporting both blasters and stunners.

"Your business, citizen?"

"I'm not a citizen," He drew back the cloak to reveal his diplomatic blacks.

"Your business?" repeated the woman, not knowing or caring what the uniform meant.

"Nathaniel Whaler, Envoy of Accord. Fourteen-thirty appointment with Ms. Ku-Smythe."

"Your I.D."

The Ecolitan handed it over.

"One moment, Lord Whaler."

The guard tapped several keys on the console screen.

She seemed startled at the result.

"You're expected!"

"I knew that before you asked," he said flatly, knowing he was being snide, petty, and nasty, but tired of all the potshots, literal and verbal. "Room, 104 A-6?"

"Yes, sir."

"Thank you."

The gate opened. Hoisting his datacase, he went through. The gate buzzed loudly.

"Weapons, sir?"

"Just a stunner." He fished it out of his pouch and handed it to the guard.

"You can pick it up on the way out."

Ten to one, by the time he left it would have been rebuilt with a complete snoop and trace system inside. He decided to "forget" to pick up the stunner. He also wished he could get rid of the datacase—the damned thing was always getting in the way. He was used to having both hands free. Room 104 A-6 was a small, functional reception area with two maroon pilot chairs, a table, indirect lighting, and a receptionist.

For the first time, it seemed, the receptionist was a woman, small, coming to his shoulder, with long black hair and brown eyes, olive skin, dressed in a maroon and cream tunic with matching maroon trousers.

"Lord Whaler?"

"The same."

"You are early, but Ms. Ku-Smythe will be with you shortly. Please have a seat. Would you like anything to drink?"

"No . . . but do you have the latest faxtab?"

"Standard, Ministry, or Court?"

"What's the difference between Ministry and Court?"

"Not much. They have the same columns and gossip."

"What do you recommend?"

"The Privy Council reads the Ministry edition."

"And the Court edition is mainly for socialites and appearances?"

The receptionist smiled, one of the first genuine smiles the Ecolitan had seen since he'd arrived in New Augusta . . . except perhaps for Sylvia.

"I'll take the Ministry edition."

She tapped several studs on her console, and with a series of buzzes, three pages burped forth, which she delivered to Nathaniel.

"There you are, Lord Whaler."

About half the faxtab consisted of factual briefs a paragraph or two long in relatively simple Panglais. Fifth Fleet dispatched to Sector Eight in support of the Sector Governor on Byron. Would Senator Rysler retire and turn over his Agriculture Committee to Ngnoma?

Failure of the synde bean crop on Ferne II and the need for Imperial aid. Possible breakdown of the Parthanian Cloud talks. Need for tax reform more urgent and might appear on the Emperor's Legislative Calendar for the new Senate. Repeal of the sex determination ban to be brought up again by the pro-choice faction.

Nathaniel skipped to the "personality" section or "Scandalous Sam."

Nothing mentioned about Accord or one Envoy Whaler. That was a relief after such bits as: ". . . should we tell you which Assistant Deputy Minister, after being seduced by his luscious receptionist (what a man!), asked his contractmate for a dissolution?" Or ". . . it's rumored that the coronary arrest suffered by the Delegate from Greater Srik Nord wasn't."

"Lord Whaler?"

"Yes?"

"Ms. Ku-Smythe will see you now. Through the portal on the left."

He folded the faxtab, laid it on the table, slipped to his feet, picked up his datacase, and strode through the left portal.

The office, with cream wall hangings and a sweeping panoramic window, was three times the size of either his own office as Envoy or that of Courtney Corwin-Smathers.

Marcella was attired in a formal cream tunic and matching trousers, with a set of gold Commerce pins on her collars. A single maroon ring circled each tunic cuff. Her hair was upswept, severe, and she stood behind her wraparound console, formally, not advancing to meet him.

The console, at the far end of the office, allowed Marcella to survey both entry portals and the window.

He bowed and could feel the portal shut behind him.

"Greetings again, Nathaniel."

"Greetings to you, Marcella."

She gestured to the padded antique leather wing chair across from her console. He wondered at the real age of the chair with the new maroon leather, but sat down with the datacase at his feet.

"How's the business of Commerce with the Special Assistant?"

"As well as can be expected. What about you?"

He hesitated. Should he tell Marcella anything?

He let his face show some indecision.

"Not terribly well received somewhere, is that it?"

"More complicated than that. I'm not sure where to begin, and beginning at the beginning would take much time."

He pulled at his chin. "This business is getting more involved than I'd anticipated, and did I not think I would have any illusions about the degree of difficulty."

Marcella sat back in the swivel, waiting, seemingly ready to let him take his time to get to the point. He doubted she had that much patience. But she was capable and a good actress to boot.

"Yesterday, Courtney Corwin-Smathers suggested I come by today to discuss Senator Helmsworth's interests in trade negotiations. I arrived at the appointed time, was warmly greeted, explained our interests in arriving at a favorable settlement without antagonizing any of the parties involved, and left her a copy of our preliminary proposal."

He thought Marcella's eyes narrowed slightly, but went on.

"Rather politely, and oh-so-pointedly, Ms. Corwin-Smathers suggested that while I certainly could let the Ministry of Commerce see such a proposal, I would be well advised to put my faith in the Senator."

"Did she put it exactly that way?"

Marcella leaned forward in her swivel, brushing a strand of sandy hair back over her ear.

Nathaniel chuckled. "Are you serious? Let me see if I can recapture the essence of the conversation. I am not much on innuendos, you know, but try I will."

He composed his face into a stern mask.

"I do wish you luck with your contacts . . . we're regarded as poor innocent bystanders . . . and Commerce could certainly ratify your agreement if that is *really* what you want . . . Ms. Ku-Smythe would surely be pleased not to deal with other influences . . ."

"She mentioned my name?"

"As I recall."

"Did you say you were coming to see me?"

"No. I made a point of being vague about my appointments, but she seemed to know I had an appointment with you. And that leads on to the next thing, which was even stranger."

"Stranger?"

"I took a tunnel cab over here from the Senate Office Tower and was dumped out in the tunnel outside the concourse—"

"Outside the concourse?"

"Outside the concourse. With a stunner, a woman strange to me tried to attack me. The tunnel cab took flight."

"Obviously, you survived."

Nathaniel shrugged and spread his hands. "Some luck, I think. But left I in a hurry. So why should someone be after me? If Senator Helmsworth wanted one set of terms . . . if you another . . . and External Affairs another . . . but before anyone has said anything? This it would seem would mean that someone wants no talks."

Marcella frowned. "I'm not sure I understand."

"Why would you have me assaulted? I would think you would want to see what Accord had to offer. Is that not so?"

"That's true. It wouldn't make sense, not from my point of view."

"That implies that more than one point of view there is within the Commerce Ministry."

Marcella looked straight at him.

"I have this feeling you've been underestimated, Lord Whaler. I'll try not to make the same mistake."

"Lucky I have been, so far." He leaned back in the leather chair. "Secondary to something else are questions of trade, and to some facet of Imperial politics not immediately obvious to outsiders." The Ecolitan bent down and lifted the datacase into his lap.

"Imperial politics do become somewhat involuted," added Marcella, "and could be rather confusing to an outsider."

Nathaniel didn't like Marcella being patronizing any more than he had Courtney Corwin-Smathers, but he only opened the datacase and pulled out a trade folder before closing the case and returning it to the floor. He stood abruptly and leaned toward her, watching her hands flick down toward the edge of the console. Ignoring the danger, he read the private line numbers and memorized them.

So . . . the console had a full protective system, and dear Marcella didn't trust him all that much.

"Here's the folder with our proposal," he said as he extended it slowly. "I'm sure you can handle far better than I the intricacies of Imperial politics. After you study it, I would be most interested in your thoughts."

"After we study it, I'll be happy to talk with you."

"You know, Marcella, you can trust me or not. But if you really need a console protective system, the controls ought to be in the arms of the swivel."

He bowed to her. "Your leave, Marcella?"

He could see the play of emotions under her tightly controlled face. No secrets there at the moment. He'd gotten to her, and she wasn't pleased about it.

"You do me honor, Lord Whaler."

"The honor is mine, and outside the questions of diplomacy."

She flushed ever so slightly at the compliment, but so quickly he almost missed her reaction.

He gave a mental shrug as he walked out through the portal, case in hand, to the reception area.

"Lord Whaler?"

He looked at the receptionist.

"Did you leave anything at the security gate?"

"I do not believe so."

"Ms. Ku-Smythe arranged for your return transportation in one of our tunnel vehicles to spare you the rush period congestion. I am to escort you."

"Indebted I am."

The small woman led him through a corridor vaguely familiar. He caught a glance of a receiving hall, and the memory jibed. This was the hall he'd come up to meet Rotoller and Marcella.

They stopped in front of the small lift/drop shaft.

"Now where?" he asked.

"We'll go down to the Commerce official concourse."

"Indeed a step up over the public transport," he commented inanely.

While several guards patrolled the corridor, none seemed to take notice of either Nathaniel or the receptionist.

She stepped into the shaft, assuming that he would follow.

He did.

As he exited, the receptionist handed him a small flat envelope.

"I think you dropped this in the shaft. It floated past me."

Nathaniel hadn't.

"Thank you. I was careless."

He surveyed the guards around the concourse, both men and women, as they walked to the embarking platform.

An electrocougar was waiting.

The receptionist stayed until he was inside with the door closed.

The car was upholstered in maroon, but the fabric was less yielding than that in the official car that had brought him to his meeting with Rotoller.

The male driver was in a plain maroon tunic.

As the car pulled away, the receptionist waved before she turned. No one had done that before, not on Terra. He turned the envelope over,

The heavy cream paper was without name or address, except for three intertwined initials on the reverse flap, and was barely sealed . . . just at the tip of the flap. The three initials were MKS.

Before opening the envelope, Nathaniel looked up at the back of the driver's head as the limousine dropped down into the tunnel. Nothing he could tell.

Holding the envelope gingerly, feeling stupid about his qualms, he used his belt knife to flick it open. He turned the envelope, and a small card fluttered out onto the seat cushion.

A single word appeared on the blank card, handwritten: CAREFULLY.

He resealed the envelope and card and put them in his belt pouch.

The writing might be Marcella's, but since he'd never seen it, how would he know?

And for Cloud's sake, what specifically was he supposed to be careful about? He was already too cautious.

The more he found out, the more he didn't know.

XXIII

ALERT TO THE possibility of another tunnel cab incident, Nathaniel spent the ride back to the Diplomatic Tower fully ready for anything. The Commerce Ministry electro-cougar delivered him to the Diplomatic Tower without mishap.

"Your destination, sir."

"My thanks."

Despite all his suspicions, he made it up the lift shaft and to the

Legation's front entrance without an obvious tail, and without anyone else attempting to take any potshots at him.

"Good afternoon, Lord Whaler. Were your meetings successful?" asked Heather as he walked past.

"Everything went as expected."

He didn't recall telling anyone he had a single meeting, let alone two. He sighed audibly. In New Augusta, if more than one person knew a secret, it wasn't a secret.

"Greetings, Lord Whaler," added Mydra, as he paused outside his office.

"Any calls for me?"

"No. Things are relatively quiet here. Have you seen the faxnews?"

"Too busy have I been. Why?"

"I wondered if anyone else from Accord was in New Augusta. The afternoon casts reported a strange man in black assaulted an Imperial Intelligence agent in a tunnel, broke her leg, stunned her, and escaped. The Imperial Intelligence Service is denying the report. No one has seen anyone in black in the area."

Mydra was giving him a calculated look.

"You know, Mydra, after days like today, sometimes one would wish to be more violent. But professors, we are not known as such. Today I have talked to too many who say, 'Maybe yes. Maybe no. Let us think about it.'"

He went on. "I do not think I should like to meet such an Imperial Intelligence agent. I hear most competent they are."

"I'm glad to hear that, Lord Whaler. After the report hit the fax, I called a friend of mine. She's an office manager at I.I.S. I asked her about it. She couldn't say much, but the agent who was allegedly attacked was one of the best. The next time they go after that fellow, they'll go with lethal weapons, I understand."

"Most interesting. Does this happen often here?"

"I don't believe I've ever heard of another case."

The Ecolitan shrugged and entered his office.

The room had been searched, thoroughly, and more than once. Items were fractionally out of place, and the datacase on the table had been moved. He scanned the case with the belt multitector. A rather large mass was inside, doubtless something unpleasant and explosive.

Sergel had left his report in the in-tray, and Nathaniel swept it up as he walked back to the portal and began to scan the office.

Two new full-scale snoops showed, one right above the console and the other almost over his head, plus a fluctuating energy concentration right between the two.

He'd seen the pattern before.

Not waiting to see the needle peg off the scale, he dove out the doorway and into the main office.

"Down! Hit the floor!"

The first explosion cut off his words, and then the gimmicked datacase followed with a roar, the second explosion bulging the wall outward.

As Nathaniel picked himself up, he ran a quick sweep of the staff office. Three standard snoops, period.

He hadn't been back in the Legation for more than ten minutes, and he'd been delivered three messages—two explosive ones and a veiled threat through Mydra.

Was Mydra working for the Imperial Intelligence Service or someone else? Was the I.I.S. telling him they didn't care what he knew? Was the military behind Sergel . . . and the bomb he'd planted?

Mere trade negotiations couldn't be that explosive, could they?

"Lord Whaler! What happened?" demanded Hillary West-Coven, her left arm bleeding from a long scratch.

"Fortunes of trade, Hillary. Fortunes of trade."

Mydra was standing at the door from the hallway to the staff office. How much coincidence had her temporary absence been?

Nathaniel almost shook his head.

"Mydra, my office has been somewhat damaged, and to my quarters I will repair. Would you arrange for the necessary repairs?"

He marched out, going straight through his shattered office and into his private quarters.

Once inside, he swept the rooms for snoops, but found only a single additional visual. He used his tool kit to disable it.

After that, he turned up the background music and used the private comm.

"Ms. Du-Plessis' office."

"Lord Whaler, Accord Legation. Is she in?"

"I don't know, sir. I believe she is in conference."

"Find her. That is, if she expects either to retain her position or to have some trade talks with Accord."

An ivory-skinned, black-haired woman of the indeterminate age range that had characterized Courtney Corwin-Smathers appeared on the screen.

"Lord Whaler, aren't you overly free with the positions of the Ministry and their disposition?"

"Ms. Du-Plessis, the situation is deteriorating and called for drastic measures."

"Oh?"

"Madam, Accord, you, and I are running out of time for reasons unclear to me. I do not have time to fence with words, nor words to fence with. How many times have you tried to reach me, and what were you told?"

"Five or six, at least, and I was told you were behind in returning your calls. I told . . . I mean . . . Lord Jansen also called and received the same response, which was most puzzling."

"I can see that it would be, considering I'm here to talk with you and Lord Jansen. Where is your office? External Affairs Tower?"

Janis Du-Plessis nodded.

"What room?" snapped the Ecolitan.

"Uh . . . room 203, C-4."

"I'll meet you there as soon as I can get there."

"But—"

"Madam, you will be there."

"I don't understand, and I don't like orders from outsiders."

"Ms. Du-Plessis, I do not think you want to understand. Or you are putting me on. I have been on this Imperial planet less than one standard month. During the past two days, there have been two attempts on my life. Before that, an assassin almost needled me on the day I arrived. A bomb just destroyed my office with me almost inside it. And you don't understand.

"All my calls to you have been rerouted, and you indicate that yours to me have been blocked. Now . . . do you understand my urgency?"

"I find this rather difficult to believe."

"Then let me explain it again . . . in person."

Nathaniel broke the connection and checked his belongings. So far as he could tell, nothing had been tampered with.

He picked up Sergel's report again and folded it inside his tunic. Still he hadn't had time to read it.

He left the datacase in the study, only pulling out the remaining trade terms file. No more lugging around unnecessary baggage when all the warnings had been laid out.

The private comm line buzzed. He debated answering, finally jabbed the Accept stud.

"Whaler."

The face on the other end, filling his screen, was that of Sylvia Ferro-Maine, slate gray eyes, dark hair and all. She was not smiling.

"Lord Whaler, since your office line is strangely out of order, I thought I might be able to reach you here."

"Yes. My office line is out of order. As a matter of fact, Sylvia, my entire office is out of order. An explosion of rather large dimensions has rendered it nonfunctional."

"You're all right?" Her tone was perfectly even, as if she were asking about the weather.

"Fortunately, I seem to be together." He paused. "And to what do I owe this call?"

"I had only wanted to let you know that you made quite an impression on Ms. Corwin-Smathers, and that she will be taking up the matter with the Senator shortly."

He repressed a sigh.

"Glad am I that such an impression was created. Unfortunately, such impressions seem to be spreading, since the explosion within my office was not of an unplanned nature."

"Given those circumstances, Lord Whaler, you are indeed fortunate."

The Ecolitan did not respond immediately, just looked back at the woman. She could be anything—the staff aide she said she was, an intelligence agent, the brains behind Courtney, or the representative of yet another party.

Today, she wore a formal dark blue tunic with a high collar that set off her high cheekbones and delicate features, and added an elfin edge to her image. He could almost smell the scent of oranges.

He shook his head.

"You seem most doubtful, Lord Whaler."

"More to everything on New Augusta is there than meets the eye." He smiled. "But I appreciate your interest, your concern, and your news, and hoping I soon will see you am I."

"I would hope that matters would work that way, Lord Whaler, but those determinations are over my head and with you and the powers that be."

Sylvia's control relaxed enough for a faint smile to escape onto the screen before it went blank.

The Ecolitan shook his head again, more violently.

Something more than trade was riding on the trade talks, at least for the Imperial players. The question was what.

He stood and looked down at the console, then turned away and checked himself. Dart tube and darts, belt fully charged, file folder on the trade talks . . . he was as ready as he could be under the circumstances.

He let the private portal to the corridor edge open, half-expecting to see the Diplomatic Police, an Imperial Monitor, or the Imperial Marines. With none of the agents of Imperial authority present, he marched out and down to the drop shaft and into the high speed descent lane. He had decided on a tunnel train, much as he disliked them, because there was less chance of either the Imperials tracking him closely or waylaying him.

"Still paranoid," he muttered as he waited in the concourse for the train.

Finding it hard to believe that it was still afternoon, he checked the time. 1550. Things were moving, probably too fast, and he wasn't having much of a chance to think them over. Neither were the other players, but they didn't have to. They just had to eliminate one Nathaniel Firstborne Whaler.

No obvious snoops or tails were planted on him, but after the day's events, they would be the best and virtually invisible, and he certainly didn't have the time to check out every speck of dust after every time someone got close to him.

Nathaniel had been trained for war—guerilla, conventional, and total—not for espionage. He felt more and more out of his element with each new addition to the cloak-and-dagger routine.

The tunnel train hissed up to the platform. The Ecolitan took a single seat in a row between the two doors. When the train had left the Diplomatic Concourse, half filled with what seemed to be Imperial supplied staffers to various Legations, he pulled out Sergel's report and began to read.

After the first quick skim, from what he could tell, at least three groups were involved. Sergel claimed he had been contacted by Sylvia Ferro-Maine's direct superior, Alia Herl-Tyre, because of the interest of the External Relations Committee of the Imperial Senate. Alia claimed that the Ministry of Commerce might act unilaterally on the Accord question and cut out the External Relations Committee . . . and the Senate. A Commerce agreement was not a treaty and did not require Senate approval.

According to Sergel, Ferro-Maine had previously been attached to the Imperial Intelligence Service. The I.I.S. was not under the control of the Emperor, but reported to the Senate directly. More precisely, to the staff of the Majority Leader, the Elected Consul. The separation was designed as a check on the powers of the Emperor and on the military branch.

At the first stop, the Ministry of Ecology, the Ecolitan took a quick look around the train. A few more junior bureaucrats climbed aboard, but the majority of passengers kept staring into space or reading folded faxtabs.

Sergel claimed he had not received anything for the routine information he provided to Alia and Sylvia, but did so to open up a "two-way communications flow."

Nathaniel didn't believe it. Sergel was about to get sent on a one way trip to Accord, provided Nathaniel survived the next few days to do the scheduling.

Courtney had hinted that there were two aspects to everything, and Marcella had told him to be careful. Both conversations would indicate that neither of those obviously powerful women were totally in control of the situation.

He shook his head. Despite his recognition of the female control angle of Imperial society, he still didn't have enough information. He doubted that Janis Du-Plessis would have any answers or be willing to share them, but he needed to complete the first round and to ensure all the players were fully involved.

The train hissed to a second stop—Ministry of Defense—where several nonuniformed types marched aboard with a bearing that contradicted their civilian attire.

For an Imperial capital, Nathaniel hadn't seen much evidence of the military, outside of the ceremonial Imperial Marine guards and the scattering of military types in the Emperor's throne room, receiving hall, whatever it was, when he had presented his credentials.

For an Empire with ten major fleets, and Forest Lord knew how many strike forces, it seemed odd that none of the military had surfaced directly on the trade questions. And odder still that so many indirect leads seemed to point to the scarcely visible Ministry of Defense.

The third train stop was the Ministry of External Affairs. A handful of passengers left with Nathaniel—a white-bearded man in a russet cloak, a pregnant woman in a ministry tunic he did not recognize, two youngsters in glittertights, and a man and a woman who appeared to be tourists from Sacrast, from the sticker on the carrying case the woman shouldered.

Nathaniel outpaced the lot to the lift shaft and took the high speed center lane to the two hundred and third level.

The Security Gate was just beyond the exit stage portal.

"It's after hours, citizen," announced the guard.

"I know. Nathaniel Whaler, Envoy from Accord. I have an appointment with Ms. Du-Plessis."

"They don't give appointments after 1530, citizen."

"I'm not a citizen, and I do have an appointment."

"I'm, sorry, citizen, but I'm not allowed to admit anyone. Orders, you know."

The Ecolitan studied the guard. Male, mid-aged, sagging slightly in the midsection, armed with both stunner and blaster, lounging back in the chair.

Nathaniel leaned forward so that he was half over the console, eyeing the layout.

"Quite a control board you have here," he observed, noting the open channel and input plates. The guard began to sit up and lean forward.

"What would happen if I," asked Nathaniel, as he reached over and tapped out Janis Du-Plessis' number, "called Ms. Du-Plessis to see if she were still here?"

The guard grabbed for the stunner. Nathaniel half vaulted, half circled the console and pinned the security man's arms in place.

"Why don't we just wait and see if she answers?" he asked as the guard began to struggle.

The screen unblanked and displayed the features of Janis Du-Plessis.

"Guard, what's going on?"

"This citizen—"

Nathaniel let go of the man with one arm, keyed the screen, then used his forearm to choke off the guard's response.

"I apologize for the direct approach, but this guard was interpreting his orders so literally I found it impossible even to announce my arrival."

The guard broke one arm free and grabbed for the laser blaster.

Regarding that as a uniquely unfriendly move, Nathaniel shifted his hands, caught the nerves behind the man's elbow and twisted.

"Yiii!" The laser skidded from the guard's limp fingers across the permatile.

The Ecolitan observed the surprise on Janis' face as she saw the weapon.

"Perhaps," gasped Nathaniel as he half lifted, half turned the guard from the chair and slammed a stiffened hand into his opponent's solar plexus, "I'm being over-dramatic, but I do believe that either you or someone else doesn't want me to see you."

"Not me . . . not—"

"Fine. Are you in room C-4?"

"Yes."

"I'll meet you there."

"What about the guard?"

"He'll be fine . . . at least for now," commented Nathaniel, looking down at the slumped figure. He hadn't hit the man *that* hard. "Now, would you send whatever signal is necessary to open the gate?"

"Oh, of course."

The gate opened. Nathaniel broke the screen connection, yanked the semiconscious guard out of the chair, hoisted him over his shoulder, and marched through the gate. It buzzed but shut behind him anyway.

C-4 was less than fifty meters away, but the guard's weight had the Ecolitan breathing heavier than he would have liked by the time he got there.

Janis Du-Plessis was waiting, open-handed, as he marched up.

Without a word, Nathaniel dumped the guard into one of the chairs. By now the man was nearly alert.

"I apologize, madam, but I need to ask this gentleman a question or two. While I do, you might want to study this folder, which someone doesn't want me to deliver to you."

He pulled the folder from under his tunic.

"I also apologize for its slightly bent condition, but I feared I might need two hands on the way over, and, unfortunately, I was correct."

She stood there, black hair slightly mussed, in her rust and tan tunic, as if she did not believe the spectacle of an Accord diplomat having to fight his way through her own guard for the sake of one thin file.

"I find this whole . . . episode . . . rather disgusting."

"So do I, madam. So do I, but apparently these trade talks have been escalated to a level beyond mere diplomacy."

He turned his full attention to the guard.

"All right, time for a few answers."

"Can't," protested the man.

"Who told you not to let me in?"

The guard just smiled. Nathaniel reached down and grabbed the nerves at the back of his neck, applying pressure. The sensation should have been acutely unpleasant.

"Who told you . . ." The Ecolitan stopped. The man was unconscious.

He shook his head and reached for the guard's belt stunner. Pulling it from the holster, he set it on mid-range.

"*Strumm!*"

"What happened? Why did you do that?"

"He's been pain conditioned. Any attempt to get information from him through tiredness, torture, pain, and he'll immediately black out. There are ways around it, but not without time or special equipment. It's very effective for this sort of thing."

He centered his attention on the Special Assistant to the Minister of External Affairs.

"Do you know most of the guards? Is he someone new?"

"I don't pay that much attention, but I don't recall seeing him before."

Nathaniel looked up to make sure the portal to the corridor was still closed.

Janis Du-Plessis had once been pretty. With her ivory complexion and long black hair, she was still attractive, but her cheekbones and nose weren't prominent enough for her to retain her prettiness as she grew older, despite the cosmetology of the Empire.

"Ms. Du-Plessis, as you may have noticed, my safe time in any one location appears to be limited."

"Why don't we go into my office?"

Nathaniel dragged the man in with him, laid him out by the doorway.

The woman was standing by her console, as if waiting for him to finish.

"Lord Whaler, I would appreciate some background. You place calls to me and to Minister Jansen but won't accept the return calls. All of a sudden, you claim it isn't your fault, give me some outlandish story about two attempts on your life, and insist on disrupting my private life in order to personally deliver what seems to be a quite routine set of terms for a trade agreement. It seems so reasonable on the surface that everything else seems totally unreasonable."

Nathaniel nodded, hoping she would go on.

"I decided to cancel my evening and see what would happen, but I certainly didn't plan on you attacking one of my guards, dragging him in here, questioning him, and having me cover up for you!"

"Madam, I don't expect you to cover up anything. I came to New

Augusta assuming we had a mutual economic problem which could be solved. I have been assaulted twice, not counting the attempt by your guard to incinerate me when he failed to stop me from getting through to you. My calls to you—and I have called several times—have apparently not gotten through. In return, your calls to me were blocked when I was in my office waiting for them.

"Just this afternoon, someone successfully bombed my office. Fortunately, I was walking out the door at the time, but there were *two* explosions. Either someone, or several parties, is taking a great deal of explosives to warn me to depart, or they merely want to eliminate me. I care for neither possibility."

The hard expression on Janis' face softened.

"I can understand your concerns, but I don't understand why all . . . this . . . violence . . . is involved with a simple trade matter."

"I was hoping you could tell me. The Ministry of Commerce is interested. The Imperial Senate is interested, and for all I know, so are those planting the bombs."

"The Ministry of Commerce?" she snapped. "They don't have any business in trade terms with independent systems outside the Empire."

The pieces came together with a click.

"I think they're interested in the impact changes in the trade terms will have on Imperial commerce. What about the Senate?"

"That's got to be Courtney again, always wanting the last word on everything before the terms are even considered. I can take care of that." The fire in her eyes indicated she intended to try.

"I think you have everything in hand," he offered, rising from the pilot chair.

"Lord Whaler, you still haven't told me why your entrance had to be so violent."

"I don't know. One reason might be that the Commerce Ministry has no confidence in the process and would like different terms. That's one guess. But it is only a guess."

He frowned.

"Is there any way you could register our proposal in your records, so that it could not be erased? Even if anything happened to you?"

"Are you suggesting something?"

"No. But I wasn't attacked for nothing, and you just told me that you did not know the guard who attacked me."

"I see what you mean. If the effort was to cut us out, we really don't have it until it's in the data banks under seal. Certainly, registering it couldn't hurt and might well reduce the . . . uh . . . unpleasantness."

She sat down at the console again, rapidly touching keys, placing the proposal facedown across the screen in order.

A soft chime sounded.

"We're done. Locked in and sealed."

Nathaniel bowed.

"You have been gracious at a time when few have been and more helpful than you can possibly imagine."

"You do me honor." She flushed, color momentarily replacing the flat ivory of her skin.

"No more than is your due."

A long moment passed before the Ecolitan cleared his throat.

"We still need to deal with some leftover unpleasantness. I suggest two things. First, that you escort me to your private drop shaft. That way I can get to the tunnel train level without going through the main concourse. Second, that you return here and find the guard lying in the middle of the office. You will, of course, be most upset and call Imperial security."

"I was coming back and found him?"

"Exactly. He'll be out for several hours. He can't possibly explain what happened without being probed. So he'll have to invent some excuse, which will say he was investigating something when he was stunned, and he doesn't know what happened."

Nathaniel dragged the man into the middle of the reception area while Janis locked her console and office.

The rust and tan corridors to the private drop shaft of the senior staff and Ministers were deserted, the lights at half level.

"This doesn't go down to the tunnel train level, just to the Ministry vehicle concourse, you know." She touched the drop plate.

"Can I get to the trains?"

"Yes, but you'd have to walk back through the tower and another gate to catch the public shaft."

"Hmmm . . ." He pulled at his chin.

"Why don't I just send you back in a Ministry pool car?"

"That would be appreciated."

He couldn't see Janis doing him in, not when she had nothing to gain.

The electrocougar from the Ministry of External Affairs seemed identical to the one he had ridden in from the Commerce Ministry, with the same plasticloth hard seats, except for the colors of the car and the driver's uniform.

His driver was a petite black girl, perhaps the youngest driver he'd had.

He watched Janis standing at the dispatch point as the electrocougar whispered into the tunnel.

"Isn't she too old for you?"

The question jarred him.

"Oh . . . I suppose so . . . if it were personal."

"Business this late? You're an outworlder. You're used to working longer."

"How about you?"

"Way to get credits after classes. Besides, after-hours drivers usually just sit. Good time to study. Where you from?"

He wondered if she worked for someone. It didn't matter.

"Accord."

"Should have known from the black. Don't always apply what you learn when you see it in real life. You don't look like you poison planets."

"I never have. We haven't done anything that severe in centuries."

"How come you're here?"

"Trade talks."

"How come that's not in the faxtabs or casts? That ought to be big news." She grinned impishly, and Nathaniel caught it in the reflection from the front bubble. "Planet poisoners here to talk trade."

She dropped the grin. "Guess that's unfair. Professor Ji-Kerns says we've done worse to some systems, but he's a man."

Nathaniel ignored the slam to his sex.

"What are you studying?"

"Second year in law. Out-space legal systems. We haven't gotten to Accord yet. Working on Halston."

"Why did you pick law?"

"Mother, she's the head of tactics at the Ministry of Defense, wanted me to go to Saskan, but I didn't like all the rules. Rather make them."

"Saskan?"

"You know, that's the Imperial Space Academy where all the Fleet officers are trained."

"I suppose she, your mother, I mean, doesn't like your doing this?"

"She doesn't mind. If I wasn't meant for the Eagles, I wasn't meant. This way, I can pretty much pay my own way. That's important. Lots of youngers don't, just collect basic and snerch. Guys are the worst, always talking about being Ministers, as if the Ministers ever did anything. Who does the work? You and me."

Nathaniel nodded, although he didn't think she was really looking for a response.

"Bet you work for a fancy-pants Envoy. Here you are working, and he's probably luxing it up. First man I've seen working so late since I took the job, and you're an outworlder. Figures."

She shook her head.

Nathaniel didn't bother to correct her misimpression. "I wouldn't be surprised if anything and everything went on here. Or is it just boring because nothing happens after hours?"

"Pretty dull. Wouldn't dare to talk to any woman, and I don't rate standby for a Minister or Deputy. All of them sit and stare, or sit and read. Not like Perky. She's got the same job at Commerce. I got the idea from her, that is, driving after classes. She's Class I now, even got Lord Mersen last week.

"Told me the other day she drove three Fleet Commanders back from Defense to Commerce. Nothing like that happens here."

The car slipped out of the tunnel.

"Want the public or private concourse?"

"Wherever I'm less likely to get noticed."

"Public side, this time of day. Still crowded. Be like a tomb on the private side." A pause followed. "What are you worried about?"

Nathaniel couldn't help laughing. The girl was one of the first real people, without a mask, that he'd talked to.

"Tell you when I get out."

"Here you are."

"Thanks for the ride."

As he climbed out of the backseat, she poked her head through the top opening in the front bubble.

"You forgot to tell me."

"I'm the Envoy, and someone keeps trying to assassinate me."

Her mouth dropped open.

"Not everyone wants those trade talks."

It was probably unfair to leave it at that, thought Nathaniel as he ducked away and into a public fresher stall on the concourse level.

With the belt detector he went over his clothes thoroughly for tracers or snoops. One minute speck on his collar registered, but it could have retained static charges. Otherwise he seemed clean.

He put on the rust film cloak over his blacks and left the fresher.

A woman talking to another woman on the far side of the corridor looked up as he passed, then looked back at the closing door to the fresher. She began fiddling with her pocket calendar, but centered her attention on the fresher, totally disregarding Nathaniel.

He took the lift shaft to the corridor for the private entrance to the Envoy's quarters. Under the cover of the cloak, he checked the entrance as he approached. The snoops had been replaced, of course, but they were standard. No energy links to the portal showed.

XXIV

ONCE INSIDE, AS he folded the cloak and surveyed the apartment, he swept the area again. The disabled visual snoop had not yet been replaced.

He marched into the study and eyed the comm unit.

With a sigh, he sank into the all too plush swivel and thumbed for the directory, keying up some background music at the same time. While whoever had links to the comm unit would know what he was asking, perhaps some of the other players wouldn't get all the information yet.

He tapped out the number for the Diplomatic Reference Library, assuming that it was either automated or operated around the clock. It was both.

"State your interest area."

"Interstellar law."

"Choose from among the following . . ."

The gist of the answer to his long question was that the Ministry of External Affairs had jurisdiction over trade and treaty matters involving nonempire systems.

"Query: authority of the Ministry of Commerce to enforce trade agreements within the Empire . . ."

The Commerce Ministry could request the Imperial Fleet to apply sanctions.

"Query: does an agreement between a former Empire system and the Ministry of Commerce constitute a legal basis for resumption of Imperial Jurisdiction?"

According to the library computer, there were precedents on both sides.

Nathaniel pulled at his chin, looked down at the screen.

"Query . . ." What else could he ask? He signed off.

Leaning back in the swivel, he gazed out the window. Sunset would be coming soon, and for the moment he was going to watch it. Maybe think while he watched it, but watch it he would.

A few high and thin clouds dotted the sky, deep blue as he saw it through the panoramic window, and yellow white of the sun was turning golden as it dipped toward the tree-covered hills on the western horizon.

He'd seen the holos of the blighted forests created by the Secession, and the Terran casualty figures in the billions as the result of the ensuing starvation.

He'd also seen the slag that had been Haversol City and holos of the asteroid belt that had been Sligo before the Empire pulverized it.

Both sides were people, people like the girl who had driven him, people like Sylvia, like Marcella, even people like Janis Du-Plessis, who set in motion the bureaucracies that created the violence that appalled them.

The high flare of a shuttle in the distance over the port winked like an evening star early in the sky and was gone.

The shadows over the hills lengthened, and the lights in the other towers glowed stronger, and the sun dropped. He supposed he should finish what was necessary, what he could.

Some could wait until morning; some could not.

Seen in perspective, the whole thing was obvious. The Secession itself had created a terrible convulsion for the Empire. Fifty odd systems ripping themselves away, using the Accord grievances as an umbrella for a myriad of reasons, denying the government that had helped them stand alone.

In the beginning, the Empire had hesitated to use maximum force, planet busters, because of the closeness of the ties. It's hard to murder your cousin because he wants to stand alone, and the internal political outcry that had risen after the First Fleet had busted Sligo had rendered that option unusable.

Four hundred years later, no one thought in those terms. Accord's allies had gone their own way, some to their own small empires, big enough to give the old Empire pause. And Accord was considered Outie, an outland system. Relations were minimal, sometimes nonexistent, and the question of attacking "relatives" was moot. Twelve generations of Imperial schoolchildren had been raised with horror stories about Accord.

If the Empire decided to use force, no public outcry would be raised, and Accord could count on few allies. In return, the Institute could send out the death ships, and if everyone was lucky, perhaps ten percent of the population of a thousand systems might survive.

The Accord House of Delegates ignored the enormous growth in the massive destruct weaponry of the Empire. The Empire was totally ignorant of the potential biological and ecological disasters created by the Institute and already dispersed to where not even total destruction of the Accord Coordinate systems could stop the rain of lingering death.

From what he'd seen, neither side would believe the other's power, although Accord had acknowledged the Empire's fleets somewhat.

So what could he do?

He turned to the console and punched out the office number of Courtney Corwin-Smathers, leaving his own screen blank.

"Courtney here. What's wrong with your visual?"

"Whaler here. Call off the dogs, Courtney. You've made your point. The preliminary terms have been registered officially with External Affairs, and you'll have to coordinate with Janis Du-Plessis, but I think you can handle that.

"The other thing you should know is that Defense is also playing. We don't need that, and neither do you."

"Oh . . . ?"

"I still will have to stay around, making polite speech after polite speech, and committing Accord to nothing until you get your ions flared. Or do you have a better suggestion?"

"Your prudence is commendable, if belated, but Ms. Ku-Smythe might request a quiet elimination if the I.I.S. or the Ministry of Defense haven't already done so."

"That's a chance I'll have to take."

He tapped the stud and cut the connection.

His next call went to Marcella's direct office line. He got a recording with a smiling face.

"I am out at the moment. If you would leave a message, I will return your screen when I return."

"Whaler here. The Ministry of Defense has decided to shove Commerce directly out of the picture by eliminating me. You might also be interested to learn Alia Herl-Tyre paid off some of my Legation staff to stall you. At the same time, Defense exploded my office and removed one of my staffers. External Affairs thinks you played them for nulls."

Again leaving his own screen blank, he tapped out Sergel's private number, and got another recording requesting a message.

"Sergel. You'd better be gone tomorrow, or on your way, or have a damned good story. The External Relations staff knows you played them false, and the Ministry of Defense knows you failed."

He tapped out another number, with a blank screen. He didn't have a private number, but the External Relations Committee number for Alia Herl-Tyre. Another recording.

"Ms. Herl-Tyre. My name is Nathaniel Whaler, and we haven't met. Sergel Weintre used to work for the Legation, until he claimed that you were paying him to spy on us, and we discovered that he was also being paid by the Ministry of Defense to spy on you as well as us.

"Under the circumstances, thought you'd be interested."

With a sigh, he leaned back and touched the wide belt, running his fingers along the side, splitting the layers and removing a thin flimsy.

The code system was crude, but unbreakable without either the flimsy, which would last for less than a standard hour after he touched it, or the Prime's personal diary, of which there was one copy. The system was one way, but that didn't matter.

After the ten minutes it took him to code what he needed, he picked up the draft and opened the door from his private quarters to his office. The walls to the staff office still were jagged and bulged in places, although the steel portal door remained untouched.

He palmed the plate, and the portal irised open. The deserted staff section had the lighting at half bright. He slipped behind Mydra's console, congratulating himself on his professional ease until he barked his knees as he pulled the chair up to the console.

The first job was to send the message to the Prime.

He accessed the direct comm line, feeling the charges ring higher and higher as the message ran out.

He hoped it would get there, and since the Legation was paying for the direct shot, it had a chance.

He staggered out from behind Mydra's console and back to his own office.

The next step would be trying to break the media blackout on the talks, which he suspected was due to their dull sound, rather than any conspiracy. After all, what self-respecting faxcaster in the capital of the Empire was interested in tariff and exchange terms negotiations between the Empire and a former colony, particularly when the Ministry involved hadn't told anyone and when the others didn't want anyone to know?

From the New Augusta directory, he got the numbers for Galactafax and Faxstellar.

"Greetings. I am the Accord Trade Envoy, Nathaniel Whaler. And a statement to make on the bombing of our Legation I have."

"The what?" asked the duty faxer at Galactafax.

"The bombing of our Legation by forces opposing the talks on trade—"

"Hold it! Hold it! Let me catch it all on flux. First, who are you? For the record?"

"Envoy Nathaniel Whaler, Acting Legate and Trade Envoy for the Legation of Accord."

He paused and cleared his throat.

"This very afternoon, my office was bombed. Two devices. Bystanders, several were hurt. Good faith we came in, but the Imperial Senate and Imperial Ministries respond not, but question who has jurisdiction. No one pays attention."

"Hang on there, Lord Whaler. Let me see if I have this straight. You were invited here for trade talks. The Imperial Senate and the Ministries are arguing over jurisdiction, and this afternoon your Legation was bombed, and people were injured. Is that the idea?"

"Essentially correct, that is. Diplomatic Police come, say they will look. Nothing happens."

"You mentioned a jurisdiction problem . . ."

"External Affairs should have control, but has done nothing. Commerce Ministry presses for answers but has no jurisdiction. Most confusing. Senate External Relations Committee staff is also interested, and Senator Helmsworth and the S.I.I. are involved somehow, I am told."

The Ecolitan wondered if he were carrying it all too far, but the young man on the other end was drinking it all in.

"The S.I.I. . . . S.I.I.? You mean the I.I.S., the Imperial Intelligence Service?"

"That is what I understand."

"Lord Whaler, where can we reach you?"

"At the Accord Legation is where."

He gave the office and the private line, not wanting Mydra blocking the calls if the faxers waited until morning.

He repeated the process with the young woman who answered for Faxstellar. Her reaction was much the same.

Within twenty minutes, a distinguished-looking woman from Galactafax had gotten back to Nathaniel.

"Marjoy Far-Nova, Lord Whaler. I've seen the tape of your announcement, but I wondered if you could possibly supply a few more details for us about the trade talks and any possible connection this might have with the bombing."

"Connection I know not. Here I am, poor Envoy, wanting to ease relations with Empire. Here am I, empowered by my government to reduce some tariffs and eliminate others. But for this, right after we circulate proposals, my office is bombed. The situation is strange, but whom should I tell?"

"Let me get this down. After you circulated your trade proposals, your office was bombed. At the same time, no one in the Empire seems willing to act except those who you think should not be involved. Is that it?"

Nathaniel could only shrug and gesture to the bulging wall to his right.

Shortly thereafter, he went through a similar performance with the call back from Faxstellar, declining to speculate beyond the facts.

Once again, he headed to the deserted staff office and Mydra's console, this time not banging his knees as he sat down.

He set it for a voice scrambled tape and began to speak.

"To Scandalous Sam, the Gossip Man of New Augusta . . . Have you heard about the awful runaround they're giving that poor Envoy from Accord? They bombed his office, not once, but twice. And none of the Ministries will talk. His staff has been profiteered . . . and you should listen in on the snoop network, like Sylvia, Marcella, Alia, Courtney, and a few others do. One even we dare not name. His calls are blocked by his own staff. Call him, and they tell you he's behind in returning his screens. He doesn't know it yet. More to follow . . ."

Nathaniel wound it up and sent it off into the local faxdelivery.

A similar set of faxes went to other sources, as well as a scholarly letter under his own name to the pure print media.

That done, he closed down Mydra's console, trying to leave it exactly as he found it.

He was hungry, and officially and unofficially, all he had to do for a while was wait and play dumb.

He locked the portal into his private quarters and headed for the hygienarium, where he stripped and took a steaming fresher. He dressed slowly, choosing a dress green outfit and a rich, matching green cloak.

According to the belt multitector, the clothes weren't snooped or tagged, but the snoops outside his private entrance were fully functioning.

After a quick walk to the lift shaft, he took the slow outside lane all fifty levels up to the Legate's private dining rooms.

The head waiter was ready, this time.

"Lord Whaler . . . a pleasure to see you. Table in the main dining room or the portico?"

"The portico, if you please."

Through the wide expanse of unbroken permaglass he could see the shadows of the towers, their lights like beacons, and the dark outlines of the hills beyond. He was seated at a table for two at one end of the windowside tables.

Not much on the silver printed menu appealed to him, but he finally settled on the scampig with a salad, and liftea.

The liftea arrived immediately. Either he looked tired or the staff had been briefed on the fact that liftea came first on Accord, not last.

He sipped the tea, watched the lights glitter, took in the occasional shuttle flare in the evening sky.

"I beg your pardon." The man's voice was lightly accented Panglais. Nathaniel pegged the speaker as Frankan.

He looked up to see a man standing by the table.

The Ecolitan rose, half bowing.

"At your service," he responded in Frankan.

"You honor me," replied the other diplomat in his own tongue. "Not many would immediately recognize my background or make the effort. But none of the formal nonsense. May I introduce myself?" He presented a diplomatic I.D. and miniature credentials identifying himself as Gerard De Vylerion, Legate of Frank. "Gerard De Vylerion, soon to be returning to Wryere."

Nathaniel sat and gestured to the seat across from him.

"Nathaniel Whaler, Envoy from Accord and acting Legate," he continued in Frankan.

"You do know Frankan. I must confess I knew who you were. After this afternoon, everyone wanted to talk to you, but your Legation indicated you were out of touch."

Nathaniel motioned for De Vylerion to go on.

"I've been here five standard years, full tour, and I've never heard of violence against a Legation. There aren't even any records. What did you do? Was it an accident?"

"Accident? No, I doubt it was an accident. I was leaving my office when they exploded. Two, one right after the other. We informed the Diplomatic Police, who came and went." Nathaniel shrugged. "Nothing so mysterious was happening. We circulated preliminary proposals, and I felt that everyone who was interested should be informed. I did not want to say much about the explosions until I had a chance to think."

"I could not be that calm," answered the Frankan Legate, sipping from the glass he had brought with him.

"I waited to see if there were any reaction. But I will wait only so long."

"And?"

"I finally told the faxcasters. Was that how you found out?"

"No. My staff told me of an explosion on the three hundredth level, and I asked a friend of a friend. He told me an accident had occurred in the Accord Legation."

"No. Not an accident. Someone does not like what I am doing. Someone does not want, apparently, a peaceful trade treaty."

"Lord Whaler—a friend of mine, Lord Naguti, from Orknarli, is also interested." The Frankan gestured to his larger table where two others, a man and a woman, sat. "We could join you, but . . ."

"Alas, I see my table is too small."

The Ecolitan got up, beckoned to the waiter. As the man approached, he turned to De Vylerion, "Have you eaten?"

"Yes, but we would be honored. Have the waiter serve you at our table."

Probably a breach of etiquette, thought Nathaniel, but the chance to spread a little distrust of the Empire was too much to resist.

"Tables I will be changing," he told the waiter in Panglais, "and there would I like to be served."

The waiter nodded and retreated to his post.

The other two stood as the Ecolitan approached.

"Lord Naguti, acting Legate from Orknarli, and Lady Persis-Dyann. This is Lord Whaler, Envoy from Accord."

"I speak no Orknarlian," Nathaniel explained in Panglais, "but more fluent am I in Frankan, Old American, or Fuardian."

"We all understand Frankan," clipped Lady Persis-Dyann, who seemed too young and too sharp-featured to be an Imperial Lady.

"Then I will continue in Frankan," observed Nathaniel, switching languages with relief. "It is a pleasure to meet you, Lady Persis-Dyann, and you, Lord Naguti, although under somewhat surprising circumstances."

"Lord Whaler has just informed me," added De Vylerion smoothly, "that not only was his Legation bombed, but that no one seemed terribly interested. He called the faxcasters himself."

"Oh?" asked the Lady.

"Most interesting," mused Lord Naguti.

Nathaniel took a sip of his tea.

"I'm puzzled," he began slowly. "I arrived thinking progress would be slow but steady and that a trade agreement could be worked out. It's not that big a problem. It deals with certain microtronics. But nothing happened. So I requested audiences and began direct contacts. Remember, the Empire requested us to come. I was perhaps too aggressive. Yesterday, it begins to appear someone does not want a treaty. Today, there is an explosion in my office."

He looked around the table. Naguti was nodding. Persis-Dyann seemed bored, and De Vylerion wore an expression of mild interest. He stopped and waited.

"If the treaty's so minor, why would anyone want to stall it?" asked Persis-Dyann.

"My thoughts exactly," answered Nathaniel. "That leads to an interesting point. Haversol came to New Augusta to negotiate and had the same trouble. Now . . . the similarity I cannot prove, but . . ."

Naguti nodded again.

"You men all talk in mysteries," observed the Lady.

"Not so mysterious, Lady Dyann," responded Naguti. "The Imperial Fleet attacked and reduced Haversol because Haversol refused to negotiate with the Empire. If what Lord Whaler says is true, negotiations were stalled by the Empire to give the impression of Haversolian recalcitrance and to give the Empire the option of using force."

"And because it was veiled in semilegality, the Federated Hegemony, the Accord Coordinate"—and there the Frankan De Vylerion inclined his head toward Nathaniel—"the Fuardian Conglomerate, and the other independent systems chose not to make an issue of a minor planet like Haversol."

"That is true," added Nathaniel, leaning back from the table as the waiter delivered his roast scampig. "Another disturbing thought occurs. Haversol was a minor system, and no one protested. Not even Accord, I admit, at least not beyond a simple protest. But Accord is not, shall I put it bluntly, the most admired of the smaller multisystem governments. And so, if the Empire creates a technicality on which to base the use of force against Accord, who will protest?"

Nathaniel cut into the roast scampig, wrinkling his nose as the steam escaped.

"Isn't that basing a lot on assumptions?" cut in the Lady.

Nathaniel wondered which Ministry had bought her. Despite her sharp nose and piercing eyes, she was attractive and had a nice figure beneath the gold-trimmed brown tunic.

"Assumptions, yes," he continued after swallowing, "but could you explain why there have been two attempts on my life, including exploding my office, and bribes to my staff?"

"Bribes to your staff?" Naguti asked.

"A minor official, but I caught him and actually got a written confession that an Imperial Ministry was paying him to spy. Not unusual, I would guess, although since the Empire supplies most of my staff, I would question why they would need to approach him."

"What do you think, Neri?" De Vylerion asked.

"I think we may all have a problem. While I earnestly hope that the incidents which had befallen Accord and Lord Whaler are merely isolated coincidences, I have grave doubts that they are. You know, don't you, that the Fifth Fleet was dispatched yesterday to reinforce the Sector Governor on our borders?"

Gerard took another sip from his near empty glass. Even Persis-Dyann was silent. Nathaniel took advantage of the lull to finish the scampig and salad.

"I regret my story has depressed you. Perhaps the lady is right. Certainly, there is no hard proof."

"In our business, Whaler," said Gerard softly, "and since you're still young, you may not always remember it, motivation and past actions are more important than scraps of proof. Hard proof often arrives just before the warheads."

"Our debt, Lord Whaler," offered Naguti, rising, "but I must be heading back to my Legation. May I escort you, Lady Dyann?"

"So far as our paths coincide."

Nathaniel struggled to his feet as the pair left.

"Very nicely done, Whaler, but do you believe it?" asked the Frankan as soon as they were alone.

"I've made it a bit more clear-cut than it really is, but, in essence, it's all true. True, but complicated, and the stakes are far higher."

"I can guess why. Perhaps we are all fortunate Accord sent you and not another." He rose. "I, too, must leave, but I appreciate your candor."

The portico was nearly empty by then, with only two other tables occupied. The Ecolitan caught the eye of the waiter.

"All right is it if I return to my first table?"

"Yes, sir."

"A Taxan brandy, please, and clear water."

He sat down and stared out through the permaglass, watching the shuttle flares and the stars, so much thicker here than in the skies of the Rift planets, where an arm of blackness clove the center of the night heavens.

The brandy arrived, but he ignored it, still drawing in the stars.

It was like operating in a vacuum. Little or no feedback. Lord of the Forests! He didn't know whether he'd touched the people he'd met or whether everything he did was blocked just outside his ability to observe.

Perhaps the faxcasts or the morning faxtabs would show something. If they didn't, he wasn't sure what other studs he could press, what other people he could try to manipulate.

Destruction was easy. It was the refraining from destruction that was hard.

He picked up the brandy and watched the stars till past midnight.

He was cold sober and holding an almost full glass of Taxan brandy when he stood again. Every other table besides his was set in morning gold. His was still in evening silver.

As he strode back to the drop shaft and fifty levels down, he wondered, idly, whether he would find anyone waiting by or inside his door—whether an assailant or a Lady.

Finding neither Sergel nor Sylvia, or their like, he locked up and slipped into the large bed alone, and into sleep.

XXV

NATHANIEL WOKE EARLY, and gratefully, out of a nightmare where Imperial battlecruisers fractured planets and where Ecolitans on black wings sowed death down the Milky Way, turning the stars dark as they stepped from sun to sun.

A hot fresher helped begin to burn away the depression, as did the cup of liftea which followed from the tiny kitchen.

He had not been standing in the shambles of the Envoy's office, dressed in a set of crisp blacks he'd never worn before, for more than a few minutes before Hillary West-Coven scurried in from the front desk.

"Sir . . . Lord Whaler, there are two fax crews outside, and they say you personally called them. Ms. Da-Vios isn't here yet." Her tone conveyed that he was personally responsible for some catastrophe and that Mydra could have avoided it had she been present.

"Why, I did call them. Let them in, so fax the damage to our Legation they can. Talk with them I even will."

"Yes, sir. You *will* talk with them?"

"If they desire such."

"But . . . but . . ." Seeing Nathaniel's broad smile, she capitulated. "Yes, sir."

Nathaniel left his console to place himself firmly in front of the damage. The three women and one man who represented the media walked in. The two well-groomed women, with the hand-held directional cones and belt paks, were the commentators. The other two wore shoulder mounted fax units.

"You're Lord Whaler?" demanded the smaller of the two interviewers, who was dressed in a silver jumpsuit that flattered her slender figure and dark hair.

"Lord Whaler, I am." He beamed.

"Fine. Please stand over there out of the first shots while we get a panover of the damage. Marse, start at the right and sweep up toward that hole.

"Check-shot. Canning, two, three, and go."

The other interviewer nodded to her faxer, who followed the same pattern.

The once-over of the damage was followed with detailed close-ups of the two blast areas.

Nathaniel stood at one side, feeling somewhat neglected.

"Ms. West-Coven," asked the smaller interviewer, "can you tell us what happened?"

"One instant we were working. The next there was an explosion, and Lord Whaler came flying from his portal there. I remember seeing him standing there just before the blast, and I guess he was lucky. He was walking out when it happened."

"That was his office?"

"Yes."

Nathaniel cleared his throat, but no one was paying any attention. Both faxers were training their units on Hillary.

"How did it happen?"

For the first time, Hillary looked bewildered. "You'd better ask the Envoy."

"Lord Whaler. Stand right there."

The Ecolitan complied meekly. The media commentators were more peremptory than the bureaucrats.

"Do you know why the Legation was bombed?"

"Someone does not want the trade treaty. When I first arrived, attacked was I. Now comes the bomb."

"Isn't that stretching things?"

"Aren't you being overdramatic?"

Nathaniel shrugged as expressively as he could and pointed to the blast-torn wall. "That. That is not dramatic?"

The faxers were off Nathaniel.

The smaller commentator wound the segment up.

"That's the story at the Accord Legation. Trade talks, an explosion following an attempted assassination. Frian Su-Ryener for Galactafax at the Accord Legation."

The taller woman positioned herself by the worse section of the bulging wall and smiled.

"For the second time in as many days, violence in New Augusta. Yesterday, the I.I.S. refused to comment on why a fully armed agent was assaulted here in the capital. Last night, this explosion, and an Envoy who wears the diplomatic blacks. The rumored assailant of the I.I.S. agent also was reported to wear black.

"Now we learn that trade talks with the Empire are involved, and the Envoy involved has already been attacked once before. Why? Whatever it is, it's sparked the first bombing in New Augusta in three decades. This is Kyra Bar-Twyla for Faxstellar."

"Is that right about the I.I.S.?" Hillary asked.

"Worse than that," interrupted the other commentator, "if you believe the rumors. Defense had five agents in the area, and three don't know what happened and two are now walking nuts."

"No confirmation," clipped the taller one, "no story."

They both nodded to their faxers, and the four left as quickly and abruptly as they had arrived.

"What did they mean?" the Ecolitan asked Hillary.

"There's some rule by the Ministry of Communications. You have to have at least two witnesses to any rumor you fax, and three or two plus documentation if you present a fact and if it involves official Imperial business."

"You know that rule from where?"

Hillary was spared a response by the arrival of Mydra.

"Lord Whaler, do you think it was wise to let those . . . those . . . rumormongers in?"

"Wise, I know not. But what would they have said if I had said no?"

"You may have a point there, but sensationalism could affect the trade talks."

Nathaniel nodded politely and waited until the two were looking at him.

"Later, I think, we should talk. Right now, some communications I must make. Repairs, will they be made?"

Mydra retreated to her console without acknowledging the question.

The Ecolitan sat back down behind his own console and began to compose a faxletter for transmission to the Legations of the independent majors, the Federated Hegemony, and the Fuardian Conglomerate.

When it was completed, he buzzed Mydra.

"Yes, Lord Whaler?"

"In my console stored is a communication I need improved for transmission. As soon as possible in the formal way."

"I'll get right to it."

"See it I would like before you send it."

"Yes, sir."

As she was completing the text, he wandered out into the staff office and began to peer over her shoulder at the text screen. Much as he had suspected, the message bore little resemblance to what he had set out originally.

"Forgot you the part about Haversol."

"So I did. Do you think you should mention such an unpleasant incident so bluntly?"

"Find you a more politic way to express, and pleased I would be."

He waited as she revised the language.

"Need the part about the appearance of delay causing misunderstandings that could be avoided. Say it most politely, as you do."

Mydra nodded.

When it was completed, the faxtext from the acting Legate of

Accord was a polite, understated account of the difficulties faced by one Nathaniel Whaler, with even politer implications about how precedents unfavorable to all non-Imperial systems could be set if current patterns continued.

It has to be good, thought Nathaniel. Mydra doesn't like it a bit.

"Show me, please, how it is sent."

Mydra touched several studs, and the dispatch plate turned red. She did not touch it.

Nathaniel bent over and tapped it.

"Do you not finish by this?" he asked naively.

"That's right, Lord Whaler."

He watched while she sent off the other twenty-three, knowing she was getting frustrated by the surveillance.

He retired to his console to authenticate the routine correspondence. The debris had been removed, but the repairs had not been started nor were any workers in evidence.

After running through the material, he decided to see if anything he had attempted to plant had showed up in the faxtabs. At the three buzzes from the console as it burped forth the faxtab, Mydra looked up sharply at him through the open portal. She seemed to relax as she saw him lean back in the big swivel and began to read.

The factual side of the news hadn't changed that much.

The First Minister of Orknarli protested the "maneuvers" of the Fifth Fleet. Repercussions of the synde bean shortage on Imperial trade balances. Ministry of Defense requests for greater funding. Prince Heuron dedicates H.M.S. *Gold Prince*, flagship of the newly dedicated Eleventh Fleet.

Scandalous Sam was at the end of the faxtab, and Nathaniel hesitated a moment before checking the gossip, not sure he wanted to see if any of the bait was there.

Explosive news . . . should we tell you which diplomat had his office explode . . . after seeing a very special assistant . . . and yet he's so very hard to see . . . Which playboy of the court rolled his airchair over his chef? And don't forget . . .

Nathaniel let the flimsies drop. Unless the Imperials were onto every innuendo, Scandalous Sam's gossip needed a few more kicks to keep the interest in the Imperial treatment of Accord going.

At 1153, his private line buzzed, and out of the corner of his eye, he saw Mydra go bolt upright.

"Lord Whaler?"

"The same."

"Alexi Jansen, here, and my valued assistant for External Trade, Janis Du-Plessis. I understand there has been some confusion, some rather strange occurrences." Jansen was a big blond man with skin the color of leather, and he laughed as he finished the sentence.

"Of that, some," admitted Nathaniel.

"I do hope we can help."

"Our proposal submitted to Ms. Du-Plessis, and rapid consideration of those terms would be helpful." Nathaniel shrugged as dramatically as he could. "What can I say? Come for trade, get explosions. Come to talk, and . . ."

"Lord Whaler," commented Janis Du-Plessis, "we hope we can clear these up as soon as possible."

"Janis, here, told me about your visit. It seemed rather unusual, but she checked up on things, and that guard . . . he was wiped. Strange."

"Guard? Wiped? I had difficulties but did not understand the reasons." Nathaniel shook himself and smiled into the screen. He went on, "Your courtesy I surely appreciate and look forward to hearing from you." The Ecolitan half bowed. Alexi Jansen bowed in return. "When we have finished an analysis of your proposal, Lord Whaler, we'll be back to you."

The screen images blanked.

Nathaniel cleared his throat loudly and thoroughly, stood away from the swivel, and strutted over to the open portal where he could peer down at Mydra.

"Mydra? Where is Sergel?"

"I don't know, Lord Whaler."

"He is supposed to be an Information Specialist, and never do I see him."

"I'll try to locate him, but I imagine he's quite busy at the moment."

"And busy doing what?" The Ecolitan turned and marched back to his swivel, clearing his throat again for effect.

He had decided he should be somewhat unreasonable; at least some of the time, and occasionally petty until he could see how things were shaking out.

Dropping himself into the swivel, the black and green swivel, with an audible thump, he twisted the chair to watch the low clouds swirl above the towers. At the angle he chose, he could keep an eye on Mydra without seeming to. The layout of the office had been designed to let her keep tabs on him, and the thought that he could reverse it gave him some small amusement as he saw Mydra keying things out using her console.

While he couldn't see the screen itself, she was faxing a number of individuals, from what he could tell.

At one point, her back stiffened, and he figured she'd been told something she hadn't expected. After that she made two or three more calls.

With a snapping movement that flipped out the back of her short black and tan tunic, she stood and entered his office.

Nathaniel returned his full attention to the storm clouds outside, watching the white-gray tops of the cumulus clouds race toward the patches of blue above.

"Lord Whaler?"

He swiveled back from his window view and put both feet on the floor directly behind his console.

"Yes, Mydra?"

"I can't seem to locate Mr. Weintre."

"Was he not in someone's custody the day before last?"

"You had him released."

"Fruit a little rotten can only get more rotten . . . it is hard to translate sayings into Panglais, but you understand?"

"A partly spoiled fruit can only rot? Is that what you meant? What does that have to do with Mr. Weintre?"

"Sergel has gotten rotten. First, a little trouble, now perhaps more trouble. Who guards troublemakers?"

"Here in the tower, the Diplomatic Police."

"Elsewhere?"

Nathaniel had a solid idea where Sergel was: in the hands of "specialists" at the Ministry of Defense who would be questioning him thoroughly, mind-probing him in depth. But the Ecolitan didn't want to voice that, just lead her along that track.

"The Imperial Monitors."

Nathaniel shrugged to indicate his ideas were exhausted and went on as if to change the subject. "All the difficulties we have, Mydra, and the Envoy from another system last night told me military people caused his problems. Is that possible?"

"Everyone likes to blame the Eagles, Lord Whaler, but they stay out of New Augusta for the most part."

Nathaniel shrugged again. From the momentary gleam in her eyes, she'd gotten the thought he'd wanted to plant, the military aspect of Sergel's disappearance and the Legation's troubles.

"I understand. Force Command is strong on Accord, and I wondered if the military was also on New Augusta."

Mydra gave him a smile that was equally warm and patronizing.

"The Empire's not quite like any place else in the galaxy, I suspect, Lord Whaler."

"How true. Yet people are people." He looked out the window and leaned back again. "Not always do I say well what I think. Panglais is a lovely language but too flowery for a simple teacher of trade and economics. I came to New Augusta hoping people would see that agreement is possible always and that all lose when war comes.

"When the more powerful is stubborn, the small fight. Knowing they will lose, they fight, and before they perish, many would poison the water the victors would drink. Fighting is always so."

Nathaniel looked at Mydra, efficient in her brown and tan.

"A scholar could express that better. The point is the same. Your Empire is . . . complex . . . many towers, many Ministries, many people, many battlecruisers, many troops. Accord is simple. Few people, few ships. The only defense we have is the power to destroy the ecologies of the galaxy, strewing death across the suns before we perish."

He shrugged.

"Can I tell the Empire, with thousands of ships, that little Accord can sow such vast death? Who believes? Can I tell our House of Delegates, who know they can sow such death, that the Empire does not believe? To prove our power, must millions die? And so, I sit and talk, sit and hope. Hope they have not forgotten."

He looked blankly out the window.

The room was silent. The clouds swirled outside, and Nathaniel watched. Watched, hoping the snoops had gotten it all, hoping that Mydra had understood it all, and hoping that both thought he wasn't playing to the unseen audience.

"Lord Whaler," Mydra asked softly, "may I go?"

He nodded.

The waiting was the worst, whether it was waiting in the darkness of space, in a full-blanked needle-boat, knowing that another needle-boat waited, knowing that whoever moved first was dead, or whether it was lying flat in the jungle outback of Trezenia, listening for the slight change in pitch of the treehoppers' song to signify someone, something, was out there moving, or whether it was sitting behind a modernistic console waiting, debating whether to take stronger action, when too strong an action might unleash the disaster that needed to be contained.

He leaned further back in the swivel, half noting that the clouds were clearing, that the westernmost towers were glistening in the jacket of moisture lit by the noon sun.

The signs were there—the overt absence of military influence coupled with the continuing references to the "Eagles" and the large military bureaucracy; the gentle and total control of the population; the small stories about the use of the Fleets in pressuring out-systems; the dedication of the new flagship of the new Eleventh Fleet; the routine acceptance of the dispatch of the Fifth Fleet to intimidate Orknarli; and, of course, the example of Haversol.

The Imperials liked to play the diplomatic game as politely as possible, without overt violence, and using the threat of the immense force of the Empire as the major tool. The use of violence in New Augusta didn't fit, not unless Accord was a real threat to something being planned, not unless the conditioned fear of Accord ran deeper than he thought.

The intercom buzzed. He ignored it, trying to pin down the elusive angle of the bombings.

The intercom buzzed twice.

He wondered if Marcella had anything to do with the explosions. Why her warnings? Or Courtney's veiled references? And Sylvia . . . With that thought he wondered if he detected the faintest trace of orange blossoms in the office.

He shook his head.

His fingers headed for the console control studs as he swung back to face the bank of plates and lights. Finally, he touched the plates and tapped out the codes.

"Senator Helmsworth's office."

"Nathaniel Whaler for Sylvia Ferro-Maine."

"I'm sorry, Lord Whaler, but she and Ms. Corwin-Smathers are on the floor with the Senator."

Floor? Floor of what?

Charles caught the confusion on Nathaniel's face and flashed his professionally engaging smile at the Envoy.

"The floor of the Senate. The debate on the ad valorem tax changes has just begun." The receptionist paused.

"Would you like to leave word that you called?"

"No . . . not right now. Thank you."

Nathaniel absently looked down at the console where the intercom plate still flashed.

Of course the lady was busy. Weren't they all? He shook his head again.

The intercom buzzed twice more, and this time he decided against ignoring it.

"Lord Whaler, the repair crews are here."

"Fine."

"They're likely to make a great deal of noise."

"Noise? Ah, yes, noise."

"Perhaps now would be a good time for you to eat?"

Nathaniel scratched his head, then nodded.

"Lunch, I suppose, I will have now."

He stood and looked out at the hills, now beginning to show a golden tinge. He wondered if the color shift were seasonal or merely the result of little rain.

XXVI

"HE'S A DANGER for two reasons."

"Two? The first is obvious. If he succeeds in getting that trade agreement, we lose the most favorable chance in generations to remove the Accord influence. But what's the second?"

Three officers sat in the small sound-and snoop-blanked room, and the special construction absorbed each word even before the next was uttered.

"His success fuels the myth of Accord's invincibility."

The third officer, a woman wearing the uniform of a Vice Admiral, frowned, tapped her fingers on the soft top of the table. "Can you honestly say that the average citizen knows, or cares, about whether Accord can hold us off? Who cares? When you get to that level of argument, it's a leadership discussion. The whole universe knows Accord is not an aggressive force. The more subtle danger is overlooked."

"Subtleties yet," snapped the First Fleet Commander. "How subtle is it that our traders are effectively blocked from the entire Rift? How subtle is it that fifty systems followed Accord into rebellion and still look to the black and green for leadership?"

The Rear Admiral shook her head. "For you, it's not subtle. But who in the Imperial Court really follows the trade flow on the Imperial borders? Who understands that Accord's example will leave us boxed on all borders? Or that stagnation is bound to follow? N'troya understands that. He should, since he's the Emperor, but he also claims that the use of force begets force, and that force will lead to the Empire's downfall."

"The Grand Admiral hasn't bought that."

"Not yet. That's the position her daughter is staking out at Commerce, and a successful trade treaty with Accord could bolster both the Emperor and young Ku-Smythe. Not incidentally, it would further strengthen Accord."

The Vice Commander spoke up.

"For generations, they've bluffed us, claiming their Institute could poison all the worlds of the Empire. It's just not possible, but everyone goes along with the blackmail bluff and nods."

The Rear Admiral looked at the two younger officers, the Fleet Commander and her Vice Commander.

"Bluff it might be, but if we get the go-ahead from the Grand Admiral, you'll have literally only standard hours in which to bake the entire system. Who knows what they have hidden on the outer planets, on asteroids, parked in orbit . . ."

"That can't be done, unless—"

"That's right. Even so, the nova front would take hours to get to the outer orbits, which means that you'd have to maintain a picket line until nearly the last minute."

Silence, deeper than before.

"But no one would ever challenge the Empire for generations . . . would they?"

XXVII

"MYDRA, COME WITH me."

"Lord Whaler, I couldn't."

"No?"

Mydra looked around the staff office as if for moral support, but Hillary had scurried out toward the front desk.

"I do have a great deal of work," she protested.

"Which can wait, can it not? Besides, the repair crews will make a great deal of noise, will they not?"

She almost smiled but managed to keep a straight face.

"Let me get my cloak."

He nodded, knowing she was surely going to do more than that, wondering whether the stops were for cosmetic touch-ups, snooper equipment, or to report to whomever she reported to, or all three.

Ten minutes later, she reappeared, wearing a deep brown cloak trimmed in cream, and with every dark brown hair in perfect place.

At the Legate's dining room, Nathaniel announced "the portico" and was rewarded with the same table he had had the night before.

"Have you dined here before?"

"Once or twice with Legate Witherspoon."

"A drink?" inquired the waiter.

Nathaniel inclined his head toward Mydra.

"Sperlin."

"Liftea."

"Do all Accordans like liftea?"

"A planetary vice it is, I fear." He gestured to the sweep of the windows and the towers. "Never would I tire of such a picture."

"I never do, either. You know. These are the only towers left on Terra."

"So was I told by someone."

"Tourists come from the underground cities all around the globe to see the views." There was an edge to her voice.

"They do?"

"The war with Accord, you know," she explained, "drove us underground. It's only been in the past century that any real aboveground excursions have been permitted."

"Not well liked are we, then?"

"I wouldn't say that, Lord Whaler, but Accord isn't the most popular system outside the Empire, either."

"That will affect trade talks, doubtless."

"It may, but that's your field, and I certainly wouldn't presume to guess."

The liftea and the white wine Mydra had ordered arrived with the menus.

As if to cover his confusion, Nathaniel immediately buried himself in the printed selections.

He'd already decided on a light salad after having checked his weight that morning. New Augusta was definitely too rich for Ecolitans, both in the complexity of the political systems and in the caloric content of the food.

He put down the menu and looked out the window, knowing as he did so that he was looking out windows far too much just in order to avoid talking.

"Lord Whaler?"

"Hmmm . . ."

"Earlier, you mentioned something about Accord and your worries. Are you still that worried?"

"Yes, Lady dear. Worried and a little tired. What can I do but wait? Terms have been suggested."

"I know that, but . . ."

The Ecolitan beckoned to the waiter.

"Yes, sir?"

Nathaniel waited for Mydra.

"I'll have the flamed shrimp, with the fruit salad."

"This salad here," added the Envoy as he pointed to the entree.

"Saying you were . . ." he prompted.

"I was wondering," she said slowly, "about what you said. You seemed so . . . weary . . . tired . . . and so sure that Accord and the Empire would end up destroying each other."

The Ecolitan let his shoulders sag slightly, then took a sip of the liftea.

"You know what I am. A professor of trade, an Ecolitan, and someone who is not a politician. Complicated diplomacy that seems separate from what I know to be true I have trouble with. A large Empire also needs many Ministries and people, but I understand not why they do not have the same purposes. But you have them and we, small system that we are, must deal as we can."

Mydra's right eyebrow twitched slightly.

As he paused, he could see the portico was beginning to fill with other diplomats and their guests.

"To us, we looked for simple negotiations. We proposed alternative terms—"

"I understand that, Lord Whaler. I do sympathize with the confusion which has occurred, and I suppose all Empires have problems with their bureaucracies, but that doesn't seem to be what bothers you. You seem almost haunted."

"Haunted?"

"Possessed. Bothered by an image of something terrible, as if the Empire were some ogre hanging over Accord."

"Did you not say that Accord was not liked? Should I not worry? Should we not worry? Should the people of Haversol not worry? Should the people of Orknarli not worry?"

He took another sip of his liftea.

Mydra followed his example and sipped her wine. He could sense the frustration she was feeling at his avoiding the real thrust of her question.

"You think I do not understand what you ask?" He shook his head. "I understand. Simple questions do not always have simple answers. Let me answer your questions with questions." He stopped to take another sip of the tea. "Is not the Empire more powerful now than before the Secession? Does not the Grand Admiral control more than ten fleets? Is not each of those fleets bigger than the entire Imperial Navy of the Secession time?" He waited.

"Yes. You said that already. You said that the Empire could destroy Accord. It was the other things you hinted at . . ."

"About the little people . . . about those who will not give in even though they would be destroyed?" He cleared his throat. "Accord did not win freedom with battlefleets, did we? Why does the Empire think we should turn to big ships and big fleets now? Why should we abandon our own ways of warfare? As the Empire has strengthened its weapons, would not poor Accord have done so as well?"

He shrugged, then finished in a lower tone. "Planets that cannot grow foods cannot support Empires. Any planet must support itself, except a very few, such as New Augusta. And to disrupt the balance necessary for such is not difficult for Accord, though the results would not be immediate. These weapons cannot be tested—not obviously—cannot be paraded through streets, cannot thunder through skies. Very quiet, and no one sees. The Emperor does not see the danger, nor does the Grand

Admiral. And Accord does not understand that the Empire does not see. For me, it is dangerous even to hint at such, and dangerous not to."

He forced a smile. "We cannot dwell on this, but do our best to work it out."

"Work out?" stammered Mydra, her mind apparently fixed on the implications of what he'd said. "You're not saying that Accord would literally wipe out life on hundreds of planets for better trade terms?"

"No. Accord does nothing first." He spaced his words firmly and deliberately. "Remember. The Empire attacked Haversol over the terms of trade, not the other way. The Empire stalled trade talks, then used delay as an excuse. I see delay. I see me trying to get around that delay, and I see someone trying to kill me."

He looked away from her and at the sunlit western hills. "I have done what I can. You should enjoy the shrimp and the view."

Nathaniel plunged into the salad which had been delivered during his monologue, discovering he was hungrier than he'd thought.

Mydra ate silently.

After he'd finished the salad down to the last morsel, including the bitter garnish, he straightened and studied the other tables.

The spacing became apparent. What amounted to a circle of empty tables surrounded his. Was he persona non grata, or did no one want to consort with the next victim of Imperial expansionism?

Even as he debated, a tall woman dressed in yellow stood up at one of the far tables and swiftly crossed the dining area toward him. A matriarch of Halston, he identified her, probably the Legate from her bearing and age.

He rose.

"Envoy Whaler? Berthea of Carthos." She spoke in Panglais.

With Mydra present, he decided against replying in Halstani.

"Your honor. May I present Ms. Mydra Da-Vios of the Legation staff?"

"My pleasure, and may I invite you both to join us?"

"Delighted we would be," Nathaniel answered quickly.

Three women, all attired in some shade of yellow trimmed with dark brown, and one man, dressed in a similar yellow tunic and trousers piped with the same dark brown, all came to their feet when Nathaniel, Mydra, and Berthea returned.

The women were Carin, Lynea, and Deirdre. The man, younger than Sergel, trimmer, blond, clean shaven, and regular featured, was Arthos.

Berthea wasted no time.

"Understand you're having trouble getting straight answers from the Empire."

The Ecolitan launched into his whole explanation, starting with his arrival, his meetings, and the ensuing strange events.

". . . and I am waiting, hoping that the situation can be resolved."

All five of the Halstanians nodded.

"That's the story we'd heard, but I wanted to get it direct from you," snapped Berthea. "Sounds like a replay of the Haversol situation."

From the corner of his eye, Nathaniel could see Mydra sitting on the edge of her chair.

"Have you had any pressure from the Eagles?" asked Carin.

"Only that they sent a battlecruiser to escort me. Strange that none of the military have contacted the Legation."

"That fits," noted Berthea, gray eyes resting levelly on Mydra. "They stay in the background, just dispatch their fleets to do the talking. That Admiral Ku-Smythe, she's a cool one."

"Ku-Smythe? Special Assistant at Commerce, I thought."

"That's the daughter. Just as cold as the mother, I hear." That was Lynea's comment, who looked to be close to the same age as Marcella.

"Halston has had similar difficulties?"

"Not yet. We'd rather it didn't get that far. Orknarli's too close."

"Divide and conquer," chipped in Carin, who earned a frown from Berthea.

Nathaniel just nodded.

"For someone who's sitting on top of flamewasps, Lord Whaler, you seem rather detached."

"Not detached, just waiting, hoping that upon reflection the Empire will accept our very reasonable terms of trade."

"If they don't?"

"Then Accord will do what it must."

"I was afraid you'd say that," the tall Legate said softly.

Lynea flashed a puzzled look at her Legate.

"Check your histories, Lynea. Only fools, idiots, or men pick fights with the . . . with Accord."

The Ecolitan wondered how she had almost described Accord.

"My apologies, Ms. Da-Vios," added Berthea in a cold tone, inclining her head toward Mydra.

Nathaniel spread his hands in a gesture of appeal.

"In this, if you would convey our situation to any whom you think could be of value . . ." He let the sentence trail off.

"Will do. Understand your position. Probably would have to handle it in much the same way. Hope the Empire understands. Good luck."

Nathaniel understood as well and rose to his feet.

"Mydra, we need to return to the Legation."

Three strangers were working in his office when he returned. In the two plus hours since he and Mydra had been gone, plastic sheeting had been laid over virtually all the furniture and the carpeting. The workers were beginning to cut out squares from the walls where the damage had been the heaviest.

In passing through to his own private study, Nathaniel saw enough to know the snooping equipment had been replaced and improved.

Back in his quarters, he dropped into the smaller study swivel and stared into space.

Finally, he turned to the screen on the comm unit and began twisting through the public channels but only picked up dramas, song and dance shows, music programs.

The fax channels had news somewhere. Was the two position switch to the right of the selector for such a distinction?

It was. The blue was for news and factual material, the red for lighter fare.

After fifteen minutes of flipping back and forth, he found one quick segment on the Accord-Empire situation.

A commentator in silver sat behind her console, green eyes somehow enhanced, silver hair flashing, both professional and alluring at the same time, in a way that reminded him, distantly, of Marcella.

"Newest developments on the Accord trade talks."

Flash to a shot of the Accord seal on the Legation's front portals, then to the tattered wall of Nathaniel's office.

"Earlier today we showed you the bombing damage to the Accord Legation and an interview with the Envoy there, who insisted the Empire was stalling trade talks."

The screen shifted back to the commentator for an instant before displaying another scene, this time of a slender, gray-haired woman in brilliant yellow.

"The Matriarch Princeps of Halston today requested that the Emperor favorably consider the terms of trade offered by Accord and stated that delay would not be in the best interests of either the Empire or other systems. No amplification was forthcoming. Neither the Ministry of Commerce nor the Ministry of External Affairs would comment."

The screen flicked back to the commentator.

"In the meantime, Imperial Intelligence still denies one of its agents was injured while involved in the Accord case.

"Explanations are missing. The Accord Envoy has none, and no affected Imperial Ministries would comment.

"Next . . . a special report on the impact of the synde bean shortage—"

Nathaniel switched off the screen.

The media hadn't forgotten . . . so far.

He tapped the intercom.

"Mydra! Any word on Sergel?"

"No, sir. He doesn't answer, and he hasn't called in."

"Then please officially report that he is missing."

"So soon?"

"No. So late."

He cut Mydra off and accessed the Faxstellar number.

The receptionist was male, blond, regular featured, even if his chin was weak.

"Nathaniel Whaler, Envoy of Accord, this is. More interesting information have—"

"Yes, sir. Ms. Bar-Twyla said to put you straight through."

"Kyra Bar-Twyla . . . Lord Whaler. What a surprise! How can I help you?"

"Perhaps we can each other help. A person from my staff is missing."

"Are you serious?"

"Most serious. Mr. Sergel Weintre, my Information Specialist, is not in his quarters, has not reported to work, and was supposed to be here early this morning. Now is late afternoon and no Sergel. I would not worry about so trivial a matter, but after these past few days . . ." Nathaniel shrugged.

"Why do you think his disappearance is connected with the trade talks situation?"

"Suppose I should not say, but if you check with the Diplomatic Police, several days ago Mr. Weintre was found unconscious outside my quarters. He could not explain what happened or why. Now he is gone."

"Is Mr. Weintre a native?"

"Native?"

"Is he from Accord?"

"Yes. From Accord."

"That is very interesting. I appreciate it. Thank you."

Nathaniel was left staring at a blank screen.

The intercom buzzed.

"Lord Whaler?"

"Yes."

"I've just gotten a call from the Diplomatic Police. They've located Mr. Weintre."

"Where?"

"He was wandering around the Diplomatic Concourse, they said."

"Wandering?"

"Well . . . yes . . ."

"Why did he not come to the Legation?"

"He couldn't."

"Why not?"

"Because . . . because . . . he's been partially mindwiped. He thinks he's eighteen standard years old and coming home from summer training. He doesn't understand how he ended up in New Augusta ten standard years older."

"I see. I see." He sighed. "Anything, anything there is that you can do, please arrange for Sergel." He swung his head from side to side.

"Yes, Lord Whaler."

Nathaniel shuddered. The Ministry of Defense did not like Accord, that was certain.

He faxscreened Galactafax.

"Lord Whaler at—"

"Yes, sir. Marjoy Far-Nova would like to tape you, sir."

"Lord Whaler, you have new developments?"

"Yes, Lady. Unhappily, I do."

"Unhappily?"

"My Information Specialist, Sergel Weintre, has been missing since yesterday. He has been found. Just found, but he thinks he is eighteen standard years, and part of his thoughts are gone."

"He's been mind-wiped?"

"That is the term."

"What did he know? Where can I confirm this?"

"I cannot say what he knew. I feared he was not to be trusted, and yesterday I ordered Mr. Weintre to see me this morning. I thought he might have been connected to some information losses, but he never arrived. Now the Diplomatic Police have him."

"Let me get this straight. You discovered, or suspected, that Mr. Weintre was not to be trusted, then the Legation was bombed. You tried to reach Mr. Weintre to question him. He disappeared and turns up mind-wiped?"

"That is essentially correct."

"Oh, sister! Will this . . ." she caught herself and turned her full attention back to the Ecolitan.

"Thank you, Lord Whaler."

With the blank screen again facing him, Nathaniel realized how secondary he was to the need for instant fax reporting.

He wondered belatedly if he were being strung out. What if Mydra had fed him a baited story?

He fumbled with the directory codes until he obtained the number for the Diplomatic Police.

"Lord Nathaniel Whaler," he announced.

"Yes." The cold-eyed dispatcher waited.

"Understand you have one of my staff, one Sergel Weintre?"

"No."

Nathaniel felt himself stiffen, even while trying to keep calm. Had he been set up to be discredited? Left to hang himself with the media?

"Sure are you? Report had I that—"

"We did have Mr. Weintre, Lord Whaler, but on the instructions of your office, we have already begun the transfer to the rehabilitative center."

"Thank you. Thought I that you were not quite so quickly acting. That number, do you have it?"

He took it down, his heart still beating fast. He had to remember that he couldn't necessarily trust anyone. So easy to forget that in the isolated and pleasant surroundings of his quarters.

Then he called Kyra Bar-Twyla back and relayed the latest developments on Sergel.

She took the details quickly, and once she had the facts, cut him off.

He shrugged. Envoys didn't carry much weight with the Imperial media, that was for certain, nor with many others either. Not in New Augusta.

If the Empire didn't agree to trade talks, he hoped the stories in the faxcasts would have at least some of the independent systems asking questions and further doubting the Imperial good will.

The graceful way out would be negotiations . . . if the Ministry of Defense would accept a graceful way out.

XXVIII

THE ECOLITAN FROWNED, slammed his clenched fist into his right palm, once, twice . . . three times. Finally, he looked out into the darkness where the lights of the towers sparkled.

"Flame! Flame! Flame!"

"They want negotiations. There's every reason to have negotiations. But it isn't happening."

He glanced down at the small comm unit of the study.

"Why? Why doesn't anything happen?"

He should have been in bed hours earlier, but the sense of danger, the nagging, dragging tightness in his gut had not let him rest.

Instead, he had cleaned up and dressed, pulling on a green tunic and trousers, along with his belt and the rest of his easily concealed infiltration equipment.

He took a last look at the view from the small study at the lights of the towers and then tapped the lockplate on the portal into his Legation office.

The first sliver of light from the opening warned him. He drove through the portal even before it was open.

The four figures who seemed to turn in slow motion toward him all had masks slung around their necks, not yet in position. Three were women. The fourth, on the far right, leaning against the big official console, was a man. All wore uniforms.

The first two women sprayed away from the Ecolitan, slammed into the wall by his attack. The third Marine went down as Whaler arced his elbow across her throat.

The man had a nerve tangler halfway from his holster before the Ecolitan slashed it from his hand.

Seconds later, the man in green looked down at the unconscious Marine and looked around the office.

Surprisingly, all four Marines were still breathing, and one of the women on the far side of the office was beginning to scrabble toward the stunner that lay about a half meter from her outstretched hand.

Nathaniel reached it first, readjusted the setting from its near-lethal level, and used it, first on the one conscious soldier, then on the other three.

The masks meant that someone was about to gas his quarters, and the fact that the Marines were in his private Legation office meant someone on the Legation staff, besides the unfortunate Sergel, had been in on the operation.

He worried his tongue between his teeth for a moment, tried to think, while moving toward the portal to the staff office.

He had a stunner in each hand. While their high-pitched *strumm* was noisier than he liked, they were quick. If another crew were waiting, he would need all the edge in time he could get.

Before activating the portal, he adjusted the stunners' focuses to almost a point.

He looked at the portal, took a deep breath, shook himself gently, then tapped the lockplate.

Again, he came barreling through the portal, low and fast, even before it was fully open.

His first shot dropped the single Marine guarding the next doorway. His second paralyzed Hillary West-Coven's right hand before she could touch the console studs.

"You move, and I'll put the beam right above your heart."

She froze.

No one else was in the staff office.

"Stand up and move back from that console."

Nathaniel hadn't realized how olive her complexion was until he saw the whiteness beneath the skin tone.

"Lord Whaler, there must be some mistake."

"Right. I was mistaken."

Her left hand drifted forward.

"Strumm!" The needle width of the beam singed the back of her hand.

Hillary jumped backward a half step.

"Don't listen, do you?"

His eyes traveled the room. He didn't have much time. For all he knew, whatever Marines had been at the other door to his quarters were already inside.

Where could he go?

He smiled, and Hillary backed away yet another step until her back was almost to the wall.

"Sorry," he said.

"Strumm!"

The woman crumpled.

Nathaniel eased open the door to the hall which led to the reception area. It was empty, and he picked up Hillary and threw her over his right shoulder, stuffing the one stunner into his belt, leaving the other in his left hand.

Although Hillary was lighter than he expected, he set her down beside the portal to the reception area and took out the other stunner.

Shaking his head, he thumbed the portal access. Imagine, having to fight his way out of his own Legation!

This time he waited until the portal was three quarters of the way open before snapping three quick shots. He dropped both Marines who waited—one officer, one squad leader.

Once into the reception area, he made another check but found no other employees or bodies. Hillary had to have been the duty officer.

The reception console's screens showed that the exterior corridor was empty, except for the two tunnel buggies that bore the crest of the Diplomatic Tower, and except for the two men dressed in repair uniforms.

Nathaniel snorted.

With a series of quick movements, he laid Hillary out on the couch closest to the exterior portal and pulled off the officer's tunic and beret. Both were too small to fit him. He slit the tunic up the back and slipped it on over his own. The beret came next.

He cradled Hillary in both arms, her weight on his forearms while he still held the stunners, shadowed by her.

He would not be able to carry her that way for long, but long enough to do what was necessary.

He stepped outside and turned toward the "repair" buggies. Neither "repairman" looked up until he was within five meters.

"Sss . . . what?"

"Have a problem?"

"Strumm! Strumm!"

Both crumpled, their faces blank.

He placed Hillary in the nearest buggy, climbed in, and began to guide the vehicle toward the service shaft that the maps had indicated was at the far end of the corridor.

He wondered if the level were temporarily blocked off or if it were merely deserted in the hours between midnight and dawn.

The service shaft was vacant, and he steered the buggy onto the drop platform, setting the level destination for the one hundred twenty-first level.

He hoped he could do what he wanted, since he intended to get back to the three hundredth level shortly . . . if he could.

Pulling Hillary off the buggy at the one hundred twenty-first level, set it on remote and programmed a course that would take it back toward the main lift shafts.

The service shaft took them another three levels down, where he half lifted, half dragged Hillary out. There he wadded up the beret and the tunic and let them drop into the shaft.

Hillary was beginning to wake up. He used the stunner again, at low power, to nick her larynx. While there was some danger it might permanently damage her voice, at the moment he felt less than charitable, and he needed Hillary able to walk.

He gently tugged the gold film cloak from his belt and let it billow around him and partly over Hillary. With his arm around her tense body, he said, "You can't say a word, but if you try to escape, I'll trigger the stunner against your spine. You might not ever walk again, at least not without a *long* rehab."

He gave her a gentle shove.

"Now, we're just a loving couple headed back for my quarters . . . right?"

He could feel her reluctant nod.

"That's right, dear," he added.

They ambled toward the lift shaft. Once or twice, he bent toward her, as if to embrace her, stopped, and looked down into her eyes, which burned green hatred back at him.

He smiled back at her.

They reached the lift shaft and slipped into the slow rising lane.

The Ecolitan could see a few others in both drop and lift shafts, which indicated that the tower had not been sealed off for the attack on his quarters, which led to even more interesting speculations.

As they stumbled off at the three hundredth level, Nathaniel checked the stages quickly but could see nothing out of the ordinary.

Sergel's quarters were even further from the shaft than Nathaniel's, but in the opposite direction. Once there, it took the Ecolitan less than a minute to manipulate the fields and slip inside.

The three rooms were a mess, everything totally out of order, with abundant signs that at least several intruders had pawed through the rooms.

Without warning, he pressed the nerves in the back of Hillary's neck and let her slump unconscious.

He needed the time to change the lock fields to keep anyone else from repeating his trick and to see what he could find, assuming the other searchers had left anything.

Point by point, centimeter by centimeter, he went through the three rooms—the living area, which had a small nook for food preparation; the sleeping room; and the hygienarium. The previous searchers had removed virtually all personal effects, outside of a few small console reference tape discs, clothing, four solidio cubes, some of Sergel's calling cards, and a package of blank and old-fashioned notepaper. Whoever had searched the quarters had apparently wanted every possible clue to the Information Specialist and to his psychology.

The Ecolitan finally straightened, pulled at his chin, and looked blankly at the wall. Sergel had not rated an exterior view, and the lack of windows made Nathaniel uncomfortable.

He sighed, checked Hillary, then stretched himself out on the other couch across from her, willing himself to wake in three standard hours or at the faintest sound.

In seconds, he was asleep.

When he awoke Hillary was still out. The Imperial standard time was 0700. He stretched and got to his feet, pacing back and forth in the cramped space for a few minutes. Finally, with one eye on Hillary he washed his face and cleaned up as well as he could.

Once he was fairly presentable, he moved back into the living quarters to keep a closer eye on Hillary, shaking his head as he tried to think things out.

Some things were clear. Some were not. The attempted "replacement" of the Envoy of Accord and the use of Imperial Marines in a clandestine attack on his quarters pointed toward a military involvement; and, to some degree, the fact that it was not being kept terribly quiet added to his concerns.

Yet it wasn't public, which meant that someone besides Accord wasn't supposed to know all the grisly details. Since the Terran public could have cared less about the fate of either trade talks or the Accord Envoy, the military didn't seem to want someone else to know, and if it weren't the head Admiral . . .

That left another question, which led to another answer.

He frowned. Who could he trust? Sylvia? Could he really trust her?

He didn't have much choice. He needed someone with the kind of access she could presumably provide.

With that, he tapped out the code.

"Senator Helmsworth's office."

"Nathaniel here, for Sylvia."

"Your business?" asked Charles, not really even looking into the screen.

"Personal."

"Thank you."

Sylvia's image snapped into place.

"Where are you?"

"Where I am, dear Lady. Two questions for you. First, are you loyal to the Emperor?"

"What does that mean?"

"It means what I asked. Whoever is after me isn't. That's why they're after me."

"Can you prove that?"

"Someone used a Marine detachment to raid my quarters. They weren't quite successful."

Sylvia's gray eyes widened. Nathaniel half ducked and turned, but Hillary was still out cold.

Sylvia drew in the chaos of Sergel's room and the figure lying on the stained scarlet couch.

Nathaniel shrugged.

"You've probably managed to trace where I am . . . which means I'll leave. So . . . where do I meet you?"

She laughed.

"The best place would be the Legate's dining room in the Diplomatic Tower. We could have a late breakfast there. That's possibly the one place where almost no one would dare to create a scene. If what you have to say isn't that compelling, however, you might have some trouble when you left."

Nathaniel shook his head from side to side. "So simple. I'm inclined to agree, and a friend will I bring, one with whom your friends might have much to say." He paused. "By the way, you never answered my question about the Emperor."

Sylvia frowned. "You know the answer, whether you know it or not. Otherwise, why would you have faxed me? Yes. Of course. How else could it be?"

This time, she waited to see what else he had to say.

"What can I say?"

He took a last look at the woman in the screen, who wore her hair down and swept back above a yellow and white tunic. Nathaniel decided he didn't like the yellow on her as well as the darker colors.

He smiled after the screen went blank. She would look good in either black or in the dark forest green of the Institute.

Once again, Hillary was beginning to stir, and he didn't really want to stun her another time.

He waited.

"Are you ready to head out?"

She jerked her head from side to side.

"You should be able to talk now, or whisper."

"No," she half croaked, half whispered.

"Why not? Just because you're part of this crew out to discredit the Emperor doesn't mean you aren't hungry."

"You men!"

He scowled. That was the second time around. First had been the agent who'd tried to zap him in the tunnel. Now Hillary was using the same phrase.

Stunner in hand, he gestured to the hygienarium.

"Clean up."

She glared at him but went ahead with her necessities, despite the lack of privacy, and finished up by brushing her short black hair.

The Ecolitan checked over his equipment a last time, then unlocked the door fields and ushered Hillary out before him. Although a few pedestrians strolled by Sergel's door, the area did not appear to be directly monitored, and Nathaniel and Hillary reached the main drop shaft without incident.

"Keep walking," the Ecolitan said lightly as they passed the drop and lift shafts.

Hillary only missed one step before continuing onward.

"I thought we were going to breakfast . . ."

Nathaniel almost missed his step. He had not said anything about breakfast, except to Sylvia, and that meant Hillary had been feigning sleep. And that could mean trouble for Sylvia.

"I did mention that but not exactly when."

Nathaniel did not miss the newly stationed pair of Imperial Marine sentries before the Accord Legation, but since his destination was further down another corridor, he and Hillary only saw the pair from the far side of the shaft area.

At least one passerby gave the evening gold film cloak a strange look, but then shook her head and continued on. Possibly the Diplomatic Tower was the only section of New Augusta where outré clothing rated but a passing frown.

The Ecolitan could feel the tenseness mounting in Hillary as they began to circle back toward the private entrance to his personal quarters.

When he saw that there were no outside guards, he frowned. Were they inside? Would they expect him to strike back so quickly? Did he dare risk it?

He nearly laughed aloud.

Did he dare not to? Within hours, the omnipresent Imperial machine would have located him, and he couldn't keep dragging Hillary along.

He marched up to the portal and slapped his palm on the lock.

Even as the portal began to open, he tensed, then in a single fluid movement scooped Hillary up and tossed her through the portal.

He followed, stunner drawn.

"*Strumm!*"

"*Strumm!*"

Nathaniel was quicker, barely, and the single Marine pitched forward out of the stool and onto the tiles.

Hillary, who had absorbed the first shot, was flat on the tiles next to the Marine.

The Ecolitan felt sorry for her. Too many jolts to her system. But he had already left the entryway behind.

The bed was mussed, in the way that indicated it had not been slept in, but the quarters were vacant.

Nathaniel palmed the lock to his office and snapped a shot through the barely open portal to the spot behind the console.

He followed his shot, low and to the left, rolling and firing.

"*Strumm!*"

Another damned Marine!

"*Strumm!*"

A line of fire burned down his right arm.

The stunner dropped to the floor from his numb right hand. He shifted the aim of the stunner in his left hand.

"*Strumm! Strumm!*"

Nathaniel's first shot spun the female Marine to the carpet, and the second stilled her twitching.

He stood momentarily over the bodies, looking down at the second face of a man who looked like him. For a moment, he studied the patched wall, yet to be fully repaired from earlier explosive events.

He checked the portal to the staff office, decided that it would hold and took out the two small probes. The one he held in his right hand clattered to the floor. Even with full concentration, his pain conditioning could not override the jangled nerves in his right arm. With the single probe in his left hand, it took several minutes for him to lock the portal, though it would hold against anything less than a military laser cutter.

"Hope they don't have that handy."

"Strumm!"

He gave another jolt to the Marine before holstering the stunner and bending to drag his double back into his own private quarters through the still open portal.

He smiled as he glimpsed the ragged thunderclouds through the vista of the office window panorama.

Definitely prophetic. Definitely.

Back in the entryway of his private quarters with the three unconscious bodies, he knelt down, rolled Hillary over, listened to the heartbeat.

He was no doctor, but he didn't like the sound.

Still . . . he had to make a few changes.

First, he focused the stunner and burned out all four visual snoops. When he finished, he laid the stunner aside. The charge was exhausted.

With his good hand, he pulled the diplomatic blacks off his double and stuffed the man into the greens he had been wearing—minus the equipment belt and gear, which he retained. Then he hurried into a set of his own blacks, pocketing the I.D.s and other "official" credentials carried by the false Envoy.

Finally, he wiped off the useless stunner and tucked it into the other's belt holder.

The remaining stunner was down to about twenty percent charge, but he decided to keep it until he could replace or recharge it.

He straightened his stiff shoulders.

He hadn't been thinking clearly. Too long since he'd slept well. The easiest way out was the direct way.

After a sigh, he took a deep breath. With a grunt, he stooped and swung Hillary over his shoulder, lugging her through his quarters before setting her on the couch in his office.

Next, he dragged his double back into the office and laid him out in a position on the floor, and put the exhausted stunner in the unconscious man's hand.

Finally, he unlocked the portal and hit the emergency stud.

First through the portal from the staff office was Mydra, followed by another Marine.

"Whoever he is," snapped the Ecolitan, "he attacked through my private quarters, he used poor Hillary as a shield, and managed to get both guards as well."

He glared at the Marine. "Some protection you are!"

"But, sir . . ."

"But nothing. All's well that ends well, I suppose. Now . . . the woman . . . I mean . . . Hillary. She's in a bad way. Probably needs emergency medical care. Handle that immediately. Then there's the other Marine in my quarters, plus that one over there. You'd better post some guards *outside* my private exit this time. Damn the gossip. Enough's enough."

The Marine saluted and thumbed his belt comm.

"Lord Whaler . . ." began Mydra slowly.

He nodded at her.

"What do you intend to do with the intruder?"

"Take him to breakfast, of course. Under guard."

He could see the effort she was making to keep her jaw in place.

He chuckled, which he had never done in front of her before, and added, "Since I seem to require armed guards these days, they might as well carry my friend with me to my morning appointment."

XXIX

SYLVIA, IN THE yellow and white that did not become her, was waiting for him in the outer lobby of the Legate's dining room.

Nathaniel watched her eyes widen as he walked in, flanked by three red-coated Imperial Marines, two of whom supported a semiconscious figure. The Ecolitan opened and closed his right hand several times, blocking away the pain. He had full control back, but it would be several hours before he would be able to relax his controls.

"I apologize for being late, dear Lady, but I had a great deal to accomplish since we talked, as I am sure you realize."

He gestured. "This gentleman might be of some interest to you, since he was attempting to be me."

He turned to the three Marines.

"Wait here with this gentleman. I fully expect you to be here when I return. Then we will deal with the problem."

"But . . . sir . . ."

"But nothing. I am certainly safe within the Legate's dining room, especially if you are guarding the entrance and exit. True?"

He offered his arm to Sylvia, faced the waiter, and nodded.

"Nathaniel Whaler, Envoy from Accord. A table for two on the portico."

The man's dark eyes widened fractionally, but his thin and clean-shaven face did not shift expressions.

Nathaniel turned his head toward Sylvia.

"And this time, dear Lady, I would appreciate it if you did not sneeze. To repeat our luncheon would create an additional strain I would rather not face—not right now, at least."

She stopped, right in the middle of the empty main dining room, and let go of his arm.

"I think you owe me an explanation."

"I do. You're right. I unreplaced their replacement of me, and I'm doing the best I can to get that replacement into your hands. So far, everyone either believes or is playing that I'm the replacement, rather than me. It won't last very long. So if you can have a team pick up that gentleman . . . fine. If not, then the Marines will take him away. They will interrogate him and discover he is indeed not me."

"How in Hades can I arrange that—right out from underneath the Defense Ministry—in the middle of the Legate's lobby?"

"I don't know, but the waiter is coming back, and we'd better get along to our thoroughly bugged and snooped table."

Sylvia smiled and the gray of her eyes seemed to lighten.

"I could make it so the snooping wouldn't work."

"Fine . . . and then they'll be even more suspicious." Her face darkened.

"For Cloud's sake . . . you've already blown any cover I had. You think those Marines won't recognize me and tell the Admiral?"

His shoulders drooped slightly. "I should have thought of that. Too much going on, and I'm not used to the wheels within wheels."

She took his arm, and he could smell the faintest hint of the orange blossoms he had remembered. They strolled through the nearly empty outer dining room toward the waiter.

"If I hadn't recognized the risk, dear Envoy, I wouldn't have agreed to come."

Sylvia disengaged herself from his arm and let the waiter seat her. Nathaniel pulled out his own chair and seated himself. His fingers flicked over his belt, and the readouts were clear. The table was snooped to the hilt.

The view from the portico was obscured by the swirl of dirty gray clouds that dipped below the tops of the towers, and the murkiness of the light reminded Nathaniel of the mountains of Trezenia. The tightness in his gut was the same, despite the opulence of the morning gold table setting, the white and gold dishes, and the gilded table utensils.

"Would you like menus, Lord Whaler?" asked the waiter, hovering at the table edge between them, looking from one face to the other.

"Not I. I would like liftea, some fruit, if you have it, and any sort of breakfast pastry. Sylvia?"

"Just cafe, thank you."

"Already eaten?"

She nodded, put her elbows on the table and leaned forward, her eyes studying his face intently.

"Yes. You're you." She leaned back. "That's good, I think, but you realize we can't keep meeting this way." Again, he caught the glimpse of her smile, but only the glimpse.

"That, dear Lady, have I realized. And some plans I have to take care of that . . . if you would care to listen."

"In a moment . . ."

"I see. In the meantime, what do you think of the view?"

"Frankly, I would prefer a few words on how a senior professor ever obtained the background to be able to have survived the amazing set of coincidences that have befallen you."

"We academics have hidden reserves, particularly when fueled by necessity." He paused, cleared his throat, and looked into the dark gray slate of her eyes. A moment later, he looked away.

"Most of us on Accord have taken early survival training through the Institute. I liked it, as well as the academics, and one thing led to another. Only the government or the Institute have the funds for out-system travel, and there was much I wanted to see. The comparative po-

litical economy and economic history which are my academic specialties do not rate field trips . . . meant that I had to maintain and upgrade
my survival skills to obtain the Institute's backing for my academic
studies . . ." He shrugged. "Call me the reluctant Ecolitan . . . or maybe
the cowardly professor."

"Cowardly?"

"I'm afraid of everything. So I must prepare for everything."

Sylvia squinted and looked at her timestrip.

"In a few seconds, there will be a power failure."

His eyes darted toward the floor beneath the nearest table and back
to Sylvia.

She nodded once, slowly.

"That seems a bit unusual for New Augusta."

"Even we have switching failures and equipment malfunctions once
in a while."

"But—"

The entire room went gray, lit just by the light from the windows.

Nathaniel dropped and rolled under the table to his right in time to
miss the bolt from the waiter's stunner.

He rolled further and yanked the man's feet from underneath him,
but the waiter dropped like a dead weight.

"He lost his balance," observed Sylvia as Nathaniel looked up from
the floor at her.

The Ecolitan scrambled to his feet and surveyed the rest of the portico. The other table in use was occupied by three Fuards, and none of
the three—at the far end of the room—seemed to have noticed the
disturbance, although all three were gesturing about the lack of lighting.

"Shall we return to our table, Lord Whaler?"

"If you so suggest."

Two new waiters appeared, gravely picked the figure off the floor,
and disappeared.

Nathaniel shook his head.

"You do arrange things."

"I hope it's worth it. Now," and her voice hardened, "you have
roughly five minutes to say what you need. Quickly."

He cleared his throat.

"Besides what you've already done, I need access to a console
which can transmit messages directly to the Grand Admiral and to

the Emperor. Second, I need to be able to walk through the most secret Defense sections you can get me into in the Defense Ministry Tower. Not any information—just walking the halls will be sufficient. The sooner the better. The longer it takes, the more likely the Admiral will think up something else, and I honestly don't know how many more of her traps I can avoid. They almost got me last night."

"You seem awfully sure that it's the Grand Admiral."

"Couldn't be anyone else, could it?"

Sylvia gave him a rueful grin, and he had to return the expression.

"No, but if you knew that, why did you ask me if I were loyal to the Emperor?"

"To let you know where I stood."

Her mouth opened in a slight O.

"You're more devious than I suspected, dear Envoy."

He looked straight at her, liking what he saw, but pressed with the sense of the minutes ticking past, he raced on.

"Look. There's every reason for a simple trade agreement to be ratified. The credits aren't *that* significant. But it isn't. Instead, another fleet is building, and every time it looks like I move another step forward, someone with a military bearing or connection appears to stop me. When it gets right down to it, you can't trade with an incinerated system. That means only the military has a reason for stopping things cold, and they will, if—"

"You can't do something to stop it. What do you have in mind? Why do you need to walk through the secret sections of the Defense Tower?"

"To deliver a message that can't be delivered any other way."

"No other way?"

"This time, you'll have to trust me. Will you help?"

The Ecolitan became aware of how quiet the room was. Even the Fuards at the far end seemed to be conversing in whispers.

Sylvia seemed to be thinking over his request, but her face revealed nothing.

Finally, she looked up.

"I don't see how what you've asked is that unreasonable, under the circumstances. To set it up will take several hours, and you will have to leave with me. Right now."

"What about the Marines? Can I dismiss them and tell them to return? I'm a bit reluctant to disappear again so officially."

She frowned momentarily.

"That might be better."

He handed her a small capsule.

"Swallow that."

"Why?"

"Because the information in the Imperial data banks is wrong, and because it will make your life a great deal more comfortable."

"What are you planning? Not some sort of murder campaign?" Her voice rose fractionally.

"Forest Lord, no. But a lot of people will be very uncomfortable, and I'd rather you weren't among them." He didn't like twisting the truth, even a little, especially when talking to Sylvia, but he didn't have time to explain. "Please."

"All right."

She swallowed the capsule with a gulp of water.

Nathaniel realized that their food had not arrived.

"No breakfast . . ."

"I'll see you get something later—while we prepare." She rose, and added, "I'll wait here, while you dismiss your guards—or jailors."

XXX

THE GRAND ADMIRAL glanced back at the faxsheet that lay before her on the console.

For the fifth time in as many minutes, she picked it up again and read it through. Then she put it down.

Were her hands shaking? Nonsense!

She turned in the noiseless swivel and beheld the outer world. From her double thickness permaglassed view, she looked down and out over the golden plain, her eyes focused beyond the dome that contained the Imperial Palace.

Not looking at the words, she picked up the thin white sheet once more, and finally turned back to the console. She reached for the communication studs, then drew back her hands and read the fax message, this time slowly, and word by word.

J. KU-SMYTHE
GRAND ADMIRAL
MINISTRY OF DEFENSE
NEW AUGUSTA, TERRA
XVX-URG-CODE ONE BETA-SKV

YOUR INTEREST IN THE ACCORD ENVOY HAS BEEN NOTED.
THE ECOLITAN INSTITUTE UNDERSTANDS YOUR INTEREST, AS
DOES THE EMPEROR N'TROYA.

IN VIEW OF YOUR POSITION AS HEAD OF IMPERIAL DEFENSE
AND SECURITY, THE SUCCESS OF ANY FURTHER ACTS AGAINST
EITHER THE EMPEROR OR ACCORD DIPLOMATIC PERSONNEL
WILL BE REGARDED AS A PERSONAL FAILURE BY YOU TO CARRY
OUT YOUR RESPONSIBILITIES.

IN AN EFFORT TO BE HELPFUL IN THIS REGARD, WE OFFER
THE MOST RECENT PROJECTIONS AT HAND. THESE PROJECTIONS
INDICATE THAT MORE THAN 80% OF ALL INHABITANTS OF THE
MINISTRY OF DEFENSE TOWER WILL SUFFER A LOW-GRADE VER-
SION OF GERSON'S DISEASE. FOR ROUGHLY 2%, THE INFECTION
WILL UNFORTUNATELY BE FATAL. NO PRECAUTION YOU CAN
NOW TAKE WILL BE EFFECTIVE.

THIS TOTALLY SPONTANEOUS OUTBREAK HAS BEEN PRE-
DICTED BY THE EPIDEMIOLOGISTS OF THE INSTITUTE, AND
WHILE TOTALLY COINCIDENTAL AND WHILE WE REGRET IT IS
TOO LATE TO PREVENT IT, WE HOPE THIS ADVANCE NOTICE WILL
BE HELPFUL AND INDICATE OUR INTEREST IN FRIENDLY AND
NONMILITARY SOLUTIONS TO PROBLEMS, SUCH AS TRADE.

WE ALSO HOPE THE EMPIRE IS NOT SO INDISCREET AS TO
BELIEVE THAT WAR IS THE MOST SUCCESSFUL MEANS OF DEAL-
ING WITH ECONOMIC REALITY.

THEREFORE, THE SUCCESS OR FAILURE OF TRADE TALKS WITH
ACCORD WILL ALSO BE REGARDED AS YOUR PERSONAL RESPONSI-
BILITY. IF YOU HAVE ANY QUESTIONS, LORD WHALER, THE SE-
NIOR ECOLITAN AND THE ENVOY FROM ACCORD, WOULD BE
MOST HAPPY TO EXPLAIN. A COPY OF THIS MESSAGE HAS ALSO
GONE DIRECTLY TO EMPEROR N'TROYA.

No diplomat had written it, nor any functionary from any of the
other Ministries. But how had the writer gotten her personal codes,
down to the final and hidden authentications?

Not even the Emperor had those.

She did not doubt that the copy had in fact gone to the Emperor.

The fax was phrased as a public interest warning but was nothing more than a threat. And yet . . . even if she published the entire text as she had read it, who would believe it? If they did, wouldn't she be adding to Accord's credibility with the nonaligned systems?

She paused, then asked the console the question.

She returned to looking at the eastern plains, thinking, and waiting for the system to supply the answer.

Buzz.

"Gerson's Disease. Pathology. Informal name for influenza polioencephaliomyelitis (D-strain), an acute, infectious, virus disease characterized by inflammation of the gray matter of the spinal cord, and of the brain, coupled with respiratory inflammation, headache, fever, muscular pains, and irritation of the intestinal tract. Mortality in an untreated and susceptible population approaches ninety percent, but baseline T-type populations have normally demonstrated an immunity that approaches unity . . . immunization requires a series of injections . . . spread over roughly three standard months . . ."

The Admiral read the listing on the console screen twice, and the furrow between her eyebrows deepened into a gouge by the time she had finished.

The message was either a colossal bluff, or . . .

The Grand Admiral picked up the faxsheet and quietly tore the message to shreds.

Then she tapped out two instructions on her console.

If the fax had been correct, Accord not only possessed the ability to infect the most secure structure in New Augusta, but also to modify a disease in two separate aspects, a modification currently beyond Imperial medical technology.

Only time would tell, but at least for that time, any more of the attacks against the Ecolitan Envoy would have to be postponed. The risk was too great, even for her, particularly if the Emperor had a copy of the fax. If the Ecolitans had her codes, she had no doubt they had the Emperor's.

She repressed a shiver and turned back to the view of the plains, leaning back in the swivel. For a time she regarded the grass and the distant line of clouds above the horizon.

At last, she tapped a code, waiting . . .

"Marcella?"

XXXI

NATHANIEL STRAIGHTENED HIS tunic in mid-stride, not pausing in his steps but matching his pace to Sylvia's.

"I'm still not sure why this has to be done," said Sylvia in a tone that was half statement, half question.

The Ecolitan inhaled deeply. The air in the corridor was still, with a metallic trace scent to it, the first hint of oil and machine he had smelled since he arrived in the indoor world of New Augusta.

"Metallic smell," he commented.

"The filters and recyclers are about ninety-nine and nine-tenths percent effective. The circulation here in the deeper parts of the tower isn't quite as effective as elsewhere."

"That's why we need to stroll through as much of the Defense Tower as possible. The relatively accessible corridors will do."

Sylvia straightened her own military tunic and frowned.

"You still haven't elaborated. But not now."

Nathaniel sighed. "Have I asked you all your secrets?"

She laughed, a short gentle sound, "Touché."

The first security gate was staffed by a single guard, enclosed in a permaglass booth.

Nathaniel ran his eyes over the enclosure—guarded against energy weapons and projectiles, but not airtight.

"Let's see your passes." The woman's bored tone echoed in the emptiness of the deep corridor. Despite the standard lighting, the lack of ornamentation and the metallic edge to the air gave the area a tomblike feeling.

Sylvia placed two square cards facedown on the scanner.

"And your I.D.s and thumbprints," added the Defense sentry.

The three waited momentarily in the silence.

Nathaniel caught the green flash reflecting in the permaglass behind the sentry and almost shook his head. Bad design. A really alert intruder could take advantage of the warning.

"You're cleared."

The gate swung wide enough to let them pass through one at a time, then clunked shut. The sound reminded Nathaniel of a coffin lid falling shut.

He wondered whose coffin—Accord's or the Empire's?

"This way." The corridor branched, and Sylvia touched his hand, led him to the left.

Signs of greater activity began to appear as well as portals in the sides of the corridor and a military figure or two heading in one direction or another, some in uniforms similar to those he and Sylvia wore and some in the plain jumpsuits he had earlier suspected of being of military origin.

He nodded to himself.

Wheels within wheels . . . but all he had to do was to walk through the tower.

True—he could have planted the dispersers on Sylvia and asked her to do it, but that option bothered him. If Accord had dirty work, then he should be the one doing it. He knew his decision was irrational, and he hoped the Coordinate and the Institute didn't end up paying for it.

To be discovered as the Envoy from Accord within the top-secret sections of the Ministry of Defense might be more than embarrassing. It might prove fatal.

He almost laughed, and had he done so, the sound would have been grim. Were he to be discovered, he wouldn't ever be found. The last thing the Empire could afford would be an admission that Accord could breach Imperial security at will.

After three more turns, the corridor, now more of a thoroughfare, widened further into a lift/drop shaft concourse.

"We're ordered to the fifth level," Sylvia said in a tight and controlled voice.

He nodded and followed, presuming, although she had said nothing on the subject, that every word within the Defense perimeters was monitored or at least computer scanned.

He straightened automatically, keying in a military posture, and let himself follow Sylvia. They had a lot of corridor left to cover.

XXXII

HIS FEET HURT. He had walked further, hiked through the high plains of Trezenia, through the Parundan Rain Forests of Accord, and done it all with a standard field pack. He had forgotten how many extended marches he had led his trainees through, whether in rain, snow, or blistering sun. But now his feet hurt. And the muscles in his right arm still ached.

Nathaniel looked down at the omnipresent permaplast floor tiles. While they gave slightly under foot, they were hard, and he and Sylvia had walked more than ten kilos through the Defense Towers and the caverns beneath.

From the corner of his eye, he could see the portal to the Legation, and the pair of Imperial sentries.

"Here's where I leave you, dear Envoy. I hope things turn out the way you hoped."

"So do I." So do I, he added mentally.

Sylvia was gone even as he watched her melt into the passersby. He shook his head and trudged toward the portal, flinging back the film cloak to reveal his diplomatic blacks.

"Lord Whaler . . . we've been—"

"The same," he responded to the Marine with a smile, and he marched into the Legation.

"Lord Whaler, we've been a bit worried . . . what with the power failure and the disappearance of the man who attacked you. Then you dismissed your guards and went off by yourself." Heather Tew-Hawkes had moved around the reception console to greet him.

"How's Hillary?"

"They got her to the health center in time. It was close, but she should be back in a few days. She rambled a lot and kept insisting that there were two of you, and how she wasn't sure which one you really were." Heather smiled a tight smile, one obviously put on, and waited a moment before going on, as if to see whether Nathaniel would respond.

He didn't, just stood there, meeting her gaze levelly.

"She seemed more worried about you, but she's going to be fine."

"I'm glad of that." And he was. At the same time, the guilt and sadness rose within him.

Shortly, thousands of relatively innocent individuals would sicken, and some of them would die. Had there been a better way? Had he missed it?

He shook his head, forgetting where he was. How long, how long . . . ?

"Lord Whaler, are you all right?"

Heather's voice lost its tightness. Her tone of concern brought him back to the small Legation reception room with its mismatched lorkin wood furniture.

"Yes, Heather," he said slowly. "I'm all right. Tired, but all right."
As right as can be, now.

He straightened.

"By the way, Heather, would you get someone to clean up my office.
If I had an intact office, I might actually stay in it. Especially now, I
might stay there."

A puzzled look flitted across the redhead's face, but she answered
without questioning. "Mydra has already made the necessary arrangements. Maintenance has just about finished the repairs. They should be
complete tonight, and your office will be ready in the morning."

The Ecolitan shifted his weight from one sore foot to the other. Perhaps it had been the weight of the special heels on his boots. They
might have changed the pattern of his stride just enough.

Shaking his head again, he turned toward the portal that led to his
office and to his quarters.

"Lord Whaler?"

He turned back to the tentative sound of Heather's voice.

"Would you like me to order something for you to eat?"

"No, thank you, Heather. I appreciate it, but I'm not hungry right
now. Perhaps later, perhaps later."

He gave her a short smile that felt false, then went through the portal and down the hallway toward the staff office.

Mydra was standing by her console.

"The maintenance staff is finishing up the repairs to your office."

"That's fine. I won't be using it tonight anyway. Where are the
guards?"

"They're stationed outside the Legation and outside your private
doorway."

He nodded an acknowledgment.

"Lord Whaler, you look tired."

"I am tired. Tired beyond . . ." He broke off. Who would really
understand?

Instead, he took a deep breath, inhaling the odor of wall solvent, and
gathered himself together.

"You're right. I am tired, and I need a good night's rest. I will see
you in the morning, Mydra." He paused, then finished in a softer tone.
"And thank you for getting this mess cleaned up."

He had turned even as she said, "That's only my job."

The crew of three women and two men did not look up as he passed through his office. Thin blue plastic sheeting covered the carpet, the console, and the furniture. His boots left a line of tracks through the whitish powder that lifted at each step.

His quarters were empty—and clean. Even the private entryway tiles had been repolished to a beige glaze, with all the scuffs and bootmarks removed.

He took out the two probes from his belt and began to work on the portal controls. After several minutes, he stopped. The newly replaced control units were more complicated than the originals. His right hand was trembling too much to finish the alignment he needed.

Putting down the probes, he sat cross-legged on the tile next to the wall portal, concentrating on holding back the waves of fatigue, while trying to let his arm and finger muscles relax.

At last, he got back on his knees and completed the changes.

With a sigh, he closed the access panel, leaned to his feet, and trudged back through the quarters to the exit portal between the private study and the office.

Again, he changed the fields to lock totally the portal. This time he had to stop twice to rest.

Finally, with another deep breath and a sigh, he headed to the sleeping quarters, forcing himself to take off his clothing piece by piece before collapsing onto the bed.

Just before the darkness washed over him, he wondered if he had smelled orange blossoms.

XXXIII

THE CONSOLE BUZZED.

"Admiral, there's some disturbing news you ought to know."

"Such as?"

"Well . . . it's hard to explain," stammered the Commander on the other end of the screen. "It looks like an epidemic, but there hasn't been one . . . here . . . in ages . . . not with the air recirculators and purifiers." Her eyes dropped along with her voice.

"What sort of epidemic? How widespread? New Augusta? Planetwide?"

"Not exactly, Admiral. Not exactly. So far ninety percent or more of those reported cases are Defense Ministry personnel."

The Admiral looked squarely into the screen. The indirect lighting of her office had gradually brightened as the day had waned. The touches of gray in her dark hair looked silver, simultaneously gave her a harder appearance.

"Let me know if anything changes or if the outbreak should spread." She broke the connection.

The most senior officer of the Ministry of Defense of the Empire of Light stood away from her console, away from the five banners fanned on the inner wall, away from the gilt-framed honors on the side wall, and turned to look at the horizon to the east.

She wondered if Accord's sun, invisible to the best of Terran optical telescopes, including the orbital observatory, would be above or below the visual horizon, were it visible.

"Accord . . . one man," she whispered softly. "One man."

The goal of a lifetime was gone. Perhaps she had never had it. Perhaps her daughter had been right all along.

She studied the plains grass below, then the darkening sky to the east.

Finally, she squared her shoulders and turned back to the console.

There was more to the Empire than the Rift, and more to the Ministry than the Eleventh Fleet.

Her fingers unstacked the messages, and she began to scan them as they flashed across the screen.

XXXIV

THE ECOLITAN ENVOY stood by the swivel and studied the plush office for at least the tenth time in the last hour.

The day had been long. No one had faxed. No messages on trade had arrived. No fax commentators had followed up on any previous events. Perhaps all the quiet had been for the best. Just in the past few hours had reports of a mysterious illness at the Ministry of Defense begun to surface.

The fax commentators had announced the tower was closed until the entire structure could be totally sterilized, and that all victims were being treated in isolated facilities. So far, there had been nearly a hundred fatalities, out of ten thousand cases discovered.

Nathaniel shook his head.

It had been so easy, and the Empire had been so secure in its smugness . . . and would probably continue to be—except for the few who knew. Knowing the ways of empires, he wondered if that knowledge would die with its possessors, until a generation from now no one would remember and Accord would again be faced with the same dilemma. Why did it always take sheer power?

Restraining power was always the hardest part. It would have taken far less effort to have decimated the entire population of New Augusta than it had to engineer the limited impact on the Ministry of Defense.

The private line buzzed, interrupting his self-probing.

He jabbed the accept stud.

"Lord Whaler." He hated using the "Lord," and it was all he could do to refrain from the simple "Whaler" he would have preferred.

The caller was Marcella Ku-Smythe. Nathaniel had never given her his private number, not that he recalled, at least.

"Lord Whaler?"

"Yes."

"I was wondering, upon reflection, how you saw the trade talks progressing."

He shrugged, wondering what she wanted. "I have done what I could do to persuade the Empire. I hope those who count are persuaded, but after the strangeness with Mr. Weintre . . ."

"What strangeness?"

"Mr. Weintre, the Information Specialist, disappeared some days ago. When he was recently found, his memories were gone."

"All of them?" Despite the question, her inquiry was matter-of-fact, as if she knew the answer and wanted to get to something else.

"He thinks he is eighteen standard years."

Marcella's always perfect hair was not, but slightly disarrayed, and a faint smudge showed beneath her left eye.

"I see." She stopped, and the tip of her tongue touched her upper lip. "Lord Whaler . . ."

"Yes?"

"I feel that there may have been some misunderstanding. In no way would the Ministry of Commerce wish anything but a speedy resolution to the trade talks, and one which would be of mutual benefit."

Nathaniel almost whistled. He was getting the closest thing to an apology possible from the always-efficient Marcella.

"Dear Lady," he lied, "no misunderstanding. Your position and your efforts toward meaningful trade agreement have always been recognized, and for that I thank you and wish you well."

While her face remained composed, the Ecolitan could sense her relief through the screen.

"At the same time," he continued, "so far have I not seen any movement from the Empire." He shrugged again. "And without such movement . . ."

"While I cannot promise anything personally, Lord Whaler, I would suspect that your terms are being studied carefully and that within a short time the Empire will respond positively and much along the lines you originally suggested. You have been most persuasive, I understand. Most persuasive."

"Dear Lady, I do appreciate your call and your courtesy in keeping me informed."

"Thank you, Lord Whaler."

The screen blanked.

The Ecolitan frowned. Beneath the facade, the Lady had been upset. Upset indeed.

Then it clicked. Obviously, her mother the Grand Admiral had briefed her on the warning and on the ensuing epidemic. Perhaps the information would last more than a generation. Perhaps . . . but all he could do was wait. Wait and hope.

He decided against any more great debates, mentally filed the information, and locked up his office to retire to his private quarters.

Dinner would be whatever he could get out of the tiny kitchen, followed by a full night's sleep. Sleep he was shorter on than food.

Still . . . after he finished the small salad and meat patty smothered in a too-sweet sauce, he sat and watched the tower lights from the small and private study, punctuated as they were by the occasional shuttle flare, until he was tired enough to head for his bed.

He woke refreshed, despite the recurrence of the nightmares about the death ships and the Imperial fleet.

This time, the Imperial Fleet Commander had been Marcella Ku-Smythe, except she'd been older and black haired. Doubtless, his subconscious was picturing her mother, Admiral Ku-Smythe.

What was her father like?

He dismissed the question as he got out of bed and staggered into the kitchen for a cup of liftea.

A melon supplied by hidden means followed the liftea.

Next came the hygienarium and a complete fresher.

After dressing, he settled behind the small console in the private study of his quarters, turning to watch the early morning clouds scatter and the golden sun lift a silver dew off the towers. As he looked out through the wide window, he marveled at the fact that the day was basically his.

No matter how he'd gotten steamed up about things, the Empire was on its weekend break, and negotiations would not be held. Period.

At the Institute, somehow, he'd never gotten into the habit of a regular division between work and play.

Still . . . his time on New Augusta would be limited. Should he go sight-seeing?

Alone? With whom?

Would Sylvia consider showing him some sights?

He recovered her card from his pouch and studied it, checking the time on the console.

Too early to call anyway.

He passed the next hour by studying the figures on the trade balances, mentally calculating the amount of increased Imperial tariffs Accord could absorb and which of its own tariffs Accord could realistically drop below the levels in the proposal to the Empire.

The parameters were simple enough, but he'd have to wait for the actual negotiations to see what the Empire might accept, assuming that Marcella was right and that he would see some progress in the next few days.

He put the papers back into his datacase and stretched.

Finally, after letting his fingers stray toward the console and onto the keystuds and pulling them back twice, he punched out the New Augusta directory on the screen, requesting the listing for Sylvia Ferro-Maine.

A single number was listed, Private Tower Orange.

He tapped out the number, wondering if she would stay on the screen once she saw his face.

The faxscreen chimed four times, but there was no answer and no recording.

Could she actually be at work?

He tried the Senator's office.

"Senator Helmsworth's office."

The face that appeared on the screen was another woman, black, with curly brown hair, strong nose, and flashing teeth.

"Lord Whaler, from the Accord Legation. I was looking for Sylvia Ferro-Maine."

"Just a moment, Lord Whaler."

Sylvia appeared shortly, wearing her casual yellow-striped tunic, the top two buttons undone, and with her dark hair loose.

"Working are you?"

"We work most days, Lord Whaler."

"Is there any chance that I could persuade you otherwise? To show me a few sights later in the day?"

"I'll be tied up until early afternoon."

"That would be fine. Early afternoon, I mean. Should I meet you somewhere?"

"Why don't I meet you at your Legation around 1400. You have a duty officer who can call you?"

"There is one. Always," he added ruefully.

"Then at 1400, dear Envoy."

Nathaniel found himself staring at a blank screen.

He leaned back.

In the meantime, what could he do? Why was he so restless?

He let his eyes traverse the console.

Stir the pot with a few more anonymous tips?

He smiled. Snooped or not, his hidden watchers couldn't stop his communications.

"Sam," he began on the keyboard, "have you heard the latest about the Envoy from the black planet? His staff is losing their minds. At least one did, wiped all the way back to age eighteen, poor fellow. He's the one who visited the Envoy's office just before the fireworks exploded. Rumor has it that he was on three separate payrolls, and only one was Accord's."

Nathaniel knew it was weak, but it would keep Sam's mind on the Accord issue and might get a phrase or two in the gossip section. He sent it off and found himself pacing around the study, which felt too small, looking at the time on the console, wanting 1400 to arrive.

He debated running through a workout but rejected the idea.

Compromising, he sat down back in front of the console and accessed historical information on New Augusta, deciding to see if he could learn anything new while he waited.

Surprisingly, the Empire apparently had no problem with open library files. The index alone was massive. That whetted his interest and encouraged him to dig in.

"*Buzz!*"

He barely resisted the urge to jump before tapping the plate on the screen.

"Lord Whaler?"

Heather was on the screen.

He looked for the time. 1407.

"Yes?"

"A lady in the reception area says you are expecting her."

"Ms. Ferro-Maine? Ah, yes. I'll be there shortly."

He shut down the screen. So far he'd gotten through the founding of New Augusta and the events leading up to the creation of the Empire from the wreckage of the Second Federation.

Realizing he was still in a set of undress greens, he retreated to his bedroom for a quick change to a tan tunic and matching trousers.

Sylvia rose when he entered the reception area. Since the morning, she had changed into a short-sleeved, dark blue tunic trimmed with white, with corresponding slacks. The color imparted a fragile, almost elflike cast to her face.

"I understand you were hard at work."

"Just background research. Not work."

"Please don't tell Courtney that," she mock-pleaded.

"Our secret." He looked over at Heather and shrugged. "When I will be back, I do not know."

"Don't worry, Lord Whaler." The redhead smiled. "You need to enjoy yourself."

As they stepped out into the corridor, he turned toward Sylvia. "Where would you suggest we begin?"

She came to a stop and faced him.

"What do you have in mind this time?"

He ignored the hint of bitterness in her tone.

"To look, to sightsee, perhaps to have some dinner at a place you suggest. Just to enjoy the afternoon. Or did I not make myself clear?" he asked.

"I wasn't sure. Wanted to know where we stood. Have you seen the fire fountains at the Gallery?"

"I knew of neither. Where?"

"Let's go. We'll take the drop and the tunnel train. The Gallery is where the most noted art from all through the Empire is displayed. They change exhibits almost daily, and some of it is fascinating. There's also a section of pre-Imperial art dating back to the dawn."

She reached for his hand and half skipped, half ran down the corridor toward the drop shaft.

With the pace she set, it seemed only minutes before he was being dragged into the Gallery.

The circular main hall was larger than the receiving hall where he had met the Emperor and more than twice as high. In the center a bronze wall, fully three meters high, circled an area fifty meters across.

Behind and above the wall the fire fountains played, colors interweaving, shimmering, rising, falling—the rough image of a dying angel, superseded by the angry red bursts that suggested the usurpation of grace by a demon and the fall of the demon in turn.

Green, green, the first real green he had seen inside the corridors and tunnels of New Augusta, showered up in the eternal triumph of spring, measured in instants, followed by the darker green of summer and the red and gold of fall, the gold fading into the dead white of winter.

Standing there, entranced, the corners of his eyes filled with his reaction to the green images and the flow of seasons.

"You miss Accord?"

"Yes. You have so many endless tunnels and walled-away vistas from the towers where one can see, but not touch."

She reached over and touched his hand.

"Let's go see the old Hall of Sculpture."

Again, she skipped off, catching him off balance as he watched her dancer's gracefulness leaving him flat-footed.

He had to remind himself that she had once been and still might be an agent of the Imperial Intelligence Service.

No, he corrected, doubtless still was. How else could she have gotten the materials which gained them access to the Defense Tower?

"This one dates from before the age of atomic power. It's called the Thinker."

"They had trade negotiations then, I see."

"Less of the diplomat, dear Envoy, and more of the artist."

"I cannot draw even straight lines."

Sylvia drifted toward the next sculpture, a representation of a man breaking out of a sphere. Nathaniel studied the markings on the sphere momentarily before understanding, belatedly, that the sphere was Terra and that the markings were the outlines of the continents.

The sculptor had captured a steely look of determination, one that the Ecolitan had seen more than once on the faces of his Institute troops, along with the hint of hope, a suggestion of something faraway and unattainable.

"*Flight*, circa 100 A.E.F.F. Sculptor unknown. Recovered from ruins at DENV."

The Ecolitan nodded. Sylvia, on her way to the next figure, didn't fully appreciate what the artist had meant. He did. Maybe that was the problem between the Empire and Accord. The Empire stood for containment, whether in New Augusta's corridors or within the sector boundaries drawn from star to star.

He left *Flight* and rejoined Sylvia at the next statue, a dancer poised on one toe, impossibly balanced on that single point.

"You miss the dance?" he guessed.

"You don't ever get it out of your blood."

"Why did you not continue?"

"I wasn't good enough. Not for the Imperial Court, with its pick of the best from hundreds and hundreds of systems. Oh . . . I fought it, but in the long run, you accept the decision of the Arbiter."

"Arbiter?"

"The Arbiters of the Arts, who judge who gets into the artistic professions."

"That is important?"

"Dear Envoy, for an artist, it's everything. If you aren't accepted by one of the Arbiters for the arts or for a profession, you've got two choices—emigrate or join one of the services."

"I see. And you?"

"Foreign Service . . . barely." The undercurrent of bitterness was there.

"Why did you not emigrate to where you could dance?"

"It doesn't work that way. Emigration is randomly assigned. Otherwise the children of the well-connected would all end up on places like Calleria and Einstein, and the unknowns and those out of favor would be out on the worlds of the Alparta. The one thing that's been kept absolutely fair is the emigration lottery."

Nathaniel doubted that, but kept his mouth shut. How the Empire kept order on New Augusta was becoming much clearer. He changed the subject.

"Do you still dance?"

"As a hobby, a spare-time pursuit, but enough of that, dear Envoy."

He patted her shoulder, not sure exactly what else he could do.

She walked out from underneath his second pat, touched his hand, and was on her way to the next exhibit.

The rest of the Hall of Sculpture was a blur. His thoughts kept going back to the statues of the man emerging from Terra and to the dancer.

As they emerged from the Gallery, Sylvia halted in mid-skip, and pointed to the miniature garden they had passed on the way into the main hall.

"Are the flowers on Accord much like that?"

"Those few we have are from Terra, but there aren't that many except for the fruit trees."

He hoped she would let the statement go, knowing at the same time she wouldn't. How was he going to explain, without lapsing into pedantry, that while Accord was a product of parallel evolution, the principal plant families were more like the year around, nonflowering gymnosperms than the deciduous trees of Terra. After two millennia, the imported Terran stock was beginning to predominate over much of the Accord native flora. The hardier breeds and the crosses developed by the Institute could hold their own against the Terran plants, and, in some cases, were reversing the trend.

The drier high steppes were totally indigenous and would remain that way since Terran cacti and plains grasses had not been among the original imports.

"No flowers? Except on fruit trees? We're limited because of ecological problems. You're free to walk your planet, but there's nothing bright to see?"

"Not exactly. The finger tree, with green and yellow striped fronds, can be spectacular in the dry seasons."

"But what about flowers? Just plain old flowers beautiful to look at?"

Nathaniel shrugged. While he enjoyed the finger trees and the spring greenbursts of the corran forests as much as anyone, he hadn't placed the need for a large variety of flowers at the center of his aesthetics.

"Maybe that's why," she mused.

"Why what?" He was annoyed, not knowing why.

"Why you don't understand the starkness you present, why the black and the dark forest green you wear so often fit you so well. Flowers and dance go together with sunshine and open air. You have the open air but not the flowers. We have the flowers." She looked down at the blooms. "Now's not the time for any more philosophy. You need to see more before you go, and I can't imagine you'll be the one to stay and sightsee once your talks are complete. And it won't be all that long now."

She started off, with more a brisk walk than a skip.

"Next, you ought to see the Maze of Traitors."

He repressed the urge to ask her how she knew the talks wouldn't last too long and clamped down on his tongue. Sylvia seemed to flit from point to point and subject to subject with annoying rapidity, not ever quite finishing anything.

Maze of Traitors? he wondered.

Sylvia was still moving quickly, and he had to quick-step to catch her.

"Can tell your military background, dear Envoy, you know?"

"Military?"

"You don't ever amble or skip or run. You march or quick-step, and if you really got behind, I'd bet on a military jog or a flat-out sprint."

"Maze of Traitors?" he asked, not wanting to touch on the question of his background.

"Dates from the First Foundation. Legend has it the Directorate built it under Alregord. He called the fallen oligarchs rats, but any rat who could run the maze could emigrate. We can get there from the Concourse at the Ministry of Defense."

The history of New Augusta hadn't mentioned the Maze of Traitors, and the rise of the Directorate under Alregord had merited two brief paragraphs.

Sylvia flung herself into the drop shaft and assumed he would follow, which he did but without the same reckless abandon.

The Maze of Traitors had been sanitized and covered with perma-glass, on which tourists could walk and trace the paths beneath the transparent flooring. The Maze was deserted, only a man and two children wandered ahead of them.

Each of the hazards beneath was marked with a plaque and announcing stand.

"Station six," declared a disembodied voice as Nathaniel approached. "This is the delayed drop trap, which was counterweighted so that it did not drop until the body weight was a full meter onto the surface. According to the records, less than twenty percent of the criminal victims ever escaped this section.

"Station nine. As you can see, this appears to be a gentle incline which leads to a cul-de-sac, but the surface is specially treated to be directionally friction sensitive, making a return climb back up the ramp impossible for all but the fastest."

Nathaniel did not ask what happened to those who could not make the climb. The two paragraphs about Alregord had been specific enough.

"Station thirty-six. This is the false exit, identical to the real exit except for the seal of the Directorate beneath the lettering. Each victim was shown a picture of the real exit before being placed in the entry area, but no special emphasis was placed on the need for absolute identity. As a precaution, the incinerator units in the walls, like the other weapons in the Maze, were disconnected when it was restored by the Emperor H'taillen."

Fast as he'd been in touring the maze, Sylvia had gone ahead and was waiting.

"Why did you think I should see this?"

"Just did. Call it for my own reasons. No more questions, dear Envoy, please. Now, how about the observation platform at Tower Center?"

He'd heard of that—the circular permaglass platform on the tallest tower in the center of New Augusta where it was rumored that you could see three hundred kilometers. Unless the towers were taller than he suspected, three hundred kilometers seemed a bit far. He supposed he could have figured out the math, but assuming that the earth was flat, technically a two-kilometer tower would have allowed a look at flat ground more than six hundred kilometers away, although the angle would be so flat as to be useless. Probably the maximum distance would be closer to one hundred kilos. In any case, the view might be worth it.

As at the Maze of Traitors, he and Sylvia found few tourists or others on the observation platform, even though there were no restrictions on entry, no cost for entering the high speed lift shaft, and plenty of space atop the tower.

As the morning had promised, the sky was clear. In the growing dusk of the late afternoon, the shadows of the towers spilled over the Imperial Palace to the east. The western mountains were black, the sun behind them, with sparkles of light flashing from behind them.

"You can see the glitter from the ice," he observed.

"I like to see the shadows across the plains grass," Sylvia answered.

He eased his way around the absolutely clear walkway to the eastern side and looked at the Imperial Palace again. Seen from the tower, it was a low mound of lusterless gray metal anchored by five squat golden towers, none of which reached half as far into the sky as the lowest tower of the city.

Somehow, Nathaniel would have expected the highest tower of all to have belonged to the Emperor.

"On stormy days, you can see the plains grasses dancing with the wind, and the patterns change as the winds play through the towers."

Sylvia must have used a scope. Either that or she watched from a lower vantage point. His vision was supposed to be excellent, but he could only make out the general bending of the grasses from his office.

"After the Ecologic Rebellion, all of this had to be restored square by square. Just a hundred years ago, my mother said, there were bare patches you could see from the towers."

Sylvia twirled and looked up at him. "I'm hungry. What are you in the mood for?"

"Something simple ... something you like ... something ... somewhere an Envoy would not discover."

She grinned, and there was a hint of wildness in the gray eyes.

"But not too dangerous," he added quickly. "Food and danger don't mix. Not without poor digestion."

As they dropped down the shaft, he wondered if he had let himself in for more than he should.

After a long tunnel train ride, well past the Port of Entry, and a long walk, punctuated with a drop shaft, followed by another long walk through the first angled and jointed corridor he'd seen on Terra, he was certain of it.

He kept his fingers playing over the detectors in his belt, but no energy foci were registering.

At irregular intervals, hallways joined and branched from the main corridor, and a few local residents hurried on their ways, not bothering to look at either the Ecolitan or his escort.

The flooring was harder, and the sound of footsteps echoed more than in the tower corridors.

"This is one of the older residential areas. People who don't like the towers, mainly. It dates back to right after the Rebellion."

Sylvia led him off the main corridor and around a gentle curve in the hallway to a dead end, but it took him a moment to realize it.

At first glance, he thought it was a garden plopped into the middle of the rabbit warren they had scurried through. His second look took in the umbrellaed tables under the low trees and soft lighting. People were seated at most of the tables, but Sylvia led him along a gravelled path through a hedge and to a table for two, set by itself.

"Astounded . . . amazed . . . speechless . . . almost," he muttered, "but not quite."

"I hope so." She laughed.

"Whatever you say, dear Lady. I am in your hands."

And he was, because as flighty Sylvia had flitted through the afternoon he had lost sight of the fact that she was a perfectly competent intelligence agent.

She pointed to the table. "A seat?"

He sat, and she settled herself across from him, taking the napkin, real cloth, Nathaniel noted, and putting it in her lap.

"I would like to set the record straight, dear Envoy." She looked squarely at him, and the scatterbrainedness was gone, her eyes cold like slate.

"One, I understand the impossible situation you face. Two, you have behaved like a perfect gentleman while being a total bastard. Three, you asked me to trust you, and I did, and a lot of people died. It was necessary, but I don't like it. Four, I helped you do it, but I don't want to talk about it. Five, I can't help liking you. Six, dinner is my treat."

The Ecolitan managed to keep his face nearly expressionless, even with the sinking feelings that settled in the pit of his stomach.

Sylvia smiled. The coldness was gone, as if turned off by a switch.

"This garden was planted blade by blade, stem by stem, by the owner. It's unique in Noram, maybe anywhere on Terra. And the food is as good as the atmosphere."

"May be the only one in the galaxy," commented Nathaniel. "Never seen one like this with such flowers, paths, trees, especially totally indoors."

A young woman, black-haired and black-eyed, edged through the hedge and looked at Sylvia, who nodded.

The waitress departed, to return with two slender crystal glasses filled with a golden liquid.

"Sniff it first," urged Sylvia.

He did. He couldn't place the bouquet, but the warmth of it

recalled a summer's evening and seemed to relax the tension in his back and legs.

Sylvia took a sip of hers. After a moment, he followed. The taste was stronger than the delicacy of the bouquet suggested, but the warmth of the trickle that eased down his throat was totally without a sting or hint of bitterness.

"Arranged everything, have you?"

"Absolutely everything. Memories are the most important thing you'll take back to Accord. I want you to remember this dinner."

"And the Empire, too?" he queried, teasing.

"Empires are people, as I think you once said, and we all share the same stars."

"With such artistic interests and concerns, how did you get from the study of dance to the Foreign Service and to the Senator's office?" And to the Intelligence Service along the way? he wondered as well.

"That's a long story, and not one to tell tonight. Let's just say I don't like doing the same thing for very long, except dancing, which I can't for reasons we've already discussed. So I change as I can. Maybe I'll emigrate, but emigration is a one-way ticket. You don't do that without a good reason."

The waitress reappeared with two thin china plates, each containing a salad. Nathaniel touched the edge of the plate.

"Real china," confirmed the dancer/intelligence agent/woman across the table from him.

The lighting dimmed in the garden, and the small lamp on the table came to life with a flame of its own.

Nathaniel took a last sip of the liqueur. Sylvia had already finished hers and started on the greenery. He followed her example. The small salad was as good in its way as the drink had been.

"Lord Whaler?"

He started.

"What do you really think of the Empire? In your heart of hearts?"

"That you ask of a diplomat? Or an Ecolitan?"

She just looked at him.

"It's difficult to put the feelings of a lifetime into words, and not in my own language, but I will try."

"Take your time. I'll listen."

"The Empire is different, so different. It's large, always pressing at

Accord. Some fear the Empire because it is big. Some wish it would go away. Some want to destroy it . . ."

"You?"

"The Empire is dead at heart, I fear, although no one, or few except the Emperor himself, knows it."

He took another bite of the salad before going on.

"Dreams, aspirations, are the shadows of the future. Art, also. At the Hall of Sculpture, there were only a few people. You saw the dancer. I wondered at the man breaking free of the earth. But where were the other dreamers? The Emperor's Palace does not soar to the skies but buries itself in the earth."

"But what about the growth, the new systems, the explorations, the success in battles?"

"They are not from the heart of the Empire. The young of the outer systems bleed and strive. Like Accord, they will some day want to dream their own dreams. I hope the Empire is wise enough to understand when that time comes. But I doubt that."

She shivered, though the air was warm.

"You paint a dark picture, and your words are compelling. I suppose that's why—" She broke off as the waitress came through the hedge to remove the small plates.

He wondered where she'd been heading, but before he could ask, she threw another question at him.

"Why did you take the job?"

"I was asked by the House of Delegates."

"Were you required to accept?" Her tone was dry, a slight curl at the corner of her mouth. In the dim light, he wasn't sure if she was masking lightness, a mild skepticism, or out-and-out disbelief.

The slight breeze carried the faintest hint of orange toward him as he waited. Finally, he spoke. "No. But duty, responsibility . . ."

"Does everyone on Accord take duty so seriously?"

He laughed. With her put-on seriousness, it was impossible not to.

"Does everyone here take duty as seriously as you do?" he countered, hoping for a laugh in return.

He got it.

"Touché, dear Envoy. I suppose I deserved that."

Another set of china plates appeared from the hands of the waitress, as if by some sort of magic.

The main course was equally simple, a single slice of meat under a golden sauce, and a side dish of long slice beans, sprinkled with nuts and a clear sauce.

"What is it?"

"My secret."

He waited until she started before venturing a bite. Like the salad and the liqueur, the meat was excellent, with an almost cristnut flavor that lingered after each bite.

"Gentle men are the most dangerous, don't you think?"

"What?"

"They give the impression of weakness, of confusion, and they often let themselves be pushed on minor matters because they're only willing to fight for the most important things."

"Perhaps. But is such a person gentle?"

"Would you consider yourself a gentle person, Lord Whaler?"

"In those terms, no. I would not."

"I would, I think," she mused, looking, but not really looking, at him with an unfocused expression.

He waited, not willing to commit himself.

"Why?" She paused. "Because power is only a means to an end, rather than the end." Her eyes focused on him, but the seriousness was gone. "How do you like the food so far?"

The Ecolitan couldn't answer, his mouth full, and finished the rather large bite he had taken.

"Delicious."

"The dessert is heavier. But I do admit to a sweet tooth, and I've selected an old favorite."

The dinner plates disappeared at the magic hands of the waitress and were replaced with crystal bowls filled with a brown pudding like substance topped with white fluff.

The taste was distantly familiar . . . chocolate. He'd had it once before, years ago when he and Raoul had done student drops on Fioren. A real luxury, chocolate, at fifty Imperial credits a gram. His estimation of the cost of the dinner rose further.

Whatever it cost, he was enjoying it.

The chocolate dessert was followed with two small snifters of Taxan brandy.

"Never have I been so royally treated."

"I hope not. I hope not."

Over the low hedge, he caught sight of sparkles in the air. Sylvia glanced in the same direction, then back at him.

"Marchelle can overdo it. Replica fireflies. Real ones can't be brought into the tunnels."

He sat there in quiet, the subdued hum of conversation from other tables barely audible, wondering why Sylvia had gone to such lengths. Wondering if she had set him up for a rude surprise.

"Time to depart," she announced. "Time to get you back to your Legation and me back to my cubbyhole before I turn into a scull again. Ci'ella complex, you know."

Not understanding a word, he nodded, his fingers dropping to his belt and still finding no energy fields, no snoops, no other devices in the vicinity.

Nathaniel left the grassy lawn, the hedges, and the tables with a feeling of regret, not sure why.

"Always hate to leave," Sylvia murmured, "but there's a purpose for every time."

Pleasure or not, dinner or not, Nathaniel forced himself into combat alert, mentally ticking through the checklist. If ever there were a time to be alert, now was that time, when he didn't feel the slightest bit like it.

He stayed next to Sylvia, through the curves and lift shafts back to the tunnel train, alert for any deviation from the route by which they had come.

The train was almost empty, and that worried Nathaniel.

Sylvia wore an amused smile but said nothing.

"Few use the train," he commented halfway back toward the Diplomatic Tower, feeling the silence weigh on him.

"Right now. Too late for most and too early for the real carousers. Aren't many of them any longer."

With his newfound understanding of the Imperial population control techniques, he understood why.

He lapsed back into silence. Never had he mastered the art of small talk while keeping thoroughly alert. That was for espionage types, not Ecolitans.

A few souls were in the concourse of the Diplomatic Tower when the two of them swung off the train, but, again, he could find no trace of either tails or energy concentrations.

Finally, they reached the portal to the Legation, which was opened by the duty officer as they approached.

"Here's where we part company, dear Envoy." She took his hands in hers.

He stiffened, unsure of what to do.

"You're expecting the worst, have been all afternoon. You're too ethical. Even when you play dirty, you play fair."

Turning to face him full on, Sylvia stood on her tiptoes, brushed her lips across his forehead and stepped back, still holding his hands.

"Good night."

She was gone, gliding toward the drop shaft before he could open his mouth. When he did, he left it open because there was nothing to say.

What could he say? Obviously, he was more transparent than he thought.

He closed his mouth and turned toward the still-open portal.

Heather stood inside behind the console.

"Still here, Heather?"

"All day, Lord Whaler. I trust you had an enjoyable outing."

"Enjoyable but puzzling. Most puzzling." He shook his head as he started toward his private quarters, still alert, still checking.

Neither his office nor his quarters had been touched, further snooped, or otherwise tampered with so far as he could tell.

He was still shaking his head when he finally climbed into bed. Another social encounter with the women of the Empire was unlikely, for a while at least. Another might well undo him totally.

The faintest hint of orange blossoms drifted into the room as he closed his eyes, but when he looked, the space was empty. He turned over and willed himself to sleep.

XXXV

EVEN AFTER A full day more of studying the history and development of New Augusta from the viewpoint of the Imperial historians, followed by another night's sleep, Nathaniel felt he had only a slightly more than superficial grasp of the motivations of the people with whom he was dealing. He understood better some of the phobias of the Imperial citizenry, such as the dislike of the color black, which, interestingly enough, had been the color adopted by the Directorate after Alregord.

Perhaps Accord had been wrong to let the Institute choose the combination of military expert/scholar. Were his well-intentioned machinations leading the way to disaster?

Despite his elementary precautions, Sylvia could have set him up for assassination or an incident which could have totally embarrassed him or reduced his credibility. Instead, she had treated him to a charming afternoon and evening, while making clear she knew exactly what he was up to. But she hadn't explained her reasons. Maybe they were supposed to be obvious, but to him they certainly weren't.

He shrugged as he donned his blacks. The week ahead was going to be interesting enough without adding worry on top of worry.

Should he get into his office early? Too early, and Mydra would be suspicious. Too late, and she'd glare.

He laughed at himself for the thoughts. Like the generally unseen Imperial men, he was reacting to the pleasure and displeasure of the Imperial women.

The hell with it! Forest Lord take the foremost. He liked being at work early, and he was going to enjoy it.

He took a cup of liftea in his tiny kitchen and eased through the apartment quarters into his office. The shadows of the westernmost towers reached the foothills below the mountains, but the rational side of his mind questioned what his eyes told him. Were the towers that tall?

The sky was cloudless, as it was so often, and he enjoyed the blue heights. The skies over the Institute displayed clouds more often, in keeping with the generally wetter weather he was used to.

He leaned back in the swivel, debated whether he should try to finish the Imperial version of the history of New Augusta or enjoy the view.

The view won.

"Lord Whaler?"

Mydra stood in the open portal from the staff office.

"Beautiful morning, Mydra, is it not?"

"If you say so." She looked at his console. "I'll be feeding some communications which need authorizations into your console. If you could take care of them this morning, I'd certainly appreciate it."

"Fine. Will do them as soon as they're ready."

So much for the history of New Augusta and the view. Duty called. He drained the lukewarm remainder of the tea.

With a touch on the power stud, the second faxscreen lit and projected the first communications.

Most were either letters back to students, supplying information or referring them to the Institute for more detailed studies. Another batch was composed of routine denials of emigration requests from Terra to Accord.

He found himself amused that the facsimile of his signature remained as the principal validation of communications after centuries of electronic transmission methods.

"After all this thinking machinery, someone still has to read and authorize this junk."

Midway through the program stack, the intercom buzzed.

"Lord Jansen for you."

Moderately surprised that a call through the main office was actually being routed to him, he jabbed the stud.

"Lord Whaler."

"Alexi Jansen, Lord Whaler."

"Good it is to hear from you."

"We've had a chance to go over your proposal, Ms. Du-Plessis and I, and I was wondering if you and your staff could talk over some of the points raised."

"Most happy to do so."

Jansen cleared his throat and waited.

Nathaniel waited also, then realized that Jansen was in a difficult position. The Minister couldn't really demand that they meet over at the Ministry of External Affairs, nor did he want to talk in the leaky confines of the Accord Legation.

Nathaniel cleared his throat in return, gestured around his office. "Alas, not terribly suited are my spaces, but pleased would I be if no other space is available."

The Ecolitan could see the relief on the Deputy Minister's face.

"Our offices are not that much more spacious, but if you would like to come here, I would be more than pleased to send Ms. Du-Plessis and put a tunnel limousine at your service."

"That would be most gracious. I regret our situation, but you know the damage we have suffered."

"I understand, Lord Whaler. I certainly understand."

"A time we have not agreed upon."

"There is a saying about striking while the iron is hot," responded Jansen.

"Cancelled my appointments because of the damage, since I knew not when it would be repaired. I am free today."

"Right after midday? We could meet and settle some of the points."

"That would be fine."

After another ten minutes of phrases within phrases, it was agreed that at 1230 Janis Du-Plessis would arrive to whisk one Nathaniel Whaler off to the tower housing the Ministry of External Affairs.

The Ecolitan leaned back in the swivel momentarily. Then he leaned forward and began to rummage through the remaining datacase, the one that hadn't been blasted to shreds by Sergel and his friends. Enough files and holo slides remained for his purposes.

He went back to the authentication of student comms, obviously foisted off on him by Mydra. Envoys weren't supposed to look out windows and enjoy the views.

A standard hour later, he'd finished and turned the screen back to his history studies of New Augusta. Before he reached the last few centuries of the glorious and stupendous history of the capital of the Empire of Light, the intercom buzzed.

Nathaniel shook his head. The closer to the present the text got, the preachier it became.

"Ms. Du-Plessis has arrived."

Nathaniel did not acknowledge the announcement but picked up the datacase and marched to the portal door.

"Where is she?" he asked Mydra.

"At . . . the main desk."

"See you somewhat later."

He interrupted a conversation between Heather Tew-Hawkes and Janis Du-Plessis at the front desk with his sudden appearance.

"Ready to go?"

"Uh . . . is anyone else coming?"

"Not immediately," lied Nathaniel.

"Later?"

"Later," lied the Ecolitan, "and shall we go?"

"Yes, Lord Whaler."

As he left for the drop shaft with Janis, he could see the puzzled look on Heather's face from the corner of his eye.

Janis Du-Plessis did not make a single comment during the drop to the concourse level or on the way to the External Affairs electrocar, except a curt, "This way."

The driver was not the black youngster he'd had before, Nathaniel observed with regret, but an older woman with short cut black hair flecked with silver.

He couldn't tell whether the color was natural or applied.

Janis sat on the far side of the rear seat of the limousine and point-edly stared out the window at the murals as the electrocougar dipped into the tunnel.

"Amazing it is how things are governed by impressions and appear-ances," mused Nathaniel. "Sometimes, the slave is the master, and sometimes the master is the slave, and sometimes both master and slave think they are the master."

He wasn't getting a reaction and didn't expect one. He just waited.

"How did you get selected as Envoy, Lord Whaler?"

"That is a rather long story. An authority on trade was required, but one not indebted to the bureaucracy or to either political party. I was available. The Empire indicated the matter was urgent, and I was sent."

The Assistant shifted her weight and turned to face him, her face pale in the dim light of the electrocar.

"Always, it seems as if Accord is cloaked in mystery."

"It is not that mysterious. I am concerned. One of my staff has been mind-wiped. I have been attacked and bombed."

Nathaniel cleared his throat, pulled at his chin, and said nothing further.

The car hummed onward through the tunnel.

"You indicated your staff would meet us. How can we finalize the agreements?" Her voice rose slightly as she finished.

"Staff is a luxury."

"A luxury?"

"Does the lion tell the owl his business? Does the star-diver instruct the glide-ringer?"

Janis displayed the puzzled look he had seen all too often over the past few days. He wondered how she had gotten as far as she had. Was her mother a General of the Marines?

He let the silence draw out, wrapping the stillness around him like a blanket.

The official electrocar began the climb out of the tunnel and into the concourse area of the Ministry of External Affairs.

"What will I tell Lord Jansen?"

"That everything is under control. That you have the situation in hand. That is true . . . is it not? Of course it is."

Four ceremonial guards in rust and tan, three women and one man, waited at the private concourse entrance.

Alexi Jansen stood by the door of the conference room on the one hundred forty-first level. Through the portal, Nathaniel could see a projecting faxscreen and two technicians.

"Greetings, Lord Whaler."

Jansen looked at Janis, who returned the glance without expression, then back at Nathaniel.

"Will . . . uh . . . others . . . be joining us?"

"I fear that some misimpressions may have been conveyed. While others might wish to be here, I am indeed the expert on trade, and we can proceed, I assure you."

Jansen raised both eyebrows.

"Do you think that wise . . . that is . . . without supporting technical staff?"

"Lord Jansen, I am empowered to act solely, if I so choose. Let us go ahead, and we shall see what we can work out."

The Ecolitan marched around Jansen and into the conference room. Janis looked at Jansen with a look that said, Don't blame me.

Nathaniel placed his case on the table in front of the chair that was his, letting the case push a green and black name placard into the middle of the polished wood surface. He opened the case and removed four of the files, snapped the case shut, and put the datacase on the carpet next to his chair.

"Shall we begin?"

Jansen, who had followed the Envoy into the room but still stood, opened his mouth, shut it, opened it. Finally, he closed it and nodded.

Janis Du-Plessis handed a card to Jansen and sat down.

"The first item," she announced in a businesslike tone, "is the proposed schedule on microminibits."

The technician fiddled with the controls of the projecting faxscreen, and a holo of the list appeared above the end of the table.

"That is the schedule as it presently exists. You will note the Imperial tariff is the highest on the combined minibits, though still very low under the circumstances—around eight percent of assessed valuation—and decreases with complexity to a low of four percent on the single minibit."

The holo projection changed to show a second set of figures, displayed in green, next to the first set.

"The green figures represent the change suggested by the Coordinate of Accord. Those maintain the present rate of graduation, but increase the top rate to ten percent and the lowest rate to around six percent."

The Ecolitan looked at his file and checked his figures against those on the screen. They matched. He'd known that immediately, but if he hadn't made the overt comparison, his lack of response would have been misinterpreted as knowing the numbers inside out. He knew all the figures cold, and the real and allowable leeways, without consulting the folders, but Jansen and Du-Plessis wouldn't have believed it. If they did, they would ask rather embarrassing questions.

"Correct those figures are," he announced in a self-satisfied tone.

"External Affairs," continued Janis Du-Plessis, "would like to suggest a further change, increasing the rate of graduation and raising the base scale to eight and a half percent so that the full rate of twelve percent is first assessed on quintuple units, as is now the case."

The latest projection added a set of figures in red beside the green figures that had bordered the original tariff rates in black.

Nathaniel pointedly looked at the holo chart, then bent down and retrieved his datacase, from which he extracted a miniputer. He began entering figures into the instrument, either frowning or nodding as the results came up.

He stopped for a moment and let his eyes flick around the room, from the rust hangings to the nondescript tan fabric-covered walls to the rich dark wood of the conference table, then back across the faces around the table.

Lord Jansen wore a politely bored expression, sitting back with no real interest in the various projection figures.

Janis Du-Plessis twitched as his eyes crossed hers. Nathaniel realized she had been studying him. The other staffer, not the fax technician, was running numbers through a small console, which had to be linked with the main External Affairs data banks.

The projection tech's expression matched Jansen's, but on her the boredom looked contemptuous as well.

The Ecolitan glanced back at the figures. The Empire, or External Affairs, reasoned the more complex the minibit, the greater the advantage that Accord possessed, the reason underlying the graduation of the tariff schedule. A twelve percent tariff rate effectively meant a fifty percent increase in the rate.

"A twelve percent rate means, dear friends, an increase of fifty percent in the tariff rate."

"These figures were developed after long consultations with the affected Imperial industries and with regard to the calculated rate of return to Accord's suppliers."

"A twelve percent rate will reduce many imports to nothing, and the purpose of the talks was to further trade, to make it fair, but not to stop it."

Actually, Accord's industry could make money so long as the top rate stayed below fifteen percent. In any case, the minibits were important but not the entire battle.

"Lord Whaler, here are the supplementary figures. Chart One B, please, Devon."

Chart One B appeared in place of the microminibit tariff schedule. On it were the volumes of Accord exports to Terra, the existing tariff rates, the revenue to the Empire, followed by a second column showing the volume of imports from Accord projected under the External Affairs proposal.

"As you can see, even with our proposal, the volume of imports from Accord will decrease only ten percent, but the increase in the effective price will give our manufacturers enough leeway to compete."

The problem with the External Affairs proposal was that it put too much duty on the more complex minibits, where the emerging and continuing market was likely to be, and too little on the simpler, lower profit minibits. Plus, accepting the idea of a more steeply graduated schedule left the door open for further steepening and set a dangerous precedent.

Nathaniel dug a memorandum from his datacase. Stripped of all the technical nomenclature, it basically stated that the Accord microprocessing industry had developed the capability of producing triple minibits which could do the work of Imperial quintuple minibits produced by the Noram microprocessors. The terms triple and quintuple were misnomers, since a single minibit referred to a million gate choice, and each level multiplied by ten.

He handed the memorandum to Janis.

"As this indicates, there is likely to be a problem of description."

He sat back and waited for her to read the two page technical summary.

After Janis read it, she passed it on to the console staffer, who scanned both pages into the data banks and passed it on to Lord Jansen.

"He's right," announced the data tech after several minutes at the console.

Jansen, beginning to lose his bored look, started to lean forward in his swivel.

"This could set us back to square one, Lord Whaler. Why did you even bring it up?"

"Several reasons. First, not to bring it up risks the Empire declaring that we have bargained in bad faith. Second, the information points out the error in using a graduated tariff based on an artificial distinction. Third, the problem has to be resolved."

"See your point," observed Jansen.

"So what do you suggest?" snapped Janis. "You brought the problem to our attention. You must have some suggestions."

"Already, it appeared likely some questions were arising over the point at which the maximum level of the tariff should be assessed. Is that not true?"

"That's true. That's a question on any graduated schedule. What does that have to do with this?"

The Ecolitan shrugged, as if the answer were obvious, even to a dullard like the Envoy from Accord.

"Simple Envoy that I am, it seems obvious that the problems lie not in the articles being taxed but in the tax structure. If the schedule is not graduated, then using different names for equipment all doing the same job will not matter."

"Are you suggesting a flat rate for all minibits?"

Nathaniel avoided a direct answer. "What would be the average of costs to Accord, given a flat rate of nine percent?"

"That's low," answered Janis, "but let's see it, Devon."

Nathaniel already knew the answer. Under the current trade flows in microminibits, a nine percent rate would reduce the tariffs Accord paid the Empire by about two percent. Assuming a decrease in Accord exports to the Empire of ten percent, a tariff rate of nine and a half percent would give the Empire a comparable increase in tariff revenues.

The numbers flashed up into the midair holo display.

"You'll get even more of a break at nine percent," protested Janis, "and the present situation is already unacceptable."

"Nine and one half," offered Nathaniel.

No one said anything until the next display appeared, showing the figures outlining the results of his suggestion.

"That would be somewhat of an improvement, but I hope that Accord would be somewhat more flexible," said Jansen, "particularly given the higher volume of trade in multiple minibits."

Nathaniel began to play around with his computer, finally threw up his hands.

"What about ten percent?"

At the ten percent rate, the Imperial figures showed close to a twenty percent reduction in imports from Accord, and slightly more revenue to the Imperial treasury.

Nathaniel's estimation of the economists at the Ministry of External Affairs took a nosedive. No commodity was that price-elastic over a half percent. Plus, it was apparent that no one had calculated the impact of technological change.

He frowned.

"Nine and three quarters as a final offer?" he asked.

"Ten!" Jansen declared before Janis could say anything.

"But the loss! A true increase in tariffs . . . this represents nearly forty percent . . . but—" protested Nathaniel.

"Lord Whaler, for several years now, many of our microprocessors have been suffering because tariffs were too low. It's not just the present situation the Emperor must consider. There are many other factors . . ." Janis let her voice trail off.

"Ah, yes, I understand 'other factors.' While I would prefer the nine and three quarters rate, for the sake of agreement, we will accept ten percent. What else can I do?" The Ecolitan shrugged.

"For the sake of making progress, let us close the discussion on this item," suggested Jansen. "Of course, we will have to clear this with the Emperor and the full Ministry staff."

Nathaniel made appropriate notations on his file.

"I will also check."

"The next item," droned Janis Du-Plessis, "is . . ."

Nathaniel fumbled through the files again. It was going to be a long afternoon.

XXXVI

THE NEGOTIATION SESSIONS went on and on, with weekend interruptions, scattered breaks for "clarifications," then, like everything else in New Augusta, ended abruptly on a mid-week day.

The whole agreement had been packaged and readied for transmission to the Imperial Senate and the tender mercies of Senator Helmsworth and his colleagues.

Nathaniel found himself behind his Envoy's desk with a full day looking at him. After more than a standard month, Marlaan was still on vacation, and Witherspoon, reputed to have just finished his "consultations" on Accord, was planning to take home leave before returning to Terra.

"They certainly gave me enough vine to swing cliff clear," he muttered to no one in particular.

He glanced out the wide window at the clear sky, absently wondering why the Imperials had preferred to negotiate in a windowless room, then looked back at the faxscreen and the authentication lists for the outgoing communications. He suspected that Mydra piled up the lists whenever she thought he spent too much time staring out the permaglass.

The intercom buzzed.

Nathaniel looked up from the second faxscreen, punched the accept stud.

"Marcella Ku-Smythe for you, Lord Whaler."

"Thank you."

He jabbed at the flashing plate.

"Ms. Ku-Smythe?"

"Yes, Lord Whaler. Let me be among the first to congratulate you on the progress I hear you have been making with External Affairs."

"Only talks, dear Lady, long and involved, wherein everyone must check with everyone." He shrugged. "And progress? Who can tell?"

"You're too modest."

"A mere fumbler with numbers am I."

Nathaniel glanced up at the bare wall, out through the open portal to the staff office, looked back at his fingers, and finally clasped both hands before looking back into the screen.

Marcella dropped her eyes for a moment.

"How long do you think it will take you to complete the talks?"

"If nothing unforeseen arrives, if no further difficulties are observed, then most of the work is done," he hedged. "But for your sake and mine, I hope nothing unforeseen occurs."

"For my sake?"

"We are what we are, Lady, not what we would like others to see or what they would like to see. Me . . . a mere fumbler of numbers, a professor doing what he can. You . . . a most competent Special Assistant."

"Were the Commerce Department to take a more active role?"

"I defer to your superior knowledge and to that of your associates and family. Doubtless you know best. For my part, humble as it is, so long as the talks result in the mutual agreement of Accord and the Empire on tariffs and the continued independence of Accord, your presence would always be welcome, whether in an official or in an unofficial capacity."

He half bowed to her image on the screen.

"Thank you for your graciousness, Lord Whaler. While I could not accept under the circumstances, I appreciate your understanding."

He looked at the blank faxscreen for several minutes, shook his head. Desirable woman but definitely the strong-willed type.

He shook his head again, violently. Enough wool-gathering. Getting involved with anyone, Sylvia or Marcella, at this stage of the game, while the final terms of the agreement were hanging before the Senate, could be highly counter-productive, to say the least.

He flicked back to the scan screen and the list of authentications Mydra had dredged up. They had helped fill the hours, not necessarily pleasantly, while External Affairs had wrangled with the staff of the External Relations Committee to ready the package for full Senate consideration.

He tapped on the intercom.

"Yes, Lord Whaler."

"Sergel? Isn't he due for release shortly?"

"I checked this morning, and he could be sent back to Accord any time now."

"Would you make the arrangements? For later this week?"

"I'll take care of it and let you know."

The Ecolitan froze the seemingly endless stream of authentications on the second screen, putting them in temporary storage, and flicked on one of the faxnews channels.

". . . in one of the more surprising developments during the hearings on the Purse, Senator Helmsworth proposed close to a fifty percent increase in the budget for the Imperial Intelligence Service. Helmsworth, when questioned, cited reasons of Imperial security and offered to display evidence in secret debate. For the first time in more than a generation, public debate was halted for the secret session. The sole outsider present was Grand Admiral Ku-Smythe. After the presentation, the chamber was opened, and the motion passed unanimously."

The screen switched from a view of the Senate chambers, hung in shimmering red and paneled in dark wood, to a mid-aged woman wearing the cream tunic with the red slash of an Imperial Senator.

"Senator Re-Lorins, before the secret session, you questioned the need for such an increase in funding. Yet you voted for the increase. Why?"

"Both the Senator from Noram and the Grand Admiral showed evidence of a persuasive nature. Rather startling and shocking evidence, I might add, even to me."

"Can you reveal the nature of that evidence?"

"No. I cannot."

The screen cut back to the commentator and her studio console.

"That was the only statement from Senator Re-Lorins, Chair of the Intelligence Committee. No other Senator would comment, including Senator Helmsworth."

The screen filled with a panorama of dying plants in their fields.

"The synde bean virus is still on the move. These bean fields on Heraculon are the latest victims of the gypsy virus which seems to appear at random. Botany pathologists are puzzled at the spread of the resistant species of the virus, which was formerly controlled with a derivative of antoziae."

The next scene was an empty warehouse.

"At this time of year, the warehouses on Heraculon are normally beginning to reach full capacity. As you can see, that's far from the situation now.

"Bryna Fre-Levin on Heraculon."

As the screen switched again, this time to an orbit scene centered on an Imperial battlecruiser, martial trumpets blared in the background.

"Admiral of the Fleets, Jorik Ypre-Tanelorn, transferred his flag to H.M.S. *Gold Prince*, which will lead the new Eleventh Fleet through its shakedown cruises before it takes station.

"Admiral Ypre-Tanelorn," and the screen featured a still shot of a black-haired, thin-faced man with a pencil mustache and black eyes under bushy eyebrows, a picture of perfect formality with the Admiral in his dress red and gold uniform, the starburst of the Empire above his left breast. "The Admiral declared the Eleventh Fleet will serve as the vanguard for continuing peace and stability for the Empire and its allies."

The screen dropped back to the studio.

"Back in New Augusta, the Empress welcomed an unusual delegation, a talking centaur troupe from Alpha Megara—"

Nathaniel flicked off the faxnews and leaned back in the swivel.

He wondered if he should let the media take another shot at Sergel's situation. They'd probably take it, but he shook his head.

Sergel's example was tragic but not permanent. And Sergel might well turn out better the second time around, in any case.

The late afternoon sunlight through the filtered permaglass warmed his no longer quite so crisp diplomatic blacks, yet the selective polarization let him see the golden disc of the sun hanging over the western hills without requiring him to squint.

The other towers rose, dark gold, before the western hills, like so many obelisks, or so many pillars of dark fire shedding flickers of reflected light.

He put his feet up on the console, leaning further back in the chair to watch the play of light over the towers.

The intercom buzzed, and he sat up quickly, realizing that over an hour had passed as he had let his thoughts drift.

"Ms. Corwin-Smathers for you."

"Lord Whaler."

Courtney was wearing a cream tunic with rust piping and banded scarlet flecks at the cuffs.

"My pleasure, Lord Whaler."

"And mine also, to hear from you, although I am puzzled at the reason for your courtesy."

"No real reason, Lord Whaler. Senator Helmsworth would have liked to call himself, but right now things are rather hectic over here."

"I heard about the Intelligence Service . . ."

"That was just another incidental, for which, by the way, we thank you. Your actions were most instrumental in helping the Senator, though not in the way you probably intended. That and the synde bean problem . . ."

"Coincidence has been helpful to many throughout history."

"But that was not the reason I called on behalf of the Senator, you understand. He did want me to convey our appreciation for the way in which the trade negotiations have been handled and to let you know that we look forward to an early ratification vote in the Senate."

"Only doing my humble best, dear Lady, and without the help and advice you and others have provided, indeed I would have been lost. You are most kind, and I look forward to a successful vote."

"Lord Whaler, you are too unassuming."

He shrugged his now-habitual shrug. "We do what we can, and hope for the best for all."

"The Empire is doing its best also, Lord Whaler, and Senator Helmsworth and I, and the Emperor, I'm sure, look forward to the successful and peaceful resolution of the trade talks in the weeks ahead."

"Your concern and reassurance lift my spirits."

"That's all I really wanted to say. The Senator wanted you to know that the agreements will be coming before the Senate shortly and to convey that to your government. We all understand your talents and your sense of restraint, and wish you well."

"Thank you."

Courtney nodded, and once again, Nathaniel was left looking at a blank screen. One thing he'd never get used to, no matter how long he stayed in New Augusta, was the abruptness with which most friendly fax calls were terminated.

The synde bean thing . . . was that something the Institute was involved with? If it were, he'd be the last to know, sitting on Earth. Certainly, that sort of mutation was well within the capabilities of the Institute. If it had been the work of the Ecolitans, and the Emperor thought so, so much the better.

He wondered if the offhand reference he'd made to the synde bean situation had been construed to mean more by Courtney. Not beyond the realm of possibility.

With a quick tap, he called Mydra on the intercom.

"Why don't you finish up the authentications tomorrow, Mydra?"

"All right, Lord Whaler. If you say so."

"Is there anything special I should do?"

"No. Not really."

"Then to your superior judgment I defer."

Nathaniel turned back to watch the late afternoon change into evening and to watch as the evening crept from beneath the hills toward the base of the westernmost towers like an incoming tide of darkness. So unlikely his return to New Augusta would ever be that he wanted to fix the spectacular images firmly in his mind.

XXXVII

NATHANIEL TOOK ANOTHER look around the Envoy's office. His three bags and datacase were stacked up by the exit portal, ready to be picked up.

The signing ceremony at the Emperor's Indoor Garden had gone off without a hitch, although he'd been surprised to find himself greeting Lord Fergus, rather than Lord Mersen or Rotoller. For whatever reason, neither Janis nor Marcella had been at the Indoor Garden. Nor Sylvia, though there was no reason why she should have been.

For that matter, neither had the Empress, which probably reflected her feelings about provincials from Accord.

"Lord Whaler?"

He turned.

Heather Tew-Hawkes, Hillary, and Mydra were standing in the doorway.

"The Marines will be here in about an hour for you and your luggage," said Mydra. "May we come in?"

"Of course, dear ladies."

He gestured to the chairs and couch.

The three women walked into the office but did not sit down. Mydra, in the center, had her hands clasped behind her back.

"Lord Whaler," began the office manager, "I have a confession to make."

Nathaniel nodded.

"When Legate Witherspoon left and when Mr. Marlaan abruptly took leave, I was deeply concerned about the continued effectiveness of the Legation—"

"As you had a right to be," interrupted the Ecolitan gently.

"And I couldn't help but wonder how an inexperienced professor from an out-planet university was going to deal with a complex set of negotiations. When you first came in, I thought my worst fears had been realized." Mydra paused.

"Mine too," chimed in Heather.

Hillary smiled a shy smile of agreement.

"After your arrival, things just got worse. The violence, the bombings, and all the strange goings-on, not to mention the dreadful thing that happened to poor Sergel, all of those were enough to make me want to leave."

Nathaniel nodded again. "But you did not, and stayed to help me through the difficulties."

"You were so calm, even when you were certain the Empire was courting disaster, and so determined to work things out for everyone." Mydra gave a sheepish grin.

Heather was smiling also. "I heard from my friends who work in some of the other Legations how much people who really count were impressed with what you did in such a short time. I don't think any of us here really understood all that was going on."

I hope not, thought the Ecolitan as he listened. I hope not.

"At first," Mydra went on, "I wondered why no one had been sent to check on you. But that became obvious later on."

"When you were the one who stayed and picked up the pieces," added Heather.

"Especially after the bombing and when someone tried to kidnap you," added Hillary.

"Do what we must."

"That's true, Lord Whaler, but we did want you to know that we, all of us on the staff, understand how difficult your job has been and how careful you had to be. We wanted to give you this before you left." Mydra brought her hand from behind her back and opened it. On her palm was a small black box.

"But . . ." he protested.

"Go ahead. Open it," prompted Heather.

"It won't explode." Mydra laughed.

He opened the jewelry case gingerly. On the green velvet was a collar pin, done in black and green, a miniature of the formal crest of the Ecolitan Institute.

He studied the pin, realizing that it was not enamel or lacquer, but that the colors came from the depths of the two metals themselves.

"Beautiful . . . but . . . I don't deserve such . . . such a magnificent . . . not I . . ." he stammered.

"Everyone here chipped in," said Heather.

They had to, and then some, realized the Ecolitan. The pin was solid lustral.

"For doing my duty, I could not accept something like this. Not something so beautiful."

Mydra gave him an even broader grin. "You can't refuse it. Gifts of personal jewelry authorized by the Emperor are acceptable. Failure to accept such a gift would amount to an insult to the Imperial Court."

Nathaniel turned the pin over.

"From the staff, Accord Legation, and from His Imperial Majesty. J.L.M. N'troya, in sincere appreciation."

A tiny imprint of the Imperial Seal appeared beneath the inscription.

Why would the Emperor add his name in "sincere appreciation"?

"Why would the Emperor . . . ?" he asked out loud.

"That's the second part of my confession," admitted Mydra. "That afternoon when you were so depressed, when you were talking about how the Empire didn't understand Accord and its abilities, and how Accord couldn't understand how the Empire didn't understand . . ."

"Yes?"

"Well . . . I recorded it. I couldn't say it the way you did. So I recorded it, and I sent what you said to a friend who has direct access to the Emperor." She spread her hands. "I know I shouldn't have, but you wouldn't have admitted it in public, and if you'd said it straight out, no one would have believed it. And you were so right and so depressed."

"Don't be either. Just accept it," advised Heather.

"We wanted you to have something, and it almost wasn't ready in time," added Mydra.

"Go ahead. Pin it on," insisted Hillary.

He started to, but his fingers felt a meter wide.

"Here," said Heather, "let me help."

"Looks good on your blacks," observed Mydra as Heather stepped back.

"Bet it will go with his greens, too." That was from Hillary.

"He's blushing, Mydra. He's really blushing." Heather giggled.

Nathaniel shrugged, knowing he couldn't do anything about the flush that spread across his face.

"What can I say?"

"Nothing. Nothing at all," answered Heather. "Just enjoy it."

"You deserve some recognition, Lord Whaler. I doubt that Legate Witherspoon, Mr. Marlaan, or anyone on Accord will fully understand all you did for them, and the rest of the Empire certainly won't either."

The Ecolitan stood there helplessly.

"Come on, ladies. We've still got a Legation to run. For once, we've left the Envoy speechless."

All three were smiling self-satisfied smiles as they marched out of his office.

Nathaniel collapsed into his swivel, wondering how much they really knew, and more important, how much anyone else knew. The answers would be largely academic, since the trade agreement revisions had been signed and approved by the Empire, and the House of Delegates wasn't in the mood for suicide by refusing to hold up Accord's end.

He switched on the faxnews. One channel was discussing the synde bean shortage. He flicked the selector.

". . . in a quiet ceremony at the Indoor Garden, the Emperor signed the new trade agreements with the Accord Coordinate. While observers termed the agreements 'routine,' the talks literally exploded earlier this year when the Accord Legation was bombed.

"Although the investigations by the Imperial Intelligence Service and the Ministry of Defense failed to uncover the reasons for the bombings or the individuals involved, the evidence uncovered led to a revamping of the Intelligence Service and the resignations of Lord Rotoller and Lord Mersen from the Commerce Ministry . . .

"The revised tariff and trade terms are expected to benefit the Imperial transport and microprocessing industries—"

Nathaniel flicked the newsfax program off the console. Time to go. As soon as the Marines arrived, he'd be on his way to the port and the shuttle that would carry him to the Accord courier that waited for him. Three subjective weeks, and two objective days, and he'd be home, along with the agreement to be ratified by the House of Delegates.

He fingered the collar pin, possibly the most expensive personal possession he'd ever owned.

The private circuit on his console chimed. He debated not answering, but touched the plate with his forefinger.

"Lord Whaler."

The caller was Marcella Ku-Smythe.

"Congratulations, Lord Whaler."

"The same to you. All is going well with you?"

"I think it will. I'm working with Lord Fergus now, and I learned a lot from watching you."

Very convenient system, reflected the Ecolitan. Change the figure-heads and leave the structure, with the women still in control.

"You're leaving soon?" She pointed through the screen toward the bags behind him.

"A short while."

"I'm very glad I reached you. You know, I'm scheduled for a trip to Accord later on to close down our section of the Imperial Legation in Harmony and to make a final evaluation. Perhaps I could look you up."

"Anything is possible."

"And," she looked straight at Nathaniel, "I expect some explanation of your specialties."

"My specialties?"

"How to sell nonexistent tariff reductions, for one. I just finished analyzing the final terms. You eliminated the Accord duties on all Imperial microprocessors. Very generous, but how will that help? We can't compete here on Terra. Then there was the increase in Imperial multichip duties to ten percent. The market is so competitive that nothing less than a fifteen percent rate would offer any real protection. All two hundred plus reductions and changes follow the same pattern."

She smiled and waited for his response.

"You do me far too much credit. I only followed my instructions to the best of my ability. You are far more expert than I am."

"Perhaps I am overstating the case. But I really do admire you. There's always the tendency to underestimate men these days, no matter what we say, no matter what I told you about not underestimating you. But no hard feelings—you did what you had to, and as delicately as possible, all things considered."

"I fear my understanding is limited."

"Oh, Lord Whaler, you're still the cautious one. I can't blame you. If there was a lot you didn't know about us, there was more we didn't bother to look up on you. A senior practicing scholar of the Ecolitan Institute, flawlessly fluent in at least five languages, including Panglais. A man considered one of the brighter economists on Accord and who is a trained military specialist who normally spends an hour a day practicing hand-to-hand combat. No wonder you looked bored and restless! We had it all in the file and didn't bother to notice the inconsistencies once you blundered in, stumbled over your tongue, and bored the devil out of us all."

She grinned at him, and there was no mistaking the openness of the humor.

"Before we could figure that out, you make fools out of some very competent security agents, among others, and the media starts asking us very embarrassing questions.

"Lord Whaler, loyal and obtuse, stumbles along trying to explain that 'he is trying to help,' but no one is interested. The faxhounds keep asking about bombings, secret agents who failed, jurisdiction, and why the Empire can't get its act together when Imperial industries are suffering. Now we have a trade agreement which gives the Empire sufficient short-term gains to quiet everyone, while reinforcing Accord's long-term position and independence."

Nathaniel cleared his throat. Loudly. "Too kind, much too kind, gracious Lady—"

"And," Marcella plunged on, "since the treaty doesn't cost the Empire too much and avoids the possibility of getting involved in another ecological war, no one is about to admit that a bumbling and stumbling Envoy from a third-rate system is really an extraordinarily capable agent from the only independent, first-rate power of a nongovernmental nature. Besides, and this is strictly personal, it serves Janis right."

The Ecolitan relaxed fractionally. Marcella wasn't talking about the real military aspects behind the treaty, but she'd definitely picked up on the power of the Institute, which was interesting since most of Accord's House of Delegates didn't understand that. And since Marcella didn't have to bear the final responsibility, as Janis might, she would let things slide.

"I guess that's it, Lord Whaler. Don't be too surprised to hear from me."

The screen blanked.

Nathaniel shook his head.

He supposed he ought to feel sorry for Janis Du-Plessis. She was outclassed by virtually everyone, from Mydra to Marcella to Sylvia, who, in her own quiet way, was the class act of the lot.

Sylvia!

He glanced around the console, then jabbed at the controls, letting his fingers flicker over the keyboard to pick out the information he needed.

He smiled as the screen printed up the answers he was hoping for.

While he waited for the system to dredge up the last responses to the questions he had posed, he looked out again through the wide window, out at the mountains in the distance, at the blue of the sky, and at the thunderclouds piling up over them.

The intercom buzzed.

He ignored it while the screen scripted out the last of the clearances he had requested.

"Whaler," he muttered, "you're assuming a lot."

He shook his head.

"You're also being impetuous, which is not at all healthy in your line of work."

Having refused to persuade himself, he committed the clearance numbers and codes to memory, then, as an afterthought, jotted them down on a note sheet, which he folded carefully and placed in his belt pouch.

That done, he stabbed the intercom stud.

"Lord Whaler, the Marine Guard will be arriving shortly."

"Thank you, Mydra. I'll let you know the final arrangements shortly."

He tapped out another number, one he wasn't supposed to know.

"Ferro-Maine . . . Lord Whaler!"

"Nathaniel," he corrected softly, taking in Sylvia's face, the wide clear gray eyes, and the strand of dark hair dropping over her forehead.

"What . . . can I do for you?"

"Where are you?"

"At the office . . . you know that . . . that's where you called," she stammered. "I thought you were leaving."

"I am. That is, I may be shortly. Please stay where you are, dear Lady." He grinned happily and broke the connection. On the screen he could see the confusion running across her face as her image faded.

"Mydra, please have my luggage delivered to the shuttle port by the Marines and tell them that I will meet them there."

"But . . . Lord Whaler! You can't do that!"

"Dear Mydra . . . I have to . . . but don't worry. Not this time."

He was already moving toward his private quarters and the outside exit when he tapped the intercom stud.

By the time he raced through the quarters and into the corridor toward the drop shaft, he was nearly running. He slowed only after he was actually dropping toward the concourse and the tunnel train station below.

The platform concourse at his destination station—the Imperial Senate Tower—was moderately crowded but melted away from him as he marched toward the lift shaft.

"Seem to draw back from an Ecolitan on the march," he mused as he watched a number of citizens edge away from his path.

Sylvia's office was only fifty meters from the exit stage.

"Lord Whaler, how good to see you," burbled Charles, the friendly receptionist, half rising from his chair and leaning toward a small panel on the console.

Nathaniel reached the man before Charles' hand could hit the warning plate.

"This is a friendly visit, Charles," announced the Ecolitan as he hoisted the other away from his console.

"Friendly?"

"As a matter of fact," noted Nathaniel, he tapped the flat plate labeled, F-M.

"You're here? Here?" asked Sylvia on the small screen.

"Nowhere else. Do you want to come out or invite me in?"

"I'll be right out."

Nathaniel returned his full attention to Charles and set the receptionist down in a swing chair away from the main communications console.

"Lord Whaler?"

"Yes, Charles."

"Why . . . I mean . . . to what do we owe . . . ?"

"To a happy occasion, I hope."

Nathaniel kept his eye on the console and on the portal from the staff offices, wondering if he should have charged all the way through, hoping that Sylvia wasn't ducking out whatever back ways existed.

"Happy time?"

"I hope," the Ecolitan added under his breath, wondering what he was doing literally hours before he was to catch his shuttle home.

His head snapped up at the whisper of a portal.

Charles looked at the console, then at Whaler, and decided to stay put.

Sylvia was wearing the same blue and white trimmed tunic she had worn when they had gone sightseeing together. Did he smell the faint tang of orange blossoms? What was he seeing in those gray eyes?

He shook his head.

"I'm impressed. You came to say good-bye in person."

Her voice was polite, but he could sense an undercurrent, exactly what he couldn't identify.

He shook his head again.

"No. I didn't."

"You didn't?"

"Not to say good-bye." He shifted his weight, looked at her for a long moment, then at the floor, before finally taking the slip of notepaper from his belt and handing it to her.

She unfolded it.

"This is supposed to mean something, dear Envoy?"

"Nathaniel," he corrected automatically. "Sylvia, you know I'm not good at speeches . . . and there's not much time—"

"So don't deliver a speech. Say what you have to and go."

"Those codes represent your visa, your clearance, and your immigration permit to Accord."

From the corner of his eye, Nathaniel could see Charles' mouth drop wide open.

"Me . . . an ex-Imperial agent?"

"No. You . . . the person . . . the woman . . . Flamehell! We've got less than three hours to catch the shuttle."

"For what?"

"For Accord. For us."

Sylvia smiled, and her expression was guarded. "Why us?"

"Because I want you to come with me!"

The guarded look was replaced with a fuller, yet somehow more tentative smile.

"You haven't asked me."

"Would you please come with me?" He finally managed to grin himself. "Even if you hadn't planned to emigrate for a few more years yet?"

"But I'm scarcely—"

"Sylvia."

"Yes."

Without realizing what he was doing, Nathaniel reached for her, only to find she had the same thing in mind. They collided in mid-step, grabbing at each other to keep from falling.

"I think this time you beat me to it," he murmured in her ear.

"Not now. We've only got three hours to catch the shuttle."

She kissed him slowly full upon the lips and then stepped back from his arms.

Charles shook his head from side to side as the tall man and the dancer walked from the office, hand in hand.

THE ECOLITAN ENIGMA

For Eric, Phyllis, and Alex

"Though fraud in other activities be detestable, in the management of war it is laudable and glorious . . ."

Niccolò Machiavelli
[pre-Ecollapse writer . . . dates unknown]

"Conflict is always rooted in ecology, and rational scholars spend careers denying this precept, because it precludes the possibility of cultural transcendence."

Kristen Janes-Cornet, *Compilations of the Primes*

"The most cost-effective war is that waged by others on their own lands at their own cost. Strive always for such . . ."

Fleet Admiral Gorham, *Memoirs*

"A *good* economist is worth a dozen spies and two fleets. Unfortunately, the fleets and spies are far easier to come by."

Alexi Lederman-Meier, *Economics of Conflict*

PROLOGUE
SECESSION, ECOLOGIC (3647–48)

THE WAR LEADING to the independence of the Coordinate of Accord [See also Ecologic Rebellion, Accord, Ecolitan Institute].

During the years 3645–46, Imperial relations with the Fuardian Conglomerate became increasingly strained, and a number of colony systems protested the ad valorem and ad personam taxes levied by the Empire to support the infrastructure necessary to restrain the Conglomerate. Among the discontented colony systems were those of Accord (Imperial Sector Five) and Sligo (Imperial Sector Seven).

Accord used high-technology sabotage and commando tactics to destroy key military fueling and staging bases (Haversol, Cubera, Fonderol) at a time when the majority of Imperial forces were deployed in Sector Two to counter the perceived Fuardian threat. The Accord sabotage limited to an even greater extent the ability of Imperial warcraft to reach Accord's isolated location on the Parthanian Rift.

Unable to deal with potentially extended conflicts on three fronts, the Empire reduced Sligo, where casualties exceeded fifteen million, despite an initially published estimate of only three million [See Lies for the Popular Good]. Following the Empire's destruction of Sligo and all installations in its system, the provisional government of Accord launched a successful ecologic attack on Old Earth in 3647, primarily using the resources of the Ecolitan Institute [See The Black Institute].

The resulting Ecollapse eventually fragmented the terran ecology. The Empire retaliated by sending a full fleet to the Accord system. Innovative and suicidal tactics developed and spearheaded by Ecolitan [later Prime] James Joyson Whaler [See Wright-Whaler Controversy] resulted in the total destruction of that Imperial fleet in late 3647.

The Fuardian Conglomerate then unveiled a new series of warships of performance and armament vastly superior to existing Imperial craft [See CX Affair] and seized former Imperial systems in Sector Two (the Three System Bulge).

With the Empire weakened by the increasingly unstable political climate and mounting death toll from the Ecollapse on Old Earth, the potential of further ecological devastation from the Ecolitan Institute, and the clear technological superiority of the Conglomerate, Emperor Jynstin II recognized the independence of Accord and shifted all Imperial forces and battle groups to Sector Two, leading to the Truce of Tierna. Under the Truce, the Conglomerate retained the Three System

Bulge, except that the then-undeveloped system of Artos was ceded to New Avalon, and the Empire ceded the undeveloped system of D'Sanya to Chezchos, later the Federated Hegemony.

The perceived failure of the monarchy led to the Senatorial Reformation [See N'Trosia Catalyst] and the political restructuring of the Empire . . .

Dictionary of Imperial History
K. J. Peynon
New Augusta 4102

FILLED WITH THE faint odors of oil, hot metal, and recycled air, the down-shuttle from Accord orbit control to Harmony was less than half full. In the left front couch sat a tall sandy-haired man wearing the formal greens of an Ecolitan. On his left uniform collar was a black-and-green lustral pin—a gift from the Emperor of the Hegemony of Light, more commonly known as the Terran Empire. The pin was a contradiction in terms because the substance of the lustral represented a small fortune and the form was a miniature of the crest of the Ecolitan Institute. Beside the Ecolitan sat a dark-haired woman in a blue jumpsuit.

Sylvia glanced sideways at Nathaniel as the Ecolitan fidgeted in the hard passenger seat of the Coordinate shuttle.

"Iffy approach," he said.

"And yours haven't been?" The slender and dark-haired woman offered a smile.

"Mine?"

"Yours." The smile broadened.

"Which kind are you referring to?" he countered, trying not to grin in return.

"Any kind, most honorable envoy."

"I'd hope mine, especially in shuttles and needle-boats, were less rocky," he finally said, squelching a frown as the buffeting shuttle tossed him against his harness.

"Do all pilots find other pilots' approaches questionable?"

"Probably. We hate being passengers."

"It sounds like you're all control addicts." She offered a softer smile.

"That's probably true, too."

"I still wonder." She shook her head. "This is so sudden. I hadn't planned to emigrate so soon. And certainly not to Accord. Your clearance officers on the orbit control station—they barely looked at me. Do all Ecolitans have that kind of power?"

"Hardly." Nathaniel laughed. "It wasn't me, but the Prime Ecolitan's access codes."

"Just codes? Could any Ecolitan do that?"

"Not unless the Prime gave him the codes." The sandy-haired man swayed in the seat as the shuttle banked onto what Nathaniel hoped was the final approach. "They're held tightly."

"Does that happen often?"

Nathaniel shrugged. "Every few years, maybe. This was important to us." Still, he had trouble believing his mission as an agent/official envoy was over, and that he had actually managed to avert what could have been an interstellar war between the Coordinate of Accord and the Empire. Although he'd sweated and worried, especially when it had looked as though the Imperial fleet had been ready to deploy, now it seemed almost too easy . . . and as if he'd missed something. He refrained from shaking his head. At least he'd gotten Sylvia off Old Earth. But did she want off?

"You'd already gotten the trade agreement before you left Old Earth," Sylvia continued. "You didn't need me. Why was I important to your mission? Or afterwards?"

"Because I think so." He grinned. "Because you made it all possible, and because—"

"Please remain in your seats. Shuttle Beta is on final approach to Harmony. Please remain in your seats."

"—you'd be an asset to the Institute."

"They'd take me on your recommendation?"

"Not automatically, but I can't recall when the recommendation of a senior professor was last rejected." He cleared his throat and raised his voice above the roar of the landing engines. "That's because we don't make many, and we're held responsible."

"How many have you made?" Sylvia asked with a smile.

"You're the first. I don't know of any professor, or even the Prime, who's made more than three. Some never have."

Her eyes dropped to the green of the bulkhead before them. "You make me sound extraordinarily special, and I'm not."

"You're not? How many people would have had the background, the understanding, and the willingness to help me—and to prevent the deaths of billions of human beings?" And that was just where an interstellar war could have led.

"I'm not that special."

"We'll talk about that later, Ms. Ferro-Maine," Nathaniel said as the shuttle's tires screeched on the permacrete of Accord and he lurched against the harness. "Way too rough . . ." he murmured more to himself than Sylvia.

Even before the shuttle lurched to a halt, prompting another sour look by Nathaniel, the announcement hissed through the passenger compartment.

"Please pick up your bags or any luggage on the way out of the shuttle. You are responsible for carrying your own luggage unless you have made prior arrangements. Please pick up your luggage on the way out."

"Self-sufficiency begins from the moment you set foot on the planet, I see." After the final lurch, Sylvia eased out of her harness and stood, stretching.

Nathaniel watched for a moment, enjoying her grace, still half-amazed that she had not been good enough for a professional dancing career on Old Earth.

"Dancing takes more than grace."

"How did you—"

"You've said it enough, especially every time I stretch." Another warm smile crossed her lips. "Time to become pack animals."

"With what little you brought?"

"I had very little time to choose, as you may recall?"

"Sorry. I'll see that you get a stipend for that." And he would, even if it came out of his pay.

"You aren't responsible for everything, dear envoy."

No, he thought, *we Ecolitans only think we are.*

One of the uniformed crew members—a woman in olive greens standing behind the baggage racks—looked sharply at the two for a moment as they retrieved their bags, two field packs for Nathaniel and two oblong black synfab cases for Sylvia.

Once they stepped out of the shuttle and into the shuttleway to the port terminal, Nathaniel took a deep breath. "Smells better than ship air."

"It smells like burned hydrocarbons to me," confessed Sylvia.

"Professor Whaler?" asked the redheaded young woman in plain greens, waiting by the end of the shuttleway.

"I'm Whaler," Nathaniel acknowledged. "And this is Ms. Ferro-Maine. She's accompanying me to the Institute."

"Trainee Luren, sirs," offered the youngster, probably a fourth-year trainee, Nathaniel suspected. "The Prime sent a flitter when he got your message." Her rust-colored eyebrows lifted just slightly. "If you would follow me?"

"Thank you." The Ecolitan did not answer the unasked question. Few Ecolitans got private flitters on returning to Accord. Most carried their own luggage and took the monorail.

As they trailed Luren, Sylvia murmured, "I thought you said we'd have to take the monorail."

"I couldn't count on a flitter . . . didn't want to disappoint you."

"You won't be disappointed that you aren't flying it?" She raised her eyebrows.

"A little, but into each life some rain falls."

"Please . . ."

Luren paused by a narrow doorway. "We're down the steps and across the permacrete."

Nathaniel squinted as they stepped out into the bright sunlight of Harmony, if a shuttle port nearly twenty kilos south of Harmony could be considered part of the Coordinate capital.

"There it is, sirs," said Luren.

Nathaniel glanced toward the green flitter as he eased the field packs through the doorway, then looked back toward Sylvia, whose mouth opened.

Scritt! Scritt!

Nathaniel scarcely felt the needles that slammed him around, not after Sylvia threw him behind the slight cover afforded by their bags. For a moment, he just lay there. On Accord? With an Institute flitter less than a hundred meters away? How could an assassination attempt take place? And why? He'd already done his job, and nothing would stop implementation of the trade agreement.

Nathaniel squinted through his sudden dizziness at the sprawled form of the trainee and then toward the flitter.

Thrummmm . . . thrummm . . . Almost as quickly as the stunner bolts flew from the Institute craft, two figures in greens sprinted from the flitter toward the three sprawled on the permacrete.

Eeeeeee . . . The sirens seemed to waver in and around Nathaniel from a distance as he slowly eased himself into a sitting position.

His entire side was a mass of fire.

"Are you all right?" Sylvia asked.

"Will be . . . need to get to the Institute." He struggled to stand, then found himself being helped by both Sylvia and a young Ecolitan.

"Whoever it was is gone, professor. We've alerted the Prime, but we're to get you home double speed." The young crewman turned to Sylvia. "You, too, Ms. Ferro-Maine."

Nathaniel forced his legs to carry him toward the still waiting flitter, although it was more of a stagger than a walk. Still, he knew every pace was worth more than antique gold, especially if the needles had carried nerve collapse toxins. He blocked the pain and kept walking, but the permacrete and the flitter began to swirl around him.

"Catch him."

THE FUARDIAN OFFICER wearing crimson-trimmed formal grays and a silver hawk on his shoulder tabs stepped inside the spacious office. "Ser?"

"I don't have time to read forty-page reports, colonel. Answer me simply. Are your operations going as planned?" asked the gray-clad officer behind the desk.

"Ah, sub-marshal . . . yes. We had not foreseen the Accord trade negotiations, but the Coordinate's conduct there has sharpened the Grand Admiral's concerns. The use of an Ecolitan as a trade negotiator has definitely put the laser on the Rift. The devastation of the synde bean plague on Heraculon has reinforced those Imperial concerns . . ."

"How strongly?"

"The death toll is over four million so far. The Empire has had to divert most of its spare cargo capacity for food concentrates. They've even sent in military power systems from reserve units."

"Good. And?"

"There are still murmurs about Accord. We don't have the analysis yet, but those could be pushed by the trideo initiative. Either way, the laser points directly at Harmony. We've taken some additional steps there as well to point back at the Admiral . . . or others. We had to divert a fast courier, but . . ."

"That's secondary, though, for now. Do we have enough seed stock for the next phase?"

"Yes, ser, and the next phase will target both the anchovies and the algae. Anarra, the Matriarchy, then Imperial Sector Four. We've established the probable secondary vectors if it were a natural plague, and those will be planted over the next few weeks, using the commercial trade system."

The sub-marshal nodded curtly.

"What about the transfer arrangements?" asked the colonel. "Our contacts have asked about that."

"We do not have to deliver anything—especially warcraft—until the Ninth and Eleventh fleets are transferred to the Rift, or two other fleets in the sectors bordering the Three System Bulge are shifted along the Limber line." The senior officer smiled. "When that occurs, the general staff will be more than happy to approve the transfer. More than happy.

After we occupy the systems, particularly . . . shall we say . . . those of the priggish Avalonians."

"Yes, ser."

"And colonel?"

"Ser?"

"Next time, send a summary with the report. It will save us both time."

■■■

NATHANIEL LOOKED FROM his bed at the dark-haired dancer, her left arm in a sling and covered with a nerve regeneration sheathe. "I didn't expect . . . such a welcome here in Harmony."

"Neither did I." Sylvia offered a wry smile. "It was even more dramatic than your welcome to New Augusta."

"No one seems to want me to go anywhere, even home." He swallowed. "Are you all right?" As close as Sylvia sat on the straight-backed wooden chair, he couldn't miss the dark circles under her eyes. Behind her, through the wide window, he could see the low hills to the west of the Institute, their treed lower slopes a deep green.

"You're asking how *I* am?"

"I know how I'm doing. I'll live, and nothing permanent's damaged."

"On Old Earth, you'd be dead, I think." She frowned. "I knew the Institute had good medical techniques, but knowing . . . and experiencing . . ."

"This is Accord." He forced a soft laugh, ignoring the wave of pain that the sound sent down his side. "But I wish you hadn't gotten the experience firsthand."

"You are impossible."

"How are—" he asked.

"I'm fine. The arm hurts, and the nerves burn all the way to my neck sometimes, but the medtechs say that's normal and there's no lasting damage."

"Good." Nathaniel offered a smile. The last thing he wanted was for her to arrive on Accord and be crippled . . . or worse. But why had someone been after them?

"Has anyone—" He had trouble concentrating, his thoughts skittering from one image to another, reinforced by the tightness in his stomach that kept insisting that something was very wrong.

"Your Prime Ecolitan talked to me, while they were still working on you." Sylvia smiled. "He was more forthright than anyone from the Empire would have been."

"And?" Nathaniel tried to bring up the relaxation techniques to reduce muscular tension and pain, and eased himself back against the pale green sheets—sheets, soft as they were, that felt like hundreds of pins where his bare skin brushed them.

"The needles were Imperial military issue—the ones they use for Special Ops. They're transparent to everything. They found a dead Coordinate trooper, minus his uniform and equipment, just off the Dehar base—"

"DeHihns," corrected Nathaniel. "Named after the first planetary chairman."

"They think he'd only been killed a few hours before."

"It couldn't have been an Imperial Special Op." Nathaniel shook his head momentarily, then stopped as a line of fire slashed up his left side. He closed his eyes against the light from the window. Even that seemed to glare.

"I'd agree." Sylvia smiled ironically. "I'd like to know why you think that, though."

"First," he said slowly, "it's unlikely one could pass the screens, but if he or she did, they'd be good enough that one or both of us would be dead. Second, they'd have had a better opportunity on Old Earth. There, the timing would have been far better . . . easier . . ." He took a slow deep breath, letting the relaxation techniques blunt the pain.

Sylvia nodded.

After all, Nathaniel reflected silently, for an Imperial Special Operative to get to Accord before they had in time to set up an assassination attempt meant that it had to have been planned almost before Nathaniel had completed his trade negotiations. "Third . . . it's too obvious."

"It was meant to be obvious."

But why? That was the question. His vision blurred.

Sylvia stood quickly and stepped up beside the bed, touching his forehead with her good hand, with fingers that were cool and soothing. "Just relax . . . you need to rest."

He tried to smile, but found blackness looming over him.

IV

As he had the last time he had visited the Institute, Delegate Minister of Interstellar Commerce Restinal paused outside the open door.

"Come on in, Werlin," called the Prime Ecolitan's cheerful voice. "Remember, we don't stand on ceremony. We don't even sit on it."

Restinal forced a genial smile and carried his datacase into the lorkin-paneled office, bowing to the silver-haired man who stood by the wide table that served as his desk.

"Take a seat." Without waiting for Restinal to follow the suggestion, Gairloch Pittsway, Prime of the Ecolitan Institute, sat down in the hand-carved armchair behind the table.

Restinal eased into the chair closest to the door, his datacase on his lap. "I wished to convey personally my thanks to you and to the Institute for its willingness to relinquish Ecolitan Whaler to the Ministry. His efforts as Trade Legate to New Augusta were most effective." Restinal smiled again. "Most effective."

"I'm glad you recognize that."

"I was sorry to hear that the Empire rather belatedly also recognized his expertise and effectiveness."

"Professor Whaler will be incapacitated for a short while, no longer, and I am sure he will appreciate your concern, Werlin. Even if I did have to force him on you." The Prime's smile was faint.

"I bowed to your wisdom then, and I still do."

"Werlin, you only bow to superior force of one type or another, and we both know it." There was a slight pause. "You didn't come all the way out here just to offer congratulations and condolences. What did you have in mind?"

Restinal shifted his weight on the chair, already hard. "I understand that Professor Whaler is a highly regarded expert on development economics, and especially economic infrastructures."

"That is his specialty," acknowledged Pittsway.

"We understand that New Avalon may be requesting our assistance with such a matter on Artos." Restinal kept his voice even. "We are to prepare a report on the economic development structure and possibilities of Artos . . ."

"We? The Coordinate government doesn't have either the expertise or the impartiality. Why did you agree to this before talking with the Institute?" asked Pittsway, his voice equally level.

"We are well aware of the Institute's capabilities, as are the Avalonians."

"Minister Restinal . . . for whom did you agree to do this report, and why?"

"Officially, the report will be prepared for submission to the Commerce Ministries of both New Avalon and the Coordinate."

"I see. And what . . . emphasis . . . do you expect this report to highlight, Werlin?"

"I would like to see the report as factual and impartial as possible," Restinal answered earnestly.

"You're aiming this toward Whaler like a point-tailed retriever. Why? The poor bastard deserves a rest. We do have other experts in the Institute."

"The Ministry has gained a great appreciation of Professor Whaler's skills, even in dealing with our own bureaucratic structures, and, alas, even we have those . . ."

"Oh?"

"You may not have heard, but he was successful in . . . encouraging a young . . . professional, from the External Affairs Committee staff of the Imperial Senate to return to Accord with him. In some fashion, he obtained clearance from both governments, or documents which represent such a clearance. Especially those endorsed, even indirectly, by the Prime Ecolitan." Restinal shrugged. "It's not exactly politic to question successful Legates, especially those who have outmaneuvered the Empire, on such a relatively minor matter."

"I'm well aware of Ms. Ferro-Maine, and you knew that before you headed out here. You wouldn't be bringing it up, Werlin, if you weren't angling for something. What mess have you got stewing with New Avalon? Is this some involuted scheme Torine designed?"

"You misunderstand me, Prime. It's just that I would scarcely want to have the Institute embarrassed by the arrival of an Imperial citizen who might be linked to the I.I.S."

"Restinal, you are behaving more and more like Torine every day. Or Quaestor and Verlingetti. I understand that Elder Torine has only a thin working majority, and that you Normists wish to retain power. That's politics. The Institute doesn't care for most of your games, but every society and government ends up with political intrigue. What we resent is your attempting to conceal that intrigue when you're asking the Institute for something. So, if you don't start thinking and leveling with the Institute, I'll be forced to suggest that you take your portfolio and place it somewhere very private and very dark."

Restinal felt himself flushing. He rose.

"Sit down. We, or Ecolitan Whaler, saved your precious posterior. For Torine to send you out here to insist on a dubious study with a clear second purpose and then to threaten either one of us shows little gratitude and less sense. That's particularly true given what Whaler's been through. Further, if I made public what you just implied, you and Torine would suffer more than the Institute, and you don't have that many seats on your side of the aisle to spare. You'll have even less if Elder Quaestor or Verlingetti or one of the Orthodoxist radicals hear this. Now, what do you really want and why?"

Restinal tried not to clamp his lips together too hard as he reseated himself.

The Prime waited, a half smile upon his lightly tanned and lined face.

"All I can say is that Artos is mentioned in some materials we are not supposed to have. There is also a strong possibility for some agricultural-technology transfer trade."

"Werlin . . ."

"Honestly, respected Prime. That is all I can say because it's all we know."

"There has to be some context," pointed out Pittsway.

"Artos appeared in some standard business communiques from a New Avalon factor with a less than savory reputation. We *think* the copies were sent to our woman in New Avalon by a Hand of the Mother. The context was merely a listing of cargos and agricultural techpaks destined there."

"Since these are of themselves no value, I presume you brought copies," said the Prime.

Restinal nodded slowly.

"But you don't feel comfortable turning them over to me unless I agree to send Whaler on this fool's errand?" The Prime Ecolitan glanced at the datacase in Restinal's lap. "You know better than that. After we see the communiques, and after Professor Whaler is recovered enough to review the materials . . . if he's interested, he can make that choice. He deserves that after saving your posterior. Agri-tech trade indeed. Do you think Artos is just a pretext? Have you any idea of where this insignificant system is?"

Restinal sat silently.

"Werlin?"

"It's a fringe system of New Avalon."

"And?"

"It's the closest system to the Three System Bulge."

"My . . ." Pittsway drew out the word. "What a coincidence. The Fuards hold the Three System Bulge, which they took from the Empire during our war of secession, and they're flanked by Artos, held by New Avalon, by the Federated Hegemony, and by the Frankan Union, and by, of course, the Empire. And you blithely suggest that there's nothing beyond some cargo manifests and an economic study?"

Restinal looked at the smoothly finished wood floor.

"Didn't you learn anything from the last mess, Werlin? First, if you have those communiques, so does every intelligence service in the Galaxy. Second, whoever it was that leaked them to you knows you'll have to go to the Institute, and they'll be watching. That means someone wants us to do something they can't do, won't do, or want to blame us for. We still have to do this . . . study—and I presume it's something you have worked out as a tacit cover that the entire Galaxy will know is a cover. And we'll have to do it well, even while doing your dirty work. Our problem here at the Institute is that we live in the same system as you idiots do, that we have a fondness for Accord, and that, unlike some, we attempt to live up to all our codes—and that means we don't play politics. Not your way." Pittsway smiled. "So . . . do you trust us, or are you going to take your papers home and fold gliders out of them—which is about what they'll be worth if you leave without giving them to us?"

Restinal held in a sigh. Why was Elder Torine always putting him in such impossible positions?

"Torine puts you in those positions, Werlin, because you're basically honest, and no one else in the Delegate Ministries is both honest and intelligent. You're also expendable because you got the portfolio through expertise and not political capital."

Restinal did sigh as he opened the datacase.

"You're handing us a mess, Werlin, but it's not nearly that bad for you."

Restinal was sure it was worse, far worse, and that his troubles were just beginning. He handed the flimsies across the desk.

V

NATHANIEL FIRSTBORNE WHALER bowed as he stepped inside the door, ignoring the twinges that intermittently traveled the nerves of his left side. "Prime?"

"Come on in, Nathaniel." The silver-haired Prime Ecolitan stood by the wide table with the single drawer that served as his desk. As usual, the office was free of clutter. Two hard-copy files lay on the corner of the immaculate blond Ecolog-style desk-table. The louvered shutters were open, and a cool breeze wafted through the office.

Nathaniel paused between the two carved and high-backed wooden chairs.

"Sit down." Gairloch Pittsway's green eyes twinkled. "After your ordeal, I wouldn't keep you standing—not yet, anyway."

Nathaniel took the chair on the left side of the table and waited, his eyes on the older man.

"Solid work you did on Old Earth." The Prime took the other carved chair in front of the desk. "Your return proved that."

"Thank you." When the Prime began with a compliment, trouble lay on the course ahead. Nathaniel also didn't like the idea that an attempt on his own life proved his value. That was almost like saying he wouldn't be appreciated until he was dead. That kind of appreciation he could do without.

"Your unvarnished description of Imperial politics was refreshing, if not unexpected. In view of your earlier efforts, you might be interested to know we took steps with regard to the elections on Hernando. The Popular Front had some setbacks in the balloting, and the Conservative Democrats have consolidated their government. They no longer need the Socialist Republicans." The Prime Ecolitan leaned back in his chair. "Would that our own citizens were as perceptive. Or our own honorable representatives."

"What did the House of Delegates do?" Two compliments, reflected Nathaniel, meant real trouble.

"At our prompting, indirectly, of course, they sent a communique to the Imperial Senate strongly suggesting it was in everyone's best interests if Hernando remained independent. The Imperial Secretary of External Affairs sent a reassuring response, and the Elders are patting themselves on the back, conveniently forgetting that the Institute carried everyone's oil. It works better that way." Pittsway grinned. "You did manage to terrify a few of the Imperials. That was obvious." The Prime glanced toward the green hills framed in the window. "I am not referring to the needle-gun attack."

"I hadn't thought so."

"We'll get to that in a moment. Even on Old Earth, you were obviously overtly formidable."

"The synde bean plague on Heraculon helped." Nathaniel raised his eyebrows and waited. "Probably a great deal."

"Nasty business, there. I've started a team on that." The Prime frowned momentarily. "I suppose you couldn't afford to disclaim it."

"I didn't claim or disclaim it. I didn't think so, but I didn't know."

"Matters would have to degrade considerably for us even to think about a return to ecological weapons with that broad an impact. You know how the Institute feels about ecologic warfare except as a last resort. One of the lesser benefits of the Secession. Besides, we'd have the entire galaxy up in arms if we did. It's perfectly all right to wage wars, manipulate trade and agriculture, and starve or kill millions, but ecological warfare . . . horror of horrors. That's another reason why the Charter and the Iron Rules were codified by the first Whaler. You're some sort of relation, aren't you?"

"You know the answer to that," said Nathaniel with a smile. "About as distant as one can get."

"You ought to read his papers, if you haven't. They're sealed, but the access is in your debrief file. I'd appreciate it if you would at least read through the entries I coded. You might also consider some of his exploits as a basis for revising your contingency plans. You managed the trade negotiations with minimal use of force. You may not have that option on your next assignment. I'm afraid the Fuards or the Federated Hegemony, or both, are setting up trouble."

Nathaniel refrained from swallowing. References to force and the first Whaler? The one who had a reputation for drastic action? For the Prime to suggest such was definitely a bad sign. "Could I ask why you think so?"

"There are three reasons, or perhaps they're the same. The next request for your services, the attack, and your friend. Or is she more than a friend?"

"I have hopes, but that has to be up to Sylvia. I think she'll be an asset, one way or another."

"I'm sure of that." Pittsway offered a wry grin. "After the way you bent both our system and the Imperials' to get her here, she must be quite a person."

"She is. I wouldn't have been able to do it without her."

"Is that true or a justification?"

"True," Nathaniel admitted. "She provided access and insight." He didn't want to admit out loud that Sylvia's ability to get him inside the Defense Tower on New Augusta had made possible his distribution of the Institute-modified Gerson's disease that had forced Admiral Ku-Smythe to accept the trade negotiations. Besides, the details in his report should have told the Prime what he needed to know.

"Hmmm." The Prime nodded. "You have her in the intensive indoctrination courses already."

"We thought that advisable."

"More than advisable, as I'm sure you're beginning to understand, after the past few weeks."

Nathaniel waited.

"You know that the needles used on you were military Empire-issue, spiked with a nerve toxin used only by the Empire, and nastier than anything anyone else uses. It was touch and go for a bit, for both of you, and for the trainee."

"Sylvia didn't tell me that."

"That increases my considerable respect for her—and for your choice of her." The Prime steepled his fingers briefly. "What do you think about the attack on you being backed by the Imperial military?"

"It couldn't have been. They have to know that, if we revealed the details, that would put the Defense Ministry at direct odds with at least two Imperial Ministries and the Emperor." Nathaniel paused. "That would be an embarrassing situation. It could have theoretically been the work of a lower-level commander who was angry at Admiral Ku-Smythe . . . a set-up to embarrass her and get her removed so that in the future, the next Defense chief would be ready to attack the Coordinate. But I don't see anyone senior enough to order it being that stupid." The sandy-haired Ecolitan cleared his throat. "Or it could be designed to provoke us—or you. Or it could be an Halstani ploy . . ."

"Or an Orknarlian or Fuardian or Federated Hegemony effort—or one by New Avalon," pointed out the Prime. "Or even a subtle move by the Frankan Union. I'd discount that, but not dismiss it."

"New Avalon?"

Pittsway nodded. "While you were recovering, our friend Werlin

Restinal paid a visit. You have been requested to visit Artos—in your academic capacity."

"The Delegate Minister of Interstellar Commerce?"

"The same. He requested that you do a study on Artos. It's a recently planoformed colony planet, and he provided some fanciful story about your expertise on infrastructure economics and the possibility of agricultural-technology trade. He also provided some odd shipping manifests, and he looked worried."

That had been where the Prime was leading. Nathaniel wanted to groan.

"You may recall that he's also the shadow minister for Coordinate intelligence, such as it is."

The Ecolitan professor managed not to groan or sigh—barely. "Do we know what the problem is?"

"Torine hasn't told him what the problem is. And Torine isn't about to tell us, if he even knows the details." The Prime shrugged. "Restinal doesn't have any way to get anyone onto Artos. Not anyone he can trust. Everyone *knows* the Institute can't be bought by the Coordinate government—anyone else from Accord would be automatically suspect, and Artos is three sectors away. Who from here would ever travel that far to a planet barely out of planoforming? Except an Institute economist or a Coordinate intelligence operative?"

"So why Artos?"

"We don't *know*, but it's on the edge of the Three System Bulge, and we do know that both the Federated Hegemony and the Fuards, and lately the Frankans, have all been increasing their arsenals, although not there. I find the absence of military activity around the Bulge more disturbing than its presence." The Prime smiled wryly. "We also have a very nervous politician on our hands, and he—or someone—has dummied up a study to get you to Artos. The study has to be real—and first class. And he's got a deal with Camelot, one he won't reveal."

"But it's an obvious cover—even to the Avalonians."

The Prime nodded.

"How obvious and how nervous was Restinal?"

"Obvious enough that more than a few will know everything about you before you leave. Restinal was nervous enough to mention that Ferro-Maine might be considered an Imperial agent by some, and an embarrassment to the Institute. I told him to take his portfolio and place it somewhere very private and very dark." The Prime smiled.

"I'll have to tell her."

"I thought you would. I also thought she might like to accompany you to Artos, but that has to be her choice. She is welcome at the Institute in your absence, and would be accorded full staff privileges."

"I'll have to ask her." Nathaniel paused. "How does the assassination effort tie into New Avalon?"

"I have this feeling that the Avalonian Commerce Ministry was pressured into requesting the study. Someone doesn't want it done, and Werlin was sent out here to make sure it was . . . and that you were assigned to do it. Someone knew that before Restinal did."

"An infrastructure study? They don't kill people over the allocation of energy and transportation resources." Nathaniel shook his head.

"Unless that allocation ties into something else rather nasty. Then again," said the Prime, "it may all be an elaborate scheme to get you isolated away from Accord."

"I find that hard to believe."

"So do I, but—" the Prime shrugged "—some people take defeats as very, very personal, and you made some very powerful people look very stupid. Right now, we don't know, and by the time we do . . ."

"It could be rather late."

"Exactly. But I feel, as you'll see in the briefing materials, that it's much worse than that. Far worse. Possibly far worse than what you just concluded with the Empire."

Nathaniel pursed his lips. He'd hoped for a respite—and the chance to get to know Sylvia better—when he'd returned home.

"You don't have to go to Artos."

"I don't know that I'd be any safer here—not if the assassin could penetrate Coordinate security."

"They won't penetrate the Institute."

"And I'm supposed to remain under Institute restraint for months or years? No, thank you. I'd rather go to Artos."

Pittsway smiled wryly. "I thought you might. There's a full briefing package on file for you."

"Thank you."

"Don't thank me. This is doubtless another one of those insurmountable opportunities that Strongarm's memoirs cites."

"I'll remember that."

"And I think you'd better review your contingency portfolio. I've also granted you the full credit and authority of the Institute."

"The *full* credit?" The younger Ecolitan wanted to whistle. He hadn't even gotten that on his trade mission to New Augusta.

The Prime nodded. "I've also instructed our representative in Camelot that your authority is as mine, not to be questioned or obstructed."

"You suspect . . . ?"

"I suspect everything, and if my suspicions are correct, this will be even nastier than your last effort. And you may not have much time to act if it comes to that. I hope not, but I'm already half-convinced that we're past hoping. As I indicated, the details are under seal in your briefing packet." The Prime rose. "After you review that, if you have further questions, we can talk. I would also suggest that you inform new Ecolitan professor Ferro-Maine that the situation is uncertain, but that it could be quite hazardous, for reasons we can only suspect, and that you would prefer to limit her briefing to the facts in order to get her unvarnished judgment."

"Yes, Prime." Nathaniel stood, belatedly.

VI

THE TWO FIGURES in field greens sat on the bench in the middle of the Institute's formal garden.

"You know," offered Whaler, "this garden dates back to the founding of the Institute. And this bench was where the first Whaler fell in love." The sandy-haired Ecolitan grinned, simultaneously being fully aware of the faint orange-trilia fragrance that seemed to emanate from Sylvia. It was already hard to believe that he'd met her over a dose of fidelitrol, trying not to tell the truth, or not too much of it, while she was doing the same.

"This very bench?" she asked with a smile.

"One like it, I imagine. Even our benches don't last four hundred years. There are other parallels. He was an Imperial Special Operative. She was an Ecolitan field agent, and probably a far better operative than he was. His specialty, according to the material the Prime gave me, was destruction on a large scale."

"You haven't done that badly."

Nathaniel suppressed a wince, thinking about fifty deaths from a mutated virus that was supposed to have a minimal fatal impact. "I wish I hadn't had to do what I did."

"That makes two of us." Sylvia paused. "Sometimes, our choices are only between the lesser of evils."

"That's one thing that worries me about this Artos assignment," the Ecolitan said quickly. "I have a feeling that nothing good is going to come of it, no matter how we handle it. So does the Prime, and he's granted me a lot of authority. Too much. But we're all just speculating."

"Is it real?" she asked thoughtfully.

"The Prime thinks it is. I don't know. But I worry about your coming." He glanced at her, then added, "On your own, you're probably better than I am at avoiding difficulties. You showed me that on Old Earth."

"Don't humor me."

"I'm not. I couldn't have done it without you."

She shook her head, her slate gray eyes momentarily ocean cold. "Fifty-one deaths. Over three hundred people with permanent nerve damage, and you couldn't have done it without me."

"That's not what I meant. I was talking about Artos. If you went somewhere alone . . . you'd be better off than with me. But they've requested an economist, and a study that has to be good, even if it's a cover. And that means one Nathaniel Whaler. I want to spend time with you, but I don't want to make you a target. I told you that this could be very hazardous."

"You're perfectly willing to be a target, dear Nathaniel. And it appears as though we both already are—again."

"I knew that came with the territory. Has for a long time."

"You don't think I didn't know it came with the territory when I left everything to come to Accord—even before that mess at the port? I think I love you, Nathaniel, but I still won't be a kept woman." Sylvia's slate gray eyes caught Whaler's, held them. "I know I can help." She offered a faint smile.

"You *think* you love me? You came all this way . . . and you think . . ." The sandy-haired Ecolitan shook his head.

"You didn't ask me for a contract. You didn't even say you loved me. You provided everything, and I know that . . . I know you care. I had to choose, then. There wasn't a second chance. Was there?" Her lips quirked upward. "There almost wasn't a first chance."

"You could have . . ." He paused. Would the I.I.S. really have let her go, if they'd had time to find out and react? Would the Coordinate authorities have been so lenient if he hadn't just delivered an agreement that staved off an interstellar war? He pursed his lips, then shook his head. "You're right."

"That's one of the many things I can say I love about you."

"What?"

"Behind that secret-agent-economist front . . . you actually listen."

Nathaniel wondered. Did he?

"You do, and I'm going with you."

"So long as you keep up your lessons on what you don't know about Accord."

"That's another thing I like about this place." She offered the tentative smile that he always found so enchanting.

"The lessons?"

"People take me at my word."

"Not everyone on Accord does. Ecolitans try to. People in Harmony or on the Peninsula are pretty much the same as in the Empire. Maybe a little more open, but it makes sense to trust people at first. Most of the time, anyway."

"That's an odd way of putting it."

"Not really. It's something the Prime emphasizes. I guess every Prime has. It goes with the job. If you distrust people, they pick up on it, and that leads them to distrust you. Since human society is based on trust, and since the greater the reinforced trust, the freer a society can be, it makes sense to create a society where trust is reinforced. That's one of the perpetual conflicts between the Institute and the politicians."

Sylvia raised her eyebrows, gray eyes inquiring.

"Politicians want to nail everything down. If there's a murder or a scandal, they immediately want to make another law, conduct another study, do *something* to prove it isn't their fault. All those laws reduce freedom and trust."

"How does the Institute handle it?"

"We tell the truth. If we don't want to say more, we don't. We try not to mislead."

"That's why you limited my briefing to the actual facts?"

"The Prime was insistent that you not have his speculations or mine. He's worried enough that he wants you as an independent check, and that means that the stakes are high. He's afraid our background may mislead us."

"A definite backhanded compliment." Sylvia's lips quirked. "And what does the Institute do to its own members who violate such high principles?"

"Effectively, either exile or death, depending on the severity of the problem. We impose the same standard on the politicians."

Sylvia winced.

"Look, if you want people to trust one another, you have to protect them from those who abuse their trust. Personal profiles indicate most people don't change, and you have to base a society on the most probable patterns. Trying to create formalized exemptions only encourages people to find other ways to abuse trust legally. The Institute has to set and maintain a higher standard. That's part of the reason why we don't engage in politics. That's why an economic study that's a cover still has to be first rate."

"The other parts?" she asked.

"No matter what anyone says, politics doesn't work without compromise. Most people aren't strong enough to not be affected by the continuing pressure of daily compromise. Politicians are generally worse than the average person because they need the adulation, and that makes them more susceptible to ethical compromise and abuse of the public trust. The Institute acts as a brake, partly by example, and partly because the politicians know we reserve the right to protect the public interest. That's why we have to follow the Iron Rules. That's the Ecolitan Enigma—the riddle of how to maintain enough power to ensure ethics, yet not to be corrupted by that power."

"You reserve the perpetual right to overthrow the government? That's worse—"

"No. Not the government. Not the form of government. We reserve the right to remove any politician who abuses public trust or who would narrow the institutional freedoms set forth by the Charter."

"That's worse meddling in politics than running for office."

Nathaniel shook his head. "It's happened five times in four centuries. The Institute doesn't like to exercise that power, and every Prime who has done so resigned immediately. Two voluntarily exiled themselves."

"The threat of such a power has to be chilling. I don't know."

"It is chilling," Nathaniel admitted. "It's intended to be. The first post-Secession Prime made the point that government must always serve all the people, not just a handful and not the other way around, and that the Institute would guarantee that balance."

"I still don't know." Sylvia shook her head.

"You're right to question. I did at first." Nathaniel hesitated, wondering whether to hit her with the rest of it. He swallowed before he spoke. "There's more."

"More?"

"The Institute reserves the right to act first, as we did on Old Earth." He rushed on, wanting to get it over with. "Look, historically, governments and people are reactive. They have to depend on popular consensus of some sort. That means that when a tyrant or a madman or a system looks evil, they have to wait. It's been the same throughout history. There's this feeling that you can't use applied or deadly force to head off a disaster because you can't absolutely prove there will be a disaster. So . . . Accord couldn't act against the Empire in the Secession until the Empire destroyed the entire planet of Sligo and millions of people. In the Marundan rebellion, the Empire couldn't act until after five million Mareks had been slaughtered in Marunda's processing camps. Yet Marunda had published a manifesto detailing his plans. There was already documentation of over fifty thousand deaths. The Imperial Senate refused to act." Nathaniel shrugged.

"You're telling me that you—the Institute—has the almighty wisdom to predict the future?" Her eyebrows rose.

"Not always. Sometimes. We . . . assassinated two dozen radical political operatives being supplied by the Empire on Hernando. It prevented a coup and bloody civil war. The system is regenerating." He shrugged. "It seems to me that doing that was better than military action after thousands were killed."

"That's like playing god."

"Is it? Is it worse to do nothing so that you can claim you are justified to act after thousands or millions die? When even more people die and suffer?"

Sylvia shook her head. "Delusions of grandeur."

"Why do you think the standards are so high for Ecolitans? We don't take it lightly. We're willing to take responsibility for acting before the fact. Sometimes, we're wrong. So is everybody. But if we're wrong, a few people die. Following the traditional course ensures that thousands and millions die."

"I can't believe you're saying this." She glanced out across the flower beds. "Governments can't do that. They're designed with checks and balances."

"The Institute isn't a government, and we are a check on governments. The checks on governments are largely designed to preserve their institutional acceptability to the public. That means a government can do anything its people don't actively oppose—like massacring millions of dissidents, taking over powerless adjoining systems, and killing any troops that oppose them."

"You're implying that people are responsible for the actions of their government, no matter how despotic and tyrannical."

"Sylvia, has any government ever stood against a people where a majority were actively willing to fight against it? There isn't an instance in recorded history." He shrugged. "If a people has the means to stop a slaughter, warfare, or whatever . . . and doesn't . . . if they allow the government to carry out atrocities, don't they share in the responsibility?"

"How would they know?"

"There's no legal system anywhere, that I know of, where participation in a crime is excused out of ignorance."

"Either you're crazy, or I am." Sylvia shook her head. "I don't know."

Nathaniel forced a laugh. "Sorry. I'm too much of an ethical evangelist, and I'm throwing too much at you too quickly. Back to the Artos problem?"

His question got a nod from Sylvia . . . a very tentative nod. She was clearly stunned at his statements, but saying more wouldn't help, not now.

"I can't believe that the Avalonians want an Ecolitan economist, except as a cover, and we don't know what the study is a cover for. Who uses economic studies, anyway?" Nathaniel shifted his weight on the bench, all too conscious of the mixed fragrances of orange and trilia.

"They don't say *why* they need this study."

"No, they don't. There are several possibilities. First, the government needs an outside evaluation that will be impartial. The Institute's impartiality is recognized, enough that almost fifteen percent of our income is derived from that sort of consulting."

"That much?"

"It's not widely talked about because those who use us don't want to admit they can't trust their own people to be objective and because if we advertised, that would destroy some of the basis of that impartiality." He offered a wry smile. "Second, it's a test for something bigger, to see how good we are and to give them a feel. The Institute hasn't done any projects for New Avalon in more than a century, and there may be some hard feelings from the Trezenian mess."

"Accord backed the rebels, rather successfully, I recall."

"No, the Institute did. The Coordinate looked the other way."

"How? Why?"

"The New Avalonian government had imposed an Imperial-style re-education team on the planet. We don't like that, and the local merchants offered to pay us and grant an open-trade agreement to the Institute and Accord. We insisted on a veto power over any provisions of their proposed constitutional charter we thought were too restrictive."

"You do meddle in other people's politics. All the time, it seems."

"Not exactly. We don't insist on copies of our system. Our price is always the same. Freedom of the people to choose their government, but with the unconditional freedom of people to leave."

"That's meddling."

"I suppose so, but we make no secret about it. Those are our terms up front. Anyway, the fact that the New Avalon government would hire us—or even allow us on Artos right now—either means that they have a large economic problem or that they want somehow to use the study against the Institute or that there's an even bigger problem lurking in the background. That's what we suspect, something to do with all the systems bordering the Three System Bulge. But we don't *know*. Or there's something we haven't figured out yet. Or some combination of the above—all of which pose serious external diseconomies."

"You're sounding like an economist again. But you keep skipping over the other more personally nasty options."

"Such as?"

"Providing a way to get rid of you permanently. Or setting you up to prove how dangerous Accord really is to the entire human Galaxy. You've just admitted that the Institute is the most dangerous institution in the Galaxy to every single government."

"You think big," he said with a laugh. "But I'm not that important. Even the Institute isn't."

"It's more deadly than I ever imagined, and I'm not exactly sheltered, Nathaniel. If these unknown forces can show that as a symbol . . . symbols move people, and even the Institute couldn't stand against the massed forces of the Empire and its neighbors."

"Do all former associates of the I.I.S.—"

Sylvia firmly and gently put her forefinger to his lips. "You said my past was past, and you're assuming too much."

"All right," he said as his fingers closed around hers and removed them. "With all these nasty options, do you still want to go to Artos?"

"Of course. I told you I intended to pull my weight. Besides, some-one has to go along and put a check on your delusions of grandeur.

Finally, you're not used to the subtleties of prolonged intrigue, and this sounds like it's very intriguing."

"Terrible pun."

"Awful, not terrible."

"I did all right on Old Earth."

"After you confused people with a great and excessive amount of applied force." Sylvia forced a grin.

He shrugged. "I stand corrected. As usual."

Sylvia leaned over and kissed his cheek, almost fraternally. "I like that about you, too. In spite of your misguided ethics."

Nathaniel wanted to kiss her back, more enthusiastically. Instead, he returned the kiss, equally fraternally. Despite her facade of warmth and charm, he'd definitely upset her. But if he didn't let her know, up front, then the eventual disillusionment would be worse, far worse. Once again, which was the lesser of the evils? He'd taken the Ecolitan way, preempting the issues, but would she see it in that light?

VII

"THINGS DON'T LOOK that much better, even with the Accord mess defused," announced the I.I.S. Director, her eyes flicking around the small circular conference table to each of the three others in turn.

"Why not?" asked the redheaded man whose eyes the Director had caught last.

"We still have the Matriarchy, Orknarli, Olympia, and New Avalon talking about formalizing their informal mutual defense agreements. The Franks and the Federated Hegemony have all but finalized a customs, infotech, and defense union. And the popinjays in Tinhorn haven't changed in four hundred years."

"So whom do you think that the Grand Admiral will push against next?" asked the blond.

The Director tapped the terminal plate and waited.

"With the simplified assumptions noted in the appendices, the probability of some form of armed conflict between the Empire and an out-system coalition within twelve standard calendar months approaches unity." The terminal voice was melodic, yet firm, but the words were too evenly spaced to be human.

"Rank the probabilities," ordered the Director.

"Probability of conflict with Halstan-Reformed GraeAnglish systems thirty-seven percent. Probability of conflict with RomanoFrank systems twenty-eight percent. Probability of conflict with Coordinate of Accord twenty-five percent. Probability of conflict with Fuardian Conglomerate twenty-three percent. Other conflictual probabilities individually are less than five percent."

"I *know* probabilities aren't additive," said the redhead, "but I get nervous when they total more than a hundred percent. The probability for Accord bothers me. Why is it that high after everything we just went through? Is that the Grand Admiral's influence?"

"Admiral Ku-Smythe is an old-style, power-is-everything militarist, but the Admiral has some basic political sense," answered the dark-haired woman. "So long as the Admiral holds the eagles, that will reduce the probability of conflict with Accord."

"The Admiral also has a daughter with more than basic political sense . . . and connections," added the Director. "And they talk."

"The way the younger Ku-Smythe eased out that idiot Rotoller and got him replaced by Fergus was brilliant."

"Envoy Whaler took care of most of that," pointed out the Director. "He also alerted every outsystem to Commerce's power play, and strengthened the Emperor's hand."

"I don't like the way he manipulated Ferro-Maine into going with him," said the blond.

"That wasn't manipulation. It was love, and more intelligence has been torqued over by hormones than we'd want to integrate. Even the Imperial Intelligence Service can't stop love." The Director's tone was dry. "If she had to go anywhere, better Accord than Halstan."

"Love or not, I don't like it."

"What additional harm can it do?" asked the dark-haired assistant director. "He's a part-time professor, part-time agent who's pulled off a major coup for Accord. She's a former dancer and part-time agent who's wanted to get off Old Earth for nearly a decade. Good as he is, and much as she knows . . . there's no problem out there that's likely to draw them in. And if there is, who else would you rather have involved? Accord doesn't want war, at least the Institute doesn't—"

"What about the probabilities of the Coordinate government trying to dump the Institute?"

"They're high," admitted the Director. "We can't quantify that, but," she added with a laugh, "the Coordinate politicians have been trying that ever since the Secession. So far, the Institute's outmaneuvered or outpowered them."

"It's scary how much power the Ecolitans wield," said the redhead. "There's no way to touch them?"

"They have the capability to annihilate the ecology of every human world in the Galaxy. Their ships and bases are so small and so dispersed over so many systems and light-years that no one could find them." The Director paused. "Would you care to take them on?"

"That just makes them worse."

"Accord would be even scarier without them. That nut Quaestor would hold their House of Delegates and have the whole Rift in conflict. However, I'm more worried about what we don't see." The Director glanced around the table. "Like the Hands of the Matriarch, or the goose-stepping popinjays in Tinhorn, or the separatists in the Federated Hegemony."

"What about Marshal Illydara and his fixation on expanding the Three System Bulge?" asked the blond. "Won't that drag in New Avalon?"

"The Fuards have been agitating about that since before the Ecologic Rebellion. What else is new? Besides, it's three sectors away," said the assistant director.

"I just have a feeling."

The Director gave the slightest of nods, but remained silent.

"We can't afford to go on feelings," answered the assistant director.

"We still need to consider the Matriarchy problem first." The Director glanced around the table. "Stats says that infotech traffic between New Avalon and Anarra has increased by nearly fifty percent over the last two years. The traffic between the Fuardian conglomerate and New Avalon is also up, but only about twenty percent."

"Those are big jumps in information technology transfers."

"They are, aren't they?" asked the Director dryly. "Infotech transfer increases of those magnitudes usually go with trouble."

VIII

NATHANIEL STEPPED OUTSIDE the shuttle flitter into the glare of Artos, automatically slitting his eyes and studying the sun-bleached white permacrete that intensified the nearblinding light. His fingers touched the shoulder strap of the datacase.

"It's bright here," said Sylvia.

"Too bright." His eyes slowly adjusting, the Ecolitan took the two steps down off the shuttle and onto the permacrete. Less than a hundred meters away stood the receiving building, white-walled with a vaulted roof. Artos had a bare-bones orbit control station, enough for only four ships, and just a handful of comm-relay satellites, indications of the relative poverty of the system—and another part of the enigma behind the infrastructure study.

Matching Nathaniel's longer strides, Sylvia moved across the permacrete. Both wore the lightweight field greens of the Institute.

He took a deep breath, then another, wondering if he hadn't recovered as thoroughly as he had thought, before he remembered. Sea-level atmospheric pressure on Artos was only eighty-five percent of T-Norm, and oxygen content was a shade over sixteen percent. Carbon dioxide levels were triple those on Accord but well below any concern for acidosis. In short, he and Sylvia shouldn't expect good performance in running marathons.

Behind them came Geoffrey Evanston, the New Avalonian businessman, in a summer jacket, cravat, and white knee shorts and socks above matching white sandals. After Evanston ambled Jimson Sonderssen, the agricultural-technology factor from the Federated Hegemony, and the half dozen others that had come down from the *Elizabeth the Great*, former flag of the Wendsor Lines now reduced to outsystem colony traffic.

A light and hot wind blew out of the west, carrying the odors of dust, decaying vegetation, half-burned hydrocarbons of some sort, and an unidentifiable fruity odor.

"Pungent, too," Nathaniel added.

"The fruit smells like berries."

Not exactly, but Nathaniel couldn't identify it, and his eyes flicked to the building ahead on the edge of the permacrete apron.

A squat man in a white uniformed jacket with silver epaulets, also wearing white shorts and socks and glistening white shoes, stepped forward out of the shade as the two Ecolitans neared the portal under the Receiving and Customs sign. "Professor Whaler?"

"The same," replied Nathaniel in formal English, rather than the more colloquial and divergent Old American of Accord.

"I am Robert Walkerson, the Port Chief here at Artos." He offered a shallow and stiff bow. "Minister Spencer-Hawkes has requested that I do everything possible to assist you in your study."

"Most kind of you." Nathaniel paused. "Minister Spencer-Hawkes? I was under the impression that—"

"Quite right, sir. The Commerce Ministry requisitioned your study, but the coordination of arrangements for an outsystem dignitary falls under Defence Security. Port Authority falls under Defence."

"I am but an economist." Nathaniel belatedly turned to Sylvia. "This is Ms. Ferro-Maine, my assistant. Her specialty is institutional structures." Nathaniel added, "I know. The traditional wisdom is that developing economies have no institutional structures. They do. What they do not have is labels."

"You are also a dignitary, a former Trade Envoy to the Empire, and someone Artos is pleased to welcome." Walkerson offered a perfunctory smile. "If you would please follow me. I must apologize, but Artos is less than a century out of stage two planoforming, and rather primitive. Also rather . . . quiet. Very little occurs here."

"It is far more structured than many places I've been," answered Nathaniel. He could use some quiet, but he wondered if they'd actually get it.

"You are too kind. Too kind." Walkerson cleared his throat and stepped through the open doorway.

Inside, out of the glare, Walkerson nodded to the uniformed man and woman behind the inspection consoles. "The Ecolitans are cleared."

Both nodded stiffly as the three walked past the consoles and to the far end of the long room where a moving belt inched along in a circle. Beyond the belt was another set of consoles, each with two uniformed figures, each armed with stunners.

"As soon as your bags arrive, we shall be on our way. You'll be quartered at the Ministry Guest House—much better than at the Blue Lion. That is our local hotel, and not much better than an outback horse station."

"Horses?" asked Sylvia.

"We use them in some regions. They are ever so much more efficient than fuel-burners in certain applications, and there is certainly more than enough fodder here. There will be for centuries to come, although we do hope that you two will be able to pinpoint areas to speed our industrialization process."

"Infrastructure economics does not always promise speed," Nathaniel answered. "We hope to identify optimal resource use patterns and suggest structural change options for developmental alternatives." He shook his head. "I have been in the classroom too long. We will attempt to discern the least expensive manner in which to reach your goals. Not one that is penny-wise and pound-foolish, however."

The Artosan port officer gave a barking laugh. "Quite so. Quite so."

With a thump, a field pack appeared on the black fabric of the belt, followed by a second thump and second bag. The Ecolitans picked up their bags, Nathaniel using his right hand, Sylvia her left.

"If you wouldn't mind just putting the bags under the scanners there . . . ?" ventured Walkerson. "And your cases?"

"Not at all." Nathaniel slipped his pack, then the datacase, under the right hand scanner, as Sylvia did the same under the left.

"Clean, sir," said the woman scanner operator to Walkerson.

"Good." The Port Chief nodded toward the old-style glass door behind the scanners and the four security types. "Shall we depart?"

Nathaniel held the door for Sylvia, using the moment to survey the area outside the receiving building. He didn't need a recurrence of his arrivals on Old Earth or Accord. The belt multitector showed no energy concentrations, and he could see nothing apparently out of the ordinary for a landing field—just a cracked permacrete circle of road, flanked with low bushes he didn't recognize, that led out to another highway. A long bus, repainted pale green, and two groundcars were parked in the circle.

The sky was bluish green—greener than that of Old Earth and bluer than that of Accord. Gray clouds piled up over the mountains to the north, and a hot wind blew out of the south, carrying a mildly acrid odor similar to ozone.

"The first car," said Walkerson.

The pale green groundcar waited, its engine idling—liquid hydrocarbon—fueled from the smell—the rear doors both open, as was the trunk.

"Your luggage can go in the boot," offered Walkerson.

"Thank you." The Ecolitan lifted his field pack into the trunk, or boot, as did Sylvia—not that either had that much luggage—a datacase and an Ecolitan fieldpack each. He fingered the boot release—a simple lever, without even a lock—then closed it, checking to see if it released at a turn. It did.

He caught the glint in Sylvia's eyes that said, "Suspicious man," more clearly than words, and answered, "Always."

"Good."

Walkerson smothered a quizzical look. "Then we're ready to depart?"

"We are proceeding into Lanceville?" asked Nathaniel, holding the rear door for Sylvia.

She offered a smile and slid across the bench seat to allow Nathaniel to sit without walking around the groundcar.

"Just outside Lanceville." The port official eased himself into the front seat, and nodded to the uniformed driver. "The Guest House, Helverson."

"Yes, sir."

"I'm glad you introduced me relatively early this time," Sylvia murmured.

"An absentminded professor am I, remember," he murmured back in stilted Panglais. "Though I try."

"That won't work here."

"Want to bet?"

Sylvia raised her eyebrows and bent close to his ear. "After he pointedly noted your accomplishments as an envoy to New Augusta?"

She was probably right, Nathaniel decided, but it was still worth a try to lower local expectations. The proverbs would help . . . he hoped.

As the driver eased away from the port building, from which none of the other shuttle passengers had yet emerged, Walkerson turned in the front seat to face the two Ecolitans.

"I really don't know what ship time you might be on, whether it's midday or at the end of three sleepless days."

"Near the end of one long day," said Sylvia after the briefest of pauses. "A very long day."

"A long day makes for deep sleep," added Nathaniel.

"We won't make it too much longer," promised the Avalonian.

Nathaniel looked out the scratched and tinted window, blotting his forehead and wondering when the groundcar's cooling system would kick in, or if it even had one. To the right of the highway was an expanse of low plants, with narrow dark green leaves and clusters of greenish purple globes—synde beans. "Are all your hydrocarbon needs provided from the beans?" he asked. "Or do you supplement them with other organics?"

Walkerson cleared his throat. "You know, professor, I couldn't say. Around the port area, we grow and process a lot of beans. There's a fuel-processing facility southwest of Lanceville, but I don't know what else they process or where it might come from. I just have the groundcar refueled."

"I did not perceive any broadcast power grids." Nathaniel tried again.

"We're still on a local area fusactor system. There are a number of areas not much beyond the oxy-creepers, second tier soil-fixing. They say we'll need another ten to twenty years of iron-feeding the seas to stimulate algal oxygenation."

"You could get too extensive a bloom."

"They talk about that, but so far the basking shark-mods are taking care of that. They are ugly and rather large."

"Rather large?" asked Sylvia. "Is that Avalonian understatement?"

As he blotted his forehead again, Nathaniel continued to smell fuel—raw hydrocarbon. His fingers flicked to his belt. "Stop the car! Out!"

After a quick glance at the Ecolitan, Walkerson nodded to the driver.

Nathaniel jumped out, almost before the groundcar eased to a halt on the highway shoulder, next to a ditch that separated the highway from the synde bean fields. He fumbled open the boot and grabbed the field packs. Almost on the run, he threw the packs behind the car, yanked open the front door, and jerked the Port Chief from the front seat.

"What the—" Walkerson looked more bewildered than angry.

Crack! Whooshhh! The bonnet erupted into a sheet of flame that flared across the entire front of the vehicle.

Sylvia dashed toward the driver's side, then abruptly darted back. She slipped toward the driver again, then retreated and crossed behind the vehicle, rejoining Whaler and Walkerson and shaking her head.

"Dead?" asked Nathaniel.

"Helverson is? He couldn't be. That wouldn't be proper," protested the Avalonian. "Not at all."

"I'm afraid he is," Sylvia said. "It looked like shards of something across his neck and chest. There was blood everywhere." She swallowed and looked at the ground.

"It can't be!" Walkerson circled the blazing vehicle and dashed toward the driver's door . . . once, twice, before returning to where the Ecolitans stood by their packs on the shoulder of the road behind the blazing mass of plastic and metal.

"You were right," the Port Chief admitted, "but I don't see how something so awful could have happened like that."

As the rest of the groundcar burned hotter, the three backed away farther, the Ecolitans lifting and carrying their field packs another twenty meters back toward the shuttle port facility. Walkerson circled the groundcar again, then looked back down the highway toward the shuttle port.

"Was it wise to go for the packs?" asked Sylvia in a voice shielded by the crackling of the flames.

"This was an accident. So it had to be a fuel spark of some sort, except that synthoil takes a high jolt. And I prefer my own clothes."

"I think you prefer everything your own way."

"Don't we all?" he asked with a harsh laugh, wondering if he should have pointed that out.

Walkerson rejoined them. "The bus should be along momentarily. It has a comm unit, and it goes right past the Guest House. I'm most awfully sorry about this. Poor Helverson. How . . ."

"It was certainly not your fault," Nathaniel pointed out. "I am most sorry about your man."

"I just do not . . ." Walkerson shook his head again. "An engine fire . . . but an explosion . . . I . . ."

A long green shape appeared on the permacrete.

Whhheeeppp!

The bus pulled up, and the driver leaned out. "What happened, chief?"

"Some sort of engine malfunction. The entire front bonnet went to flames. I fear Helverson was killed instantly. We tried, but couldn't get him out. Professor Ferro-Maine tried and so did I, but he was dead on the spot." Walkerson wiped his sooty forehead. "Might I use your comm, N'Trosian?"

"Hop on. I'll drop you at the Guest House, and you can ring Cen-Comm from there."

"Your comm is still malfunctioning?" asked Walkerson.

"Still, chief? I've been on you about that for weeks. No spares. No spares ordered." The dark-skinned driver nodded to the Ecolitans. "Folks, best you climb aboard. There's nothing else going your way."

Whaler and Sylvia sank into the narrow plastic-covered seat in the third row, behind Jimson Sonderssen, the Hegemony agri-tech factor. Nathaniel blotted his still-sweating forehead and looked down at his field pack for a moment.

The deeply tanned, tall and lanky factor, whose hair was half blond, half white, turned in the seat and gestured toward the smoldering groundcar wreck that the bus was leaving behind. "Hot enough for you, was it not enough already?"

"It was hot enough." Nathaniel admitted, shaking his head. "Far too hot, and this sort of event we do not welcome or need."

"And you?" Sonderssen inclined his head to Sylvia.

"I agree with the professor."

"You see, Professor Whaler, Professor Ferro-Maine, the sad state of our transport infrastructure," offered Geoffrey Evanston from several seats back. "What groundcars we have are few and in poor condition, yet the government will neither ship more nor sanction deep minerals development or asteroid drops to support local manufacture."

"I will keep your observations in mind."

"All other things being equal?" asked Evanston.

"But of course," answered Whaler with a smile. "I am not a one-handed economist."

"Perhaps there should be some."

Sylvia smothered a quizzical look with a bright smile.

Port Chief Walkerson sat on the seat behind the driver, looking stolidly at the white strip of permacrete ahead, glistening in the afternoon sun as the bus rumbled eastward toward Lanceville.

The Guest House boasted white plastered walls, a pale red-tiled roof, and a cooling system, Nathaniel noted with relief as they stepped inside the white-lacquered front doorway.

"This is the Guest House, such as it is," announced Walkerson. "The lounge is to the right, the dining salon to the left. The stairs lead to the quarters. If you don't mind the haste, I'll get you to your rooms, and then leave you for a bit while I deal with the accident."

"Of course."

They followed the Avalonian official up the antique tiled steps to the second floor and to the far end of the polished tiled floor. Each of the ceramic tiles bore the imprint of a horned beast.

"These are rather unique tiles," Nathaniel offered.

"Unicorn tiles, made here on Artos." Walkerson halted between a pair of white-lacquered doors with bronze lever handles. He opened the door on the right and then the left. "Two adjoining rooms, with separate refresher facilities—that was what you requested."

"Exactly," said Nathaniel.

"Thank you," added Sylvia.

"I imagine you two would like a chance to refresh and change. Then, I'll join you for tea in the small lounge, and then, shall we say, a briefing on our situation here." Walkerson flashed another perfunctory smile. "I need to report on the accident. Terrible thing. Terrible thing." He turned to Whaler. "You said you smelled fuel?"

"I perceived some odor when we entered the vehicle," Nathaniel said, pulling at his chin thoughtfully. "I considered that it might have been my imagination after all the space travel or that it might have been the vehicle engine. We employ electro-vehicles for ground transport, and I am not familiar with fuelburners. After we had proceeded a ways, however, my perceptions become noticeably more distinct. That most assuredly should not have occurred. That was when I suggested that we depart the vehicle. At that point in time, I thought I saw an electrical spark or the equivalent, but I was not absolutely certain. That was when the hood was enveloped in flame." The Ecolitan shrugged.

"Did you see anything else, Ms. Ferro-Maine? Or should I call you Ecolitan Ferro-Maine?"

"Whatever's comfortable, Mr. Walkerson, or is it captain or chief?"

"Most call me Walker or chief."

"Walker, then," Sylvia offered. "I can't add much. There's something in the air here, allergens maybe, and I'm not smelling things very well. I did see a glint of flame or sparks, and I ran up to try to help your man out, but . . . I told you. He was already dead. There was a huge gash in his neck, and . . ."

"I'll have the maintenance team check it out." Walkerson shook his head. "I still can't believe it."

Nathaniel had the sinking feeling that he could, at least to the degree that disaster seemed to be following him. How could he anticipate and act when he still hadn't figured out who was involved?

"Until tea, then."

"Until tea," Sylvia confirmed.

Nathaniel stepped into the first room, which contained a large bed with an off-white comforter spread, a table that could double as a desk, two pressed-wood armchairs, and a large window framed in white curtains that matched the comforter. Sliding doors concealed a closet, and an open door showed an old-style fresher room.

He played the belt detector around the room. Surprisingly, the room registered clean, except for the equipment concealed in the sides of his own datacase and Sylvia's.

"Adjoining rooms?" Sylvia raised her eyebrows.

"Someone told me that she thought she loved me, and I didn't want to rush matters."

"Who said I even wanted adjoining rooms?" A mischievous smile flickered across her lips.

Nathaniel threw up his hands. "A poor struggling professor am I," he said in Panglais, "and arrangements I make the best I can."

"You still might pull that off." The smile vanished, and Sylvia shook her head. "I don't like it."

"No snoops?"

She nodded.

"This actually might be what they contracted for."

Her eyebrows went up again.

"Foolish of me to think that, I suppose?"

"Not foolish, but improbable."

In addition to the door from each room to the hallway, an inside door connected the two rooms. Nathaniel stepped toward the interior door.

"I see," said Sylvia, looking pointedly at the interior door that had been left ajar.

"I didn't say a word. It's the polite New Avalonian way of covering all alternatives." Nathaniel momentarily raised his hands in protest as he stepped into the second room with his belt detector. "Clean here, too," he added after a moment.

"I like this less and less."

"Maybe it's not the Avalonians," Nathaniel murmured.

"The native Artosans here? Or the long arm of the Empire? Or some outsystem?"

The taller Ecolitan shrugged. "As a poor struggling professor must I consider the alternatives."

"A small amount of that dialogue travels a long way."

"Yet journeys of light-years, they begin with but one pace."

Sylvia mock-glared.

Nathaniel grinned.

"I'm cleaning up, dear Envoy. You may do as you please, but I do not intend to continue to look like a frump." She gestured toward the connecting door.

"The message I have received." He backed away, then stepped through the door, which closed with a distinct *thump*. The Ecolitan shook his head. The way everything was going, resolving the trade wars between the Coordinate and the Empire and getting Sylvia out of the Empire had been simple. Now, they not only had to worry about conducting a study and resolving the problems behind it, but he had to worry about Sylvia's mindset that morality required millions of dead bodies before drastic action could be taken.

He'd been at the Institute too long. That was the way most people thought, and being reminded of it by someone you cared for was a shock.

He pursed his lips.

Or was it that the current unsolved problems always seemed more insurmountable than the past difficulties that had already been resolved? He took a long, slow, deep breath before heading for his own fresher.

Later, with a clean set of greens on, a smooth face, and all the grime removed by a fresher spray not much more sophisticated than a ancient shower, Nathaniel rapped on the connecting door. "Time to head down to the lounge."

"In a moment."

"Let me know." He'd barely seated himself in one of the chairs when Sylvia stepped through the door, carrying her datacase.

"I'm ready for high tea. I'm hungry."

"Also am I," he offered in mock seriousness.

She rolled her eyes.

Whaler picked up his own case, then opened the door, noting that the room had no external locks.

"Trusting types, or they want us to be trusting," said Sylvia.

"Colony planets are often that way. They just execute thieves. It has a rather convincing effect on honesty, even if a few innocents pay as well."

"Someone always pays."

Their boots echoed on the polished unicorn tiles as they walked toward the steps and down them to the main floor.

"The lounge is to the left," he offered.

"I recall."

Why was he always putting his field boots in his mouth? Sylvia knew where the lounge was. He'd just been making conversation, and he was coming off as incredibly patronizing.

"I'm sorry," she said softly, reaching out and squeezing his hand. "You didn't mean it that way."

"Thank you." He smiled. "I was trying to fill the awkwardness, and . . . I'm not very good at small talk that's not intellectual, and there . . ." He shook his head.

"Unless you're playing a role," she added. "You're good at that, but I get the feeling you don't enjoy it with people you like."

"Right."

Sylvia knew more about him from a relatively short period of casual observation—or was it casual?—than he'd ever expected.

They stepped through the green-curtained archway into a room that could have been transported from centuries past, with dark wooden tables and matching chairs upholstered in a green velvetlike material. A silver tea service sat upon the wooden cart beside the white-linened circular table, where Robert Walkerson sat facing the doorway. The other tables were vacant.

The port officer rose as they entered the room. "I can see that you two are looking more chipper."

The two Ecolitans took seats on either side of Walkerson, who sat down and gestured toward the tea cart. "Tea or liftea?"

"Liftea," answered Nathaniel.

"The same," murmured Sylvia.

"It's not the same as real Avalonian tea."

"Nothing, I have heard, quite resembles the tea of New Avalon, nor the effect it has on those who are unused to it." Nathaniel inclined his head.

"Try some of the cakes." Walkerson nodded toward the circular platter in the middle of the table.

"Did you find out how it happened?" Nathaniel glanced at the handful of cakes in the middle of the green-rimmed, off-white china platter. Two were round and white, several were dark and square, and one had white icing with green stripes.

"Ryster-Jeeves found what looked to be a leak in the fuel line. With all the damage and the heat, it's hard to tell, but he thinks it was metal fatigue. Our groundcars here aren't new, and you know what it costs to ship them. We don't have that kind of manufacturing up yet."

"There's not much in the way of mining," said Sylvia. "How much of a problem is that?"

"Artos doesn't have satellites and no real hydrocarbons in its geologic past. Metals mining has to go deep." The Avalonian lifted his cup and inhaled the steam. "We do get some good tea, but it's chancy yet, and it's from under plastic."

"That looks to be good china. Might it be local?" asked Nathaniel.

"It is. Off the highlands of the back continent. Gheric-Shrews found it, but it's more of a hobby for her than honest commerce."

Nathaniel tried a small brown cake, the one with green-and-white striped icing, forcing himself to eat it slowly, while not gagging on a texture that seemed heavily saturated with a rather raw substitute for rum.

"Potent, those are."

"I agree." The Ecolitan took a long sip of liftea.

Sylvia tried a white cake, and from her polite and small mouthfuls, Nathaniel suspected her choice had been little better than his.

"Did they determine what occurred to your man?"

"The explosion drove glass fragments through him. Ugly. Very ugly." The Port Chief shook his head. "I can't believe Helverson's dead. He seemed such a nice young fellow, and he was fresh from New Brista."

"Most tragic." Nathaniel shook his head. "All too often, inadequate capital investment is paid for in the currency of human life."

"That would be an odd way of putting it." Walkerson's tone was even, almost flat.

"Governments are fond of that," Nathaniel answered. "It is often easier to explain away loss of life with greater facility than investment of credits and resources. When they do not wish to provide sufficient capital assets—whether groundcars, flitters, or fusactors—those under pressure to complete the task at hand are put at greater risk. Some die who would not do so otherwise." The Ecolitan shrugged. "All those involved shake their heads sadly, decry the tragedy, and continue to undercapitalize the venture."

"You've seen it before, I see."

"In many places," Nathaniel agreed. "Gold makes honest men thieves."

"Do you share your colleague's cynicism, Ecolitan Ferro-Maine?" Walkerson turned to Sylvia.

"I'd have to say that Professor Whaler is being extraordinarily polite in his phrasing. Governments prefer to spend lives rather than credits." Sylvia took a sip of her liftea.

"About this survey," ventured Walkerson after the silence had filled the lounge. "Where will you begin?"

"With a quick survey of the transportation infrastructure, the broad infrastructure, and that of energy supplies and distribution."

"Dare you say you won't find anything out of the ordinary for a place just out of planoforming. I'd guess it shouldn't take you that long." Walkerson offered a chuckle. "You're high-priced, and I'd wager that means you'll hurry."

"It can be difficult to estimate a timetable even before the field work begins." Whaler smiled. "With the high cost of interstellar transport, we certainly can take the time necessary for a thorough effort. To do less would not be cost-effective, and as an economist . . ." He offered a shrug, trying to ignore the smothered smile from Sylvia.

"Of course, of course. We wouldn't expect anything less from the Institute and the Coordinate."

A woman in a green-and-maroon tunic appeared in the curtained doorway. "Any time you are ready, dinner is available."

"Old Reeves-Kenn sent over a side for dinner." Walkerson offered a strained grin. "I trust you two won't mind if I join you."

"Not at all." Sylvia returned his grin with a smile. "Not at all."

The Port Chief rose and touched the back of Sylvia's chair. She let him slide it away from the table before rising in her dancer's gracefulness.

The dining room was almost the same in layout as the lounge, and as empty—except that the tables were set with antique silver, and more china.

A small wilted green salad smothered in oil lay beside each diner's plate, and on each plate was a green napkin. Nathaniel slipped his napkin onto his lap, feeling the slickness of crude polyester fabric.

The serving woman slipped large china platters before the three, beginning with Sylvia. On each plate were heaped slabs of rare meat and an old white lump that looked like a fallen souffle.

"Local beef," said Walkerson. "Say it's better than the best even on Olympia. One of the few organics that people will pay to transship, and not much of that."

Nathaniel nodded. "There never was much bulk cargo traffic, and it seems like there's even less these days." He cut a small bite of the beef, and chewed, not that he had to work, since the meat practically melted in his mouth.

"It's all ultra-tech or information technology traffic. We wouldn't have that except jumpshifting's a few hundred years faster than beam traffic."

"Why was Artos planoformed in the first place?" asked Sylvia. "The records aren't exactly clear . . ."

Walkerson finished a mouthful of the beef. "Who could say these days? It was started back under the House of Spenser, when there was the hope that the Barna-Barltrop jump generators would allow cheaper travel. They did . . ."

"But not enough," finished Nathaniel.

"Then land got so expensive on New Avalon, Hibernia, and the older planets that the agricultural processors pushed for Artos."

"Foods won't pay for planoforming. They can't even be shipped profitably, except as a luxury good, and you can't ship enough beef or anything agricultural to create a fraction of the revenue—" said Sylvia.

"Perhaps it was the way of life," offered Nathaniel, glancing at the Avalonian.

"Right on, professor. The old agricultural types ran the system, and they persuaded the High Council . . . and the rest is history." Walkerson hacked off another chunk of beef and chewed heartily.

"They are not so powerful . . . now?"

"No," mumbled Walkerson. "High-tech interests, like everywhere . . . they hold the High Council now, not that you could prove it."

Nathaniel wanted to nod and shake his head simultaneously. As with everything else he'd ever done for the Institute, the complexity was building faster than his understanding.

"With the current emphasis on direct-data injection," Sylvia said, "I imagine that agricultural concerns on a planet barely post-planoforming take a low priority in Camelot."

"You saw the state of our groundcar," pointed out Walkerson. "It's like that with everything we can't manufacture here. Some of the locals, like Reeves-Kenn, are putting credits into developing more of the infrastructure, but there aren't enough credits in a small economy to do everything that's needed, and Camelot hasn't cared for generations."

Nathaniel nodded and took a last bite of the tender beef. Hungry as he had been, he found himself unable to finish the huge slab of meat on his plate. Sylvia had eaten less than half of hers. Walkerson had left nothing, not even the soggy mass meant to have been a facsimile of ancient York pudding.

"You didn't finish it all. Good beef, Reeves-Kenn has. Right proud of it, he is, and with reason. His grandsire was the first to make it work—

started with embryos, he did, and made a fair shilling when there wasn't much else edible but hothouse sawdust and plasticframe soy."

"He sounds very successful," observed Sylvia.

"He is. The family owns twenty percent of ConOne here. The hydrocarb facility is mostly theirs, although a bunch of the other growers put up the credits, too."

"I had thought we might look at that facility. It might be a good place to commence." Nathaniel leaned back in his chair, feeling far too full. He'd barely gotten his weight back under control from the beating it had taken on the Old Earth mission, and that probably because of forced starvation in the Institute hospital, and here he was, overeating again.

"As you wish, professors." Walkerson glanced toward the archway.

Nathaniel took the hint. "We must not keep you too long, and we do need to recuperate ourselves."

"You've been most kind," added Sylvia.

"Only my job. But I should be running along. Madeline will be worrying." The Port Chief smiled and stood.

So did the Ecolitans, and the three walked slowly out of the apparently empty dining room and toward the main entrance.

"The replacement groundcar will be here tomorrow after breakfast. It's at your disposal until you leave, professors." Walkerson bowed. "A pleasure meeting you both, and I would hope to see your report, once it's completed."

"We will ensure you are among the first to see the infrastructure report." Nathaniel inclined his head.

With an overly broad smile, the Avalonian nodded and turned.

After the door closed, Nathaniel turned to Sylvia. "Tired? Ready to get some sleep?"

"Yes and yes."

The two climbed the stairs side by side, not meeting or passing anyone.

"I get the feeling that we're the only guests."

"I'm sure we are," Nathaniel answered. "I don't imagine Artos has that many official government-sanctioned visitors." He paused before opening the unlocked door to Sylvia's room, then held it, and stepped into the room behind her. "It was a good meal, better than the tea." He fingered his chin, not quite looking at her in the dimness—the only light diffused into the room from the hall lamps through the half-open door.

Sylvia pressed the plate at the base of the lamp on the table, set her datacase down, and turned back toward him. "And?"

"The beef—it shouldn't be that good, but I couldn't say why."

"You're thinking like an economist, trying to quantify everything."

"I am one, you know."

"A very good one, according to the official bio."

"A tired one," he admitted, closing the door to the corridor, sliding the bolt to the locked position, and looking toward the half-open door that joined the rooms.

"Me, too."

"Leave the door unlocked—the one . . ."

"I know which one you had in mind." She raised her fine, dark eyebrows.

"I worry."

Sylvia hugged him, then kissed his cheek. "I know, and you're right, and I won't lock it. But I'm tired, and . . . let's leave it there right now. Please?"

Nathaniel hugged her. "All right." He let go slowly, and her lips brushed his cheek again.

"Living happily ever after doesn't work as easily as the trideos say," she offered with a smile.

"I'm discovering that." He touched her hand, squeezed it briefly.

"Good night." Sylvia's words were warm, but firm.

He closed the door between the rooms gently and then groped his way to the light, shaking his head as he did. Stupid! He was behaving like a love-besotted bull, and it could get him killed. He set down his datacase on the table and looked to the bed where he'd left his field pack.

It had been searched, as he'd expected, and not well.

Later, with the lights out, Nathaniel lay back on the too-soft bed, simultaneously appreciating the cool air provided by the antique air conditioning and ignoring the continual whirring.

They'd been on Artos less than a day, and already someone had targeted them, with a well-planned "accident." Unlike the assassination attempt he'd weathered on his first day in New Augusta on Old Earth, which had been half attempt and half warning, the groundcar accident had been no warning. Then, neither had the attempt in Harmony.

Why? What was it that they weren't supposed to find—or see? And how many other accidents were waiting to happen? What could possibly be hidden on a colony planet barely out of planoforming? It couldn't be anything obviously technological or military. EDI concentrations could be spotted from orbit, and would be all too apparent. Besides which, the planet clearly didn't have the industrial basis to support a military establishment, and, even if it did, New Avalon certainly had the right to put military establishments wherever it pleased.

Rebels? That didn't make sense, either. The government wouldn't allow a survey if it were trying to hide a rebellion, and would have asked directly for assistance if it weren't. Then, was there an outside influence that New Avalon couldn't afford to note publicly? That didn't make sense. At least, he didn't feel it did, even if Artos did happen to be the key to controlling the Three System Bulge.

Or were Sylvia and the Prime right? Was someone out to get him? Or the Institute?

He shook his head slowly. He just wasn't that important. Anyone doing the "survey" would have been targeted. Wouldn't they?

He blinked, then yawned. Finally, he closed his eyes.

IX

IN THE MORNING, another pale green groundcar waited in the shade of the portico of the Guest House, the window of the driver's side open. A round-faced young man, black-haired and clean-shaven, sat behind the wheel, his eyes on the doors.

As the two Ecolitans stepped outside, the driver bounded out of the car and stepped around the bonnet to greet them. "Sirs! I'm Glubb Bagot, and the chief sent me to be your driver." The young man wore the white shorts, socks, and shoes of the port authority, but a green-and-white striped uniform shirt.

"Nathaniel Whaler, and this is Ecolitan Sylvia Ferro-Maine." Nathaniel tried not to wrinkle his nose at the pungency of the Artosan atmosphere—or was it because the Guest House was down-wind of some industrial or agricultural facility?

"The chief said you were in charge, professors. Where do you want to go?" Bagot offered an open smile.

"The synde bean fields, to see some in all stages, and from thence to the processing facility."

"Lots of bean fields, professor. They start over there, and they go for kilos in every direction." The driver gestured out past the portico and in the general westward direction. Between the edge of the road and the field, less than a hundred meters from the west side of the Guest House, two men worked on a fuel-burning tractor in the clear morning light.

Although his eyes followed Bagot's gesture, Nathaniel was well aware that his belt detector pulsed. He and Sylvia exchanged glances. More surveillance, but who . . . and why? Those handling the spying had to be locals; they were too obvious to be anything else, and that meant the Prime had been right about the study not being entirely desired by New Avalon—or by someone.

"Are there more toward Lanceville? Or are the majority farther out?"

"Some in just about every direction, sir." Glubb Bagot offered another guileless smile.

"Start toward Lanceville." Holding his datacase in his right hand, Nathaniel opened the rear door with his left, letting the detector scan the groundcar, but no energy flows beyond the normal registered.

With a bored expression, Sylvia slipped inside, sliding across the worn plastic to seat herself behind the driver and letting her datacase rest on her lap. Nathaniel took the other side of the rear seat, closing the door.

"Toward Lanceville it is, sirs." Glubb Bagot closed his own door and started the antique internal combustion engine. Gray smoke puffed from behind the boot.

The mechanical wheezing from under the bonnet, and the faint hint of air that was lukewarm as opposed to hot, indicated that the ground-car possessed some rudimentary cooling system. Despite the comparatively lightweight greens, Nathaniel blotted his forehead even before the vehicle was on the permacrete headed eastward.

The low, dark green plants filled roughly half the fields on both sides of the narrow road. In those fields not filled with beans grew falfamut, the legumelike nitrogen- and soil-fixing plant that also doubled as animal fodder. The combination provided an effective two-crop rotation that continually strengthened the soil and the atmosphere—provided that the rotation was equal, not something that always happened.

Ahead, Nathaniel could see a low and irregular skyline, shapes in various shades of gray—Lanceville.

"If you would pull over and halt here?" Nathaniel ventured.

"Sir?"

"Over by the field side," the sandy-haired Ecolitan said. "You halt the groundcar so I might inspect the beans."

"Yes, sir." A faintly quizzical expression crossed the young driver's face.

Once the car rumbled to a stop, Nathaniel slipped out and walked over to the row of synde beans, bending and studying the narrow, dark green leaves and clusters of greenish purple globes. The globes seemed the same as those varieties he'd seen at the Institute in his training years. Still, with a quick motion he flicked the tiny vidimager from his sleeve and, as he touched a leaf or two gently, recorded a series of images for future study.

Nathaniel walked back to the car, nodded to Sylvia, and then asked Bagot, "Are they harvesting anywhere?" He took out the large green kerchief and blotted his sweating forehead once more.

"Up near the lower Reeves-Kenn spread, I heard. That's a good hour."

"Fine. That will be fine." The Ecolitan stuffed the overlarge kerchief back in his pocket.

"You're in charge." With a quick look up and down the empty per-macrete strip, Bagot eased the groundcar one hundred eighty degrees back in the direction that they had come, easing the speed up, enough so that Nathaniel could actually feel a greater flow of cool air from the overworked cooling unit.

"How long have you been on Artos, Bagot?" asked Nathaniel.

"All my life, sir. Father worked for the Port Authority, too."

"I imagine you've seen a great deal of change."

"Not really, sir. Most of the bare ground is gone . . ." The driver paused as the green bus from the landing field lumbered past and eastward toward Lanceville. "Fewer shuttle drops these days."

"That usually happens when a planet first comes out of planoforming," Sylvia said.

"Sure has happened here, miss . . . I mean, professor. Except for a few times a year, like last winter when the new ag stuff came in, it's slow. Most times, it's weeks between ships. Sometimes months."

"New seed types?" asked Sylvia, "Or technology-transfer templates?"

"I wouldn't know. Probably seed or clone stuff. We don't have many manufacturing places that can take tech-templates. I heard Chief Walkerson talking about that once."

"They do on New Avalon," Nathaniel prompted. "I would consider it only prudent to invest in a limited capacity on Artos."

"Limited is right, sir. We're most limited here. The ocean fellows—

the Evanston family—they've put in a small tech-forming facility in Lanceville, but it's all for ocean farming. Lord, I'm tired of algaeburgers."

"I understand you do not sample the beef of the Reeves-Kenn establishment?" asked Nathaniel.

"Sample? That beef is for them and for the aristos and any outsystem wealthy enough to pay for it."

"But they do not have a tech-transfer facility," mused Sylvia.

"Don't want one, to my way of thinking. They still use horses on the wilder parts of their spread. That'd be what Jem is doing right about now."

"Jem?"

"My older brother. He's a rover for George Reeves-Kenn." Bagot shook his head.

For a time, Nathaniel just watched the fields blur past, noting that the vast majority were either synde beans or falfamut, although they did pass fields of other crops he did not immediately recognize, except for the ripening wheat. Then there were the tall green plants.

"Is that corn?"

"Maize? That's the tall stuff. We don't grow a lot of it. According to something I saw, it really upsets the water balance, and you've got to grow falfamut for three years out of four. Most of it's for the export beef—Reeves-Kenn outfit."

"Chief Walkerson said there was a lot of that exported."

"Not so much as when my dad worked at the port. I guess transstellar rates have gone up or something. Jem told me that last Boxing Day."

A long groundlorry, its gray metal cab pitted and rusted, rumbled past them, headed back toward Lanceville, three hopper pods on its flat trailer. The car swayed in the rush of air from the ag-carrier.

"Really moving, he is." Bagot shrugged.

"Haste, it makes waste," pontificated Whaler.

"They think they own the permacrete. I suppose they do. Not many groundcars left."

"Were there many when you were young?" asked Sylvia.

"More than now, but I don't guess there were ever a lot. My dad had one, because he was a checker, and he got called at odd hours. Maybe I thought everyone had one."

Nathaniel kept a pleasant smile on his face as they sped westward and as a second lorry whooshed past heading eastward and rocked the car once more.

The dust rising over the fields indicated the harvest efforts long before the groundcar was close enough for the Ecolitans to see the actual machinery. Sicklelike blades cut the plants perhaps twenty centimeters above ground. Oil pods and greenery dropped into a hopper-sorter, and from the hopper-sorter dropped a dark powder, the residue of the vegetation, while the pods went into the cargo bin. Behind the harvester-sorter came a cultivator-shredder that turned the soil and shredded the bean roots and stalks into fragments then reburied them, and seeded the falfamut for the next growing cycle. The machinery looked as ancient as the groundcar from which they observed it.

"Let us travel to those unharvested fields there." Nathaniel gestured to the west.

"We're getting low on fuel, professor. I hadn't thought we'd be traveling this far from Lanceville."

"A little farther, a kilo or so, that will not make much difference, I do not believe."

"Yes, sir."

Another kilo farther west, Nathaniel cleared his throat. "If you would halt again . . . ?" Nathaniel offered a smile.

"Of course." Bagot slowed the groundcar gently.

Nathaniel stepped out, still carrying the ubiquitous datacase, wishing he could have both hands free. Sylvia followed him as he walked from the shoulder of the road toward the nearest row of synde beans.

The dull *thwop thwop thwop* of a high-flying flitter drew the Ecolitan's eyes from the white permacrete to the eastern sky. Was the flitter tracking them? Why would someone on an energy-poor planoformed globe use a flitter? He shook his head slowly. Clearly, he hadn't escaped from his indoctrination of paranoia from his months on Old Earth.

Sylvia's eyes followed his, but she smiled faintly. "It's nice to have friends." The word "friends" was gently stressed.

Was she right—or even more paranoid than Nathaniel?

He bent down and studied the closest row of beans. Were the globes more purple than the varieties he'd seen at the Institute years earlier? Again he slipped out the miniature vidimager and recorded a series of images for comparison and study.

"I take it they're not just beans?" murmured Sylvia.

"Don't know yet. I have some suspicions." He laughed. "I always do—except about you."

"You had suspicions about me. You just didn't listen to them—until you realized you could be in deep trouble."

"Good thing you were ethical."

"I wasn't. If I'd been ethical . . . I wouldn't be here."

"Ethical in a deeper sense," he offered.

"No. I wasn't that either, dear professor, and I'm glad I wasn't. Even after trying to make sense of your . . . morality . . . I'm not unhappy to be here."

"I am glad of that." Nathaniel fingered the thin, dark green bladed bean leaf a last time, fixing the image in his mind, then straightened. He still felt Sylvia was far more ethical than she credited herself as being, but the continuing questions about his morality bothered him. How many other cultural and background conflicts were likely to surface as they worked together?

The two walked back to the groundcar and Bagot.

"The hydrocarb processing plant is where we should go next," announced Nathaniel, flourishing the enormous kerchief and blotting his damp brow as he stood in the heat by the open door.

"That's back in Lanceville, sir."

"Is there anything of a transport nature here, or around here?" asked the sandy-haired Ecolitan.

"Ah . . . no, sir." Bagot shrugged. "You're in charge, and the chief said not to worry about the fuel bill—but . . . oh, well, they'll comp the tank at the plant."

Bagot almost flew the groundcar back eastward, passing two of the big lorries along the way. With the speed, the cooling system actually reduced the interior temperature to a semblance of comfort, although when Nathaniel touched the window, he could feel the exterior heat.

The synde bean processing plant looked like a processing facility, with windowless and blotched ferrocrete walls. A thin line of steam swirled from one roof pipe, while a grayish mist seemed to wreath the entire building. Although the facility was set in the midst of level ground, fields alternating in synde beans and falfamut with infrequent swatches of maize, the whole facility seemed to descend eastward in blocky steps from the raised western end that appeared to hug an artificial mound.

As Bagot slowed the groundcar, they passed a side road with a small sign bearing a single word: Haulers. Just beyond the permacrete, a groundlorry strained to climb a long inclined ramp toward a series of loading docks that protruded from the elevated west end of the facility.

R-K Fuels—ConOne facility announced the sign by the main entrance.

"I do not suppose that R-K stands for Reeves-Kenn, does it?" asked Nathaniel.

"It probably does. They own most of ConOne." The driver offered another of his guileless smiles. "Where might you want to go?"

"Wherever the office or supervisor might be. It would be best to inform them."

"As you think best, sir." Bagot eased the groundcar to a halt by a double door at the eastern end of the facility.

"Thinking is far indeed from knowing, and he who knows nothing doubts nothing."

"What?" muttered Sylvia.

"A proverb spoken is a proverb learned." After considering for a moment, Nathaniel finally touched several points on his datacase, then left it on the floor of the rear seat. It would take more than Bagot had to open the case, and the Ecolitan didn't like the idea of entering a strange building without both hands being free. Sylvia frowned momentarily, but followed his example.

Several vehicles were clustered near a smaller side loading dock. One of the men who had been working on the tractor outside the Guest House stood by a small groundlorry, wearing a green deliveryman's jumpsuit. Nathaniel checked his belt multitector. Besides the electronic gear in the equipment belt, the deliveryman carried at least one stunner and a needler, according to the Ecolitan's belt detector.

More interesting was the pseudodeliveryman's focus.

"He's not watching us," murmured Sylvia as they walked toward the double door. "He's focused on the plant."

Nathaniel nodded, then held the left door for Sylvia.

"Always the gentleman. I could hold it for you, you know."

"You could, but this impression works better." His words were low, and he presented a faint smile. "Seeing an attractive woman first . . ."

"And I thought you cared."

Nathaniel suppressed a wince, stepping inside and waiting a moment for his sun-adjusted vision to readjust to the comparative gloom of the building.

"Sorry. That was a low blow, and . . ." Sylvia stopped as a blocky man in a maroon singlesuit marched down the dingy, half-lit corridor toward the two. The corridor smelled like diesel or some variant.

"Greetings!" called Nathaniel. "We are here on behalf of the Ecolitan Institute. We're doing an economic survey—"

"This is a private facility, and we're not open—where did you say you were from?" A frown crossed the black-haired man's bronze face, and his eyes took in the green uniforms.

"The Ecolitan Institute on Accord. We're doing an infrastructure survey here on Artos. I am Nathaniel Firstborne Whaler, and this is Ecolitan Professor Sylvia Ferro-Maine."

"Marcus Stapleson-Mares, facility shift manager." The dark brows furrowed. "Don't suppose you'd be here from New Avalon?"

"We arrived yesterday from Harmony, through a transship or two."

"What do you want?"

"We had hoped for an informal tour of the facility. We are not interested in processes or anything proprietary," said Nathaniel.

"We're detailing energy flows and how they impact the infrastructure economics," added Sylvia.

Stapleson-Mares glanced from one Ecolitan to the other. "Wait . . . follow me, please."

"Of course." Nathaniel inclined his head.

They walked silently down the corridor into a small office with little more than a desk, three utilitarian plastic chairs, and a row of antique filing cabinets that covered the entire outside wall, except for the space for a single narrow floor-to-ceiling flexiplast window. The desk had only a narrow flat screen—blank—upon it.

Stapleson-Mares tapped the screen and then several studs on the compact keyboard on the screen frame.

"Yes?" came a crackly voice as an image swirled into place on the screen.

"Boss . . . there's two professors in green here. Claim they're Ecolitans doing some sort of economic survey."

"Put them in front of the screen, Marcus, if you will." The voice was hoarse, almost raspy.

The shift manager nodded at the Ecolitans, and they stepped in front of the screen.

"Nathaniel Whaler, and this is Sylvia Ferro-Maine."

For a moment, the thin gray-haired man studied the two, his eyes flicking sideways several times as if comparing the faces to a flat picture or solideo cube.

"You look like the folks old Walk said were coming, and I can't see as there'd be two sets of you running around in those strange greens. I'm George. What do you want at the facility?"

"If it meets your approval, just a general tour, and some basic figures," answered Nathaniel. "We would like to see the process flow, and how the hydrocarbon feedstocks are fed in, processed, and distributed. A general idea of the energy equivalence of the output would be appreciated, and the general sectoral usages of that output."

"In short, how the facility works, how much raw energy we take in, and how much of the fuel goes where?"

"That would be the general idea," Nathaniel admitted.

"Where else might you be visiting?"

"Every significant energy and transport producer and consumer on Artos, as we can. The wider the net, the better the information."

George's weathered hand touched his chin, and the faint hiss of static mixed with what seemed a sigh.

The two in greens waited.

"Marcus?"

"Sir?"

"Tell Wystuh-MacDonald and Hensburg-Kewes that the Ecolitans are here, and have Jimmy give them the standard tour—the one that he gives the Empees when they come. You can give them the briefing packets. They're in the red folders in the second—"

"Yes, sir. I know."

The green eyes turned back to Nathaniel. "I trust you'll find every number you could possibly desire in the packets, and some you won't." A wintry smile crossed the man's face. "What have you seen on Artos?"

"Little besides the port, the Guest House, and the fields have we viewed thus far." Nathaniel inclined his head.

"I take it you haven't seen our spread?"

"Ah . . . unless it constituted some of the fields . . ."

"Why don't you come out here the day after tomorrow? There's more to the economics and infrastructure of Artos than energy and transport." The smile warmed slightly. "Get a flitter trip from Walkerson. It's a lot faster."

"If that would not be a difficulty . . ."

"No difficulty at all. Might save us all some grief. Rather have you get the whole picture. You Ecolitans have a lot of clout with your reports, I know." The green eyes flicked toward Marcus Stapleson-Mares. "Give them the direction sheet, too, the one with the beacon codes."

"Yes, boss."

"Have a good tour."

"Thank you."

"Thank you." Sylvia's words lagged Nathaniel's only fractionally.

The flat screen blanked to a dark gray.

"If you'll just wait here, I'll be getting Jimmy." The shift manager glanced toward the door.

"Fine. Fine."

Nathaniel studied the office for a time, then watched Sylvia as she slowly walked around the office looking carefully at everything. He enjoyed the grace of her movements.

A wiry man hurried into the officer from the corridor. "Jimmy Hensburg-Kewes. Quality control and plant safety. I also get to be the designated tour guide. Marcus told me you're here for the grand tour." A smile crinkled the safety officer's face.

"We had asked for a general overview," ventured Nathaniel.

"It'll be pretty general. Most of the lines after the ovens are closed. You can follow the piping, but all you'll see is the equipment."

Sylvia smiled brightly.

Stapleson-Mares reappeared. "You wanted the data packages?"

"Could we get them after the tour?" asked Nathaniel.

"Of course, sirs." The shift manager inclined his head.

"We'll start at the loading docks," Hensburg-Kewes said, then turned and stepped into the corridor. The Ecolitans followed.

The west end loading docks were just that—docks where the bean pods were dumped into bins that fed them into the shredders and crushers.

"Pretty simple operation," said the safety officer. "The pods are unloaded and shredded. From here they go into the ovens. At the end of the ovens are the big screens . . ."

Sylvia studied the inclined trough that vibrated just enough to shift both pulp and liquid down its length into metal-clad ovens that radiated heat even through the heavy walls. "How do you heat the ovens?"

"Raw hydrocarb from the stage-two gross filters. It's fed back. We have to use wider nozzles, but it works, and we don't have to worry about conversion losses."

"What is your conversion ratio?"

"We do pretty well. About eighty percent of the pods are usable, but only about half is hydrocarb oil. We get hammered on the stuff that gets reformulated for flitters, but all the lorries run on filtered oil. Fuel economy's half, two-thirds that of fossilized petroleum, but you can't regrow that. 'Sides," added the wiry man with a grin, "we don't have any on Artos."

After the ovens, the raw hydrocarb fluid was carried through two parallel, heavy metal pipes each half a meter in diameter, which climbed at a thirty degree angle. Less than ten meters beyond the ovens, the pipes branched and distributed the feedstock into eight large, apparently identical tanks.

"Second stage filters."

From the base of the tanks the smaller exit pipes merged back into three pipes—two large lines and a smaller one. The smaller line ran back toward the ovens.

Hensburg-Kewes gestured to the right where the two large lines ran down the center of what was essentially a covered walkway. "Now, we go to the filter building—that's where we separate the keroil and base. Centrifuge. Crude, but it works."

The three followed the walkway and pipes for nearly fifty meters. The safety officer opened a heavy door, holding it until Nathaniel and Sylvia had passed through. He closed it with a thud.

Unlike the equipment in the earlier sections of the plant, the filter building appeared newer—and far cleaner. The stainless steel of the four centrifuges glimmered in the indirect light from the fifteen-meter-high ceiling. The permacrete floor was smooth and dustless. Each of the three outside walls had a door set exactly in the middle, and by each door was racked a set of large chemical extinguishers and a heatsuit.

For a moment, the only sound was that of a high-pitched, continuous whine.

Nathaniel walked up to the bright red line on the floor, set almost five meters back from the centrifuge, and studied the equipment, noting the apparent tap levels and separate off-feeds.

The safety officer gestured toward the centrifuge. "This is the real heart of the plant."

Behind him, Sylvia appeared to be checking the paint of the outside wall. Nathaniel tightened his lips, stepping back and moving toward Sylvia, who was frowning.

"Really watch this, we do, sirs—"

Nathaniel felt, rather than heard, the explosion that slammed across his back like a torch, carrying him toward the wall. He danced sideways against the heat and grabbed Sylvia, holding his breath and trying to cushion the blow as they were dashed against the wall.

Somehow, he managed to struggle along the wall to the exit door, and thrust Sylvia out before him.

Crummpttt!

The force of the fire and explosion propelled him after her, and he staggered across the rougher exterior permacrete. They turned.

Flames belched from the open emergency door. A jet of white-hot flame burned through the plastic roofing of the synde bean filter station, and black smoke swirled into the blue-green sky.

The crackling of the flames rose higher. Abruptly, there was a shrilling hiss, and white foam cascaded from the walls. The entire small building was almost instantly enshrouded in a cocoon of foam, although the plumes of greasy smoke spread skyward before diffusing into a haze.

A handful of figures in heatsuits scurried inside the filter building. Shortly, one of them brought out a limp and charred figure into the pitiless sunlight.

"Let's see your back," suggested Sylvia abruptly.

"I think it's all right."

"Let me see."

Nathaniel shrugged.

"Your greens look untouched." A hint of amazement colored her voice.

"Very good fabric." She shook her head. "Was that why you wanted me in greens?"

"One of the reasons."

"And the other?"

"You look good in them."

One of the suited figures pulled back his hood and trudged across the permacrete toward the Ecolitans, sweat and grime streaking his face and dark hair.

"Terribly sorry, sirs." Stapleson-Mares wiped his damp forehead. "Terribly sorry. The heat detectors should have registered sooner." He shook his head. "Poor Jimmy. He took most of the blast."

"He seemed most knowledgeable," Nathaniel answered.

"No one knew the system better. It's hard to believe." The shift manager shook his head dolefully. "Hard to believe." He straightened. "Do you have any idea what happened?"

"No," answered Nathaniel. "We had just entered the filtering area, and Mr. Hensburg-Kewes was explaining about the centrifuges. Then . . . I felt a blast of heat . . . I looked for him, but I could not see him."

"You wouldn't have, not the way . . . never mind." The manager shook his head.

"I take it that there are problems with the filter operations?" asked Sylvia. "Recurring problems?"

"How—yes."

"It's a separate building almost," Sylvia answered the unspoken question, "and you've obviously taken a number of precautions."

"We've still got impurities in the soil, and the beans were gene-designed for both cleansing and hydrocarbon output. Easier to filter . . . but we're using high-speed centrifuges because it's faster and a lot cheaper for the speed. Diffusion would be even harder to handle, and this is the only facility on ConOne." Stapleson-Mares wiped his forehead again with the back of his hand.

The odor of chemicals and ashes drifted across the pavement on the light wind. Nathaniel eased out the large kerchief and blotted his own forehead, then replaced it in his pocket. "There is one on the second continent?"

"No. It's too far south and too cold. ConTrio has a facility, but it's only got a capacity a third of ours." The dark-haired manager glanced at the foam-covered structure. "The fire shouldn't have gotten that far. That's what the alarms and foam systems are for."

A green groundcar eased around the end of the plant and headed toward the group on the permacrete.

"Yours?"

"I believe so," answered Nathaniel.

The groundcar drew up beside the three. Bagot peered out the now-open driver's window. "Are you all right, sirs?"

"We have survived," Nathaniel responded, pulling out the large kerchief again and blotting away yet more sweat and soot. "I should have asked. Is there anything we can do? Any information we could supply?"

"If there is, I know where to find you." The shift manager inclined his head. "If you don't mind, I'll have someone bring over those packets later. Right now, I need to talk to George and let Lindy know about Jimmy. They've got three daughters. The oldest is eight."

"I don't envy you," said Sylvia. "Is there anything I could do?" Her voice was gentle.

"No, professor." The shift manager's voice softened. "There isn't. Appreciate your asking. We've lost a dozen men over the years here, but it's never easy."

"I am sorry it happened, but I do not know what occurred," added Nathaniel. "One moment we were looking at the centrifuges . . . then . . ." He shrugged.

"It can only take a moment. That's why . . . why . . ." Stapleson-Mares shook his head. "We thought we'd covered everything."

Nathaniel waited. So did Sylvia.

"There's nothing you two can do." The dark-haired man forced a wry expression. "Not good at dealing with this. If you need anything more, or if you remember something that might help, please let me know."

"We will," promised Sylvia.

Nathaniel turned to the manager. "I fear I am famished. Is there somewhere in Lanceville where the food is recommended?"

"We're not much for gourmets," said Stapleson-Mares coolly. "Elizabeth's has good food. Not fancy, but good."

"Thank you." Nathaniel smiled politely. "Thank you."

"Take care," added Sylvia softly.

"Thank you, professor." Stapleson-Mares did not look at Nathaniel, even after the two Ecolitans had entered the groundcar.

"Lanceville," said Nathaniel.

"Yes, sir." Bagot's voice was formal.

Nathaniel held back the wince. He'd probably overplayed it . . . unless he happened to be right.

THE METAL-POVERTY of Artos became more pronounced as the groundcar neared Lanceville. Every structure was comprised either of stone, brick, or synthetic hydrocarb building sheets—or some combination of the three—and the majority of roofs were of the faded red clay tiles similar to those on the Guest House.

"Where might the road lead?"

"If we took it another kilo, we'd be at the R-K piers, professor."

Nathaniel nodded—Lanceville was a port city, both for sea and space. He gestured toward a large blue building ahead to the left. "What might that be?"

"That's the Blue Lion. Most visitors, except for Empees or folks like you, stay there," offered Bagot. "We'll pass it on the way."

"Empees?" questioned Sylvia.

"Members of Parliament . . . from Camelot." Bagot flushed.

Facing west, the Blue Lion's facade sported four levels fronted with tinted glass that stretched perhaps one hundred meters. The hotel was half that in depth, and was separated from the street by fifty meters of browning grass. The blue-tinted glass panels of the facade were smeared with dust and rain-splotches. On the north side was a carpark with perhaps a half-dozen vehicles. Scarcely the outback station cited by Walkerson, not unless an outback horse station were a great deal more on Artos than the name implied.

"There are not many visitors at this time of year?" asked Nathaniel.

"Not many at any time anymore, except for the Agricultural Exposition. The Ag Expo's the big thing in the fall. We get people from all over—Halstan, the Fuards—they look stiff in those gray outfits. You name the system . . . someone's here."

"Even from Accord?"

"I've seen people in greens like yours," Bagot said. "Didn't know where they came from, though."

Nathaniel glanced at the first cross street past the Blue Lion, as wide as the highway from the Guest House and shuttle port. "Where might that go?"

"That's the road out to Gerick."

"What's in Gerick?" prompted Sylvia.

"The big fusactor station's there, and the facility where they make all the synthetic panels for building. Some other stuff, too."

"Other stuff?" Sylvia's tone was gentle, but persistent.

"I don't know everything, professor, but there's the permacrete place and a place that makes electrical stuff. That's what the chief said. And a bunch of job shops—plumbing, pipes . . ." Bagot shrugged. As the groundcar squeaked to a stop outside a small free-standing building with small windows and a double door—synthplast treated to look like oak—he added, "Here's Elizabeth's."

Nathaniel slipped out and held the door for Sylvia. He carried his datacase. So did she.

"If it's all right with you, professors, I'll be back in a standard hour." Bagot looked expectantly from the open window.

"Fine that would be," answered Nathaniel.

With a nod, Bagot was gone.

"Did you have to be such an ass?" whispered Sylvia as they stepped toward the maroon awning. "That man was killed."

"I'd rather have you be the good person," Nathaniel murmured.

"Why does anyone have to be the bad one?"

"We already are to someone. That means there's no way they'll see us both as nice or acceptable."

"You really can play the ass. If I didn't know better . . . those proverbs—where did you dig them up?"

"*The Dictionary of Proverbs*. I made some modifications."

The hint of a frown crossed her face as Nathaniel opened the door, nodding his head. Yellow polyester cloth covered the eight tables in the brightly lit room. Five tables were filled. The air carried the odor of fresh bread and spices.

"Smells good," murmured Sylvia.

He glanced across the small dining area. Three of the tables held couples—neither young nor old. One held three men in the shorts and formal shirts of Avalon, and one held an older man—who sported a brush mustache—in a grayish singlesuit. Only the three men looked up at their entry.

A heavyset, gray-haired woman stepped out of the doorway that led to the kitchen and walked forward. "Two for luncheon?"

"Yes, please."

"You look familiar—or your uniforms do, but I can't place them," said the local, looking toward Sylvia.

"The Ecolitan Institute—Accord," said Sylvia, after a quick look at Nathaniel.

"That's a far jump from Artos. Might I ask what brings you here?"

"We're doing an economic study."

"Economists?" The server laughed as she gestured toward the corner table. "You're almost too graceful to be an economist. You . . . never mind me. I chatter too much." As they seated themselves, she added, "The special today is basking-mod souffle, and it's a good seafood souffle. That's five and a half." With a smile, she inclined her head. "I'll get you some water. Would you like me to get you anything else to drink while you are looking over the menu?"

"Have you liftea? While it is not so good as your own, I fear . . ." Nathaniel shrugged.

"We can do liftea—and you're not alone in that, sir. And you?" She looked at Sylvia.

"Real tea, if it's not steeped quite forever."

"We can do that, too."

After the server left, Nathaniel studied the menu.

"What are you having?" asked Sylvia.

"It appears I have a choice between algae protein and reformulated synde bean protein, disguised in some form or another."

"So it does. I'd bet the algae pasta tastes like pasta, though."

"I will throw myself on the mercy of the kitchen." He took out the overlarge kerchief and blotted his forehead.

"They may not have much mercy, especially if—" Sylvia's gray eyes glinted, but she broke off her sentence as the server neared.

The gray-haired woman set the tumblers—real glass—on the table and then the two mugs. "Have you decided?"

"What might be good?" he asked.

"It depends on what you like," answered the waitress. "Most outies like the spice dishes. Liz is good at disguising algae and bean protein. I've even used some of her tricks at home. That's those that don't take forever. The souffle *is* good, but it is fish, and some don't like that."

"The special pasta," said Sylvia.

"The souffle, with an extra side of the special sauce, if that is possible?"

"It's possible, and you won't regret it. Liz does good sauces." With a smile, the server was gone, only to return in moments with a small basket. "I forgot your breads."

Nathaniel offered Sylvia the basket.

"They smell good."

He hoped they tasted equally good.

The souffle was fishy, but the extra tomato herb sauce helped disguise it, although he didn't finish everything, unlike Sylvia, who left none of the pasta.

"It was all very good." Nathaniel offered the twenty pound New Avalonian note to the server.

"It usually is," said the gray-haired woman as she made change with the oblong, off-red Avalonian notes and several coins. "We do hope you'll come again."

"Thank you," said Sylvia softly.

"Good food is nourishment for the soul," he added.

A nod, and the server slipped back toward the kitchen.

"You remember what Stapleson-Mares said about Elizabeth's?" he asked, leaving the gratuity. All Avalonian planets retained the antique tradition, except it was more than a tradition, since it really represented the server's pay.

"Oh . . . that the food was plain."

"Did this strike you as plain?" He rose.

She shook her head with a smile as she slipped gracefully out of the chair.

"Does that mean he didn't want us here?"

"I don't know. I think it meant he was angry at you. Mostly, any-way." Sylvia tilted her head slightly in a pensive gesture.

Nathaniel could accept the anger, but he still wondered, even as his eyes lingered on Sylvia's profile, then toward the street outside.

Thwonkkkk! Nathaniel turned toward the sound of the horn.

Bagot waved from where he was parked in the shade across the empty street. "Here, sirs!"

Nathaniel looked both ways out of habit, but the street was empty of traffic. A hundred meters south of Elizabeth's he saw a uniformed fig-ure, or a guard of some sort, in a bright blue uniform, walking briskly around the corner.

"What are you thinking?" asked Sylvia.

"Oh, I couldn't say. More of a feeling, but I can't place it. There's something . . ." He shook his head and followed her to the car.

"Might we see the piers?" asked the Ecolitan as he closed the rear door and settled himself in the back next to Sylvia.

"Anywhere you say."

A circular drive fronted the harbor, a drive constructed of heavy-duty permacrete and wide enough for three of the heavy ag-lorries side by side. But the sole vehicle in sight was theirs.

Bagot pulled up the groundcar in an empty carpark lot overlooking the water at the foot of the center pier. The R-K piers were just that—three stone piers jutting out into the gray waters of the harbor. Each pier was less than a hundred meters long and not more than twenty wide.

Nathaniel stepped out into the damp heat and swallowed—hard—at the humidity and the acrid odors that swirled around him. He immedi-ately turned and studied the streets behind him.

Three of the wide permacrete highways fanned out away from the harbor drive. As far as he could see, all were empty. Yet the pavement around the harbor bore the signs of hard usage.

Was Artos on a downhill economic slide—or were they missing something? And why had the study been commissioned? He turned back and let his eyes turn toward Sylvia. At the northern-most pier were two long barges. The eastern one, closest to the open sea, appeared half-loaded with plastic crates and containers. For a time Nathaniel studied the synthplast-hulled barges.

Then, Sylvia nodded abruptly and began to walk out on the empty center pier before her, datacase in hand. Nathaniel followed.

She paused at the end of the pier and glanced back north again. "That's heavy equipment of some sort."

"It could be."

"Look at how high the second one rides compared to the first. Yet the cubage of the cargo isn't that great."

"It could be processing equipment."

"It could be."

"You don't think so."

"No . . . but it's only a feeling."

"Let's walk over there."

They got halfway down the north pier before two men bearing antique slug-throwers appeared.

"Hold it, you two!" ordered the shorter man. He wore a maroon singlesuit with a plastic badge on the chest bearing the emblem of a long-horned bull and the initials R-K.

"What is the difficulty?" asked Nathaniel.

"This pier's closed." The stocky man gestured with the rifle.

"We were only observing. We are conducting an economic study—"

"The pier's closed—study or no study."

"This isn't a public pier?"

"Friend . . . you and your lady better go someplace else. This belongs to R-K. You want to look around—I need an authorization from Sebastion or George. No authorization, no look-see. That's it."

"As you wish." Nathaniel inclined his head and turned to Sylvia. "Shall we depart for more hospitable climes?"

"And none of your fancy words, outie."

The Ecolitan glanced at the slug-thrower. While he doubted the stocky man could have stopped either Sylvia or him, there wasn't much point to pressing the issue. So he nodded again.

He could feel the eyes on their backs all the way down the pier.

"Score one or more for your feelings," he murmured.

"You were itching to teach him some manners."

"I thought about it—but only for a moment. No percentage in it."

Bagot stood by the groundcar as they returned. "That Gershon—he's a nasty one."

"Gershon? Was he the short one?"

"That's him. Jem took him apart in school. Gershon tried to club him down from behind. Jem didn't take to that." Bagot smiled. "Gershon limped for years."

"Well . . . I can understand your brother's feelings," said Nathaniel, opening the rear door for Sylvia. "We might as well get moving, onto another aspect of infrastructures."

From the piers, they headed out past the Blue Lion toward the industrial facility the driver had mentioned. Both used their datacases for detailed notes.

The area was exactly as described, Nathaniel reflected on the way back to the Guest House—a fusactor power plant, lots of electrical distribution towers, and a dozen fabrication facilities of various shapes and sizes, all housed in structures built of grayed hydrocarb-based plastics.

The highway back to the Guest House was lined with synde bean fields as well, younger plants than those they had seen earlier, and seemingly of the more purple variety. The Ecolitan frowned, but said nothing, just watching until Bagot brought the car to a halt outside the Guest House.

"We'll see you in the morning," noted Nathaniel.

"Yes, sirs." Bagot nodded.

"You were quiet," Sylvia noted as they walked through the late afternoon heat toward the Guest House door.

Nathaniel blotted his forehead again with the overlarge kerchief. "I was thinking. I'd really like to study those figures we didn't get—the energy usage ones."

"They'd only be for transportation."

"But they'd tell a great deal." He paused and looked around the foyer of the Guest House—empty as usual.

Back in his room, after washing away the grime from his face and hands and sweeping the room with the detector, Nathaniel set the datacase on the table.

He slipped the tiny vidimager into the slot in the side of the datacase and called up the images, comparing one set of green-leaved beans to another. Different—subtly different, but different. Was that significant, or just good agricultural practice in having different variants available?

The bean plants with the narrower leaves and darker shade seemed smaller. Did that mean they were an older variant? He wanted to shake his head. Instead, he flicked through the other images while appearing to riffle through the flimsies in the case in search of something.

There was a rap on the door.

"Yes?" Nathaniel closed the datacase, stood, and walked to the door.

"Professor? There's a linkcall from Chief Walkerson for you."

The Ecolitan opened the door.

A sandy-haired woman stood there, holding two red folders. "And these were dropped off for you as well."

"Thank you."

"You'll have to take the call below."

"I'll be right there." He stepped toward the connecting door, rapped, and peered into Sylvia's room.

"What was that?" Sylvia looked up from the table and her datacase.

"There's a call from the Port Chief. I'm headed downstairs to take it. You might look at the . . . material . . . in my case while I'm gone. Also we got folders from the hydrocarb facility."

She raised her eyebrows, then nodded. "I'll look at both."

"Good." He went back to the half-open hallway door, stepped out and closed it behind him, and followed the Artosan woman down to a small room off the front foyer, a room containing little more than a desk and two chairs.

"Right there." She pointed to the utilitarian gray unit on the corner of the desk.

Nathaniel sat and faced the screen where Robert Walkerson waited.

"Ecolitan Whaler . . . I'd heard from Bagot that there had been a little problem at the hydrocarb facility. Are you two all right?"

"We're fine. These things happen." Especially around me. "I was sorry that our escort was killed. Most sorry."

"They've had problems out there before, Ecolitan. I'm sure it had nothing to do with you."

"I would hope not. Still . . . it was most distressing." Nathaniel bobbed his head up and down. "Most distressing."

"I am sure the accident was just that. They've had more than a few at the facility. More than a few." Walkerson flashed a smile across the screen. "How are you doing with your study?"

"Just beginning. A good study is not done in a few days. And then we must cross-check the data and the correlations. Then . . . but you do not wish to hear about academic details."

"You can tell me about them tomorrow, if you wish." Walkerson paused. "There's a small get-together tomorrow night. It might do you and your . . . associate good to meet some of the locals you wouldn't run across otherwise. Nineteen hundred at the Blue Lion—the Unicorn Room. Not too formal."

"The best we have?" asked Nathaniel.

"People will understand . . ."

"We have formal greens."

"Good-oh."

"By the way, could you lend us the use of a flitter?" asked Nathaniel. "For the day after tomorrow?"

"The day after tomorrow?"

"We have an invitation to visit the Reeves-Kenn operation."

"You must be special. Not many get those. Well . . . with our little get-together and his invitation, you'll be meeting most of those of import on Artos." Walkerson laughed briefly, then pulled at his whisker-shadowed chin. "I don't have many pilots right now."

"I am qualified in most flitter classes and types."

"Are you . . . I suppose you are, or you wouldn't be here. It's a Welk-Symmons, old model, like the Empire's twelve twenties."

"I can handle that, but, if you would feel better I will stop by tomorrow for a check ride with your people."

"That might be better . . . I couldn't say what the differences might be between our old vibrator and what you've piloted."

"Nine hundred?"

"That would be good. I'll have Jersek expecting you. Do you need any gear?"

"Helmets, or headsets."

"We can take care of that. Good luck, and let me know—or let Bagot know. He'll certainly relay any messages."

"Thank you."

After the screen blanked, Nathaniel headed back up to his room.

Sylvia sat at his desk, looking through the case. She smiled. "What did he want?"

"To express his concerns and to see how we were doing."

A minute headshake greeted his not-quite-sardonic words.

"Also to invite us to show off our most formal wear at a small party for the local elite tomorrow evening."

"You must have been impressive."

Nathaniel shook his head. "He wants us to meet someone."

"But he doesn't want to say so?"

Nathaniel nodded. "So I took the opportunity to request a flitter for our trip out to visit George Reeves-Kenn."

"He wasn't too enthusiastic?"

"No. He said he was short of pilots, and I offered my own services for us. I'll have to get a check-out tomorrow morning."

"Is it wise?" she asked.

"Probably not, but I trust me flying more than I trust others."

"We don't have to go . . ."

Nathaniel raised his eyebrows.

"Not by flitter."

"If anyone's serious, all it would take would be a large lorry running over our groundcar, and no one would notice. Sabotaging a flitter would at least have a higher visibility."

Sylvia nodded slowly, then asked more loudly, "Are you ready to eat?"

His stomach growled. "I think I am."

She smiled. "I heard that."

Except for the serving woman—the same woman who had knocked on the door to tell Nathaniel about the linkcall—and them, the dining area was empty.

"Strange . . ."

Sylvia nodded. "There's more support for visitors than visitors. Unless it's a seasonal thing."

"It could be."

The serving woman in the green-and-maroon tunic bowed slightly as they neared the only table set for dining. "Beef stew this evening, professors." She straightened, and then inclined her head. "And a good stew it is."

"Thank you."

Nathaniel waited until the server had departed before saying, "Tomorrow, we should eat at the Blue Lion."

"You think the ambience . . . ?"

"I need a better feel. It's lovely here, but we're isolated."

"That's not an accident, either."

The sandy-haired server returned with wilted salads, followed by the stew. Nathaniel had to admit that the stew beef was more tender than some gourmet steaks he had enjoyed in many locales. The local lettuce of the salad tasted more like algae than algae.

They ate quietly, and Nathaniel found his thoughts flitting from one thing to another. Comparatively high-volume roads led to an almost empty port. A largish hotel for a backwater planet had an empty carpark. A relatively modern hydrocarb processing facility had a record of accidents—and one just happened to occur when they visited. A "plain-food" restaurant had anything but plain food.

"You're thinking."

"Yes. I'd rather not say . . . yet. I'd like your thoughts after another day or two when we can compare notes. Don't want to influence your opinions."

"That makes sense." Sylvia paused. "The stew was good."

"Far better than the salad."

They both laughed softly.

No one was in the front hall or lounge as they walked back upstairs and to their rooms in the dim light of twilight. Nathaniel opened the door to his room, ears alert, but the room was empty, and the detector, as usual, registered no activity.

Sylvia closed the door. "I know we didn't do that much besides look at things and take notes, but I am tired. And you need some rest before you do whatever you need to do with that flitter tomorrow morning."

"It's just a check-out."

"I just need some time to myself. I'll see you in the morning." She paused, her hand on the connecting door to her room.

"All right." He forced a smile. Still . . . she probably did need to be alone. They were spending almost every waking moment together, and there was probably such a thing as too much togetherness.

He flicked on the lights in his room, then sat down in front of the table that held the datacase. Someone had fumbled with it, but not opened it. He nodded, and touched the entry points.

He had some reviewing and some thinking to do.

Later, much later, Nathaniel slipped through the connecting door and into the bed.

"What—"

He covered Sylvia's mouth, and whispered, "Shhh. . . . I'm not up to anything nefarious, but we need to talk, and I'm not sure that eavesdropping isn't what's going on, rather than electronic surveillance."

"Oh . . . it strikes me as a convenient . . ."

"Sylvia . . ."

"I'm just teasing," she murmured. "You are *so* serious, and this is humorous, if you think about it."

Nathaniel had been too aware of her warmth and desirability to think about too many things simultaneously, but, with her words, he had to laugh softly. He couldn't get close to her romantically, and here he was in her bed.

"We've had two 'accidents' in as many days," he murmured, "and someone is watching everything we do."

"Are they watching us? Or are they watching for whoever's after us?"

"I don't know, but I think you're right." Nathaniel touched her shoulder, as if to hug her.

"Careful . . ."

"There aren't many groundcars, but they're more fuel efficient than flitters. It's as if the permacrete highways are more like a heavy-duty transport system with all those big ag-lorries, but the numbers of lorries aren't enough to justify the investment," he pointed out softly, almost nuzzling her ear.

"Careful there." Sylvia inched back from him ever so slightly. "You're right about those highways, from what we've seen so far. There are five that come into Lanceville."

"And they have had heavy use."

"Do you think they were loading military equipment on the barge?"

"I don't think so. I'd guess, if I had to, that it was heavy industrial equipment."

"But Bagot was talking about how little real industrial equipment there was on Artos."

"That he had seen . . ."

"Oh . . . but why?"

"I don't know. There was also something that waitress said that bothered me."

"About the Ecolitan greens? You said it had been a long time—"

"Exactly. Well before her time. But a waitress wouldn't make that up. It's a big Galaxy . . . but I don't know anywhere else where they wear greens beside Accord."

"I haven't studied uniforms and heraldry, but since the . . . Secession—"

"You almost said 'rebellion.'"

"I'm working on it," she whispered back.

"The piers are short, but there are three. Why not one long one?"

"You think that they're sending military equipment to different locales?" Sylvia asked.

"I don't know why. It had crossed my mind."

"Private armies?"

"That could make it nasty."

"Nastier," she added.

Nathaniel feared she was right.

"I did have one question," she whispered in his ear, after a silence.

"Yes?"

"Where did you get that ridiculous kerchief?"

Nathaniel almost choked. "It gives a certain effect."

"You might pull it off here, even. But I don't believe it. Even with those damned proverbs." Sylvia pursed her lips, and shook, holding in what Nathaniel suspected were giggles.

"A professor I am and remain."

"Oh . . . please," she whispered.

He shook his head, swallowing his laughter.

"Sweetheart," Sylvia said loudly enough for any possible eavesdropper, "you are sweet, but I'm just too tired. I'm sorry."

Slowly, slowly Nathaniel swung himself out of the bed. "Good night." He bent over the bed, as if to kiss her a last time, although there hadn't been a first time.

Her arms went around his neck, and her lips were on his, warm and soft. After a moment, she eased her lips away just enough to whisper, "You are sweet . . . and I appreciate it more than you know." She gave him a last kiss. He tried not to be *too* enthusiastic in his response.

Nathaniel shook his head as he left the door between rooms slightly ajar and headed for his own cool sheets. He was missing more than a few things, both with Sylvia and their ever-stranger consulting assignment, but he was having trouble focusing on anything more than how warm Sylvia's kiss had been. He'd been around the Galaxy, and more than a handful of women had found him attractive—in and out of bed—yet he was almost trembling, not a good sign. Definitely not a good sign.

XI

AT THE FAINT beep, the Grand Admiral touched the stud. An image formed on the small shielded screen, an image coming over a secure Defense Ministry scrambled line. "You called?" The screen held the image of a sandy-haired woman.

"I did. How do you feel about Accord now, Marcella?"

"You mean the algae and anchovy kills on Squamish? Why would they change anything?" asked the Special Assistant to the Imperial Minister of Commerce.

"They've also appeared on Anarra. The Matriarch sent a query to us and to the Coordinate. Of course, the Coordinate denied everything . . . but who else has that kind of biological capability?"

"It's too obvious, especially this soon after the trade talks. Accord isn't stupid."

"Unless they're counting on everyone thinking that," pointed out the Grand Admiral.

"They've shown a better grasp of politics than that." The Special Assistant's eyes narrowed. "They also have issued a warning every time before they've employed ecological tactics."

"That may be, but the Senate is already debating investigating and sending the Eleventh Fleet to Sector Five." The Admiral's voice was almost flat. "They also haven't shown that courtesy when they've undertaken more conventional covert action."

"Is the Senate really that stupid?" The Special Assistant shook her head. "Are you going along with it?"

"Politics, Marcella. Politics. If half the Empire wants to blame Accord, and wants action, that's where the eagles have to go. I can't oppose the wishes of the Senate."

"Even if they're based on images in cheap trideo that show Ecolitans as devils without horns. Even if half the human Galaxy ends up an ecologic or radioactive or nova-seared waste? Is your position worth that?"

"It shouldn't come to that." The Grand Admiral smiled.

"It shouldn't?"

"Accord might be persuaded to stand aside on Hernando."

"You've already lost Hernando."

"No loss is permanent."

"What are you really planning?" asked the Special Assistant. "What do you want?"

"You've already provided it. You've confirmed that you don't believe Accord is behind this covert ecological warfare."

"Couldn't you have just asked? They aren't."

"Then who is, Marcella? According to both Defense intelligence and the I.I.S., no one else in the human Galaxy has that kind of capability."

"That's not quite true. No one else has ever demonstrated that kind of capability, and they certainly wouldn't, not while they can keep the laser aimed at Accord and the Empire."

"Fine. Who is it? The Fuards? Olympia? Halstan? The Federated Hegemony? Orknarli? The Frankan League? New Avalon? Every one of them would like to see Accord and the Empire at each other's throats again."

"The Franks probably wouldn't, and New Avalon is too . . . traditional . . . to keep anything like that secret."

"That leaves quite a few—and you're assuming Accord is innocent." The Grand Admiral frowned. "Most senators will quickly point out that only Accord has ever employed large-scale ecological warfare."

"That argument cuts both ways. It makes a perfect case of why it wouldn't be Accord. Also, as I pointed out, they've always delivered a warning, and it's been after we've done something. We haven't acted against them, and there's been no warning."

"You may be right, but I cannot oppose the Imperial Senate, not if it decides to send the eagles against the Coordinate. Not without any proof. Do you have any?"

"You know I don't."

"Then contact your tame envoy and ask him . . . if you can find him. You might also ask why he barely returned to Harmony before they sent him off to Artos—that's a colony of New Avalon, recently planoformed." The Admiral smiled politely. "I'd appreciate it if you would think about it."

"I will. I always do."

"I know."

The Admiral's smile did not vanish until the screen blanked. Then she frowned, pursing her lips.

XII

"YOUR FLITTER CHECK-OUT was uneventful?" Sylvia's gaze crossed the expanse of blue that was the dining room of the Blue Lion—blue table cloths, blue carpet, and blue-tinted light from the blued glass windows. The linens and the carpet were new; the blue-upholstered chairs were not. The china was also new, as was the blue fabric covering the interior walls, but images seen through the facade panes had the slightly indistinct appearance created by aged glass.

"Very uneventful—thankfully. It must have been one of the first Welk-Symmons built, and from its pristine condition, it was shipped by slow-cargo asteroid in a high sublight transit." Nathaniel took a sip

of the vinegar that passed for wine, then cleared his throat. "Jesting I
am not." He pulled forth the big kerchief and blotted his brow.

Sylvia winced. "How many of those do you have?"

"Enough, dear lady. Enough. One even matches my formal greens."

Sylvia winced again. "Why do you like to play the eccentric professor, the buffoon, almost?"

"I am eccentric. That you should know. Besides, eccentric is
regarded as dense, and that helps. I need all the assistance I can get." He
cleared his throat. "I also tried to get a tour of the R-K marine establishments. I used the comm units in Port Chief Walkerson's offices."

"And?"

"'Most regretfully, professor, we are undergoing rebuilding and
maintenance, and such a tour will not be possible for at least several
months. I will send you the documentary background we have supplied
to Camelot and to all interested parties.'" Nathaniel smiled wryly.
"That was the honorable Sebastion Reeves-Kenn himself."

"You pointed out you were from Accord?"

"He was still politely firm."

"Interesting . . ." mused Sylvia.

"Very interesting, I thought. I wonder if Chief Walkerson has any
orbit photos or scans. We'll have to ask about some."

"I wonder what they're hiding."

"Anything and everything." With a glance around the half-filled
dining room of the Blue Lion—and the three dozen or so other diners—
Nathaniel glanced at the antique paper check again, less than six
pounds for lunch for the two of them. He showed it to Sylvia.

"I know why Stapleson-Mares sent us to Elizabeth's," she said with a
laugh.

"Why? Because it's the most expensive restaurant in Lanceville, and
because he thought Ecolitan economists had to be stingy?"

"It might be. It does shows a restrained sense of humor . . . or
something."

"You're probably right." The sandy-haired Ecolitan raised his hand
as the short-haired, graying waiter passed, then pressed eight pounds
into the man's hand. "A good day to you."

"Thank you, sir." The waiter bowed just slightly, then continued on
past the table.

The two Ecolitans rose, and Nathaniel said, "I think he expected
more than twenty percent."

"Probably."

"The service wasn't worth it." Nathaniel stepped out of the Blue Room into the main lobby—also blue, from the recently ground and re-polished blue synthstone floor to the glittering blue vaulted ceiling to the pale blue lion that crouched in the frieze above the concierge's semikiosk.

"More power lines?" asked Sylvia.

He nodded, his eyes going to the pair of security guards by the door, each in smart, brilliant blue uniforms, each short-haired, and each with a holstered stunner.

"You got all those power figures from the manager at the fusactor station, but you still feel we have to travel every road on ConOne?"

"Not every road—but enough to get a feel." Were the Security Guard uniforms the same as the one he had seen the other day near Elizabeth's?

"A feel?"

"If you just rely on numbers you'll get it wrong. You need . . . well . . . I need a feel, and numbers alone don't provide that. Besides, using numbers assumes a certain accuracy, and I'm not sure about local figures. Our informal survey should either confirm the figures or suggest we look further," Nathaniel added as they stepped back into the midday, midsummer heat. "Even so, you're right. The fusactor plant figures are probably far more accurate than any rough estimates we could come up with."

"But you worry?" she pressed.

"I couldn't even tell you why," he admitted. "I just feel that way."

"You're not particularly trusting." The gray-eyed woman smiled.

"From what you've seen, should we be?"

"They don't look any less trustworthy than anyone else."

"That means I should be skeptical."

Sylvia laughed.

Glubb Bagot stood beside the groundcar in the carpark, a resigned smile fixed upon his face.

Nathaniel wondered if the resignation were because of all the synde bean fields, the power relay units, and the highway measurements they'd taken after his check-out stint at the shuttleport. The Ecolitan shook his head, not wanting to think about all the other quantifications they had left to do.

"Where to, sirs?"

"To the piers, and then we will follow the south highway for a time."

"Yes, sir."

Nathaniel closed the door for Sylvia and circled the ground-car as Bagot started the engine and the exhaust belched partly burned hydrocarbons. The Ecolitan could hardly wait to tally more power lines and highways and industrial facilities.

XIII

"BACK INTO THE blue world," said Nathaniel as they crossed the lobby of the Blue Lion.

"People used to write songs about blue; the ancients did," answered Sylvia.

"They must have been awful."

"They were."

As the two Ecolitans stepped toward the open door, above which was a synthstone frieze of a blue unicorn, Robert Walkerson stepped forward, his bald spot glistening in the light and the short jacket and formal shorts making him appear even more squat.

"You look stunning, Professor Ferro-Maine." Walkerson bowed to both Ecolitans, but his eyes were on Sylvia.

"Thank you. A uniform is a uniform, formal or not."

"It becomes you."

"It does indeed," added Nathaniel. "I've said so, but the opinion of a colleague counts for less than that of someone less involved in such matters."

"Your colleague is correct," responded Walkerson. "But let me introduce you to a few people who had hoped to meet you." He gestured toward the door, leading them inside the Unicorn Room, where perhaps two dozen people stood talking in small groups. Half turned as the Ecolitans entered.

On the left wall was a long table, covered in white linen, and bearing trays of various foodstuffs.

"The wine table is on the other side. Local—but I'd recommend the Kenward. It's rather like Sperlin, if sweeter."

"Thank you," murmured Sylvia, as Nathaniel nodded.

"You may recall Mr. Evanston."

Nathaniel inclined his head slightly.

"Good to see you," offered Geoffrey Evanston, lifting a wineglass. He wore black shoes and long formal socks and shorts. The short evening jacket was white with green piping, and a green bow tie matched the piping. "Might I present my wife? This is Ecolitan Whaler, Vivienne, and this is Ecolitan Professor Ferro-Maine. Hard to believe, isn't it, but they're economists."

"Economists? How charming! That is so much more . . . appropriate than agricultural factors and scientists, or marine agronomists, or whatever they're called." The slender blond woman pursed her lips. "I do hope you are not agricultural economists."

"No," said Nathaniel. "Infrastructure economists—transportation, power systems—those sorts of matters."

"You did not bring Madeline, Walker?" asked Evanston.

"She is a little under the weather."

"Ah . . . terribly sorry. Perhaps next time. She has such a delicious wit." Evanston nodded.

"Indeed she does. And she is so forthright," added Vivienne, turning toward Nathaniel. "An economist? You look more like an athlete, even with that slight graying at the temples."

"We do a great deal of walking in infrastructure economics, and in conducting studies, one must always walk before running, so to speak."

Sylvia looked at the blue carpet underfoot.

"You are both in excellent condition, I see," continued Vivienne.

"We're not quite adjusted to the atmosphere yet," protested Nathaniel.

"One would scarcely guess that."

"If you will excuse us, Geoffrey . . . Vivienne?" said Walkerson. "I'll let them return shortly."

"But of course."

"I do hope we can talk," said Vivienne, leaning slightly toward Sylvia.

"I do, too."

Walkerson plowed toward a taller man—also in formal jacket and shorts who stood momentarily alone.

"Governor General Eden-Danby. He's my ultimate superior." Walkerson nodded. "Governor General, might I present the Ecolitan professors? Nathaniel Whaler and Sylvia Ferro-Maine."

"Delighted!" The round-faced official sported neatly trimmed gray hair. Almost as tall as Nathaniel's 191 centimeters, he rocked forward onto the balls of his feet. "Delighted! We don't get scholars from so far. I hear you're studying our infrastructure. What have you found so far?"

"A state-of-the-art hydrocarbon conversion facility and a great number of well-built transport highways," offered Nathaniel cheerfully. "Also a good restaurant and an impressive harbor."

"A warm welcome," added Sylvia.

"With our summer, it is warm indeed, yes indeed." The Governor General coughed. "Well . . . I'm sure it will be a good study. It's good to see you. I certainly hope you enjoy your stay on Artos. Don't let me keep you." With a chuckle and a vague gesture, General Eden-Danby dismissed the Ecolitans.

"Is that the wine table?" Nathaniel turned to Sylvia. "Would you like some?"

"Please."

The Ecolitan eased around two men in gray jackets talking in low voices.

". . . beastly heat—worse than last year . . ."

". . . still say that George is diverting too much of the runoff . . ."

". . . how else can he get the credits for tech-templates?"

A blue-jacketed attendant turned to the Ecolitan. "Your pleasure, sir?"

"Two glasses of the . . . is it Kendall?" Nathaniel tried to pick up the rest of the conversation between the two men in gray jackets.

"Kenward? The sparkling white?"

"That's it."

"A moment."

The Ecolitan carried the two crystal wine glasses slowly, more slowly than necessary, toward Sylvia and Walkerson, easing behind the two men, who glanced toward Sylvia.

". . . more to Artos than beans, beef, and basking mods . . ."

"You forgot algae." A laugh followed.

". . . so I did . . . seen the guests?"

". . . she's beautiful . . . other one . . . here somewhere . . . looks too military for my taste . . ."

"Still think R-K would have . . ."

An elbow in the ribs stopped the conversation.

Nathaniel nodded politely and eased up to Sylvia, presenting her with a glass. "The Kenward." He turned to Walkerson. "Might you know the two gentlemen in gray behind me?"

"Ah . . . I believe the taller is one of the Hailshams—Durward, I think."

"Who are the Hailshams?" Sylvia sipped the sparkling white wine. "A trace sweet, but good."

Nathaniel took a sip of his own—far too sweet for his taste. Then Sylvia was probably being diplomatic.

"Durward . . . hmmmm . . . I do believe he handles the permacrete business—mostly highway construction, that sort of thing."

"You make it sound like the Hailshams have a commercial empire."

"They do have some ties there."

Nathaniel smiled, then turned abruptly and stepped back over to Durward Hailsham. "I say. I'm Nathaniel Whaler, from Accord, you know. Chief Walkerson was telling me that you must be the local construction magnate."

Hailsham swallowed. "Scarcely a magnate, professor. Artos is barely large enough for a small permacrete facility and the equipment to lay it."

"We're looking into infrastructure economics—you might have heard about our study—and permacrete supports highways, which are infrastructure."

"I suppose they are." Hailsham eased back a step.

Nathaniel stepped forward, just into the edge of Hailsham's personal space. "You produce permacrete for other things?"

Hailsham looked at Nathaniel blankly.

"There isn't much other use," admitted the square-faced second man. "I'm Keiffer DeSain." He chuckled. "If Durward is a permacrete magnate, then I'm . . . I guess you'd have to call me the local piping magnate."

"Do you produce large diameter piping for water? I'd imagine you must, with so little ground water," pressed the Ecolitan.

"We have worked with Durward to produce some two-meter permacrete conduit for the Jier Project, but it's mostly water piping—some for commercial uses here and on ConTrio. You don't realize how big even a small continent is until you get contracts for hundreds of kilos of pipe for houses or irrigation projects." DeSain laughed. "I'll dream about pipes until I die, even if I never extrude another one."

Nathaniel turned back to Hailsham. "You have heavy equipment?"

"Not enough. And what I have is ancient. Making permacrete's the easy part. Transporting and laying and fusing it is where the problems are. You need tech-template equipment and metal . . . and we're always short of that."

"Always . . . there is something in short supply. Economics is the study of such shortages. There is an old saying—whatever be not there is rare." Nathaniel turned back to DeSain. "The piping—do you use Sir Hailsham's permacrete for other than huge water conduits?"

"No. It's too heavy for most applications. We mostly use hydrocarbon synthetics."

"You make your own feedstocks—or purchase them from the facility?"

"I wish I had my own feedstocks." DeSain shrugged. "But that takes credits and grower contracts—or fertile land—which also takes credits. We purchase from R-K and make do." He offered a tight smile. "That's all anyone can do anywhere, I'd guess."

"So it is. So it is." Nathaniel offered his own smile. "If you would not mind, gentlemen, we would very much like to discuss your contributions to the infrastructure of Artos and what you see as the planet's future needs. Perhaps Professor Ferro-Maine and I might visit you at your facilities in the days ahead?"

"Ah . . . ," began Durward Hailsham.

"Fine with me," said Keiffer DeSain with a short laugh. "I'll tell you more than you ever wanted to know about piping."

"Thank you both for your patience and forbearance." Nathaniel bowed, and eased away, to catch Walkerson blotting his forehead. The Ecolitan suppressed a grin and pulled out another of his overlarge kerchiefs. "Ah . . . it is warm, and I see I am not the only one who finds it so." He could sense Sylvia's concealed amusement and refrained from looking directly at her.

"A bit warm. A bit warm," conceded the port official. "Over there is Detsen Oconnor." Walkerson lifted his left hand toward a clean-shaven, brown-haired man in a dark blue jacket and shorts. "He's fond of you folks from Accord."

"And he is?" asked Sylvia.

"The head of the government biomonitoring laboratory. Very important, you understand. We're not that far out of planoforming."

"Of course."

Oconnor turned even before the three reached him. "Ecolitans. I recognized the uniforms. Good to see you."

"We're pleased to meet you, sir," said Sylvia.

"Fine work you people do. I keep abreast of all the journals out of Accord. I even did a seasonal residency at the Institute after I got my doctorate. Years ago . . . too many years ago, but I do my best to keep in touch. Dr. Hiense and I still trade abstracts, and he was most helpful when . . . oh, he's been helpful so many times, I'd be foolish to single out one instance." Oconnor beamed over his long nose at Sylvia. "Are you as good economists as your ecologists are?"

"Probably not," said Sylvia with a grin, "but we try. Professor Whaler is well known for his infrastructure work. I'm not."

"Ah . . . it all ties together. You cannot have a working economy without a working ecology, and there's a deplorable tendency to avoid

biodiversity in post-planoforming situations. I keep pushing for it, but
the growers keep telling me 'output, Detsen, output.'" The monitoring
official snorted. "Output—as if they'd have any output at all with a
monoculture approach—"

"Mostly synde beans for the hydrocarbon plants?" asked Nathaniel.

"First, it was luxury beef, and then there was the furor over the alba-
clams because the algae detritus—"

"Fascinating, I'm sure, Detsen," interjected Walkerson. "Would you
mind terribly, however, if I spirited the Ecolitans away for a moment?
I'll bring them back later . . . but a number of people . . ."

"Quite so." Oconnor smiled warmly at Sylvia and then at Nathaniel.
"You must send me a copy of your study. I'm asking now, because I
always forget. Hazards of the profession, you understand. So much to
watch, and so little time. You won't forget, will you?"

"You'll get a copy," promised Whaler.

"So good of you." Oconnor bowed. "I'm in the harbor building of the
ministry."

The Ecolitans followed Walkerson back in the direction of the food
table, and Nathaniel paused to take another small sip of the too-sweet
Kenward.

"Ah, the Ecolitans!" exclaimed a blond-and-white haired, lanky figure. Beside Jimson Sonderssen, a thin-faced man in long gray trousers
and a matching formal cutaway, piped in red, bowed from the waist.

"You will not mind that we . . . intruded upon your . . . occasion,
Port Authority Chief?"

"Your expertise in such matters is well known," said Walkerson
stiffly.

"Let us not be too curt, especially before the lovely Professor Ferro-
Maine." Sonderssen bowed again.

"The noted agricultural technology factor from the Federated Hegemony, Jimson Sonderssen." The Port Chief inclined his head but barely.

"My thanks." Sonderssen smiled, and turned. "My friend, Fridrik
VonHalsne, my counterpart in the Conglomerate," announced Sonderssen. "He says little, at least in any of the Anglo-derived tongues."

"Pleased am I to meet you," said Nathaniel ponderously in Fuardian.

For a moment, VonHalsne did not speak. Finally, he replied in
Fuardian, "You have the better of me. Not many on Artos speak Fuard."

"Not from Artos am I. Do you claim Tinhorn as home?"

Sylvia's eyes flicked from Whaler to Sonderssen. Beside her, Walkerson smothered a frown.

"No. I was born on Perugonia, although I live, when I'm not in the field, on the outskirts of Tinhorn." The Fuard inclined his head. "You are far from Accord."

"Where our studies take us . . . that is where we must go. What is your expertise—that of hydrocarbon plants? Or grains?"

"I . . . must attend to all those."

"Especially the beans and the legumes, would I not imagine," said Nathaniel, more slowly than he could have responded.

"Fridrik knows them all," said Sonderssen in English with a laugh. "If it grows, he knows it."

"My friend, Jimson, he knows far more than I," protested the Fuard in his own language.

"You both know a great deal," interposed Walkerson. "And I am sure that you will have more time to display that knowledge to the Ecolitans in the future. This is a social occasion tonight."

"But of course." Jimson Sonderssen bowed. "A pleasure to see you both again." He extended a card. "It has my local office."

Nathaniel pocketed the card.

The Fuard bowed silently, and both agricultural factors eased away.

"No sense of propriety, those two. None at all." Walkerson straightened his formal jacket.

"Robert," said Vivienne Evanston, appearing at Sylvia's elbow, "you must let me insist. I promised to introduce the Ecolitans to Kennis." The blond woman with the sparkling eyes and animated face turned to Sylvia. "That's Kennis Landis-Nicarchos. Kennis, you know, owns most of Lanceville, even the Blue Lion and the fusactor power concession," offered Vivienne, leading them toward the tall, slender red-haired man dressed in a deep blue outfit of formal jacket and shorts, with a pale blue ruffled shirt. "He is one of our leading lights."

"Great lights cast often equally great shadows." From his first glance, Nathaniel didn't care for the industrialist, not that he could have said why, but he'd come to trust his feelings. About people, intuition was often far better than reason, probably because it was based on whole-body intangibles and not just facts.

"You, too, have a forthright wit," said Vivienne with a bright smile, "and a discerning eye."

Nathaniel shook his head. "Not I. I am a man with a blunt wedge for wit."

"You are too modest, professor." Vivienne turned. "The Ecolitans,

Kennis. You said you wanted to meet them." Vivienne offered a smile and a head-bow.

"Kennis Landis-Nicarchos, at your service." The local industrialist, taller than Nathaniel, bowed deeply to Sylvia.

"Enchanted." Sylvia smiled politely.

"I am the enchanted one. I had no idea that such attractive Ecolitan professors existed, and an economist yet."

"Nathaniel Firstborne Whaler, and I am most pleased to meet you, Sir Nichos-Landarchos." Nathaniel offered a deep bow. "You must be most fond of blue."

"A failing, I must admit." Kennis turned back to Sylvia. "I could easily become fond of gray."

Nathaniel suppressed the simultaneous urges to grin and break the redhead's knees. "Gray is most becoming, especially upon the discerning."

"How did you become an economist?" the industrialist asked Sylvia. "Such a prosaic title . . ."

"I found that there was far more substance in economics than met the eye," said Sylvia.

"A woman of imperial substance. That I like."

"Kennis always knows what to say," added Vivienne. "And he is so charming. Everyone finds him delightful."

Nathaniel refrained from differing. The term "imperial" hadn't been lost on him, or the message. He glanced around the Unicorn Room, noting that the numbers had slowly shrunk. The two men in gray had vanished, as had Sonderssen and the Fuard and the Governor General.

"Now . . . Kennis . . . you'll have to relinquish your attentions for now," suggested Walkerson. "The professor has others to meet."

"I hear and obey." The industrialist bowed, then flashed a whitetoothed smile at Sylvia. "Until we meet again . . . and we will."

Walkerson guided them away from both Kennis and Vivienne. "Next you should say a few words to Laurence, there. He manages the Artos operations of the Bank of Camelot."

The three stopped before a round-faced man with a short white goatee.

"Professors Whaler and Ferro-Maine, Laurence. The Ecolitan infrastructure specialists."

"Laurence Karl-Abbe, pleased to meet you." The banker smiled. "We actually have some numbers, and if you'd like to stop by in the next few days, perhaps I could assist your study."

"You're most gracious," offered Nathaniel.

"I should be. We share a common plight. No one is totally comfortable with either economists or bankers. Do you know why we turn off the climate control in the bank after customer hours? Because reptiles don't need it." He gave a belly laugh.

"Do you know why losing a hand represents total disability for an economist?" countered Nathaniel. "Because he can't say, 'On the one hand . . . '"

"Enough . . ." said Sylvia with a forced laugh.

Walkerson shook his head sadly.

Nathaniel barely managed to retain the last names and faces as they circled the room and spoke and made small talk. Abruptly, he found himself clutching an empty wineglass and looking around a nearly deserted Unicorn Room.

"There," said Walkerson, in a self-satisfied tone. "I've gotten you properly introduced to almost everyone who is anyone in Lanceville, and your jaunt tomorrow should take care of the rest."

"I take it that this was the creme de la creme?" asked Sylvia.

"Precisely."

"Thank you. It's not the sort of thing we could have managed," Nathaniel said.

"My pleasure." Walkerson bowed. "My pleasure."

Nathaniel managed to avoid rolling his eyes, at least until they were outside the Blue Lion.

Bagot had the groundcar waiting for them. "The Guest House, sirs?"

"Please," offered Nathaniel, his eyes and detector scanning the area and both coming up empty.

He slumped into the rear seat beside Sylvia, shaking his head. "Receptions are worse than interviews."

"Because no one says much? And tiptoes around everything?"

"Putting together a study is a puzzle. You need numbers, but the numbers you get aren't usually the right ones. So you have to combine and analyze, and then everyone faults your methods. The people you talk to come in two kinds: those who are in charge—and they either don't know the details or won't say—and those who aren't, and they're afraid to tell you anything. So we dance around asking questions designed so that any answer will provide some information, and they dance around trying to provide as little as possible, unless they have an axe to grind, and that means the data is skewed, and we have to figure out how before we can use it."

"You *are* cynical."

He sighed. "Sometimes."

The foyer of the Guest House was vacant.

"Do you have this feeling that people are avoiding us?" asked Sylvia as she started up the stairs. "It's as though we have to be acknowledged, but that we're not people, not really."

"The way I felt in my audience with the Emperor when I first arrived on Old Earth."

"Was it that bad?"

He nodded.

"You never mentioned that."

"Outsiders are treated that way most places. It's nothing new." He opened the door to his room, but heard or saw nothing unusual. The bed was turned back, the draperies drawn, and the light on the bedside table on.

Nathaniel closed the door and paced across the room, noting that, once again, his case was not precisely where he had left it and that the closet door was fractionally ajar.

"More surveillance?" murmured Sylvia.

"To be expected."

"What did you think of Walkerson's little gathering?"

"Two things of interest," mused Nathaniel. "The gathering was almost a teaser of sorts, and those present were mostly male, and Chief Walkerson did not have his wife with him—or a feminine companion."

"Neither did Kennis."

"I noticed."

"Are you jealous?"

"I could be very jealous . . . except you're free to make your own choices and you didn't seem terribly interested in him—as interested as he was in you." He paused. "I also enjoyed your comment about a warm welcome. Interestingly, there was no reaction."

"Kennis wasn't really interested in me. He also didn't seem to notice when you scrambled his name. For most men, that would merit at least a quiet correction. He was more interested in delivering that message that said he knew who I was and feeling out whether I'd be interested in him."

"Another indication that we're part of a setup, but no indication of who actually created it."

"You don't have any idea?"

"He's not in any of the background material. He's not Avalonian, and not Imperial. We can ask around." Nathaniel frowned. "I didn't like him, even before he started flirting."

"He doesn't feel quite right. His come-on was too strong, and that bothered me."

"Good."

"Oh, Nathaniel . . ." Her lips brushed his cheek, then touched his lips, and her arms were around his neck. After a long kiss, she eased back. "You offer so much more than he does."

"He owns most of Lanceville," responded Nathaniel with a wry tone. "I own the clothes on my back, some few securities, and a little in savings."

"I'm not after possessions. You should know that." Sylvia frowned. "You said the gathering was a teaser."

"I didn't expect much more. The political heads of organizations seldom reveal much. You have to look at numbers, or count traffic or power lines. There were always hints about things here and there, but Walkerson was clever enough to let the hints surface, but never to let us hear the rest. And his forthright wife . . . ?" The sandy-haired Ecolitan spread his hands.

"They have wives—a rather hidebound and traditional society, I gather. But she wasn't there."

"Exactly." Nathaniel glanced toward the connecting door, still ajar. "We'd better check your room."

"You won't find anything."

"Probably not . . . just like we're not finding anything with our study." He slipped through the door to find her room a mirror of his—empty, the bed covers turned, draperies closed, and bedside light on.

He looked up from the detector as Sylvia eased back beside him. Her fingers squeezed his free left hand.

"I much prefer you." Then her arms went back around his neck.

XIV

A HIGH HAZE covered most of the sky, and the hot wind, bearing fine grit and bringing the odor of hydrocarb fuel and dust, blew out of the south. Nathaniel studied the waiting flitter.

"You forget how small these are," Sylvia said.

"Small? This must mass eight tonnes. Some things I've flown . . ." he shook his head, and unlatched the turbine cover. "I need to preflight this. You can get settled on that side."

Sylvia nodded and slid open the copilot's door.

Nathaniel just looked at the craft for a long moment, then moved toward the port turbine where he undid the catches.

"Sir?"

Nathaniel turned his attention from the uncovered port turbine to the approaching pilot. "Yes, Jersek?"

Jersek fingered his trimmed salt-and-pepper beard. "Well . . . I just wanted to tell you. I would have been out here when you came, but the factor and his friend stopped by, wanting to know about heavy lift flitters." The Port Authority pilot shook his head. "With all this flat land, we need to think about those? Anyway, wanted to tell you I had the tanks topped off this morning. If you're headed straight out and back, you've got enough for that with a good margin. You do sight-seeing around George's place, and you'll want to top off there. Use the good stuff—there's a tank buried by the windsock, and I'd let the pump run a moment before you put any in the tanks." Jersek paused. "You know about the stub tanks?"

"Right—they won't draw if the mains are below thirty."

"She's a good old bird, sir. Seen me through a lot."

"And she'll see you through more." The Ecolitan forced a grin.

The Port Authority pilot and maintenance chief nodded, then turned and ambled toward the building that held his office and Walkerson's.

Nathaniel methodically scanned the turbine, then fastened the cover, checking the catches. He repeated the process with the starboard turbine, and then used the pull-out steps to get to the rotor deck.

Sylvia had long since been strapped in by the time Nathaniel returned to the cockpit and began the checklist, murmuring the items to himself as he went through them.

"Sequencers . . . check. . . ."

"Diffusor . . . check . . ."

"Ignitors . . . check . . ."

He slipped on the helmet.

"Intercom . . . can you hear me?"

Sylvia nodded, and her helmet bobbed.

"The red button there—press it when you want to talk."

"I hear you."

"Good. Comm freqs . . . set . . ."

Finally, he touched the port ignitor.

Wuuuffff . . . eeeeeee . . .

Once the port turbine was up and in the green, he started the starboard one, completed the checklist, then released the rotor brake. The flitter swayed as the heavy rotors began to turn.

"Rotors . . . engaged."

He checked the instruments one last time, then triggered the comm. "Artos main, this is Port Angel two, ready to lift."

"Angel two, cleared to the southwest, radian two eight five. Report the river on departure."

"Stet. Two here, lifting this time. Will report the river."

Nathaniel eased power to the thrusters, and the flitter slipped onto the air cushion. He air-taxied slowly until he had the old Welk clear of the Port Authority hangar. The Ecolitan swallowed back a touch of bile—the unburned exhaust gases weren't wonderful for his digestion. With spacecraft you smelled ozone and hot metal, but not exhaust fumes.

From the copilot's seat Sylvia studied the patched permacrete and the hangar walls that were an alternating pattern of old and new synthetic hydrocarbon building sheets.

Once past the hangar, Whaler added power to the thrusters and lowered the nose slightly, keeping the flitter on its air cushion as the speed built up. At one hundred fifty klicks, he eased the stick back and let the flitter climb.

From the air, the shuttle port looked like a permacrete X imposed on different-sized squares of varied green, across which ran the tan lines of the shuttle landing strips. To the east was the gray line of the ocean, a darker gray blot that was Lanceville, and the tiny blue dot that was the Blue Lion.

"Tower, Angel two, clearing the river this time."

"Stet, two. Report the river inbound on return. Same freq."

"Stet, tower." Nathaniel eased the flitter onto the outbound two nine five radial and continued to climb, scanning the instruments. The heads-up display had long since ceased working—as was the case with most of the older Welk-Symmons.

"How far is the Reeves-Kenn spread?" Sylvia's voice crackled through the earsets of the helmet.

"Two hundred fifty kilos, give or take a few—almost due southwest." He inclined his helmet slightly.

Once past the river, the ground beneath began to slope upward, and to dry out, showing traces of grayish sand that grew more prominent with every kilo. "The midplateau desert, according to the maps." His voice sounded scratchy in his own earset, and he hoped it was just the set. "Badlands . . . mostly."

"They didn't planoform it, so close to Lanceville?"

"It's mostly lava of some sort—I don't know the term, but it's the stuff that you get on hotcore worlds with no oxygen and no way to reduce it. Give it a few thousand years, and it'll be fine. Right now it isn't worth the trouble."

"People won't wait that long."

"Probably not, but it takes money, and that's something in short supply here on Artos."

The terrain below had become one of rough stone hills, joined by sweeps of gray sand. Nothing grew in the ocean of stone and sand where the only movement was that of wind-swept silica particles, not anything large enough to see from the flitter cockpit.

"Desolate," Sylvia said after a time.

"Gives an idea of what Artos was like centuries ago."

The sky was clear—and empty—like the desert beneath.

"Do you have any better idea why we're doing this study?" asked Sylvia after a long silence.

"No. It's getting clearer that the government in New Avalon wants something from it, probably for us to reveal something that they can't afford to disclose and need an impartial source for. Either that or support for some program. They want to be able to say that it was Accord's—or the Institute's—idea. That means politics, and trouble. But I don't know what they want, only that someone doesn't want us to find it, whatever *it* may be. I'm hoping this little trip will shed some light."

"You don't sound certain it will."

"I'm always a skeptic when you get to politics."

His words drew a laugh, and he smiled to himself, even as the silence drew out and as he checked the nav screens.

"On course . . . beacon's clear."

After another stretch of silence, he cross-checked the ground beacon readings. Supposedly their destination was less than twenty kilos ahead. With that reminder, he re-checked the main tanks—down twenty percent—and switched the fuel transfer pumps on. Later Welk flitters didn't have that problem. They had others, generally harder to resolve because they used more microtronics, and higher technology wasn't always suited to conditions of high mechanical stress. Flitters incorporated high mechanical stress, and always would, at least until antigrav units were finally developed that would work planetside.

To the southwest, beyond the gray and tan of sand and rock appeared a hazy line of grayish green that grew more distinct.

Nathaniel kept his scan moving—instruments, horizon, ground ahead—as the flitter carried them toward the green, absently flicking off the transfer pumps when the main tanks registered full. He doubted that the automatic cutoffs worked, or worked well.

Beyond desert came the first flush of green, interspersed with gray sand, then the river, still flat and wide and smooth, and then more green. A long strip of permacrete road ran northwest from the cluster of hilltop buildings until it intersected a long arrow-straight section of the wide permacrete main road that presumably made its way back to Lanceville.

"Kenn base, Port Angel two inbound."

Sylvia jerked in her seat. Had she been dozing? Nathaniel didn't blame her. The flight had been anything but intriguing, and he personally hadn't been that scintillating. Then, pilots with sparkling personalities in the cockpit, like bold pilots, usually didn't live to be that old.

The Ecolitan waited, then triggered the transmitter again. "Kenn base, Port Angel two inbound."

"That you, Jersek, still flying that antique?"

"Negative. Ecolitans Whaler and Ferro-Maine, inbound to see George Reeves-Kenn."

"Stet. Do you have the strip and the wind indicator?"

"That's affirmative."

"Set her down there. See you after touchdown."

"Not the most formal place," Nathaniel said.

"After last night?" she asked. "That gathering was so formal everyone creaked. And you and all those proverbs . . ."

"I've got several hundred more . . ."

"No . . ."

"You see . . . they're working." He eased off power from the turbines and brought the nose back as he eased the flitter into a left-hand turn to bring it into the wind, then past the fluorescent green windsock and onto the cleared claylike strip that ran the length of the low ridge. He settled the craft into a hover and air-taxied toward the spot where a single figure waited by a small shed a hundred meters or so east of a long low stone house.

"You make that look easy," said Sylvia.

"I've had some practice," he admitted.

When he stepped from the flitter, Nathaniel's hands were empty, since he'd reluctantly decided to leave his datacase in the Guest House—not that there was any information that wasn't available one way or another to New Avalonian intelligence, or the Federated Hegemony, or whoever. Sylvia slipped the strap of her case over her shoulder and closed the transparent permaglass door on the copilot's side of the flitter.

They walked toward the waiting man.

"George Reeves-Kenn." He was rail thin with a tanned and leathery face. The green eyes were hard, and the white-gray hair was short.

"Nathaniel Whaler."

"Sylvia Ferro-Maine."

"Welcome to Connaught. Understand you two wanted a look-see at how our operation runs. That's what old Walk said, anyway." Reeves-Kenn waited. "Thought economists just looked at numbers and paper." He frowned. "Can't say as you look like an economist—more like a trooper. Guess you Ecolitan types are always part military."

"We've been called that," Nathaniel said. "I can send you a copy of my latest monograph, if you'd like, *The Unrecognized Diseconomies of Decentralized Metals Refining*."

"In plain talk . . . what was it?"

Nathaniel shrugged. "In basic terms, it's an exposition that quantifies how much more asteroid mining costs than people recognized. But it sounds more impressive to academics if all the title words are long."

Reeves-Kenn smiled, briefly, and turned to Sylvia. "And you look more like a dancer . . ."

"I was, once, before I found happiness in economics." She gave the beef grower a warm smile.

"Best we get started. It'll all make more sense if you take a ride first." Reeves-Kenn began to walk toward the corral just below the landing strip. Adjoining the corral was a barn.

The Ecolitans exchanged glances and followed.

Reeves-Kenn halted at a fence post made of formed plastic and gestured toward the black horse on the other side of the plastic composite "wire." "This is Wild Will."

Nathaniel looked at the horse. The horse looked at Nathaniel. The Ecolitan glanced toward Sylvia, who seemed to share his reaction.

"You not familiar with horses?" asked Reeves-Kenn.

"Not really," admitted the Ecolitan. "I've ridden a few times, but I'm certainly no expert."

Sylvia just shook her head.

"We've got gentle mounts." The rancher gestured toward a figure on the shaded north side of the barn. "Jem?"

"Sir?" Jem ambled out of the shade of the shed. He was dark-haired, clean-shaven, wearing long trousers and half-calf boots, brown and scarred.

"Our guests are Ecolitans—they're economists, not rovers. Professor Whaler and Professor Ferro-Maine."

Jem bowed. "Pleased to meet you."

"Jem here—he's one of my lead rovers, and he'll be happy to show you around." George Reeves-Kenn smiled. "Get them mounts—Happy and Pokey—and give them the short tour, and then we'll have a late lunch at the house." The rancher turned to the Ecolitans. "Screen-work and bureaucracy—we still have too much here, and I need to catch up on it." He nodded, grinned at Jem, and departed with long strides, back toward the house.

"If you'll wait here," said the rover, "I'll bring out your mounts."

"You don't look happy about the horses," said Sylvia.

"I worry about riding something that has its own mind and masses five to ten times what I do." Nathaniel glanced toward the barn and the wide door, through which Jem led two saddled horses.

"Five times," said Sylvia absently.

"That's enough." He grinned. "You think all the time, and she that thinks seldom finds ease."

"No more . . ."

"Here you go—Happy and Pokey, gentle as you'd ever want."

"Do you have a brother who works for the Port Authority?" asked Sylvia.

"GB? He works for Chief Walkerson." With deft movements, Jem tied the reins to the sole hitching rail—also heavy plastic—outside the corral gate. "All he rides is a groundcar. I could never stand being cooped up in a pile of metal, or a building, not me. Now, professor, Happy likes ladies better." He gestured toward the dark chestnut.

"And I get Pokey?" asked Nathaniel.

"He's not that slow. He just doesn't like to gallop." The rover hurried back to the barn, returning riding a gray.

"What's in the red pack?" asked Sylvia, pointing at the circular object behind her saddle. There was one behind Nathaniel's saddle as well.

"That's a desert kit . . . survival kit, in case you get stranded. We all carry them." Jem reined up, waiting. "Artos is still wild in places." The rover cleared his throat and looked at the two Ecolitans and their mounts.

Nathaniel got the message and untied Pokey, then climbed into the saddle, and watched as Sylvia did the same—more gracefully, he suspected.

"We'll head out to the end of the ridge," announced Jem, turning the gray to the southeast.

Sylvia lifted her reins, and lurched in the saddle as Happy slow-trotted after the rover. Nathaniel gingerly flicked the brown horse's reins, and Pokey lumbered after the other two, losing ground with every step.

Jem reined up and waited with Sylvia until Nathaniel's gelding carried the Ecolitan to the end of the rise. Grass-covered hills stretched southward, and a line of trees to the west of the ridge that held the house and buildings outlined the course of the river.

"The spread runs another two hundred kays south along the river. Most is like this, grass and hills, but we got a couple stands of woods, and a few more set. 'Course, it'll take another thirty years before they're much."

Horned cattle—nearly a hundred—grazed beside the pond below.

"What kind of animals are those?" asked Sylvia.

"Cattle—modified Tee-type longhorns. They did something to their genes—George told me, but I don't recall. It allows them to digest the grass better. They're tamer, too. Don't have big predators here." Jem started the gray downhill toward the cattle.

Around the pond, the grass had been churned into a muddy mass, an area that Jem gave a wide berth.

Nathaniel suppressed a frown. "What feeds the pond?"

"It's pumped from the river. We've got ponds across the spread. That way, we can rotate where they graze. Got a bunch of herds. Someday, we'll get natural ponds. Till then . . ."

Up close, the cattle were larger than they had seemed—monsters whose shoulders were level with Nathaniel's waist on horseback and whose horns spread more than two meters.

"You're certain that they're tame?" the Ecolitan asked, noting the pointed horn tips.

"So long as you don't whack their nostrils. Even then, they'd just knock you aside."

Just being knocked aside by something that weighed nearly a tonne would be painful, if not worse.

"We'll ride out to the river, if you can hang on that long."

"As long as we don't gallop," said Sylvia.

"No hurry. This beats riding fences or herding strays out of the sand. Gets hotter out there."

Nathaniel felt for the big kerchief, blotting his forehead. "Rather hot here already."

"This is cool compared to that." Jem laughed. "We can't go too far into the desert anyway."

"Is that because of the heat?"

"The heat's part of it, but the ground's unstable, too. George or Terril could explain that better than me. I'm just a dumb rover."

The three rode abreast across the flat expanse of grass, leaving the herd behind.

"No beans—that sort of thing?" asked Whaler.

"Got to have some hydrocarb source, I guess, but George says that it won't be on this spread, not ever. Feels strong, he does. Even the maize for fattening the steers comes from the boss's commercial lands closer to Lanceville."

A series of flies buzzed around the horses and riders as they neared the river, but Nathaniel would have bet that the planoforming had left out mosquitoes.

The river was about a hundred meters wide, smooth-flowing dark gray water, bounded by willowlike trees and taller grasses on either side.

"Marsh grasses," said Nathaniel, glad to recognize something that fit ecologically.

"Yeah . . . George doesn't like it much, but he says we got to leave the grass and trees. Dr. Oconnor says we'd have the river ripping up all the grasslands without them. Used to be straighter, I'm told, but it'll find its own path over time, and there's no good way to change that." Jem turned in the saddle. "You're ecologic folks. That true?"

"Pretty much," admitted Whaler. "The optimum is to work with natural flows and not to combat them." He managed not to wince at the pedantry of the words.

"Got some fish in there, but we can't catch 'em yet. Too many heavy metals to eat. Some day, they say."

The two Ecolitans nodded.

"Seen enough?" asked Jem. "We ought to head back."

Sylvia and Nathaniel exchanged glances. He nodded. "Fine with us."

As they rode back toward the rise that held the ranch house and the flitter, Nathaniel studied the cropped grass, noting the absence of bushes and competing vegetation, trying not to shake his head.

The air was still, and the sun hotter yet. Nathaniel blotted his forehead several times more as Pokey followed the other two mounts back.

"I haven't seen anything like a cattle processing plant." The Ecolitan glanced at the stone walls of the ranch house and then at the long stone barn that finally appeared above them. "Is that in Lanceville?"

"Hardly. George doesn't like things outside the spread, not unless it's crops."

"But . . ."

"George likes his views." Jem laughed. "Everyone knows that. Not much to the plant, but I can show you. We'll go this way." He turned his mount westward.

The three circled the base of the rise that held the main house until they entered a swale between the long ridgelike rise and a much smaller hill.

"That's it." Jem gestured to his left and grinned.

A permacrete strip, wide enough for a lorry, if not much wider, ran down from the top of the rise and through the swale where Jem had reined up and then to a heavy lorry dock set in the side of the lower hill.

"Under the hill?" asked Nathaniel.

"It makes sense," said Sylvia. "George likes his views. So he built the processing plant under an artificial hill."

"Not just the plant, professor," Jem added. "The slaughterhouse and everything."

Sylvia grasped the antique saddle horn, leaned toward Nathaniel, and murmured. "Not another word about underground stuff."

"All right," he said amiably.

She lurched in the saddle for a moment before managing to straighten up.

"Careful there, miss . . . I mean, professor." Jem shrugged. "That's pretty much it. I mean, the grasslands go forever, but all you'll see is more grass and more steers and the river. 'Sides, I need to get you back to the main house." The rover flicked the gray's reins.

After a moment, with a last look at the hill that concealed a processing plant, the two Ecolitans followed.

George Reeves-Kenn was waiting as the three rode up to the barn area from where they had started.

Nathaniel eased himself out of the saddle, wondering if he might not have been in better shape if he'd walked or run. Sylvia descended with more grace and less obvious stiffness.

"How did you like it?" Reeves-Kenn grinned.

"It's awesome," admitted Sylvia.

"Impressive. Most impressive," added Nathaniel, massaging his backside slightly. "Most impressive is the skill to ride horses."

"It takes some doing, but you can learn. Jem there—he'd never seen a horse up close, and he rides like he was born to it." The rancher nodded. "Ready to eat?"

"I could manage that," said Sylvia.

"I also."

The dining room was at one end of the long stone house, with the entire north wall comprised of tinted glass. A single table was set for three people, all three places on one side, facing northward and looking out.

Reeves-Kenn nodded toward the center place. "The rose between two thorns."

"Sometimes I feel thorny . . . but thank you." Sylvia took the center place, and all three sat.

"We don't get outworlders here at Connaught that often. They take a look at Lanceville, the fusactor system, the harbor, and the hydrocarb processing plant, maybe Sebastion's marine farms and assimilators, and they think they've seen Artos." The white-haired rancher handed the basket of still-warm bread to Sylvia. "This is Artos." He gestured toward the hillside below the expansive glass windows, toward the grass-covered ground, and the river, and the desert in the distance to the northeast.

"It's beautiful in a stark way." Sylvia took a chunk of bread and passed the basket to Whaler.

"Your family had much to do with creating Artos as it is now, I understand," offered Nathaniel, breaking off a chunk of the crusty bread.

"Most folks choose to forget that, Ecolitan. We're just inconvenient leftovers now that the synde beans and the marine projects have taken off. Blood-mare! It was the credits from luxury beef that kept us going. Now, they talk as if beef . . ." George shook his head. "They don't know what sort of gene-tinkering it took. Too much arsenic and other stuff in the land and grass. How do you get steers that can ingest it and still produce edible beef?"

"It took some doing, I'm sure," Nathaniel offered, taking some of the warm bread. He had the feeling he was going to be sunburned, maybe brightly burned. He reached for the water.

"Doing? The gene-plan alone was more than ten million."

An older woman stepped across the dining room with a green platter that she eased onto the center of the green linen.

"Thank you, Estelle."

Estelle nodded.

"Try these. Marinated beef. Guarantee you've never tasted better—even if I raised the steers."

Nathaniel waited for Sylvia, then helped himself. He cut a piece, then chewed slowly. If anything, the marinated beef strips were even more tender and tasty than the steaks and stew served at the Guest House. "They represent the best I have tasted."

"Me, too."

"Told you so. Can't raise this in a tank." The rancher took another mouthful before speaking. "What did you think of the Unformed Desert?"

Nathaniel looked at Reeves-Kenn's weathered face.

"That's what they call the badlands between here and Lanceville." The grower shook his head. "My grandsire—he said he could recall when most of Artos looked like that."

Nathaniel thought the rancher was stretching. Planoforming was a far longer and more arduous process. But he nodded. "It makes you think."

"Think? No one thinks anymore." The rancher snorted. "The environauts in Camelot think that ranching takes too much land, and that all of this should be left and allowed to develop naturally. Naturally—there's not a damned thing natural about any of it. We built it. The redistributionists think we're dinosaurs, and want us to become extinct quietly, so they can give every soul in the commonwealth his thirty hectares. No one remembers that we're the ones whose fathers and fore-fathers lived in domes and choked on ammonia and . . ." He stopped and offered a sheepish grin. "I get too upset about this. I'm sure you don't want to hear a diatribe."

"It's interesting, and part of Artos," Sylvia answered.

The three ate quietly for a time, the only interruption that of Estelle replacing the empty basket with another one—again full of hot and fresh bread.

"According to your rover, you have a well-integrated facility here," said Nathaniel. "It appears most modern, yet there are those who find you less than enthused about technology."

"Folks think that technology means change, that you have to do something just because you can or because it's a shade cheaper." Reeves-Kenn shook his head. "Look at Jem. He's a first-class rover, and a horse is better than any flitter or scooter for what he does. But we put high-tech survival packs on every horse, and we use the latest technology in slaughtering and packing. I believe in being the master of technology, not its slave. Those idiots in Camelot—all they want to know is what sort of tech-transfers you can develop and what kind of transstellar credit you can develop. I was talking about Jem. He rides a horse, and his brother pilots flitters and groundcars. Ought to be room for both, but you can't have both if you break up the big spreads."

"Why not?" asked Sylvia. "Doesn't everyone say you can?"

"They don't know what they're talking about. Smaller bean growers—take them—they have to share mechs, pool transport—all that means more technology. That means a bigger tech base. To support a bigger tech base means growing more hydrocarb sources and more tech-transfers. More hydrocarb crops means plowing under the grasslands, because no one wants to go through what my grandfather did—they just want to take the results. They'll do that over my dead body." The rancher snorted. "Not that it will come to that. But all those tech-transfers mean more metal drops, or deep coring, and those cost. To pay those off requires more emphasis on technology—and then Artos'll be trapped, just like New Avalon is. Once you get on that spiral, you never get off."

"Such has occurred on more than a few planets—that the Institute has seen." Nathaniel sipped the cold water, realizing that he'd effectively stuffed himself, and pushed back his plate fractionally, to remind himself not to eat more than anything. He probably felt stuffed because there hadn't been any vegetables or greens either.

"How did you folks escape that?" George refilled his water glass.

"Luck—and isolation—and a war that left most systems reluctant to trade high-tech concepts." The Ecolitan shrugged. "We had to limit technology to interstellar transport and the directly related infrastructure. By the time we escaped that need, the cultural patterns were established."

"We haven't had that kind of luck. Doesn't look like we will, but I guess we're the type of folks that have always had to make their own." He paused. "Would you like some tea?"

"No, thank you," said Whaler. "Not another item could I eat. It was all delicious . . . but . . ."

"Absolutely," added Sylvia. "If I ate like this every day, I'd look like your steers."

"Never, professor. Never." The rancher's leathery face cracked in a grin.

"I think not either," said Nathaniel.

Sylvia shook her head. "You're both kind, but I know better."

"I suppose you need to go, and I need to get back to checking on a few things." The rancher glanced at Sylvia, then rose.

So did the Ecolitans.

"Lovely view," said Sylvia as they walked from the dining room.

"It is. I'd like to keep it."

"Do you think changes are occurring that rapidly?" asked Whaler.

"Quicker than that. That Landis-Nicarchos fellow is buying up Lanceville faster than folks can sell, and they're moving to ConTrio. But what will they do there when their money runs out? Come back and work in whatever tech-slavery he's got set up? Or push for more welfare? That means you run a tech surplus, and you can't do that without metals mining and more hydrocarb growth." The rancher shook his head as he held the outside door.

"That amount of credits has to come from somewhere," pointed out Sylvia.

"They do. No one's said, but some come from Camelot, some from the Federated Hegemony, and he's promising the politicos in Camelot that he'll buy out the low-interest long-term development bonds in return for concessions."

"Is there any . . . documentation," asked Nathaniel, stepping around a small water spigot that fed a low trough.

"Of course not. He's too smart for that, but it's what he's doing."

"Without some form . . ."

"I know. I know." A note of weariness crept into Reeves-Kenn's voice. "Other than that . . . how will this visit affect your report?"

"Everything affects our report." Nathaniel laughed.

"Everything," added Sylvia, "including outstanding marinated beef."

"I hope so. Hate to lose all this. Hate to see my grandchildren lose it and have Artos turn into a miniature of the rodent-mill in Camelot."

Nathaniel picked up one of the red survival kits beside the shed. "Might we borrow this?"

"You can have it. We can spare that." Reeves-Kenn grinned. "Call it a souvenir. Call it a reminder that you have to master technology, not let it master you."

Nathaniel nodded. He agreed with the beef grower's points, but felt that there was more left unsaid—a great deal more.

As Sylvia strapped herself in place, Whaler walked around the flitter, then pulled out the step brackets and climbed up to check the gearbox and rotor—and the control links. From what he could tell nothing had been touched.

He opened the turbine cover, trying not to shake his head. He couldn't see that anything was out of place, but that, unfortunately, didn't mean much. While he knew spacecraft systems from at least a cursory maintenance point of view, his understanding of internal combustion turbine systems was more limited.

The ducts to the antitorque difusor were clear—a malfunction there would be great fun!

The remainder of the craft's preflight seemed normal, and he strapped himself in and began the preignition checks. After he finished them, he lit off the first turbine. The power system registered normal. Then he brought the rotors on line, and, after a wave toward Reeves-Kenn, lifted the flitter into a hover, checking all the indicators and systems again before beginning a true liftoff run.

As the craft swept over the cattle herd and eased into a climbing turn to the northeast, Whaler's eyes went to the permacrete highway to the north, the stretch that was arrow-straight for nearly four kilos and twice as wide as any other stretch.

Then he swallowed. Because of the hills, the prevailing winds would almost always be out of the south. The damned highway was nothing but a shuttle runway—or it could be. Was he getting too suspicious?

He took another look, first at the artificial hill that held the processing plant. He swallowed and took the flitter into a wide circle of the main complex.

"Sylvia . . . look at the hills around the house."

"I'm looking." After a moment, she added, "I'm not a geologist, but that pattern doesn't look normal. He's got a lot hidden there, and I thought he might, if you recall . . ."

"You were right. But what?" He eased out the vidimager and took a series of shots. They'd probably end up blurred, but he had to try.

"It could be anything. Supplies, a tech-transfer facility, an armory . . . who knows?"

At the end of the single circle, he straightened the flitter on a heading of one zero five, not quite a reciprocal of the outbound course line, then leveled off. "What did you think about George Reeves-Kenn?"

"Gracious . . . defensive about being a beef-grower . . . or rancher . . .

very handsome, I'd bet, when he was younger. A good host, even for an Avalonian."

"The more handsome the host, the dearer the reckoning . . ."

"Cynical. If you react like that . . . I won't tell you."

He turned his helmet toward the copilot's seat, then grinned back as he saw the smile beneath the tinted face shield.

Beneath the flitter, the Unformed Desert scrolled past, the same wasteland of unchanging rock and sand, rock and sand.

Even as he checked airspace, orientation, and instruments, Nathaniel could feel all sorts of inchoate thoughts swirling through his mind. Reeves-Kenn seemed both straightforward and somehow deceptive, but the Ecolitan couldn't quite put his finger on anything specific, only on a feeling—and he hated relying just on feelings, especially when they had to produce a hard-copy report.

Abruptly, the pilot cocked his head, listening.

Thwop, thwop . . . thwop, thwop, thwop . . .

The rotors sounded normal, but the faintest screeching had surfaced beneath the roaring whine of the turbines. His eyes went to the antique engine instruments, catching the slow rise in EGT and the fractional power loss off the left turbine.

He kept listening.

A second faint screeching added its supra-audible noise to the first, and the second EGT began to inch upward, matching that of the first turbine. A quick or casual scan of the instruments would reveal neither—not for a while.

He looked out across the midplateau desert—they were nearly seventy kilos from the Reeves-Kenn spread, with another sixty to go before they reached the river by the shuttle port. He began to ease slightly more power into the rotors, trying to calculate the trade-offs. If the damage were calculated, he'd need the altitude.

There was no way they'd be able to cross forty or fifty kilos of desert in midsummer—assuming that they could walk away from the wreck that was about to occur.

Should he set it down? He shook his head. The rotors were fine, and so were the control links. Sabotaging those would have been too obvious, and too easily detected by the most cursory of preflights. So that meant a fire on touchdown or flare.

He wasn't sure about the form of the sabotage, but he had an idea that the turbines would seize rather abruptly, and the key to their survival lay in his shutting them down just before they seized—and not being in the driest part of the badlands.

From what he recalled . . . he eased the craft into a gentle turn to bring it onto a west-northwest heading.

"Isn't Lanceville that way?" asked Sylvia.

"We may be having some mechanical trouble, and, if we do, I don't want to set down in the middle of this wasteland."

"Accidental trouble, or assisted trouble?"

"If it's accidental, it's all too convenient." He cocked his ears again, straining. Was the abrasive whine louder? He shook his head. How could he tell? "Lock your harness. We're going to lose power, and when we do, we're going down fast."

"Locked."

"Good." He scanned the terrain below, noting each possible landing site, hoping for hard and flat rock. Sand was too uncertain, and could conceal too much, though he'd take sand over sharp rocks.

"We'll need to clear the cockpit as soon as the rotors stop. Can you make sure you take that desert kit?"

"I've got it here."

The Ecolitan kept scanning the instruments and looking westward toward what he hoped was a darker gray—the river and the planoformed lands that bordered it. The flitter continued to gain altitude slowly, as Nathaniel tried to calculate the strain and altitude trade-offs, as the river neared imperceptibly.

An almost subsonic vibration began to shake the fuselage, but not the rotors—a sure sign that the vibration was coming from the turbines.

Abruptly, the EGTs pegged, and a sheering sound lashed through the cockpit. Even before the sound vanished, along with the sound of the turbines, Nathaniel had dumped all the pitch off the rotors, and dropped the nose, aiming due west—for a slightly inclined sheet of what seemed to be rock.

As the flitter dropped abreast of his hoped-for landing site, he eased the craft into a slight bank, trying to keep the flitter in balance to stretch every meter of altitude.

"Too fast," he muttered to himself. "Slow . . . ease it back . . . check the altitude."

Two more red lights blazed on the panel—fire lights.

"Easy . . ."

At a hundred meters, he leveled the nose, and at thirty, brought back the nose and pulled full pitch, then flattened the flare as the flitter's sickening drop slowed.

"... tail straight ..."

The ground still seemed to rise too quickly, and he could see small jagged edges in the rocky plain. The smell of hot metal and smoke was seeping into the cockpit as he pulled full collective, trying to milk the last bit of lift from the slowing rotors.

Thudddddd ... Clunnkkkkk ...

As the flitter swayed on the uneven, rocky ground, one hand went to the overhead rotor brake, while the other slashed along the electrical switches.

He unfastened his own harness, and when he could see the front blade quiver to a halt, he slid back the door and grabbed the kit from under the seat, not knowing what was in it.

"Run! Straight ahead! Get behind that hump!" His feet were pumping as he stumbled out of the cockpit.

Sylvia was in front of him and opening space between them.

They both half-crouched, half-skidded behind the low line of boulders, Sylvia first.

Whoooshhh!

Even from behind the small outcropping, he could feel the heat wash across the air above them, but he just lay on his back gasping. "Out of shape ... can't believe ..."

"Give ... me ... some ... credit ..." She gasped back.

"Lots ... wasn't talking about you."

As he lay there, he opened the kit he'd pulled from beneath the seat, reading the label. "Emergency pilot supplies ..." he murmured, "New Avalon military issue." He looked through the items. A plastic flask of water—that would help, as would the floppy sun hat. He set the desalinization kit aside and pocketed the three-shot miniature stunner, as well as the pencil flare set. That might have other uses.

Finally, he rolled over and peered out. The flitter's intense initial fire-burst had subsided to a mere roaring fire. "Are you up to a short fifteen kilo walk?"

Sylvia sat up and brushed the short dark hair off her damp forehead. "I assume it's necessary?"

He gestured back at the burning wreckage. "I doubt that the locator beacon is operating, and there isn't a satellite surveillance system. Besides, do we wish to accept the hospitality of those most likely to find us?"

"When you phrase it that way . . . which direction?"

"That way." He pointed west.

"Isn't Lanceville in the other direction?" She shook her head. "I'm an idiot. So is a lot of sand."

"Fifty kilos, give or take a few."

"And you figure how many going west?" asked Sylvia.

"Ten in the sand, four or five beyond that."

"I was getting out of shape anyway. I would complain about eating too much." She adjusted the desert kit into its pack form and shouldered it.

Nathaniel did the same with the supply kit.

The hills weren't that high or steep, not to the eye, but they had crossed only half a dozen before Sylvia stopped, panting. "My legs ache already."

"Mine, too. More CO_2 in the air. System has a harder time flushing out wastes," said Nathaniel in between deep, heaving breaths.

They looked back to where a thin line of smoke circled into the cloudless green-blue sky.

"No one is looking yet."

"Not yet. They wouldn't want to find survivors. That would be embarrassing."

"Then we'd better keep moving."

"Try to avoid the sand . . . takes too much effort."

"Fine with me," Sylvia answered over her shoulder, as Nathaniel struggled to catch up.

Having more mass also had its disadvantages, he reflected as he finally drew even with her, trying to keep his feet from sinking into the deeper sand.

That was the pattern—three or four small hills and a rest, then three or four more.

After several dozen hills, Nathaniel found himself squinting—because the sun was hanging just above the western horizon. "Where . . . did . . . the . . . day . . . go?"

"Happens . . . when . . . you're having . . . a good . . . time." Sylvia panted as she stopped at the hill crest.

He offered her his water bottle, taking out the kerchief and blotting his forehead. Forest lord, late afternoon or not it was hot! The sun hat helped, but not a lot.

"Why . . . the . . . the flitter?"

"Because," Nathaniel glanced at the low hill beyond the one where they stood, "they were doing double duty—crippling Walkerson's resources and getting us."

"Who? The smaller growers? Kennis What's-his-name? Or . . . it isn't the Empire . . ."

"Probably not, but who knows?" He laughed, and the sound was harsh because his throat was dry, despite the water. "It's almost as complex as New Augusta. Let's go. We need to reach the river. They've got boats there. Maybe we can get a ride to Lanceville."

"How far to the river?"

"Another eight kays—that's a guess."

A faint *thwop-thwop-thwop* echoed across the stillness of the Unformed Desert. Both turned back east, toward the dark spot in the sky.

Sylvia took a deep breath. "We'd better get moving."

Nathaniel nodded. "They shouldn't see us from here, but we'd better keep an eye—and ear—out for them."

By the time he finished and took a deep breath, he had to hurry to catch up with Sylvia.

XV

"NOW WHAT?" ASKED Sylvia, water dripping down her face, a face Nathaniel knew was red like his, although seeing the sunburn was difficult in the late twilight as they knelt by the edge of the river.

He splashed his face again, with water that smelled slightly medicinal. Iodine in the water, or some other trace? The background infopaks had said the waters were fishable and swimmable, but how fishable and swimmable? Jem had said the fish weren't edible. He shrugged. "The road's on the other side, and I don't see any bridges. We could rest, and then swim across."

"It's deeper than it looks."

"Any other ideas?"

"We could follow it for a while. We certainly won't die of thirst or dehydration now."

"We can rest for a bit," he said, walking toward one of the larger of the small willow trees and sitting down with his back against the trunk.

"I could . . . stand a rest." Sylvia sat down almost beside him. After a moment, she asked, "Is it always like this with you?"

"What . . . like the flitter? No . . . sometimes it's dull. I remember one time when all I did was sit in an orbit station and scan screens and dump data into a matrix to determine technology-transfer trade patterns." He laughed. "For two standard months."

"Were most of your 'consulting' assignments like that ?"

"No. Most are like this. We never get the easy ones. The Institute charges too much. So . . ." He shrugged.

"I'm tired."

"Me, too."

From the darkness and quiet came the sound of insects, and the gurgle of the river, and even the rumbling of a groundlorry on the distant highway.

Nathaniel jerked awake, realizing he must have dozed off.

A set of reddish lights seemed to float on the river. He squinted, trying to make out the shapes, then staggered up, putting a hand out and steadying himself on the willow trunk. Every muscle in his body seemed to protest as he touched Sylvia's shoulder and made his way toward the most solid section of the bank.

"Hello . . . the riverboat . . ."

The lights veered slightly toward the shore.

"Can you give some stranded travelers a lift?" he yelled.

"If you can get aboard, you're welcome to the ride," came back a scratchy voice. "I'll slow the pack, but that's all I can do."

The two Ecolitans dashed through the knee-deep water, splashing in all directions, then bounced through the deeper water, and finally swam to the dark hull of the barge, feeling their way along the hull until they found a ladder. Sylvia half-vaulted, half-climbed onto the barge, while Nathaniel levered himself up after her, scraping his forearm in the process.

"Just walk along the catwalk there. It'll take you back to the crossplank," called the gravelly voice from the dark shape of what seemed a pilot house. "You all on board?"

"We're on," said Nathaniel, dripping and glad for the first time that it was summer and not cold.

The barge bucked slightly, and the sound of the engines dropped to a purr.

Sylvia led the way aft, across the catwalk, and then up to a raised and covered pilot house. A handful of instruments glowed in reddish light.

"Anna-Marie FitzReilly," said the square-faced, gray-haired woman at the wheel. "Guess I qualify as the master or whatever of this puttboat and barge assembly." Her eyes never left the river or the instruments. "You two look like soaked muskrats. There's stuff in the locker, if you want to change till yours dries. Won't take long, not in summer."

"Thank you. I'm Sylvia Ferro-Maine, and this is Nathaniel Whaler. We're from Accord, and we're doing an economic study—"

"On that side of the river?"

"We walked out of the desert."

"The desert? Walking out of the desert? Not much economics in that, is there?"

"We had a little trouble with our flitter," Nathaniel said.

"Good thing you didn't get caught too far in. Lots of suckholes there."

"Suckholes?" Nathaniel felt stupid, as though he were off balance and reacting too late. Then . . . wasn't he?

"Suckholes . . . big holes covered with powdery sand. You step on the edge and down it all does, sucks you down so far no one ever find you. There are little ones, too, I hear, but folks don't worry about those."

"You were right about the sand," said Sylvia.

"How about lucky?"

"You still didn't say what you were doing out there. New Avalon send you?" FitzReilly's eyes narrowed.

"No. We're professors at the Ecolitan Institute. The Institute is being paid to do the study, and we were the lucky ones chosen."

"What's to study?" snorted the boat pilot, easing the wheel slightly to starboard, her eyes remaining on the river.

"Infrastructure, things like power sources, highways, harbors . . . barges, I suppose, except nothing we had on background mentioned barges." Nathaniel cleared his throat. "You don't have a comm set of some sort, do you?"

"Me? You got to be kidding, professor. This is a low-budget operation. Besides, just what could a set do? In a real emergency, someone could get here with a groundcar or a flitter—most of the time the road's within a few kilos of the river, sometimes closer."

Nathaniel looked at the covered bins in the barge. Then he grinned. "Well . . . you're part of the transport infrastructure. Mind if we hitch a ride back to the Lanceville area and interview you along the way?"

"I'm not going anywhere. Just stop talking when I tell you. There's a tricky part of the big bend in a while." She eased the wheel slightly.

"What do you carry?"

"Beans—synde beans. What else is there on Artos? Falfamut is fodder or plowed under. Maize is for the aristos. Lorry garden stuff—there's not enough."

"It seems that all the big groundlorries carry beans," ventured Sylvia.

"We do the little growers," growled FitzReilly. "They got a co-op thing, store their crops until they get a barge full. Synde beans don't spoil that quick, but it's usually only a few days anyway. Most live way south of that aristo plaything they call a spread or a ranch or whatever. Barging is cheaper than selling to the freelance haulers, and R-K costs more than that 'cause they want to drive out the smaller ones. My husband and me—we sell to R-K, and they're pretty fair—that's because we haul all their precious beef—the live ones—down to the harbor. Guess groundlorries upset their digestion."

"You don't hear much about the smaller growers." Nathaniel stifled a yawn.

"Why would you? No one cares for them. The Reeves-Kenn people are scared they'll find some way to take their spread. Rumor is they won't let them near the place. The tech-transfer crowd doesn't bother them, but doesn't see much future for 'em."

"What about the marine farms?"

"That's a black hole. Always promising cheap protein, but it's mostly algae. Personally, I think old George Reeves-Kenn just shovels credits at his little brother so as to keep Sebastion off his cattle lands. Quiet now . . . wait till we get round the bend." FitzReilly turned the wheel deftly, checking the riverbanks, a dim set of green-and-red lights, and the instruments. Her left hand flicked across the throttles, and the purr of the engines rose to a muted roar, then dropped back to a louder purring.

Nathaniel glanced around the pilot house—stark plastic, utilitarian, with nothing in it but the basic instruments, and the high-back stool behind the wheel where FitzReilly sat.

Once the barge and push boat straightened out below the bend, the pilot nodded in the red-lit dimness. "So what else you want to know?"

"What's the capacity of the barge?"

"Close to six hundred tonnes, but that's mass, not cubage. A load of beans like this runs maybe four hundred tonnes, and that's all I'd want to take most times with the draft. Big harvest times, we'll run both barges."

Nathaniel tried to wrestle with the numbers mentally—perhaps the equivalent of well over 150,000 litres in hydrocarb fuel equivalents, or had he misplaced a decimal? He rubbed his forehead. "How long does the run take?"

"Two to three days. Josh and I alternate,'cause one of us has to run the depot."

"Three runs a week."

"Sometimes."

"All beans?"

"Except for a beef run or two. They pay all right, but we do that to keep R-K off our backs."

Nathaniel wanted to shake his head. The *small* growers were shipping the equivalent of more than half a million litres of synde bean oil feedstock a standard week. Then . . . it really wasn't that much if the oil were the energy supply basis for everything except fusactor-powered electricity. Even with all its alternative power sources, Accord used something like a half-million barrels of hydrocarb feedstocks a day.

"You're carrying a lot of value for them."

"They're supposed to trust R-K or the gouging haulers?"

"Any of this ever come to violence?"

"Not so far, but it's gotten uglier in the last few years. Attacks on the growers' small hauling van. Some of the small growers got stunners and slug-throwers—smuggled in somehow, and they're not cheap."

"You think George Reeves-Kenn knows that?"

"He has to. He knows damn near everything. More high-tech stuff hidden in that simple ranch house of his than in most of Lanceville, and he plays at being a poor dumb grower trying to hang on to his heritage." The pilot snorted.

"You're not painting a cheerful picture."

"What is . . . that's what is. We're trying to make a living and make Artos a better place, but sometimes you got to wonder."

"You mean," said Sylvia, "why people always think that the other side won't bring in heavy weapons, too."

"Haven't seen any of those, but I wouldn't bet against it if this keeps up."

Nathaniel took a deep breath.

"I've talked too much, and you look beat, professor."

"He's had a long, hard day," said Sylvia.

"Get some rest. The blankets are in the locker over there. I'm not going anywhere. You have more questions when you feel better, you know where to find me." FitzReilly laughed. "Be midday before we get to the dock at Lanceville, and you won't sleep that long once the sun's up."

Sylvia tugged at Nathaniel's elbow. He just stood there, trying to concentrate.

She went to the locker and pulled out two blankets, then returned. "We need some rest. Now."

"Be more comfortable below here in front," suggested the boat captain. "Use the pallets hung there."

"Thank you," offered Sylvia, taking Nathaniel's hand.

He followed her down the short ladder to the main deck. The two Ecolitans sat on the two pallets, wrapped in rough synthfibre blankets, listening to the gurgle of the water past the hull, and the hissing chirps of some unknown insects.

"Tired . . ." mumbled Sylvia.

"So am I."

"This whole business is exhausting. I thought Impies were unpopular, but Ecolitans seems even less welcome. Around here anyway."

"Around anywhere. We're pretty impartial, and no one likes that." Nathaniel yawned again, "In fact, it's hard to figure why anyone really wants this study. It's almost like . . . I don't know . . ."

"As though people were using it to flush out everyone else?" suggested Sylvia.

"Something like that . . . I guess." He yawned.

"We'll think about it later." Sylvia blinked her eyes, then stretched out.

"As if we had much choice," he muttered to himself, letting his eyes close, knowing he'd missed more than a few questions and hoping he could dig them up when he was rested and could think.

XVI

NATHANIEL'S CHIN WAS stubbly, and his greens smelled of smoke, oil, sweat, and the faintly medicinal odor of the Green Knight River. Sylvia didn't smell much better. The two paused in the corridor of the Port Authority building outside the door with the sign saying Port Authority Office of the Chief of Port.

"Will the receptionist or whatever let you in?" Sylvia asked.

"I think so."

They entered the main office, and Bagot looked up from the console, his jaw dropping slowly.

Nathaniel's hand slashed across the console, knocking the man's hands away, even as he moved around the console and yanked the driver back from the gear. "Easy, Bagot. I just want a word with the Port Chief." Without looking at Sylvia, he asked, "Would you keep Bagot company, and ensure he stays quiet? I'd rather not be interrupted."

"Don't get too violent." She grinned at Nathaniel.

"Me, violent?" Nathaniel picked up the smaller man and set him on one of the straight-backed plastic chairs.

"It has been known to happen." Sylvia turned to Bagot, miniature dart gun in hand. "We're not very happy at the moment. You'd better just sit there quietly."

Bagot opened his mouth.

"No." Sylvia's single word was like liquid nitrogen, and Bagot seemed to shrivel in the seat.

Nathaniel nodded, then opened the door to the back office and stepped inside. "Good morning, Port Chief."

Walkerson jerked upright at the console. "Whaler! Where . . . they said you were killed in the flitter crash." His eyes narrowed at the small stunner in the Ecolitan's hand. "Ah . . ."

"I'm not too trusting at the moment. I do hope you understand. And who said we were killed in the flitter crash? They weren't very observant. We left ten kays of tracks across the Unformed Desert." The Ecolitan leaned forward. "Just who are 'they'? You seemed to have someone in mind."

Walkerson's hand wandered toward the console.

Thrum!

The Port Chief winced and looked down at his numb, temporarily lifeless hand. "Whaler . . . I don't care who you are. You can't do this sort of thing."

The Ecolitan smiled. "I strongly suggest that you not tell any Ecolitan what he or she can or cannot do. Especially one who's had a flitter sabotaged under him."

"What?" Walkerson massaged his hand.

"Now . . . who are they?" pressed Whaler.

"Sabotage?"

"We'll get to that later. Who are the people who suggested we were dead?"

"When you didn't come back, Jersek took out the second flitter. The smoke was still obvious. He called Reeves-Kenn, and they sent a team out. This morning they confirmed that there appeared to be no survivors."

"The reports of our death are somewhat exaggerated." Nathaniel paused. "Jersek has a maintenance certificate, does he not?"

"He has to, but he inspects. He doesn't do the repairs. You can't do both. That's for safety reasons."

Nathaniel nodded.

"You aren't suggesting . . . ?"

"I suggest nothing. Deeds are the grain, words the chaff."

"How did you get back?" Walkerson ventured.

"We had to take a boat ride to get back from the Reeves-Kenn spread. Much safer it was. Rivers run, even planoformed ones, as rivers run."

"You didn't have to do this." The Port Chief kept massaging his hand. "I'm on your side."

"Sorry. Wouldn't you be a little jumpy? We had your groundcar explode on us and your flitter fail. That doesn't count the processing plant explosion. That's three attempts to murder us in four days."

"The groundcar was a mechanical failure."

"Enough of a failure to explode glass into the driver?"

"I'd have to say that is a trace strange, but it's also getting a bit embarrassing, Whaler. First, the groundcar and now our best flitter. You said you were a qualified pilot."

"I am. If I weren't we'd be dead, which is what someone wanted."

"I am willing to accept some things, but that seems a bit farfetched just to avoid . . ."

"Taking blame?" Nathaniel shook his head. "No. I've got some vidimager shots of the instruments. I thought they might come in handy. Show the EGT temps identical and equal at max. They also show a few other things." He shrugged. "They're not conclusive, but they'd be enough to convince most aero engineers. Now, I understand your problems, Port Chief, but I really don't think that sabotage comes under pilot error."

"There isn't any way to prove that . . ."

"All you have to do is check the turbines. They're spot welded in place. The crash fire won't have changed that. It will have destroyed the liquid metal injector they used—or whatever."

"You knew this and took the flitter?"

"No. I deduced what was happening when it had already started in the middle of the damned desert and after I blew the turbines to put us someplace besides where they wanted us to be."

Walkerson cleared his throat. "Whaler. You have every right to be upset and, as you put it, chap, jumpy. But would you listen to some reason?"

The Ecolitan waited.

"First, we've got exactly two working flitters. It will be years before we get a replacement for the one that crashed."

"It didn't crash. I landed it in the Unformed Desert. It caught fire after that—and the fires were planned, and not by me."

"Why would either Jersek or I make our own life even harder? I have to strain to make ends meet here, and everyone snipes at the Port Authority."

"All right." Nathaniel kept his voice even and the smile off his face. "Then who would benefit by hurting you—and saddling you with our deaths? If you're right, that's the game."

"Unfortunately, a very great number of people." Walkerson took a deep breath. "Could you point that somewhere else?"

"I'm listening. Who would benefit most?"

The Port Chief massaged his limp right hand with his left. "Sebastion Reeves-Kenn for one. He'd address three problems—his brother, me, and your study."

"Go on."

"Your study should show that his marine enterprises add very little to Artos. The Counter Tories would use that as an impartial analysis to cut the subsidies he's been getting." Walkerson licked his lips. "George has been reluctant to keep pouring credits into R-K Marine, but, if your murder were pinned on George—or the finger pointed in that direction, at the least, George would have other more pressing problems than Sebastion, and at the most, Sebastion would take over all of R-K."

"And you?"

"We're required to submit an annual report to Camelot, assessing the use of the port and the probabilities for growth and future utilization. The last report was quietly critical of R-K Marine, not, you understand, even in direct words, but in suggesting that the export of luxury goods would remain stable, and that significant future growth toward full self-sufficiency would have to be based on greater tech-transfer and industrial infrastructure."

"So . . . essentially, we're here to validate or refute your report?"

"I was never told. Only that I should provide all support and assistance within our abilities." Walkerson touched his chin with his good hand. "I assume there is some connection."

"Do you have orbit scan photos of Artos—recent ones?"

"The last set is a year old. Orbit control is in a geocentric station."

"I'd like a set."

"Ah . . . after this?"

"That"—Whaler pointed to the Port Chief's limp hand—"wouldn't have happened if you'd been a little more forthcoming. I apologize for the misunderstanding, but, as the saying goes, few days pass without clouds."

"You Ecolitans aren't the most likeable folks."

"Probably not. But remember, your people wanted us to do something that was difficult and nasty. It's hard to survive and be likeable after three attempts at murder." Nathaniel forced a smile. "I mean, would you be in the best of moods?"

"I guess not," admitted Walkerson.

"Now . . . who else would like to see us disappear?"

"Kennis Landis-Nicarchos. Your death would probably cause a lot of instability. Property values on Artos are already declining since the Commons decided to cut the colony subsidies, and more uncertainty would depress values."

"Is that stretching? I don't like the man, based on one meeting, but . . ."

"He's a lizard." Walkerson laughed. "He'd kill his mother, except he probably already has, to shave an additional five percent off the cost of a chunk of property. I'm assuming that your report would show that Artos has too many roads, too great an investment in marine development, but that it's basically sound. Kennis wouldn't like that. It would encourage people to bargain or hang on. Artos doesn't have a bad trade location—it's near the Three System Bulge, and we can trade with the Frankan Union, the Hegemony, the Empire, and the Conglomerate. That makes for a good long-term investment." Walkerson rubbed his hand. "Some feeling coming back."

"Who else?"

"Any number of outsystem reps—Sonderssen for one. They can live high here—the suites in the Blue Lion cost less than a small conapt on Nieustron. If Artos develops, they lose that luxury."

"Rather petty motivation, I would think."

"I was on Trezenia, Whaler, before your bloody Institute got involved, and I saw the locals sell their daughters—or little boys—for a whiff of Elysium, or for the price of a wooden hut. Don't tell me that

Sonderssen wouldn't be above arranging a murder to keep living high on the steer. He's in the Blue Room—or Elizabeth's—every night."

"And the Fuards?"

"Obvious, isn't it? Tactically a good locale, but they're not usually that devious. I'd expect them to show up with a small fleet and just annex us."

The Ecolitan slipped the stunner into his belt. "So, what do you recommend?"

"Not stunning your allies." Walkerson shook his hand. "Bloody hurts."

"You hadn't shown you were an ally. I won't do it again."

"I wish I had more confidence in that."

"Oh, you do. How else can we get off-planet?"

Walkerson grinned, then laughed ruefully. "I see your point." Then he frowned. "I can't say much—except I'd be certain to have a talk with Karl-Abbe."

"I'd planned on that. And how do we avoid more 'accidents'?"

Walkerson took another deep breath. "I truly don't know. Can you believe that I wanted to lose a groundcar and our best flitter?" He paused. "Or a driver. Do you know how much difficulty that will create for our operations and budget? Were I after you, likeable chap that you are, I would scarcely employ ways that slit my own gullet. And I had no intention of letting anyone else abuse our equipment. Jersek checked that flitter twice that morning. I looked once, and I do know something about them."

"Well . . . I certainly don't do emergency landings in the middle of unknown deserts for the joy of it."

"All I can say, Professor Whaler, is that I will be careful, and you should be careful. And I will let you know anything that bears on this. I would hope you will do the same."

"What about the small growers? I heard that they were getting upset with R-K Enterprises. Would they be desperate enough to try to frame George Kenn-Reeves?"

"Some of the younger hotheads might. I don't know how they'd get access to the flitter . . ."

"Perhaps they didn't. We've assumed that all of these were from the same person or group."

"I do hope things are not that bad, Whaler. That is a horrifying thought."

"Just crossed my mind. As the saying goes, it's best not to look for a golden life in an iron age." He looked down at his stained, rumpled greens. "Could we prevail upon Bagot to take us to the Guest House? We could use some cleaning up."

"We?"

"Professor Ferro-Maine is outside, entertaining Bagot. She's been with me every step of the way—often in front."

"I see." Walkerson shook his head slowly from side to side. "You two are rather formidable. Well . . . if Bagot is willing . . ."

"I think he should drive us everywhere. He is from Artos."

"That wouldn't stop some."

"Any port in a storm . . . and I definitely sense heavy weather."

"I still don't think you're all that likeable a fellow."

"It's hard to be likeable when people are trying to kill you." Nathaniel offered a patently false smile and gestured for the Port Chief to rise. "Perhaps you should explain this to Bagot."

"I suppose so."

Bagot glanced up expectantly as Walkerson and Whaler entered the outer office. Sylvia stepped back so that she could use the dart gun on either Avalonian.

"Bagot . . . it appears as though we and the Ecolitans are on the same side, and the other fellows are getting rather rough. I'd like to have you serve as the permanent driver and aide to them until they leave."

"Yes, sir. Whatever you feel is best." Bagot did not look extraordinarily pleased.

Then, reflected Nathaniel, he didn't look horrified either.

"So . . . we're friends and allies, now?" said Sylvia in a low voice as they followed Bagot out to the carpark.

"Allies, for now. He needs us, and our survey, and we need to finish and get out of here while he still does—before we release our results." Nathaniel answered in a lower voice, then added, "I can't wait to get cleaned up."

"Me, too."

"And then we need to visit a few people."

Sylvia nodded.

XVII

"WE NEED TO talk to this banker, Karl-Abbe, and then maybe you can loosen up the piping magnate and that permacrete supplier." Nathaniel reloaded the vidimager, then slipped it into the sleeve harness of his second pair of greens. The first was being washed by the Guest House staff, along with Sylvia's. He touched his face, reddened and warm to the touch. "You've got a better touch with people."

"I'm glad you find that useful."

The Ecolitan frowned at the coolness of her voice. "Let me go downstairs and use the comm to see what I can arrange. Then I'll see what we can fit in for the rest of the day."

"All right. Let me know when you have everything arranged." Sylvia eased to her feet from the straight-backed chair and slipped through the connecting door into her own room.

Nathaniel closed the datacase, then frowned again, and opened the connecting door to see Sylvia disappear into the corridor. He hurried after her, finally catching her at the top of the stairs.

"Where are you going?"

"For a walk." She did not turn, but continued down the steps, each foot precisely placed.

"Can I come?"

"I don't know." She jerked her head toward the side of the foyer, where Bagot had risen expectantly. "You'd better talk to Bagot."

Nathaniel turned to the driver. "It's going to be a little while, Bagot. Something's come up."

The driver's eyes followed Sylvia through the front door, and his face blanked. "Sir?"

"If you wouldn't mind waiting . . ."

"No, sir. It's cool here." Bagot looked toward the door as a puff of warm air drifted into the foyer.

"Thank you." Nathaniel nodded and walked quickly through the door and after Sylvia, his eyes watering against the bright sun. He stumbled on the edge of the drive before his vision adjusted to the afternoon sun.

Sylvia had reached the edge of the fields behind the Guest House and was striding up one of the wider rows between the low synde bean plants by the time Nathaniel again caught up.

She did not turn.

"You're angry."

"How did you ever guess?"

"What did I do?"

That got no answer, except for Sylvia to increase her pace. Both were breathing hard.

"Forest lord! What do you want from me?"

"I don't know." Her pace increased again, almost to a jog.

"Whatever I did . . . I'm sorry."

Finally, at the end of the row, a good six hundred meters long, she stopped, almost panting, and turned.

"I said I was sorry. Even if I don't know why."

She took several deep breaths, then fixed his eyes with hers, cold and gray. "Nathaniel . . . I don't know why you even asked me to come— except to be a decorative side piece. And I don't know why I agreed. You're used to doing things your way. Oh, occasionally I'm useful—for an insight, to cover your back. But that's not my idea of either life or a relationship—personal or professional." She shook her head. "I should have known. That was the way it started, and why would things change?"

Nathaniel looked at the low bean plants—still in the hot and windless air—and wiped the sweat off his forehead with the back of his hand. He'd left the kerchief behind. "I'm sorry. I didn't think."

"I'm not blaming you. Not much. In your line of work—this part of it anyway—you don't have much time to think."

He swallowed. "Maybe I should."

She turned to him and smiled faintly. "Why? You've gotten results."

"First, because you've saved my life and neck a couple of times. Second, because I want to, but have trouble figuring out how, and third, because what I'm doing hasn't really gotten results." He pursed his lips. "People are still trying to kill us, and we don't know who or why."

"You—we're—still alive. Most people wouldn't be. You're good at surviving."

"I want more than that."

"So do I."

For some reason, he thought of the scent of orange and trilia, and his throat and guts tightened, and he looked down at the dark ground between the plants. "What would you do next?" he finally asked.

"Don't humor me."

"I'm not. I'm at a loss. Oh, we need to talk to that banker, but even if he has every banking number on Artos, what will that tell us?" He waited.

"Do you honestly want an answer?"

"Yes."

Sylvia was silent. She glanced out at the low bean plants for a time. When she finally spoke, her voice was low, and Nathaniel had to strain to hear.

"People aren't numbers. I'm not an economist, but numbers can justify anything. We've looked at power plants and roads and harbors. We've looked at hydrocarbon production and conversion. We've been introduced to almost everyone who is anyone." She shrugged. "What do we know about the people, beyond their positions and statistics?"

"Not much," admitted Nathaniel.

"Where have we learned the most?"

"Probably from George Reeves-Kenn and FitzReilly, the boat pilot."

Sylvia stopped and glanced out over the rows of beans. "Doesn't that tell you something? People have dreams, desires. The only people whose dreams we know are George Reeves-Kenn and Anna-Marie. Why did I go with you to Accord?"

"Dreams . . ." Nathaniel nodded. "I'm sorry."

"I should have talked to you. But, I'm not an agent . . . not this kind. I don't know how to land an exploding flitter. Or drop onto a strange planet and pretend to know everything about its economy."

"You know people, better than I do."

"You're just saying that. You did fine on Old Earth."

"No, I made a lot of mistakes, and people died. I was lucky, and I found you. And now . . . now . . . I think I'm in over my head."

"You . . . over?" Sylvia shook her head. "I was going to be unfair."

"I've been the unfair one."

"Nathaniel . . . we can't fight. Not and get through this."

"I . . . don't want to fight."

"Neither do I."

"But you don't . . . I think I understand." He swallowed.

Sylvia touched his wrist. "It's all right."

After a moment, he swallowed again. "So we need to get people to talk more about who they are and what they want?"

"That's one thing." She turned to him and put a hand on his shoulder, lightly, before dropping it. "I'm overreacting. The numbers are important, too. It takes both. You can't change things without resources, and the numbers should show where those are."

"But," Nathaniel said slowly, "if there's no reason for change . . ."

"It doesn't happen."

"I think." He took a deep breath. "I think it's time you decided what we do next. I've managed to get people stirred up enough to try to kill us three times, and we don't know much more than when we landed."

"We do . . . except we don't know what we know." She paused. "No. We don't know how what we do know fits."

"Because we don't know enough about people's motivations . . ."

"Exactly."

"So where should we start?"

"The banker, and Vivienne Evanston. She knows people." Sylvia turned. "We ought to head back. Poor Bagot is probably confused."

Not as confused as he'd been, thought Nathaniel, not nearly. He wanted to shake his head. Sylvia had every right to be upset. She was intelligent and competent . . . and he was far too used to operating alone. He needed to change, and that wasn't going to be easy—not at all.

They walked back toward the Guest House slowly.

"I'll try to do better," he said in a low voice as they stepped into the shadows of the portico and up beside the empty groundcar.

"So will I." She squeezed his hand momentarily. "You call the banker."

"And you call Vivienne."

They exchanged smiles.

XVIII

"I HOPE YOU don't mind," ventured Sylvia.

"It works out better this way. Karl-Abbe said it would give him some time." Nathaniel glanced up as Bagot turned the groundcar onto a long drive that wound out along a ridge bordered by water on both sides. From the midsection of the ridge, below the manicured, grassed, and gardened grounds around the house, and above the rocks that bordered the gray water, grew trees—one of the few forests that the Ecolitans had seen.

"You couldn't find a locale like this on Old Earth," she murmured.

"There aren't many left on Accord, either. Not unless you are very well off," he answered, studying the flowers and plants that bordered the permacrete drive.

"This is the place, sirs." Bagot eased the groundcar under the high-roofed extension that shaded the entry to the house.

The Evanston house was a two-story copy of something from pre-Ecollapse Old Earth. At least, reflected Nathaniel, that was what it looked like, with stone columns, and a blue tile roof, a balcony overlooking the ocean and what seemed to be a closed courtyard on the landward side. The long structure sat on a small promontory north of Lanceville.

As he got out of the groundcar, Nathaniel glanced toward the flat gray water, nodding to himself. Without a moon, and without strong winds, there wasn't likely to be much in the way of waves. Were some of Sebastion Reeves-Kenn's problems linked to a form of oceanic stagnation? Could they find out from the monitoring official? Nathaniel couldn't remember his name. Did it matter? As Sylvia had pointed out, if Sebastian thought he had a problem . . . he did. Still, it would be nice to confirm it. He refrained from shaking his head. There he was, going after hard facts again.

"Nathaniel? Are we going in?"

"Sorry. I was thinking."

Vivienne Evanston stood outside the double front doors, her slender form concealed by a loose-fitting short-sleeved tunic and matching pale green trousers. "It's so good to see you both."

"It's good to see you," offered Sylvia.

Nathaniel smiled and half-bowed.

"The balcony is lovely today. Why don't we sit there?" Without waiting for an answer, the blond woman turned and opened the ornately carved wooden door.

The Ecolitans followed her through a high-ceilinged foyer with an inlaid parquet floor and down a wide corridor which separated a formal dining room from a large salon. At the end of the corridor was another set of double doors that opened onto the covered balcony.

Three chairs were spaced around a table covered with cream linen. On the side table were a tea service and a tray of pastries and small sandwiches. "I do hope you don't mind if I took the liberty of having tea. I also have liftea. That's in the gold-rimmed pot."

"You're very thoughtful," said Sylvia.

"It is most kind of you," added Nathaniel.

THE ECOLITAN ENIGMA 343

"Here . . . you two take the chairs that face the ocean. I can enjoy the view all the time. Too much, some times."

Nathaniel touched the back of Vivienne's chair, then eased it into place as she sat.

"Thank you."

He turned to Sylvia, but she had already seated herself. She smiled at Nathaniel. As he eased around the table to seat himself, he realized that the angled balcony was visible from the covered portico and that he could see a servant carrying a tray out to Bagot. He nodded, not surprised. Vivienne Evanston was the perfect hostess.

"It was so nice of you to remember that I did want to chat with you. Geoffrey will be jealous, to say the very least. He's out on ConTrio today, Salisville, I think."

"You're kind to see us," said Sylvia.

"Oh, you're kind to visit me. We see so few offworlders, and I know you both must be so very busy, with . . . whatever you are doing."

"It's an economic study." Sylvia smiled warmly. "But that wasn't why we came."

"Gracious. I would think not. I know nothing of economics. Not much anyway, although I did take a few courses at the university, but that was years and years ago." Vivienne paused. "Would you like tea or liftea? The tea is the milder Grawer, not at all like that awful stuff at the Blue Lion."

"Tea, please." Sylvia smiled again.

"I will try the tea." Nathaniel hoped it would be mild, but he was following Sylvia's lead.

"You are brave." Vivienne Evanston laughed melodically, and filled three china cups, transferring them from the serving table to the linen. Then she set the silver tray of pastries and miniature sandwiches in the middle of the table. "There . . . please do help yourself, or I will be forced to eat them all, and I will bulge out all over the place, and Geoffrey will not be pleased at all."

"Somehow," ventured Nathaniel, "I think not. I cannot imagine you being one who would bulge."

"You don't know my weakness for sweets, professor."

"I imagine it can get lonely this far out of Lanceville," observed Sylvia.

"It can be lonely here, at times, but I like the quiet. I work with the flowers, and three days a week, I assist at the public clinic. Years ago, I was a practicing physical therapist, and this keeps my registration current. Geoffrey laughs at me, but I could support myself if I had to. Gracious, not on this scale, but . . . I think it's practical, and besides, who would they have without me?"

"If Lanceville cannot afford a therapist . . . it is really small, isn't it?" said Sylvia. "Did you come here from Camelot?"

"Not from Camelot. I went to school on New Avalon, but on Sofssex. The University of Pierce. That's in Exton, and then I went to work at the Medical Centre hospital. That's where I met Geoffrey. He'd been in a flitter accident. Silly way to meet your husband, I suppose . . ."

Sylvia darted a grin at Nathaniel, who almost choked, considering that he and Sylvia had met over drugged sparkling wine.

"Exton isn't that big," continued Vivienne, apparently unaware of the byplay, "but that corner of Sofssex has more people than all of Artos."

"That's hard to believe."

"When we came here, Geoffrey was so confident that Lanceville would grow." Vivienne laughed softly. "Like Kennis is now."

"Kennis does seem rather confident," replied Sylvia, "but from what everyone says, he has done a lot. The Blue Lion is being refurbished."

"In blue. He favors far too much blue," offered Vivienne. "Even his security force—those bright blue uniforms—they look more like soldiers. Security forces . . . we scarcely need those here. If dear Kennis feels they are so necessary, they should be clothed in something . . . less obtrusive. He won't, though." She laughed. "He's an overgrown boy, almost playing at soldiers."

Nathaniel listened, trying to pick up something from the way the Avalonian woman spoke. There was something . . . he wanted to shake his head.

"You've scarcely said a word, Professor Whaler. I do hope we're not boring you."

Nathaniel smiled and shook his head. "No . . . an economist by trade am I, and most likely the boring one. It is good to listen to something besides external diseconomies or the cross-subsidies of interlocked transport, or the marginal disutility of heavy highway lorries." He shrugged. "People are far more interesting." He sipped the tea, carefully—far stronger than liftea, and the Grawer was considered mild.

"Professor Whaler, you are so cautious with your tea."

"Beverages are milder on Accord. But this is good."

"In small doses, I think you mean." Vivienne smiled indulgently.

"The more precious the taste, the slower the drink," he answered.

Both women smiled.

"You sound like an economist."

Whaler hoped so.

"Can I ask what use your study might provide?" Vivienne rose and refilled her cup, looking toward Sylvia. "More, dear?"

"Please." Sylvia looked to Nathaniel.

"Precisely, I could not say, dear lady. We do not create the reasons for studies. Usually, however, studies such as ours are used to plan."

"That worries Geoffrey, you know. So much of what happens here on Artos is dictated elsewhere. Geoffrey is worried that the Commons will cut the colony subsidies again."

"And you think our study might provide a rationale?" asked Sylvia.

"Politics . . . I could not say."

"If anything," Nathaniel injected, "I would say that, on a preliminary basis, a very preliminary basis, you understand, there needs to be more emphasis on infrastructure diversification. And more trees."

"That has a lovely sound, infrastructure diversification. So do trees, but Geoffrey once explained that to me. Something about the more immediate needs, except where nothing else will grow, as on the rocks here." Vivienne gestured vaguely in the direction of the sea and then to the silver tray. "Please have one. They absolutely won't keep, and then I will feel obliged to eat more than I should."

"Could you give Vivienne an idea of what you mean?" Sylvia paused to sip her tea. "I mean about how diversification would affect the subsidy."

"That is difficult to predict. I would say we will submit a good study, but," he laughed, "fair words feed but pride, and pride goes before a fall. Now, here on Artos, the infrastructure is solid, but narrow. Transport is by land, and the permacrete highways are wide and well built. Energy comes from one fusactor complex here on ConOne and from the hydrocarbon processing plant, and the feedstocks are synde beans." He paused, concealing a shiver as the full import of what he had said struck him, but adding a shrug. "All these are tested and common. But there is no provision for alternatives. An earthquake, and how good are the highways? An major accident at the processing plant or the complex?"

"You make it sound as though such disasters could happen easily," said Vivienne.

Nathaniel shook his head. "They happen seldom, but economists are paid to outline what might go wrong, and to quantify the trade-offs." He straightened in the chair. "To ship in more flitters, and big cargo flitters, would ensure transport under more conditions, but shipping and building such is expensive. Growing other feedstocks—that is possible, but none are so cost-effective as the synde bean. Governments do not like to spend resources far from the majority of those who vote, but they also do not wish to be blamed for troubles. So . . . they will take our report and read it, and decide whether keeping the subsidies and increasing the infrastructure will measurably reduce the possibility of troubles without increasing the taxes on those who are close."

"You make it sound so cold, but then, I do suppose it is." The blonde set her cup on the saucer with a faint clink.

"Politicians do not care for warmth, except as an impression. In the end, the politicians look after self-interest, while pretending to be warm," said Nathaniel.

"Most people pretend to be warm, and some are," said Sylvia. "Geoffrey seems like a warm person."

"Beneath that courteous businesslike exterior, he is very warm. He is not always the best politician. Kennis, as I am sure you noted, has a very warm presence. He is also a very good politician, I am told. Me—I would be lost in politics, and I have told Geoffrey that." Vivienne offered a warm laugh. "Are you sure you will not have a pastry?"

Nathaniel had to grin, and he leaned forward and took a small cake. "My arm has been gently twisted, ladies." He lifted the cake dramatically, then ate it in two bites. "Excellent." He took a sip of tea. "I may have another, if you would not mind."

"Mind? Please, please do. And you, professor . . . could I call you Sylvia? Wouldn't you . . . ?"

"Sylvia is fine. I'm not nearly so senior as my colleague." Sylvia opted for one of the tea cookies.

Nathaniel barely managed to keep from choking on the Grawer he was sipping.

"Geoffrey will be so pleased . . ."

Nathaniel continued to listen, and make a few comments, as the conversation drifted more toward shopping, the lack of amenities, and the proliferation of synthcloth.

Sylvia finally straightened. "I do fear we've taken too much of your time, but you've been so very gracious."

"I've taken your time, and you were so delightful to come all the way out here. As I said, Geoffrey would have liked to have been here, I'm sure, but I'll certainly pass along your words." Vivienne rose gracefully, not quite so gracefully as Sylvia, Nathaniel thought, and the Ecolitans followed her example.

The three walked back through the house and to the front portico.

"It has been an interesting conversation, and I hope we will see each other again, if not on this trip to Artos, then in the future." Vivienne offered a slight bow as Nathaniel opened the groundcar door for Sylvia.

"We'll look forward to that." Sylvia smiled.

Vivienne waved as the car pulled away, and Sylvia waved back.

"Did you have something to eat?" Nathaniel asked Bagot. "I should have asked before we left."

"Yes, sir. Quite a lot, actually, and it was very good. I know Anne-Leslie, too. We talked for a bit." Bagot cleared his throat. "Ah . . . where to, sirs?"

"The Bank of Camelot office in Lanceville."

"Yes, sir."

"Gracious lady, she is," offered Nathaniel.

"Very much so," agreed Sylvia.

"I imagine Geoffrey Evanston is also quite a gentleman." He looked at Bagot. "Does he have a solid reputation?"

"Yes, sir. The family's been here for a long time. They treat their people fair, they do. Started out as cotton factors, I heard, but cotton didn't do well. They've got a small manufactory that makes cookware and electrical supplies and some other stuff . . . probably a lot of things I don't know."

"Never do we know everything," said Nathaniel, taking out his large kerchief and blotting his forehead.

Sylvia covered her mouth and her grin.

The Lanceville office of the Bank of Camelot looked like the caricature of an ancient Old Earth bank—small windows, thick stone walls.

"I can't imagine there have been any bank robberies here," offered Sylvia with a look toward Glubb Bagot.

"Not since I was a boy." The driver paused. "Should I wait? Or come back later?"

"Wait, I think. This will not be long, and then we will retire to the Guest House and ponder." Nathaniel slipped out, but Sylvia had her door open before he could get around the vehicle.

"I'll be in the shade across the way."

The two Ecolitans stepped into the dimness of the bank.

"May I help you?" asked a square-faced, white-haired woman.

"Ecolitans Ferro-Maine and Whaler. We're here to see Laurence Karl-Abbe."

"He's expecting you."

As she spoke, the head banker strode from a door at the back of the main office. "Professors!"

"It's good of you to see us on such short notice."

"Nonsense . . . nonsense. This way, if you will."

"This looks like a fortress." Nathaniel stepped into the office behind Sylvia. A broad, old dark wooden desk commanded one end of the long, rectangular office. Behind it was a tall maroon reclining chair, and on the desk was a modern compact console. In front of the desk were three straight-backed plastic armchairs, upholstered in maroon matching the recliner.

"It was one of the first buildings in Lanceville—the walls are over two hundred years old. The winds and weather were more severe then." The banker's eyes twinkled as he closed the door to the office. "We have updated the interior. It's only a century old. Please have a seat."

"We really didn't have much of a chance to talk the other night," began Nathaniel.

"It's just as well." Karl-Abbe offered a faintly twisted smile. "I'm sure Kennis has every word on solideo or the latest technology whose name I don't even know."

"He seemed rather charming, in a cool way," said Sylvia.

"He is charming, and cool. And very calculating. He got his immigration permit as a major investor, you know. He's Argenti—that part of the Hegemony really has never accepted the Federation."

"He never spoke to Sonderssen the other night," said Sylvia.

"They have different views."

"One the industrialist, the other the agriculturalist?"

"There is that," said Karl-Abbe. "I was actually thinking more about their employers. Kennis works for himself; Sonderssen, for all that he works for AgriTech Galactic, works for the Hegemony, and partly for Tinhorn."

"Tinhorn?" asked Nathaniel, surprised in spite of himself.

"AgriTech is technically an equal partner, joint venture between Agricultural Specialties—that's the big Hegemony agricultural technology supplier—and Technical Agronomics—they're a big seed and DNA template firm based in Tinhorn." The banker snorted. "I know their funds patterns. So do the politicians in Camelot. They lose credits—big credits—every year."

Nathaniel nodded. "But no one says anything because it amounts to a subsidy of Artos?"

"I couldn't speculate on political motivations. Bankers cannot afford to speculate, but . . ."

Sylvia and Nathaniel exchanged glances.

"You said you had numbers." Nathaniel waited. "What kind of numbers?"

"Mostly bankers' numbers, but a few others. We have to do economic projections for headquarters—probably nothing compared to your sophistication, but we manage. Average monthly pay, deposits, savings, all for the past twenty years."

"Those have to be hard to come by," said Sylvia.

"Honestly, yes," answered Karl-Abbe with his round-faced smile. "But statistics aren't honest, and neither are we. We can tag pay deposits and then separate out the total and average them. Likewise, we can estimate savings, and the changes, from average monthly balances. We do most of the nonmajors' construction financing—I couldn't tell you what R-K built, or what's on George Reeves-Kenn's spread, but their stuff is big enough that a comparison of any good satellite holos would show that sort of construction."

"Confidentiality?" murmured the sandy-haired Ecolitan.

"Oh, these are all aggregated figures. There's nothing in them that would reveal anything at variance with the New Avalon commercial code. So . . . here you go." Karl-Abbe handed the hardcopy report across the desk. "There's also a console disk inside the cover, but I didn't know whether you had access to a console—the Guest House is more private and discreet, but it lacks some amenities."

"Discretion is useful," said Nathaniel.

"Very useful, but it's not exactly something that one can count on in our modern age, or for that matter, even in older times, such as those represented by the Guest House." The banker sat back in his chair. "I don't know as I can provide any more hard data than you have there. And I certainly am in no position to speculate."

"You're being very helpful." Nathaniel understood. Karl-Abbe had said what he was going to say, and his numbers would say even more.

"What do you hope to accomplish with your study?"

Nathaniel smiled faintly. "That would depend on others. I suppose those who benefit will try to use it, and those who do not will attempt to have the findings set aside. And if it changes nothing . . . then everyone will applaud with relief and call it a wonderful study."

"You are cynical beyond your face and years, professor."

"What do you think the study should accomplish?" asked Sylvia.

"I am a banker. I would like to see the study show the need for more capital investment in Artos, and the promise that such investment will be repaid."

"Artos has become your home."

"After thirty years and three children and a grandchild, it has." Karl-Abbe smiled sadly. "I make no secret of it, and that makes my judgment suspect to my superiors in Camelot. And I worry about the future of Artos, because politicians and bankers are attempting to make decisions on numbers, and numbers, no matter how good they may be, never reveal everything."

"No," agreed Sylvia. "They don't show dreams or determination, or hatred and hostility."

"Or the ambition of outsiders," added the banker. "Or the temptations placed before outworld systems. Depressing, isn't it?" His lips curled into an ironic smile, and he stood. "You'd best go, before I really get on my antique soapbox and depress you both. It also might bias your study if anyone found out that you spent long hours with such a hidebound financial antiquity."

"Thank you." Nathaniel stood, as did Sylvia.

The ride back to the Guest House was quiet, and Bagot left them with a promise to return the next morning—a smile on his face. Nathaniel suspected that the driver and the groundcar just might be visiting a young lady named Anne-Leslie.

"After we unload this stuff and wash up, let's take a walk," Nathaniel suggested.

"A walk?"

"I'd like to talk to you, without . . ."

"In a moment." Sylvia smiled.

After completing their respective ablutions, they walked down the empty stairs and through the empty foyer, across the empty pavement to the empty fields, where they followed the path through the bean plants again.

"He wanted us to have these numbers, almost desperately," said

Nathaniel. "But he didn't want to say much. Except about the joint intelligence operation that AgriTech apparently is."

"Our briefing materials didn't show that."

"I know, and that bothers me. I have to wonder what else others think is common knowledge that we don't know."

"That's why we're here," she reminded him. "You Ecolitans—we Ecolitans, I guess—can't know everything in advance."

"He cut off the interview pretty sharply," mused Nathaniel.

"He did. He said that discretion wasn't possible even in the most antique of surroundings. What is more antique than that bank building?"

"Everywhere, the walls have ears."

"And eyes."

"The more we learn, the worse it gets." Nathaniel stopped, turned, and looked back toward the Guest House, but nothing moved, not even on the permacrete highway south of the bean field. "Someone wants us dead, and someone else wants our report, badly enough to ensure we get numbers that would be impossible to get elsewhere. I'd guess they're accurate numbers, too."

"They're accurate," affirmed Sylvia, "and that's going to cause trouble."

"Someone could charge the numbers are cooked. How would we know? In gross terms, we can provide cross-checks, but for some things . . ." he shrugged. "Who else would know? I doubt that the Bank of Camelot on New Avalon would fully approve."

"They might—if the numbers showed Artos could become independent."

"That's true—because they could cut the subsidy and retain the ties, eventually ask for support for the defense forces . . . whatever."

"Then there was Vivienne's parting message," mused Sylvia.

"I missed that."

"She as much as said that we shouldn't meet again."

"Odd . . ."

"Not really. She told us a lot, but visiting her again would draw too much attention. Did you notice that the tea table was placed where Bagot could see us?"

"I hadn't thought about that either. That is interesting." Nathaniel blotted his damp forehead. "Nothing like working up a sweat just to get a private talk."

"They could use directionals."

He glanced around the empty fields. "Even the I.I.S. would have trouble here, I think."

"Especially the I.I.S. Its charter is restricted to the Empire, and the eagles make sure of that."

"I suppose we should head back. We can split up the data, see what we can find, and then trade."

The dark-haired serving woman—was she the entire staff of the Guest House—greeted them at the door. "Port Chief Walkerson wanted you to call him, sirs. He said it was urgent. The codes are on the pad by the unit."

"You come, too." He nodded at Sylvia.

Sylvia sat out of sight of the screen while Nathaniel inputted the codes. Walkerson was waiting for Nathaniel.

"Whaler . . . have you heard?"

"Heard what?"

"George Reeves-Kenn—he was out riding this afternoon, and some-one killed him. I thought you might like to know."

"Forest lord! No . . . we didn't know. That's not good," mused Nathaniel. "Not good at all. Does anyone know who did it?"

"Long-range military needle. Looks Imperial."

"That means it's not."

"I know that, and so do you, but most people don't, and even if they do, that only leaves local dissidents, business rivals, and about four major outsystems that flank our starspace." Walkerson cleared his throat. "I don't expect you to do anything, Whaler. I hope you won't. But you also deserve to know. I hope you can wind up your study before long."

"We are progressing, and we may be able to do that in another week."

"A week?" Walkerson's face sobered.

"Perhaps longer. We will do as we can."

"Do that. I need to go."

As the screen blanked, the Ecolitans looked at each other.

"Not a dull moment," he said slowly.

"Around you, no."

They both glanced toward the foyer and stood, silently.

"We should get ready for dinner."

XIX

THE I.I.S. DIRECTOR surveyed those around the conference table before gesturing at the hard-copy reports before each person. "This is a report on an attempted murder on New Avalon. It bears on our problem with the Coordinate and the Empire. This trade factor Bannon took a needle through the lungs, a second one through the shoulder, and a third along the side of his skull. Enough blood to make anyone think he was dead."

"What kind of needles?" asked the dark-haired assistant director.

"Imperial military issue, of course," answered the Director.

"The same kind that was used on Whaler?"

"You have to ask?" The Director's eyebrows rose.

"Who wants to pin the blame on Defense? And why?"

"Only about half the known Galaxy." The Director's voice was dry. "The picture's getting clearer. Every intelligence service *knows* 'we'— the Empire, that is—tried to assassinate the Accord negotiator who made a fool of us, and to kill the Imperial agent he seduced."

"We didn't, though," pointed out the redhead leaning back in the chair across the table. "Neither did Defense, even if the Admiral would have liked to."

"Everyone also knows this Accord agent-vanished on some other mission, along with the Imperial agent. In the meantime, this synde bean plague is rampaging across almost all the planoformed Imperial planets, and anchovy kills are beginning as well. Both are spilling into other systems. The Matriarchy is marshalling a fleet, and we've gotten a stiff note from Orknarli. The Senate is talking about sending the Eleventh Fleet to Sector Five. What's the impression?"

"That Accord and the Empire are teetering on the fringe of an all-out war." That came from the blond who sat beside the redhead.

"Right. We know that. We've been fighting that impression for weeks," said the assistant director, "but why did you bring up this report on a minor importer/fixer from New Avalon? Why would anyone want him dead? And how do we know? We don't even have any firm links there."

The Director held up a thick envelope. "We have this. I *think* it came from F.U.I.—Frankan Union Intelligence. It's a complete file on New

Avalon and Artos, a recently planoformed colony planet. Whaler and
Ferro-Maine are doing an economic infrastructure study on Artos, by
the way."

"The Frankans—they wouldn't share solid information with us."

"Not with D.I., but occasionally we do share material. We didn't ask
for this. I've been able to verify some of the material independently, and
it seems genuine."

"Oh . . ." murmured the redheaded man.

The Director nodded. "They see trouble. Enough trouble that
they'll contact the I.I.S. That means they know the Empire's being
manipulated."

"Doesn't that solve the problem?" asked the blond. "If we know and
they know . . ."

At the sounds from the others in the conference room—snorts, guf-
faws, and a bitter chuckle—the blond flushed.

"The Admiral knows," pointed out the Director, "but she'll still have
to send the eagles where the Senate demands. The Senate Intelligence
Committee knows, but with starvation and energy shortages on two
dozen planets, they have to do *something*, and that something may well be
military action against Accord. What else can they do politically, with
over five million dead on Heraculon? The Matriarch knows, but she's got
problems with all the fish kills and hungry people and economic unrest,
and that means Halstan will jump to whichever side is advantageous."

"That still doesn't say why the Frankans alerted us to an attempted
murder in Camelot." The Director leaned back in her chair. "And,
according to these background reports, about half of New Avalon
would weep crocigator tears if Flash Bannon died."

"It doesn't make sense. This Bannon has to be more than a minor
importer," mused the dark-haired woman.

"He is. He's almost interstellar class as a keyboardist, either
directlink or manual. He's got a doctorate in infrastructure economics
from ChicLandan University, and he owns the seediest Cuberan pub in
Camelot. He's also the head of both a trade factoring firm and a consulting firm."

"That makes him hated? Or a target?"

"Besides the fact that he's big, belligerent, and nasty to anyone he
doesn't like, and doesn't like anyone for more than a standard week? He
uses his consulting firm—and that's an economic consulting firm in
only the broadest sense—as an intelligence brokerage. Except we can't
call it that. He knows everything about everyone."

"What about the factoring business?"

"That seems legitimate. So legitimate that what exists in his consulting firm is probably fine rice compared to the trade business. He has tech and ag transfer lines with all the major outsystems from Tinhorn to Accord, from Orknarli to Anarra."

"Agriculture?"

"Interesting, isn't it?" asked the Director. "That seems to be the common thread. Even to the Federated Hegemony."

"You think Bannon became a target because of agriculture?"

"That's the implication. He either knows something or shipped something or both."

"His firm ships *everything* . . ."

"Makes it difficult. I've asked stats to analyze the cargo manifests we got earlier, but I wanted you all to think about it. We'll meet later."

"New Avalon—they're pretty repressed there. They make the Halstani matriarchs look like extroverts."

"This is getting nasty," added the redheaded man.

The Director held up the hard copy of the file. "This just might be the reason why—if we can figure it out. Except we don't have ships and outsystem operatives."

"Sylvia?"

"She's committed to the Institute. Let's hope she can help them."

Several heads nodded.

"Or we'll be facing a bigger mess than the Secession. Even the Grand Admiral would wish it were just the Secession."

XX

NATHANIEL AND SYLVIA walked slowly toward the front doors of the Guest House.

"I still worry . . . especially after yesterday," said Nathaniel quietly.

"The flitter 'accident'?"

"I meant Reeves-Kenn's murder. That means, I think, that someone decided since they couldn't set George up for a fall, they needed him out of the way. I wish we knew who . . . or why." Nathaniel looked around. "You be careful."

Sylvia nodded. "I'll be careful. You, too."

"I will." For some reason, one he couldn't put a finger on, he worried more about her, and it wasn't just male protectiveness. At least, he didn't think so.

"DeSain seemed willing enough to see me . . ."

"I would hope so. Ravishing you look." Nathaniel mock-leered at her as he held the door. "And smell."

"And he hinted at having lunch."

"I don't know. Perhaps you should go now." Nathaniel frowned, then shrugged. "I still worry."

"So do I, but we can't find out things without going out."

"No," he agreed.

"It is nice to hear you care." She touched his arm as they walked toward the groundcar. "Hailsham begged off seeing me. He pleaded the press of an ongoing urgent project."

"I probably upset him too much. Too pushy for a reserved Avalon-ian." Nathaniel glanced toward the east and the advancing gray clouds. Even the light wind was cooler, for once, and a hint of dampness and the vaguely metallic scent associated with water on Artos drifted across the permacrete drive.

Glubb Bagot hopped from the vehicle, and Nathaniel couldn't help wondering if the chipperness arose from the young lady at the Evanston's. Lucky man, he thought, except the finding of the special lady was the easy part. Keeping her was much harder. That he was discovering.

"What are you going to do?" asked Sylvia. "While I see DeSain, I meant."

"Walk. Walk the streets and roads of Lanceville. I need a better feel." He grinned momentarily. "I might even discover something."

"Like the time you cruised the Defense Ministry Plaza?" Sylvia shifted her grip on Nathaniel's datacase, hers for use in her interviews, since her own had perished in the flitter crash.

"You weren't supposed to know about that." He gave a dramatic sigh as he opened the groundcar door for Sylvia. "Even then, I had no secrets."

"You had enough, dear envoy."

Bagot looked momentarily puzzled at the reference to Nathaniel's previous assignment, but then smoothed his face and reseated himself behind the wheel, waiting.

"Drop me by the piers, Bagot, and then take Professor Ferro-Maine where she needs to go. I'll meet you two back at the Guest House. There are taxi services of some sort?"

"Yes, sir." Bagot grinned. "Pyotr's. But you'd better plan to wait a while. They don't hurry."

"I'll keep that in mind." The Ecolitans bounced as the vehicle lurched out toward the main highway.

"Sorry, sirs."

"That's all right," said Sylvia.

Outside of scattered trees, all planted near residences, Nathaniel again was reminded how few he had seen, except for a handful of small wood lots, all with trees that had to have been less than fifty years old. He wanted to shake his head. The more he looked, the more he realized how unbalanced the later stages of planoforming had been—a sure sign of stinginess or lack of funds from New Avalon.

"Unbalanced planoforming," he murmured to Sylvia.

"I wondered, but I'm not an expert. It seems like there's a lot missing."

More than a lot was missing. Could Dr. Oconnor shed some light on that? Oconnor was another contact he'd failed to follow up on.

"Has anyone ever talked about the problems of planoforming Artos?" Nathaniel asked Bagot.

"There's been talk since . . . ever since I can remember. The big things were trees and predators. R-K stopped the big predators. They said that luxury beef was all that kept Artos going, and they didn't need anything that killed cattle. The trees . . . I don't know. They just talked about it."

"Was there anything else?" prompted Sylvia.

"Water . . . there's always something on the vidfax about water. It gets so you don't pay any attention." Bagot put both hands on the wheel, but the groundcar still shivered as another big lorry whipped by them, headed away from Lanceville.

Water? Jem had mentioned the water table. Probably there hadn't been free water on Artos long enough to build that, not when aquifers and the like took thousands of years to charge and recharge on most T-type planets. Whaler took a deep, slow breath, trying to sort out all the miscellaneous facts that ought to have told him more—and hadn't.

He still hadn't any more answers when Bagot pulled up by the harbor piers.

"This do, sir?"

"Fine. Thank you." He turned to Sylvia, bent toward her, and said, "Be careful."

"I'll be fine." She squeezed his hand warmly.

As the groundcar rumbled off, the Ecolitan turned and studied the harbor. All three wharfs were empty, and low waves barely lapped at the stone columns that served as both supports and bollards.

Dust swirled off the harbor drive, carried by the ocean wind, and the only sound besides the whisper of the wind was the scraping of a small section of plastic sheeting as it twisted along the permacrete.

Nathaniel edged over toward the white-and-red square of plastic. Then he had to run as a sudden gust of wind lifted the sheeting past his extended arm. He finally grabbed the errant plastic in the middle of the deserted highway, a good thirty meters west from where Bagot had let him off. The plastic looked to be a fragment of heavy-duty shrinkwrap, the kind that was proof against the cold of space, and bore a part of a logo—the stylized initials SAI, and, underneath the initials, some jagged points of black running from one ripped edge.

"SAI?" The initials sounded vaguely familiar, but he couldn't place them. So he folded the roughly oblong sheeting into a small packet and slipped it into the hip pocket of his greens, checking the hidden loops in his belt that held the dart gun and the miniature stunner. Then he walked back across the permacrete highway, clearing it just before a small lorry with the name "Evanston Electric" rolled past in the general direction of the Blue Lion.

As he neared the center piers again, he walked past a small square building with barred windows and two locked roll-up doors for tractors or loaders or the like, and then strolled down the empty central pier, past the empty kiosklike watch post and the sign that read, "No Entry Without Permission. R-K Ocean Enterprises."

Black marks on the permacrete slabs that comprised the top of the piers testified to the recent presence of some vehicles, probably loaders.

At the seaward end of the pier, the Ecolitan looked for a time at the ocean with but a trace of whitecaps and waves, despite the darkening clouds that filled more and more of the eastern sky. The sea breeze smelled faintly metallic.

Finally, he turned and surveyed the waterfront and Lanceville beyond. Outside of the blue rectangle to the north that was the Blue Lion, the buildings that fanned out along the main highways that converged on the harbor were all low. And all were sand colored or brown, with generally the same red tile roofs. Not more than a handful of trees even reached much above the equivalent of two stories.

The Ecolitan took a deep breath and began to walk back in from the end of the pier toward the southernmost highway—empty except for a few vehicles moving there intermittently.

Immediately back from the harbor drive, the grayish ground was bare for almost a hundred meters. Nathaniel lengthened his stride, but found himself breathing heavily even before he reached the first set of buildings, a line of windowless bricked structures with heavy synthplast doors large enough to accommodate trucks and loaders—warehouses of a sort. But the Ecolitan did not discern many traces of recent use.

With a shrug, and a few deep breaths, he continued following the southern highway, past another line of unused warehouses and an empty cross street. He looked both ways, watching as the light breeze skittered sandy dust across the permacrete.

The next cross street contained a half-dozen squat houses. A bent old man sat on the steps of the second, perhaps seventy yards from the Ecolitan, and stared at him. The windows on the nearest house were open a crack, to let in the breeze, but Nathaniel could hear nothing from within.

The next cross street contained a larger building, what seemed to be a small market. A twenty-passenger electrobus was pulled up by the entrance, just beyond a bicycle rack that held nearly twenty bikes. A woman pushed a wheeled plastic basket-cart down the street away from the Ecolitan. An ancient electrocar whined jerkily into the carpark.

Nathaniel kept walking, and, slowly, the structures he passed became better kempt and larger, but he saw very few people about—except for the playground of the school where the shouts and calls of more than a hundred children echoed through the cloudy afternoon.

In time, he reached a solid, three-story structure on the corner of another cross street. He paused, taking several deep breaths, trying to flush the carbon dioxide from his system while he studied the building. It was almost as far south from the highway that led from the shuttle port and split the town as the Blue Lion was to the north. Although the structure was clearly new, it was built in the same fashion as the Bank of Camelot—stone and solid, with barred, small windows. The glittering plaque on the left side of the covered, arched entryway bore the intertwined letters LN. That and the two guards uniformed in bright blue told him more than enough—Landis-Nicarchos. Without looking back toward the building and the guards, he crossed the broad street after waiting for a single battered groundcar to pass. On the other side was a series of smaller shops. The first, on the corner, held a small bakery. The name "Aimee's" was stenciled on the wide glass. A faint smell of pastries seeped outside. Nathaniel found his mouth watering, and he checked the time—actually past noon. How far had he walked? He turned and looked back—probably three or four kilos.

The second shop was vacant, with off-green plastic sheeting covering the windows. The third was a small eating establishment. "Jerry's Grub" was burned into the plastic simulated-wood sign which swung slightly on plastic brackets outside the scarred door.

The Ecolitan stepped off the street and into the dim room.

"Drink or grub?" The warm voice came from a hard-faced woman in a brown singlesuit, her white-streaked red hair in a tight bun.

"Grub, mostly."

"Any of the empty tables on the wall. Menu's posted. Keep away from the rockfish."

"Thank you." The Ecolitan took a small table for two covered with a clean but faded blue synthcloth, next to the larger vacant table in the back corner. He squinted for a few moments while his eyes readjusted and he could read the single-sheet menu.

"What would you like?" The trim older woman in brown stood by the table.

"What would you recommend?" he asked.

"The meat pie. There was a big to-do over at the Lion, and Jerry got a quarter of the good beef."

"Fine. I'll try the Grawer."

"You're new here." A smile traced itself on her lips.

"The Grawer's that bad?"

She laughed gently. "No. Best brew we have, but I know everyone, just about. Lived here for . . . let's say long enough. I'm Elna, short for Elinor."

"I'm Nathaniel. No one ever shortened it, and you're right. I'm new. I was walking around, feeling things out."

"Sooner or later, everyone comes here." Another quick smile flitted across her lips.

"Elna!"

"I'll get your brew." In three long strides, Elna stood by the table where a white-haired, balding man held up a teapot.

The Ecolitan studied the room. Besides the older man, the various heavy-formed plastic tables held a young couple, two men in grease-spattered blue singlesuits, a mid-aged man in Avalonian dress shorts and high socks, two graying women, and three blue-clad security guards.

"Here's the brew." Elna set the teapot and a mug before him.

"Thank you."

"Be a bit for the pie. It's worth the wait."

The three blue-uniformed guards sat at the front corner table. One continually looked toward the LN building. Nathaniel listened.

". . . think we were real groundpounders . . ."

". . . Girhard . . . says . . . doesn't want . . . empty uniforms . . . do what he wants . . ."

". . . been sore for weeks . . . training never ends . . ."

". . . better pay than in the marine pens . . . bastard Sebastion . . . bleed dry . . ."

". . . say we're . . . heavy weapons . . ."

". . . careful . . . careful . . ."

"All right. Swarzee . . . really marry Elise?"

". . . figured she'd get someone . . ."

The three laughed, then stopped as one rose. "Greener's car . . . let's go . . . take a bit for him . . ."

The three were still laughing as they left Avalonian notes on the table and hurried out, talking, without even a look in the Ecolitan's direction, striding quickly toward the heavy-walled building.

The beef pie was worth the wait, almost as good as the marinated beef at George Reeves-Kenn's, and the heavy sconelike biscuits were hot.

Nathaniel discovered how hungry he was only after he looked at the empty plates.

"Need any more, Nathaniel?"

"No. I probably ate too much, but it was good."

"Isn't always, but I told you." Elna smiled, then left the paper check on the table. "Come again."

"Thank you." He didn't want to promise too much, but he did leave a hefty tip—the Artosans had kept that Avalonian custom. Then he used the public comm to call the taxi. He waited for a time even for the comm to be answered, but was assured Pyotr was on the way.

The Ecolitan burped, as quietly as possible, as he stood outside Jerry's, waiting for Pyotr's taxi, ignoring the mistlike rain that intermittently fell. On the far corner, one of the security guards in bright blue studied Nathaniel for a time before retreating back into the two-story building.

The multicolored, multipatched groundcar that growled up to the restaurant sported a hand-painted starburst in the center of which were scrawled orange letters spelling out a ragged "Pyotr."

"You the fellow who called?"

"That's me. The Guest House."

"The Guest House—the one on the highway to the shuttle port?"

Nathaniel slipped into the plastic-covered rear seat. "That's it."

"That's five."

"Fine."

"You're the chief." That was all the driver said, and the Ecolitan left the window open, out of self-defense against the odor of rancid spices emanating from the driver and ill-burned hydrocarbons from the engine.

Back at the Guest House, for a time he sat in his room, going back over the figures from the conversion plant, then taking those from Karl-Abbe and running some correlations and drafting some rough tables.

He rubbed his forehead and studied the hand-drawn tables again. He'd have Sylvia look at them, to make sure, but even from the outdated published figures on Artos, from the plant numbers, from the Bank's financial assessment, and from what they'd seen, the ConOne hydrocarbon facility not only had the capacity to process double its current output, but current output was somewhere well above current Artosan fuel needs—unless the ag sector on the outcontinents were disproportionately large—and the facility on ConTrio was supposed to handle such needs.

He shrugged. Right now, the figures were too rough to be absolutely conclusive in the economists' sense. But no manager/owner anywhere ever overstated capacity or output—especially to government overseers. So that meant that the numbers were conservative, that they had been exaggerated for other reasons, or that he and Sylvia had gotten cooked numbers.

The banking figures were worse. Free credit balances were building, even as average wages were almost stagnating. And where had Karl-Abbe gotten the import duty figures? Was the bank the holder? Someone was importing a lot of something, but the aggregations didn't say what.

He blinked and rubbed his forehead. He'd seen enough. Every number looked worse, and they all felt like they were in the right sector—and that gave him a uneasy feeling. All of Artos gave him a very uneasy feeling.

He snorted. How much of that was because someone had tried to kill them three times? He stood and checked the time. Fifteen hundred.

Sylvia should have been back earlier.

Finally, he stacked up folders and papers and went down to the empty foyer. No Sylvia. No messages on the comm unit. He called Detsen Oconnor at the New Avalon Monitoring Laboratory and got his assistant, but managed to set up an appointment for the next morning. After he broke the connection, he wanted to shake his head. He should have done that earlier. He should have tried to understand Sylvia earlier. It was hard to remember that she came from a far more repressed background than he did, and one where everything was involuted and convoluted. Add to that his own reserve. He shook his head. He should have done a lot of things earlier—that seemed to be life.

After pacing the foyer for a good fifteen units, he went outside under the portico and watched the misting clouds drift land-ward over Lanceville. Still no Sylvia.

When studying the rain palled, he went back and checked the comm unit. No messages.

He went back outside and watched more rain and clouds, until the rain dropped out to a trace of mist, and even less, and the clouds thinned.

A distant purr-rumble pricked his ears. Finally, out of the mist rising from the permacrete, the green groundcar lumbered in under the portico.

Sylvia smiled as he opened the door for her.

"I was getting a little worried."

"I'm fine. Keiffer DeSain is talkative."

Nathaniel nodded and stepped up to the groundcar window. "Bagot?"

"Sir?"

"Where's a good place to eat? Not as fancy as Elizabeth's and not as crowded as the Blue Lion? Someplace you'd like to go."

"Well . . . there aren't many places. The Old Tower used to be my favorite, but old lady Tuer died last spring, and they closed. Jerry's is all right for lunch, but they close early. Faro's, I'd guess."

"Well . . . you're our guest for dinner, and, if you like, you can invite a friend, as well."

"Sir . . . I wouldn't . . ."

"You've been very kind, and very helpful, and it's the least we can do." The driver looked toward Sylvia. She smiled. "It's little enough."

"And you can tell the chief that we insisted."

"Sir . . ."

"Anyone you'd like—brother, friend, lady—and we'll see you at eighteen forty."

"Yes, sir." Bagot grinned. "Yes, sir."

"A walk?" Nathaniel asked as the groundcar roared off and as they stood before the Guest House doors.

"It's a little damp, but we don't have much choice, do we?"

"Not really."

As they stepped out from the covered portico, a light breeze ruffled the summer-weight greens.

"It won't be bad." He glanced toward the west, where the heavier clouds that had passed the Guest House earlier had almost reached the horizon.

"That was nice of you, to ask Bagot, even if your motives aren't totally altruistic."

"Thank you. But they're partly altruistic."

"And the rest?"

"I just want to hear him talk. Sometimes, we don't listen to the right people."

Sylvia nodded. "You still surprise me."

"Me?"

"You." She leaned closer, then kissed his cheek, before stepping aside and into the row between the lines of bean plants.

He bent to check the ground at the edge of the field—barely damp despite the earlier light rain—and looked at the plants more closely. "Most of the young ones are this variety." He straightened. "But I wouldn't know why they'd grow one variety as opposed to another."

"Such an Ecolitan."

"I'm an economist, not an agronomist. What did you find out from the piping magnate?"

"DeSain seems like a likeable enough person, and he works hard, I think. He showed me the facility. It's pretty simple. They've got a small tech-template module that can turn the synde bean feedstock into a couple of different plastics. They're all handled by a small continuous extrusion mill, which is adjustable for pipe diameter. Simply sophisticated, I guess I'd call it."

"See anything interesting?"

"They've expanded recently. He showed me the addition. It's not that big."

"So . . . some growth, but not of the magnitude you'd expect at this stage of postplanoforming, if he's as good a businessman as he seems and you think."

"My thoughts as well." Sylvia brushed a strand of dark hair back off her forehead and tucked it behind her ear. "He's worried. He didn't say anything, but I could tell, and I don't think it's about business."

"Did he mention our good friend Kennis?"

"No. Why?"

"The good businessman has what looks like a fortified headquarters on the south side of Lanceville, and more than a handful of those blue-uniformed guards. I ate lunch at their hangout. One mentioned heavy weapons and intensive training and got hushed up."

"Private army—that confirms what Vivienne was telling us." Sylvia frowned. "Have you heard anything more about George Reeves-Kenn?"

"No. I didn't talk to Walkerson. The people at the monitoring laboratory—we're going to see them tomorrow morning—didn't say anything. There's not a vidfax at the Guest House."

"Karl-Abbe was right about the minimal amenities. I wonder if that's to keep official visitors isolated?"

"Could be. I don't like Reeves-Kenn's death, either, not that I like any death, but right now, I don't know what to do . . . or what we could do. There's a lot boiling around under the placid surface of Artos. Too much."

"You think that's why we were sent?"

"Probably—but I still can't figure why the House of Delegates has any interest in what's beginning to look like civil unrest on a colony planet three sectors away. I can see everyone else's potential interests . . . and there are so many."

"Too many," Sylvia said wryly.

"Then, the piers were empty, but there are marks there, heavy black marks. A lot of heavy stuff has been loaded or unloaded recently." Nathaniel shook his head. "Did you find out anything else?"

She lifted the datacase. "I've got some numbers on piping. You might be able to fit them into the puzzle. I also got him to say a few words about your other friend—Durward Hailsham."

"And?"

"Durward is as dense as he seems. The business was founded by his father. The older Hailsham made a lot building the road system, and he built well enough and big enough that his son is struggling and doesn't know why. Basically, Hailsham Enterprises is doing private surfacing, mostly for R-K Enterprises, and for some others."

"He probably built the LN building—or the armory beneath it." Nathaniel cleared his throat. "I'm guessing about the armory."

"LN building?"

"Kennis's headquarters."

"Oh . . . anything else?"

"Ever hear of an outfit called SAI?" He unfolded the red-and-white sheeting and handed it to her. "The chime's familiar, but I can't identify the melody."

"SAI . . . I should know that." She frowned.

"That's shrinkwrap for heavy equipment. I couldn't say what. It could be tech-transfer machinery, ocean processing gear, armaments, or just tanks of hydrocarbon feedstock."

"Armaments . . . SAI. Maybe . . ."

"Maybe what?" he asked.

"Sasaki Armaments, Interstellar . . . you've heard of them, haven't you?"

"They're in the Nippon sector of the Orknarlian Union, I think."

"And they're the biggest manufacturer of armaments outside the Empire. They'll supply anyone—but you have to supply the shipping."

He took the fragment of shrinkwrap sheeting back from her and looked at it again. "SAI . . . could it be the same . . . or just coincidence, some other little outfit with the same acronym?"

"Unlikely, but it could be. I don't know their logo or their design, but isn't that the edge of a multipointed star?"

They both shrugged.

"We've got a little problem."

"A little problem?" Sylvia raised her eyebrows.

XXI

THE SANDY-HAIRED SPECIAL assistant pursed her lips tightly. Her green eyes were dark, and she waited for the blank screen to clear.

Cling!

The image of a uniformed admiral of the fleets filled the screen, square-faced, with dark-circled green eyes and black hair shot with silver.

"Yes, Marcella?"

"Thank you," said the special assistant. "I had hoped you, or your staff, had a chance to review the materials we sent."

"We reviewed the materials very closely, and I personally found them persuasive. So did the D.I. staff."

"Yet you're going to transfer the Eleventh Fleet out to Sector Five, as well as pull the Third Fleet from Sector Two?"

"I cannot comment on that, Marcella, even on a secure line." The Grand Admiral met the special assistant's eyes.

"I understand. Has it crossed anyone's mind in the great and glorious Imperial Senate that Sector Two contains the Three System Bulge? And that, even though both the Conglomerate and the Hegemony have not increased their presence there, the total resource investment in defense has increased steadily over the past decade?"

"I have been informed that the First Fleet remains there, and that it has been some four centuries since there has been an armed conflict in Sector Two."

"In short, the starvation, the fish kills, and the spread of the bean plague have pushed the Senate absolutely to require a show of force in the Rift? Or is it worse than that?"

"You know I can't comment on that, Marcella."

"I sent you a complete analysis of the economics. Accord isn't gearing for war. They're at the lowest level of war footing in centuries. The science analysis shows that the gene structures in the bean plague aren't typical of Accord-structured types . . ."

"You are suggesting that the Imperial Senate is misguided?" The Grand Admiral's tone was ironic. "Have you seen the latest polls about Accord? According to UGI's latest survey, Accord is rated as an immediate and deadly danger to the Empire by fifty-one percent of the population."

"That's a trideo creation. Like those ridiculous shows that portray Ecolitans as green-coated evil monsters assisted by dancing fluffheads."

"Those trideo viewers vote, Marcella, and those they elect control the Senate. And the Senate dictates where the eagles go, even over the Emperor."

"You know it's a mistake."

"I am required to carry out the orders of the Senate. These fleet shifts are resource-intensive, as you know, however, and it may take several weeks, or longer. If matters should change, or some absolute documentation should arise in the meantime . . ."

The special assistant's shoulder's dropped. "I understand."

"Until later, Marcella."

The special assistant looked at the blank screen, her lips tightening.

XXII

THE DARK-HAIRED YOUNG woman in the front seat turned as Nathaniel and Sylvia settled into the back of the groundcar.

"Anne-Leslie, these are the professors," said Bagot, turning as well. "This is Anne-Leslie Hume."

"Nathaniel Whaler, and this is Sylvia Ferro-Maine."

"It's nice to meet you," offered Sylvia.

"I saw you at Madame Evanston's, but . . . I was busy, and I did want to make sure GB got something to eat."

As Bagot eased the groundcar out onto the highway toward Lanceville, a groundlorry rumbled by in the twilight headed westward.

"He's in a rush," observed Bagot. "Probably wants to get home."

Nathaniel wondered.

"What's Faro's like?" asked Sylvia.

"It's nice." Anne-Leslie wore a dark green jumpsuit and a white scarf. "I've been there once or twice—with the family. You can get things besides fish and algae, and Faro has his own still, where he makes his own stout and beer—his brother is a small grower way south. They say that he makes more by growing barley for Faro than what the big growers pay for beans." She looked at Sylvia, almost asking if she'd said too much.

"What have you eaten there that you liked?" asked Sylvia. "Is there anything especially good?"

"I don't know as there's . . . well . . . they say that the pork changa is good, and I liked it."

Nathaniel laughed good-naturedly. "I cannot say I've ever heard of pork changa. This sounds like an adventure. Might you enlighten me?"

"Stop sounding like an economist," teased Sylvia.

"But that is what—"

"Not tonight." Sylvia smiled indulgently and looked at Anne-Leslie. "I haven't heard of it either, but it sounds good."

"It is. It's all wrapped up in a crust, covered with real cream sauce, and filled with just about everything—peppers and seasoned pork and onions . . ."

As they entered Lanceville, a second lorry roared by, once more shivering the old groundcar.

"Can you drive by the piers on the way to Faro's?" asked Nathaniel. "Not stop. Just drive by?"

"Sure, professor. That will only take an extra couple of units. Lanceville's not exactly huge." After a moment, Bagot added, "If I might ask, sir . . . ?"

"I wonder whether something's being unloaded at the port."

The two in the front exchanged glances, but neither spoke.

"Can't you ever stop the economics?" asked Sylvia, squeezing Nathaniel's hand reassuringly, even as she let out a long sigh.

"I will try. After the harbor, I will try."

"Try harder," suggested Sylvia in a wry tone.

A faint smile creased Anne-Leslie's lips.

"How about desserts?" asked Sylvia.

"I like their chocolate rum tort," said Bagot.

Anne-Leslie shook her head. "You would."

"That means it is strong and large," suggested Nathaniel.

The young woman in the front seat nodded emphatically.

Bagot turned onto the harbor drive and slowed the groundcar. "Do you need me to stop?"

All three harbor piers were lit, and two held tugs and barges. A third tug, pushing a high-riding barge, appeared to be steaming seaward. On the two piers, loaders lifted a variety of crates onto waiting groundlorries. Four other lorries waited at the foot of the empty center pier.

"No. That will do. They do what they do, and—"

"Enough," said Sylvia firmly, a glint in her eye.

"Thank you, Bagot. Let's go eat."

"Thank you, honored economist and professor," said Sylvia.

Faro's was less than a kilo from the harbor—in what looked to be a converted store. The windows were blocked with dark, louvered interior shutters, and the floor was a polished gray stone.

After stepping into an atmosphere of muted incense, spices, and cooking oil, the four waited a moment. Most of the nearly twenty tables were taken.

A heavyset woman wearing a floor-length full maroon skirt and an orange blouse scurried toward them. "Four? We have a large booth . . ."

"That's fine," said Nathaniel.

The booth was lit, dimly, by a hanging ceramic oil lamp that shed almost as much smoke as light. The two Ecolitans took the seats with their backs to the wall.

After checking the menu, and tentatively deciding on the pork changa, Nathaniel turned to Bagot. "You grew up here, and your father worked for the Port Authority. My father was a datamanager, and the last thing I ever wanted to do was manage data. How did you end up at the same place?"

"I guess I never thought about it that way."

"What would you gentles like to drink?" asked the server, a slightly thinner version of the hostess.

"A glass of Kenward," said Sylvia.

"I'll try that," added Anne-Leslie.

"Stout," said Bagot.

"Grawer."

"Soon as I get those, I'll take your order." With a snap of her head she was gone.

"That's . . . you know . . . ?" offered Anne-Leslie.

Bagot frowned.

"Susanna . . . the one . . ."

"Right oh. I didn't recognize her."

"I'll bet you were one of those boys who drooled after her."

Bagot flushed.

"Be easy on him," said Nathaniel. "We all make mistakes."

"Like that blond one in New Augusta?" asked Sylvia with a broad smile.

Nathaniel winced.

Anne-Leslie and Bagot laughed.

"Here you are." Susanna set two wineglasses, a tumbler, and a mug down on the brown synthcloth. "And what would you like tonight? The special's sea-grilled baskmod."

"Would you suggest the pork changa or the house pie?" asked Sylvia.

"They're both good. Depends on how spicy you like things. The pork's pretty spicy."

"The house pie."

"Pork changa" came from Anne-Leslie, and then Bagot.

"The same," added Nathaniel.

"You were saying how you ended up at the Port Authority," prompted Sylvia, after a moment of silence following the server's departure.

"Jem wanted me to be a rover, said he could get me on at R-K. It never grabbed me. There was talk about opening a branch of the University of

Camelot here, but it didn't happen. Pa said the growers were against it . . ." The younger man looked at the glass of stout, then sipped it.

The Ecolitan refrained from wincing at the thought of drinking anything alcoholic and warm.

Susanna dropped a longish basket of bread on the table, barely hesitating as she passed, and Nathaniel offered it to Sylvia, then to Anne-Leslie.

"I imagine growing up here was difficult," said Sylvia, looking toward the younger woman.

"We were pretty lucky, I guess. Better off than some." Anne-Leslie sipped the Kenward. "It's better now, a little anyway. I can remember the year everything came out of plasticpaks."

"After the tox-rain?" Bagot shook his head and looked down at his stout, then took a quick swallow, almost draining it.

"I'm sorry," apologized the younger woman.

"It happened. Can't change that."

Nathaniel and Sylvia exchanged quick glances.

"I walked by the school the other day. Was that the one you attended?" asked the older Ecolitan.

"Same one. Both Anne-Leslie and I went there. That's the only one there is, really, here on ConOne. Never got away with much, not after Ma started working there." Bagot laughed.

"It sounds like your mother didn't let you get away with much anywhere."

"She still works there, and she still doesn't."

"So . . . you went to school there, and then you went to work at the port."

"They owed him that, what with his father," interjected Anne-Leslie.

"How did your father end up with the Port Authority?" asked Sylvia gently.

Bagot looked at Anne-Leslie, then at Nathaniel, who sipped the too-strong Grawer.

"He was with the Fusiliers, the Green and Tans. That's what Ma says, anywise. Pa never would talk about it. After New Avalon took Hibernia, they offered him . . . 'cause he was such a good pilot, I guess, they offered him a job anywhere he wanted except Hibernia." Bagot hurried another swallow of stout.

Nathaniel had the feeling that someone other than Bagot would be driving the groundcar.

"Here you go, gentles, and a good go it is!" Susanna spread the plates around the table, then set a small dish at each plate filled with a scoop of something. "And there's your pinko." She looked at Bagot's empty glass.

The younger man nodded.

"What might be pinko?" asked Nathaniel after the server left.

"It's a kind of local sherbet, some mutated raspberries, and it tastes pretty good." Bagot snorted. "One of the few things besides cattle that taste good, and pinko's the only one that's cheap."

In the lull after Susanna provided another glass of stout to Bagot and as they began to eat, Nathaniel picked up fragments of conversation at the adjoining table.

". . . sure he's the young fellow from the port . . . other one might be his brother . . ."

"Too tall . . . Bagots are short . . ."

". . . new to me . . ."

The pork changa was mild, and the Ecolitan wondered. "Is the house pie . . . lightly seasoned?"

"Bland," murmured Sylvia.

He offered her some of the pork.

"That's good," she murmured after eating a mouthful.

He took a small spoonful of the pink sherbet and had another. "The changa's quite good, and so is the pinko," he announced loudly. "A good recommendation." He nodded to Anne-Leslie. "A good recommendation."

The young woman flushed slightly.

"How do you find working for the Evanstons?" asked Sylvia quickly.

"Madame Evanston is easy to work for. She tells me what she wants, how she wants it done, and, if I don't know, how to do it." Anne-Leslie smiled. "The best parts are that unless I mess up, she leaves me alone, and the food is good and free, and there's plenty. Sometimes, she'll even send some home with me. And clothes for the little ones."

Sylvia looked at the younger woman inquiringly.

"Martha-Elizabeth and Laura-Olivia . . . they're the youngest. Clothes out of anything but synthcloth are still hard to come by."

"The big growers don't like sheep. I heard tell that there's a small herd on ConTrio, but that wool doesn't get here." Bagot took another swallow of the stout and finished the second glass, holding it up for a refill. "Nothing gets here."

"Another?" asked Susanna, sweeping by and taking the glass.

"Another."

Anne-Leslie glanced at Bagot, but the younger man avoided her eyes.

"It seems like things are improving somewhat," began Nathaniel. "The Blue Lion is being redecorated and refurbished."

"It looks nice," said Anne-Leslie, "but they don't pay very well."

"Your stout," announced the server, setting it in front of Bagot. "Would anyone like dessert?"

"The rum cake," said Bagot.

"The nut cake," added Anne-Leslie.

"I think I'll pass," said Sylvia.

"I also." Nathaniel knew, again, that too much food was tightening his trousers.

"I still can't believe you drooled after her," commented Anne-Leslie after the server disappeared into the kitchen area.

"It was . . . a long time . . . ago." Bagot took another hefty swallow of the warm stout.

"You were saying that the Blue Lion does not pay well," prompted Nathaniel, recalling the disappointed waiter there.

"No. I looked there."

"No one pays well on Artos, 'cept the Port Authority," added Bagot.

"They only hire men." Anne-Leslie's eyes glinted.

Bagot looked down into his half-full glass.

Susanna dropped the two deserts before the two younger diners. "Need anything else?"

"Just the bill, if you wouldn't mind," said Nathaniel quietly.

The server nodded, then slipped the paper oblong onto the table.

After she left, Nathaniel asked, "Did you know Helverson very well?"

Bagot swallowed a large mouthful of the dark cake before answering. "Didn't know him . . . mush . . . at all. The chief . . . said he was a former grenadier, special services . . ." Bagot looked up and offered a wide and sloppy grin. "Just for you . . ." The grin slowly faded.

Anne-Leslie's hand went to her mouth.

"That's all right," said Sylvia. "We thought that might be the case. He's one of the few not born here on Artos, right?"

"Thass . . . right. You . . . win the prize, professor." Bagot slowly ate another bite. "Good . . . cake . . . good . . . food . . ."

Abruptly, Bagot grinned even wider, and then put his head on the table, right beside the remnants of the chocolate rum cake.

"GB . . . oh, GB."

"Perhaps we should go." Nathaniel rose.

Sylvia nodded.

After paying the check and including enough for a tip, Nathaniel simply lifted the slight form of Bagot right out of his chair and carted him to the groundcar.

"What will happen to him?" asked Anne-Leslie as Whaler eased the limp figure into the backseat beside her.

"Not a thing. Because he didn't say anything at all. Not that I heard," said Nathaniel.

"You planned this." The young woman looked from one Ecolitan to the other.

"No. He only had three glasses of stout. I had no idea he was that sensitive to alcohol. The only thing we planned was to get him to talk about Artos."

"That doesn't make sense."

"Yes, it does," said Sylvia while Nathaniel shut the door and slipped behind the wheel. "People who live someplace take their world for granted. You need stories about friends, family, little things that happen to get a better view."

"That's what Madame Evanston says . . . but you're professors."

Nathaniel wanted to slam his forehead. The term "madame" finally registered, and he knew what his subconscious had been trying to tell him about Vivienne Evanston. She had to be Frankan.

"We have a study to do," said Sylvia. "In the end, economics is about people, and the numbers don't make sense without knowing about people. Professor Whaler spent most of a day just walking through Lanceville, looking and listening."

"Oh . . ."

Nathaniel eased the car into the street. "Where should we drop you off?"

"No," said Sylvia. "I think we should drop GB off first—if Anne-Leslie can show us where."

Nathaniel nodded. "Fine. GB first." That made sense, especially given how worried the young woman was.

"We don't live that far apart, really. GB still lives with his family. So do I."

"In town here?"

"Yes. Three streets ahead, turn left."

"That's a long bicycle ride out to Madame Evanston's. I assume you ride," said Nathaniel.

"I do, but it's flat and easy, and in the morning it's cool. If they have a big party or something, I stay there for the night."

"It's another five long blocks to his house." Anne-Leslie turned in the seat and glanced down at Glubb Bagot. "Are you sure he'll be all right?"

"He'll be fine." Sylvia reached back and touched her shoulder. "Except for a splitting headache."

Nathaniel concentrated on driving the heavy antique, following Anne-Leslie's intermittent directions.

The small boxy house was like all the others on the street, brick with a red tile roof and a small stone stoop.

Nathaniel lifted the snoring form from the rear seat and headed up the low step.

"Oh . . . what happened? Is he all right?" The gray-haired woman with the lined face wore faded trousers and a shirt—clean—that was gray from too many washings.

"He should be fine, except for a headache. He drank three glasses of stout too quickly," explained Nathaniel, as he followed Bagot's mother into the front room.

"Best you put him on the sofa there."

"Tell him I'm sorry, but I'll bring the groundcar to the Port Authority in the morning."

"The Port Authority in the morning?"

The Ecolitan nodded, then stepped outside and walked swiftly back to the groundcar. "And now you, young woman."

"Turn left at the corner."

Bagot's dinner partner lived just south of the main highway that bisected Lanceville.

"Thank you for dinner," said Anne-Leslie as Nathaniel pulled up outside another square brick dwelling. "I'm sorry . . . about GB. It's just that . . ."

"We're sorry," said Sylvia. "We certainly didn't mean . . ."

"No . . . you wouldn't know. I didn't know." She flashed a warm smile. "I'll check on him on the way to work." With that, she slipped from the groundcar and walked swiftly to the darkened door of the house and inside.

"So . . . what have we found out?" asked Sylvia as they pulled away from the boxy brick house where they had left Anne-Leslie.

"Helverson was there to protect us, and Walkerson was probably ordered to ensure we finished our study. Walkerson's ambivalent about it, because he's worried that Helverson might be checking on him as well."

"Do we really know that?"

"No. That's a guess, but Walkerson was more upset about the lost equipment than about Helverson, and Helverson was one of the few recent arrivals from New Avalon—if not the only one."

"Sebastion's moving heavy equipment out to the ranch—military stuff?" asked Sylvia.

"That's a guess, but it's probably either that or construction equipment that could be used as such." Nathaniel turned the groundcar back to the south at the next cross street.

"Ah . . ."

"I want to drive by Kennis's armory. Or what I think is an armory."

"You are worried."

"Yes."

Nathaniel let his breath out slowly when he saw that, except for the entry, the LN building was dark. "We've got some time."

"How much?"

"I don't know. Days at least. Maybe weeks."

"What are we going to do?"

"Stop a Galactic war . . . somehow."

"From a backwater colony planet? With an economic study?"

"Not just from here. Tomorrow we need to plan when to leave for New Avalon. We don't want to be on an Avalonian ship or a Fuardian one, and I'd really not want to travel on a Halstani vessel either."

"My . . . aren't we picky."

"Picky?" Nathaniel eased the groundcar back onto the main highway heading for the Guest House.

"I'm sorry. But you're doing it again. This is like New Augusta. You spew forth all of this and expect me to follow along."

"I'm sorry. I didn't mean to, but I suppose it sounds that way." He took a deep breath. "All right. There's a civil war—or a rebellion—brewing. Everything points that way. I can't prove it, but I'd bet on it." He laughed harshly. "In fact, I am. Our lives probably. Artos can't produce the resources necessary to fight such a war, nor enough productive equipment, but I'd guess they're here somewhere, and they didn't come from New Avalon. They also have an oversized bean conversion facility that produces too much liquid fuel, but prices remain high, and that doesn't happen if there's a true surplus."

"Fuel and energy for combat vehicles?"

"That's another guess. And someone has been shipping them in, probably to both Kennis and the R-K bunch."

"I see." Sylvia's voice was low in the darkened car. "That means some outside interest wants to create a civil war, and then use it as a pretext to take Artos. New Avalon has been feeling the pinch for a long time and doesn't want to plough any more capital investment into Artos, and because they don't, that's created the opportunity."

"I'm guessing, but that's what I see. Oh . . . and I'd bet that Vivienne is Frankan, and that she's still got ties there. That just dawned on me."

"You didn't realize that?"

"No."

"So who's behind this civil war?"

"I wish I knew. We've seen traces of the Federated Hegemony, the Frankan Union, and the Conglomerate." Nathaniel shrugged. "I don't know. I'd bet it isn't the Franks, but I couldn't say why. Then, my guesses aren't doing that well now. I do know that we have to get to New Avalon before it blows. Am I being too obscure?"

"No. Although, for an economist, dear, you certainly get involved in some interesting situations."

That wasn't the half of it, not even half, he feared.

XXIII

NATHANIEL EASED THE groundcar away from the portico of the Guest House, then turned west toward the shuttle port. "Sebastion was transferring a lot of equipment and gear last night, and the more I think about it, the more I'd bet there are weapons involved, a great number of them."

"I wouldn't bet." Sylvia laughed softly, but not gently. "You think they're building for a showdown with the small growers?"

"I don't know. That's certainly what comes to mind first, especially after George's murder. But the fact that Sebastion is moving equipment seems to mean that he has a lot to do to take over the establishment at the ranch. I wonder just what's in those underground installations."

"Enough to make everyone unhappy," predicted Sylvia. "Especially if it's a setup by Kennis, to play the large and small growers off against each other."

"That's true," admitted the sandy-haired Ecolitan, "but I would have expected more activity around Kennis's headquarters last night."

"Unless he's really as devious as he seems," pointed out Sylvia.

"Or unless someone else has the same idea. This is at least a three-way power struggle."

"Did you have any luck with the transport center?" she asked.

"There's a Frankan ship due some time in the next few days—probably the day after tomorrow. The Fuard cargoboat has three spaces, and the Wendsor liner won't be back for another week."

"You wanted a Frankan ship, anyway, didn't you?" asked Sylvia.

"Better than anything else, although an Orknarlian or an Imperial vessel would have been better." Nathaniel eased the groundcar onto the drive to the shuttle port.

"Imperial?"

"Very tightly run."

"I'm glad you approve of something Imperial."

"I approve of other Imperial . . . items." He grinned.

"You're still impossible."

"Absolutely."

As Nathaniel drove up to the Port Authority building, both Walkerson and Bagot came out to meet the Ecolitans.

"Hoped we'd have a moment to chat," said the Port Chief. "We can do that while Bagot gets the beast here serviced."

"We're here," said Nathaniel.

Bagot didn't look at either Ecolitan and kept his eyes averted as he slipped behind the wheel of the groundcar and eased it toward the maintenance building several hundred meters south of where the three stood.

"It's like this . . ." began Walkerson. "The hoops are getting tight. The constabulary, such as it is, has no idea who killed George Reeves-Kenn. We don't either." Walkerson's eyes went from one Ecolitan to the other. "I suppose I should ask where you were on the afternoon of the day before yesterday."

"As I am sure Bagot has told you, we visited Madame Evanston and then the Bank of Camelot." Nathaniel smiled pleasantly.

"I know. That's a formality, but had to ask. Now . . . you've seen a number of people over the last few days, and some rather strange happenings have taken place. Do you have any ideas who might have murdered George?"

"No," said Nathaniel.

Walkerson's eyes shifted to Sylvia. "And you, professor?"

Sylvia shook her head, then added. "From what little we have seen, a number of people would have some potential reasons. Isn't that so?"

Walkerson coughed and looked at the permacrete underfoot for a moment. "Unfortunately . . . you have the right of it. I was hoping you might shed some light."

"Every light brings shadows, sometimes more shadow than illumination."

"That seems to be the case here."

"Tell me, Chief Walkerson," continued Nathaniel, "everyone talks about the smaller growers, but never have we heard a name. We have heard about the larger growers by name, the bankers, the scientists, the traders . . ."

"That's another problem. We know all the small growers. There are maybe two hundred. But none of them are leaders. No one ever steps forward. They come to some meetings, and they all protest the tax levies." Walkerson shrugged. "But I couldn't call a single one a leader."

"Does that mean they have none, or that they protect whoever is their leader?"

"If I could find that out . . ."

"You'd know," suggested Sylvia.

"Exactly." Walkerson smiled as the groundcar pulled up. "Thank you. I do hope that you'll let me know if you should chance across something."

"Of course." Both Ecolitans smiled politely.

Walkerson watched impassively as they seated themselves in the rear seat of the groundcar. The Port Chief was still watching when Bagot drove by the main entry building and the groundcar passed out of Walkerson's sight.

"Bagot," said Nathaniel, "don't worry about last night. I don't think Chief Walkerson's that upset, and we aren't."

"Don't know what came over me, sirs."

"Good food, good drink, and good company," suggested the sandy-haired Ecolitan. "And probably not a very high tolerance for alcohol. Some of us have to be careful." He paused. "Anne-Leslie was worried about you. She seems like a nice young woman."

"She is. Came by early this morning." The driver cleared his throat. "I'd forgotten how nice she is."

"I'd do something special for her," suggested Nathaniel. "Special women are hard to find." He squeezed Sylvia's knee slightly.

"Yes, sir."

"That's not an order." Nathaniel laughed.

"Where to, sir?" Bagot slowed as the vehicle neared the main highway.

"The biomonitoring station—Dr. Oconnor's operation?"

"That'll be on the south side." Bagot turned right and headed east.

Even more ancient than the Bank of Camelot, the thick-walled biomonitoring laboratory squatted on the low bluff on the north side of where the river entered the ocean, scarcely a kilo south of the harbor piers.

Bagot glanced at the Ecolitans. "I'll just park on the shady side and take a nap, if you don't mind."

Nathaniel suppressed a smile. "That's fine."

Oconnor was waiting for them. "Professors, professors. Ah, let us use the lounge, such as it is."

The short corridor he led them down was plain brick and aged, and the stone floor bore thin traceries of cracks.

"Sit down. Sit down." Oconnor gestured to the threadbare couch under the two high narrow windows. Without waiting, he perched on the plastic stool opposite it. "What can I do for you? It seems silly to be asking that."

"I had hoped you could brief us on the ecologic status of Artos."

Oconnor pushed a longish lock of brown hair back off his forehead. "I don't know as I could tell you anything you don't already know. You Ecolitans wrote the books on ecology."

"Some Ecolitans did." Nathaniel smiled. "We are economists, however, and we are investigating the interrelations between ecological development and the infrastructure of the economy of Artos."

"You are wise enough to see what you see," said Oconnor.

"That the job was never really finished," suggested Sylvia when Nathaniel did not answer.

"The atmosphere is correct and improving," answered Oconnor, his voice neutral.

"Was it lack of funds or the political pressure of the old age interests?" asked Nathaniel.

"I'm not one to speculate, and I'm not in a position to," said the biomonitoring official.

"All right. Then perhaps some ecological questions. What is the largest predator on Artos?"

"I'd have to say the wild dog. Some escaped early on, but the ranchers shoot them on sight."

"And after that?"

"There is a juaranda cat—maximum of eight kilograms—but its principal prey classes are all rodents."

"No snakes? No large mammalian or reptilian predators?"

"No." Oconnor smiled under the long straight nose.

"What about plant diversity?"

"Above the microbic level, the diversity drops off more than in the normal pyramidal distribution."

"I've also noticed almost a monoculture in terms of major crops, a heavy emphasis on synde beans."

"Four crop families, if you will, comprise about eighty percent of all cultured areas. Tops are the synde beans, but that's to be expected on any planet at this stage, both for the energy requirements and for the supplemental soil scavenging and the oxygen enhancement properties."

"Grass and food crops—maize and wheat."

"Zima grass, and the others are as you observed." Oconnor touched his chin. "To reduce the coverage of those eighty percent in a balanced fashion to a more normal distribution would require an annual investment of close to a billion credits for at least a decade. The large growers have been subsidizing forestation at a level of nearly fifty million, but . . ." The monitoring chief lowered his shoulders.

"It's not enough, and it appears unlikely that they can continue that level of investment. You mentioned earlier, an emphasis on 'output' by the growers."

"That's their favorite word. 'Output, Detsen, output.' Given the constraints they face, I must give them credit for the ecological contributions they have supported."

"Anything extensive besides the forestation?"

"G-H Factoring has begun a small rain forest effort on ConTrio. That's very promising."

"Is there anything else?" asked Sylvia.

"This is a large planet." Oconnor chuckled. "Even a small planet is large, ecologically speaking. It takes time." He hopped off the stool.

"Have you talked to any of the outsystem agricultural factors recently?" asked Nathaniel quickly. "Sonderssen or the Fuard?"

"I talk to all of them at one time or another," responded Oconnor after a pause.

Nathaniel wanted to nod, but asked instead, "How do you think the ecological development, ideally speaking, ought to go from here?"

"More forestation, diverse forestation. I'd like to see a stronger base in the marshlands. You get good solid marshlands, integrated properly, and established marine diversity, and an ecology can take a great deal of disruption."

"You've made that point forcefully enough," said Nathaniel with a chuckle. "Even George Reeves-Kenn's rovers know it by heart."

"I'm glad someone does." Oconnor glanced toward the closed door. "I shouldn't keep you any longer, but I'm glad you stopped by. If you run across Professor Hiense, please give him my best."

"We will," promised Sylvia.

Outside, some scattered cumulus clouds were forming out over the eastern ocean, but the sun remained bright.

Nathaniel blotted his forehead.

"Not that again." Sylvia laughed.

"Yes, this again." He put away the overlarge kerchief. "He's not as forthcoming here as he was at a totally snooped party. Interesting."

"He doesn't worry about Kennis. Here . . . he worries."

"You think the Avalonian government has put a thumb on him?"

"Someone has."

"One of the factors?" asked Nathaniel.

Sylvia lifted her eyebrows.

"You'd rather not speculate?"

"You aren't," she pointed out.

"I can't. It can't be his superiors—there haven't been any Wendsor ships since the reception, and that means no messages or messengers. Local, then, and probably commercial, and some form of personal pressure, but I can't figure out why."

"Neither can I." Sylvia frowned.

Nathaniel rapped on the side of the groundcar.

"Wha . . . ? Oh, sirs!" Bagot rubbed his eyes and sat up.

"Do you know where the trade factors have their offices or warehouses?" asked Nathaniel.

"Yes, sir. All of them are at the shuttle port. They have to have one there, anyway. That's a Port Authority requirement."

"Back to the shuttle port, then."

Bagot dropped them outside a door in a long building. Beside the door was a blue-and-red plaque: AgriTech Galactic, Sonderssen & Company, Representatives, licensed factors.

Jimson Sonderssen stood from behind a small console as the Ecolitans stepped into the comparatively dimly lit room. "The Ecolitan economists . . . I do believe." The lanky man bowed from the waist. "And you were lucky, if that is the word, to find me actually here. In what might I be of service?"

"I find myself somewhat confused," began Nathaniel. "You are an agricultural factor, but trade in agriculture is usually unprofitable between star systems, except for new species or breeds of agricultural animals. Is this not so?"

"The basics you have correctly, professor," answered Sonderssen.

"And you have been a factor here for several years?"

"That is correct. Eight, almost to the day."

"Ecologically, Artos is less advanced than some planets still in planoforming, and agricultural diversity is low."

"Also true."

"Yet diversity is necessary for trade."

"That is an accepted fact." Sonderssen bowed slightly.

"I understand you've recently been talking to the biomonitoring office."

"Recently? That is so." Sonderssen offered a dazzling smile. "I often consult with them. Who else could advise this poor factor?"

"Do you handle the luxury beef for the Hegemony?"

Sonderssen spread his hands. "You can certainly surmise that I do. There is no one else accredited to the Hegemony."

"Yet the beef trade has been falling off."

"You would like to know what a poor factor such as I might do to justify his existence in economic terms?"

"You're obviously prosperous," pointed out Sylvia.

"Good I might be at appearances."

"Neither the Hegemony nor its merchants reward appearances," suggested Nathaniel.

"A wit you have, professor." Sonderssen smiled. "And that is rare among Ecolitans and economists."

"You seem very close to the Fuardian factor, Fridrik . . ." Nathaniel could see Sonderssen would only say what he wished to say.

"VonHalsne. Yes."

"He wears an informal dress uniform."

"So do you, professor. All Fuards in semiofficial capacities outside the Conglomerate are representatives of the state. For sure, is that not known to all?" Sonderssen smiled. "And why am I close to him, when our governments are, shall we say, less than perfect friends? Because I adhere to an ancient maxim. It is better to hug your enemies closer than your friends, for it is difficult to lift a blade when held tightly."

"You're also good with the words." Sylvia's laugh was almost bell-like.

"Is your friend Fridrik around somewhere?"

"His office is the third down, but he is not there. I believe he has returned to Clava for several weeks." Sonderssen looked at the door. "It has been pleasant seeing you once more."

"And you, too," lied Nathaniel.

Sylvia offered a slight bow, which the trade factor returned.

Fridrik VonHalsne was not only absent, his office was closed and locked.

"Not good," murmured Sylvia.

"Not at all. So . . . was it Sonderssen or Sebastion or Kennis that put the touch on Oconnor?"

"What do you think?"

"Sebastion. I think he told Oconnor that he'd never see another cent from the growers or the big ag interests if he said a single meaningful word to us. That's only a guess."

"I'd have to second that, but it's only feel."

"What a pair! Guesses and feelings, and the sky's about to fall."

"At least we know that."

They exchanged wry smiles.

Port Chief Walkerson was waiting by the groundcar when the Ecolitans returned. "Things are getting nasty, Whaler. You didn't catch your boat ride with one of the FitzReillys, did you?"

"As a matter of fact, we did. Why?"

"Someone just fired their barge this morning while they were loading. They were both killed, and it's a flaming mess—raw synde oil in the river, a grass fire . . ." He shook his head. "Sebastion Reeves-Kenn denies being involved, but he claims that it's a blessing in disguise, that the pods carried this synde bean plague. He says it's been ravaging the Imperial planets, and even Halstan. You know anything about that?"

Nathaniel pursed his lips. Synde bean plague on Artos? How had it ever gotten across four sectors?

"You look like you know something."

"Oh . . . I do. There's been a bean plague in the Empire—Heraculon, as I recall—but I couldn't figure how it could get here, and none of the plants I saw looked diseased, although I wouldn't know one plant disease from another."

"Well . . . Sebastion wants me to set Oconnor on it, and quarantine the small growers' fields. He was almost screaming."

Nathaniel shook his head. Now what?

"And by the way, old chap, just for the record, where have you been today?"

"We spent most of the morning at the biomonitoring station—or going to it and returning. We had a long discussion with Dr. Oconnor." Whaler didn't mention the visit to Sonderssen's small office, or the attempt to see VonHalsne, although Walkerson could certainly see where they had been.

"Good. Good. Terrible business, this. Do you two know anything more about this?"

"The FitzReilly woman told us that they carried cargoes for both the small growers and beef for R-K Enterprises. She said that the larger haulers overcharged the small growers."

"That's all?"

"We got a lot of information on barge traffic patterns and capacities."

"Port Chief," added Sylvia, "you might remember that we had walked some fifteen kays before we found the barge, and it was the end of a long day. We collapsed and slept most of the trip back to Lanceville."

"Right . . . forgot about that. Well . . . let me know if you think of anything." He paused. "Are you sure you don't know more about this bean plague thing?"

"Walker," said Nathaniel tiredly, "I told you. I'm an economist. I wouldn't know one plant disease from another."

"Well, I had to ask."

The Ecolitan just nodded.

"Now what?" asked Sylvia, as Walkerson marched back toward his office.

"We might as well get something to eat. Bagot needs it, and so do we."

They needed more than that, but a solid late lunch was a start.

XXIV

NATHANIEL SLIPPED INTO the bed in the darkness.

"Not again," whispered Sylvia. "We talked over everything before."

"You know I think we need to get out of here while it's still relatively safe and possible. Do you think I'm overreacting?" He touched her shoulder.

"Yes, but you're male." Then she giggled and whispered. "I'm sorry. I couldn't resist, and I don't mean that the way you think."

"How did . . . do—"

"After four attempts on our lives, is anywhere safe?"

"New Avalon is likely to be safer than it will be here, once open fighting breaks out."

"You don't think this is really a fight between the large and small growers, do you?" She twisted, and her lips brushed his ear. "Really?"

He tried not to shiver, and forced himself to concentrate on his words, not her warmth and closeness. "It is, but they haven't all the resources they need. Sebastion's as worried about Kennis as he is the small growers. I think the outsystem types who do have the resources don't want to complicate things at the moment. They'd rather pick up the pieces. That's what I'm gambling on. Things will have to get messy. New Avalon won't want to spend the credits . . . so they'll get messier."

"And then someone will step in with their snow-white ships of mercy, so to speak?" Her hand massaged the back of his neck, and he tried to resist the impulse to draw her closer.

"I believe that's the agenda. So the sooner—and safer—we can get to New Avalon, the better our chances to head this off."

"I thought you—we—were here to do a study. Not in my bed, either."

"I'm sorry. I couldn't sleep, and I wanted to talk this over."

"That's not all you want."

"No. But I'm not asking or insisting on anything else." He took a long slow, quiet breath.

"Stop puffing in my ear."

"Sorry." He swallowed. "We will do the study, but . . . we're also here to stop what could turn into a mess, with the Institute being blamed for it all."

"You're stretching." Sylvia shook her head, close enough to his face that he could smell the trilia . . . and her. "Just how does this impact Accord and the Institute?"

"Someone wants the study. We show up. A revolt or something starts. The bodies of two Institute members are found. One has a nasty reputation, and the other is a former I.I.S. agent. Whoever's behind this then accuses New Avalon of throwing in with the ecologic butchers of Accord and the Empire, and uses that to justify liberating the poor oppressed small folks."

"You really think people will fall for that?"

"Smart people won't, but there aren't many of them in any society, and politicians live by the numbers." He found his hand massaging her shoulder and moving downward. "Besides, rationality is usually only used to develop logical arguments to support existing beliefs and prejudices."

"You are cynical."

"Realistic," he whispered.

"About some things."

"We'll also not tell Walkerson until we have to."

"That's realistic," she conceded.

"Very realistic."

Her fingers ran along his cheek. "Things are going to get worse."

"Probably."

"I think so, too." Then her lips were on his.

XXV

AT THE RAPPING on the door, Nathaniel crossed the room from the fresher wearing his greens but still barefoot.

"Who's that?" Sylvia peered through the connecting door. She was already fully dressed, so efficient that he felt sluggish.

He shrugged and said in a low voice, "I don't know." Then he raised his voice: "Yes?"

"A call for you from the Port Authority, sir."

"I'll be right there." He sat in the chair and yanked on socks and boots.

"The Port Chief said it was urgent."

"Just a moment," whispered Sylvia. "Hold it a moment." She vanished through the door.

He frowned, but waited, then stepped to the side of the door, before starting to edge it open.

Thrummm! A line of fire seared his lower right arm.

Even as he kicked the door shut, he could hear another dull thump, then quiet. Waves of pain radiated up his right arm, and he paused to take a deep breath before easing back toward the door.

"You can open it now." Sylvia's voice came through the heavy wood clearly. "I got her."

With his left hand, he pushed the lever handle down and opened the door. Sylvia stood above the limp figure of the serving woman in green-and-maroon tunic and green trousers. The dark-haired Ecolitan lifted a stunner and smiled at Nathaniel. "It's Imperial issue, set pretty far up."

"I know." He massaged his lower right arm with his left for a moment. "Let's get her inside."

"Good idea." Sylvia slipped the stunner into her waistband, and they dragged the woman into Nathaniel's room and laid her flat on the floor.

He watched closely as Sylvia locked the doors of both their rooms, but the woman still seemed unconscious. He began to search the woman, starting with the bulge in a capacious hip pocket.

He lifted the small, flat slug-thrower. "Another toy."

"Stunners work better through doors or at odd angles."

"And this was meant to finish the job."

"Maybe . . ."

He straightened. The woman carried nothing else of import, except the groundcar placard that he set on the table. Somehow he couldn't see a weapon being concealed in the tube of lip gloss or the package of tissues.

"Quite a wake-up call," Sylvia observed, settling into one of the straight-backed chairs.

Nathaniel set the slug-thrower on the table next to the placard, sat on the edge of his bed, and looked down at the Artosan woman, then at Sylvia. He massaged his throbbing right arm. "Forest lord—I should have seen."

"You were meant not to. Who pays any attention to servants, especially in a GraeAnglo culture? Especially to women servants. And she figured you'd probably be less alert this morning." Sylvia's lips tightened. "I don't like voyeurs."

"I'm sorry."

"That's not your fault." Her expression softened momentarily. "I don't regret last night. If anything, this just shows I was right. But I don't have to like people watching." She paused and glanced toward the door. "The question is, now what do we do with her?"

"I can handle that." The older Ecolitan fumbled out the miniature dart gun.

"Murder—that's not—even for this."

"No." Nathaniel said. "The darts have a mild nerve toxin—mimics some forms of influenza, the violent ones. You may recall these. She'll have seizures and a pretty significant memory loss for today and maybe yesterday."

"This isn't another case of 'trust me,' is it?"

He winced. "I deserve that. No. All the ones I used darts on while I was on New Augusta recovered—except for several days of memories." He paused. "We must be close to something. I just wish I could see it."

"We really still haven't discovered anything. We don't know for sure who's behind the attempts on our lives, or why everyone's so threatened by this stupid study, or why there's an arms buildup and civil unrest on a planet with nothing on it."

For a moment, he just sat there, thinking about four attempts on their lives. Thinking about the fact that he'd walked around Lanceville totally exposed, that he'd been exposed when he'd gone to find Sylvia just before he'd left New Augusta, thinking about the dark-metalled slug-thrower on the table.

"Oh . . . no." How could he have missed it? How could he have been so self-centered? He wanted to pound his head. He swallowed and looked at Sylvia. While he knew she wasn't, that she was tougher in many ways than he was, she looked somehow . . . vulnerable.

"What?" Her eyebrows lifted in a gesture of annoyance and amusement.

"I'm sorry."

"If you're going to apologize for last night again . . . I told you—"

He shook his head. "I think you and I have misjudged all of this. Or I have. I really did. Kennis What's-his-name was the key, but I should have seen it sooner."

"Seen what?"

"Someone's after you. They have been all along, but I was included so that we wouldn't realize that. Ecolitans like me are dangerous, but we don't really know anything. You're knowledgeable, and you still presumably have access to Imperial sources, and someone definitely doesn't want you to use them. I'm just a target to cover the fact that they're after you."

"That doesn't make sense. I don't know that much."

"You do. You have to, because . . . I can't explain it totally logically, but they're after you. That's why the stunner. A message for you wouldn't have been plausible."

"Maybe it does make sense."

"It makes very good sense, and so many people could want us out of the way that it'll be hard to eliminate suspects. We need to get out of here even faster. Confined as it is, orbit control would be better because whoever it is won't want to take out a whole station . . . yet."

He lifted the dart gun and fired into the slumped figure.

"What . . . ?"

"I've been telling you my speculations, and I don't want her remembering it, even subconsciously. I'll tell you as we pack."

"You're serious."

"Yes." Trying to ignore the throbbing in his arm, as well as the voice in his head that kept reminding him that he'd been stupid, he managed to lay out his field pack on the bed and slowly fold his clothes.

Sylvia dumped all her clothing on the other side of his bed, then brought in her own field pack and the datacase.

"Oooohh . . ." The serving woman moaned, and then twitched.

Sylvia glanced down.

"I didn't say it was painless, but neither is my arm."

"You can move it?"

"It hurts."

She shook her head. "Most people couldn't function with that kind of nerve pain."

"I don't have much choice." He rubbed his forehead—damp—and then resumed folding his clothes, slowly.

"What's the event horizon?" Sylvia asked. "The real issue?"

"It's got to be the Three System Bulge. It belonged to the Empire until the Secession, and then the Fuards took it and fortified it, but it's a dagger at the side of the Empire. If Artos falls to the Empire, then that flanks the bulge, and the Fuards are paranoid anyway. Artos is on the end of the Avalonian drift, and not much use to Camelot, but would strengthen either the Hegemony's position or the Union's. And to complicate matters more, the Empire doesn't want any of the three to have Artos, I'm sure. So . . . if our study and investigations reveal that Camelot is effectively capital-starving Artos, the ArchTories—or someone, because I'm guessing at the internal politics—are going to suffer because the Empire will put the screws on New Avalon to beef up Artos to keep it strong and inside New Avalon. That's where you come in. You could ensure the report gets to the right people, and that they believe it. More important, from your point of view and safety, someone believes you're here to ensure the Empire's interests."

"It could look that way." Sylvia paused. "If they think that we're a joint Imperial/Accord team . . ."

"They want us removed. Exactly."

"You're convinced that most Avalonian politicians would quietly let

Artos go?" Sylvia closed her pack, and then stepped up beside Nathaniel, folding his remaining set of greens. "I can do this faster."

"No. They'd wail and wring their hands and moan and complain loudly—but can you imagine them going to war over a single colony outsystem against the Hegemony, the Conglomerate, or even the Frankan Union? So . . . unless I'm missing something and unless we can be very successful on New Avalon, there's going to be a disaster here. Invasion, starvation, plague, rebellion, a declaration of 'independence' backed by Kennis's private army, or all of the above."

"And we can't do anything here?"

He shook his head. "With what? Either of us could assassinate Kennis. That would just allow Sebastion to do the same thing, and he would, and then the small growers would really revolt. If we removed Sebastion, then . . .'"

"Kennis takes over with his private army and fights it out with them, and then the Federated Hegemony, the Union, or the Fuards bring in fleets and light up the sky."

"And what will the Grand Admiral do at that point?"

Sylvia winced.

"Add to that two dead Ecolitans, one tied to the I.I.S., and the Empire is effectively neutralized—at least long enough for Artos to fall."

"It could be worse than that," mused Sylvia as Nathaniel closed his field pack.

"Oh?" He rubbed his forehead, then reached out and pocketed the ignition placard for the groundcar.

"The fish kills and the synde bean plague—that screams to the Galaxy that Accord is trying to weaken the Empire on all fronts, even using an economic study to foment rebellion in another area that would weaken the Empire. Without you and me around to get the real message across, what will the Senate do? What can they do but bring some sort of force against Accord?"

"Which means they won't have forces near New Avalon and Artos."

"Which will make an outside takeover of Artos rather easy." Sylvia gestured toward the door. "I suppose we're going to steal a groundcar?"

"I prefer the term 'borrow.'" The sandy-haired Ecolitan shouldered his field pack. "Anyway, all this leaves one nagging question. Why in creation did the Institute and Accord ever get sucked into doing the study? What did New Avalon promise the House of Delegates? Or vice versa?"

"That's one reason—"

"We're going to Camelot. You've got it." He paused. "I'm sorry. Do you know why? I cut you off."

"No . . . and thank you." She leaned closer to him and kissed his cheek.

Nathaniel opened the door gingerly. The corridor was empty, but his pack was over his right shoulder, and the dart gun back in his left hand. Sometimes it was a real advantage to be left-handed, although he was as close to ambidextrous as training could make him.

"You're going to leave her?" Sylvia glanced back at the slightly twitching figure on the rug. "And the slug-thrower?"

"Why not? Even if no one finds her, she'll be all right. Besides, my arm hurts. And we couldn't get a metal weapon through the detectors."

As they passed the foyer, Nathaniel nodded to the room to the left. "Would you duck in there and call Vivienne? Suggest that the weather's likely to be cold and that she and Geoffrey should consider a short vacation at some warm place—off Artos—without saying it directly? Would you mind?"

"No, I wouldn't mind, and that makes sense. Just a moment."

Nathaniel scanned the area, ears alert as well, but no one appeared until Sylvia popped out of the small office.

"She was most gracious, and said that they had considered such a vacation, perhaps on one of the tropical islands on Altours." Sylvia opened the front Guest House door for Nathaniel.

"Frankan . . . that figures. The groundcar ought to be on the side. Can you drive?"

"Of course."

"Good."

The mottled gray groundcar tucked up beside a nondescript bush made Pyotr's taxi look like a luxury model.

"You can pick transport." Sylvia laughed.

"At least we're driving, or you are."

The field packs went in the flat space behind the front bench seat—there was no rear seat, just a flat slab of stained blue plastic.

Clouds of dark gray smoke billowed from the rattling engine as Sylvia eased the vehicle onto the lane out to the main highway, and the entire body of the groundcar shuddered.

Another heavy-cargo lorry rumbled past, empty and heading for Lanceville.

"More equipment being unloaded?" Sylvia turned right and headed west for the shuttle port.

"Probably."

"You're sure there'll be a shuttle today?" asked Sylvia.

"There's a Hegemony vessel due today, and a Frankan one late tomorrow. That's a little strange, too. Bagot was talking about how few ships there usually are."

"More than a few things are a little strange."

"How true," mused Nathaniel.

Sylvia stopped the borrowed groundcar right at the entrance to the Port Authority offices. "We can leave this here?"

"Of course. Chief Walkerson will certainly know what to do with it."

They both laughed, even as their eyes scanned the area before they entered the building.

Bagot looked up as the two, field packs on shoulders, entered the outer office.

"Is Chief Walkerson in, Bagot?"

"Ah . . . yes."

"Good. He put in a call for us, so I'm sure he'll be expecting us."

Furrowed brows revealed the driver's puzzlement, but by then Nathaniel had his hand on the inner office door.

Sylvia bestowed a dazzling smile on the driver. "Take good care of Anne-Leslie, and listen to her. She has good judgment." She entered the inner office and clicked the door closed behind her.

"What are—" began the Port Chief.

"We're returning your call of this morning in person," Nathaniel announced.

"Ah . . . my call?"

"Perhaps we were mistaken, but we got a message that you'd called. Then one of the staff started firing a stunner at me." Nathaniel offered a broad and false smile. "So we decided to return the call in person."

"Stunners? That's preposterous."

Sylvia held up the weapon. "It's even Imperial issue. We left the slug-thrower behind on the table. I'd bet it's Imperial issue, too."

"It's amazing," added the other Ecolitan. "Artos is so tech-poor, can't even manufacture its own groundcars, yet all these weapons keep showing up. And there's not an Imperial on the planet, but all the weapons come from the Empire."

"I'm quite afraid I don't understand," protested Walkerson.

"You don't have to," declared Sylvia. "We're just going to keep you company for a time, Port Chief, at least until the next shuttle to orbit control arrives later this morning."

"You're leaving so soon?"

"Let's just say that we've completed as much of the study research as we can while here on Artos," replied Nathaniel. "The next phase will take place on New Avalon."

"You're going to Camelot?" asked Walkerson.

"That's the idea," said Sylvia sweetly.

"But why?"

"I think you know why." Nathaniel smiled, ignoring the throbbing in his arm. "Why do you think we're going?"

"I couldn't say . . . after all, you are the Ecolitans."

"In technical terms, then, you can tell everyone that too much of Artos' infrastructure is tied up with that of New Avalon." Nathaniel's voice went cold. "While we can certainly point out areas where improvement is necessary, even vital, it makes no sense to recommend remedies that are mere technical exercises and cannot be implemented politically." He smiled politely. "As you may recall, the Institute is known for its emphasis on *practical* solutions, and we are going to be working very hard for a practical solution. Not that there seems to be much interest on Artos in a practical solution, since everyone seems quietly bent on setting up to destroy the other fellow, in order to ensure that you all lose."

"You've totally lost me, Whaler. You've gone absolutely batty."

"Me? The infrastructure economist and diplomat selected for the high-profile fall? Dragging down Professor Ferro-Maine in the process?"

Walkerson turned to Sylvia.

Her gray eyes were like cold stone. "I don't care much for men who declare they have a duty when they ignore what is really happening."

"I do have work to do . . ." Walkerson looked helplessly at the office door.

"The most important business you have," said Sylvia, "is to stay with us until the shuttle leaves. Otherwise . . ."

"Also, once we leave," added Nathaniel, "you might want to check up on your help at the Guest House. They've gotten into rather nasty habits lately."

Walkerson swallowed. His forehead dampened visibly.

"Now I know," continued Nathaniel, "that our arrival placed every-one in a rather tense situation. After all, it would be most embarrassing to New Avalon to have a civil war—or was it going to be a war of independence—break out while we were here."

"I am afraid I don't understand, old chap."

"You understand, Port Chief Walkerson," said Sylvia. "That's why we're going to be very close together until the next shuttle lifts. Very close." She smiled.

Walkerson swallowed.

XXVI

NATHANIEL WALKED ON Walkerson's right, Sylvia on his left, as the three headed across the permacrete of the ramp to the waiting orbit shuttle.

"It has been an interesting time, Port Chief, especially for a place that you called quiet when we arrived."

"So quiet that there have only been four attempts on our lives—just about one every other day." This time Sylvia smiled. The smile was not pleasant.

"You had a little time to think." Nathaniel studied the hangars to the south where the two remaining Port Authority flitters were hangared. "In view of everything that's occurred, is there anyone you would suggest we contact while we are in Camelot?"

"I couldn't tell you who would help with your study."

"Walker!" snapped Whaler. "Can't you get it through your thick Avalonian skull that your usefulness to just about everyone is limited? If New Avalon manages to hang onto Artos, you'll be the scapegoat, along with us, probably, because we brought an unpleasant mess to everyone's attention when they wished it would go away. If not, how many people are going to be happy with the lead representative of New Avalon's Defence Ministry?"

"You really are serious, aren't you, old chap?"

Nathaniel wanted to roll his eyes. Instead, he glanced at Sylvia.

"Some men are particularly dense." She emphasized "men" just slightly.

Walkerson swallowed. "Not that I believe you—I think you're overreacting terribly—but you might pay a call on Minister Spencer-Hawkes or his Deputy, that's Alsion-Welles. Alsion-Welles might be better, really."

"We will make the contact." Whaler smiled. "Of course, there's no guarantee they'll want to take this seriously, either. But there are others that will." I hope, he added mentally.

Nathaniel and Sylvia paused at the ramp to the orbit shuttle, where Nathaniel handed the two datablocs to the crewrep who waited.

"Well . . . professors, it has been . . . enlightening. I'd like to see a copy of your report when it's finished. I would be quite interested to see your conclusions and recommendations." Walkerson offered a nervous smile. "And the supporting documentation."

"It has been enlightening." Nathaniel nodded, taking the data-blocs back from the crewrep.

"And you'll have a great deal of proof even before then, I think." Sylvia offered a cold smile. "You'd better hope you don't, but I'm not terribly optimistic, Port Chief."

Both Ecolitans nodded, and then stepped up the ramp.

Walkerson looked dumbly after them, then shook his head, finally wiping his sweating forehead as he turned and walked back toward his office.

The ramp swung up, and the shuttle engines began to whine.

XXVII

"I JUST HOPE this Frankan ship arrives on time." Sylvia lurched slightly with the gravity fluctuation as she stepped through the open reinforced arches that joined two sections of Artos orbit control, past the concealed pressure doors, and into section two, distinguished from section one by a darker gray shade of the plastic spray that coated the bulkheads.

Even alerted by Sylvia's lurch, Nathaniel still found himself staggering through the slight change in gravity. He shook his head—just another example of slow decay. Grav-field generators were comparatively large, expensive, and needed constant maintenance, power, and tuning—and the closer they operated to a planetary field, the more they needed of all three, one reason why they weren't practical for atmospheric use.

"We slept better—" he began.

"Safer, not better." Sylvia rubbed her neck. "I still feel like a pretzel."

"I stand corrected." His own shoulders were tight, but how much of that was from uneasy sleep and how much from constant surveillance of their surroundings was another question.

They passed a flat expanse of plastic on the outboard side of the corridor, thin enough that Nathaniel could make out the outlines of what had once apparently been a ship docking area. At the edge of the comparatively newer plastic were large globules of gray.

Did the panels beneath his feet flex more than they should? The Ecolitan wasn't sure. Once he started doubting, he got skeptical of everything, and they had plenty to be skeptical of at the moment.

His eyes flicked ahead to the sign that read Lock 3. Lock three was empty, with seal-tite across the access doors to the lock itself. The handful of plastic benches were scarred and darkened with age.

They passed under a ventilator that puffed warm metallic air at them with intermittent wheezes.

"What are we looking for?" asked Sylvia.

"More indirect evidence, although I suspect we've already seen enough."

"As someone once told me, by the time the evidence is solid, you'll be too late to do anything." She flashed a brief smile.

"I wonder who said that?"

"I wonder who."

He paused as they passed two older, hard-faced women in Halstani singlesuits. Both were nearly as tall and muscular as Nathaniel.

After the women had passed, Sylvia turned and raised her eyebrows. "Hands of the Mother?"

"Probably former Hands. They train some as pilots. No one shipjacks a Matriarch vessel."

"I wonder why." Sylvia laughed harshly, then frowned as they passed another blank expanse that might once have held a receiving lock. "The whole station's pretty run-down."

"Not exactly the picture of an up-and-coming colony planet about to become prosperous and independent." Nathaniel's tone was low and wry.

"No."

"Ready to return to Clyde's Cafe?"

"Since I'm hungry, and since we've got a few more hours to kill, and since there's nowhere else to eat . . . why not?" Sylvia flashed a bright smile that showed too much tooth.

"It's a bit safer here."

"Except from maintenance failures."

They both grinned.

XXVIII

NATHANIEL SLIPPED THE pocket tools from his field pack and fastened them to his belt, then glanced around the three-by-four-meter cube that qualified as a standard cabin on the *Omnia Gallia*.

"I thought a Frankan ship was going to be safer." Sylvia glanced at the tools.

"I thought so, too. But you said the head steward recognized us somehow, or showed some sign of recognition."

"I said I *thought* he did."

"That's good enough for me. I'll trust your instincts any day." Nathaniel grinned at the dark-haired former dancer and agent.

"Don't blame this—"

"I'm not blaming. I'd do it anyway, but your senses are solid confirmation."

Sylvia smiled, briefly. "I can see why a lot of people don't like Ecolitans. You don't spend time presenting logic and facts."

"That's a good way to get killed. You have to be prepared a long time in advance."

"You brought those tools, planning this?"

"Not exactly. The tools are there to carry out a number of contingency plans. I've also got a mental listing and their specs, in case I'd lost these."

"I still don't know . . . I have trouble with the Institute's act-first philosophy."

"Most of the Galaxy does. People would rather see a lot of people hurt and a lot of damage before taking drastic action. That way they can rise in righteous revenge and be justified."

"If everyone has that much trouble with the Institute, why are you all still here?"

"Because our resources are dispersed, and because we do act faster than our opponents. If someone decides to gather a fleet, the entire universe knows, and they know that we know, and they also know that we wouldn't hesitate to destroy their entire ecology." Nathaniel laughed. "Of course, we haven't done anything that drastic in four hundred years, but they all fear we could. So they don't."

"That just could be what caused this mess," suggested Sylvia.

He nodded. "I'd wondered about that—covertly dragging the Empire and Accord into war to avoid facing the Institute and its sanctions. It's clever, and unless we can do something, it just might succeed."

A hiss of something came over the small speaker above the plastic cabin door. "We will be approaching the first jump point in approximately thirty units. Passengers have ten units to return to their cabins. Passengers have ten units to return to their cabins."

Nathaniel smiled briefly and glanced at the narrow door. "We'll wait about two or three units."

"And . . . ?"

"We'll find the chief steward. Or he'll find us, and somehow, I'll bet he's wearing a stunner. They're not supposed to, but most do."

After the scurrying in the corridor subsided, the two Ecolitans slipped out of the minuscule cabin.

"Which way?" asked Sylvia.

"Aft . . . there."

"I know which way—"

"Sorry."

The blue-clad steward hurried forward to meet them, his shoulders squaring as he neared.

Nathaniel waited.

"Ecolitan . . . I must insist that you both return to your cabin." The steward's hand dropped toward the stunner even before he finished speaking.

Nathaniel's leg and foot were faster. As the big man doubled over, the Ecolitan's knee caught his chin, but the steward's hand still clutched the butt of the stunner, and his body turned sideways.

The steward slumped. Nathaniel looked up to see Sylvia massaging the side of her hand.

"Out of shape for this."

"Thank you." Nathaniel wrestled the stunner from the steward's hand and reversed it.

Thrumm!

"That should hold him." He extended the stunner to Sylvia. "Cover me. Stun anyone who looks this way, even if it's the pilot or an officer."

"I suppose you could pilot this, too." Sylvia glanced up the empty corridor.

"Yes. So don't worry if you put someone under. What we have to worry about is the mess down underneath." He knelt on the rubberized mat, looking for the releases.

"You're sure there's a mess there? I don't want to even think about what they'll do to us if you're wrong."

"I'll find someone to blame it on."

"You just might."

"Not really. You get a feel for these things, and when we both feel the same way . . ." He shook his head, then inched back up the corridor toward the ship's stem, mumbling, "Hope this is a standard design." He felt the mat, then jerked. The access plate to the ventilator was there. In quick motions with the hex wrench he unfastened the plate, then laid it aside. He felt the smooth sides of the ventilator tube, then nodded and sheathed the wrench, coming up with the cutter. Five quick motions, and he held a plastic oblong, grinning. "Keep guarding."

Another set of motions, and he had a second oblong, and an opening into the drive section.

"What . . ." Despite her comment, Sylvia's eyes remained on the passageway, stunner ready.

"I'm going into the drive section—this is modeled on an old corvette design." Nathaniel slipped his legs through the hole he had cut and eased his way into the dim light below, careful to stay to his left. The last thing he needed to do was bruise one of the supercon lines . . . or get fried if someone else already had.

The lines were clear, gleaming dusty silver in the dim light of the drive section. First came the converters, with no obvious goodies attached or out of place. Then he turned to the lines from the firin cells—also unbruised silver.

Thrummm!

At the sound of the stunner, he called, "You all right?"

"I'm fine. Another steward. Just do what you have to."

"That's what . . . I'm doing." The Ecolitan turned to the various field generators, hoping no one had tampered with the grav-systems. They seemed fine, with no gratuitous hardware, and his eyes flicked to the shields. What looked to be a cutout switch had been attached to the controller. He nodded to himself—easy and standard.

But dropping the shields alone meant nothing. He followed the spider thin line to the inner hull plates where it split. Each section disappeared into an off-color circle, presumably running to the outer hull plates as well.

What else?

The seal on the emergency signal generator had been replaced, badly.

Nathaniel eased around the generators to the backup, sealed drive controls, ripping the plastic off the intercom. He tapped the square red stud. "Captain, this is Ecolitan Whaler. I'm down here in your drive section, and I've found some rather interesting equipment here. My associate is guarding the corridor, but I'd suggest you trigger the exterior locks on the passenger compartments."

The return squawk was almost unintelligible.

Whaler shook his head and repeated the message in Frankan.

"What? How are we supposed to believe you? We'll be at the jump point in less than five standard units."

"If you jumpshift, you'll emerge with no atmosphere and no shields. Needless to say, I'll stop you if you try it—at least until you send the engineer down. Oh, and I suspect you'll find a deep space suit in the lead steward's quarters. I just don't know who else might be with him. Don't worry about him, though. We already took care of that problem."

"You . . . Ecolitans . . . you think you know everything, do you not?"

"Hardly, Captain. I thought a Frankan ship would be safe." Nathaniel eased toward the silvered apparatus beside the supercon line to the converter. Beyond them, looking at an angle, he could still see where the two hull plates had been altered. "Are you going to pull the jump-generators off-line, or have me do it? I can read the backup indicators as well as any engineer."

An exasperated sigh came over the intercom. The green lights on the small board went to amber. Nathaniel took a deep breath. He had at least ten units, because it would take that long for the repowering sequence.

"Sylvia! One engineer should be headed our way. Just one. Stand back and let him come down here. If he tries anything else, stun him, too."

"Stet!"

While he waited, the Ecolitan cut away the seals and wires locking the drive backups. "You don't trust anyone, do you?" he murmured to himself. "As if you should, these days."

"Easy . . ." Sylvia's voice drifted down to Nathaniel.

Nathaniel watched as a large pair of shipboots filled the narrow opening in the ventilator. The bearded young Frankan officer swallowed as he saw the dart gun.

"They don't register on detectors. Pardon me if I'm a little suspicious these days. I'd like you to look at the device under the emergency signal plate. It doesn't look like any signal generator I've seen. You might also check the plate just abaft frame forty." Nathaniel eased back.

The Frankan opened the plate cover. He swallowed, and his eyes went to the plate. He swallowed again.

"Now, look at that handy-dandy cutout switch on the shield generators."

The bearded man studied the cutout, laboriously tracing the microfilament line to the hull plates. He stiffened, then looked at the Ecolitan. "Might I, sieur, might I call the captain?"

"Be my guest. That's a good place to start."

A ham-sized hand depressed the red stud. "Sieur . . . the Ecolitan . . . he is correct. There is a strange device—"

"Shaped charge," Nathaniel murmured.

"A shaped charge . . . in the signal generator."

"Put him on, Faquar."

The engineer stepped back.

Nathaniel gestured with the dart gun. "Over there."

The engineer eased away from the Ecolitan.

"Whaler here. You want to believe me, now?"

"It is my ship . . . might I change positions with my engineer?"

"I'll send him right up. That way, he'll be able to report without coercion." Nathaniel nodded at the engineer. "Go on back to the control room."

"Go?"

"Of course. I'm as interested as you are in getting to New Avalon in one piece. Maybe more interested." He raised his voice. "Sylvia! One engineer coming up."

"Stet."

The engineer glanced from Nathaniel to the opening cut in the ventilator, then struggled up and out of sight.

The captain appeared, seemingly almost immediately, scanning the drives and generators before turning to the Ecolitan. "Claude Muerotte, Captain of the *Omnia Gallia*."

"Nathaniel Whaler, Ecolitan Institute."

Captain Muerotte glanced at the signal generator and then shook his head. "Why me?"

"Because I'm on your ship. Now . . . I can defuse that . . . if I can have the manual. The polarities differ depending on the installation, and I'd rather not guess."

"If I might?" Muerotte gestured toward the intercom.

"Be my guest." The Ecolitan lowered but did not put away the dart gun as he stepped back.

"Faquar? Send down the manuals. Number three, I believe, with the blue band, which deals with the signal system . . ."

"Captain . . ." began another, lighter voice. "There was space armor in LaTour's room . . . what about energy loss . . . we're past—"

"Bousie, just cut back on the drives to headway, and deliver the manuals." Muerotte stepped back, glancing warily at Nathaniel.

"As I told your engineer, I have a great interest in arriving at the New Avalon orbit control station in one piece. There are those who don't share that interest, including those who bought off your steward. Of course, they didn't intend for him to live either." Nathaniel inclined his head toward the signal generator.

"Captain," a voice called through the hole in the deck, "could we open the main hatch?"

Nathaniel shrugged sheepishly.

A faint smile cracked the captain's lips.

Light flooded over the standby drive controls, and the engineer stood above the ladder. Nathaniel caught a glimpse of Sylvia, standing well back, stunner trained on the bearded engineer.

"You get the manuals," said Nathaniel, "and find the schematic for the generator." He added. "And could you have the engineer tie up the two stewards?"

Muerotte stiffened, then shrugged. Nathaniel could sympathize. Captains didn't like being ordered around on their own ships. But they liked the idea of losing the ship even less.

"Faquar . . . tie them up."

"First the signal generator . . ." murmured Nathaniel after tracing the schematic and turning to the colored circuit lines. "Like so."

He took a deep breath. "One down."

Muerotte moved aside as the Ecolitan went back to the shield generators and the cutout switch.

"Hmmmm . . . could be simple . . . and it might not . . . still . . ." Nathaniel removed the cover with the tiny long-bladed hexdriver. "Double bypass. So . . . there." He took a second breath, then moved back to the backup drive controls, and flicked the overrides back to the cockpit, then rewired the shutouts.

"Let's head upstairs."

Muerotte cleared his throat. "I appreciate this . . . assistance . . . but . . ."

"You're not in the clear yet, Captain. We need to reroute your jumps." Nathaniel gestured to the ladder.

"There's no way, not without going into Conglomerate space."

Nathaniel took a deep breath. "What if we increase the power to the jump generators? Cut out the grav-draw?"

"Do you know what the passengers will do once we dock?"

"Do you know what the Fuards or the Hegemony will do if you come out anywhere close to your normal jump points?" countered the Ecolitan.

"But we have a transspace agreement with . . ."

"Whoever it is will blame the other—or Accord or the Empire." Nathaniel's eyes turned cold. "I really must insist, Captain. You can file protests with anyone you want, but I'd like to have us all get there so that you can." He paused. "You head up. I'm going to enable the cross-connects. Tell the second that's what I'm doing. Otherwise those amber lights on the board will upset her."

Muerotte pressed the intercom stud. "Bousie, the interlock safeties are coming on. It's not a failure. Just stand by."

"Yes, Captain." The resignation carried above the slight crackle of the intercom speaker.

Muerotte picked up the thin manual, then looked at the Ecolitan. "Why did they select the *Gallia?*" He started up the ladder.

When Nathaniel stood in the low-grav of the corridor, he answered. "Because we selected your ship, and that means someone wants two Ecolitans to disappear along with an entire Frankan craft." He paused. "Since we're all going to be in the cockpit, Captain, I'd suggest these hatches be closed." He extended the hex wrench from his belt to Faquar. "This will handle the nuts for the access plate."

Muerotte nodded to the engineer.

"You wait," said Nathaniel to Sylvia. "In case anyone gets any ideas . . . just stun all of us. The ship will hold until I wake up. When the engineer's done, you take the rear position in the cockpit."

She nodded.

"You trust few, I see," observed Muerotte as Nathaniel followed the captain forward.

"So far, this makes the fifth or sixth attempt on us in the last two standard weeks. That might explain why I'm somewhat skeptical."

"You must know something very dangerous." Muerotte laughed harshly.

"That's the strange part. I'm an economist."

Muerotte shook his head again, then punched the cockpit access stud and the combination.

"Leave it open until the engineer and Sylvia rejoin us."

"As you wish." Muerotte dropped into the vacant pilot's couch.

Nathaniel nodded toward the second's position.

"Move aside, Bousie," ordered Muerotte.

The redheaded second pilot glanced from the captain to the Ecolitan in greens, then eased aside.

"Over there," suggested Nathaniel. He didn't want anyone behind him. Bousie complied, if with a slight frown.

"If I might . . ." offered Muerotte.

"Go ahead." Nathaniel slid into the second pilot's seat, scanning the instruments and holding the input set, watching both the second and the engineer.

Two other figures entered the cockpit, Sylvia the last, stunner still in hand. The cockpit hatch closed with a dull *thunnkk*.

"The Ecolitan discovered a rather elaborate set of devices in the drive chambers. They could not have been placed there since he boarded at Artos. I suspect the maintenance crew, but that is not the question. He has suggested certain precautions. I agree, but I will cross-check his implementation of those precautions." The captain raised his eyebrows. "I am presuming neither you nor Faquar had any part in this, since you would have been in the cockpit when we lost all atmosphere and shields."

Bousie swallowed. Faquar shook his head. Behind them, Sylvia kept the stunner pointed at the second pilot.

"Now that we have it understood," Nathaniel said, "I'd like to start on getting us to New Avalon." He slipped on the online input set. The ship scanned clean.

The jump calculations took another ten units and five for Muerotte to confirm with a brusque nod.

"Would you announce to the passengers that they should strap in for low grav and jump?"

"Bousie," ordered the captain. "From the engineer's station."

The second bent toward the small console behind the captain's position.

"We will be approaching the first jump point in less than five units. We will be going to low-gravity just before jump. Passengers should be firmly strapped in at this time. Passengers should be firmly strapped in at this time."

"Good," murmured Muerotte.

"Cutting gravs . . . brace yourself. Five to jump." As his guts floated into his throat as the gravity dropped to near nothing, Nathaniel kept talking. "We can do this in two jumps . . . instead of three . . . and we'll arrive two stans plus ahead of schedule. That should also offset any welcoming arrangements."

Muerotte nodded, slowly. So did Sylvia, braced against the closed hatch that led to the passenger section, her stunner still on Bousie.

"Let's do it." The Ecolitan swallowed. "Countdown to jump . . . four, three, two, one . . . jump."

As he touched the jump stud and sent the impulse through the input set, the entire ship turned inside out, and white was black, and black white . . . for that eternal moment that seemed endless and yet was over before it began.

A slight shiver, and the *Gallia* was back in norm space.

The screens showed a solar system, with the normal EDI indications of a technological and populated area.

"Czechos?"

"It checks." Nathaniel avoided wincing at the inadvertent pun, and began inputting the figures for the second jump while the power built up.

"EDI buildup at two eight zero," noted Muerotte.

"Class two patroller, insystem only. Probably a lot of power with a fusactor system." That meant no jumpshifting systems and a lot of torps. He checked the range and closure. "We'll be clear."

"The Union . . . alliance . . ." the low words came from either Bousie or Faquar.

"Alliances are only for brief periods of convenience," said Sylvia dryly from where she was tucked against the closed hatch.

Nathaniel wiped his sweating forehead with the overlarge kerchief, since the dampness beaded all over his face in null-gee, then rechecked the systems and power buildup. "Better announce another jump, so that some passenger doesn't start wandering around."

"Bousie, go ahead," ordered Muerotte. "Less than five units."

"We will be approaching the second jump point in less than five units. We will remain in low-gravity until after all jumps are complete. Passengers should remain firmly strapped in at this time. Passengers should remain firmly strapped in at this time. Do not unstrap until ship gravity returns to normal. Do not unstrap until ship gravity returns to normal."

"Good," said Muerotte. "Log that, too. Heavens forbid, if there's a claim, the warning will help."

Nathaniel nodded, then rescanned the systems as he waited for the sequence to run.

"Countdown to jump . . . four, three, two, one . . . jump!"

Reentry was normal, and Nathaniel eased the drives to full, ensuring they were stabilized, before restoring ship grav.

"Smooth," observed Muerotte, "but we're plus five on the ecliptic."

"Right. We'll angle down. The dust buildup will be greater at the end, but we'll get there faster, and not by the normal route." The Ecolitan pointed to a signal on the EDI screen. "I wonder who that might be. The drive tuning would say either Hegemony or Fuard—maybe Orknarlian—but it's not Imperial or Avalonian."

Muerotte swallowed.

"Almost cruiser size, just outside the formal system bounds," continued Nathaniel. "I'd say just about where we would have been. Justifies my faith in human nature."

"As if you had any left," quipped Sylvia from the rear of the cockpit.

Nathaniel eased from the seat. "Your ship, Captain. We would like to remain here until you lock in—in case we can provide any additional assistance." The Ecolitan smiled as Bousie slipped past him and into her couch. "Although we all hope it's totally unnecessary."

"Shipping headquarters won't be happy."

"They'd have been a lot less happy with no ship at all," pointed out Sylvia. "Remind them of that."

XXIX

THE LEGATION OF the Coordinate of Accord in Camelot was not on Embassy Boulevard, but a block south, across a narrow street from an unnamed grassy square. The building itself was of gray stone, three stories high, with a green tile roof, and golden wood shutters that actually were hung on antique wrought-iron brackets and could be closed against the driving rains that still occasionally drenched the temperate capital city of New Avalon.

The parquet-floored foyer held only a single console centered on a green patterned carpet. At the console was a thin-faced young woman. Her eyes widened fractionally at the sight of the pair in Ecolitan greens, but she only asked, "May I help you, Ecolitans?"

"Yes. I'm Ecolitan Professor Whaler, and this is Professor Ferro-Maine. We've been conducting a study on Artos, and I'd like to set up some appointments with the commerce section chief and his staff. I'd also like to see Ecolitan Swersa as soon as possible."

"Let me contact Ecolitan Swersa, first." The receptionist/screener touched the console, waiting momentarily. "Ecolitan Swersa, there's an Ecolitan Whaler . . . yes, sir, I'll send them right up."

The hint of a smile crossed Sylvia's face.

"You're expected, sirs. Take the stairs there"—she gestured over her left shoulder—"to the next level. Ecolitan Swersa's office is at the back. I'll check with the economic section while you're with the Ecolitan."

"Thank you."

The two Ecolitans lugged their field packs and the remaining data-case up the stairs.

A trim but muscular white-haired woman in greens met them in the second-floor corridor. "I'm LuAn Swersa. It's good to meet both of you." A broad smile creased her face. "I understand the Avalonian bureau-rats actually let bonafide economists onto Artos. I'll wager that Clerigg and his crew will want to spend hours grilling you. Come on in." She stepped inside the corner office, holding the antique wooden six-paneled door.

The office overlooked a small garden courtyard, but both large corner windows faced blank brick walls. "It's got light, but not much of a view. Typical of our operation here."

Swersa closed the door, then stepped toward the console, where her hand flicked three switches. "All right. We're blocked, but I won't guarantee that even with the random screens that it will hold for longer than a quarter stan. This place is almost as bad as I hear New Augusta is. So let me tell you what I know. Sit down." She gestured toward the armchairs opposite the console.

"That bad?" Nathaniel set down his pack and sat.

"I could be exaggerating. It seems that way." Swersa coughed once. "First, the Fuards have begun to pour men and materials into their Three System Bulge bases and developing staging areas. The Hegemony and the Union are beefing up their adjoining systems. Second, the Imperial Senate is almost certain to require the Eleventh Fleet to move to Sector Five adjacent to the Rift, and there's talk of reassigning the Ninth and Third Fleets—"

"I thought the trade talks . . ." said Sylvia.

"There have been massive algae and anchovy kills on five water planets, including on Anarra. Squamish and Kaneihe inside Imperial Sector Four. The synde bean plague has spread to another dozen

Imperial planets. That makes twenty affected now, all of them planoformed."

"No natural hydrocarbons," ventured Nathaniel.

"Exactly, and Heraculon has already lost more than five million people to starvation. That's in the latest briefing files."

"Five million?" whispered Sylvia, paling.

"There are resistant strains, aren't there?"

"Of course, but most produce less, and it will be two years before they're mature. The lag time, you know. And everyone believes it's our doing," Swersa said. "As if we were that stupid. Or cruel."

"We didn't. I talked to the Prime about it. He wished, and I do now, that I'd made that clear when I was on Old Earth." Nathaniel shrugged. "But I didn't know." His shoulders slumped slightly. "And I wanted to use every tool possible."

Sylvia gave a low whistle.

"So the Empire is convinced that the trade talks were a cover while we undermined them ecologically?" asked Nathaniel.

"It's more political than that," suggested Sylvia. "D.I. and the I.I.S. have to know better, but the Senate reacts to public perception, and the eagles have always wanted an excuse to go after Accord."

"That's the way I'd read it," affirmed Swersa. "Is Artos as bad as I'd guess?"

"Worse," suggested Nathaniel. "It's fragile ecologically and worse economically . . ." He quickly sketched out their findings, the varied assassination attempts, and their trip to Camelot. Sylvia added what he forgot.

"Whew," murmured Swersa. "Worse than we'd guessed. Your thoughts about the politics here are pretty much right on. The system's teetering on bankruptcy or economic collapse, and they've got their heads tucked inside wormholes to avoid seeing that they're going to lose half the Commonwealth systems if they don't finish what they started—but they don't have the capital or the drive."

"Who's the Legate here?" His briefing documents had noted that the position was being filled. "Has one been appointed?"

"The honorable Morton Spamgall. He was the temporary Legate, and the House of Delegates confirmed him about the time you went to Artos."

"That bad?"

"He's a political type. Brand-new and placed by Verlingetti, or so I've been led to believe. After we're done here, I'll take you up and introduce you."

"Who is Verlingetti?" asked Sylvia. "Remember . . ."

"Sorry," said Swersa. "He's the deputy minority leader in the House of Delegates—the one who handles all of Elder Quaestor's dirty work. And the Orthodoxists have been known for less than spotless political tactics and techniques."

"How does the minority get to place people?"

"It's a complex rotating system. Actually, all appointments are worked out by both parties on a consensus basis. New Avalon's not considered important, compared to other places, so . . ."

"That's where the minority's choices go?" suggested Sylvia.

"Here, Orknarli, maybe Olympia."

A series of red lights played across the console.

"Here they go. I'd guess another ten units," said Swersa. "What else?"

"We have another problem. We need to finish and release our report, and we'll need some quantitative backup, and lots of impressive-looking graphs and tables. I can set them up, but we've only got a few days. Do you think Clerigg and his team can handle it—both technically and from a security point of view?"

"Is this study that hot?"

"Not on the surface," said Nathaniel. "But it's critical that it be finished before we leave Camelot, and we'll have to leave in the next week, maybe sooner."

A faint frown crinkled Sylvia's forehead, but vanished.

"If you're that pressed," added Swersa, "you probably ought to be staying here. We've got some guest suites on the fourth level . . . not huge, but more secure."

"More secure sounds wonderful." He frowned "How secure is the Legation?"

"Physical security—as good as anywhere in Camelot except a Defence installation. Snooping? I wouldn't yell, but the guest suites don't have any powered equipment, and they're centered. Stay away from the windows, and it's pretty good."

"Do you have two with adjoining bedrooms?" asked Sylvia.

"The main suite is free. That's got a center sitting room with bedrooms on each side. Separate freshers." Swersa glanced from Nathaniel to Sylvia.

"That's fine," said Sylvia. "Especially the separate freshers."

More red lights flicked across the console. Swersa rose and tapped a series of studs. "Let me call Farlen, and tell him to get the Legate ready for you." Nathaniel looked toward the two field packs by the door.

"You can leave your luggage here for the moment. Farlen . . . the Ecolitans are ready. We'll be right up." Swersa broke the screen link as fast as she had established it.

The Legate's office was on the top level, and looked out through wide sliding glass doorways on a roof garden. The entire decor was Ecolog Secession, proving a sense of spareness that seemed to clash with the slightly pudgy man in a dark blue tunic and trousers who waddled forward to meet them.

"Welcome, Ecolitan Whaler, Ecolitan Ferro-Maine. You have no idea how marvelous it is to see faces from home. No idea how marvelous." Morton Spamgall offered a broad and charming smile under short, wispy blond hair. His blue eyes remained distant.

"It's a pleasure to be here," Sylvia offered.

Nathaniel just bowed.

"It is too bad you could not have come earlier in the fall. Simply marvelous, and the Landing Fest is something you must experience to believe." Spamgall extended his hand toward the roof garden, pointing toward the shimmering building on the hill. "If you have the chance, you should visit the Commons Hall. Such tradition there." He offered another smile. "Farlen tells me that you have come from Artos. You have been doing a study there. Economics of some sort?"

"Infrastructure economics. A contract from the Avalonian Ministry of Commerce."

"Good. It's about time they brought in some experts. Clerigg has been urging that for years, I understand. You haven't met Clerigg yet, have you?"

"No," offered Sylvia.

"Good man." Spamgall gestured toward the table, set with two tea services. "Some tea—or liftea?"

"That would be good," said Nathaniel.

Swersa nodded, as did Sylvia.

"Oh, help yourself, and take a seat. We're not much on ceremony here. Certainly not the way the Avalonians are. I've never seen a people with so many ceremonies."

Nathaniel waited for Sylvia and Swersa to pour their tea, then offered to pour for the Legate.

"No. I'll get mine. I mix them, you know. The Avalonians think it's a terrible thing. It almost would make me want to do it, even if I didn't like it that way." Spamgall laughed, a deep booming sound. "How did you find Artos?"

"It's a recently planoformed planet," Nathaniel said. "Backward in some ways, but you expect that."

"And you, charming professor, what did you think?"

Sylvia finished a sip of her liftea before answering. "I enjoyed seeing the open land and meeting the people. Some of them were very nice."

"And the others?" asked the Legate with yet another laugh.

"The others were like people everywhere."

"Like people everywhere . . . ha, ha, ha! You should be the diplomat. Yes, you should." Spamgall lifted his cup. "To the successful conclusion of your study!"

"Thank you."

"You aren't the Whaler who worked out that trade agreement with the Empire, are you?" asked the Legate, as though the thought had belatedly crossed his mind.

"Yes. They needed an economist there. The issues were somewhat . . . intricate."

"You do get around. Then, I guess that's the business of Ecolitans . . . getting around, that is."

By the time the tea was over, Nathaniel felt wrung out.

"The Legate can be overpowering," said Swersa as they headed back down the stairs. "His personality is formidable."

Nathaniel suspected that Spamgall's political cunning was also formidable, but that the intellect was somewhat less impressive, although assuming that might be decidedly dangerous.

"I take it he concentrates on impressions," said Sylvia, "so that others forget his intelligence."

"His personality obscures a keen mind," confirmed Swersa.

Nathaniel decided to bury his observations, as well as to change the structure of the study somewhat.

"Here we are—third floor, possession of the substantive folk." The white-haired Ecolitan turned toward the front of the Legation, leading them into a long narrow room with high windows. A balding, stocky man with a brush mustache stood up.

"Clerigg, Professors Whaler and Ferro-Maine."

"Delighted to meet you both." Clerigg smiled broadly as he stepped forward and bowed, then inclined his head to Nathaniel. "It's not my area, but I did enjoy your piece on the external diseconomies of deep space mining. I'm not sure outsiders would have understood it all."

Nathaniel hoped not. "Thank you. Professor Ferro-Maine is a specialist in applied infrastructures and policies. She has special expertise in large bureaucracies."

"It's good to see you both." Johannes Clerigg motioned to the two most comfortable-looking armchairs. "I can't believe they actually let a trained economist onto Artos, let alone two. I mean ones who aren't owned by the Commonwealth."

Nathaniel refrained from noting that the two economists in question weren't ever supposed to leave Artos, merely saying, "We were fortunate."

"Very fortunate," added Sylvia with enough irony that Clerigg paused momentarily, before he slumped into a straight-backed chair across from them. Swersa tucked herself into a corner chair, effectively guarding the door.

"Is there any possibility that you might be able to share your findings with us?" asked Clerigg.

"I'll make you an even better offer," said Nathaniel dryly. "You and your team help us write it, and you can be the ones to release it."

"You aren't . . . you mean that?"

"Absolutely. You get the best of both worlds. Our names are on it, with the Institute seal, and you get to tell the Galaxy about it."

"You sound as though this isn't the greatest offer," said Clerigg.

"It isn't," admitted Nathaniel. "I'll need almost every member of your staff full time for the next three to four days. In return, you can copy all the data and use the study—immediately."

Clerigg laughed once. "Since you could commandeer us all, or Swersa could on your behalf, you're being more than fair. When do we start?"

"Tomorrow," said Sylvia. "Today's been long enough, and we need to sort out some things."

Nathaniel turned cold inside. Had he been too domineering? Probably. Had it been necessary? Probably not. Was he going to stop digging holes for himself? He hoped so. He took a slow deep breath, then looked at Sylvia. She inclined her head.

They both stood. So did Swersa.

"Thank you," offered Nathaniel.

"Until tomorrow," returned Clerigg.

Once outside the economic chief's office, Swersa gestured toward the stairs. "We need to get your packs from my office, and then I'll get you settled in the suite, and you can do what you need to do."

The packs were where they had been left, behind the apparently sealed office doors, and looked and felt untouched to Nathaniel, not that there happened to be anything particularly unique in the packs, just the information in the datacase.

"Now, back up two levels," said the Legation Ecolitan.

At the door to the main suite, Swersa extended two small datablocs. "These were just recoded. The Legation mess is on the lowest level. It's open until nineteen thirty, and opens in the morning at zero six forty-five. If you want to go out, there are a number of decent restaurants in the blocks behind the Legation. I'll have you coded into the entry system in the next few units." Swersa paused. "If there's anything else I can do, let me know."

"There will be, I'm certain," Nathaniel confirmed, trying his databloc. The door opened, and he stood aside.

With a quick smile, Swersa was gone.

Once the packs were inside, he closed the door and studied the sitting room—two desk consoles, two sofas with matching upholstered armchairs, all arranged around a low wooden table with a large spray of fresh flowers.

"Luxury accommodations." Sylvia looked at Nathaniel. "Status for a former envoy?"

"More like luck and a friendly Ecolitan," he answered. "I doubt my status entitles us to this."

Nathaniel hugged Sylvia.

"I'm not in the mood . . ."

"I know," he whispered. "Hug me back and listen. Your turn is coming. That's why we have to finish the study here and now. Can you get it through the Imperial embassy and to the I.I.S. and the Defense Ministry?"

Sylvia relaxed slightly and bent toward his ear, nibbling it slightly, but scarcely sensually, before answering. "Until I try, I won't know, but I think so. Do you think the Legate will let the report go?"

"He can't overrule an Ecolitan, but he also has to know what's in it. If he's the typical political appointee, he'll only want to see the executive summary, and that's just about all he's going to get, certainly not any of the appendices, not until it's spread across the entire diplomatic community here, and to the New Avalonian Ministry of Commerce, which has to get the first copy. You and I are going to do one of the appendices. It will have a title something like, 'The External Diseconomies of Artosan Spacio-Graphics.'"

"Meaning that it will spell out everything?"

He nodded.

"That won't stop this . . . war."

"No. But it will slow down the Empire, I hope, while we find a way to stop the war."

"Us? Just us?"

"Us."

"That scares me," she whispered.

"If it's any consolation . . . it scares the frig out of me. And I do love you, you know." He gave her a last hug. "Now . . . let's get freshened up and then get something to eat. Is that all right?"

"I am hungry." She lifted her field pack. "Let me put this in the bedroom. Which one do you want?"

"Why?"

"I want the same one."

"But . . . ?"

"That was to keep you in line." She kept her face straight for a moment, before smiling wickedly.

"I think you're doing just fine." He lifted his own pack. "You pick."

XXX

"WHAT ABOUT THESE tables?" asked the young man with the goatee, easing up beside Nathaniel's console, where the Ecolitan continued to struggle with the wording of the executive summary. "Do you want frequency distribution or a geometric mean?"

"Both," decided Nathaniel. "Label them 'Thirty A' and 'Thirty B.'"

"Stet, sir."

No sooner had the goateed staffer departed than Clerigg reappeared.

"Fascinating figures here. Quite a story."

The Ecolitan nodded, waiting.

"I don't quite understand what you meant in this direction," confessed the Legation economist, showing Whaler the table he held, and the note hastily scrawled earlier by the Ecolitan.

"Wasn't as clear as I could have been, probably," said Nathaniel. "Take the energy production figures, both liquid fuels and fusactor output, converted to quads, and show total production and per annum rate of growth. Then I'll need a separate chart that breaks out per capita liquid fuel production, with two subcharts, one showing per capita production, and one that takes per capita production of say, five years ago, and increases it by the percentage of economic growth for the whole Artosan economy. On the same chart, the second one, show the surplus. Now . . . these second charts go in a separate appendix we're working on. You put the gross power charts in the infrastructure appendix."

"You're saying that there's a considerable increase in liquid fuels sources, far more than accounted for by population demand?"

"Something like that, but we'll let the figures speak for themselves."

Clerigg nodded. "Fascinating."

Nathaniel hoped so.

"You're generating some strange-looking figures, Ecolitan Whaler," offered the third staffer, easing three hard-copy color graphs onto the flat area beside the console. "Are these what you wanted?"

"Leave them. I'll let you know in a moment." He looked over at the second console, where Sylvia was inputting text for the appendix. "How's it going?"

"Slow."

"Me, too. The summary's got to have just the right flavor."

She shook her head.

They both looked up as the door to the long office opened.

"This just arrived," announced the fresh-faced receptionist, "by courier from the Frankan Legation."

"Frankan?" Nathaniel pondered.

The parchment envelope with the Frankan Union seal in the upper left corner bore two names, scripted regally in black ink:

> The most honorable Nathaniel F. Whaler
> The honorable Sylvia V. Ferro-Maine

The sandy-haired Ecolitan walked over to where Sylvia struggled, watched as she pushed a strand of dark hair behind her ear. "Here. You open it." He watched as she studied the names. "What does the V stand for?"

"Vittoria."

"You never told me."

"I don't recall that you asked." Then she smiled, reached out, and squeezed his fingers before she opened the envelope, only to find a second inside. Within the second envelope was a card, also neatly scripted.

The honor of your presence is requested at The Salisbury Club, the eighth of November, at 12:30 P.M., for a luncheon.

The signature beneath was that of Gerard De Vylerion.

"Who's De Vylerion?"

"He was the Frankan Legate to New Augusta."

"Then we should go." Sylvia looked at the screen and the lines of text. "That's tomorrow, and I'll need a break from this."

"We'll be mostly done by then."

"You will. I won't."

"We will."

"Promise?" she asked.

"I promise."

"Good. How anyone . . . could like being an economist."

Nathaniel chose not to point out that his being an economist had brought them together. Instead, he murmured, "It's a living."

"So long as it keeps being a living," she answered dryly.

They both laughed, ignoring the puzzled looks around them.

XXXI

"ECOLITANS?" VENTURED THE thin-faced woman at the Legation's front console.

"Yes?" Nathaniel and Sylvia paused.

"Legate Spamgall suggests that if you are going out, today would be a good day to see Gerry Adams Park. It's quite a spectacle, you know, with all the speakers and posters."

"Thank you," said Sylvia.

The two hurried down the steps of the Legation toward the waiting groundcar and driver.

"It'll have to be after lunch," Nathaniel said. "We're cutting it close. I know. It was my fault, but I wanted to get those last graphs right. As if anyone will read them." He snorted. "The economics make it obvious, but if you say it in plain language, it's suspect because it's too simple, and if you use the proper terminology everyone's eyes glaze over."

"There's another problem," ventured Sylvia. "More wars have been caused by economics than by any other factor, and almost no one recognizes that even after five millennia of constant proof." She opened the groundcar door and slid across the seat.

"The Salisbury Club," Nathaniel added as he closed the door.

"Yes, sir."

"While we're being philosophical," Nathaniel continued, "I'll add another thought. Everyone thinks that conflicts are caused by politics or personalities, but they're not. They're caused by massive forces. That's why personal diplomacy is generally only good for buying time while the forces are rearranged."

"As you did in New Augusta?"

"I'm getting this feeling that the forces weren't rearranged . . . the big problem is that individual diplomacy and economic studies usually aren't sufficient to offset public opinion and basic economic forces." He laughed harshly. "Dramas and trideos and books and their sappy happy messages to the contrary."

Sylvia smiled wryly. "Whereas economic disruptions and war are sufficient?"

"Or their equivalent. And then everyone protests, saying, 'You didn't have to do that.'"

"You've been writing too many economic studies."

"Absolutely."

They reached the Salisbury Club at twenty-five minutes past noon.

"Might I be of service, sir and madame?" asked the figure in the antique black formal jacket and black bow tie, looking coolly at the green uniforms.

"Sylvia Ferro-Maine and Nathaniel Whaler. We were to meet Gerard De Vylerion . . ." said Nathaniel.

"He has arrived. If you would follow me." The maître d'hôtel bowed and turned, leading them through the half-open dark oak doors and past a false leaded glass window showing the first landing at Camelot, framed by deep maroon velvet hangings.

"He knows where to dine," murmured Sylvia.

"He knows a great deal more than that."

A tall, almost ascetic, figure rose from the table in the paneled, velvet-framed corner of the room. "Gerard de Vylerion, Lady Ferro-Maine . . . a pleasure to see you again, Lord Whaler."

At the terms "lady" and "lord," Nathaniel caught the faintest stiffening in the posture of the black-coated maître d'hôtel, and the Ecolitan held in a smile, even while returning Gerard's bow.

"You're very kind," answered Sylvia.

"I'm an economist, not an envoy," protested Nathaniel.

"A most distinguished one. Did not the Emperor himself provide that collar pin?" An amused smile played across Gerard's face momentarily.

"Ah . . . well . . . yes."

Sylvia turned to Nathaniel. "I don't believe you mentioned that."

He flushed. "I had more important matters on my mind at the time. I was trying to get clearances . . . for a colleague."

She flushed.

De Vylerion nodded past the Ecolitans, and the maître d'hôtel slipped away quietly.

"Please . . . please . . . be seated." De Vylerion eased out the chair to his right for Sylvia.

As the two sat, a server in white carrying a silver pitcher filled their crystal water goblets, then retreated.

De Vylerion reseated himself. "I have been enjoying a glass of Lexin—very similar to Imperial Sperlin—but slightly drier. Would you like some? Or could I order something else?"

"The Lexin is fine." Sylvia smiled.

Nathaniel nodded.

"And you will pardon my emphasis on titles, but it is so amusing to see the Avalonian reaction. Accomplishments, and you both boast considerable accomplishments, mean little in Camelot. Only the titles matter, and that, my friends, is why New Avalon's days are numbered. I should not be so philosophical, but I am so glad you two could spare a moment for a luncheon with a broken-down old diplomat."

"I would have to dispute that description," said Nathaniel with a smile.

"Please . . . I know what I am."

Another server arrived with a pair of wineglasses, and De Vylerion leaned forward and filled both.

"To your continued health," offered the diplomat.

Both Ecolitans raised their glasses.

"And to yours."

Continued health was definitely a good toast, reflected Nathaniel, as he glanced around the half-filled dining area.

The leather-bound menus arrived, silently, and the blackcoated waiter vanished momentarily.

"What might be good?" asked Sylvia.

"It is all good." De Vylerion smiled. "Perhaps not so good as I could offer you in Wryere, and I hope that in the future you will be able to visit me there. Caroline would enjoy meeting you both. This was to be a short trip; so she was unable to accompany me." After a sip of the Lexin, the diplomat added, looking at Sylvia, "You might have been her sister, years ago."

"She must be beautiful," offered Nathaniel.

Sylvia flushed again.

"He does you and her justice," suggested the diplomat with a gentle smile. "I do admit I am prejudiced after all these years." He looked at the menu as the waiter bowed. "Have you decided?"

"I think I'll try the scampig," said Nathaniel.

"How are the spicetails?" Sylvia glanced at the waiter, offering a dazzling smile.

"They are good, madame. So is the deep crab."

"I'll try the deep crab."

"Just the Shienmez salad for me," added De Vylerion.

The waiter nodded and collected the menus.

"Once I had heard you were in fact in Camelot, I hastened to send an invitation, although one must not appear too hasty, especially in these times. That is why it was so formal."

"Formal or not," answered Sylvia, lifting the crystal glass, "it was appreciated."   •

"You were most helpful on New Augusta." Nathaniel smiled and turned to Sylvia. "Gerard is the one who told me that hard proof arrives only just before the warheads, or words to that effect."

"You have a good memory, an outstanding memory. I only quoted an ancient writer. Very cynical, but accurate. How do you find the Lexin?"

"This is excellent, if not quite in the class of Remoc." Sylvia inclined her head as the silent waiter set a green salad before her, then before Nathaniel, and finally De Vylerion.

"It is not, but it is close," affirmed De Vylerion.

Nathaniel knew that was something he didn't know. He could taste bad wine, but the subtleties between very good and great wines were far beyond him. "I wish I had your taste, both of you."

"You have other expertise." Sylvia's eyes were warm as she glanced at him.

"Indeed he does, as do you, lady."

"So do you," suggested Nathaniel. "Such as being in the right place at the right time. I somehow doubt that your presence here is a happy coincidence. You were headed back to Wryere, as I recall?"

"I was." De Vylerion set his fork on the side of the pale green porcelain plate.

"So why are you in Camelot?"

"There was a temporary vacancy here for a Legate, and I was asked to fill the position for a few months. I had thought to retire . . . and that made me above politics, as if anyone ever is." The Frankan laughed self-deprecatingly. "For reasons of my own, I accepted."

"Reasons of your own?" pressed Sylvia.

"I could say that I have taken an interest in your careers, and that would certainly be accurate. Accurate, but not wholly truthful."

"My career? An infrastructure economist?"

"A low-level Imperial political staffer?"

"An infrastructure economist with a tendency toward, shall we say, accomplishment? Accompanied by a lovely and talented lady whose looks belie considerable experience in understanding convoluted machinations and who possibly retains contacts with the only organization within the Empire capable of understanding the situation in which she and her companion find themselves?" De Vylerion smiled. "Surely, you are aware that practically the entire Galaxy knows about your study."

"We had that feeling." The Ecolitan took a last bite of the salad, then sipped the Lexin.

"A pity that the New Avalonian Arch Tory government fell. You know, I assume, that the commission of your study was about its last official act?"

"No, I didn't know that." Nathaniel could sense Sylvia stiffen and swallow hard.

"The Arch Tories succeeded in being voted out because they suggested, and attempted to carry out, a program which reduced social benefits in order to fund greater infrastructure development on the outplanets. They argued that greater development would eventually reduce the drain on New Avalon." De Vylerion paused and sipped his Lexin. "Any economist or even broken-down functionary could understand that. The voters did not."

The salad plates vanished into the hands of the silent server, and were replaced with the entrees. The aroma of apple-roasted scampig drifted up to Nathaniel's nostrils, and he could feel his mouth water—a definite improvement over ship fare and the mess at the Legation.

"And?" prompted Nathaniel.

"Your study was commissioned, and funded, as a means to embarrass the new government."

"Will the people care?" asked Sylvia.

"No," said Nathaniel, "not until the next elections. Then someone will drag out the study to show the new government's failings."

"If there remains a government," added De Vylerion, "or a problem with Artos."

Still listening to De Vylerion, Sylvia took a small bite of the crab. "This is very good."

"I am glad." De Vylerion glanced at his salad. "I doubt that Minister Smeaton-Adams will be quite so enthused about your findings, although Harding-Eames will be. He's the shadow minister, now."

"How did this change of government affect overall New Avalonian policies?" asked Nathaniel.

"Let us offer an analogy. New Avalon resembles a stately spaceliner whose drives have failed and which circles a black hole in a decaying orbit. I have some doubts that changing the captain alone will effect any significant difference in the eventual outcome."

Sylvia took the smallest of sips of Lexin, then reached for the pepper.

"You have doubtless observed the decline of New Avalon." De Vylerion gestured around the oak-paneled and velvet-hung room. "Although that decline is far from obvious in present surroundings. Camelot has much to offer, even in its present slow decline. Some might suggest you wander through the Gerry Adams Park today. That offers a view of Camelot unlike any other. Myself, I would think you would find the park inhospitable today. It might be chilly . . . unwelcoming. Perhaps on a warmer day," De Vylerion suggested.

"*Aaachew.*" While Sylvia's sneeze was muted, both men paused for an instant.

"Sorry." Sylvia rubbed her nose. "I overdid it on the pepper."

"That is easy to do. I have done so often." De Vylerion nodded politely. "As for the park, no one quite knows where the name came from, but I would surmise that she was an early politician, somewhere. It's quite amusing really, and sometimes informative. Perhaps the only place on New Avalon where one can speak in public and be totally ignored."

"Or in New Augusta," suggested Nathaniel.

De Vylerion laughed politely.

"Only visibly ignored," added Sylvia.

"True," admitted Nathaniel. He set down his fork, not believing how quickly he'd demolished the scampig. "How do you see the situation on Artos?"

De Vylerion lifted his wineglass, sipped, then offered an almost imperceptible shrug. "There will be a struggle for control of Artos. That has been obvious to those near the Three System Bulge for some time. Yet, except for the Empire, and for New Avalon itself, those likely to be affected are locked in a delicate balance of force. We of the Union have an alliance of mutual survival with the Hegemony against the larger forces of the Conglomerate and the Empire . . . although we share little else." He raised his eyebrows. "Very little else."

"You think that New Avalon has any awareness of the situation?"

"Awareness . . . most certainly. The will and ability to commit resources? Most certainly not. So we shall see." De Vylerion paused. "Oh, by the way, I understand that you prevented some considerable unpleasantness on the *Omnia Gallia*." De Vylerion laughed gently. "Captain Muerotte did not see it that way initially. But he does now."

"Thank you."

"No, most honored Ecolitan envoy, the Frankan Union owes you. At this time, to have a ship disappear on jumps through Hegemony territory . . ." He shrugged. "That would be destabilizing, to say the least."

"It would seem that everything points toward destabilization," began Sylvia, lowering her wineglass.

"Yes, Lady Ferro-Maine, and the name suits you, much points toward such destabilization. Much indeed."

Sylvia waited expectantly.

"And of that, there is the Empire. Alas, I fear that the Imperial eagles would employ any excuse to begin a conflict on the Rift. That could, unhappily, divert Imperial forces from our sector here." De Vylerion shrugged. "I mentioned that to my Imperial counterpart, Legate Wu-Reginald, but he was less concerned than I. Could you speak to the feelings of the Accord Legate?"

Sylvia nodded at Nathaniel, who stalled by sipping the wine. Good . . . but was it excellent? How would he know? Or ever know?

"Legate Spamgall has expressed some concerns about the economics of the situation." That much was true, and it was about all Spamgall had said in three days. "He has avoided commenting beyond that."

"That would seem politically wise . . . for anyone but a representative of Accord."

"Legate Spamgall is a politician appointed by politicians," Nathaniel pointed out.

"As are all too many Legates." De Vylerion laughed ironically. "Would you care for dessert?"

Nathaniel considered the tightness of his trousers. "Ah, I'd care, but I would regret it long after the pleasure passed."

"That could be said of many pleasures, Lord Whaler."

"He takes his duties very seriously." Sylvia's somber words were lightened by the twinkle in her eyes.

"In that, Accord is fortunate, as are we all." De Vylerion eased back his chair ever so slightly. "I do regret that Caroline was not here to meet you both, but I would hope that, once you have completed your study and the associated duties, you would be able to visit us."

"That would be a pleasure," said Sylvia.

"Thank you, for everything," added Whaler.

The Frankan Legate rose. "It has indeed been a pleasure in seeing you, and I wish you every success in your study, and in conveying the results to all interested parties. I would hope to see a copy, as we might be able to aid in its distribution."

"Thank you. You're most thoughtful," said Sylvia.

Nathaniel inclined his head as he stood. "You've always been helpful, and you have been again."

"We do live in the same Galaxy, Lord Whaler, and it grows smaller with each year. Some fail to recognize that, or that the laws of economics are not to be mocked . . . but we must try. My best to you both." De Vylerion inclined his head again as the Ecolitans left.

XXXII

THE FUARDIAN COLONEL saluted, crisply, before the wide gray antique desk that held no obvious data console.

"Your summary here was incomplete, colonel." The submarshal lifted a gray-covered folder. "The first report."

"Sir?"

"You failed to mention that the Accord agents escaped from Artos, despite your group's efforts. You knew this when you filed the report. You also failed to mention that they apparently contacted the Frankan agent on Artos." The sub-marshal's smile was cold.

The colonel stood stolidly, ignoring the sweat beading on his forehead.

"What have you done to remedy this, colonel? Anything?" The sub-marshal's tone was indolent, relaxed.

"A second team has already landed in Camelot."

"Did you know that the Hegemony's Blues failed?" The submarshal's square fingers tapped the hard gray surface of the desk. "And that the large growers of Artos are mobilizing against them?"

"I have just received that confirmation."

"Just?"

"Yes, sir. Team Two's deep agent was neutralized as well. The Frankan ship deviated significantly from its normal jump and entry patterns. I believe I mentioned that in the second report, sir."

"So you did. And why did the Frankan ship deviate?"

"We have not received the reports. I would assume that the Accord agents took control of the craft."

"Assume? Then why did they go to New Avalon? If they knew enough to understand the need to seize the ship, why would they go to New Avalon? Perhaps you can answer that question?"

"That is the closest Accord Legation."

"But no military support. For that you should be grateful. Perhaps you will do better on the next effort. There will be no third effort. Not for you, colonel. Is that clear?"

"Yes, sir."

"Good."

XXXIII

LIGHT RAIN, MORE like mist, drifted around the two Ecolitans as they walked back through the gray, chill afternoon toward the Accord Legation.

"If you believe De Vylerion, it's even worse than we thought," ventured Sylvia.

"I believe him."

"So do I."

"Is that Gerry Adams Park? The one the Legate mentioned?" Nathaniel gestured toward the walls ahead, intermittently fringed with brown bark mulched flower beds, evergreens, and bare-limbed deciduous trees that had shed leaves perhaps half a season earlier.

"De Vylerion also said something about it, but I was arguing with the pepper."

"I wish . . . oh, well . . . he did say that it was the only place where we'd hear even partway free speech."

"We can walk through it, and then turn right at the next corner. That would get us back," pointed out Sylvia. "Without taking any more time. Or much more."

Gerry Adams Park was odd, to say the least, with stone walls two meters tall on all sides, except for the wide arches at each end.

"It's hard when you change systems. It was midsummer on Artos and now it's almost winter here." Whaler eased to one side as two youths in short-sleeved shirts ran pell-mell past them. "You wouldn't know it from them."

A handful of people were gathered around a woman standing on a black box that raised her several heads above her audience.

"Do you think they care? Women, for all those rights in the Charter, are nothing more than baby factories to the ArchTories. Factories to produce laser fodder on worthless colony planets . . ."

The Ecolitans exchanged glances.

"I think I've heard this one before," said Sylvia. "Let's try the next one."

"What did you really think of De Vylerion?" he asked as they drifted toward a second speaker, a white-bearded barrel of a man.

"De Vylerion is supportive, and thankful, and it seems real." Sylvia glanced at the speaker standing on a red box framed by dark green conifer needles that were turning yellow at the tips.

". . . if you eat, you are *their* puppets. If you watch trideo, you are their puppets. You have always been their puppets. They doctor your food with chemicals. They pour what they want you to think into your brains through the trideo, and you think what they want. And you think your thoughts are yours . . . do you know how many images you cannot see? The commands that are implanted in your trideo through their schemes . . ."

"I've heard this one," Nathaniel said.

"There's a group like this in every society, pointing out how people are led to think." Sylvia shook her head. "The truth's closer to the opposite. The media and the politicians pander to the prejudices of the people, but the people, of course, always protest the opposite is true."

The two in greens walked slowly along the stone walkways flanked by turned dirt that probably held flowers in the summer.

The third speaker's box was empty, but a young man in brilliant purple stood beside it, handing out leaflets.

"Join the Purple Peace Party! The Purple Peace Party for eternal love and peace."

Both Ecolitans smiled sadly and shook their heads.

"Well . . . back to finish our masterpiece."

"Will it do any good?" Sylvia gestured back toward the barrel-shaped speaker. "When I hear trash like that, I wonder."

"De Vylerion seemed to think it would. From what he said, I get the feeling that the ArchTories want the study to embarrass the Conservatives, maybe even as something to topple another government."

"He made that pretty clear."

"Would that be enough to have someone in the New Avalon structure go after us?"

Sylvia shrugged as they turned and moved toward the middle of the park.

"Another thing," said Nathaniel in a lower voice. "Have you noticed that the modus operandi is either an accident or Imperial military needles—no matter where we are?"

"That means it's not the Empire, but it could be almost anyone else."

"Or several anyone elses," pointed out the sandy-haired Ecolitan.

"That could be . . . everyone copying the first incident on Accord."

"They're all copying the first player, which effectively conceals exactly who's involved?"

"You've got it." Sylvia glanced across the park, then slammed into Nathaniel, dropping them both to the ground.

Scritt! Scritt!

Needles splintered on the stones behind them. From the damp grass beside the stone walkway, Whaler turned his head to catch sight of one thin figure in a baggy gray coat dashing toward the end of the park, while a chunkier man struggled in the other direction.

Scritt!

He ducked again, even as Sylvia rolled off his legs and into a crouch.

"Someone's shooting!"

"Maude! Get down . . ."

Nathaniel took three fast steps to join Sylvia.

Whheeeeee! Wheee!

"Over the wall," Sylvia snapped. "You go that way . . . over the wall." Then she was gone, headed toward the far wall.

"Right." Nathaniel half-vaulted, half-scrambled up the rough stones and dropped down into the dried bark covering the flower bed on the outside of the park wall.

An older couple stared, wide-eyed.

"Training," he said, wondering why he'd bothered. Then he sprinted eastward along the edge of the park, trying to breathe deeply as he ran.

The thin man walked out of the east gates of Gerry Adams Park and across the empty crosswalk, as if he had not even been hurrying. Then he turned at the other side of the street, glanced at the oncoming Ecolitan and reached inside the coat again.

The handful of pedestrians scattered.

Squeeeekkkk . . . eeetch . . . Two groundcars tapped into each other.

The Ecolitan slammed into the gray-coated figure, staggered, then managed to lever a side-footed kick into the other's knee. The man in the gray coat crumpled, his knee shattered, but his hands still groped under the jacket. Nathaniel slammed the man's wrist, snapping away the minineedler, and probably the would-be assassin's wrist. Even as he reached for the weapon, the figure slumped, and the eyes glazed.

Without hesitating, Nathaniel searched the prone body, getting only a thin wallet folder, nothing else from otherwise empty pockets, and leaving the needler untouched. Then he sprinted back toward the park, dodging groundcars. Once past the gates, he slowed to a quick walk, eyes darting from side to side.

"Here!"

Following Sylvia's yell, he dodged more groundcars making his way across the second avenue to join her. They loped down the street.

"You didn't . . . get him?" asked Sylvia.

"Got him. Suicide bloc."

"You, too?"

"You . . . left the body?" asked the taller Ecolitan.

"Why not? All he had . . . was . . . thin wallet. Probably minimal identification . . . wad of credit . . . notes . . ."

Once around another corner, they slowed into a ground-covering walk.

"That . . . was . . . all mine had," said Nathaniel between deep breaths, wondering if he'd ever be in the shape he once had been.

"Good thing you left him. Great minds think alike. We'd better hurry back to the Legation. Who was behind this?"

"Has to be a cold outsystem. They weren't warmly dressed."

"Or paid locals," she suggested.

"But why were we there? De Vylerion told us to go."

"No, the Legate told us," corrected Sylvia.

Nathaniel swallowed. "De Vylerion said any day but today, in effect. He warned us, and I didn't catch it."

"Neither did I."

"Our own Legate . . ." Nathaniel shook his head.

"Is it safe to go back?" asked Sylvia.

"I'd bet on Swersa and the permanent staff. No one else. And we don't say a word."

They both moved more quickly, scanning the avenue, ignoring the sounds of sirens and whistles blocks behind them.

XXXIV

"NOTHING." NATHANIEL THUMBED off the trideo news. "Not a thing. Two dead bodies and toxic military needles all over the park. And not a thing on the news—except a reference to two homeless men who had heart attacks."

"You don't know about toxic needles . . . not for sure. And sympathetic blocs do cause heart attacks." Sylvia looked up from the bound copy of the report, then handed it across the sofa to him. "I'm glad we've got this suite, particularly now." She stretched. "I can't find any more typos or dumb sentences."

"Time to go with it." He glanced at the cover, scanning the title, *The Economic Infrastructure of Artos, Analysis and Recommendations*, then set it on the low table. "I'm hungry."

He stretched, then touched his cheek. It still hurt, and his legs and feet ached slightly as well. No matter what anyone said, sprinting in boots on hard pavement did nasty things to human tissue.

"You're going to have quite a bruise there. I'm sorry."

"I'm quite happy to be alive, thank you." And angry, angry at his own stupidity, angry that she could have been killed because he hadn't paid enough attention to De Vylerion. Had he missed anything else? He hoped not. He sincerely hoped not.

He glanced at the two folder wallets on the table. "False Coordinate passports. I still can't believe it."

Sylvia stifled a yawn. "I can."

"So can I. They can't lose. If the assassins get us, then Accord gets in the trideo or print news. If we get them, then two dead bodies with Coordinate identification are discovered. I just wish I knew who."

"It probably isn't the Union."

"It could be almost anyone else."

"Or everyone," she suggested.

"That possibility had crossed my mind. I almost feel like the rest of the Galaxy, including some of our own people, is running after us to pin our dead bodies on someone else's door step." He shook his head. "We've speculated and speculated, and we still don't know. All we can do is play the game." He lifted the draft report. "Let's go downstairs and finish this off. Then, all we have to do, once we get the corrections made, is worry about how we get this out of here and to your friends over at the Imperial legation."

"*We* don't, because that's one giveaway. They're looking for two of us."

"Oh?"

"I'll do it, and I know how."

"How, my more effective operative?"

"Status. I'll leave with the cleaning crew in a dingy singlesuit in the morning. Ecolitan professors don't look like maintenance types."

"I could . . ."

"No," said Sylvia. "You're too big. You can't disguise all that muscle. You're almost a head taller than most men here. That's one reason why they could follow us so easily."

"We could also post a meeting on the Legation schedule for both of us with Clerigg for tomorrow morning," he suggested.

"That wouldn't hurt, especially since there's clearly a leak somewhere here."

"A leak? I doubt there's just one." He shook his head. "Let's get this fixed. We'll need to hurry if we want to eat before the mess closes. And I'm hungry." He almost touched the bruised cheek again, but dropped his hand.

"You have the keyblocs Clerigg left?"

He nodded.

"I'll be glad to get this done."

So would Nathaniel, except he had the feeling that completing the study was only the beginning of the end, if that.

He also didn't like the fact that the Legate had sent them into ambush. Either someone had set up Spamgall or the receptionist, and that meant infiltration of the Legation, or Spamgall himself was involved in the mess. Right now, there was no way to tell which, but they'd have to assume both alternatives were possible.

XXXV

NATHANIEL PACED TO the front of the economic section office, then back to the console. He glanced up at the high windows and the gray clouds of winter that oozed across the permaglass.

She'd been gone four hours. Surely it didn't take that long, did it? But the Legations didn't open that early, did they? Probably not on New Avalon. Even the Accord Legation wasn't open to the public until zero eight thirty.

Clerigg glanced at Whaler. "I thought Ecolitan Ferro-Maine was supposed to be here."

"So did I."

Clerigg went back to his console, then looked up. "When can we send—"

"As soon as she shows up." He swallowed. "I'm sorry, Clerigg. It's been a strain. I know it's been a strain on you, too."

The Ecolitan's eyes went to the door, but it was only the messenger, who delivered several envelopes to the economic section chief.

Sylvia . . . how long could they keep it up? Sooner or later . . . He shook his head, his hand going to the bruise on his shoulder where she'd slammed him into the permacreate to save his life. He hadn't even felt that one until later. Twice so far, she'd saved his neck, and that probably didn't count the times her knowledge had averted danger. She hadn't trusted the second pilot on the Frankan ship—not at all. Nor Kennis.

But who was following them closely enough to strike in New Avalon? Was it the Imperial military? Despite Sylvia's statements, Nathaniel had no doubts that the eagles were cold enough to use sympathetic death blocs. But so were the Fuards and the Hegemony. And, where men were concerned, so was the Matriarchy.

And who had infiltrated the Legation? And, if it weren't infiltration, why was the Legate working with an outside power? Spamgall was a political creature, and that type, contrary to popular opinion, wasn't usually open to venality or bribery. Their vices were linked to power, not credits.

Nathaniel paced back to the front of the office. Clerigg glanced up, then looked away.

He kept pacing, and Clerigg kept looking at the time readout on his console.

Click.

He turned.

"It's done." A damp-haired Sylvia stood in the door in a maroon singlesuit.

For a long moment, he just looked, and his knees felt rubbery. Then he stepped forward and hugged her . . . hard.

For a moment, she hugged him back, then eased away. "It's no great accomplishment." She shook her head. "Not at all."

"It's a fine study," protested Clerigg.

"The study is good," Sylvia admitted, offering the staff economist a brief smile. "And you made it possible."

Nathaniel nodded to Clerigg. "Send them all out, regular courier, as if it were totally routine distribution."

"Just routine?"

"The fireworks come later, Clerigg. We discussed this. If we call attention to it, then we'll be accused of sensationalism."

"Yes, sir."

"I need to change," said Sylvia, "and we have something to discuss."

"I thought—" began the economist.

"We'll get to it," temporized Nathaniel. "Thank you for everything." He followed Sylvia outside into the corridor.

"Up to our room," suggested Sylvia. "There's a trideo set there."

"A trideo set?"

"Yes, a frigging trideo set."

He winced and followed her.

Even before heading to the fresher or the closet, she went to the set and slipped in a cube she extracted from a pocket. "This and a few other items were waiting for me. They knew! Frig it! They knew, and they were waiting. That report is probably headed for orbit already. Not that it'll do much good."

Nathaniel watched the holo images that rose in the center of the room, a series of people in uniforms and formal dress around a raised throne, the scene showing a vague resemblance to that of the Imperial receiving hall where he had presented his credentials as an envoy.

"That's him—the evil envoy," said the trim and handsome woman in an Imperial uniform, pointing to another figure at the far side of a huge reception hall. Then the images shifted to reveal a blocky, hard-faced figure in a caricature of Ecolitan greens, with a smooth smile and cold eyes.

"He can make the smartest people think black is white . . . or that green is beautiful . . ."

Nathaniel wanted to retch, but he kept watching.

After several units, Sylvia cut off the images. "There's three hours of cuts like this. That's what Berea said. There's even one that shows the evil envoy's traitor aide—she's a former exotic dancer who seduced her way into an Imperial bureaucracy to get the information to sell out to the evil envoy. Slander is the sincerest form of flattery, I suppose." Sylvia's voice was bitter.

"I'm sorry. It wasn't . . . I didn't."

"Don't apologize. I know all that, but it still hurts. It shouldn't, but it does."

"But why would the Empire—"

"It's not the Empire. These are all commercial productions, sponsored by TTG. That's Tech-Transfer Galactic, and one of TTG's subsidiaries is an outfit called AgriTech. It operates in the Empire, the Frankan Union, the Hegemony, and the Conglomerate. Supposedly, it's headquartered on Tinhorn."

"So Accord is getting an incredibly bad image through all these trideo dramas?" Nathaniel still wondered who would watch the dramas . . . and accept them as real . . . except he was afraid he knew.

"You've got it. And what will one economic study do to combat all the biases being raised and fanned by the entertainment industry? One excellent, factual, and dry economic study? And that's not all."

"Oh?"

"The synde bean thing. You were right. Something very funny happened here in Camelot. An Avalonian trade factor was almost killed—a hit—with Imperial style needles. It's coincidental, of course, but he had some dealings with the Conglomerate and the Federated Hegemony—and with R-K Enterprises. Several months ago, some new strains of beans went to Artos, and to George Reeves-Kenn. Berea flagged it because it made no sense. The value was minimal, but you have to log those to a planoformed system—ecological imbalance."

"The plague . . . the different beans . . ." mused Nathaniel. "There's no way to prove that, but . . ."

"It looks that way. George found out about the plague and wanted to protect himself, but that left a trail. Smack—no trade factor, and no George. Someone wanted to cover their tracks."

"And make sure the laser stayed focused on Accord."

"That's how I see it." Sylvia's voice turned edged as she added, "And there's nothing we can really prove. Berea suspects, and she's reported those suspicions, but how can the I.I.S. tell the Imperial Senate that they suspect this without proof—especially when the entire Empire *knows* Accord is out to poison it. How many millions have already died from starvation or power losses? Five, ten million so far?"

"I guess we'll have to do more to put a stop to it."

"What? Destroy half the Galaxy? That's what it would take. And we'd have to do it before the Empire destroys the other half."

"With my luck, I'd choose the wrong half," mused Nathaniel.

"I don't know. I'm soaked. I'm cold, and I need to change." Sylvia stripped off the singlesuit. "Then we'll get something to eat, and talk. Although what we can come up with, I don't know." She draped the damp suit over her arm and walked to the fresher, seemingly unaware, or uncaring, that Nathaniel watched. "A frigging exotic dancer! That crap . . . how can people . . . ?"

XXXVI

"DO YOU THINK you can go back to the Imperial Legation?" Nathaniel asked as he closed the door to the suite, wishing he'd eaten less of the heavy crepe. He burped quietly, he hoped, still wondering how a crepe could have been so heavy. "I worry that going back again . . . they might . . . not be so helpful."

"Berea was encouraging . . . and told me that they'd take anything else I could bring . . . but I don't think it's going to help enough. This whole thing has gotten beyond reason. Then, I suppose it always was." Sylvia stood and looked at the silent trideo projector. "An exotic dancer . . . that's hard to believe. A frigging exotic dancer . . ."

"I find you very exotic."

"You won't find me doing that kind of dance." She smiled briefly. "Not in public."

"Does that mean I have something to look forward to?"

"What did you have in mind?"

"A very permanent arrangement," he blurted, not believing that he'd said what he had.

"If we get through all this . . ."

"Promise?"

She kissed his cheek. "First things first . . . like survival."

"Survival isn't enough."

Sylvia looked at him directly, her gray eyes deep, for a long time before she answered. "No, it isn't, and that's the problem. We both want more than mere existence." She sighed. "We all do. But most people's desires are modest on an individual basis—and totally unreasonable for an entire society. Maybe that's why reason doesn't work in government."

"Reason can work on those in power . . . if you use it to appeal to greed, fear, and prejudice," suggested Nathaniel.

"I don't like that."

"Neither do I."

"That's what you did in New Augusta, wasn't it? And that's why you didn't tell me, either?"

"I wasn't that noble." He snorted. "I wish I had been, but I didn't want you hurt if things went wrong."

"Please don't protect me that way anymore."

Nathaniel looked at the numbers on the borrowed hand calculator, wishing he'd understood them before, but the trideo shows and the little information about the beans had been the key . . . those and the Artos study, once he'd really had a chance to investigate the data. "I won't, but it's hard."

"Go ahead." She reached out and squeezed his hand.

He took a deep breath.

"All right. Who's behind all of this? Let's take it step by step. Forget about hard proof for the moment."

"Do we really want to know?" Sylvia took a long swallow from the glass of water she held. "It's dry in here."

"I know. Can I have a sip?"

She extended the glass, and he drank before answering.

"Probably not, but it won't go away, and things will just get worse." He cleared his throat, glancing at the figures and phrases he'd scrawled out. "From what we do know, the overall effort to put the Empire and Accord at each other's throats isn't being caused by either the Coordinate or the Empire."

Sylvia nodded. "Nor New Avalon or the Frankan Union."

"Now, the attempts on Artos and here probably weren't managed by Halstan or by Orknarli or Olympia—they're too distant. Effectively, that leaves the Hegemony and the Conglomerate."

"It has to be the Conglomerate," said Sylvia.

"Why?" asked Nathaniel idly.

"Take those trideo clips. They're airing all over the Empire. Who else could afford them?"

Nathaniel laughed.

"Don't make fun of me."

"I'm not."

"You are."

He swallowed. "Let me point out something. Probably the shows paid for themselves. People like that sort of thing. But even if they didn't, what was the total cost—production, sponsors, airtime, everything?"

"I wouldn't know, but a commercial slot on New Augusta might cost a quarter million a minute. It'd be less elsewhere."

"And the show is aired twice a week . . . three times a week? Eight minutes of dedicated commercial sponsor time."

She nodded.

"All right, let's assume that they sell the commercial spots for next to nothing, but the structure works. That means that, on Old Earth, each show costs four million, or twelve million a week. That's six hundred million a year for intensive coverage. How many systems are there in the Empire?"

"One hundred sixty seven, but only ninety-some with significant populations. Voting populations."

"There's no other market that expensive. Let's assume the average cost is twenty percent of that on Old Earth. A little over a hundred million a year a system. That works out to nine billion credits. Do you know what the cost of the *HMS Black Prince* was?"

"No." Sylvia frowned even as her mouth opened.

"Eleven billion credits."

"But people don't look at it that way." She fingered the near-empty water glass.

"They don't. That's the beauty of it. People don't think in those terms, but whoever is behind this is brilliant. This is a fullscale, low-budget war. The Empire is practically ready to launch an all-out assault on the Coordinate, and it's cost the Fuards less than two capital ships, and probably less than a hundred million in bioresearch and bean plague dissemination efforts."

"You said it—"

"You were right, but not because of the money, not exactly. It's the commercial ties that counted, and the Hegemony doesn't have enough. But my guess is that the two are working together, despite the Hegemony's official alliance with Wryere."

"Sonderssen and his friend Fridrik?"

"And Kennis was trying to get his section of the pie. He'd be able to keep it under either Fuard or Hegemony rule. So he wanted us out of the way as well." Nathaniel nodded. "Another is Gerard De Vylerion. And there's a feel to all of this."

Sylvia looked at him. "Fine. We know who, but what can we do? Our study will convince the I.I.S., but they're already convinced. Oh, I had Berea make sure your friend the special assistant got a copy. She might be able to persuade her mother. Probably not, but it couldn't hurt."

"She's not exactly my friend."

"She tried hard."

"You are much superior."

"I'm glad you recognize that." She offered a brief smile. "So? What do we do?"

Nathaniel swallowed—twice. Was there any choice? Realistically, he couldn't see any. Not with the little time they had left.

"It's the whole business of being an Ecolitan—the Prime calls it the Ecolitan Enigma. I told you that before, the interaction of power and ethics."

Sylvia waited.

"It's like a puzzle. If we wait until what we do is obvious and justified, then far more people are hurt, but we can claim justification. Or we can do what needs to be done as soon as possible." He pursed his lips. "And then we're arbitrary and enigmatic . . . puzzling . . . and always called overbearing and high-handed. I suppose it really ought to be called the Ecolitan Dilemma, but the Ecolitan Enigma sounds better. And isn't that the way people do it anyway, picking whatever sounds better?"

"You're avoiding getting to the point."

"It's hard." He edged closer to her on the sofa, and lowered his voice. "Ecolitans always have contingency plans. The Prime insisted I develop some. You won't like them. They're far worse than what I did in New Augusta, far worse—"

"What we did."

"What we did," he agreed. "Here's what I have in mind. You and Swersa and I are going to raise the military and governmental stakes . . . very high . . . and very directly . . . for Tinhorn. One thing that the Institute has understood from the beginning is that you strike for the heart and at those responsible."

"That's why you hit the Defense Tower on Old Earth."

He nodded. "This is worse. I think we can take out the Conglomerate's entire command structure."

"You . . . us? No one's ever done that."

"It's been done before. It's just that most leaders avoid operations that would make them targets in retaliation . . . and there's going to be some collateral damage. Maybe a lot of collateral damage."

Sylvia swallowed as he continued to lay out the contingency plan. Finally, she held up her hand. "Do we really need to do something this drastic?"

"Let's see. We've killed two Fuardian agents; highjacked a Frankan ship; sent information and messages to most of the intelligence agencies in the Galaxy. The I.I.S. has beaten on D.I. and the eagles. In response, the Empire continues to prepare to attack Accord. The Conglomerate continues to spread bean plague and increase its military arsenal while preparing to invade Artos. All the factions on Artos are ready to explode into a civil war which none of them can win."

"That's all true," Sylvia said. "But do we need such a drastic response?"

"There theoretically might be something less . . . catastrophic. There's only one problem. We don't have those kinds of resources. We don't have a fleet at hand. Or landing battalions, or whatever." He paused and took a deep breath. "Besides, I have a moral problem with that. Our hypothetical fleet—and the people in it—is innocent. We're supposed to get lots of our people killed after the Fuards have already killed millions? As I see it, I have a choice. I can wait until Artos is in Fuard hands, and until the Empire and Accord are at full war, and until millions more die on planoformed worlds. Then, any action I take will be justified. Or, I can take immediate action to prevent a war and be condemned for being immoral and precipitous because any action I take has to be targeted and catastrophic."

He looked at Sylvia. "Now . . . I've been raised in a system that believes that early action that saves the innocent is more moral than later, more justified action that results in more deaths. And sometimes, we're wrong. And if I'm wrong now, a lot of people will die. So, first, do you think I'm wrong about the cause of the problem?"

Sylvia moistened her lips, then looked at the floor, then at the window.

Nathaniel waited.

"No," she finally said.

"All right. Can you think of any other way to stop this mess before millions or hundreds of millions die?"

"No. But that doesn't mean there isn't one."

"You're right about that, too," he admitted. "How much time do we have to come up with another solution?"

"Not much."

"How about a compromise of sorts? We work on this. If you can think of anything that we can actually implement that's less deadly . . . we'll look at it."

Sylvia took a deep breath. "I don't like it."

"Sylvia, do you think I do? Do you think I like being the point man in a universe where every time I have to act I discover that people respect only force in large quantities? Where people are more interested in self-justification than in preventing unnecessary deaths? Where I'm being betrayed or undercut by my own people? Where the same thing is happening to you?"

"You might as well get on with your plan." Her voice was hoarse.

So he did, stopping for water all too often to moisten a throat that got drier with each deadly word.

XXXVII

"WE HAVE A problem," said Nathaniel as the two stepped into Swersa's office. Sylvia closed the door.

"I thought your study was complete." The white-haired Ecolitan fingered her chin and frowned.

"The study was only the first part. It was also a cover." Whaler laughed. "It's a good study, but it wasn't enough."

"Reason and rationality usually aren't," Sylvia added with a hard and bright smile.

"Might I use your console for a moment?" Nathaniel smiled politely.

Swersa swallowed, then stepped toward the equipment, and flicked the privacy screens on. "You're not just an economist."

"I'm an economist who's been continually drafted into trying to solve problems bigger than I am."

"You're going to invoke the delegation clause, I suppose?"

Nathaniel shook his head, almost sadly, as he slipped behind the console. "No. I'm invoking the Prime clause."

As the lights flickered across the console before settling into the green, the older Ecolitan looked from one green uniform to the other, then to the grayness of brick and clouds beyond the windows. "I got the message, but . . . I hoped it wouldn't come to this."

"It has. Perhaps worse than the Prime anticipated."

In the silence that followed, Nathaniel sat behind the console and began to enter the necessary codes.

Over his shoulder, Swersa watched as the lines unfolded on the screen, and her eyes widened. Her swallow was more like a gulp.

"You want to purchase the largest interstellar cargo carrier available in the New Avalon system and want it delivered now? How can you afford—"

"The credit line is twenty billion. You should be able to get what we need for three."

Even Sylvia swallowed as Nathaniel offered the numbers.

Swersa continued to stare over the sandy-haired Ecolitan's shoulder at the screen.

"Now," emphasized Nathaniel. "The largest carrier available by tomorrow, the day after by the latest. With support boats. If not support boats, then yachts that will fit inside a cargo lock. No publicity, no notice." He began to type in the remainder of the specifications he had developed at a time that seemed all too long ago, even though it had been less than two months earlier.

"Isn't this premature? I mean, nothing's happened."

Sylvia shook her head. "By the time anything happens, it will be too late."

"This would happen to me." Swersa paused. "What about a crew?"

"Me . . . you . . . Sylvia." He paused. "You are current, aren't you, at least to be a second pilot?"

"I've got a command cert, sir."

"Good."

"But . . ."

"What is the oath?"

Swersa paled. "You can't be serious."

"Don't you think averting a Galactic war is enough justification?"

"I can't believe you—or the Prime—"

Sylvia's eyes flicked from one Ecolitan to the other.

Nathaniel shook his head and said slowly, " 'All that is necessary for evil to triumph is for good men to do nothing.' Very ancient quote. What does the oath say?"

"To do what is necessary . . . to act for the greater good . . . to put principle above politics."

"That's what we're doing." He pushed himself away from the console and gestured to the screen. "That's your charge."

"But a cargo carrier . . . how will that . . . the Conglomerate has hundreds of warships. Or will you pull out some economic miracle?"

"As all of the great villains in history have said, 'Trust me.' " Nathaniel laughed harshly. "If I'm successful, I'll doubtless join them. If not, then several hundred million more innocents will die."

XXXVIII

PRIORITY FLAME ONE
DENEAL F. KRUPKLAATU
MARSHAL OF THE FLEETS
DEPARTMENT OF WAR

FUARDIAN CONGLOMERATE
TEMPTE, TINHORN
PRIORITY FLAME ONE

TINHORN'S INTEREST IN ARTOS, AND THE SPACIAL CONCERNS SURROUNDING THE THREE SYSTEM BULGE, HAVE COME TO THE ATTENTION OF THE ECONOMIC SURVEY SERVICE OF THE ECOLITAN INSTITUTE. WE ARE DEEPLY CONCERNED AS WELL ABOUT THE MISUSE OF CERTAIN ECOLOGICAL STUDIES INVOLVING HYDROCARBON FIXING AND SYNDE BEAN OPTIMIZATION. WE HAVE CONVEYED OUR UNDERSTANDING OF THESE CONCERNS TO OTHERS WHO SHARE SIMILAR INTERESTS.

IN VIEW OF YOUR RESPONSIBILITIES AS THE TITULAR HEAD OF THE DEPARTMENT OF WAR, THE INSTITUTE REGARDS ANY ATTEMPTS TO (1) DESTABILIZE THE DOMESTIC STRUCTURE OF ARTOS, (2) IMPOSE A MORE STABLE STRUCTURE THROUGH EXTERIOR EFFORTS, (3) REDUCE HYDROCARBON FIXING ON IMPERIAL AND OTHER SYSTEMS THROUGH THE PERVERSION OF ECOLOGICAL STUDIES, AND (4) THE USE OF COMMERCIAL ENTERTAINMENT MEDIA AS A VEHICLE FOR TARGETED ADVERSE PROPAGANDA AS CONTRIBUTING TO GALACTIC DESTABILIZATION.

BECAUSE THE INSTITUTE HAS LONG VIEWED ECOLOGICAL, SOCIOLOGICAL, ECONOMIC AND POLITICAL STABILITY AS INTERTWINED, THE INSTITUTE REGARDS ANY SUCH ATTEMPTS AT DESTABILIZATION AS ECOLOGICALLY UNWARRANTED. THAT DESTABILIZATION WILL BE RIGHTED SHORTLY. WE STRONGLY SUGGEST THAT YOU NOTE THE MINIMAL USE OF RESOURCES REQUIRED TO ACHIEVE THIS RESTABILIZATION.

YOU WILL ALSO NOTE THAT ALL OTHERS WITH AN INTEREST IN SUCH RESTABILIZATION HAVE BEEN COPIED. THEY HAVE ALSO RECEIVED SUPPORTING INFORMATION THAT IS UNNECESSARY FOR THE CONGLOMERATE.

The Fuardian marshal looked at the flimsy. "They're bluffing. They have to be bluffing."

The sub-marshal waited.

"What do you say, Sub-marshal Hommel?"

"I do not have the information you have, ser."

"But?"

"Accord—the Institute—has never bluffed."

"They cannot stop us. Not even they can stop us. Not now. Continue the plan."

XXXIX

THE FOUR STOOD behind the lock hatch of the shuttle as it crept up to the wall-like hull of the former *J. M. Turner.*

"She's all yours, Ecolitan. Fully energized, with all the boats except number five." The small man wiped his forehead. "All the magtites operational except number three—you knew about that. And two weeks of standard crew fare." He raised both eyebrows.

Nathaniel nodded. "We'll take a look, of course."

"Yes, sir." Magnuson, the ship factor representing the Bank of Camelot, wiped his forehead again. "The crew fare is class one, I might add."

"Thank you."

Clunk. The shuttle shivered as the small craft linked to the cargo carrier.

"Magnuson, you're clear to take the purchasers aboard." The words reverberated from the speaker above the lock.

Nathaniel closed his helmet, as did the others, before entering the lock. The faint hissing as the pressure between the cargo carrier and the shuttle equalized was inaudible, and Nathaniel automatically checked the outside pressure gauge—a little over thirty, or about eighty percent of T-Norm. The pressure stayed there as the four entered the *Turner's* lock. Even the passenger lock was oversized, with a three meter square hatch, probably for large and delicate cargo of some sort.

Once the inner lock hatch closed behind the four and they stood—or floated—in the red maintenance lights of the passageway, Nathaniel cracked his helmet. The air was chill, both sterile and musty, although the *Turner* had only been laid into storage a month before, with the bankruptcy and collapse of Hanoverian Shipping. Three other cargo ships had also been available, but the *Turner* had the largest drives and the greatest tonnage.

"Forward." Nathaniel turned and let the others follow as he pulled himself forward.

The cockpit—except it was the bridge on commercial ships, Nathaniel recalled—was only slightly larger than on an Institute cruiser, with four couch positions, rather than five. The board before the pilots' couches was simpler, the engineering board close to identical, but a military ship had nothing to compare to the fourth board, for cargo handling and loading. Then . . . there were no weapons board, and no separate comm board.

He pulled himself down into the captain's couch, belted himself in, and lifted the input set, adjusting the clamps before easing it into place and toggling the system standbys. He could feel Magnuson wince at the power drains. *Anything* drained power on a ship so large.

"Cells . . . normal . . . converters . . . accumulators . . . shield lines . . ." he murmured as he checked the circuits to each and the readouts.

From what he could tell through the shipnets, the *Turner* was as represented, not that he could afford to reject the ship if she were basically capable of what he needed. But there was no point in letting the bank's tame factor know that. He paused, then set the gee field to minimum.

He set aside the input headset and stood. "Now . . . the drive spaces."

Magnuson nodded, and the three followed him aft, half-bounding, half-drifting in the min-gee he'd toggled into place.

The door to the drive spaces creaked as it irised open, but moved smoothly.

Each jump-generator was the size of the entire drive space in a military corvette, and there were five. In spite of himself, Nathaniel was impressed. The *Turner* might actually have the power to do what he'd planned. He pushed aside those thoughts. First things first, or he'd never get to the end.

The drives and supercon lines looked operational, as did the rest of the arrayed equipment.

Nathaniel plugged into the lower boards, running through the circuits, starting with the drives, then going to the jump-generators, and finally ending with the power leads to the magtites.

He shook his head.

"What's the matter, sir? It's just as the specs said . . ."

"The power draws for the magtites are thirty percent above specs. That wasn't specified."

"We'll rebate a hundred million."

"Make it two." Nathaniel wouldn't need to use the magtites anywhere close to capacity, perhaps not at all, but there was no sense in the Institute paying more than necessary. "With four of these beasts to sell . . ."

"All right." Magnuson swallowed. "All right. Two hundred million."

"If you would, just send it to the Legation. They can handle it. And make sure title is held by the Institute," he emphasized again.

"As you wish, Ecolitan Whaler."

He closed down the boards, shifting the controls back forward, and sealed them. Then he checked the supercon lines again, and the actual power flows. Supposedly, cross-connections were standard on every cargo carrier, but he needed to ensure that.

He finally nodded. He could shift everything into the in-system drives, every last erg of power.

"Is that all?"

"Almost, Magnuson. The boats, and then we'll be through."

There were supposed to be two boats for each hatch, ten in all, and a lifeboat, which was more like a courier. In fact, the specs were similar. One boat—boat five—was missing, as the factor had pointed out from the beginning.

From what Nathaniel could tell, the ship held atmosphere; the boats were operational; the systems worked; and the entire carrier was economically unfeasible under current economic conditions.

After checking the courier, the Ecolitan straightened. "Everything seems to be as specified . . . except for the magtites. Let's go back forward."

As the four reached the passageway opposite the forward crew/passenger lock, Magnuson fumbled out the oblong that was half clipboard, half datacase. "If you would authenticate this, and make the changes. The rebate section is at the end . . ."

Nathaniel forced himself to read through all the clauses, just to make sure of things like liabilities and contingencies, to ensure they didn't outlive the lifetime of the ship. From what he could tell, they didn't, and he finally authenticated everything, after he'd added the provisions for the two hundred million credit rebate, and ensuring that the Institute held title.

He wanted to smile. For a man who'd never made fifty thousand, spending slightly over three billion credits in a day seemed insane— but what he was planning was equally so.

"What are you going to do with her, sir, if I might ask?" Magnuson stowed the datacase, then paused by the passenger lock.

"Reinforce some of the forgotten laws of economics, Magnuson." Nathaniel smiled coolly.

"I . . . we . . . wish you well."

"Thank you."

After the ship factor's boat vanished into the darkness beyond the hull, Nathaniel took a deep breath. They had much to do, too much.

Sylvia and LuAn looked to him.

"First, we get ready to break orbit and get out of here, before anyone understands what we've got."

"What do we have?"

"A ship almost as big as the largest Imperial battlecruiser." And about a dozen times as deadly . . . if . . . if . . . his contingency plans worked. He turned back toward the bridge-cockpit. "Let's go."

XL

NATHANIEL EASED THE drives on line, then completed the checklist before squaring himself in the pilot's couch and triggering the comm. "New Avalon orbit control, this is Coordinate ship *Adam Smith,* breaking orbit this time. Breaking orbit this time."

"Coordinate vessel *Smith,* cleared outbound, radial zero nine five, remain within the orange until past beacon three. Request you remain at point one zero delta vee until clear of the home zone."

"Stet, control, holding point one zero on zero nine five this time. Point one zero on zero nine five this time." Nathaniel glanced toward the second seat where Sylvia sat monitoring his actions, trying to get some basic understanding of the board. He turned his head toward the engineering board.

LuAn nodded. "Everything's in the green."

Nathaniel stretched, but continued to scan the boards and the shipnets. While the basic layout was familiar, neither the scope and size of the ship were, and he would need a better feel before he had to implement his contingency plan.

"Feels like . . . it's big," added Swersa.

"That's the point. We need a big ship," Nathaniel said. The newly named *Smith* was big enough that there were different grav-field generators for the bridge-cockpit, and for the rest of the ship—a definite energy-saving measure for the big cargo-carrier.

Sylvia frowned.

"Coordinate ship *Smith,* this is orbit control. Interrogative destination. Interrogative destination."

It was Nathaniel's turn to frown. He wasn't about to reveal their interim or ultimate destination, but what plausible destination could he provide? Then he grinned. "Herzogov three. Herzogov three is immediate destination." A destination of the military core of the Federated Hegemony should create a little stir.

"Understand Herzogov three, *Smith.*"

"That is affirmative. Herzogov three."

"Thank you, *Smith.* Pleasant jumps."

The Ecolitan pilot went back to the boards and began a thorough scan of the systems, taking his time as he did, and interspersing his check-out with continued scans of the comm bands and the EDI. He didn't want any more deep space surprises, not after their experiences with the *Gallia.*

Nearly a stan later, he leaned back in the couch and wiped his forehead.

"All right. I've waited. Can you two let me in on the big secret?" asked Swersa.

"Yes. Sorry I haven't been too communicative, but I figured there'd be time to explain along the way." Nathaniel checked the EDIs—nothing headed their way, and a clear corridor to an out-system jump. "And there will be. We've got another three until jump point."

Swersa turned to face Nathaniel directly.

"In simple terms, we're going to destroy the Fuard High Command."

Swersa's jaw dropped. "With what? This is a cargo ship."

"Exactly. And we're going to visit a graveyard."

"A graveyard?"

"A place called Sligo. The Empire fragmented it four hundred years ago. You may recall . . ."

Swersa nodded. "I trained there, but that was years ago, and even then . . ."

"There's a lot of free metal hanging around."

"I don't think I'm going to like this." Swersa paused. "And just how are you going to turn this cargo hulk into a warship?"

"I'm not. I'm going to turn it into the biggest high-speed torp ever launched."

The older Ecolitan paled.

"I don't like it, either," Nathaniel admitted. "But the Fuards are on the fringe of starting a war between Accord and the Empire, plus a civil war on Artos. The civil war will allow them to take Artos, and begin to turn New Avalon into a protectorate. The Empire can't respond, not with the animosity created toward Accord, and not with three major fleets being shifted away from the Three System Bulge toward Sector Five."

"Just how will devastating the Conglomerate High Command stop this war? That's assuming you can even pull off this miracle."

"It will be a disaster, not a miracle," confessed Whaler. "I calculate that it will bring home three points. First, that Accord can create vast destruction without use of a single known armed vessel. Second, that governments should not be allowed to manipulate others into fighting their wars, not and get away with it. And third, that Accord is impartial enough to rescue the Empire, since the Coordinate can obtain absolutely no advantage from this, economic or military." The pilot smiled. "Except to prevent an unnecessary war."

"Won't the Conglomerate . . ."

"They can't really get to Accord, except through the Empire, or the other major outsystems, or by taking incredibly out-of-the-way jumps, which won't leave them with much energy to spare," pointed out Sylvia.

"Plus, it's very hard to carry out a war when you have no coordination and command structure left." Not to mention high collateral damage, he added to himself. Would he be part of the collateral damage? There was an awfully high risk of that.

"I don't know." LuAn touched her chin. "I don't know."

"Would you let a Fuardian fleet jump through your space? That's also assuming that they're going to want to after all the information about their little covert war is spread to every intelligence service in the human Galaxy," added Sylvia.

"Will the Empire believe this?" asked Swersa.

"The I.I.S. already does, but it can't change things under the current political climate," answered Sylvia.

"In short, the mob still wants to whack the Coordinate, and the Fuards are somehow encouraging them."

"I think that sums it up," acknowledged Nathaniel.

Swersa turned to Sylvia. "How many links to what you two do have?"

"Enough," answered Sylvia. "Enough."

"When I got that message from the Prime, I was worried." LuAn grimaced. "I don't think I understood how much I should have worried."

There wasn't much either of the other Ecolitans could have said, and they didn't.

Nathaniel dropped back into the shipnets, trying to improve his feel for the huge cargo boat.

XLI

"STAND BY FOR jump. Mark . . . four, three, two, one . . . jump."

As Nathaniel touched the jump stud, the big ship turned inside out, black becoming white, then, after that timeless and endless moment of jump, reverting to black.

Thirty percent of the power—gone from one jump, and not that long a jump. No wonder Hanoverian had gone bankrupt.

He scanned the screens. No EDI tracks, just the selectively compressed image of the representational screen showing the Sligo system—out of scale. With a slow release of his breath, he eased the *Smith* on course toward the long-abandoned asteroid metal processing facility in the Sligan belt.

"What are we doing?" asked Swersa.

"Heading in-system to the processing center."

"They just left it? Half a system away from where it was used?" asked Sylvia. "I know you said they had, but . . . that's a lot of equipment, and you look at a place like Artos, starving for fabricated metals and technology . . ."

Nathaniel went through the shipnets again, then rechecked the drives and board readouts. Except for a slow pressure loss in the aft cargo section and the exorbitant use of power, the ship seemed fine. The EDI screen was clear, and he hoped it remained that way.

"Economics again. You saw what we paid for this, and we probably got it for a third or less of what it cost to build. Relative energy costs always climb in a developed system, even if absolute costs drop. That increases the comparative disadvantage of high-cost, high-bulk transport, and transporting anything across stellar distances is costly. Smaller ships can do it cost-effectively if they carry extremely high-value cargoes. Iron or even carbon steel or specialty alloys are not that high value.

Plus, carrying all that potentially magnetic material plays hell with jumpshift generators after just a few shifts, and that increases the maintenance costs. The *Smith* probably has the capacity to supply all Artos can afford for a year—six months anyway—in one trip. All of that factors into a cost spiral . . . multiple cost spirals really . . . the bottom line is that big ships don't work, except when you're planoforming and need everything—and some government foots the bill. It's still not strictly economic, but provides the illusion that it is. Add to that the fact that there's always someone out there who thinks big is better, generally who's new to the industry . . ." Nathaniel broke off as he saw the glazed look begin to appear in the eyes of both the other Ecolitans. "Sorry. I didn't mean to go on and on."

"Just about the time I forget that you're an economist," said Sylvia with a small laugh, "you remind me."

"For an economist . . . you are . . ." Swersa groped for a word or phrase.

"Terribly bloody-minded," Nathaniel suggested as he rechecked the EDIs, which were still clear, thankfully.

". . . you're suggesting a pretty costly solution," LuAn concluded.

"In war, all solutions are costly," pointed out Nathaniel. "Especially losing. The real winner is the one who can get everyone else to pay. That's what the Fuards have been trying, and we're going to present the bill for collection."

After a glance at the two, Whaler tried again. "Look. War is economic . . . whoever spends more generally wins, except our friends who're going to receive their just desserts thought they had found a way around that law. And they probably have, and the Galaxy won't be a better place for it if anyone thinks it will work again. We're going to make sure that message is delivered."

Another silence filled the bridge-cockpit.

"We've got time," suggested Sylvia. "You never finished why the Sligans had a mining station so far from the planet."

"I'll try not to ramble on," said Nathaniel. "There are effectively two ways to mine iron—you take it to where there's power and smelt it or you take power to the iron. By using small miners—exploitation, if you will—most systems with metallic asteroids can keep costs the lowest by building a fusactor-based processing facility somewhere near the belt. It's outside any major gravity well, and you can use low-acceleration barges on long declining orbits. One load of steel or iron is the same as any other. You just keep the pipeline full. And you keep a bunch handy in case the natives, the exploited miners, threaten to hold back." He shrugged. "That's what we're after. The reserve inventory. No one's touched it. There wasn't any reason to . . . not until now."

"Just a lot of iron? That's going to make the difference? No weapons, no . . . planet-busters . . ." LuAn frowned slightly.

"Several years ago, you might recall that comet that hit Raisa, an ice and rock comet massing only a few hundred tonnes. The terminal velocity was somewhere around fifty klicks a second."

"Fairly big mess, as I recall. It wiped out a few towns, created a killer storm, and sterilized part of one continent."

"The mass of the *Smith*—empty—is well over one hundred times that. Do you have any idea what terminal velocity on drives is?"

"The atmosphere . . . it would be like hitting a barrier."

"The Fuard Command is on Tempte. It's a nickel-iron asteroid put in orbit around Tinhorn. It doesn't have much atmosphere to speak of. The shields will last a while . . . until the ship gets lower . . . low enough, anyway."

Swersa paled. "You wouldn't . . . the collateral damage from that sort of orbital fragmentation . . ."

"The last war the Empire started left this . . ." Nathaniel gestured to the screens that showed the lifeless system and the slagged fragments that had been Sligo. "There are five fleets mustering to take on the Coordinate, because of what the Conglomerate has set up. Do you have any better suggestions?"

"But, no one's declared war, nothing's happened yet."

Nathaniel took a deep breath. "Let me get this straight. If I wait until millions die, then it will be all right to unleash a terrible weapon. If I bring devastation on those who would create it, and who have already started a civil war on one planet and starved millions on others, then I'm history's greatest villain."

"Starvation?" asked LuAn.

"Oh, the synde bean plague," answered Sylvia, her voice hard and falsely bright. "That was unleashed by the Fuards or the Fuards and the Federated Hegemony together. The last hard figures we had were over fifteen million dead."

"But an entire planet?"

"The collateral damage won't impact the entire planet, but the point still holds—if I don't do something, millions more will die." Whaler's eyes flicked across the EDI screens.

"You're holding a people responsible for the actions of a few leaders."

"Exactly. Who else should be held responsible?" asked Nathaniel. "They allow the system to continue. No government can stand against its people, not if they really want to change it. So . . . any protests that they can't do anything about it are really a statement that they don't want to pay the price for changing it. Why should the rest of the Galaxy pay? Or have you forgotten our oath?"

"I haven't faced a case where the price was this high," Swersa said tiredly.

"Neither have I." Nathaniel took a long, slow breath, and went back to the pilot's board, hoping it wouldn't be that long before they reached the Sligan belt and the long-abandoned processing center.

After a few units, he turned back to Swersa. "If you wouldn't mind studying that cargo board . . . we're going to need to do some loading once we reach the processing center. It would help if someone were familiar with the equipment."

Swersa nodded. "I can do that."

Nathaniel went back to the board, then, in between scans, began to call up the specs for the ship's cargo boats.

Sylvia, with occasional glances toward Nathaniel, studied the procedures manual, while Swersa shifted to the cargo board.

Although time did not fly by, Nathaniel felt he still hadn't worked out all he needed to do by the time the *Smith* neared the shielded Institute beacon that marked the abandoned processing facility.

"We're about there."

"Wherever there is," murmured Swersa.

He ignored the comment and eased more power on the forward thrusters, watching the closure rates ever so carefully until the big cargo carrier floated opposite a flattened bricklike asteroid.

"That should do it."

"There's stuff piled all over that," observed Sylvia.

"They just used a big laser to slice and flatten it," he noted, "and then they stacked different products in different sections. Out there are tonnes of steel—or iron as the case may be— and we need to take a quick inventory and determine exactly what will fit where. In essence, we're going to transfer all those lumps of metal onto the *Smith*, or into the boats, or both."

"That's all?" asked Swersa.

"Even with the heavy magtites and loading scooters, it's likely to take a long time—several days, perhaps—for three of us to load all of it correctly. And we'll have to be very careful, because, unlike most cargo vessels, we don't have any backups."

He didn't feel the smile he offered.

XLII

NATHANIEL SLUMPED ONTO the couch. The rough blocks of iron and the shorter girders might have been weightless, but inertia and mass they had, and attempting to move them, even with magtites and the loading scooter, had used muscles he hadn't exercised in a while—a long while.

After two days, everything ached, and while the *Smith* carried as much as Nathaniel dared pack into her, he still had more work to do before they could break orbit.

"You need to eat," said Sylvia. "We all do."

"Eat . . . I suppose so." He dragged himself erect in the mingee and bounce-floated aft toward the crew room that doubled as mess and lounge.

Swersa had two mealpaks on the table stick-tights and was taking a third out of the heater. "If this is class one, I don't ever want to see class two."

"He didn't say whose class one—probably . . . I don't know . . ." Whaler eased himself onto the plastic chair that was locked into place, and sipped from the bulb—some lime-flavored concentrate drink with a vaguely metallic aftertaste. The stew goulash was better, but with too much pepper and a bitter edge. The biscuits were bland and totally tasteless, a definite improvement.

"What does economics say about food?" asked Sylvia.

"You don't make stored food taste very good, because if it is, it gets pilfered."

"You economists are such cynics," said Swersa after finishing a mouthful of something.

"That's because we quantify human behavior, and most of it's not very uplifting."

"I don't get it . . . or maybe I do, and don't want to face it," said LuAn. "We've filled the ship to the edge of its tonnage."

"Actually, somewhat over that . . . just short of its jump capacity."

"That will drain the power," pointed out the white-haired Ecolitan.

"That's right. We'll have to repower, but I've got that figured out."

"Oh?"

"Basic economics again. We're talking ten million credits or more of power. Most systems are perfectly willing to do that for an unarmed cargo boat, few or no questions asked."

"You are pretty cynical about human nature," said Sylvia quietly, lifting her drink bulb.

"I prefer the term realistic." He laughed harshly. "That way I won't be too disappointed."

Sylvia reached out and squeezed his knee. "There are good people out there."

"I know. That's who we're doing this for." He looked down at the empty mealpak. "I guess I was hungry." He eased out from the fixed chair and eased the mealpak off the stick-tight.

"We're loaded," said Swersa. "Now what?"

"If you wouldn't mind, we need to make some alterations to the boats. You could help me a lot." The pak went into the disposer.

"Fine."

"What do you need from me?" asked Sylvia.

"You need to get those packages ready for the message torps. We need the word spread everywhere we can. Not that I expect many people to understand. Most people only understand what they want to, or what they're forced to."

She nodded.

"And after that . . . we'll see."

Nathaniel and LuAn made their way aft almost silently, all the way to boat bay ten. He had decided to start aft and work forward.

"What are we doing?"

"Reconfiguring the drives and shields." He stepped into the bay and walked up to the boat, only twice his height, where he triggered the hatch. Once it opened, he reached inside and released the access cover over the drive section, then walked back to the drive thrusters. Swersa followed.

"That's what we need to change."

Just forward of the paired thrusters was what he needed—the control module. He glanced at the boat drive controls, calling up the images he had memorized so many weeks—had it only been weeks—before and comparing them to the controls.

Why had he ever thought he could convert a drive into what amounted to a large-scale message-torp drive?

Because you have the Ecolitan complex—we can do anything, convert any machinery at hand to the dirty job necessary. The unspoken words sounded bitter, and they were. Who was he to determine which planets and people lived? Except . . . if he didn't, then millions of others would continue to die as the Fuards set the Galaxy aflame. But why were politicians so stupid?

"They aren't. They want to stay in power, and that means catering to popular prejudices will mean war between the Empire and Accord."

"What?" asked Swersa.

"Sorry. I was muttering about politicians instead of getting to work."

With a sigh, he picked up the long-handled miniature hex wrench and began to remove the cover to the drive controls. "Can you loosen the other side?"

"That I can do."

Removing the override governors was simple enough—at least in theory and comparatively, since the boats were meant to be foolproof, and the governors were hardware with circuit blocs. He had to lay and bond a strip of silver between the contacts, probably overly wide, but it didn't matter that much, not for the remaining single flight of the boat.

Still, his hands were trembling after that effort, even with Swersa's help, and they had to sit on the boat hatch ramp in the clammy boat bay and rest for a moment before they went back and replaced the drive control cover. Next came disabling the power lines to the grav-field generators and the habitability module. That would allow the firin cells' power to be concentrated where it counted—drives and shields, mostly shields.

"Four adjustments . . . nearly a standard hour."

"That doesn't seem bad."

"With eight more to go?" he asked. "Hope we can do better."

They did do better. It only took half that for the next boat.

He tried not to think about the program changes to the guidance systems, so that the boats would home on a signal besides that of the *Smith* and hold course, even if the signal were eliminated.

Between drive and power reconfigurations, and the slight modifications to the homers, it was nearly a full day later, including much needed sleep, before the three settled themselves back in the bridge-cockpit.

"Everyone ready?" asked Nathaniel.

"Stet," offered Sylvia.

"Stet."

Nathaniel began to ease power to the thrusters, very, very gently. Even so, the big ship shivered, and he kept scanning the boards and the systems until he had the *Smith* on a clear outbound corridor.

Then he took a deep breath.

"I still wonder. This is insane." Swersa shook her head. "Attacking the center of the Conglomerate."

"No. That's what everyone says when you break the rules. But there's never been a good defense against attack from space—except lots of ships—and that's expensive. And if you put all your ships around your home system, then that leaves others unprotected, and you can't maintain a large multi-system government without projecting force."

"But, why hasn't this come up before?" asked Sylvia.

Swersa just winced.

"Who said it hasn't?" Nathaniel shook his head. "Both sides tried it in the Secession, except the Coordinate was more successful. It's been four centuries, and people forget because they'd rather not understand how high the stakes are and how vulnerable populations are. And no military figure or politician is about to remind them."

With that, he went back to checking the *Smith* and all the systems, conscious of just how close he'd loaded the ship to its margins. While he trusted everything was braced and solid, or more than that, there wasn't any point in not being cautious.

They reached the Sligo outsystem jump point without incident—and without any stray EDI traces.

"Ready for jump . . . mark, four, three, two, one . . . jump."

The universe turned inside out once more, black to white, and back again, for the endless and instantaneous transition between congruency points.

"We're at less than thirty percent, thanks to all that mass," pointed out LuAn.

"That's why we're headed in system here. It's as short a jump as possible from a non-Conglomerate system. We might have seventy percent when we emerge beyond Tinhorn." Nathaniel frowned, then added, "LuAn, Sylvia . . . can you two get out the power cables and make sure every one of the boats is fully charged? And the courier."

"You want that done before we repower."

"Every margin possible," he admitted.

The two dragged themselves aft, not to return until they were approaching their interim destination.

"A couple—three and seven—are bleeding power," announced Swersa.

"How much?"

"Two, three percent. That's in just three days."

"We can handle that. Thank you both."

He waited until they were back in position, not that it mattered, before transmitting.

"Galatea one, this is Coordinate ship *Adam Smith*, inbound station this time."

"Where did you come up with that name?" asked Sylvia as they waited for the Frankan outpost's response.

"He was an ancient economist who believed in the invisible hand of economics, or something like that. It's better than calling us *The Invisible Hand*, I thought."

"Coordinate vessel *Smith*, interrogative intentions. Interrogative intentions."

"Intentions are repowering and transit. I say again, repowering and transit."

"Thank you, *Smith*. Cleared to beacon one three. One three."

"We're reaching the end of the easy part," he announced.

"If this has been the easy part, can I get off?" asked Sylvia, straight-faced.

"Of course. As soon as we finish the hard part."

"Somehow, I was afraid you'd say that."

XLIII

THE SPECIAL ASSISTANT waited for the secure link to unscramble and the image of the Grand Admiral to slip into place before she spoke.

"Did you get my latest?"

"Yes. I got the report from your tame Ecolitan—and the former I.I.S. agent. My analysts and D.I. both agree that it's first rate, and probably on target, especially the apprendices. I took the liberty of sending a copy to the External Affairs Committee. They'll have trouble with that message to Tinhorn, though. They won't believe that it's anything but rhetoric."

"Even now?" asked Marcella.

"It's been too long since the Secession, and they don't want to remember. In time, it will make your life easier." The Admiral shrugged.

Marcella paused, then asked, "I assume that means there is no change in the plan to send the Eleventh Fleet along the Rift? Or to move the Third and Ninth Fleets?"

"As I told you earlier, Marcella, I cannot comment on rumors, not even on a secure link. As you know, I must follow the directives of the Imperial Senate." A faint smile crossed the Admiral's lips. "And, as I indicated earlier, such repositionings do take time, and we have uncovered several logistical problems that may add to that." A nod followed. "But, after a meeting called by the Senate Pro-Consul, I was able to assure them that the Ministry of Defense will indeed be able to carry out their directives, and stands ready to implement the wishes of the Senate . . . whatever they may be."

"Translated loosely, the idiots are convinced, despite all factual evidence to the contrary, that Accord is engaging ecological warfare on the Empire. That's even after a clear statement with evidence from the Ecolitans that the Fuards are behind this?"

"There isn't enough evidence, Marcella, not the kind that they can parade before their constituencies. Nothing that will satisfy the Senator from Heraculon, who reports more than five million deaths from energy shortage-related starvation. Of course, he also won't admit that he supported energy monoculture because of the contributions from the Agricultural Technology Alliance. Nothing will satisfy the Senator from Squamish, where deaths are nearing two million with the failure of the fisheries. Tell me. Can you transport that much food?"

"You know we couldn't, not even across a system, let alone transstellar distances. We've diverted everything we can, and it's changed almost nothing."

"Then how can I brook the will of the Senate?" The Admiral shrugged a last time. "Unless something changes the political dynamic. Right now, it's still easier to oppose Accord than the Conglomerate."

"They really would rather be reelected and see the Galaxy in flames."

"Hasn't it always been that way? Do you really expect them to behave any other way?"

"I could hope."

"Hope does not vote, Marcella. Remember that." With a swirl of colors, the Admiral's image disappeared, leaving a dark screen.

XLIV

THE *SMITH* DROPPED OUT of its jumpshift into normspace, and Swersa looked up from the screens before her to Nathaniel. "The screens are skewed. Where are we?"

"We're actually below Tinhorn's ecliptic. No one looks out here. Or down here."

"Can you explain this in simple terms?" Sylvia twisted in the second pilot's seat, but she kept her hands clear of the manual controls.

"Application of the anthropomorphic principle number three."

Both looked at him blankly.

"Nathaniel," began Sylvia. "I know what you're trying to do. That's clear. And it's clear that you're worried. But there's no one close to us—even I can see that on the screens. So, could you explain? Why are we trying to attack from here, when the system is up there—if up is the right word?"

The pilot forced himself to take a deep breath, leaving his eyes and senses on screens and shipnets. "Everyone looks up, scans up . . . or out. But we're coming in perpendicular to the ecliptic from below. By the time we register on the EDI screens, our TIV will be too high for them to have much time to react." Nathaniel smiled grimly. "And even if they do, they won't have more than a few ships with which to do it. No one puts big lasers in orbit around inhabited planets. Or large fleets. They can't intimidate other systems there. Also, people are afraid of that much power too close to home." He coughed, hoping he wasn't getting something, or that there wasn't some allergen in the ventilating system.

"In theory, anyway, it's very simple. Large and small objects at excessive rates of speed have a tendency to create large craters when they impact immovable objects. They also create great heat and climatic violence when they impact comparatively shallow bodies of water. The Fuard military command is on a planetoid which was laboriously dragged into orbit around Tinhorn. I have made some major modifications to the drives on the mining boats, and to the directionality of the shields. There are similar modifications to the drives on the *Smith*. The courier is for our departure."

"They won't let you get that close," pointed out Swersa.

"That's why we're here. Down here—anthropomorphic principle number three. Nobody looks underfoot."

"Which you just made up," quipped Sylvia.

"Right. But I'll stand by it."

"Economist and now anthropologist."

"No. Anthropomorphic principles were developed by cosmologists and physicists to explain what cold, hard science couldn't. Something like that, anyway." His eyes went to the EDI screens and the glitter of energy points surrounding Tinhorn . . . so many that, at the scale showing, the area around the planet was more of a glow than a sharp image.

They still had a long way to go, and they needed more velocity. He checked the power situation. Fifty-eight percent. Forest lord! The cargo carrier was definitely an energy guzzler, not that he'd expected anything much different, and close to sixty percent would be more than enough. More than enough, indeed.

He eased more power into the thrusters, setting the acceleration on the high end of the expected commercial range, just slightly high. Then his senses dropped back to the shipnets to monitor the stresses on the *Smith*. Outside of a faint creaking, and increased pressure on aft retaining bulkheads—compensated for, he hoped, by the internal grav-fields—nothing seemed to have changed.

Tinhorn remained a point of light, not measurably closer, nor did the EDI patterns around the Conglomerate Centre planet change as the *Smith*—the erstwhile *Turner*—lumbered "upwards" through the darkness toward the plane of the Tinhorn system. The three Ecolitans sat and watched, sat and watched.

One Ecolitan occasionally made minor power and course adjustments as slowly, ever so slowly, the blue dot that was the *Smith* on the representational screen crept closer to the red dot that Nathaniel had placed over the planet.

The nearer the *Smith* came, the more often he scanned through the frequencies, mentally regearing his mind to think in Fuardian, trying to match those on standing wave and those with direct radiation.

After a time, the signals seemed to bounce through his thoughts, as well as through the net, none quite steady enough . . . yet. The *Smith* only seemed to creep toward Tinhorn and the metallic asteroid that was Tempte, and their target, but Nathaniel had no intention of boosting acceleration since that much of a power increase could trigger increased attention. He merely wanted to create the impression, were anyone even looking, that the cargo carrier was the victim of poor piloting or jump error, and struggling back toward the ecliptic on a standard power curve.

Finally, he verified the signals he wanted, and locked them into the net. Then he turned in the pilot's couch. "Swersa?"

"Sir?"

"I want you to maintain this heading. I'll be aft. Let me know if anything strange occurs. Anything." He slipped out of the couch, and started aft.

"Are you hungry?" asked Sylvia before he reached the hatch.

"Ah . . . actually, yes."

"How long will what you're doing take?"

"Half a stan, could be a little longer."

"I'll have some of our class-one fare waiting. It's one of the things I can do for you ship jockeys." She smiled.

"Thank you." He smiled back. "I'm sorry."

"That's all right, but I want to learn how to pilot one of these. You aren't doing this again."

"You will."

"Promise?" she asked.

"Promise."

"Good."

Nathaniel paused, then turned to Swersa. "Oh, I forgot to tell you. I'll be opening the boat ports. Leave them open."

"Yes, sir."

He climbed back into his space armor and checked the tool set but left the face plate open. Again, he started with boat ten, the farthest aft.

The drill was simple enough. Enter the boat, open the port, tune the homer, set the makeshift cutout to leave the autopilot on the last homer course, leave the boat.

Nine boats and nearly a standard hour later he slumped onto the plastic chair in the crew lounge. His class-one fare—and Sylvia—were waiting.

"Just eat. You're turning white."

"Swersa all right?" He took a bite of yet another mystery protein swathed in a cheese sauce.

"She's worried. I can tell that."

"So am I." Two more bites of mystery protein vanished.

"Do we have any chance to get out of this?" Her gray eyes met his. "Straight talk."

"If things go as planned."

"If? How likely is that?"

He swallowed some of the metallic lime drink. "You need to eat, too."

"I did already, while you were working. I took some to Swersa, also. How likely?" she asked again.

"I don't know. What I've rigged up *ought* to work. But like a lot of things we do, you can't test them in advance. And I don't have the experience for this sort of thing. No one does, these days." He lifted his shoulders, then dropped them. "I'm hoping."

She reached out and squeezed his shoulder. "We don't have any choice, and I think you're doing the only thing we can."

"It's not the right thing," he said slowly. "We did all the right things, and no one listened. So we have to do this. But it still bothers me. It bothers me that numbers don't matter, that reason doesn't matter, that only force matters. And I can't tell Swersa that. I've pushed her too hard anyway."

"Greed and force—that's all most people listen to," Sylvia said.

"This is definitely force." He took the last bites of his class-one ship's fare. "I have to keep telling myself that five million innocents have already died, and several million more will die, even if we succeed. If we don't, the number goes to hundreds of millions."

"I know. Do you feel better?"

"Close to human . . . for now. I guess we'd better get back up front. Before long, things are going to get messy."

"They've been that way all along." She bent closer and kissed his cheek.

He turned and held her, more tightly than he'd intended, despite the armor he wore. He just held on as if the moment would never end—as did Sylvia.

Finally, he let go, reluctantly, and so did the gray-eyed woman. After a last kiss, they headed forward.

He dropped into the first's seat and donned the input set, setting the helmet in the holder to his left. All the boat doors remained open. Pressure leakage from the aft section had increased slightly, which probably meant the leak was in one of the boat ports, not that it would matter, not much longer.

"Nothing new, sir," reported Swersa. "Chatter, but that's been it. Seems like a lot of in-system traffic."

"It is a military base, even if most of the ships are elsewhere."

He studied the screens . . . less than an hour at current acceleration. He shook his head. They still hadn't been spotted, not yet.

Pursing his lips, he ran through what seemed to be the Conglomerate tactical bands, finding nothing of interest, not for another quarter stan when a higher-powered standing wave transmission caught him.

"CommCon . . . energy source plus ten . . . apparent heading into the red zone . . . below the ecliptic."

Nathaniel nodded and eased a trace more power to the thrusters. Total power load was down to thirty-eight percent.

". . . interrogative any delta vee . . . delta vee . . . on low ecliptic . . ."

". . . unknown vessel . . . matches cargo-carrier, class super one . . . drives tuned to Alpha scale . . ."

"That's GraeAnglo comm scale."

". . . delta vee is three plus gees . . ."

Nathaniel checked his own figures. The *Smith*'s actual acceleration had crept up to nearly four plus gees. He shuddered to think of the catastrophe that would occur should the grav-fields fail. *Then don't think about it*, he reminded himself.

Two points of light on the rep screen veered slowly on an intercept course, almost casual in their convergence.

"Interrogative your last . . ."

"This is Nordel one, correction to my last, CommCon, target at four plus gees."

Nathaniel eased more power into the thrusters, balancing the acceleration against the stress on the grav-field generators and the *Smith* itself. A momentary heaviness pressed him into the couch as the grav-fields readjusted.

"CommCon, one, target continues to accelerate."

"Unknown ship entering Tinhorn control. Request you decel immediately. Request you decel immediately." The signal smashed across all the normal traffic frequencies, as well as the emergency band.

Nathaniel winced. The same message appeared in the comm window of the EDI screen.

"They seem upset, sir," observed Swersa hoarsely.

Nathaniel swallowed, realizing he wore armor and they didn't. "LuAn, Sylvia . . . you should . . . suit up. Right now. You can leave your helmets cracked, but suit up. We'll probably lose our atmosphere sooner or later, and it could be before too long."

"Yes, sir."

Sylvia eased herself out of the second pilot's couch, her hand squeezing his shoulder as she passed.

"CommCon, two here. Intruder remains on constant bearing, decreasing range, Prime one, zone one."

"This is CommCon. Scramble all hornets this time. Scramble all hornets."

"CommCon, Hornet leader. Scrambling this time."

Nathaniel glanced back to the boards, watching as the EDI tracks of the additional interceptors began to separate from the small circle on the rep screen that represented Tempte—the asteroid base housing Conglomerate military headquarters.

"CommCon, we have intruder. Course unchanged, velocity increasing . . . mass indications off the scale . . ."

Nathaniel continued to ease power up on the thrusters, although he couldn't go much farther, because each increment also increased the grav-field drain even more proportionately, and the *Smith* was down to just above twenty percent and burning more power than a battlecruiser pushed to max gee. Then, the *Smith* massed more than any mere battlecruiser, considerably more.

Sylvia, in full suit, slipped into the couch paralleling his.

"Unidentified ship, halt and identify. Halt and identify."

Ignoring the request, the Ecolitan dropped into the datanet, running his own computations. Already, they were heading into the dilation zone, and that meant he had to think faster than the Fuards.

Before the ship came anywhere close to Tinhorn he was going to have to reduce the thrust, because the grav-fields would have to go to the shields for the *Smith* to get past the torps of the Fuard corvettes and close enough to Tempte. There was little point in getting squashed—or releasing multiple thousands of tons of steel and iron from grav-field restraint.

"Hornet leader, this is CommCon. Authentication follows. Attack at will. Attack at will."

Nathaniel snorted to himself and began to ease back on the thrusters. The Fuards were rattled—as if he could have halted. The old cargo boat didn't have enough power left to reverse the velocity she'd built, and she was centered on Tempte's underside.

The shields flared into the amber, then eased back into the green.

Nathaniel frowned. The hornets, corvettes from the EDI indicators, weren't close enough for torps, even boosted torps. The shield flare had to have been space debris—a big chunk to create that much strain on the shields.

"Suited, sir," reported Swersa.

"Stand by, no. Swersa, would you go back to the lifeboat bay and power up the courier? Get it ready for launch?"

He eased the ship's shield into more of a point, focusing the energy diverted from the thrusters into the forward shield.

"Yes, sir."

He could detect a shade of relief in the white-haired Ecolitan's voice, he thought.

Two sets of dashed lines flickered from the lead interceptors, already almost flanking the *Smith*. The torps arrowed straight toward the cargo-carrier. Because of the relative velocities, Nathaniel could see that the *Smith* would probably clear the fire zone of the first two Fuardian ships without affording another shot.

. . . *eeeee* . . . *eeee* . . .

The shields barely flickered.

"Hornet lead, target exceeding range. TIV estimated as nearing half-ell."

"Interrogative half-ell in system."

"Affirmative, Hornet lead. Affirmative."

Nathaniel half-nodded. The only thing that would stop the *Smith* now was a large chunk of real estate, and there weren't any chunks between the ship and Tempte and CommCon. The laws of inertia being what they were, the Fuards had no time to put any there, and with the speed, the shields, and the inertia of the huge cargo-carrier, nothing beside several battlecruisers would be enough to stop it. And the nearest battlecruiser was somewhere beyond the orbit of the fifth planet.

After all, only idiots drove iron-filled cargo-carriers directly at asteroids around planets at high sub-light speeds.

"Sorry about that," he murmured. "Sometimes natural laws work for you, and sometimes, they don't." Just because nothing could stop a large mass, however, didn't mean that the small entities within it couldn't be stopped.

He triggered the intercom and local comm. "Strap in, Swersa. We're under attack and the gee fields are going to oscillate." He turned his head as he checked his own harness. "You, too."

Sylvia nodded and followed his example.

"CommCon, Hornet squad commencing attack. Commencing attack."

The six corvettes appeared ever nearer on the screens, the distance shrinking moment by moment. A dashed line streaked from one corvette, then another, and then a third.

Nathaniel tightened his lips, then dropped most of the gee field power into the shields, pulsed them . . . once, twice . . .

Eeeee . . . eeee . . . eeeee . . .

The forward screens blanked with the impacts and amber lights cascaded across the board, then settled . . . slowly . . . into the green.

The Ecolitan wanted to shake his head . . . and wipe his sweating forehead. He didn't *think* anything could stop the *Smith*, but . . . he'd never tried anything remotely approaching what he was doing. And unlike his distant forbear, he had only limited training and was gambling on mass and velocity being enough—and that they would survive the pounding the cargo-carrier was about to take.

Three more dashed lines flared from the corvettes that the *Smith* rumbled toward. Nathaniel could almost imagine the fabric of space vibrating with the mass and speed of the cargo-carrier, except space didn't have that much fabric to vibrate.

Eeeee . . . eeee . . . eeee . . .

The screens flared again, three times in sequence, and only one shield even registered amber, but momentarily.

Then, almost impossibly, the *Smith* was past the second line of corvettes, and the space between the Fuard craft and the cargo-carrier seemed to widen even faster than it had closed, and Tinhorn had changed from a point of light on the screens to a disc. Tempte was finally visible as a point almost merged with Tinhorn.

Nathaniel swallowed, then noted the third line of corvettes, nearly a dozen in all.

"CommCon, Stinger squads commencing attack."

A dozen? He turned to Sylvia. "All right. Into the courier. Quickly."

"No."

He turned in the couch and looked at the gray-eyed former dancer. "Look. Fair is fair. You can't help me from here on into Tinhorn. Someone has to finish this. Once we're locked on final course, I'll get back there. Leave the lock open."

He activated the comm to Swersa. "Swersa, listen."

"Yes, sir?"

"Just in case . . . if I'm not in good shape . . . or . . . anyway . . . use a little power, as little as possible, to get the courier clear of the *Smith*. Then use a single large burst . . . and nothing for a good half stan after at least. The accumulated velocity will bat-ass you straight up at right angles to the ecliptic until you're dust-free. Save your juice for decel. You'll need it. Once you clear the dust, jump straight for the Rift. There's enough power to get us to the Coordinate."

Maybe not a lot more, he thought, but they certainly didn't want to be caught anywhere else, not if what he had begun worked. "Understand?"

"Yes, sir."

"Yes." Sylvia's voice was calm. She rose, then bent and kissed him. "If you don't come, I'm coming back for you."

"I'll come." *If there's any way at all.*

His senses went back to the screens and nets even before Sylvia cleared the bridge-cockpit. Pressure leaks were building, especially aft, and the stress meters were registering strains that the cargo boat probably hadn't been designed for.

A series of dashed torp lines flickered from the corvettes ahead, corvettes that seemed to close impossibly quickly, except that he knew that the *Smith*'s built-up velocity was the major reason for the closure rate.

"CommCon, Stinger lead. Torps away and on target."

On target, all right. That Nathaniel could see, but he didn't have the skill to move the *Smith*, not without tearing the ship to shreds. He kept hoping that velocity, beefed-up shields, and speed-induced grav-distortion would prove enough.

Eeeee . . . eeee . . . eeee . . .

With the flaring of shields and screens, the *Smith* shivered ever so slightly, and Nathaniel checked the course line and heading. The ship remained centered on Tempte, now a small disc in its own right.

Eeeeeee . . .

One of the screens remained in the amber. Nathaniel watched, even as he triggered the comm link. "Courier, this is cockpit. Comm check."

"You're clear, sir," answered Swersa.

"Good. Stand by. I'll let you know."

"Standing by."

Another torp flared past, not close enough to place any more of a load on the shields, probably a good dozen kilos wide.

"Stinger lead, this is CommCon. Intruder remains on course for Tinhorn. I say again. Intruder remains on course for Tinhorn."

Thanks for the confirmation, thought Nathaniel.

Eeeeee . . .

With yet another torp, the shields and screens flickered.

Suddenly, Tinhorn swelled, appearing seemingly *below* the *Smith*.

The Ecolitan swallowed. Was he too late? His finger flashed across the boards. "Launching boats. One . . . away. Two . . . three . . ."

The miniature points of light flared into being on the EDI screen, accelerating slowly away from and ahead of the lumbering cargo-carrier toward the asteroid that held Conglomerate military headquarters and more than a few research and repair facilities, he suspected. The boats could not have attained their speed except from the platform provided by the *Smith*, but in space, their drives were more than enough to compensate for dust density, even in system.

"CommCon, Stinger lead, intruder has released large missiles. Large missiles. Course line unknown. Course line unknown."

With a grim smile, the Ecolitan's concentration went back to the three remaining Fuard corvettes ahead, and the dashed torp lines shown on the rep screen, dashed lines that leapt toward the *Smith*.

A second series of torps followed the first, and then a third.

Amber lights flickered, only flickered, across the cockpit boards. So far, shields and mass and speed had sufficed. Would they continue to hold against the smaller attackers?

Nathaniel tried to swallow, but his mouth was too dry.

The corvette on the right flank changed course, flickered somehow. Nathaniel gulped, knowing what was coming, even before his mouth opened on the comm link. "Strap in. Impact. Strap in."

The words weren't right, but he didn't know the correct warning. There was so much he didn't know about space combat. Too frigging much.

Eeeeeee . . . eeee . . .

Surprisingly, the shudder was only slightly more noticeable than a torp impact on shields, but amber lights flashed across the entire board in a series of patterns that made no sense to Nathaniel. His forehead seemed to burst into sweat in the heat that filled the bridge-cockpit.

Another series of lights flared beyond the screens, and the outside screen panels flickered, then blackened under the energy overload. Only the center screen remained functional, and the images there wavered, distorted. Distorted by the furnacelike heat, or damage to the equipment. He struggled to check the shipnets, but the links were dead.

"Intruder is holed, leaking atmosphere. Course unchanged."

A chill wind tugged at Nathaniel's face, its cold almost comforting, and he forced himself to reach for the helmet deliberately. But his fingers still fumbled when he sealed the helmet, and then sealed his gauntlets on, his fingers already chill as the atmosphere began to shrill out of the cargo-carrier.

He checked the course line. On target, and the remaining shields still held. He hoped they would as he locked the board, then clumsily unscrambled the couch harness and struggled aft toward the lifeboat/courier bay in the dim red emergency lighting.

The deck trembled under his boots, and the atmosphere tore at him. His head ached. Partial decompression? He blinked.

Another heave underfoot—or had he tripped? Why was he so frigging clumsy? He took another step, and another.

Light flared around him. More torp bursts?

He forced another step, before the darkness rose around him, deeper than the void between systems.

XLV

VAGUE IMAGES BLURRED across his eyes, and sounds rumbled in his ears, and the sounds were like knives in his skull, the images searing as though they had been drawn with lasers.

". . . some decompression . . . burns . . . radiation . . . who knows . . ."

". . . can't hurt to keep them cool . . ."

Burns . . . burns . . . how could there have been burns? He hadn't been on Tempte . . . where thousands had to have been burned or boiled alive . . . or Tinhorn . . . with millions of casualties . . . millions . . . millions. He struggled to speak, then dropped back into darkness.

The second awakening was worse. He was bathed in heat, heat welling up from deep within, and yet his entire body shivered simultaneously, as if dipped in the space between stars.

Someone kept putting damp cloths on his forehead, cloths simultaneously too cool and too hot. And the blackness he fell back into was the steaming heat of a sealed industrial furnace, a furnace where every sinew, every bone, was seared, slowly seared, then ripped apart.

The third time, the overhead was wavering gray, with a face in it, a familiar face, except he could not make out the details.

"Tried . . . didn't . . . make . . ."

"I came and got you." The words were soft, and another cool cloth went across his forehead and his cheeks. "You didn't think I'd leave you . . . I'd never leave you. Just hang on . . . we're almost home."

Almost home? Home . . . did he have one . . . anymore? How could a mass destroyer have a home?

Her long fingers were cool on his forehead . . . cool and welcome, and he tried to hold on to her image—and failed as the heat and darkness covered him again.

XLVI

THE GRAND ADMIRAL'S shoulders squared as the image of the sandy-haired woman appeared in the screen. "I thought you'd like to know that you were right, Marcella. The Senate Pro-Consul departed a short time ago. We have been requested to pull back the fleets."

"Fact . . . mere fact, that wasn't sufficient, was it? Pages and pages of documentation, they weren't adequate, either. It only took the total conversion of the single largest military installation in the Galaxy to total energy and ten million deaths on Tinhorn." Marcella's voice was cold.

"They weren't Imperial citizens, and we didn't do it." A chilly smile crossed the Admiral's lips, one that did not extend to her eyes. "For that, the Pro-Consul was grateful, somewhat belatedly."

"And Accord?"

"The Imperial Senate has welcomed, if not with entirely open arms, Accord's offer to send scientific teams to Heraculon and the other affected planets, along with ships full of resistant bean plants and seeds. They made that offer along with their declaration against the Conglomerate. They also said they wouldn't hesitate to repeat the act against the next most-inhabited system in the Conglomerate . . . or any system contemplating commencing hostilities at this time. The message from their Prime was about as direct as I have ever had the pleasure of seeing."

Marcella shook her head. "I learned that Accord doesn't bluff from one envoy."

"Marcella, recall the jest about senators . . . five are always denser than one. There are three hundred of them."

"There isn't anything left of Tempte, and a lot of molten rock seared Tinhorn. How did they do it?"

"How? Our analysts estimate that someone drove a shielded battle-cruiser, armored to the teeth, straight into Tempte at about a half-light velocity. Do you have any idea what kind of energy that represents? They did something similar with a needleboat—several of them—except they went first and took down all the lasers and defense systems. The Conglomerate thought Tempte was impregnable. We thought so, too."

"Nothing's safe from them."

"Right now, most of the Galaxy's in shock. If it had been *any* other system besides Tinhorn, or any other attacker beside the Coordinate, we'd all be arming against Accord. Nowhere is safe against them. They've made their point, something like: By the way, would you please respect us and leave us alone?" A faint chime sounded, and the Admiral glanced to the side. "I'll have to leave in a moment for my briefing of the Emperor."

"That really isn't the point," the special assistant replied.

The Admiral waited.

"The point is that there is nothing so dangerous as directed and unrestrained action in service of principle. The Institute serves princi-ple."

"You think we should eliminate the Institute?"

"How?"

"Your point, Marcella. Besides, we might need them again. Unfortu-nately."

"Why did it take so much to convince you?" asked the special assistant.

"I was convinced a long time ago. I never doubted you." The Grand Admiral shrugged. "But . . . I doubt if anyone else could have restrained the war dogs as long as they were."

Marcella nodded. "And you hoped . . ."

"Even I hoped, daughter, even I."

XLVII

STORMS OF BOILING water, rains of iron droplets swirled around him, tearing through his thoughts, and there was heat and more heat . . . and dark-haired women running through scalding showers screaming, a blond boy looking up as he shivered into ashes . . .

Sweat poured off his forehead, searing his skin, and Nathaniel tried to open his eyes, but they failed to respond.

"Easy. Your eyes are pressure-banded in place." Sylvia's words echoed in his ears. "Don't talk. You've been through a lot."

Me? he wanted to ask. What about all those innocents on Tinhorn? Or the junior officers and men? Or the corvette pilots? How many died . . . how many . . . ?

Finally, he lifted a heavy hand, then shrugged.

"What have you been through? How about partial decompression, or metallic mist in your upper lungs, incidental radiation poisoning, burns across your eyes and face requiring a total regrowth of skin and eyes—that's why the pressure bands. Toxic systemic poisoning. You almost didn't make it. Swersa is a very good courier pilot, and the Institute had everything ready. You've been under sedation for nearly two standard weeks."

Nathaniel wanted to shake his head, but feared any motion might jar something loose. His face itched, and so did the top of his shoulders, and his head. Every muscle was stiff—if not totally pummeled out of shape.

"She's in better shape, but not wonderful, either," added a second voice, Swersa's. "She took a heavy dose of radiation dragging you through the passage and lock to the courier."

"What . . ."

"Please don't talk." A hand—Sylvia's?—gently covered his mouth.

But what about all the people? What had he done?

"You need to rest," added Sylvia. "They're going to put you back under for a while, but you needed to know we made it. Your subconscious won't struggle so much."

A cool tingling massaged his arm, and he could feel the relaxation spreading. But there was so much she hadn't said . . . so much . . .

"Oh . . . and it all worked. The Empire backed away from the war, and we're helping repair the ecologic damage there. You're going to look a little different, I'm told, more like one of your ancestors. So don't be surprised. The screen images show you'll be just as handsome . . . in a more exotic way."

Her fingers were cool on his forehead . . . cool, even as the images of a boiling planet surged through his thoughts. What had he done?

XLVIII

THE DIRECTOR LOOKED down the long and formal conference table. "Perhaps . . . perhaps . . . some of you will understand why the I.I.S. has always opposed any conflict with Accord, and particularly with the Ecolitan Institute."

"They have little regard for human life, that is certain," murmured the blond on the right at the far end.

"They ought to be tried for war crimes!"

The Director turned to the redhead. "Who do you propose would try them? War crime tribunals are usually something foisted on the loser by the winner."

"But to let them get away . . ."

"We've already lost ten million, or more. They stopped the Conglomerate and punished them. Do you suggest we take up a war against Accord when we have more than fifty planets that individually contain in excess of four hundred million people? Just how would we protect them? Or do you propose that we attempt to do them one greater and attempt to wipe out all their planets? And what would protect our people in the meantime?"

"They'll get away with it?"

"Probably," admitted the Director. "Just like the first users of nuclear weapons in ancient history did. Any other system that has the resources to retaliate—including the remainder of the Conglomerate— still has far more to lose than does Accord."

After a long silence, a hand lifted at the end of the table.

"Can you tell us how they translated a battlecruiser that close to Tinhorn?"

"They didn't. From what we can determine, they purchased an obsolete cargo-carrier, loaded it with something of high density, and then accelerated it into Tempte at high sub-light speeds." The Director paused. "Any other questions?"

"Ten million people . . . the debris and residue killed ten million people . . ."

"Correct," affirmed the Director. "That's not even a new record. The Empire murdered a mere fifteen million when it destroyed Sligo four hundred years ago. Those who are counting can take consolation in the fact that Accord concluded one of the relatively less-costly interstellar conflicts—and we lost nothing. The Emperor and the Senate should be mightily pleased."

"How . . . could anyone do that?" asked the dark-haired assistant director. "How could anyone knowingly murder that many people?"

"I doubt the Institute set out to murder any civilians. They set out to destroy totally an insane military regime. They succeeded. The collateral damage was some of the population on the planet beneath. There is a difference between debris—even large chunks of debris—killing bystanders as a result of a justified military action and targeting civilians directly."

"I didn't realize they were that bloody-minded."

"I don't think you understand. The Institute, for better or worse, operates on principle. They try to avoid small wars because the costs are disproportionate with no benefits . . . and they'll do that by deceit, assassination, or economic warfare. They will try any type of small-scale tactic to avoid war. They always back the right of an indigenous people to their own government, and the right of people to leave. That's the good side." The Director paused again. "The other side is that when they do fight, they ensure they don't have to fight that enemy again. I ask you all. Is it clear, finally, why we have opposed war with Accord?"

"But ten million innocents . . . ?"

"Those ten million were among the hundreds of millions who allowed their government to kill, through indirect biological warfare, more than fifteen million of our people in twenty systems, and another five million in the outsystems. They almost precipitated a war between the Empire and Accord that would have killed who knows how many tens or hundreds of millions more."

"But the people on Tinhorn didn't deserve that. They didn't start a war."

"They didn't?" The Director's voice was cold. "If what the Conglomerate did isn't considered a war, would you want to be around when they got really serious and started what *they* would call a war?"

"But . . . ten million civilians?"

"Do you want to tell the senator from Heraculon that it shouldn't have been done? The death toll there is nearing eight million. We're going to lose more than ten million ourselves, all told, the Halstanis several million, and associated outsystems another five to eight million from Fuardian ecological efforts. That's not a war?" The Director's eyes traversed the table. "That is all . . . for now."

XLIX

WERLIN RESTINAL WALKED up the polished wooden stairs slowly, feeling like a man headed for an execution.

"Do come in, Werlin." The Prime's voice was firm, but not exactly welcoming.

The Delegate Minister of Interstellar Commerce and shadow minister for intelligence—since the Charter forbade an official intelligence ministry—stepped into the sparsely furnished office. With the Prime was a slender dark-haired woman, also in Ecolitan greens.

"Werlin, this is Ecolitan Sylvia Ferro-Maine. She was the one teamed with Ecolitan Whaler on the Artos economic study." The Prime inclined his head to the chairs, and the woman sat immediately.

Restinal sat more slowly, turning toward Ferro-Maine's thin face. Her cold gray eyes drove right through him. He'd dreaded seeing the Prime again, but Ferro-Maine was somehow worse, and he didn't know why.

The Prime lifted a thin bound volume. "As Commerce Minister, and in your other capacities, Werlin, you have certainly read this study."

"Of course, Prime Pittsway." Restinal's lips felt dry.

"Minister Restinal, you must have been aware that New Avalon was systematically cutting off capital and technology to Artos. That was obvious on the first day we were there. The Commons certainly needed no study to confirm that." Ferro-Maine's voice was cooler than her eyes.

"No . . . until I read the study, I was not aware of that."

"Who actually requested the study?"

"I was told of the need for the study by Elder Torine."

"Who told him?" pursued Ferro-Maine.

"Prime, I must protest . . . a minister being grilled . . ." Restinal glanced at Pittsway.

"Werlin, well over twenty million people across the human Galaxy have died in this fiasco. Some of that occurred because you and Torine wanted to protect your precious and precarious government. You can stand a little grilling." For the first time, an edge appeared in the Prime's voice. "Do you wish me to announce to the entire Galaxy that your actions began this disaster?"

Restinal looked down momentarily. "I honestly do not know . . . or I didn't, for certain." He paused, more aware than ever that he sat like a rat between two cliff eagles with sharp beaks and even more powerful claws. "Subsequent events led me to believe that Delegate Verlingetti was the one who pushed for the study."

"Do you know why? Or suspect why?"

Restinal shrugged.

"Werlin," began the Prime softly, "I am well aware of your other portfolio. Surely, you have employed some of its attributes subsequent to recent events."

"I'm not certain—"

"Werlin . . . why don't you just tell us what you know about Gaetano Verlingetti? Skip the age and marital status, office, and electoral district."

Restinal glanced from one Ecolitan to the other. Both still resembled hungry and impatient cliff eagles. "Ah . . . you know about his political career. His only hobbies we know of are boxball and bird-watching. He travels a great deal to note rare species. He's on the board of a number of foundations on Accord—mostly in the education and political awareness fields. Ah . . . the Good Government Coalition, FORT—that's the Foundation for Restoring Traditions—the Business Support Fund . . ."

"They all contain politically aware and active individuals, I assume?" asked Ferro-Maine.

"Oh, very politically aware and active."

"And financially solvent, too," added the Prime. "Does Verlingetti solicit for them?"

Restinal wanted to wipe his forehead, but did not. "That is not certain."

"What is certain, Werlin?"

"Contributions to their efforts have increased since he joined their boards."

"Do you have any idea what kind of contributions?"

"All kinds. Businesses like Flinsew and AgriTech, wealthy individuals like Linsin and Bastien . . ."

"Why would Verlingetti be interested in an economic study on Artos? His interests are all linked to Accord and public policy and ecology matters here in the Coordinate." Ferro-Maine's eyes were hard as she watched Restinal.

"We . . . I don't know, Ecolitan. It might have been a political ploy. We were in a difficult position. Elder Quaestor suggested that with Ecolitan Whaler's status, he might consider a study beneath him . . . after the trade agreement. The implication was that the government . . . thought helping a smaller outsystem was beneath us."

"And you swallowed that?"

Restinal shrugged. "What harm could an economic infrastructure study do? Who pays any attention to economics?"

"As opposed to a charge of running an arrogant and highhanded government that cuts deals with the Empire and ignores small systems who have nothing to offer?" asked the Prime.

Restinal nodded.

"Can you add anything else about the study?" asked Ferro-Maine. "Why did Elder Torine agree?"

"He said he couldn't see any harm in an economic study."

Restinal did wipe his forehead, as the questions continued, seemingly endlessly.

L

NATHANIEL SHIFTED HIS weight in the inclined hospital bed and adjusted the lightweight dark goggles that protected his eyes. Lightweight or not, they tended to dig into his nose and cheeks. Sylvia had said she would be back—but not when. Why had the Prime wanted her this time? Then, while he'd been recovering, Sylvia had been spending a lot of time with Pittsway.

"Jealous . . . ?" he murmured to himself. Why? It was clear she loved Nathaniel, both from actions and words. "Insecure?" Definitely. He wasn't the dashing effective Ecolitan, just an invalid, and he hated being an invalid. Especially one with too much time on his hands to brood.

The nightmares continued—boiling rain, screaming people, and various other imaginary, yet realistic scenarios—and he had few doubts that they would continue for a long time. Yet . . . given all the circumstances, what else could he have done to guarantee that the Conglomerate's evils were stopped?

"Great—create an evil, larger evil . . ." His head turned at the faint click.

The door opened, and Sylvia—and the Prime—slipped inside, but not before Nathaniel saw the guards that had accompanied them.

"Guards . . . oh, of course."

"I can no longer afford to travel unaccompanied," said the Prime in a humorously dry tone, "now that my anonymity has been destroyed." He gestured toward the inert trideo set in the corner. "They're just about everywhere, and I understand that some faxcasters are flocking in from across the entire Galaxy. To get a profile on the leader of the most villainous Institute in human history."

"I'm sorry . . . oh, sorry, is such . . . what does it mean? You didn't do it, Prime. I did. I took the ship—"

"Ecolitan," interrupted Pittsway, firmly, but not harshly, "I told you to make contingency plans. I ensured that the Secession plan for the Old Earth mission was in those briefing books. I ordered you to take whatever steps you thought necessary. And I told you not to take half-measures. Did I not?"

"Yes, sir. But I was the one—"

"You were the one to follow orders. That's correct. And you will pay for that . . . in due time. You will always share in that responsibility, and I could not lift that from either of you. Nor would I, nor will I. At the moment, however, we have an even more immediate problem, and that is to determine who on Accord facilitated the Conglomerate's efforts." He smiled sardonically. "We just finished an intriguing, but highly inconclusive interview with Werlin Restinal that sheds more light, but not more proof, on the situation."

"And our study," added Sylvia, "which was a setup, plain and simple. We suspected that, but Restinal confirmed as much."

"This just wasn't someone trying to uncover—" began Nathaniel.

"No," said Sylvia. "The study was designed to cover up what really happened by tying the Institute to the bean plague and the rebellion on Artos."

"Well . . . there was a rebellion," pointed out Nathaniel.

"It didn't turn out quite the way most people planned, either," added Sylvia. "I can't imagine Camelot likes the idea of a Frankan system there."

The Prime looked toward the door and cleared his throat. "That can wait . . . for now."

Sylvia nodded.

"Then where did the study fit? Why did it trigger everything?" asked Nathaniel. "Did you find out who wanted the study—for real?"

"Quaestor's number two, one Delegate Verlingetti," answered Sylvia.

Nathaniel turned. "He's the one who placed Spamgall."

"I told the Prime. We were supposed to get killed, and then the bean plague that had already started on Artos would be linked to us, and the Institute."

"And another seed would have been planted discrediting the Institute." Nathaniel wanted to shake his head at the inadvertent pun. "And strengthening the Empire's resolve to take military action."

"That would have also discredited Elder Torine and the Normists," pointed out Pittsway. "Because they would have been tagged as the Institute's lackeys. That would have caused the government to fall, and Quaestor and Verlingetti and the Orthodoxists would have taken over."

"But why did Torine go with the suggestion? Or Restinal?"

"We don't know, but I can surmise," said the Prime. "Torine respects the Institute. His hold on the House is too fragile to survive the next election, but he knows that the Institute usually delivers. So he had nothing to lose. He gambled on agreeing to it."

"Verlingetti?" prompted Nathaniel.

"That is interesting. He and Quaestor had to know that they stood a good chance of winning the elections, but they worried that Torine might pull something out of a wormhole." The Prime frowned. "This is speculation now, but I surmise that was the way Verlingetti suggested the idea of the study to Quaestor."

"There's more." Sylvia turned to the Prime.

"After you left, I put a team on the bean plague," added the Prime. "I've followed their progress, and we've got a couple of resistant strains. But it's a nasty bug, one that's there's no effective remedy for, once it hits an area. All you can do is replace the beans with the resistant strains. There's already a resistant strain out there, and we've tracked it back from Camelot . . ."

"Through an outfit called AgriTech." Sylvia's eyes were bright. "Which has a small office in Harmony."

"Who sold out?"

"We can't prove it yet, but it seems clear that Verlingetti somehow got access to someone who could develop the bean plague and later, maybe even access to plague-resistant synde beans. What about Dr. Hiense?" asked Sylvia.

The Prime nodded. "Once you mentioned the contact, I had it followed up. There's nothing there—not directly. Hans Hiense is a noted authority on post-planoforming adjustments, but not on plant genetics. He's considered one of the best anywhere. The same contract for fifty years. Three children—all with the Institute, all with outstanding records. Liu Hiense is a martial arts instructor—applied hand-to-hand." Pittsway smiled.

"What aren't you telling me?"

"Hiense and Verlingetti play boxball twice a week—regularly. But that's all."

"That might be enough," mused Sylvia, "at least to give Verlingetti an idea of who else to subvert."

"I thought so, too. We're still checking. There are also some credit transfers from AgriTech to several foundations, and all of them have Verlingetti on the board."

"That sounds like an Imperial intrigue," Nathaniel protested. "Accord isn't like that."

"Accord isn't a come-lately society," pointed out Sylvia, "no matter how much you claim that it is. It might have been when your ancestor took on the Empire, but that was four hundred years ago, and from what all cubes and tapes I've had to digest—"

"Sorry."

"—It's been even more stable than the Empire. Stability always leads to intrigue."

"So what are we going to do?" asked Nathaniel.

"Take a trick out of your bag, dear." Sylvia smiled. "We're going to hold a conference for the media to lay all of this to rest. The Prime has persuaded the top four officers of the House of Delegates, on both sides of the aisle, plus Commerce Minister Restinal, to be on the panel with him to answer all the media questions."

"They agreed?"

"Not exactly willingly," admitted the Prime. "But I was able to per-

suade them that Accord could not afford internal dissention and squab-
bling at a time when much of the Galaxy would like an excuse to incinerate or otherwise remove us, and that we needed to get this behind us
and provide a united front."

Nathaniel didn't even want to guess at the methods of persuasion.

"It really wasn't that difficult," said Pittsway softly, "since I could
say to Elder Torine that it was clear he had personally done nothing
wrong."

"Stupid, but not wrong," agreed Sylvia.

"And how will a media conference resolve this mess? All we have
is speculation and logic—no real proof at all," pointed out
Nathaniel.

"If we're correct," continued the Prime. "The media conference
tomorrow will resolve everything."

"And if we're not?"

"Then . . . things will get resolved in another way, one not necessarily in our best interests."

"We take the fall?"

"Ecolitan Whaler," said the Prime somberly, "the Institute will
always take the responsibility. The only question is whether we are perceived as thoughtful and responsible killers or weapons-addicted,
unstable idiots. That is what tomorrow is all about. For the moment,
for the next several days, I only ask that you remain silent about anything you may have done after you completed the economic study on
Artos. Is that understood?"

"Yes, sir . . . but . . ."

"I promise you that I will explain, openly and publicly, and that
there will be no evasions, no justifications. The Institute must face this
with a responsible, united position. If, after I have acted, you feel that I
have not acted ethically and responsibly in any fashion whatsoever, you
will be in a position to take any actions your conscience dictates." The
Prime rose and nodded toward Sylvia. "Time is short, and I have much
to accomplish."

Sylvia rose.

"No. You two spend some time together. Try to enjoy it. Such
moments get fewer as life demands more of us." A smile creased his face,
and his eyes carried the same warmth for a moment. Then he slipped out.

Sylvia sat on the edge of the bed, bent down, and kissed Nathaniel's
cheek. "He's right."

"He's always right." The Ecolitan shook his head slowly. "Once . . . I thought I might like being Prime. Then you discover . . . I don't know. I just don't know . . ."

"We will have time to think about it."

"You think so?"

"Yes." Her voice was low. "A long time."

He put his arms around her, and she leaned back, her cheek against his, in the dimness of the hospital room.

LI

NATHANIEL WATCHED THE holo images in the corner of the darkened hospital room. He'd always been a day person, but he wondered if that would last with the sensitivity of his eyes to intense light. He'd start to find out when he was released within the next few days, according to the doctors.

He'd also start to discover if he could sleep better, and with fewer nightmares. He shook his head.

"Stop feeling sorry for yourself . . . you did it . . . no one else . . ." His eyes went back to the holo images.

The faxers centered on Gairloch Pittsway as he rose from where he sat behind the center of the table. The hologram image seemed to fill the corner of the hospital room.

"Before we open the conference to questions from the media, as Prime Ecolitan, I have a brief statement to make." The white-haired Prime surveyed the unseen faxcasters and reporters and who knew who else, then cleared his throat and spoke directly, without notes, without hesitation.

"This conference is not being held to allow those responsible to point fingers elsewhere. Nor is it held to allow a parade of excuses. Nor is it being held to justify actions. The plain fact is that as Prime Ecolitan of the Ecolitan Institute of Accord, I directed that certain actions be taken to forestall what I determined could lead to Galacticwide war. At the time I took those actions, tens of millions of individuals across the human Galaxy had died or were dying from what I determined was the onset of biological warfare undertaken by the Conglomerate. I did not delegate, nor did I debate. I acted to stop what I believed and still believe would have been an even greater human tragedy. And yes, I also acted to preserve the Coordinate.

"Whether the circumstances would have led to a larger war no one will ever know. Because those circumstances have been drastically changed, no one can know. I determined that actions were necessary, and I am responsible for those actions. Some Ecolitans have died, and others were critically injured. The entire command structure of the Fuardian military and roughly ten million individuals in the Conglomerate have perished as a result of my decisions and actions. It was my decision, and I stand on that decision."

The silence was absolute—but not for long.

"Prime Ecolitan, how can you possibly justify *any* action that caused the death of ten million civilians, no matter what the provocation?"

Pittsway's eyes went to the unseen questioner. "I am not trying to justify that action. I made the decision on the basis of the information I had. It is my responsibility. This is not the forum for debating justifications or morality. But in the interests of laying that issue to rest, I will answer the question—once. When people invoke morality in these issues, they haven't the faintest idea what they really mean. The most moral action would have been to take out the entire Fuardian High Command ten years ago, before twenty million people died across a hundred systems. Such an action would scarcely be considered moral. When people talk about morality in interstellar politics, what they really mean is justification. It may be justified that I ordered an action that killed ten million civilians because twenty million had already been killed. Justification is not morality. The only moral aspect is that the action I ordered prevented millions more deaths and a Galactic war." The Prime bowed slightly. "The remainder of the conference is devoted to factual questions. Next?"

Nathaniel nodded.

"Are you saying you do not have to justify your high-handed actions?"

"No. I am saying that any action which creates deaths can be debated endlessly as to its justifications. Justification is always after the fact, and, in that sense, is largely irrelevant. I gave the orders. Some people lived who would not have, and others died. For both the living and the dead, I am responsible. Next?"

"You are going to stand here and refuse—"

"I'm not going to debate whys and wherefores today. I'm responsible. No one else is. I'd like the next *factual* question please."

The hospitalized Ecolitan smiled grimly. Pittsway was what a Prime should be.

"Some analysts have suggested that the attack on Tempte was

designed to placate the Empire, rather than a response to a real threat. Would you comment on that?"

"Distribution of the synde bean plague has been traced to a Conglomerate-controlled outlet, as noted in the background materials distributed a short time ago. All Fuard planets began growing and harvesting plague-resistant beans more than a year ago. Deaths in the Empire and other outsystems are nearing twenty million people. Materials implicating the Conglomerate in this and other associated efforts have surfaced in at least three other independent systems. I seriously doubt that the Institute could persuade the Matriarch, for example, to reveal such information were it not so."

A faint laugh echoed through the hall.

"Analysts also suggest that a battlecruiser was used. The Institute has claimed it has no battlecruisers. Could you clarify that?"

"A large cargo-carrier was employed, filled with high-mass cargo. The total mass was greater than that of a battlecruiser. The Institute does not have, nor has it ever had a battlecruiser. Next?"

"Who was the pilot?"

"Until the next of kin of all those involved have been notified, names will not be released. In any case, the names are irrelevant, since they carried out my direct orders. Next?"

The predictable questions continued as Nathaniel watched and listened. The Prime remained cool under the glare of what had to be hot lighting and pressure.

"Are you claiming that a mere cargo ship . . . ?"

"Were the trade negotiations merely a pretext . . . ?"

"What effect will this have on outsystem relations . . . ?"

"How can other systems trust the Coordinate after this terrible disaster . . . ?"

Abruptly, the Prime held up his hand. "The questions for me are rehashing those already asked. I would suggest that you now ask any questions that you might have of the elected Delegates."

The images almost jerked to pan down the line of Delegates, showing the ascetic Quaestor, the hearty-looking Torine, a sad-faced Werlin Restinal, and a thin-faced—almost ferret-faced—Delegate who sipped from a glass of water a slender Ecolitan—Sylvia?—had placed at his right hand. The name plate before him read *Delegate Gaetano Verlingetti.*

Nathaniel peered forward before the images shifted back toward

Torine. Sylvia? In plain greens, with the darker green stripe of a support staff?

"Elder Torine, the briefing materials indicated that much of the Conglomerate war plot was discovered through a study commissioned by the House of Delegates. Is this true?"

Torine cleared his throat. "So far as the House leadership can determine, that is correct."

"Who suggested this study, sir?"

Torine coughed, shifted his weight before answering. "Both Elder Quaestor and I had discussed this."

"Elder Quaestor, why did you think such a study might be necessary?"

Quaestor shifted his weight as well under the glare of the lights. "While I would like to claim forethought—all politicians would—I assure you, I cannot. The idea surfaced because . . . we were seeking an opening with the new government of New Avalon . . . possibly for agricultural and technological-transfer development trade on Artos. Such trade would not make sense if the need were not there, and a study—an impartial study—was necessary."

"It's been said that Delegate Verlingetti actually suggested the study?"

"He did bring it to my attention."

The images shifted again, moving in on Verlingetti.

"Delegate Verlingetti, could you explain why you approached Elder Quaestor and suggested that the Institute conduct the economic study that apparently led to the Tinhorn . . . disaster?"

Nathaniel swallowed as Verlingetti opened his mouth, then closed it.

"Delegate Verlingetti?"

A panicked look crossed the man's face.

"Verificants . . ." murmured Nathaniel. Sylvia had dumped fidelitrol into Verlingetti's water, just as she once had to his drink—at a time that seemed so long ago.

"Was the Conglomerate involved with your suggesting the study?"

A slight flutter and sighing intruded over the unseen questioner's words before he finished.

"We . . . were approached by the Conglomerate. They had . . . an agreement with the ArchTories, but the ArchTory government . . . fell . . . before the agreement could be broached or implemented."

"Why would you consider an agreement with the Conglomerate? What would you gain personally . . ."

Verlingetti glanced helplessly into the lights, then stammered, "The leadership of the House of Delegates . . ."

"Would you explain that?"

Verlingetti bolted upright and started to move across the table behind the podium.

At the end of the table, Elder Quaestor buried his head in his hands.

The one set of images vanished, immediately replaced by the image of a young man at a console, a smile plastered on his face.

"The remainder of the conference here in Harmony has been closed to the media and public. We return you to our normal programming."

The hospitalized Ecolitan shook his head slowly, hoping that Verlingetti's inadvertent truth-telling would be enough to ensure the media followed the story to its true end.

After what he'd seen of human nature, he wasn't certain . . . but he could hope. That and wait for Sylvia to return.

In the meantime, the sooner the hospital doctors declared him well, the better . . . nightmares or not.

LII

THE WOODEN DOOR of the Institute hospital opened, and Sylvia stepped inside, followed by the trim, silvered-haired Prime, who closed the heavy door behind him with a firm *click*.

"What happened after they closed the conference?" blurted Nathaniel.

"What would you expect?" Gairloch Pittsway smiled crookedly and stepped toward the window, looking out into the late afternoon for a moment before turning back to Nathaniel and Sylvia. "Verlingetti is claiming he was drugged, and the media wants to know why he's opposed to telling the truth. Quaestor's insisting he didn't know, and Torine's saying nothing. Neither is Restinal."

Nathaniel squinted slightly as he looked toward the Prime and the window. The doctors had told him he'd always be sensitive to bright lights, and that the sensitivity would probably increase with age. He hoped the nightmares of boiling planets wouldn't . . . but he supposed he deserved those.

"The media has already figured out that Verlingetti was trying a literal coup and they're chasing him, and Quaestor for being his dupe," added Sylvia.

"Do you think Torine wanted the study done because he wanted us to discover the ties between Verlingetti and the Fuards?"

"We don't know that for certain," said the Prime. "But if he did know, Torine couldn't have revealed what he knew because, first, he got the information by less than ethical means, and second, because the Institute is regarded as impartial. If we revealed the connection, then the Normists could take advantage in the upcoming elections. If Torine had to suggest that, then it would have been an unfounded political charge."

Nathaniel winced. "He was willing to start a war, rather than lose an election?"

"What else is new?" asked Sylvia. "That's been going on since humans were all clustered back on Old Earth, and before probably."

"I hate to mention this . . . but verificants aren't legally accepted . . ."

"They don't have to be. With a statement appearing in everyone's house, the media will take it from here. Or Quaestor will, to save what's left of the Orthodoxists." The Prime smiled wryly at Nathaniel. "I'm not sure that any member of the Institute has created as much havoc as you two since your distant ancestor. Are you sure he was that distant?" Pittsway turned toward Sylvia. "Are you sure you want to be associated with such a Galactic menace?"

"Can you think of anyone else better suited?" Sylvia returned the smile.

"Oh . . . and do you still have a few copies of that economic report you completed—on the economic infrastructure of Artos?"

"Yes, sir." Nathaniel took a deep breath.

"Good." The Prime paused. "The Matriarch of Halstan has asked for a copy. So has the Imperial Ministry of Commerce. The Commons of New Avalon wants another two hundred . . . as part of the support documentation for chronicling the disaster."

"They were sent a dozen," said Sylvia.

"Those were mislaid, and now they desperately need copies." Pittsway's voice was dry. "Oh, and the Frankan Union has requested a dozen as part of their economic redevelopment effort now that they have occupied Artos. They've appointed a local—a Geoffrey Evanston—as their interim Gouverneur General. So I hope your report is very detailed, detailed enough for all such uses." The Prime winked at Sylvia, then smiled again.

Sylvia grinned.

The Ecolitan professor of infrastructure economics took a long and deep breath.

"Now . . . we get to the real business." The Prime walked toward the window and looked out at the mid-afternoon sun.

"The real business?"

The two younger Ecolitans exchanged glances.

"I have tendered my resignation as Prime. I am claiming responsibility for the destruction of Tempte and the associated damage on Tinhorn. There is a complete file in my office, and the contents will be released to the media with my resignation . . . shortly after my ship breaks orbit." Pittsway turned and held up his hand. "This is the real role of the Prime, and I was unfortunate enough to be here. Now, the documents in the file are correct . . . and false by omission. They contain my directive to destroy the Conglomerate High Command. The name of the pilot is blacked out, and there is an explanation that since the pilot did not survive the mission, his name will not be revealed for two reasons. First, that he was carrying out my orders, and second, that the responsibility was mine alone. His family should not suffer from his decision, and the blame should be mine alone.

"Any other explanation would seem as though the Institute were attempting to shift blame, and we can never allow that to occur. The responsibility is the Prime's and I knew that when you left for Artos." Pittsway smiled, openly and gently. "Your turn will doubtless come."

Nathaniel waited, mute.

"Your nomination as Prime has been submitted to the Institute—"

"Mine? After all I've done?"

Pittsway shook his head gently. "No, because of what you've done, although I am the only one who knows all that. The head of the Institute is not a politician. He or she can never be such. The Institute would not survive with leaders who followed political dictates. What ensures the Institute's continuation is not only our skills and abilities, but the absolute knowledge by every human government that we do not bow to politics, that we will not be intimidated, and that we will act when we feel necessary, regardless of the cost. That will must be tempered by the understanding of the weight of such costs. What other Ecolitan is there today who understands better in heart and mind the costs of our actions?"

"I . . . don't know."

"Your nomination as Prime will be accepted, if it has not already been, by the senior Ecolitans. You are a hero of sorts. You staved off war with the Empire twice, apparently without overt violence. You are respected as talented and diplomatic, if somewhat younger than ideal. Your economic report has already been cited as proof of why the Empire would never have really attacked the Coordinate." The Prime laughed, once. "We know that is a great exaggeration, but, after the fact, it covers everyone's reputation. So, we have already let it be known that you survived numerous attempts on both your lives in an effort to bring this Fuard conspiracy to light, although the last attempt hospitalized you both." Another dry smile crossed Gairloch Pittsway's face. "Even that is true in a way. The Fuards did do their best to kill you. All through this trial, you two have been the voices of sweet reason. That is the official position, and you *will* both ensure it remains that way."

Pittsway's eyes went to Sylvia. "You, Ecolitan Ferro-Maine, have been nominated as Director of Infrastructure Communications. That is the official title for what amounts to our intelligence training operations."

"But . . ."

"I know. You are going to make some ridiculous claim that you have limited experience. Everyone's experience is limited. The most important qualification that you possess is that you understand the consequences of intelligence operations, their strengths, and their limitations, and that you have survived all three. You are also willing to get the job done without trying to grab all the credit and blame."

The piercing eyes flicked back to Nathaniel. "I've been careful to point out that you, Prime-nominee Whaler, have only flitter and needleboat certification, not large ship experience. I and the unnamed pilot are responsible for the atrocities committed upon the Conglomerate. I did not call them such, but the unfortunate necessities of our times. However, history will call them atrocities."

Pittsway's eyes turned even harder as he looked first at Sylvia, then at Nathaniel. "Your somewhat altered appearance may give rise to suspicions that you were impersonated. You will not discuss the actual attack on Tempte, except in general terms, but you will state that you are responsible for all your actions on Artos and New Avalon. That is the way it was and the way it must always remain. No matter what happens, and how it happens, we are responsible for our actions, the Prime most of all."

"But my actions . . ." Nathaniel began.

"You are responsible for your actions, all of them, and you will pay for them. Admitting them publicly would be easier, far easier. You would either be dead, or unable to offer any productive service to anyone. You have scarcely begun to pay, as you will discover once you take on the duties of Prime. I am ensuring that you will pay for your actions . . . every day of the rest of your life." His eyes softened. "The hard part of ensuring responsibility is maintaining responsible initiative on the lower levels. Micro-managing doesn't work. Your fate is in the hands of those who serve you, as mine was in yours. Most of the time it works out well for everyone. Sometimes, it only works out well for humankind, and we pay the price." He paused. "Yes . . . we. I trust you don't think I'm being generous or kind. You, being who you both are, will pay for what has happened for the remainder of your lives, even if nothing else of this magnitude challenges the Institute." After another pause, he added, "And, unless I've misjudged greatly, you will be far more vigilant than any of your former peers could ever imagine.

"Ecolitan Swersa has asked to accompany me, and I have accepted her offer." Gairloch Pittsway shrugged. "One must know when to exit. Remember that when your time comes. But I don't need to tell you that. You both need some rest, because, after tomorrow, you won't see any for a very long time." He offered a last, almost sad, smile, then bowed. "Good luck."

In the silence after his departure, the two looked at each other, blankly.

"He's setting himself up as a target," murmured Sylvia.

"We're all targets from here on in."

"We always have been. Everyone is—they just don't know it." She sat down on the edge of the bed beside him. "How do you feel about all this? About Tinhorn, about being nominated as Prime?"

"Guilty. What else would you expect? I still don't see any other meaningful alternative that was open, but people died."

"You still think you acted morally?"

Nathaniel laughed, harshly. "That's not the question. Guilt isn't rational. I have to believe I took the only moral course open at the time, but I'll always feel guilty, probably always ask and search to fig-

ure out what else might have been possible. That's guilt. Morality . . .
I still don't have a moral problem. Oh . . . there will be plenty of people who will claim that what the Institute did is immoral. After all,
ten million innocents did die on Tinhorn, and were all those thousands
of soldiers and technicians on Tempte really responsible for the Conglomerate's actions? Weren't they just doing their job?" His tone was
sardonic.

"You are bitter."

"When people scream morality, they don't understand morality.
The Prime had it right—they're confusing it with justification, and
they refuse to see that. If the Empire and the Federated Hegemony
thought they could destroy the Coordinate without retaliation right
now, they would, and they'd call it moral. That's not morality, it's
fear. They're afraid that they'll be called on their actions before they
complete whatever new genocide they might contemplate in the
future."

"From what I've seen . . . you're probably right."

"Yet we've never acted first. We have acted before others would,
but there have still been plenty of bodies." He swallowed, then continued. "When you talk about morality, and when justice is applied
as retribution, what you really do is give people or governments a
choice. They can choose to be moral, or they can choose not to be,
and take the risk of retribution or possibly getting away with it.
When someone or something, like the Institute, even hints that it
won't wait for the immoral action to be completed, everyone cries
foul . . . unless the immoral actions are already on so vast a scale that
they can't be ignored. In practice, everyone ignores the problem
until they can't keep ignoring it. Then, and only then, do they
invoke morality."

"Thinking like that, especially out loud, will make you a target as
big as Prime Pittsway." Sylvia tried to force a smile. "If they don't find
out what you really did first."

"Who will tell them? Only four people know for certain who crewed
the ship. That's part of the burden the Prime mentioned."

She shook her head. "We need to get you out of here, to get some rest
before you become the designated target as Prime."

The door opened, and a young doctor walked in. "Ah . . . you can
go . . . any time. Any time . . ."

"Thank you." Nathaniel looked at Sylvia. "Are we ready for all this?"

"Just keep saying 'we.'"

"After all that's happened, what else could I say?"

What else indeed?

Nathaniel eased his legs over the side of the bed. His greens were in the closet. Sylvia extended an arm, and he took it, gratefully.